# DRAGON MATES

## THE COMPLETE DRAGONS OF CHAROK SERIES COLLECTION

### MEG RIPLEY

DADDY DRAGON GUARDIANS & SHIFTERS BETWEEN WORLDS

# CONTENTS

# HOLDEN'S MATE

DADDY DRAGON GUARDIANS

# 1

LEAH STRAIGHTENED HER DRESS AND DREW IN A DEEP BREATH. IT WAS just a night out at a bar with her friends. It didn't mean anything, and there was no pressure. Just because Autumn and Summer insisted on calling it a divorce party didn't mean that she had to feel obligated to hook up with someone and live the wild life like a college student again. It was going to be okay. She had even opted for a low pair of heels instead of the stilettos at the back of her closet, just to make it feel a little more like a normal night out with her girlfriends.

As she stepped up to The Parlor and raised her hand to open the door, she was relieved to see that there was no knob; she only had to push. Leah carefully chose a spot near the middle of the door—where very few people had probably touched the old wood—and stepped inside. The establishment was a long and narrow one that stretched away on either side of her. The back wall behind the bar was painted a pale shade of yellow that contrasted with the dark wood trim and gave the place a bright but cozy feel. Two bartenders worked away busily, sliding drinks down the slick wooden surface and collecting tips in a large glass jar.

"There she is!" Autumn squealed, waving Leah over to their table. "I was starting to wonder if you were going to show up."

"And I wasn't going to stop her if she decided to go find you and

She narrowed her green eyes at her friend, willing her to do as she was told.

"Maybe I should; I'd like to think I will, eventually. But you've got to admit this is one hell of a blow to my self-esteem." Leah slunk down a little in her seat, the weight of it all still heavy on her shoulders. She and Victor had been separated for over a year, but knowing that all the official paperwork had been filed made things feel much more final.

"Why? You're gorgeous." Summer leaned over and picked up several locks of Leah's dark chestnut hair in her hand and let them fall slowly back to her shoulders. "And you're fun and smart. You're everything most guys are looking for."

Leah shook her head. "It's not just that. I mean, sure, knowing that he was sleeping with that other woman definitely made me feel like I wasn't good enough. But I'm a goddamn psychic; I hang a shingle out so people will come to me to find out about their futures, but I can't even predict my own. Don't you think I should have known he was the wrong guy?"

Her mind flashed back to when she had first met Victor at a party. She had been far too drunk, and he had given her a ride home. Leah had been attracted to him, and it hadn't hurt that he was intelligent as well. To top things off, he had believed her when she'd accidentally told him she had psychic powers. It was the kind of thing that would have driven most people away, no matter what kind of relationship she wanted to have with them. No one believed that psychics were anything but con artists with crystal balls. But Victor had seemed to understand, even though he had no supernatural gifts of his own. He'd never complained that she was being foolish when she became a psychic freelancer, and he'd even gone with her to a few conventions. It was the most support she'd ever received from someone without powers, and it had meant a lot to her.

Autumn rolled her green, catlike eyes toward the ceiling as she thought. "Have you ever been able to predict things about yourself? I mean, it's not like you know when you're going to die, do you?"

Leah had to admit she had a point. "No, and I wouldn't want to. But it makes me feel like such a hypocrite. I managed to get a publishing deal for my book that claims it can teach people to tap into their own natural abilities, and then I get smacked in the face by reality. I fucking hate it."

"Maybe your spirit guides sent Victor to you for a reason." Summer blinked her wide, green eyes. "Maybe you needed someone to help you get started on the right path, but it doesn't mean you were meant to continue on that path *together*."

"Apparently not." Leah easily remembered that fateful day when Victor had come home from work and set his travel mug down on the kitchen counter. It was a simple thing, and not a gesture that should have mattered at all. But Leah had picked it up to rinse out the remains of his coffee from that morning, and her powers had instantly kicked in. The kitchen had faded around her and turned into an office. A woman was kissing her husband—and it definitely wasn't Leah. The image was so real that Leah couldn't help but watch as her own husband's hands unfastened the buttons of the woman's shirt and worked their way up her skirt. She'd watched in horror as the two of them made love on Victor's desk.

Of course, she had gone straight to him with her accusations. That was the first time Victor had ever questioned her psychic powers, calling her a paranoid liar. But she knew as soon as she reached out and touched the lapel of his sport coat that she was right. Victor's personal items didn't usually give her much information; not like they did for strangers. But then again, she had always known all of his secrets up until that point. The waitress brought Leah's drink, and she stared down at the salty rim of the glass as if it could help her understand what had happened.

"I'll have another one of those, please," Autumn asked the waitress, and then turned back to Leah. "That's okay. It just means you have the opportunity for someone new to walk down that path with you. Now you can find someone who *really* believes in you." She smiled and looked off into the distance, lost in the romance of it all.

"Victor believed," Leah argued. "It was his idea that I should start booking myself for parties, and that was what really got me started in the business. I would probably be stuck in a dead-end job somewhere in a cubicle or working for pennies at a psychic hotline if it hadn't been for him." Leah had a real talent; enough that she had been able to make a living from it. Even without sharing the bills with Victor, she never had to worry about how she was going to live.

Autumn tapped her finger on the table. "He had a good sense of business; I can't argue with that. But I'm not just talking about someone who believes you can predict the future or see into people's lives. But Summer's talking about someone who believes in you as a person. Someone who helps you grow and change into the person you were meant to be."

Summer sipped her daiquiri and nodded. "I'm sure he's out there. I believe there's someone out there for everyone, even if it's not the kind of person we're expecting."

"Well, whoever it is, I plan on taking a long time to find him. I don't want to date anyone for at least the next year. I'll just take time to be myself and figure out what I want from life. Even then, it's going to be a very long time before I get serious. If I get remarried before I'm fifty, then I want one of you to shoot me. Promise?"

The twins laughed. Autumn reached across the table and touched Leah's hand. "You're never going to make it twenty years, girl. I get it. We're in our thirties now. It's not going to be as easy as it was when we were twenty. But we're not dead yet, and you can't just give up on yourself like that."

Leah's phone beeped, and she was grateful for the distraction. No matter how much encouragement the other women gave her, she knew it wasn't going to make her feel any better about her situation. She needed time, a lot of meditation, and yes, maybe even a few drinks. What she didn't need was the text that showed up on her screen from Victor: *Hey, can we talk?*

"I don't like the look on your face." Autumn watched Leah carefully.

This was just too much. Although Leah hadn't thought she felt like celebrating, she knew she should at least be happy that all those long fights with Victor were over. He had claimed that his affair didn't mean a thing and that he still wanted to be with her, but that only made things harder. No. She wasn't going to give in. Victor would say he wanted to talk. Then he would get her to go grab a cup of coffee together "for old time's sake." The next thing she knew, she would be at his new apartment and falling into bed with him.

Well, screw that. He might be all turned on by the idea of messing around with her now that they were no longer married, but she wasn't going to be treated like his toy. She'd been used enough, and she wasn't going to let it happen again. She didn't feel very strong, but she would just have to fake it until it really happened.

Her phone beeped again, and she pointedly put it back in her purse. Leah grabbed one of the small cloths she carried with her and wrapped it around the stem of her margarita glass. She didn't even like knowing what was going on in her own life; she sure as hell didn't need to know what was going on in the waitress'. It was best to keep her psychic energies at bay for the night, at least as much as possible. Leah raised her glass in a toast to her friends. "Here's to my new life, and whatever comes with it."

## 2

Holden Reid glared at himself in the mirror. He was just so *human.* It had been one thing to take on this form back on Charok. It had served as a diplomatic common ground for all creatures who came to the Great Court to converse and work out political issues. It had kept things civil—at least for a time—since the natural powers of the inhabitants were all somewhat reduced when they were walking on two legs. But he wasn't sure he would ever get used to the sleek cheekbones covered in rusty stubble, the waves of matching hair on his head that had replaced his spikes, or the haunting blue eyes that stared back at him in the mirror. He knew he could shift back into his dragon form whenever he wanted to, but there was rarely an opportunity on Earth.

"Quit staring at yourself." Beau leaned in the bedroom doorway, his blonde hair combed back perfectly. "It's about time to go."

"I was thinking maybe I should stay home and let the rest of you go out." Holden turned away from the mirror and grabbed his shoes from the rack behind his door—awful things, but unfortunately, it wasn't acceptable to go out in public with bare feet. "I'm sure Xander would rather go out than be stuck with the children."

Beau gave him a level look that meant business. "Don't even try it. It's Xander's turn to stay with them, and we already have everything set up. We're not changing things now just because you want to be a stubborn dragon."

"Then couldn't we at least find a different place to go? These human bars have such bad energy. Everyone there is either sad, angry, or both. Not to mention the rancid smell of old alcohol. I don't see how this can ever work as a mating ritual." Holden knew how important it was that they each find their mates. They were the last of their kind, and the younglings they had charged themselves with raising needed mothers as well as fathers. But he had his doubts that human women could ever fit the bill, and he hadn't enjoyed their attempts at finding acceptable ones so far.

"Trust me. I've done a lot of reading on the subject, and this is how they do it here." He brushed a piece of lint from his black t-shirt. "Unless you want to try online dating again."

"Fuck no!" Holden roared, spinning around to glare at his friend. At the bemused look on Beau's face, he had to laugh himself. "I can't say that went particularly well last time." It had been an experiment for them, but not one that he was willing to conduct again. It seemed to draw out only the most desperate women, and they never looked the same in real life as they did in their pictures. He knew that physical attraction didn't really matter, but it made Holden feel as though they had been lying to him.

The two men went out into the living room, where Xander and Julian were keeping the children entertained. A living room of four dragon younglings seemed very full. They were younger than they appeared, already toddling about on two legs like human babies did. Xander sat on the floor with them, already in his role as sitter for the night. He had doled out snacks and sippy cups and was watching patiently as they emptied a bin full of toys. It was almost humorous to see the brawny ebony-haired man so tenderly taking care of such small children. Finn, the child that had hatched out of the egg Holden had claimed when they'd made their escape from Charok, grinned at him from across the room.

They had only been eggs when the War of Storms had broken out. The dragons had fought valiantly for the territory that had been theirs since the dawn of time, but the ogres had fought harder. The dragons still might have won if the wizards hadn't teamed up with the ogres and cast a spell that had instantly poisoned a vast majority of the great reptiles. Unfortunately, that had included their Queen, leaving behind the nest of eggs she had laid only a few months before.

"Do you ever think it was a mistake coming to Earth?" Holden mumbled. Maybe they would have been alright if they had stayed on Charok. They could have escaped to the mountains and found the tunnels of their ancestors. It would have been a primitive lifestyle, but at least they would have known that the next generation was being raised on their home planet.

"Don't get started on that again." Julian rolled his eyes and picked up Kaylee, his charge. They were the pair that looked most like each other, with green eyes, dark hair, and olive skin. It had been sheer chance, but it had worked in their favor. Nobody would ever doubt that Julian was her father. "We did what we thought was best, and there's no going back. That spell was hard, and it was a one-time deal. Besides, we would be questioning ourselves just as much if we hadn't taken advantage of it."

Holden nodded. It had been a risk, either way. And the rogue wizard who had agreed to help them get off their world and into a different one had been an old friend of Julian's. "I just wish he had bothered to tell us about how this world worked beforehand. What do you think the Queen would say if she could see her children being raised as soft little fleshlings?"

"I think she would say we're very lucky that our kind is able to shift at such a young age," Xander volunteered. "It's clear from my studies that human children who look different aren't easily accepted by their own species. If the children had any indication of their true nature— dragon scales, claws, you name it—then this entire journey would have been a complete bust. We'd be hiding in the mountains of Earth, instead."

"Are the three of you just going to stand around talking, or are we going to go out and find some mates?" Beau asked from the floor, where he was gently prying a small plastic toy out of Elliot's mouth.

"We're going." Holden reluctantly stuck his wallet in his pocket— since the humans seemed to favor little rectangles of plastic instead of the cold solidity of gold coins—and headed for the door.

The bar was just like all the other ones they had been to. It might have been laid out differently, and it might have sat in a different part of town, but it still smelled of liquor and tears. Even in human form, he found that the smell of Earth life was a noxious one anytime they were in the city. It was for that reason he had chosen a house out on the edge of town, where he had a massive back yard and plenty of fresh air. The other shifters often seemed to congregate there, and he could understand why.

"I'll bet you six coins that you can't even get a woman to look at you," Julian said to Beau, punching him in the arm.

"I'll double the wager and bet that every female you hit on busts out laughing," Beau chided back.

It was innocent, foolish talk, and Holden would have taken part, but something hit him the moment he stepped into the bar. It was an energy, a field of vibrations that wrapped around his body and refused to let go. His vision blurred, and he fought to stay upright with only two feet to stand on. Instinctively, his body wanted to shift back to its dragon form. He needed the stability of his four sturdy legs under him, balanced by his expansive wings. He needed to know he had the security of his scaly armor and the fire in his lungs. "Not here, not here," he whispered to himself as he felt beads of sweat form on his temples. The dragon inside was fighting fiercely to get out.

"What's the matter?" Julian's voice was distant, as though it were coming from the other side of the room, even though he was right beside him. "Are you alright?"

Holden gritted his teeth and forced himself to calm down. Whatever had happened was odd, but there was no choice but to control it. If he gave himself away, then it would be over for all of them, including their children. He curled his fingers into a fist and pressed his fingernails into his palm, forcing himself back to reality. "Yeah, I'm fine—or I will be. Let's just sit down."

He followed the other two men to a table on the right side of the bar, near the jukebox. It was noisy, but it meant they could talk without worrying too much about being overheard. They had found out quickly that it was hard to keep their conversation on normal Earth topics, even when they were out in public. Nobody needed to overhear them talking about spells, eggs, and life on another planet.

"What can I get for ya?" A waitress in a short skirt strutted up to their table, smacking her gum and openly admiring them. "We've got some great specials tonight." She pointed at a chalkboard over the bar with several drinks scrawled onto it.

"Just a round of beers, please," Julian said with a smile.

"What kind? We've got ten domestic beers on tap, and an entire list of imported bottles." She pointed to a card stuck in a condiment rack in the middle of the table.

Holden, still reeling from the odd experience, pointed to the first one. "We'll take those." He didn't even read it, and he didn't need to. Humans seemed to put so much emphasis on their different alcoholic drinks, but he had yet to find one that truly appealed to him. The Earthling beers were palatable, but they were nothing like the ale back home.

"Sounds great. If you boys need anything else, you just let me know." The waitress gave a little finger wave as she went behind the bar.

"I think you're going to lose your bet already," Beau scoffed, puffing his chest and grinning. "She was absolutely checking me out. And did you see those legs?"

"She was checking *everyone* out," Julian replied, rolling his eyes and laughing. "It's part of her job, because she thinks she'll get better tips."

"Oh, right. Tips. So weird." Beau watched the waitress, where she was filling glasses behind the bar. "So, how exactly are we supposed to know when we've found the right one? I've had women flirt with me, and I think I've had several chances to mate. Some of them are beautiful, other ones seem nice, but I know we can't pick just anyone to help us raise the children. I can't say I would mind having that one in my bed, though."

Holden pressed his lips together in thought. "I'm not sure, to be honest with you. Two humans might get married for monetary reasons without any consideration for love. Others might only count love, and still others seem to get married for no good reason at all. They spend their lives together, but they constantly fight. It doesn't make a lot of sense to me."

Julian crossed his arms and studied the wood grain of the table. "Back on Charok, dragons weren't together for any artificial reasons; they just knew they were made for each other. I'm not sure how easy that's going to be with humans thrown into the mix."

The waitress brought their beers, and Holden picked at the label on his bottle. "Sounds to me like we'd be better off alone. I'm not going to bring someone home to be a part of Finn's life if she has half the qualities I've seen in humans so far. He doesn't need a mother figure who might lie, cheat, steal, or be selfish. Let's face it, there's not a woman in this city—and maybe not even on this world—who has the kind of qualities we would have looked for in a female dragon." He had known brave and noble female dragons back home, and it seemed doubtful that any of the Earthling women could compare.

"They might not have shining scales or sharp teeth, but I think I've seen a few I wouldn't mind sinking *my* teeth into." Beau's eyes glittered as he cast a glance around the bar. "Who's to say we couldn't just experiment? We could mate without ever bringing them home."

Julian slapped his hand on the table. "You sound like an Earthling already, and we've only been here a few months. Do what you want, but I can promise it won't go well. I've heard about things called one-night stands and affairs, and they never seem to go well."

Beau snorted. "That's your problem. You never do anything but sit at home. You should start looking around and seeing what humans are really like in person instead of watching them on YouTube."

"I'm only just diving into this social media thing, but it's clear there's a lot to learn." His green eyes shone as he reflected on what he had discovered up to that point. "They're strange creatures, but they're fascinating."

Beau took a swig of his beer and shook his head. "Well, I prefer my education to be hands-on."

The repartee between the two men faded into the background as Holden took in his surroundings. He skimmed over the various men and women at the bar. Beau wasn't the only one who wondered how they were supposed to know when they met the right one. Back on Charok, there was never a doubt when a male dragon found his mate. She possessed him with a spell that nobody could quite explain, but it made the male want to do absolutely everything for his intended female. Holden didn't know if it would feel different with a human, or if it was even possible to find a human that could make him happy. Still, he was determined to try, even if it was only for Finn's sake. He couldn't let his doubts get in the way of his commitment.

But then his eyes landed on a woman on the other side of the bar. The layout of the pub made her seem small and distant, but he focused on her intently. Her dark hair, slightly curly, had been pulled back into a loose ponytail. She had thin brows that arched gracefully over her blue eyes, and her dark pink lips moved attractively as she spoke to the other women at her table. She was completely oblivious to him, but she had a power over him that he couldn't quite explain.

Once again, he felt the urge to shift. He wanted to let go of this human shell he had been forced to wear around and let his scales surface. He wanted to feel the way his wings unfurled from his back and took to the air. More than anything, Holden wanted to let his claws come shooting out of the ends of his fingertips and feel them sink into something.

"Holden. Holden!"

Julian's voice brought him back to the present. He'd been staring at the woman so intently that he had felt he'd been transported right across the bar until he was next to her and could smell the way her perfume wrapped around her body. He blinked. "What?"

"You might want to let go of the table." Julian gestured at Holden's hands.

Looking down, Holden saw what he meant. He had gripped the table in both of his hands with such force, he'd dug into the wood with his fingernails. They hadn't done much damage, not compared to what would have happened if he really had unleashed his claws. Fortunately, the months of self-discipline he'd had to impose on himself had paid off. He'd done little more than scratch the finish.

Beau leaned forward, squinting at Holden. "Are you sure you're alright? You don't seem yourself tonight."

Holden didn't know how to explain it. Maybe there was no good way of doing so. But there was either something about this bar or about that woman that had a hold on him. "I'm fine, it's just one of those nights. Ignore me."

The other men did as they were asked. Holden took a long sip of his beer, wishing it could affect him the way it did humans. Julian had theorized that there was something different about their metabolism, and that they weren't completely human even when they appeared to be. But the physiology of it all didn't intrigue him. He just knew that he had to find a way to talk to that woman.

## 3

THE MARGARITAS WERE TASTING BETTER AND BETTER AS THE NIGHT WORE on, and Leah was no longer sure of just how many drinks she'd had. The women had ordered small meals to go with their drinks, which helped, but she was feeling so dizzy and free that she didn't even bother wiping her fork down to get rid of any residual energies before she used it. Her psychic powers had been pushed to the backburner, and that was right where they belonged for the moment.

"So, tell me how your book is doing. It sounded like your sales were going very well those first few weeks." Even while tipsy, Autumn was all about business.

"Oh, it's good," Leah said with a smile. She had started writing the book late one night after a customer had told her she wished she had powers of her own. It had gotten Leah's mind churning, remembering all she had gone through as she was developing her gifts. There hadn't been anyone for her to talk to, and she had wished for more guidance constantly. When she looked back on it, she realized that she could have saved herself a lot of heartache and gone a lot further with her career if she had just been better educated and had known what to do with herself. It had been a long and lonely road to where she was, and she was determined to keep that from happening to others.

And so, her book had been born. *Develop Your Psychic Powers* had started out with late-night scribbles that had lasted well into the morning. When she had picked it up the next day, she hadn't expected it to be any good. But she found that she only wanted to work on it more, and before she knew it, she was typing up the final draft. Holding her breath, she had sent it to an agent to see what he thought of it. To her surprise, she had managed to not only get it published, but to get a request for a second book. The title was a simple one, but it let potential buyers know exactly what they were getting.

"I've done far better with it than I would have thought," Leah replied. "Another prediction I never saw."

"Don't be so hard on yourself. We've sold plenty of copies in our store," Summer encouraged. "You should come and do another book signing. You draw in all sorts of interesting people."

Autumn nodded her agreement. "You really should. It helps your business as well as ours, and I'd be more than happy to set up a table for you."

Leah shrugged. "Maybe, but the real challenge now is figuring out what I want to focus on for that second book. If I wait too long, the publisher won't be interested anymore. There's just a lot that I could talk about, but I want to keep it focused." It felt good to be talking about work again. Her abilities might pay the bills, but they were also a big part of who she was. Those long months of fighting with Victor and going back and forth with her attorney had pulled her so far out of her element, and she needed to find a way to get back to it. Hopefully, she would soon be able to find a good balance in her life again. It was going to be a while before she was completely used to living without Victor, but she had to believe she would get there.

"I have no doubt you'll be writing another hit before you know it. There are a lot of people in the world looking for help, and they need people like us to give it to them." Autumn carried all the confidence any of them needed. She was always the perfect person to turn to for an ego boost.

Summer had her head tipped back and her eyes closed. Her legs were folded in the chair underneath her, and she looked like she was relaxing in a hammock instead of having drinks in a local pub. "It's a shame, really. They keep going to their doctors for pills, but that's not going to help. They need to get in touch with their own souls. You wouldn't think we as humans could be so distant from something that's a part of us, but it happens all the time. I blame electronics.

People are too busy staring at screens instead of talking to each other or taking long walks in the woods."

Autumn glanced at her sister and looked like she was going to argue, but she nodded. "Yeah. I love that the internet has allowed us to grow our business. I just packaged up a shipment and sent it to Canada the other day, and our blog gets hits from all over the world. But I also wish we had more people who came in and just talked to us. I think there's a lot we could do for them."

"That's something I should put in my next book, then. I don't mean specifically that they should come here and talk to only you guys, but that they need to reach out and find in-person resources in their own communities." Leah was feeling the sparkle of creativity in the back of her brain, and she liked it. It was the same energy that kept her up at night when she had written the first book. There were other times that her abilities had kept her awake, but that was usually because of uncomfortable premonitions. Creativity was a lot more fun. "You know, maybe if I..."

"If you what?" Summer picked up her head, her wide blue eyes watching Leah carefully. "Are you alright?"

Leah wasn't sure. She'd had tons of thoughts swirling through her head. She had a good idea of what her book was going to be about, and even the chapter titles had begun emerging from the fog her brain had been in. She had just been about to fish in her purse for a pad of paper when everything seemed to dissipate. Her mind had drained like a bathtub, and now it was completely empty. "Yeah, I'm fine. I think. I just completely lost my train of thought."

"Blame the tequila," Autumn said with a vague gesture toward her glass, which had been emptied several times and now only held a few stray pieces of ice. "She's a fickle mistress when it comes to artistic expression."

Though Leah was definitely feeling the alcohol, she had a hunch it was something different. "I don't know. It seems like there was something more urgent trying to get through, if that makes any sense."

"You know I'm all about listening to your body, but I'd say the chances are good it was nothing more than the drinks. You should have finished your dinner." Autumn gestured at Leah's plate, which still held half a Reuben sandwich and handful of house-made chips.

"Thanks, *Mom*." Leah cast a frustrated glance at her meal. She'd eaten what she could, but she had to admit that she was thinking about watching her weight. Even though she claimed she didn't want to get serious about anyone, she thought she could stand to lose a few pounds if she was eventually going to be back out on the market. Besides, if she ran into Victor on the street, then he needed to know exactly what he was missing out on. "Really, though, I don't think that's it."

"The universe has lots of ways of communicating with us. I think the fact that different cultures take into account different signs from nature says a lot. If we actually paid attention to what the world was trying to say, we'd be getting messages from all sides." Summer blinked sleepily as she polished off her drink.

Leah furrowed her brow. "Then I've just had something whack me on the backside of the head. I'm just going to run to the restroom for a minute." She pushed her chair out and stood up slowly, knowing that her balance wouldn't be quite right. But she couldn't stay in her seat a minute longer, not without that nagging sensation tugging at the back of her brain. Her steps leaned a little toward the right as she made her way across the bar, but she made steady progress without running into anyone or anything. That, in itself, was an accomplishment.

She passed by the blaring jukebox and nearly stopped dead in her tracks. Something was pulling at her once again—no, it was yanking at her, demanding that she pay attention. But Leah didn't want to. She had enough going on in her life with her divorce, her book, her business, and just getting her head put on straight again. She didn't need psychic messages from the other side or someone else's drama to take up her time.

Her spiritual energy had been zapped, and that was all there was to it.

Forcing past the wall the universe had tried to put up in front of her, Leah made her way to the dark little hallway at the other end of the bar. Framed photos of supposedly famous people who had been to the pub hung on the wall, but Leah didn't recognize most of them. She glared at the smiling face of a woman just to the left of the restroom door as she pushed it open, wondering just why the hell she thought she was so important that she deserved to sign a photo and give it to the owners to display.

The restroom was a decent one, considering the kind of establishment she was in. There was a small seating area near the door with faux leather chairs and mirrors, and bottles of perfumes and lotions lined a small counter. Leah breezed toward the sinks, turning on the cold water, longing to splash it on her face, but knowing it would just cause her makeup to run down her cheeks. She settled for washing her hands and wrists and carefully dabbing the cool liquid at her temples and on the back of her neck. She shut off the faucet and leaned against the sink as she stared at her reflection in the mirror.

Fine lines had started to scrawl over her skin at the corners of her eyes and near her mouth. They were what her mother would have called smile lines, but Leah felt they just made her look old. "I should be grateful to be old and wise, considering what I've seen and done," she muttered to herself. Thirty might not have seemed so old if she hadn't been thrown into the land of being single again. Looking for something positive to focus on, she noted that her pale blue eyes were still clear and bright, and she hadn't seen any gray hairs yet. Though she definitely wasn't twenty anymore, she couldn't exactly write herself off as an old maid.

"Just because Victor didn't want me, that doesn't mean no one else will. This is his problem, not mine." Leah had learned back in high school that mantras and affirmations could get her through even the worst of times. When her powers were trying to take over her mind and body, making her feel as though she might be crazy, she only needed the power of a few positive words to help get her back on track. It was never perfect, but it helped. "There are plenty of fish in the sea, and I don't have to go fishing for them until I'm ready. I can take all the time I want."

She could, and she would have to. She definitely didn't have room for someone else in her life, and she didn't want to burden someone with the heavy emotional baggage she was carrying around. It was dragging along the floor behind her like a sack of bricks, and it was going to take a little time to learn how to let go of it.

Feeling slightly better and only a little dizzy from her cocktails, Leah made her way back out into the hall. Just as she was about to head into the main area of the bar, a man stepped in front of her. "Well, hello there, fine thing. Where have you been all night?"

Leah blinked in the dim light. The man was tall, but she didn't recognize the way the shadows fell on his face. He stank of liquor, as though he had been drinking far longer than just the evening, and his hot breath blew right in her face. "Excuse me." Leah stepped to the right to get around him.

He moved in front of her again, swaying a little as he steadied himself with one hand against the wall. "Where do you think you're going, angel face? I've been looking for a pretty little thing like you all night, and I can't let you get away that easily. My name's Pete. Why don't you at least let me buy you a drink?"

Leah had dropped her gaze, unable to look at him any longer. Pete had such bad energy surrounding him, it overwhelmed even his stench. She'd had plenty of clients come to her shop looking for help, and they weren't all good people. She was used to that. But this guy was of a particularly bad sort. She knew if she so much as laid a fingertip on him, she would see all the misdeeds he had committed. "I've had enough, but thank you."

"Oh, come on!" He stepped even closer now as she once again tried to get past him, and his voice had turned angry instead of cajoling. "You think you're better than me or something? You have a problem with me, and you don't even know me? You're just like every other bitch in here."

Her eyes snapped up to his now. She could just see the glaze over his dark eyes that had been laid there by his alcohol consumption. Leah might have felt sorry for him and assumed he was just drunk and didn't know what he was doing, but she had a strong feeling she wasn't the first woman he had talked to this way. "Is that supposed to convince me? Get the hell out of my way, asshole!" She shoved past him now, no longer able to avoid physical contact as he tried to stop her. Leah's arm slammed into the side of his, and she stumbled into the wall. Reaching out to catch herself, she knocked down two of the framed pictures.

Her assailant had her by the wrist, and he slammed her into the wall she had just clung to for support. "Nobody gets away with treating me like that!" Pete's face was in hers now, his stench so vile she thought she might vomit all over the front of his stained leather jacket.

Flashes of imagery flickered behind her eyes: an older man with a belt in his hand, a stolen CD player, a bruised woman in a bed. Leah struggled to get away, but his grip only tightened. Empty beer bottles, some sort of drug paraphernalia she didn't recognize, men passed out on a filthy floor. It was all right there in front of her as though she lived it herself, and her stomach lurched.

Suddenly, the man was brushed aside like a feather. A new man had stepped into the hallway, and he had the asshole's jacket bunched in his fists. He turned his head to look at Leah, his eyes haunted and fierce. "Is this guy bothering you?"

Leah's eyes widened, and she pressed herself against the wall in an effort to stay as far away from the altercation as possible. She nodded dumbly.

"Get out of here," the new man growled. His dark hair, the curls combed back neatly, was a burnished mahogany in the light of the bar. His jaw was square and firm, and he jutted it out toward the other man as he shoved him away from Leah.

Pete took a few steps backward, but he charged forward again. "Who the fuck do you think you are? You trying to nail this bitch or something? 'Cause I saw her first!" He shoved his palms at the bigger man's chest, but the feeble attack made no difference.

The man stood firm, tipping his jaw down to look straight-on at Pete, and there was such a ferocity in his countenance that Leah thought he might explode. "Didn't you hear me the first time? Get the fuck out of here. She doesn't want to talk to you." His voice was deep and firm, like someone out of an action movie.

Pete staggered away, but he still had a sneer on his face as though he thought he had won. "Yeah, well, you can have her. She ain't gonna put out, anyway."

The big man took one more step forward, and Pete went skittering out the front door. Several of the patrons laughed and returned to their drinks, and it was only then that Leah realized they had been watching the whole thing. She still stood with her back against the wall, and she slowly straightened as the stranger turned to her.

"Are you alright?"

Her lungs didn't work. Leah tried to say that she was fine, thank you, and move on to her table, but no part of her body would cooperate. Air was stagnant in her lungs, and even her eyes refused to blink as she took him in. He still looked angry, but there was an air of concern about him that made her feel as though she was the only person in the room. The noise, the lights, even that awful jukebox faded into blackness as he spoke to her, and yet she couldn't quite seem to respond. She was too focused on the amber stubble that clung to the strong line of his chin, the width of his shoulders, the subtle scent of his cologne that pulled at her to lean forward and force her lungs to work again just so she could inhale him.

"Hey, are you alright?" he repeated, holding out a hand.

Leah's eyes drifted down to his open palm, and without thinking, she set her hand on it. The visions were more than just flashes of imagery overlaying what she actually saw with her eyes. Leah was no longer in the bar. The pictures were vague and nonsensical, just quick pulses and feelings that melded into each other and mixed with emotions. Though she was normally a passive observer—as she had been when she'd touched Pete—Leah could tell she was a part of these visions. She didn't understand what was happening, and she knew it couldn't be this man's past, because she was in them. The two of them were together, but in places other than the bar. It made no sense, and she blinked her eyes to bring herself back to the current moment.

"Yeah," she finally breathed, fighting hard to bring herself back to the current moment. "I think so."

"Can I do anything for you? Do you need a glass of water or anything?"

Feeling the corners of her mouth turn up, she tried to force the smile to go away. She had just been assaulted by a nasty drunk in a bar. There was no reason to smile. But something had changed, very drastically, and she felt her face soften in a way she hadn't felt in years. Something as simple as an offer of a glass of water shouldn't have affected her so much. But she knew it was something that went much deeper than that.

"No. Thank you. I—I'm just going to go back to my table now." Her breath was slowly working again, and she stepped gingerly past the man who had saved her. Leah couldn't feel a drop of alcohol in her system anymore; adrenaline had driven it away and replaced it with something else. She slowly slid her hand out of the warmth of his and stepped away.

Autumn and Summer were both sitting up straight, their eyes unblinking as they watched her return to their table. When Leah said nothing, Autumn tipped her head. "What the hell was that?"

"I don't even know," Leah breathed. She smiled down at the table-cloth, feeling giddy. "This guy tried to hit on me, and he wouldn't take no for an answer. And then...and then..."

"That hot piece of ass stepped in and saved you?" Autumn gave a low whistle. "Girl, he must have been sent straight from Goddess herself. I saw how he was built."

"You should ask him out," Summer insisted. "He has a good aura. I can see it all the way from here."

"What? No way." Leah laughed uncomfortably. The feeling of awe and wonder that had filled her when she had been face-to-face with the man was slowly beginning to fade, and she was returning to reality. She didn't know why he had set her off-kilter like that, and it wasn't even worth thinking about. "He did what any decent man should have done. It doesn't mean he's interested."

Autumn tipped her head, weighing Leah's argument. "Maybe, but I think he would have been less likely to step in if he hadn't had his eyes on you all night."

"But he hasn't," Leah countered. Her mouth was dry, and she wished she had taken the stranger up on his offer. But what might a glass of water have led to? Conversation, questions, who knew? Or maybe it would have been nothing more than a kind gesture.

"I'm pretty sure he was before, and I know he certainly is now." Autumn quirked her eyebrows, pleased with herself.

Leah worked her jaw, finding it almost impossible not to turn around and see for herself. But her back was to the other side of the bar where the man had been sitting, and she wasn't about to give either him or Autumn the satisfaction. "That's only because he's concerned about me." Even concern sounded more intimate than she wanted it to. "It's just been a weird night, and he's not my type."

"You mean because he's not married to you and cheating on you? Because that type hasn't seemed to work out very well so far."

Even Summer giggled at that one. "She's got you there."

"No, that's not what I mean." Leah felt her cheeks flush hotly. Why, of all nights, did something like this have to happen? She wasn't ready to deal with men at all unless their interactions stayed strictly business. It was too soon to be thinking about anything romantic, and her friends knew that just as well as she did. But she had to admit that the guy was irresistible. He'd come swooping in like a knight on a white horse to save her. Leah had never thought of herself as weak, but her knees certainly had been when he'd turned those burning blue orbs on her. For a moment, she imagined what it would have felt like to reach out and touch that wide chest of his. He emanated warmth, safety, and something else that she wanted to discover more about. "No," she said again, clearing her throat and pushing aside the image. "I mean, he's just not what I would be looking for. His hair's too long, for one thing."

"Sounds like an excuse to me," Summer rolled her eyes.

"It's not an *excuse*. I just want to make sure that I get exactly what I'm looking for—when I do decide that I'm looking," she quickly amended. "I've never liked guys with long hair. And what kind of a person must he be if he's spending his free time in a bar?"

"So are you," Autumn pointed out. "And it's not like his hair is that long. It's only a few inches. Now if he was walking around with a pony-tail or a man-bun, I would agree with you, but you don't have a leg to stand on here."

"Let's talk about something else," Leah suggested. "Something a little easier."

The twins shared a look but complied, changing the subject to more mundane matters like how difficult it was to get white sage at certain times of the year or the new pet store that was going in right next to The Enchanted Elm.

Try as she might to focus on their conversation, Leah couldn't help but wonder if her knight in shining armor really was keeping an eye on her. She liked the idea of someone who was looking out for her, but it was ridiculous. She had been officially divorced for less than a day, and this wasn't the time for such thoughts.

## 4

Holden grumbled to himself as he fiddled with the numerous straps that kept Finn in his car seat. The child turned his blue eyes up at his foster father and growled right back.

"You might think it's amusing," Holden told him, "but that's only because you don't have to mess with these awful machines. It would be much easier to just fly out and catch our dinner in the woods." He buckled the last strap, handed Finn his favorite stuffed bear, and climbed into the driver's seat.

He'd had plenty of practice driving, but he wasn't sure he would ever get used to it. It was a strange sensation to guide a big machine around amongst other big machines and trust the other drivers, who of course, didn't always do what they were supposed to do. Holden had driven past accidents before, and he wondered how humans could pay so little attention when they were responsible for something the size and weight of a car.

"Maybe when you're old enough, I can take you outside and let you exercise your wings." Holden glanced in the rearview mirror for a moment before returning his eyes to the road. He and the other men had been lucky that the babies seemed to favor their human forms. Having not been in charge of raising the younglings back on Charok, he couldn't say if this was natural for them or a biproduct of spending their entire lives on Earth, but he was grateful, either way. Finn and the others were enough of a handful as they were, but it was something else completely when one of them sprouted a tail or extended a claw. That being said, the clan had agreed to watch each other's children as much as possible—versus relying on a sitter—to avoid a scandal.

Finn gurgled to himself in response and mashed his gums against the ear of his bear.

"I wish you could know what it's like to have fresh food instead of all this packaged crap you'll see at the store. They shove all the vegetables in cans and the grains in boxes, but that's only after they mix them with sugars and chemicals." He shook his head as he turned a corner. "It's disgusting, but that's the way humans want it to be."

Humans, in general, were unappealing. But the one he had seen the other night at The Parlor had been completely different. He'd noticed her early in the evening, but he hadn't said anything to his friends. Holden preferred to study her quietly, glancing at her occasionally and never making his interest known. His eyes had constantly drifted back to her, and he couldn't quite explain why. Even when she had gotten up and gone right past their table, he hadn't said a word. She pulled at his soul, and for a moment, he had wondered if she had felt the same way when she'd stopped in the middle of the floor on her way to the restroom.

But it wasn't until that drunken asshole attacked her that he had found himself taking action. Holden hadn't even had a moment to think about it before he was on his feet and striding over, eager for blood. It had been far too easy to dispatch the thug, and part of him wished it had been more of a violent exchange. How he would have loved to sink his claws into the man's flesh and make him feel pain for what he had done.

Things had changed, though, when the man had gone running out the doors and Holden could focus on the woman once again. He'd still been angry, but his worry for her had crept in as well. Maybe he had been too forceful, because she'd still looked absolutely terrified as she tried to speak with him. Holden hadn't even thought to ask her name, and he'd been kicking himself ever since.

He pulled up to the grocery store and heaved a heavy sigh. "Here we go, Finn. I get to load you down with all the processed food you can imagine, and nobody will think twice about it. Except me." He carried his son into the store and settled him into the cart, annoyed at the way it rattled as he pushed it down the aisle. "Seems like I spend more time strapping you into things than letting you run free," he said with a frown.

Holden paused in the aisle of boxes he had come to know as cereal. He didn't much care for the stuff himself; it was dry and powdery, and he couldn't see what appeal it had. But if he was going to be stuck on this planet, then he needed to get used to every aspect of it.

As he scanned the brightly colored boxes, a silky voice spoke next to him. "If you're looking for baby cereal, I'm afraid you're in the wrong aisle."

Holden turned to find the owner of the voice. She had long blonde hair that swung around her shoulders and vivid red lips. The woman lidded her eyes and stood with one hip cocked in what Xander had told him was part of the human mating ritual. He didn't quite get it. "I'm not."

"Oh, I'm sorry." Her face flushed slightly, and she batted her long eyelashes. "I thought maybe you were looking for something for your little one. You must be one of the guys who actually knows what he's doing with kids." She cast a quick glance at Finn and then looked back at Holden.

He watched her for a moment, his brows furrowed as he tried to understand what she was saying. Then he remembered that the males of the species weren't often the caretakers of the younglings. It happened, and Xander said there was more of a trend toward it now than there had been in human history, but it still wasn't the norm.

Looking down at Finn, he wondered how that could possibly be. The child wasn't his biologically, but he was part of Holden's clan, nevertheless. He had made a commitment to care for the little one, and he would do everything in his power to follow through. If human males weren't like that, then he felt sorry for the women who had to deal with them.

"Do you always do the shopping, or does your wife?" the woman asked.

Holden realized what was happening: he was being hit on. It was flattering, in a way, but he wasn't interested in anyone who wasn't his mate, the woman who could be his partner in life and in raising this child. He didn't know anything about this lady, but he could feel she most definitely wasn't the one.

"I do." Holden answered, continuing past the woman, down the aisle. There was a mutter behind him, but he ignored it. Holden grabbed a random box from the shelf labeled Captain Crunch and turned down the next aisle.

When he had made his way to the back of the store, he stared at the plastic packages in the meat department with disgust. There was no telling how old the food was, but it was obviously not fresh. Finn babbled constantly to himself and was getting louder and louder, distracting Holden from trying to decipher the difference between chuck roast and rib roast. "Easy there, little one," he crooned. "We'll be moving again in a minute."

But Finn continued, and he hopped up and down in the constraint of the cart seat.

Holden turned to see the boy pointing at something on the other side of the store. The child practically screeched with excitement, and Holden knew the other customers were beginning to stare. He didn't want to call attention to himself, and he definitely didn't want the impromptu help of strange women who thought him incapable of his fatherly duties. He grabbed Finn's stuffed bear and waggled it in the air. "Here you go. Why don't you talk to your bear for a minute?"

Finn quieted down for a moment, and Holden turned back to the shelves of meat. He was working his way through trying different cuts and different recipes, trying to find something that not only reminded him of the food on Charok, but would be acceptable to any humans who might decide to drop by. He'd made the mistake once before of cooking chunks of meat over an open flame. The smoke that had poured out the windows of his home had brought his neighbors running. Fortunately, they had laughed it off and chalked it up to Holden being a single dad who didn't know any better. An older lady from down the street had offered to give him cooking lessons, should he decide he wanted them, and that had been the end of it. But that wouldn't be good enough forever, and so Holden had persisted.

"La la la. La! La la! LA LA LA LA!" Finn was hollering at the top of his lungs, and he was once again pointing.

Holden was tempted to lean down and explain to the boy that it wasn't nice to point. That was what he had seen other parents do, but it didn't seem right. Finn had made it very clear that he had something to say, and Holden saw no reason to ignore him. "Alright, what is it?"

He turned around and bumped right into another shopper, stepping back instantly, and automatically apologized. "I'm sorry. I was talking to my son and I didn't see you."

"That's quite alright."

He recognized the voice. He'd only caught a snippet of it a few nights ago, and she wasn't nearly as out of breath as she had been back at The Parlor, but there was no doubt it was her. Holden blinked and found the woman he had rescued at the bar standing right in front of him. She was pushing a cart full of fresh vegetables and bread from the bakery, and she wore her hair down. The woman had stared up at him with wonder once he had chased off her attacker, but now her cerulean gaze was set only on Finn.

"What a handsome little man you are," she murmured. "Are you out shopping with your daddy?"

Finn grinned and clapped his hands, and then pointed at her once again. "La la!"

"How did you know my name was Leah?" the woman asked with a smile. It was only then that she happened to glance up at Holden, and the smile instantly disappeared. "Oh. Hi."

"Hi." Holden felt his body reacting the same way it had when he'd seen her before. He had wanted desperately to shift once he'd seen her and caught her scent, but it had been even worse once he'd jumped in to protect her. She brought out the inner dragon in him, and it was likely that she didn't even know it. He sucked in a breath and willed his body to remain in its current form. It had been a fight to stay human ever since he had arrived on Earth, and he had a feeling he would have to sneak down to the basement later that night and let his body have its way for a moment.

"I'm sorry," the woman—Leah—said as she turned to leave. "You just have such an adorable child, and I wasn't paying any attention. I'm sorry."

He was losing his chance, and there was no guarantee that he would see her again. He had her first name now, but he doubted that would be enough to track her down. Holden racked his brain, trying to remember what he was supposed to do next. He smiled and tried to look confident. "That's alright. You can make it up to me by having dinner with me tonight."

A wave of red crept up her neck, to her face, and all the way to her hairline. Leah flapped her hands at her sides and shook her head as she took a few steps backwards. "I can't. I'm sorry." She gazed at Finn for one final, long moment before grabbing her cart and hurtling down the aisle.

Holden stared after her, wondering exactly what he had done wrong. It was going to be a long time before he understood what women really wanted. "Come on, Finn," he said soberly as he put a package labeled stew meat in his cart, and then grabbed a roast as well. "We'll try something new for dinner." When he reached the checkout, he saw the same cart Leah had been pushing abandoned at the front of the store. She had been so eager to get away from him that she hadn't even bothered to buy her groceries.

# 5

LEAH PRESSED HER HANDS TO HER FOREHEAD. IT HAD BEEN A LONG WEEK, and it was one she hoped to forget very soon. She'd already been flustered when that mysterious man had saved her back at the bar, and then she had gone and completely embarrassed herself in front of him only a few days later. Leah couldn't even quite explain to herself why she had felt so humiliated. He was the one who had stepped in front of her as he turned around, and it hadn't been her fault that she'd bumped into him. She'd been so preoccupied with her grocery shopping, trying to remember everything she needed, that she hadn't even noticed him until she'd already carried on an entire conversation with his tot. Now there was a reason to be embarrassed. Leah didn't know anything about kids, and yet she had stopped and talked to that little guy like he was an old friend.

It had been weird and awkward, and she was doing her best to throw herself into her work. Living in an apartment over her office made for an easy commute to work, and she headed down the stairs Wednesday morning to put in her online hours and check her email.

A request popped up almost as soon as she logged on. A woman in Phoenix wanted to know if she should change jobs. Leah flipped on her webcam and smiled, prepared to put her mind in the right place to help her client. Video chats never gave her quite the same connection she got from meeting someone in person, but it was nice to be able to help people from all over the world.

"I think my husband might not be happy in our marriage anymore," the woman on the other end explained. She had identified herself as Vivian, although Leah knew that probably wasn't her real name. "He seems to be losing interest."

Leah shuffled a deck of tarot cards as she reached out mentally to this woman. "Even the best of relationships can be difficult," she said softly. "But we'll see what we can find out. Would you like to tell me why you think your husband isn't happy?"

Most people imagined that simply because she was psychic, she would instantly know everything about their lives. It happened occasionally, when she had the chance to touch someone who carried particularly powerful energies with them. Pete from the bar was a good example. But it wasn't always that clear, and the more she knew about a person, the easier it was to give them an accurate reading. Leah never pressured anyone to reveal details, but they almost always wanted to.

"Well, let's see." Vivian looked down at her hands. Her webcam only gave a fuzzy picture, but Leah could just make out the small apartment behind her. "He works all the time these days. It used to be that he'd come home right after work, but now he always has extra meetings or paperwork he has to do, and he doesn't get home until after dinner."

"Have you tried talking to him about it?" Leah began laying out her cards. Sometimes, people just wanted someone to listen to their problems. They didn't necessarily need a psychic to know they had issues that needed to be resolved, and they were too embarrassed to go to those they knew personally.

Vivian shifted in her chair. "Yes, but he always says I think about things too much and that I shouldn't worry. He just blows me off."

"I see." Leah felt the doors of her mind opening, letting her understand the elements of life and the universe that most people didn't have access to. She reached out across the miles to Vivian, and it didn't matter that Leah didn't know her physical address or her real name. This woman was calling to her for help, and she was able to answer.

But just as she was about to understand the truth of her client's plight, the doors shut. And they did it with such ferocity, she thought she could hear them slam, and she jumped in her chair at the noise.

"What is it?" Vivian asked nervously. "What's wrong?"

"It's nothing," Leah assured her. "I'm just having a little bit of an off day."

"Oh," the woman breathed. "I thought you might have seen something terrible in the cards."

Leah smiled. "Forgive me. I might be a psychic, but I'm still human. I didn't mean to frighten you." With no direct access to her client's energy, she focused on the cards. Sometimes they were just a showpiece, but right now, they were going to save her. "The Temperance card is in the most prominent position. This is a symbol of coming together, of two forces working together as one."

Vivian bit her lip. "Does that mean my husband and I will be okay?"

Leah was nothing if not honest, especially when it came to her clients. "Well, there are different ways to interpret this card. It can mean two people working together, such as yourself and your husband. But we can also look at it as you confronting the inner parts of yourself that you haven't been willing to bring out into the light."

"I don't understand."

"Have you always had fears that your husband would leave you?"

Her client started to shake her head, but she stopped. "Yes, to be honest. I've been cheated on before, and even though I felt like I could trust him, I was always worried that he would turn out to be like the rest of them."

"Your fears can manifest themselves if you concentrate on them too much, or at the very least, it can seem that they're manifesting. It might be that everything in your relationship is fine, but your worries make you concentrate on everything that's gone wrong. You need to sit down and really talk to him. Not right when he's come in the door or when you only have a little bit of time, but when you can really take the time to understand each other. Let him know how you feel. I have a feeling that he's not just brushing you off when he says everything is fine."

"You really think so?" Vivian had tears in her eyes.

"I really do." It was frustrating to not be able to give the fullest psychic experience possible, but Leah knew it was at least more genuine than what Vivian would have gotten if she had gone to someone else. There were plenty of frauds out there, and no one had a way of distinguishing who was real and who was just a paid actor.

She bid Vivian the best of luck and clicked off the chat window, not even paying attention to how much she had earned from their conversation. Money was great, but she was just glad that she had been able to help someone. The shutting down of her mind, though, *that* was disturbing.

Leah had the chance to redeem herself when a woman walked into her office. She was young, probably in her early twenties, and she glanced nervously over her shoulder when the door shut behind her.

"Come on in," Leah called from her desk. She stood up and came around, walking into the foyer. She had done her best to make the office feel warm and welcoming, like a trip to the spa instead of some voodoo tent full of smoke. There were a few patrons who had gone away disappointed when Leah hadn't appeared with a crystal ball and wearing a scarf around her head, but most people seemed to appreciate it. "What can I do for you?"

"I just, um, I want to know a few things." She looked at the door again.

"It's okay." The aura of fear was highly charged around this woman. She was genuinely scared, but not of Leah. "Why don't you come back here where things are more private?" Leah led her behind a partition wall and gestured for her to have a seat on a plush couch. "Start by telling me your name."

"Josey." She pulled her pale brown hair over her shoulder and wrung it between her hands. "I had a friend who told me I should come to you. Can you tell me what you charge?"

"It all depends on how much time we spend together and how in-depth we need to go, but here's a price list that should give you a general idea. You don't have to pay anything until we're done." She handed over the list, knowing that Josey wouldn't walk out without paying. No one had yet.

The new client glanced over it and nodded. "Okay. Well, I'll try to make it quick. Can you tell me if I'm in danger?"

Leah hadn't been surprised by this question, and she didn't need to be a psychic to know it was coming. She sat down across from her and reached out her hand. "Give me your hand, and I'll see what I can find out."

The young woman looked at her doubtfully. "No crystal ball?"

"Only when I need it, but I get the best results when I can actually touch someone or an object that belongs to them. Scientists call is psychometry, others refer to it as The Touch. You can call it whatever you'd like, but it seems to help." She smiled, hoping she could make this poor girl relax a little.

"Left or right?"

"It doesn't matter."

Josey set her hand inside Leah's and waited. Leah could feel her heartbeat fluttering in her wrist, and she closed her eyes. She could only hope that she didn't have the same experience she'd had with Vivian. It had been easy enough to save the day with the tarot cards for an online reading, but that would be more difficult in person. Besides, if she couldn't get a good reading from touching the client's own hand, then she really wasn't as good as she thought she was.

She took a deep breath and let her body relax. Josey's energy just needed to link into her own, and then she would know everything. She rested the fingertips of her left hand gently on the young woman's palm and supported her hand with her right. There were walls Leah put up throughout her normal day to block out the psychic energy that would barrage her otherwise. She slowly brought them down, one by one, to allow Josey in.

The first thing she understood was that she was being honest about her name. People tended to do that more often when they came in. The next thing she knew was that Josey's fears were real. She saw an image of a man, tall and broad, but not in a pleasant way like the guy from the bar and the grocery store. He was a hulk, and he carried a menacing air about him that would make anyone worry. He was fearsome enough that Leah nearly let go of Josey's hand, but she couldn't just leave her new client to deal with this on her own. There was a distinct sense of being followed, and it made the fine hairs on the back of Leah's neck stand up.

"There's a man," she murmured. "He's big, with dark hair and a scar on his cheek. He knows you well, but he's not friendly."

"I knew it. It's my ex. He's been stalking me." By the sound of Josey's voice, she was crying.

Leah nodded. "That sounds about right. He's angry with you, and you feel that he might have a right to be." The visions changed, and Leah could see Josey with a different man. "You cheated on him?"

Josey yanked her hand back, and Leah opened her eyes. The young woman's face was red and blotchy, tears streaming down her cheeks. "I didn't mean for it to happen. I just...I hadn't been happy, and I knew he wasn't either, and then Dylan took me out for dinner..."

Leah still felt the terrifying vibrations she had picked up from Josey. She didn't like them, and she wanted to flick her fingers across her skin as though she could get rid of the sensation that way. But she reached out for her hand once again. "I'm not sure that's the important part. There's more. Let's try this one more time."

But Josey kept her hands clasped to her stomach, and she had sunk so far into the couch that she looked like a small, frightened child. "I don't think I want to. I came here on a whim, but I thought you would just be some scam artist who would tell me everything would be okay. Now I'm not so sure I want to know any more."

Pressing her lips together, Leah tried to think of the best thing to say next. She would have to tread carefully, and she had a strong and scary feeling that it was vital she finish this reading. There was something going on between Josey and this man in the vision. "I understand. The truth can be hard to take. I'm not here to judge you; I only want to help. You're scared, and maybe between the two of us we can figure out how to keep you safe."

Her client jutted out her chin and shoved herself up from the couch. "Forget it. I've got a license for a gun. I'll be fine." She stormed out onto the street without another word.

Leah put her head in her hands, wondering what had gone wrong. She only had a few seconds to think about it before the bell over the door chimed, indicating that someone had just come in. Autumn poked her head around the partition wall a moment later. "I take it that reading didn't go well?"

"How did you know? Was it the tears on her face, or the way she ran out of here like I was the one after her?"

"She'd stopped in at our shop first and said she was looking for a talisman of protection. I gave her one, but I also sent her over here. I thought it might help if you could see if she was in any real danger." The Enchanted Elm was just across the street from Leah's shop, which made it easy for the women to check in on each other throughout the day or head out for lunch dates.

Leah nodded soberly, her eyes feeling heavy and tired as she stared at the hardwood floor. "I think she probably is, but she didn't give me a chance to find out for sure. Hell, I might not have been able to figure it out, anyway. It's like I've got this fog over my brain that won't go away. I had an online client who was almost completely closed off to me, and that woman that was just here is the first person not to pay me. I tried to work on my book this morning, and I just stared at the screen." She wanted to go back upstairs, crawl into bed, and pretend that the day had never happened.

Autumn frowned. "That doesn't sound like you." She was dressed more like a stereotypical witch today, with a long dark skirt and her hair down, but she still carried the air of a woman who was always cool and confident.

It made Leah a little jealous for once, since she wasn't anywhere close to feeling that way. "I know. I think it's the divorce. It didn't affect me at all while we were still going through the court proceedings, but now that it's official, it's like I can't function. I need something that will boost me back into my old talents again."

"What about the guy from the bar? I know you said you aren't ready for a new relationship, but a little fling might do you some good." She gave Leah a cat-like smile and ran her fingertips across the turquoise cabochon of her necklace.

Leah shook her head and launched herself to her feet, pacing nervously. "No! I actually ran into him in the grocery store the other day. It's weird, because I feel such a pull toward him. Every cell in my body wants me to just throw myself at him, but I can't. He even asked me out to dinner, and I literally ran out of the store."

"You should be listening to those inner voices," Autumn reminded her. "I hope you aren't staying away from this guy for Victor's sake. That asshole doesn't deserve you."

"No, but he has been blowing up my phone all week." Leah picked up her cell from the corner of her desk and poked at the screen. "Just look at all these text messages."

Autumn raised an eyebrow. "I'm glad to see that at least you aren't replying. But really, what's so wrong with this handsome stranger from the bar? You should have had dinner with him. It would be free food, if nothing else."

"I've been trying to figure that out." Leah imagined herself at a table for two in a dimly-lit restaurant with that handsome man looking at her in the candlelight. It would be wonderful and romantic. He might reach across the table and take her hand...But then she would have to tell him all about how she was a psychic—which most guys didn't seem to appreciate—and that she had just gotten divorced. "I think it's just that I have too much baggage. I'm dragging all this extra weight around, and I don't want him or anyone else to see it."

"Leah, look." Autumn put her hands on Leah's shoulders and looked her square in the eye. "Everyone has baggage. It doesn't matter if they have supernatural powers or if they're just regular people working office jobs. Everyone has something from their past that they're bringing along with them. And I'm not saying you have to go marry the guy. Just have dinner. Have fun. Do it for yourself, so you know you're still alive somewhere in there. You don't even know how much baggage he might be carrying himself."

Tears rimmed Leah's eyes. There was nothing better than knowing someone always had her back. Even when she wasn't doing a good job of looking out for herself, someone else was. She sniffled and dabbed at the corners of her eyes. "Well, he does have a kid, so maybe you're right."

"There ya go!" Autumn smiled, showing her straight, white teeth. "Just hang in there. You'll find yourself again. It's perfectly normal to feel a little off when you've gone through something like this. I think people like us feel it even more than others. Besides, you'd better get your head back in the game, since we have a séance planned for the weekend."

"Oh, that's right!" Leah instantly felt guilty for nearly forgetting. She had met Autumn and Summer in college, and they had instantly bonded over their powers that normal humans didn't seem to understand. But there had also been Naomi, a beautiful girl who didn't fit in very well with society herself. She had the power to shift forms, but a terrible accident meant that she was no longer among the living. "I'll be there."

The phone rang, and she excused herself. "This is Leah, how can I help you?"

"I'd like to schedule a reading, please." It was a man's voice, and a deep one. It seemed familiar, but Leah shook off the notion. She was just getting paranoid after that weird reading with Josey.

"Okay. What day of the week works best for you? I have a few openings tomorrow morning." She glanced over her appointment calendar. It wasn't nearly as full as she would like.

"Actually, I was hoping for something in the evening. I'd like you to come to my house, maybe Friday at six."

It was such an odd request that it took Leah a moment to respond.

"I don't normally do that sort of thing. I would have to charge my normal hourly rate along with another fee for traveling."

"Money's not an object."

"Go ahead and give me your address, and we'll go from there." It was quite possible that this client was too far away, and she would just need to offer an online consultation. Leah scribbled down the address as the man on the phone gave it to her, and she turned to make a face at Autumn. It was right there in town, and it was in the nicest neighborhood. Only rich bankers, doctors, and entrepreneurs lived over there. "I think I can make that work. I'll be there at six on Friday."

She hung up and stared wide-eyed at Autumn. "Can you believe that? Some rich guy wants to talk to me so badly he's asked me to come to his house! I've never really done house calls before, but if this works out, I might just make it a regular thing." She could just imagine all the personal items she might get a chance to touch while there. If this didn't make for a good reading, then she would just have to close up shop and go work in retail.

# 6

"I APPRECIATE YOU DOING THIS FOR ME ON SUCH SHORT NOTICE. I HOPE you didn't have any plans for tonight." Holden welcomed Beau inside and closed the door behind him.

Beau ran a hand through his blonde hair, which was slicked back and matched his five o'clock shadow. "No, not really. I was just planning on spending time with Elliott, so Finn will be a welcome addition. What are you doing tonight, anyway?"

Holden picked up Finn's bag and handed it to his friend. "I've got an appointment with a psychic."

The blonde man put his tongue in his cheek as he thought. "You mean like the people who wave their hands over crystal balls and tell you the future?"

"The very same," Holden said with a nod. "I'm hoping the experience might be something like the prophets we used to consult back home. Most of the ones I found only offered phone calls or online experiences, but I made special arrangements with a local psychic since I wanted to do it in person."

"Still trying to find some semblance of Charok on this planet, huh? Good luck with that. You ought to just focus on how things are now, and not worry about it so much."

"Maybe so, but this whole ordeal of finding my mate is driving me crazy. I don't want Finn to be without a mother; it's not right. There's one woman I've met who might be the right one, but—"

"The one from the bar?" Beau grinned, his blue eyes sparkling. "I think I see what's going on here."

"Oh, really? Then why don't you tell me?" Holden folded his arms in front of his chest, challenging his friend.

"You think she's hot, and you're looking for a good excuse to bang her. I might not have been on this world or in this body for very long, but I'm starting to understand how humans work. You don't need permission from some psychic, Holden, just go for it."

"For your information, that's not the whole story." Holden had to admit that he wanted to see what Leah was like under her clothing— more than anything. She was the most tantalizing female he'd met since they'd made their escape to Earth, and everything about her was intriguing. But it wasn't pure lust, and he knew it. "There's something that happens to me every time I'm around her. I want to shift so badly, I can barely contain it. That's what was going on when we first walked into The Parlor, except I didn't know it yet. Once I was face-to-face with her, I thought I might sprout wings, snatch her up, and fly off with her. I had this incredible need to protect her, no matter what the cost." His blood still boiled in his veins every time he thought of that greasy dirtbag trying to grab her.

Beau's look grew serious. "Do you think that means she's your mate?"

"I don't know," Holden admitted. "But I have to find out one way or another. I'm hoping the psychic can help."

Picking up Finn, Beau looked down at the child and clucked his tongue against his teeth. "I wish I could tell you. The only thing I know is that this would all be a lot easier if we could just have stayed drag-ons." He turned and headed out the door just as a woman was coming up the sidewalk.

Holden had been so busy talking to Beau that he hadn't been paying attention when the new car had arrived. He cursed himself for it; that never would have happened if he had been in dragon form. But the psychic was there, and it was time to get started. He stepped onto the threshold to wave her inside, but stopped dead in his tracks as she came closer.

*Leah.*

It was impossible, but there was no mistaking that dark, curly hair or the way her mouth tipped up when she smiled. The smile faded when she noticed the child in Beau's arms, and she was just about to say something when Beau pointed over his shoulder. "He's in there." Confused, Leah looked behind him at Holden.

His heartbeat sped up, thundering his blood through his veins and shoved the breath from his lungs. He clutched at the doorknob as he held it, feeling the metal heat up in his hand. For a moment, he wondered what she was doing there; she couldn't have just tracked him down. But when he saw the dark blue velvet bag she carried, he knew there could be no other explanation.

Leah was the psychic he had hired.

She stopped on the edge of the porch, staring at him as if he were a monster. "Am I at the right address?"

At least she wasn't running away this time. "You are. Come in."

Leah hesitated and looked down at her feet as though expecting them to make the decision for her. One of them finally stepped forward, and she came in and turned to face him. "I have to tell you I had no idea you were my client." Her throat worked up and down nervously.

"Aren't you the psychic?" he asked with a smile. She didn't see his humor, and he cleared his throat. Holden closed the door slowly, not wanting her to think he was trapping her in his house. He wanted to, if it might give him a chance to see where this was going. It was absurd to think they would just keep running into each other like this if it didn't mean anything. "I can see how this must look, but I didn't know it was you when I was making the call. I'm just looking for some answers."

Her hands clutched at the handle of her bag, and she forced a smile. Even when it wasn't genuine, it was beautiful. "I can help with that. Is there somewhere we can sit down?"

Holden could feel the nervous energy emanating from her skin as he moved past her to lead the way to his study. It vibrated against his bones and threatened to send his scales racing to the outside of his skin. "We should be able to make ourselves comfortable in here. Is there anything you require?"

"I should have everything." She stepped into the study, her eyes widening for a moment as she took in the rows of bookshelves and the comfortable leather furniture. "I just need a place where I can sit across from you, and maybe a little bit of table space if we use tarot cards."

"I can make that work." Holden picked up the coffee table and moved it to the other side of the room, pushing two of the comfortable chairs closer together. "Like this?"

Leah blushed, realizing she'd been staring at his muscular frame, and nodded. Setting her bag down next to one of the chairs, she looked up at him with those wide, blue eyes. "I've been so rude. I haven't even asked your name."

He was so focused on her beauty that he almost didn't hear. Her skin glowed with a dewy radiance that made him want to reach out and run his fingers down her cheek. Instead, he curled his fists at his sides. "Holden. Holden Reid. It's nice to officially meet you." He sat down across from her, feeling the way their bodies seemed to magnetize toward each other. Sitting back didn't seem to counteract it at all, but made him want to pull her onto his lap and run his hands over her body. He'd never thought of the human form being so attractive, but she was proving him wrong.

"I'm Leah Watson, although I guess you at least knew the first part." She blushed again, and the flame of color spread to the tips of her ears. "I have several different ways of doing readings, but the most effective way is by touch. There are residual energies on people and on their belongings that allow me to see into their lives. Whatever you're comfortable with works for me, but the best way is if you give me your hand."

Holden would have thought it was just a tactic to touch him if she hadn't been so professional, but he didn't mind either way. He gladly put his hand in hers, watching her face as she rested her fingertips on him and closed her eyes. Back home, he had always been attracted to dragons with the shiniest scales or the shapeliest wings, but it was different finding the beauty in a human. He studied the curve of her cheekbones and her neck, the way a lock of hair fell across her forehead, and the way she seemed to completely relax herself while she was doing her job.

"Can you tell me what kind of answers you're looking for?" Her gentle voice broke the deep silence that had settled over the room. "I don't want to just give you a bunch of random information."

Clearing his throat uncomfortably, Holden realized just how awkward this was. He had asked a psychic to come to his house to help him make a decision about a woman, and she was that very same woman! "I have some decisions to make, very important ones about my future. I just need some advice on that."

"Is it about your son? I can see that you love him very much." Leah smiled, her eyes still closed.

He wanted to make her smile again, but he wasn't sure how. "Sort of."

"If you can ask a specific question, I may be able to do a better job of helping you find the answers."

There was no way he could tell her the truth, not about anything. If she knew he thought she was destined to be his mate, she would think he was crazy. And she sure as hell didn't need to know his true nature. "I can't really disclose that."

"That's fine. I'll just do my best." She was silent again for another long minute, and the touch of her fingertips was a warm one. "You've been on a very long journey, but you're trying to settle down. I can see that you have your family on the forefront of your mind, but you aren't sure how to proceed."

Holden leaned forward. She really was like the prophets back on Charok; maybe even better. He had always suspected they got their information on their clients well before their appointments, and there was no true information to be had on him here on Earth.

"And I also see..." Leah trailed off, her brow furrowing. Her muscles gave a quick spasm that lurched her ever so slightly backward in her chair, but she didn't let go of his hand. "I'm sorry. I'm seeing some very strange things that don't make sense. I'm trying to sort them out."

"Just tell me," he encouraged.

"I'm seeing...dragons. They must be symbolic of something, maybe a past that has come back to haunt you or fear of the future."

"That could make sense." *Shit.* He hadn't thought this through, but he hadn't needed to when he was expecting a stranger to show up at his door. If some random person he didn't know saw dragons while doing a fortune-telling session, then he could easily laugh it off. But this was Leah, the woman who seemed to possess him without even knowing it. He didn't want to lie to her.

Leah's mouth tightened, her lips pursing together attractively. "There are a lot of dragons, and they're in a massive cave. Some of them are dying. They're—" She yanked her hands back and opened her eyes, breaking their connection. Tears glistened on her lashes, and she swiped at them quickly. "I'm sorry. I don't understand what any of that was."

"It's alright."

"No, it's really not. I've been a little off lately. I'm not sure what the matter is. I would offer to give you a tarot reading instead, but I'm worried it would go just as badly. I've never seen anything like what I just saw, and I think it only proves that I need a break for a while. Again, I'm so sorry. No charge." She snatched up her bag and shot to her feet.

Holden rose and reached for her arm as she turned away. "Wait!"

Leah paused, but she only turned her head partway over her shoulder so she wouldn't have to look at him fully.

"Can you at least just tell me what it was you saw?"

She shrugged, but she didn't try to pull her arm from his grasp. "It's crazy."

"I want to hear it anyway."

Leah turned her head completely away from him, only allowing him to see the back of her curly head and fine contours of her neck against the dark violet tone of her dress. "There were a lot of dragons, beautiful ones with shining scales, spikey heads, and expansive wings. But some of them were sick, and I think they were dying. They lay on the floor of a cave, their chins resting in the dirt without the strength to hold up their heads any longer. Their wings were draped lifelessly over their bodies like old leather blankets, and their eyes were beginning to glaze over. They weren't dead yet, but they would be soon. Even those who appeared to be healthy thought they would probably be next. I'm so sorry. I've never seen anything quite like that. I'm sure I sound like a complete nutjob to you."

"Not at all." He still had a hold of her wrist, and he could feel her heart thumping away gently under his thumb. "I think it might even have been helpful."

Looking up at him now, she narrowed her eyes and studied his face. "Either you're far too eager for some answers, or you're just being really nice."

"Can't I be both?"

"Not if I gave you a poor reading. You came to me because you wanted to understand something about your life. I've let you down."

"Not really." If only she could know just what spending this time together had meant. His wings throbbed underneath his shoulder blades, begging to come out and show off.

What he understood now more than anything was that he wasn't ready to let her go yet. His senses had been on fire all evening. He had no right to think of her as belonging to him, and yet the thought of her taking one step out of his house drove him crazy. His teeth sharpened in his mouth as his body tried to betray him once again. Holden bit down hard to keep them under control and didn't speak until he was completely normal again. "May I ask you to stay for dinner?"

She turned to glance at the door, and then looked back up at him. "I wouldn't want to impose."

"It's already made. It's been in the slow-cooker all day."

"And I thought I was supposed to be the psychic."

"Is that a yes?"

Leah bit her lip, and Holden wanted to bite it for her. "I suppose," she said slowly, "I could do that."

"Good. Have a seat, and I'll just run in the kitchen to check on things." Holden's body surged underneath his skin, and he forced himself to walk casually into the other room and lift the lid on the slow-cooker. He'd never made this particular roast recipe before. It might be absolutely awful, but there wasn't much choice. Holden finally had her here in his house, and she wanted to stay. He could tell that she wouldn't have if she didn't want to. Leah was a smart woman, and she would have found an excuse. If she'd run away from him in the grocery store, then she could have run away from him here. He pulled two plates out of the cabinet, careful not to crush them in his grip.

## 7

She didn't know what the hell she was thinking accepting a dinner invitation from a client. Yes, she did: she thought she might figure out why the universe kept pushing the two of them together. It was her job, after all, to listen to what the universe had to say. There was a distinct possibility that Holden—whose name alone was incredibly hot—had figured out who she was and hired her specifically to get her into his home. But he couldn't have planned out their other two meetings.

And she couldn't deny that she wanted to get to know him. *All* of him. He was handsome and mysterious, not that any of that really mattered. It wasn't like she was ready to start dating yet, but it was worth exploring. Autumn, at least, would have agreed with her.

Holden reappeared only a few minutes later. She couldn't help but rake her eyes down his body, taking in the well-fitted sport coat over a button-down shirt and jeans. He was the kind of guy who could save her in a bar, but he was classy when he wanted to be. "Join me in the dining room. I've got everything ready."

She followed him into the spacious room with a large oak table. It had been set with fine china, a chilled bottle of Chardonnay, and a steaming platter for the roast. Leah raised an eyebrow. "Are you sure you didn't have this planned out?"

He twisted his mouth, a good look on his full lips, and tipped his head. "I promise, I didn't. Nor did I mean to run into you the other day. You can blame my son for that one." He pulled out a chair and gestured for her to sit.

Leah couldn't remember the last time someone had been such a gentleman, but she supposed she shouldn't expect anything less from a man who would throw himself in danger's way for her. "He's quite the cutie. I'm not usually the kind of person who stops and talks to children in the middle of a store. He was just so insistent when he kept pointing at me, and it sounded like he was trying to say my name. I couldn't resist." Holden poured her a glass of wine, and she eagerly took a sip. She was saying too much already.

"Finn knows who he likes." Her host poured a glass for himself and replaced the wine in the bucket of ice. "He'd probably be sitting here chatting your ear off, but he's spending the night with my...um, cousin."

It seemed so prearranged. How could Holden have brought her to his house, scheduled a babysitter, and had dinner for two ready to go without the real prospect of a dinner guest? Sure, he probably didn't want his son sitting on his lap while he got a psychic reading, and he had to make dinner for himself anyway. But chilled wine? And china? On a whim, Leah reached out and picked up the wine bottle on the pretense of reading the label.

"It's from a local winery. Do you like it?" Holden had pulled the plate of roast toward himself and was carefully slicing it with a sharp, thin blade.

Leah let her defenses down, although there were very few of them left to her at this point. She kept her hand wrapped firmly around the neck of the bottle, right where Holden had touched it. The energies there were nervous, excited, but not malicious. If her abilities hadn't left her completely and she was right, then Holden wasn't trying to do anything but get to know her. She couldn't hold that against him. "It's very good."

He laid a slice of meat on her plate and passed her a bowl of gravy. "If the food is half as good, then we'll be lucky. It's a new recipe I haven't tried yet."

Leah took a tentative bite, her eyes widening in surprise as the tender meat melted in her mouth. "You made this?"

"You look so shocked." Holden grinned and took a bite himself. He chewed thoughtfully. "It's not bad."

"Not bad? It's amazing." Leah eagerly took another bite, trying to remind herself that it was just dinner, and there was no obligation with it. She didn't need to feel grateful, nor intoxicated by the good company. And she had to admit that Holden was good company. She'd never met someone who was such a gentleman, and Victor's few attempts at cooking had only resulted in smoke damage.

"You give me too much credit. I've been experimenting in the kitchen, but I'm not always pleased. This, at least, is palatable."

It might have been the wine, but Leah was starting to get that same strange feeling she'd had when she was at the bar, the first time she'd met Holden. Her mind didn't want to stay on track, and her body felt simultaneously relaxed and alive. It seemed impossible, like the kind of thing that only happened in a dream and couldn't be put into words upon waking. But she liked it, and the more she glanced across the table at Holden, the more she felt it. They chatted idly, discussing how adorable Finn was or how nice the weather had been. It might have been inane conversation with anyone else, but somehow, it meant something as long as she was sharing these words with him.

"Would you care for dessert?"

Leah half-expected him to whip out a homemade white chocolate raspberry cheesecake and act like it was simply a coincidence, but she didn't have any room in her stomach to find out. "I'm too full, but thank you." It was time for her to leave. She'd done her reading, she'd stayed to have dinner, and it was time to end this strange encounter and return to normal life. She stood up and pushed her chair in. "Look, I'd really like to apologize to you for that odd reading."

"You already did," Holden pointed out, "and you didn't need to. It's fine."

"I want you to know that you can schedule another one anytime you want, and of course it will be free of charge. I'd like to make it up to you. Just give me a little time to get myself together. I've been going through some things, but I'll get past it and then I should be fine again." She was stumbling over her words, feeling awkward. Their meal had been amazing, and she'd managed to forget what an idiot she'd made of herself, but it was all coming back swiftly now that she was standing on her own two feet.

Holden took her gently by the elbow and she followed him out of the dining room back into the study where her bag still sat next to a chair. His brow was furrowed over his eyes as though he was in deep thought, and it wasn't until he'd stood there for a moment on the large rug in the middle of the room that he turned to look at her again. "If you really want to make it up to me, then let me do a reading on you."

Blinking up at him, Leah tried to wrap her mind around what he was saying. "Are you telling me you're a psychic?" Her mind raced. Was this some sort of dirty trick? Did he think she was a fraud and he was trying to expose her? She'd heard of those sorts of things before.

"Not at all," he assured her. Holden took her hand in his, looking down at their fingers, and then took her other hand as well. They stood face to face, and when he raised his head to stare into her eyes the room around them melted away. "I just think I know some things that might help you."

She had come this far, and there was no point in giving up now. Leah swallowed nervously. "Okay." Her palms tingled with energy, and she felt that if she looked down, she would see blue fire crackling between them. This man was something else, but she didn't know what yet.

"You feel like the universe is trying to tell you something, but you aren't sure if you're hearing it correctly. You know there's got to be some sort of connection between us if we keep running into each other like this, but it's just so strange that you don't quite know how to handle it." His voice was gentle and smooth, the whisper of a breeze through the trees in a forest. His hands were strong enough that he could have crushed her fingers inside his own, and yet he held them like delicate flowers.

"How did you know all of that?" she breathed, feeling their bodies grow slowly together. It might only have been a millimeter, but it felt like a light year.

"Because I've been feeling the exact same way. When I saw you at The Parlor, it was like something clicked inside me. I was drawn to you, but it didn't make sense because I had no idea who you were. I wanted to absolutely pulverize that guy who tried to hurt you, and I probably would have if I'd let my instincts take over."

Leah could understand. She would have thrown herself at him and let him do whatever he wanted, but she had gotten into her own head and convinced herself that none of it mattered.

"Then I ran into you at the grocery store," Holden continued, "and I thought it was sheer chance. But you're here now, and I don't want to see you leave." He leaned forward and pressed his forehead against hers, closing his eyes. "I need you, Leah, in a way I can't explain."

Her heart throbbed, pumping blood throughout her body but not putting out the fire that Holden had lit inside it. Leah's lips worked of their own avail, tipping up so that they touched his. It was slow at first, tentative and sensual as they explored each other. He smelled of cologne, seasonings, and fire, and she hardly wanted to exhale again because she only wanted to breathe him in.

Holden's lips convinced her to open up to him, to let their tongues get to know each other, to solidify the fact that this wasn't just a mistake. His fingers moved from her hands to her hips, twining around her waist and pulling her close so that their bodies were pressed together.

Leah could feel the hard muscles underneath his shirt, and she knew the urgency from his mouth was a reflection of her own. With her hands freed, she let them slowly travel up his arms to his firm shoulders before they curled in the ringlets of his hair. Her thumb measured the hard angle of his jaw and the stubble that clung there, and the unrelenting urge to be close to him had completely taken over her. Leah needed him, wanted him, had to have him.

He had claimed to have no psychic powers, but he might as well have. He tipped his head back and broke their kiss. Holden looked into her eyes, his hands still wrapped around her waist. "Say you'll stay with me tonight," he whispered, his lips only a fraction of an inch away from hers. "Let's see what fate is really trying to tell us."

She could have run. Though he had his hands on her, Leah knew Holden wouldn't keep her there against her will. She might not have been able to get a good reading on him, but that much was clear. She could easily have broken away, grabbed her bag, and left.

But she couldn't. Not because Holden wouldn't allow her to, but because she didn't want to. There was a firestorm in her soul, and she couldn't put it out without his help. Leah pressed her lips to his once again, confirming her answer.

Holden took it, his insanely strong arms scooping her off the floor. He carried her out of the study toward the front of the house, and then turned up a wide set of stairs that led to the second story. Leah focused on the squareness of his jaw, the fine dusting of coppery hair that hinted at what was underneath his shirt, and the way she felt as if she were floating while she was in his arms. She felt like a goddess being sped to the top of a mountain by her hero, and she reveled in it.

When they reached a room at the end of the upstairs hall, Holden set her gently on her feet. He kissed her again, passionately, brutally, expressing his need as he slowly lifted the hem of her dress up and over her head. The skin on his hands was rough, but their touch was tender as he skimmed them back down her nearly-naked body.

She could feel the hardness in his jeans, and she wanted it. Leah felt her bra snap off as she undid his belt buckle and reached for the buttons of his shirt, splaying her fingers out over the wide chest that she exposed. Yet another rush of adrenaline hit her as she took in the wide chest and his finely sculpted abs, all covered with that haze of fine hairs that were so tantalizing.

As their naked bodies pressed together, she thought she might peak right then and there. His trim waist, firm buttocks, and muscular legs were like a marble statue. His manhood was hard and demanding, eager for her, and she wrapped her hands around his shaft.

Holden moaned, bending his head to pull her nipple into his mouth. "I don't think you know what you do to me."

"I think I do." Because he did it to her as well. This stranger, this man who shouldn't have been anything more than a passing acquaintance for all the time they had known each other, was her entire existence. Her core surged in anticipation, but Leah wanted this to last as long as possible. She dropped to her knees before him, looking briefly up and catching the arch of surprise in his eyebrows before she ran the tip of her tongue down the length of his erection, teasing him as she licked its head.

He held himself against the bedpost with one hand, and the other curled into a fist and slammed into the mattress as she swallowed him.

Leah wanted only to please him, and she stroked her tongue up and down as she sucked. Holden's hips surged forward, encouraging her, and she opened her jaws and pressed down with her lips to increase the pressure. Her hunger for him increased, knowing she was turning him on. She never wanted to stop as long as she knew she was bringing him pleasure.

But Holden wouldn't have it. He brought her to her feet and gently pushed her back onto the mattress, running his hands up her legs as he set her ankles on his shoulders. He looked into her eyes as he entered her, boring into her soul as their bodies melded. His cock was thick and hard inside her, filling her up and satisfying a need that she'd had for such a long time.

Leah sighed, letting her head fall back and surrendering her body to him. Holden brought his hand around her thigh and laid his thumb on her clit, rubbing in small circles that slowly built up speed. Her insides turned to molten metal as she formed around him, her muscles clenching and releasing as he pushed her towards her ecstasy. Leah panted her euphoria as he relentlessly gave her everything she needed and more, and she let out a cry as the seduction was complete.

Holden watched with fascination as she came, his eyes alight. He tipped his head just enough to plant a quick kiss on her calf, then moved his hands up to envelop her breasts. She welcomed the heat of his touch as he stroked inside her, the hardness of his body under her legs as he worked. Her core still surged with rapture, aftershocks of alternating tension and tranquility, brought on by days of thinking about this man. She threw her head back as another spasm racked her body, and it increased as Holden's hands moved down and tightened their grip on her ribcage.

"Leah..." he breathed.

Her name on his lips was like a beacon, calling to her to join him. She felt the crushing tidal wave of pure pleasure washing over her, taking her breath. "Holden!"

His girth expanded, and he grunted as he pounded into her harder. A roar bellowed up from the depths as he filled her, his body surging against hers. He pumped away until he was empty, draining every last bit of himself into her.

Leah fought to catch her breath, having had it completely taken away by such an intense session of lovemaking. Holden whisked the covers back and moved her up so that her head was on the pillow. When he climbed in next to her, he wrapped his arms around her and pulled her close. She expected him to fall asleep, but he brought his head down and wrapped his lips around her nipple. His tongue flicked the hard bud as he suckled.

"You keep doing that and I'll need you to do this all over again," she warned, feeling that now-familiar escalation between her legs. "You're going to make me want to come again."

Without a word, Holden slid his hand down her abdomen, across her hips, and to the folds between her legs. She was still slick and hot from their pairing, and it only took his touch to make the pulses start up again. Leah brought her hand up to cradle the back of his head, pressing him to her breast as she clutched his hair between her fingers, her hips bucking as his fingers moved to please her. She cried out again at his generosity.

But Holden wasn't done yet. He moved on top of her, his hands holding him above her. With her knees bent and her feet flat against the sheets, Holden settled himself in the grip of her thighs and pushed inside, his member as hard as ever.

She widened her eyes, shocked that he was ready to go again, but not willing to argue with it. There was something about having this broad, sexy man on top of her, and she wrapped her legs around his waist. He plunged her depths, sliding ever deeper, and he threw his head back as he came once again. Leah welcomed him, her body tempestuous with everything he had given her. Finally done, he settled in next to her and kissed the hollow of her neck.

Leah couldn't stop the smile that took over her face. She had completely lost track of how many orgasms she'd had, and she didn't even bother trying to count them. Nothing mattered except the heat of Holden's body behind her.

## 8

HOLDEN STRETCHED AND GRINNED WITHOUT OPENING HIS EYES. THAT had by far been the most incredible thing he'd experienced since they'd come to Earth, other than being Finn's father. Never had he imagined he would be able to find so much pleasure in a human woman. Her soft skin, the texture of her hair, the brilliance in her eyes. She was just amazing. And that thing she had done while on her knees...Well, Xander hadn't told him about that during all his lectures about human behavior.

Everything about the way the night had gone had shown him that his instincts about Leah were on target. He had tried to deny it, feeling uncertain about taking on a human mate, but he couldn't possibly deny it now. It started with the fact that *she* was the psychic he had contacted, and that had certainly made him wonder why the two of them were being pushed together so much.

Then she'd given him that reading. Poor Leah thought she'd done something wrong and seen something that made no sense, but it had made all the sense in the world to him. The scene she had laid out before him was a familiar one, with his own dragon brothers and sisters dying all around him. That was the way he remembered Charok, and it wasn't pleasant, but it had shown him that Leah knew his truth. She didn't understand it, but she had still seen it.

After that, he'd had no choice but to invite her to stay for dinner. He wanted to dine with her, to talk with her, to have a chance to accidentally touch her hand. It was such an odd sensation, because no other women had that effect on him. Holden understood what the typical standards of beauty were, but a woman simply having large breasts or a nice smile hadn't been enough for him. Leah had both of those qualities, as well as several others, that drove him wild.

Once he had her in his home, he found that the wild, raging instincts that tried to take over him at the bar and the grocery store were eased. It was as though he had brought her home, and he no longer felt the unstoppable urge to protect her. He was eager for her, but calm. There was no need to shift form just to let out his energy.

Holden stretched, expanding his entire body and relishing the effect that deep sleep had on him. He was sure he'd always been sleeping with one eye open up until that point. Rolling over, he found that the sheets next to him were empty. Cold. Leah had been gone for quite some time.

That sense of panic set in instantly. If Leah was out there in the world, then he needed to go find her and bring her back to safety. He felt a shooting pain in his leg as his muscles fought with him, demanding that he change to his reptilian self in order to do a better job of guarding his woman.

But after a moment, he realized that she was still in the house. He couldn't hear her, but he swore he could still smell her perfume. His mind seemed to have a built-in radar for her, and she hadn't gone far. Sliding out of bed and dressing quickly in a pair of sweatpants and a t-shirt, he headed down the stairs.

Leah was sitting at the dining table. She'd thrown her dress back on, but her hair laid in a tousled dark cloud around her head. Cards had been spread out on the wooden surface before her, and she snapped up her head as soon as he walked in the room.

"You ready for breakfast?" Holden asked. He'd already gotten her to stay for twelve hours, and he was determined to make it even longer than that.

But her eyes were on fire. "Do you have something you need to tell me?"

He had been about to cross the room and lay his hand on her shoulder, but he checked himself. "What do you mean?"

Leah took a deep breath and sat back. "I woke up early this morning, way earlier than I normally do. I couldn't get back to sleep, and it wasn't long before I realized why. The fog that had come down over my abilities and left me so closed off had finally lifted. Every door was open, and I could see everything." She looked down at her hands. "I was really excited at first, but then I realized there was something going on that I needed to know about."

Holden took a tentative step forward. "Just tell me."

She gestured at the cards. "Every reading I do—every *single one*—tells me the same thing: that you aren't who you say you are. I didn't want to believe it. It was easier to think that I was still blocked and that my emotions were clouding my readings. But there's a big difference in the way things feel when I'm closed off and when I'm completely on it." Tears glistened in her eyes as she looked up at him, her fingertips shaking where they were poised over the cards on the table. "Please, Holden. Just tell me the truth right now and get it over with."

He pressed his lips together. "I haven't lied to you." He might not have come right out and explained that he was a dragon from another world who had been transported here with the help of a magical spell in order to help raise the last of his kind, but he hadn't denied it, either. He couldn't explain to her what he really was, not yet. She wouldn't believe him, and then he would lose his chance at ever being with her.

Leah picked up one of the cards and slammed it back down onto the table. "Then why do the cards tell me otherwise? And it's not just the cards; it's this thick feeling in the back of my skull that there's far more going on than I understand. I don't like that feeling, Holden. I can't handle it, and as a psychic, I can't just pretend everything is fine and move on."

"I don't know what to say." Holden floundered for the right words. He nearly asked her if her powers truly had come back or if she was just hoping they would, but he bit down on them before he let them out. Insulting her wasn't a good tactic.

"Then at least tell me what my vision about the dragons meant to you." She scooped up the cards into a rough stack, tapping them sharply on the table to straighten them. "I know it has something to do with that. It's the strangest symbolism I've ever seen, and probably the most real, and that just makes it even more disturbing."

"It's...private." What more could he say? It was true that the vision had meant something to him, but he couldn't possibly explain it. Being with a human was easy when he knew what he wanted, but it was much harder when she wanted something he couldn't give.

"Fine." Leah shoved the deck of cards into their box and chucked it into her bag. "I see how it is. You invite me to stay for dinner, get your tumble between the sheets, and then you're done with me. Maybe that's how you do things, Holden Reid, but I'm not interested in some shallow relationship where no one talks to each other." The tears she had been holding back now streamed down her cheeks, and she swiped at them angrily. With her bag in hand, she turned toward the front of the house.

"Now, wait a minute," he growled, moving ahead of her so that he was in the doorway of the dining room. He couldn't let her leave. He just *couldn't*. She was where she belonged. "That's not how this is. That wasn't just a tumble between the sheets."

"But you won't tell me what's going on," she challenged. "I know we haven't shared a whole lot. I don't know how long you've lived here, what you do for a living, or even what happened to Finn's mother, but I was willing to let all the heavy stuff wait. I can't now, not that I've seen what I've seen." She glared up at him, her eyes flashing both with tears and anger.

"You have no reason not to trust me, Leah. I haven't lied to you, and I would never hurt you. If you feel like I'm not who I say I am, then maybe it's just because we don't know each other very well yet. That makes perfect sense to me. And it doesn't mean we can't get to know each other. We have all the time in the world." Just looking at her in this state and knowing he had put her there was unsettling his dragon tendencies once again. He reached out a finger to run it down her cheek, expecting it to become a claw at any moment.

But Leah batted his hand away. "Don't touch me. I've seen it, and I know it." She shoved her way past him.

"And what, exactly, did you see?" he called after her.

She turned, her face full of hurt. "It doesn't matter, because I'm done. If you need a psychic, call someone else." Leah was out the door and running to her car.

Holden knew he could catch her. He might be in human form, but he was still a dragon. He was stronger and faster than most humans, and his senses were far more finely tuned. It would be an easy thing to snatch her up and drag her back into the house. But then she would be his prisoner, and that wasn't how this was supposed to be. He let her go.

Turning away from the window so he couldn't see her car as it headed down the driveway, he sank his fist into the wall.

## 9
------

THE CUP OF STEAMING TEA IN FRONT OF HER SHOULD HAVE INSTANTLY made Leah feel better. After all, there was nothing better than a cup of tea with a good friend after having man trouble, and that was why Leah had run straight to The Enchanted Elm. Autumn was away picking up supplies for the store, but Summer was more than happy to listen.

"You know, you would think I'd be better at putting my psychic experiences into words if I'm supposed to be some sort of author, but I just can't." She concentrated on the heat of her cup, trying to slow her racing mind. "I just woke up with this awful feeling that Holden was lying to me. I reached out and touched his wrist, and I saw those dragons all over again. Except this time, Holden was one of them. He was this massive red dragon, but then he was stepping out of its skin and becoming the man I slept with last night. I have to believe that means he's living two different lives."

Summer pushed out her lips and twisted a length of pale hair between her fingers. "You know, a lot of people live dual lives, in a sense. They're usually not the same person at work that they are at home, and then they're different again when they're out with their friends."

"But this is different," Leah insisted. "I *felt* it. And I know from my experience with Victor that I needed to have more than just a feeling and more than just a vision. That's why I went downstairs and got the cards, but they just confirmed it, over and over. Whoever Holden really is, he doesn't want me to know about it. He's deceiving me in some way." It made her feel sick that she had shared such a passionate night with a man like that. "I think I could just puke."

"Then you're probably right. It's important to follow your instincts, even if you don't completely understand them." She stood up and went to a shelf. They were sitting in the stock room of The Enchanted Elm, and the shelves around them were stacked with boxes and bags. It looked like the inventory of any other store while it was still in its packaging, but Leah knew better. Summer plucked a small stone from a nearby box and handed it over. "Take this."

Leah studied the smooth chunk of rock, the gentle striations of blue and white almost mesmerizing as they shimmered. "What is it?"

"It's blue lace agate, and it helps discover the truth. That might be the truth about you or about Holden, but either way, I think it will help." She lifted a shoulder and let it fall. "It's also good for bone strength, so that can't hurt, either."

―――――

LATER THAT NIGHT, the three women gathered at Autumn's house. It was a big place with an expansive back yard full of numerous plants. The craftsman-style home had exposed timbers on the ceiling, old wooden floors that had darkened with age, and built-in bookshelves that Leah was always jealous of.

"It's been a while since we've talked to Naomi," Summer commented as she set up a circle of candles and stones on the floor. "I hope she has more to say than last time."

"She was always a bit cryptic, even when she was alive," Leah pointed out. "It wasn't until she realized who we were and what powers we had that she finally opened up. Oddly enough, it seemed even more strange that she could shift than that I could read minds or that you two could perform powerful spells." Leah clearly remembered the day Naomi had discovered the other women's abilities. They had expected her to scream or be angry—a common reaction when people didn't understand—but she had simply laughed and hugged them.

"It takes a lot more power to control the body like that. Not to negate anything we do, but we're pretty common, if you think about it."

Autumn had changed her usual professional attire out for a simple cotton dress in black. She took her place on the floor, folding her long legs underneath her and letting her hair down. "God, I wish we hadn't lost her."

"We really haven't *lost* her," Summer asserted. "We're still able to talk to her this way, which is more than most people can say when a loved one passes away."

In a circle on the floor, with the candles and stones at the center, the three women held hands and chanted their opening incantation. Leah hadn't known much about Wicca before she'd met the sisters, but they had taught her a lot. At first, she had stumbled over the numerous spells and enchantments required to talk to someone from the spirit world, but now she found that they flowed easily from her tongue. She relaxed her mind, trying to add as much of her own psychic energy as possible to the recipe.

The candle flame stopped flickering, burning as a steady light that slowly grew brighter. It turned a pale shade of blue, and then snaked up through the air. The thin column of fire squirmed as it took shape until a long, thin face stared back at them. The scales that covered the cheeks and the rows of sharp teeth didn't belong to the human form of Naomi that they usually knew, but they could still see her in the dragon's eyes.

"Naomi, we really miss you," Autumn said softly. "We've tried not to bother you too much because we know it must be difficult for you to reach out to us. But we can't help but at least check in with you every now and then. How are you doing?"

The swirling blue flames flickered for a moment and then steadied once again. Naomi nodded. "As well as I can."

"It's good to see you," Summer whispered, tears in her eyes. "We wish there was a way to bring you back. You belong here with us."

"No." The spirit's voice was soft, but it echoed oddly in the open room. "Not really. I don't belong anywhere; not anymore."

"Don't say that." Summer's emerald eyes were bright with tears seeing their old friend again.

"But it's true," Naomi's ethereal form insisted. "The place where my people came from is gone. But you need to know that some of them are close; very close." Those blue eyes stared pointedly at Leah, burrowing into her soul. "They're trying to make a new home for themselves, just as I had tried."

"I don't understand." Leah felt pain in her skull, a familiar sensation when new pathways were being forged in her mind. It was often painful, but it was a feeling that she was used to and that she welcomed. "We've never met anyone else like you."

Naomi smiled and slowly blinked. "They're dragons; shifters, actually. And they're here to find refuge after the destruction of so many of our people. Right now, it's much safer here on Earth for them."

Autumn turned to Summer and raised her brow at that.

"Do you think we'd be able to recognize them at all as we go about our day to day business? How much of our lives can you see, anyway? I mean, when we aren't in direct contact with you?"

Naomi's thin form began to flicker. "No, they're blending in with humans fairly well. And don't worry, I can only see bits and pieces, Leah." The dragon smiled, a stretch of her full, scaly lips. "I haven't noticed you playing with your pocket rocket in the bedroom, if that's what you're wondering."

The women all threw their heads back, sharing a much-needed belly laugh. But moments later, looking down at her lap, Leah admitted, "Victor and I are finally legally divorced. I know I should be happy, but my powers seem to be completely out of whack. I don't get it; I don't know what to do."

"Nothing is simple, hun; you know that."

The blue figure in the air slowly began to fade, and Leah furrowed her brow at the sight. "Naomi, wait! There's more we'd like to say."

"I'm sorry, but it's time for me to go. Next time, love. Miss you, guys..." Naomi turned to Leah once again and gave her a wink, and then she was gone.

## 10

HOLDEN PAUSED, A SOAPY PLATE IN HIS HAND. HE COULDN'T QUITE HEAR anything, at least not anything unusual. Finn and the other children were playing in the living room with the other men. Though the shifters each had their separate homes, they often spent their free time together. The company of humans had never proven to be enough for them, and they had found it was easier to parent when all the children were together. On this particular evening, Holden had taken advantage of the situation to catch up on cleaning. He hadn't ever kept a messy den back on Charok, and he wasn't going to do it here.

But he slowly let the plate slide back into the sink as a frisson of energy crackled across the back of his neck. Something was wrong. He grabbed a towel and dried his hands as he headed into the living room. "Is everything okay?"

Julian looked up at him from the couch, arching one eyebrow. "Of course. Why?"

"I don't know." He scanned the room. The children were playing peacefully if not quietly on the floor, with Finn babbling his nonsense to Kaylee about the blocks he was stacking. Xander had a tablet in his hand and was skimming through whatever internet article he'd found to be the most fascinating. Julian and Beau had started a card game on the coffee table. There was nothing unusual or out of sorts in any fashion.

"Maybe you should sit down for a while," Beau offered, gesturing at the recliner. "You've had a rough week."

Holden shook his head. There was no way he could sit down. Something needed to be done—something more than the dishes—but he didn't know what it was. "It's not been that rough."

Xander gave him a knowing smile. "No, of course not. You've only found your mate and then discovered that she basically thinks you're a bad guy. Nothing difficult about that at all."

Glaring at him, Holden regretted telling them anything. What Xander had said was true, but that didn't make it easy to hear. "That will sort itself out."

"Are you sure?" Beau leaned forward to wipe a line of drool from Elliot's chin. "Seems like it would be pretty difficult to work things out with her when she doesn't want to have anything to do with you."

"Shut up." But Holden knew the other shifter had a point. And there was definitely something pulling at him to get out of the house, to find what was wrong and fix it. He didn't think it had anything to do with his relationship with Leah, but he still needed to take some sort of action. "Can you guys make sure Finn is taken care of? I've got to go."

Xander and Julian laughed, but Beau smiled. "Of course. I'll just take him home with me if you aren't back before bedtime."

Holden nodded. "Good. I have a feeling I won't be." Grabbing his keys and heading out to the garage, he fired up his car and drove straight into town. Every sense in his body was telling him there was something wrong. There was danger out there somewhere. He would find it.

## 11

———

LEAH DROVE HOME AFTER THE SÉANCE, FEELING DRAINED BOTH physically and emotionally. It was always difficult to see Naomi, and it wore on all of them that a special friend who had completed their inner circle was truly gone. It was always difficult to lose someone, but it hurt more to know that Naomi had been so uniquely special; there hadn't been anyone else like her on Earth.

Parking in the alley that ran next to her building, Leah let herself in the side door of the store and climbed the stairs to her apartment. She carried an odd feeling in her gut, one that almost felt like excitement or fear. But there was nothing for her to be excited about. She was divorced and alone in the world except for her two close friends. Her first attempt at a new relationship had been such a rollercoaster that it had left her windblown and exhausted. She never wanted to see Holden Reid again, and if the universe was kind to her, she never would.

Flicking on the light, Leah dumped her purse and keys on the counter and peered in the fridge. She hadn't bothered to grab any dinner before the séance, but she wasn't really hungry. She felt the obligation to eat, but not the hunger. There was plenty available in the fridge, but none of it appealed to her, so she shut the fridge door and headed for the couch.

Normally, it was easy for Leah to settle in once she was at home.

Using her psychic abilities for her business had given her the deline-ation between home life and work life, and she was usually good at turning herself off so she could relax a little before bed. But tonight, she felt too restless to put her feet up on the couch and turn on the television. There was something in the air, and it was beckoning to that nervous feeling in the pit of her stomach. It made it feel as though there was someone there with her, someone she hadn't invited.

Concerned, she walked down the short hallway off the living room and peeked into her bedroom, the guest room, and the bathroom. She cursed herself for not having a weapon in the house. Her psychic powers wouldn't protect her against an intruder. But she only found shadows, and she returned to the living room.

Sitting on the edge of the couch, she couldn't resolve herself to let it go. Snagging a flashlight from a nearby shelf, she tiptoed downstairs to the shop. It was as she had left it, with the lights off and the front door locked. The partition wall made deep shadows in her reading room, hiding the couch and the oak bookshelf where she kept an array of items that assisted her in her work. But she scanned the flashlight over them and found nothing unusual.

Just as she was about to head up the stairs and force herself to go to bed, she heard a noise near the back of the building. She turned to find the back door open, the warm night air blowing in and rifling the papers on her desk.

And a hulking figure standing in the doorway.

Leah didn't need to touch the trespasser to know he meant her harm. Waves of anger emanated from him, making her take several steps back until she bumped into the wall. "Get out of here," she called into the darkness. "This is private property."

"Oh, I know exactly where I'm at." The man strode forward confi-dently. A beam of light from a streetlamp came in through the windows at the front of the store and slanted across his face, revealing a scar on his cheek.

With horror, Leah realized exactly where she'd seen that face before. She'd never met the man in real life, but she had seen him very clearly when she had touched Josey's hand. She cleared her throat. "I'm warning you to get out right now, or I'll call the police." Why hadn't she brought her cell phone downstairs with her? It was bad enough that her mystic powers were fading in and out, but now even her common sense was getting faulty.

"I don't care. I'll be done with you long before they get here." The man took another step forward and lifted his hand, revealing a sharp knife that gleamed in the light. "I understand you told my Josey to stay away from me."

Her breath was shallow, skipping along to the quick beat of her heart. "I never told her that. Whatever problems you and Josey have is your business, and not mine."

"You should have thought about that before you talked to her. You see, she made the mistake of cheating on me, but I was willing to forgive her. I just about had her back, but then *you* had to go and mess it all up."

Leah swallowed, trying to be brave. "You scared her, and that's the only reason she came here. There wasn't anything I could tell her about her relationship that she didn't already know."

"No!" the man screamed. He was in Leah's face now, his breath hot and fetid in her nostrils. "That's not true and you know it! She and I were doing just fine, but you convinced her I was out to hurt her. I went to her house just to talk, and the bitch went and called the cops. I've got a fucking restraining order on me now. How am I supposed to work things out with her when I can't get within a hundred yards of her?" His fingers tightened around her arm. "You're coming with me, and you're going to tell her that she's been wrong about me."

"It sounds to me like you have some personal issues to work out. You need to talk to your lawyer and a couples' counselor, not to a psychic." She trembled inside, terrified by the aura this man was exuding. He was going to hurt her if she didn't cooperate, and there was no doubt about it. "But you can't tell me you didn't mean any harm to Josey. You wanted her back at all costs, and that's not how relationships work."

"Aren't they? Are you going to tell me you wouldn't go to the edge of the Earth and back for someone you love?" He clamped a meaty hand around her arm and brought the edge of the blade to rest against the delicate skin of her throat. "Don't you have someone who means more to you than anything?"

Leah wished she could say that she did. And she desperately wished she could explain to this man that there was a big difference between going to the ends of the Earth for someone and stalking them. But she was afraid even to swallow, for fear that the sharp knife would slice right into her flesh. She could feel the prickle of the honed edge against her skin, and it wouldn't take much.

"She might not, but I do." This voice came from behind the intruder, causing him to spin around, knife at the ready.

Just then, the weapon was yanked from his hand by scaly red fingers, trimmed in claws. The knife clattered to the floor, and a great crimson beast threw Josey's ex to the ground. The monster's hands were on his chest, pinning him down, and his teeth were only an inch from his face as he spoke. "You will not harm this woman, not unless you want to deal with *me*. I can promise you, I know what it really means to do anything for the person you love."

The sharp scent of urine pierced the air, and the man on the ground trembled. "What the fuck are you?" he mewled. His voice had been so rough and deep a moment ago, but now he squeaked like a terrified kitten.

"I'm her protector," the monster growled. "And I will do anything to keep her safe."

Leah kept her back against the wall as she took in the creature who stood in her shop. He had expansive, leathery wings, the upper edge of which brushed the ceiling. His thick, black claws were sharp as razors as they clutched at the shirt of the assailant, and his crimson scales shone in the dim light. The entire scene before her was like watching a distant dream come to life. Not only had she seen the scarred man in a vision before, but she had seen the dragon. He was the very same figure that Holden's reading had revealed to her.

Right down to those sharp, blue eyes.

The dragon lifted his hands from the man's chest. "Go now, before I change my mind."

Scrambling to his feet, the dark-haired man was out the door and in the street in only a fraction of a second.

Turning to her, the dragon's head moved from side to side on his long neck as he studied Leah. "You don't need to be afraid of me."

Her throat worked as she tried to regain the ability to speak. The experiences she'd had with her supernatural powers had at times been difficult to take, but this was, by far, the hardest. "I'm...I'm not sure that I am." She reached out a tentative hand, touching the smooth scales on the dragon's cheek, surprised to find that they were smooth and silky. Once again, she saw the same vision of a den of dragons, with Holden stepping out of a red, scaly skin. "Holden?"

He pushed his muzzle against the touch of her hand. "It's me."

"I can't believe this." Seeing him in this form made her understand so many things. The vision she'd had of him in the dragon's den, the feeling that he was living two lives, and Naomi's message about her kind being nearby all clicked into place like puzzle pieces. Holden hadn't really been lying to her, he had just been protecting his identity. She couldn't blame him for that. But it also brought up numerous questions.

"Believe it." Holden took a step back. His wings folded, shrunk, and pulled into the flesh of his back. His thick, strong legs morphed back into very human ones. He writhed as his neck shortened and his face transformed into the one she had come to know so well. Each scale on his body tipped up on edge and sank down into his skin.

Leah's vision blurred as tears came to her eyes. She blinked rapidly, but she couldn't hold them back. They were hot against her cheeks.

"I didn't mean to scare you." Holden moved toward her, tentatively, taking her into his arms.

"It's not that." She burrowed her face into his chest, soaking up his energy and relishing his strong grip around her. She had felt so cold since she'd left his house, and she had chalked it up to exhaustion and emotional stress. Now, she knew it was just because she needed him. "I'm just so relieved."

He pulled back so that he could look down at her. "You are?"

She couldn't help but laugh at the look of shock on his face. "You have no idea."

## 12

---

"I FEEL LIKE A BIT OF AN IDIOT," LEAH ADMITTED AS SHE FLUTTERED with the tea kettle and pulled two mugs down from the cabinet, her hands visibly shaking.

"Why should you?" Holden watched her carefully as he leaned against the counter. He hadn't moved more than a few feet away from her since he'd arrived, and he didn't plan to. He had known, even from a great distance, that Leah was in trouble. It was for that reason that he'd gone flying down the road, even though he hadn't known it at the time.

"Because I should have known. When my senses are off, I can tell. They definitely weren't off when I was picking up those visions about you, and I chose not to trust them simply because they didn't make sense. It made me judge you unfairly." She watched the steady flame of the gas burner under the kettle.

"Leah." He moved so that he stood just behind her, his hand on her lower back. "There's no way you could have really understood what was going on. It wouldn't make sense to anyone, no matter what kind of powers they had." Holden wished he could have just told her about it right away, but it had been too risky.

She pursed her lips. "Maybe most people wouldn't, but someone who had met a dragon shifter before ought to."

"What?" His voice was too sharp, and he cringed inwardly. But the other men had seen Leah back at The Parlor, and none of them had mentioned knowing her.

Taking a deep sigh, Leah turned to face him. "I knew a woman back in college. I'm friends with a couple other girls who have supernatural powers, and Naomi was one of us. But while I'm a psychic and two of the others are witches, Naomi was a shifter. She had the power to change from human form to dragon and back again."

Holden's eyes narrowed slightly. He knew he should believe her. There was no reason for Leah to lie to him, not now. But when he, the other three and the four dragonlings had been transported off of Charok, they had been the only ones of their kind left. "A female? I don't understand."

Leah shrugged. "She was just like you. She never said much about why she had that ability, and we simply accepted her for who she was."

"Where is this woman? I need to talk to her." If there was a female shifter on Earth, then he had to let the others know.

But Leah shook her head. "You can't, not really. She died over five years ago. The only time we get to talk to her is when we hold a séance, and even then, her time with us is very limited."

"Could I join you the next time you have one?" Holden's mind was racing. It seemed completely impossible that another dragon had been here, and he only wished they had known about her sooner.

"Of course. I don't think it would be a problem, and my friends would be happy to meet you." Her face flushed an attractive shade of pink. "But it would be nice if I understood a little bit more about you and why you're able to turn into a big red dragon who makes grown men piss their pants."

Holden couldn't help but laugh at that. "It's a lot to explain, but I'll try to keep it simple. We're from another world. Our kind was threatened by a spell to the point of extinction, and we had no choice but to leave. A sympathetic warlock managed to send us here. We're just trying to exist, like anyone else."

Her cerulean eyes looked away for a moment in thought. "And your son?"

"He's a shifter as well. Our queen had laid four eggs before she died, and we each took one. They hatched shortly after we came to Earth, and we're fortunate that they seem to prefer being in their human forms. But I have to admit there are times that they express their dragon side, and it's not always convenient."

Leah laughed softly, a beautiful noise that made him want to be closer to her. "Typical kid, then, huh?"

He smiled. "Yeah, he seems to be. But I think you and I both know we've been dancing around what we really need to talk about."

She had been looking at him, but she dropped her eyes to his chest. "I'm not sure I know what to say. It's all so strange, but wonderful. First, I think I owe you an apology."

"For what?" Unable to resist the urge, Holden reached out and tucked a strand of her hair behind her ear. She looked so vulnerable, even though she wasn't currently being threatened by some corrupt human with an odd sense of justice.

"For running out on you this morning and accusing you of being a liar. I didn't trust myself, and it made me not trust you. I didn't know what else to do, and I was just scared."

Holden leaned forward and pressed his lips to her smooth forehead. His hands skimmed down to gently encase her hips and pull her toward him. "You didn't know. It's okay. I don't blame you at all."

Leah tipped up her head, encouraging his lips to meet hers. He didn't deny her, fulfilling the need he had been feeling himself. "I have so many questions. There are some things that make a lot more sense than they did this morning, but I still feel like there's more I should know." She flicked her tongue out, tentatively.

He responded, deepening the kiss and pressing their bodies together. God, how he had longed for her. It had been less than a day since he'd had her in his bed, but it felt like an eternity. Holden resisted the urge to dig his fingers into her flesh just to prove to himself that she was there. He needed her more than he could ever explain, and if he had his way he would never leave her side. "We have all the time in the world to talk," he said, moving his lips down her jaw line to nip at her ear. "But there's one very important thing you need to know right away."

"What's that?" Her body trembled slightly. He didn't know if it was from excitement or fear, but he wrapped his arms around her completely just in case.

"In our world, dragons mate for life. They don't get to choose their mates; destiny makes that choice for them. They know when they've met the right ones because of their reactions to them, and the way they make them feel."

Leah pushed gently at his chest, looking him in the eye. "What does that mean? Do you have someone at home that you're supposed to be with?"

He smiled at her innocence and shook his head. "No. I never had the chance, and I didn't know what that reaction felt like. But from the moment I met you, I couldn't control myself around you. My body demanded that I shift back to my natural form. It was a challenge to fight it until I was fortunate enough to have you in my home. Then I felt so calm and relaxed, like I never had before. When you left, I couldn't stand the thought of what might happen to you if I wasn't at your side. I sensed the danger you were in, and I had no choice but to come. That's how I know you're supposed to be my mate. I hope that doesn't scare you."

She paused for a moment, thinking. "I was having a lot of difficulty with my powers. Nothing seemed to be working right. When I did that reading with you, it was like everything came flooding back to me all at once. It was scary, and it was so different that I thought there must be something wrong."

"What about now? What do you see in me?"

Leah laid her hand against his neck, her thumb gently touching his pulse point. "It's not as intense, but it's still there. It's like I can shut it down when I want to, but it's never closed off to me like it had been." She smiled, her eyes grazing up from his neck to meet his. "You balance me."

"Does that mean you feel it, too? That we're meant to be together?" His very life was poised on her next words, and Holden felt that if he leaned forward too far he would fall right over. No woman had ever made him feel so dependent on her. If he'd thought about it before, he would have imagined that he hated feeling such a need. But he liked it. A lot.

"I do, Holden. I—I love you."

That was all he needed. The two sides of him that had been warring for space in his life suddenly converged. He didn't need to be a human or a dragon. He was always both, no matter how he seemed to outsiders. Most importantly, he was Leah's mate and protector, and Finn's father. Holden looked down into her eyes and knew he could become happily lost in them. "I love you, too."

Reaching behind her and flicking off the stove burner, he scooped his arms underneath her buttocks and lifted her from the floor. "And I need you. Desperately."

She kissed him as he held her, their tongues explaining it all to each other. Leah twined her arms and legs around him, holding on tight as he carried her to the couch.

Holden knew he could find the bedroom in the small apartment, but he couldn't possibly wait that long. He needed her now. He sat down on the cushions, her legs still tangled around him, and began pulling at her clothes.

Leah easily slipped out of her shirt, and Holden took a moment to admire her breasts while her black lacey bra still cupped them. He didn't always understand humans—not yet—but he could certainly appreciate the way Leah dressed. Her softness was the antithesis to his hardness, and he wanted to bury every part of his body in it.

She seemed to understand, and as soon as his jeans were on the floor Leah pierced herself on him. She was warm and wet, ready for him, and her thighs tightened pleasantly around his as she moved herself up and down on his shaft. He grabbed her waist and watched the pleasant bouncing of her breasts as she worked, then he pulled her gently so that they smothered his face.

"I really was an idiot," Leah breathed, arching her back to comply with his wishes.

"What do you mean?" He could never think of her that way. She was beautiful, smart, and knowing. She was everything, and he would never get enough of her.

"I might have deprived myself of this. If you hadn't come back here, I wouldn't have gotten the chance to be with you." Leah moaned as her core tightened around his member.

Holden grunted his appreciation. She felt so fucking good, and he had to admit he liked the idea of her being on top of him like this. He was the dominant type, and he would do everything in his power to make sure that he performed his duties as Leah's protector and mate, but she could do whatever she wanted to him. He snatched up her nipple in his mouth, sucked it until it was hard, and then let it go. "I wouldn't have let you. I couldn't just let you run away from me. I would have done whatever it took to make you understand what I had seen in us."

"Maybe that's one of the reasons you're so good for me. You see what I need even when I can't." She tipped her head back, and her dark curls fell enticingly down her back.

Holden took them in his hands, pulling gently. The action pressed her breasts harder into his face, and Holden felt the heat at his core increase. Leah cried out her pleasure. Her hair almost came down to her ass in this position, and he enjoyed the way her flesh bumped against the sides of his hands. He slid one finger down in the crevice between her cheeks, touching her in her most private place.

Leah's body stiffened under his hands. For a moment, he thought he had made a mistake. But she clamped her hands behind his shoulders and pounded her hips down onto him, burying his sword to the hilt inside her sheath. She slammed into him, extracting her pleasure as her walls convulsed around him. He had worked her into a frenzy, and he was reaping the benefits as her juices flowed around him.

"I'm sorry," she panted as she slowed down, holding onto him for dear life.

"For what?" he whispered against her neck. "For taking what you need?"

Leah nodded, small shivers running through her body as she continued to pulse slowly on his lap.

He could make her come again, and he knew it. If there was one thing he had learned from their experience the night before, it was that there was no greater satisfaction that pleasuring her. "Don't be. You take everything you want, because I promise you I'll take mine as well."

With one easy movement, he maneuvered her off him and slid off the couch. Holden pulled her down onto the floor with him and arranged her so that she was bent over the coffee table, that round ass of hers in air. He punctured her from behind, moving slowly at first to make sure she liked it.

Leah reached back, grabbed his hand, and gently brought it around to rest on her center of pleasure. Holden understood, and he moved his fingers in time to the rhythm of his hips. As he had predicted, it took no time at all for her to come again. She was a ripe fruit, ready for him to pluck at any time. She called his name as she climaxed, letting him know that he was the only one who could do this to her.

He closed his eyes as her walls spasmed around him. Fully engorged, the friction between them was incredible. Holden felt his entire body tighten just before he exploded inside her. His muscles drained of all energy as he gave it to Leah, and she owned him completely.

They collapsed on the floor together, their naked bodies an enjoyable knot as they held onto each other. He brushed aside her hair so he could kiss her forehead, her cheeks, her chin, her nose. "Leah, I knew when I came to Earth that I would have to find my mate, the woman who could tame the dragon inside me and make me the person I was meant to be. I never thought it could truly happen with a human, but you've proven me wrong. So completely wrong." He wouldn't have admitted it to anybody else, but he couldn't help but reveal his innermost secrets to her. With just a little more time, she would come to know everything about him.

She laid her head on his chest, and he could feel the contraction of her cheek as she smiled. "That's quite a lot to live up to."

"I think you can do it."

Leah moved her head so that she could look up at him. Her eyes shone, and she was easily the most beautiful thing he'd ever seen. Even the sunrises on Charok couldn't compare to her. "Can you stay with me tonight?"

"I wouldn't have it any other way." He stood and reached out his hand to help her off the floor, and she led him to the bedroom.

# 13

EPILOGUE

LEAH SANG ALONG WITH THE RADIO AS SHE CRUISED DOWN THE HIGHWAY. It was a much longer commute home than when she had been able to just jog up the stairs to her apartment, but she was finding ways to enjoy it. It was nice to have a little bit of time to herself with nothing to think about, and it helped create an even bigger separation between her work and her home. As much as she enjoyed doing readings for people, she needed to have some downtime.

And her clients had noticed the difference. There seemed to be a steadier stream of walk-in traffic lately. Some even called ahead to make appointments. Not since Josey had anybody refused to pay or stopped her in the middle of a reading. Instead, they wanted it to keep going, gobbling up all the information Leah was able to give them.

The fog that had come down over her after her divorce from Victor seemed to be permanently lifted. It had been almost painful when those celestial doors had slammed in her face and cut her off from her powers, but as the time wore on, she realized she didn't need to worry about it anymore. She was centered and balanced, and she gave the best readings she ever had in her life.

"Your reputation has been on fire lately," Autumn had told her on the phone one night. "I heard a couple of ladies in my shop talking about you. One of them said you could tell her dog Skippy had been sick lately, and she hadn't said anything to give it away. I know that's a small thing, but it really impresses them."

Leah had laughed. "I'm not trying to impress them. I'm just doing what I do."

"Well, keep on doing it, girl. It's working."

And it really was. Leah had converted the upstairs apartment to an expanded reading space, where she could let her clients come in and truly relax while they received her services. There was something about being moved a little further off the street and away from the public eye that made their minds more willing to open up to hers. It made it a simple task to give advice based on her visions. Most people wanted to know about love and relationships. Now that she was in a healthy, stable relationship, she felt more than qualified to give it.

Pulling into the garage, Leah could tell as soon as she walked in the door that the house was empty. She moved through the kitchen and out the back door to find Holden and Finn in the backyard. The boy toddled through the grass, trying to kick at a large orange ball. He missed most of the time, but he laughed and clapped every time he managed to bump it with his foot.

"How are my two favorite guys?" she called out as she stepped off the deck.

Finn looked up. The look of curiosity on his face instantly changed to one of glee. "La La! Mama!"

She scooped him up out of the grass and held him to her chest. Finn's pudgy little arms wrapped around her as much as they could, and he planted a big wet kiss on her cheek. Leah's heart ripped right out of her chest and wrapped itself around his tiny finger. She'd been so busy focusing on enhancing her powers and building her career that she hadn't thought much about starting a family. Now that she had a son, she didn't know how she had ever lived without him.

Holden came up behind her and wrapped his strong arms around the both of them. He kissed her other cheek. "We're glad you're home. I plan on grilling up some barbecued chicken."

She leaned into him, never tired of the broadness of his chest or the strength of his shoulders under her head. Holden was her anchor, and he kept her from lashing about like an abandoned boat when the seas got stormy. She had made the mistake before of thinking it would take someone "normal" to do that, someone without any powers or real understanding of them. But it turned out that she needed someone who wasn't even quite human, and that was one of the many things she loved about him. "You spoil me. I'm never going to want to cook for myself again."

"Maybe I like spoiling you." He let go, and Leah set Finn down to continue playing in the lush grass. "You deserve it, and I'd like to spoil you even more tonight."

"Oh?"

"There's a charity ball this weekend, and I bought two tickets. I thought it would be nice if we got to go out and do something a little special. Dinner and drinks are included. Besides, I'd really like to see you in a long black dress." He raked his eyes down her body and pulled her close.

"Dinner, drinks, and dancing? It doesn't sound like it could get any more romantic than that." Leah looked up at him, soaking him in. With that dark hair, square jaw, and dancing blue eyes, he was easily the most beautiful man she had ever seen.

And he was all hers.

His hand moved under the back of her shirt, pressing suggestively at her skin. "And then we can come home and make a little romance of our own." He kissed her soundly, hinting at everything they would do when the ball was over. Their lovemaking sessions had become a regular part of their lives, and Leah had found that she almost couldn't sleep unless she had at least a little private time with him. It wouldn't take a sparkling dress and a night on the town to arouse his interest, and Leah knew that he would whisk her up to the bedroom as soon as he had a chance. "I thought it would be a nice way to celebrate the release of your new book."

Those were words she never thought she would hear only a few months ago. It had been a difficult start on the second book while she still dealt with her hurt feelings over Victor and trying to understand why she kept running into the same handsome stranger. But Holden's support had given her the mental space she needed to focus her energies. Leah's agent swore that *Trust Your Instincts* was going to be the next bestseller. Even if it wasn't, it still felt like a huge accomplishment that not only validated her beliefs, but her career.

She glanced down at Finn, but he was too busy with the ball to pay any attention to them. The three of them made a beautiful family, and it was one she cherished. She loved her time at work, but she was just as eager to come home for snuggles and playtime.

"I wouldn't miss it for the world."

———

# XANDER'S MATE

## DADDY DRAGON GUARDIANS

# 1

---

XANDER MITCHELL RAN A HAND THROUGH HIS THICK, DARK HAIR AS HE rang the bell next to Holden's front door. The man answered, one eyebrow raised. "It didn't go so well, I take it?" Nora was still awake, smiling happily in Holden's arms.

Taking his daughter, Xander stepped inside. "You could say that." He focused on her dark curls and touched them gently with his fingers. He had been her caretaker since he and the other men had fled to Earth, but he still hadn't been able to get over how delicate she was. As hopeful as he had been about the evening, he found he was far happier to pick her up a little earlier than usual.

Holden shut the door behind him and stepped into the living room. His son, Finn, was sleepily cuddling a stuffed bear. "I told you it wouldn't work. Online dating was terrible for me."

"But it just makes so much sense when you look at the numbers," Xander argued. "It's a faster way to meet people. I know it's not like Nora is suffering without a mother figure in her life, but you and I both know it's only right to provide these children with the best parenting possible. From everything I've read about how life works here on Earth, and from everything we had experienced back on Charok, that means finding a mate."

"No," Holden corrected as he turned off the television and picked up his son. "That means finding *your* mate. She's got to be perfect, and you aren't going to be able to tell that by looking at her picture on a screen. Just look at Leah and I." Holden had indeed found the perfect mate for himself. Leah was a wonderful woman who was not only a good partner, but a wonderful mother to Finn.

Xander wanted the same thing for himself and for Nora, but it definitely wasn't happening yet. "You just got lucky."

Holden laughed, and little Finn giggled along with him, even though he didn't get the joke. His big blue eyes shone brightly up at his father figure as he ran his chubby fingers through the stubble on Holden's chin. "I don't know if I would say that. Have a seat and tell me what happened. Let me know how awful it was. The night is still early, and Leah is upstairs meditating."

Settling onto the couch with a sigh, Xander rubbed the bridge of his nose. "I guess I can't say it was awful, but I just know she's not the one. There's supposed to be some sort of spark between us, but there wasn't even a chance. While we were at dinner, the only thing I could think about was how much I wanted the date to be over."

"You know, things might not be *exactly* the same for you and your perfect person as they were for Leah and I," Holden theorized. "Trying to find a human to be with is likely to be far different than finding a dragon, although I suppose none of us will ever know that. I do know how I felt when I first met Leah, but it might be a different sensation for you."

Xander nodded. "Probably, but that still means there has to be *some sort* of sensation, right? I didn't feel nervous or even excited. When she touched my hand across the table, it could have just as easily been *you* touching my hand for all that it did for me." He frowned, wishing this didn't have to be so hard. The pressure of knowing Nora deserved a mother only made things more difficult. If he only had to worry about himself, then he might not bother dating at all.

"Okay. You've got me there." Holden yawned and smiled. "I have a feeling it'll happen when you least expect it."

"You know I love learning more about humans and living here with them, but you're starting to sound like one of them," Xander scolded, laughing. "Next thing I know, you'll be writing a book of platitudes."

"They're probably better than the ones we knew from back home. 'Never turn your back on a drooling ogre' wouldn't go over well on this planet. And it doesn't really sound like good dating advice."

"You've got me there. Maybe you're right; I should just let this happen." Back on Charok, the dragons didn't have a dating protocol, so to speak. They knew when the time was right and when they had found their fated mates. It created a boiling in their blood, a thirst on their tongue that couldn't be quenched by anything else—or so he had heard. The ogres had taken over before Xander had ever gotten the chance to find a female who made him feel that way. Xander, Holden, Beau, and Julian had barely managed to escape with their lives and with the last eggs that had belonged to their slain queen to start a new life on Earth. Sometimes it seemed much harder than Xander had ever imagined it would be.

"Tell you what. Leah and I are going to a community picnic tomorrow. Why don't you come with us? It'll give you a chance to get away from your studies and your worries. We can leave the kids with Beau and just enjoy ourselves."

Xander considered this. They ate outside all the time on their home planet, but on Earth, it seemed to be a novelty. "A picnic? I can't say I've been on one of those, but it sounds interesting. What does it mean if it's a community picnic?"

"I'm not entirely sure," Holden admitted, shrugging. "It's something about business owners getting together and eating potato salad. Leah assures me it's fun."

Always up for a new opportunity, Xander nodded. "Alright, then. I'll be there." He gathered up Nora's things and headed home.

As he tucked his sweet little girl into bed, he couldn't help but stand over her crib and watch her for a moment. If things had gone differently, she would be a princess of dragons. One of the last eggs laid by the queen before she was killed, Nora had been lucky enough to escape with the men and come to Earth with the help of a rogue wizard who had sympathized with the dragons. She would have had zero chance of survival if he hadn't grabbed her dark emerald egg and made off with it, but he hoped he was doing the right thing by raising her in a world of humans.

Stepping down the short hallway to his own room, Xander went into the bathroom to wash his face. He stood for a moment in front of the mirror, wondering how human females saw him. Xander had gotten used to his figure in the mirror: he was distinctly human, with a well-proportioned nose and smooth skin. Though he combed his thick, dark hair regularly, it often fought him and didn't want to stay in place, and his eyes were the color of the earth: a rich brown hue.

Even though he rarely had the chance to shift into his true form, he could still see the dragon that lay within. He knew that his filed nails would instantly transform into the sharpest of claws as soon as he began to morph, and his lips would extend back to reveal arches of gleaming teeth. Xander missed the way the heat in his chest used to vent out through his nostrils as little tendrils of smoke, along with the array of spikes that stood out on the back of his head. He was tempted to shift right at that moment, just so he could see it all again. But even though his apartment was a spacious one, there was no point in risking the damage he would do. Dragon bodies were much larger and bulkier than human forms, and it was next to impossible to control a lengthy tail in an enclosed space. No, he would have to wait for the time being.

Xander went to bed, wondering what it would be like to have a woman lay next to him night after night. Holden had assured him that it was a pleasurable thing, and he was inclined to believe his friend. After all, human females were often just as sharply-tongued as dragon females, but far softer and more pleasant. He would find a mother for Nora, even if he had to go on a thousand first dates to find her.

# 2

SUMMER STRETCHED AND SMILED. THE SUN WAS STREAMING IN THROUGH the recycled glass windows of her little cottage, beckoning her to go outside and enjoy the day. There was nothing better than being part of nature, and Summer had even lived in a tent for a while just to be as close to Mother Earth as possible. But it did get cold in the winter and she was human, therefore, she had to settle for a cottage on the outer edges of town.

It was a nice little place, though. With a Murphy bed that folded out of the wall to save space, an eclectic collection of decorations and knickknacks she had picked up in second-hand stores, and all her favorite books on a solid wood shelf on the wall, there was no place Summer would rather be.

Dressing in a pair of loose floral pants that tied around her waist and a flowing white tunic, Summer slipped on leather sandals and prepared to take her usual morning walk, but her phone rang before she made it out the door. "Good morning, Autumn," she said without looking at the screen. "Are you on the plane already?"

Autumn, the precise opposite of her twin sister, confirmed this. "Of course. The earliest flight out always has the nicest people on it. I was just calling to remind you to process the weekly report this afternoon."

Summer rolled her eyes, but smiled. This was just how her sister was. Autumn had an incredible mind for business and was far more professional than any witch who ran a new age shop was expected to be. But it meant that they were always turning a decent profit and making money by helping others, which was made Summer happy. "Don't worry. I'll get it all taken care of."

Her sister sighed over the phone. "I feel bad for leaving this week and making you hold down the fort. It can be a lot to handle, and I don't want you to feel overwhelmed."

"You're thinking of yourself, not me," Summer reminded her. She spent a lot of time meditating and keeping in touch with the universe. It was important to stay grounded and to remember what was truly important, something that Summer felt most people forgot about these days. The constant need that everyone felt to rush around and accomplish everything they possibly could in a day only caused anxiety and depression. It never mattered to Summer how much money she made as long as she was able to continue to grow spiritually and to help others with her knowledge.

"I know, I know. But there's a shipment of inventory coming in this week, and that's going to have to all be counted, logged into the computer system, and put away in the back. Make sure you at least do the paperwork side of things, but if you don't have time to integrate it into our stock, then it can wait until I get back. I've already sent in the quarterly estimated taxes, so you won't have to worry about that, and I've paid the rent for the store. But we did advertise that big sale on incense this week, so you'll need to get the signs put in the window and on the displays. Oh, I don't think I programmed the sale prices into the computer..."

"Autumn, I can handle it," Summer said patiently. She was used to her "older" sister fretting over things, and she never took it personally. "You forget that I've been running The Enchanted Elm alongside you all this time. But I'm not doing any of it until this afternoon."

"You're not opening the shop this morning? Why not? Saturday mornings are huge for us. Everyone comes into the downtown area to shop for antiques and eat at the bakeries. We'll miss out on a lot of profit."

She could hear the panic in Autumn's voice, and she felt bad for her, but Summer had things well under control. "Because this morning is the annual Small Business Association picnic."

"Oh, right. Ah..." Autumn hesitated for a moment. "Are you going to be alright going by yourself? I mean, you can skip it if you want to. I know how people can get at these sorts of events."

Though Summer was used to doing things with her twin in tow, she knew she didn't need anyone to lean on. "I can handle it. Don't worry. Besides, maybe people will be slightly less intimidated if there's just one witch amongst them instead of two." She giggled in spite of the situation.

"Okay. Well, have fun. I'm sure Leah will be there, so tell her I said hi."

"I will." Summer hung up, smiling to herself at her sister's worries. They were both very talented witches and they had shared a womb together, but they couldn't be more different.

She stepped out her door and took the shorter path for her walk now that some of her time had been taken up by the phone call. Even so, she reveled in the way the summer breeze lifted her hair off her neck and sang in the leaves of the trees that surrounded her. Summer had chosen a home that was right on the outskirts of the city limits, where she had access to the woods, but could still get to the shop without too long of a commute. She paused as she finished her walk and came around the back of her cottage to pluck a few rogue weeds out of her herb bed before going inside to shower.

———

Midtown Park was packed by the time Summer pulled up in her hybrid coupe. The parking spaces in the main lot were filled with cars, which had also spilled over onto the side streets that surrounded the park. Summer guided her car carefully along the curb, making sure she wasn't blocking anyone in or obstructing someone's driveway, then retrieved the fruit salad she had made from the passenger seat and headed toward the grassy meadow at the center of the grounds.

Clusters of businessmen in polos and khakis gathered in the shade, nervously picking at their collars or smoothing their hair while they pretended to be interested in each other's small talk. The women seemed to have their own ritual. The wives of business owners carefully placed their homemade potluck contributions in the shade on the picnic tables under the pavilion, keeping them carefully covered to thwart the insects and checking to make sure their coleslaws were thoroughly mixed. The professional women who ran their businesses themselves plunked store-bought angel food cakes, cupcakes and brownies down on the edge of a table in their containers and left to chat about marketing strategies.

Summer was somewhere in the middle, not really belonging to either group, but she was used to it; that was how life was for a witch. She was always a bit of an outsider, and she had learned to ignore the stares that came from some of the women when they realized just who had walked into their midst. "Good morning!" Summer called out, waving her fingers in the air and smiling. No doubt, they were wondering what spell she had cast on them by making that particular hand gesture. The spell was a powerful one, indeed, but it was one they had cast on themselves.

"There you are!" Leah said as she walked up. Her dark hair lay in a long braid against her back, and her blue eyes matched the dome of sky above them. "I got a call from Autumn just a little while ago. She was worried about you for some reason. Is everything okay?" Leah narrowed her eyes as she studied her friend.

"Don't start getting all psychic on me," Summer replied with a laugh. Leah ran a psychic reading service just across the street from The Enchanted Elm, and she had quite a reputation in the area for being accurate and honest. "Autumn is just doing her normal thing. She's a bit concerned about me running everything while she's gone, and she only called you because she wanted you to check up on me."

Leah smiled and set down her dish of scalloped potatoes. "I think she feels guilty for leaving town just for fun. It would be one thing if she was going to a marketing convention or doing some sort of seminar, but visiting an old college friend is a frivolous thing for someone like Autumn."

"Very true, but I'm glad she's finally doing it. She and Marla have been saying they're going to get together for years, and I was afraid they wouldn't get it done before they turned gray." She really didn't begrudge her sister for taking the trip, and she secretly hoped she could get Autumn to leave town more often. It might get her to relax a little more.

As she reflected on how to get her sister to be more in touch with her spiritual needs, Leah came up next to her and nudged her with her elbow. "There are a lot of good looking men here, you know. You should keep your eyes open."

Summer rolled her eyes instead. "No, thanks. I'm not really interested."

"Suit yourself." Leah picked up a paper plate and dished herself a generous slice of chocolate cake. "It's only a hunch right now, since I haven't done any official readings on you for a long time, but I think love is in the air."

"Just because you and Holden found each other doesn't mean you need to go around setting everyone else up," Summer replied, grabbing a stick of celery from a tray. "I can't imagine anyone in this town wanting to be with me anyway. They all know I'm a witch. That means the men either think I dance naked in the moonlight and they're disappointed when I don't, or they're terrified of me."

"Then this is the perfect opportunity for them to start getting to know the *real* you a little better," Leah pointed out. She snagged a napkin from a nearby stack and wiped the corner of her mouth. "The SBA gets together all the time for meetings and incubators, but this picnic is a completely different environment. Besides, Autumn isn't here to run the show."

"I'll tell her you said that," Summer warned with a smile.

"Go ahead. If there's anything Autumn wouldn't take as an insult, it's being called bossy."

"Yes, but even she hasn't harassed me into dating recently." Summer remembered when the three of them were in college, and how they were constantly on the lookout for a date every weekend. She'd had her share, but she'd found that none of them shared the sense of the world that she did. Summer was a free spirit, and she wasn't caught up in the hubbub of modern life like everyone else was. Besides, she was much happier just being herself than worrying about making someone else happy. It was going to take a very special man to not only make her interested, but to be interested in her.

"Then at least come and meet the new owners of the print shop. I've used them a couple of times for my business cards and flyers, and they didn't run for the back room when they saw what I do for a living. They're an older couple, so you don't have to worry about me setting you up with anyone, but they might at least turn into friends."

"That sounds like something I can handle." Summer grabbed another celery stick and followed her friend across the crowded turf.

# 3

FROM THE MOMENT HE AND HOLDEN PULLED UP NEXT TO THE PARK, Xander's body began acting up. His skin itched so badly on its underside that he wished he could scratch it off, and his chest was tight. He loosened his tie as he unbuckled his seatbelt.

"You okay?" Holden asked, studying him with one eyebrow raised. "You look like you're choking on air."

"And I feel like it." Xander tried to reach around behind him to his shoulder blades, which were burning with the need to release his wings. While it had often felt restrictive to be in his human form, it had never quite felt like this. "What the hell is wrong with me?"

Holden was grinning from the driver's seat. "I have an idea."

Xander started to ask him what he meant, but he suddenly understood. He and Holden had talked about the way Holden's body had reacted when he'd met Leah, and Xander had taken extensive mental notes. He had wanted to know exactly what symptoms to look for when he met the right woman. Hope surged in him, but it was quickly squashed by skepticism. "It might not be that."

"I'm surprised to see someone like you in denial," Holden said. "I think you've been more determined than any of us to find your mate. We already know from my experience what happens to us when we're around the right woman."

"Yeah, but it could be anything. Maybe it's a virus or something."

The world outside the window spun around Xander, and he closed his eyes to regain his composure. "Okay, maybe not. I've got to get out of this car, or I'm going to shift and tear the roof off it."

"Hey." Holden clamped his hand around Xander's arm and looked him in the eye. "Keep yourself together. I know it's going to be difficult, but if you come into this park looking like a dragon, you'll have people running for the hills. And judging by the scales around your eyes right now, I'd say that would include your mate, too."

Xander slapped down the sunshade and looked at himself in the mirror. Sure enough, tiny copper scales had emerged on and around his eyelids. He blinked and rubbed at his skin, but he knew none of that would get them to go away. Instead, he took a deep breath and tried to calm the inner beast that was fighting so hard to get out. "Just tell me that it gets easier."

Holden gave him a sardonic smile. "It does. Eventually. Come on, let's go."

The two men got out of the car, grabbed the food dishes from the trunk, and headed across the street for the park. Xander found himself staring at every woman he laid his eyes on, wondering if she was the one. Most of them didn't seem to notice him, but he knew that didn't mean anything. He felt the reptile inside him, surging and writhing, and that would be the tell-tale sign. It wasn't easy to control it, and it was ironic that he couldn't simply shift and let nature take over, but he had to do his best.

"I just thought of something," he whispered to Holden as they passed two couples chatting. "What if the woman who's supposed to be my mate is already married to someone else?"

Holden tipped his head, thinking. "Why would you say that?"

"Well, we know that humans don't have the same kind of instincts that we do. They often marry for money or convenience, even when they think they're marrying for love. And sometimes when it *is* love, it still doesn't work out. So, who's to say that the woman I'm meant to be with isn't already with another man?" He gaged himself carefully as a couple passed them, hoping he wouldn't feel the need to rip the woman out of her husband's arms and fly off with her. She gave him no more of a reaction than anyone else did, and he let out a sigh of relief.

"I guess it's entirely possible," Holden agreed after a long moment. "Leah was married before. I've talked to her about it now and then, when she was in the mood to discuss it. But she was divorced before I met her, so we didn't have to worry about that. Maybe you won't, either. Maybe whatever fates are on this planet won't be so cruel."

"I hope you're right." Xander didn't like the way this whole process was making him feel. He was usually very confident and calm, but he had a deep sense of being unsettled, like someone had shoved his heart to the wrong side of his body.

"If I'm not, then we'll deal with it. We've come a long way from home, and I'd like to think we've done alright when it comes to the children. We can handle something as simple as a marriage contract."

"Aren't you Holden? Leah's boyfriend?" A woman with short black hair stepped in front of them and held out her hand. "Do you remember me? I did the catering at the reopening of Leah's shop last month."

"Yes, of course. Lynn, right?" Holden shook her outstretched hand. "This is my friend, Xander."

Lynn had milky-white skin that shone brightly in the sunlight. Her eyes were tipped up at the corners, giving her an exotic look. She eagerly reached out to shake Xander's hand. "How *very* nice to meet you, Xander. I don't think I've seen you around before."

Before he said anything, Xander took careful stock of himself. He still had that same stinging feeling under his skin as his scales threatened to pop out, but he was in control. This woman was beautiful, but she wasn't the one he was looking for. "It's a pleasure to meet you."

"You as well." Lynn tucked a strand of hair behind her ear and didn't hide the fact that she was looking him up and down. "What do you do for a living?"

Xander had never really had trouble talking to humans before. He had been fascinated by them from the moment he and his fellow shifters had arrived on Earth, and he had been eager to get to know them as much as possible. But the subject of what one did for a living seemed to come up far too often, and he had now recited his fake credentials so many times, he was starting to believe them. "I'm an anthropologist."

"Oh, that sounds fancy." Lynn's eyes flashed, looking impressed. She still hadn't let go of his hand. "What would a man like you be doing at an SBA picnic?"

Grinning, Xander replied, "Why, studying humans, of course." He knew that Lynn wouldn't get the joke, but he still appreciated it.

"Well, you can study me any time you want to," she said, removing a business card from her pocket and slipping it into his hand. "I've got to go, but I'll be around."

"I take it she wasn't the one," Holden said quietly once Lynn was out of earshot.

"Nope." Xander casually flicked the business card into a nearby trash can. "Not at all."

"Nice one on the job, by the way. I've started telling everyone I'm a research analyst. Turns out most people don't really know what that entails, so they just nod blankly accept it. It's a much better explanation than telling them about living off the sacks of gold we brought here from Charok."

Xander had to laugh at that, even though the reaction sent one of his claws shooting out the tip of his finger. He stuffed his hand in his pocket while he got it under control again. "She must be getting closer." He could no longer deny the excitement that was building inside him. They had been on this world for a few years now, and he was finally going to meet the woman he was supposed to be with.

"Look, there's Leah."

The dark-haired woman waved from across the grass. She had another woman at her side, and the two of them were heading toward the pavilion. Xander had come to know Leah a little bit since she had become a part of the dragons' lives, but he didn't recognize her friend.

"There you are," Leah said as she stepped into the shade. She wrapped her arms around Holden's waist and pressed her lips to his. "You've just missed meeting David and Lisa Rochester who run the print shop. They're great people, and they've invited us to dinner."

Holden looked slightly uncomfortable, but he nodded and smiled. "That sounds very nice."

But Xander's attention wasn't on the couple. He stood just on the other side of a picnic table from Leah's friend, and he couldn't stop looking at her. Blonde waves fell around her shoulders, picking up elements of the sunshine and reflecting them back in colors of blue, gold, and purple. Even once she stepped into the shade, she seemed to shimmer with light. The rest of the world had completely fallen away, relegated to blurs and shadows. Her eyes came up to meet his, catlike, green, and entrancing.

"Oh, how rude of me!" Leah said. Her voice seemed too loud, breaking into the vibrations that were bouncing back and forth between Xander and the blonde woman. "I almost forgot to introduce you two. Summer, this is Xander. He's one of Holden's friends. Xander, this is Summer. She and her sister run The Enchanted Elm, and we've been friends since college."

"Pleased to meet you," Summer said, her pink lips parting into a luscious smile.

"It's nice to meet you, too." Xander extended his hand to shake hers, knowing just how dangerous it was. The two versions of himself jolted against each other, each fighting for space on this planet. He blinked to clear his vision, but it wasn't working. He had little doubt this was the woman who had triggered his reaction from the moment they had arrived, and there was no telling what might happen if he actually touched her, but he couldn't help himself. He was vaguely aware of Holden and Leah watching them, but he didn't care. Let the whole world watch if it meant he would finally get to know who he was meant to be with.

Electricity zapped through his fingertips and palms as she took his hand, but not the kind of impulse that made one jump back and shake out the pain. It was pleasant, intriguing, and erotic as it shot bolts throughout his body. His tongue ran over the backs of his teeth, expecting them to turn sharp and dangerous at any time, and he almost wanted them to. Xander wanted to give in to the dragon side of himself that he had worked so hard to suppress, letting his wings out for everyone at the picnic to see. She had set him on fire, the flames inextinguishable. He was meant to be with her, and he would be. Whatever he had to do, he would do it. Summer was his.

On the outside, he did his best to keep his calm. He clamped his teeth together and curled his toes inside his shoes, every muscle in his body tensing as it fought the battle between reptilian and humanoid. He didn't want to let go of her hand, but he knew it was the polite thing to do. "I'm afraid I haven't been to The Enchanted Elm before. What do you do there?"

"We're a new age shop," she explained, her smile widening slightly. There was something alluring even about the curve of her cheek and the tiny mole along her jawline. "We sell everything from incense and oils to customized talismans."

"How very interesting." Xander was aware of how dry and aloof he sounded, but there wasn't any other way for him to be in that moment. It was either that or do exactly what he was afraid he wouldn't be able to avoid, which was to shift, grab Summer, and swoop off with her to claim her as his.

"You don't have to say that for my sake," Summer replied. "Most people in town think we're trouble, but they secretly come to us when their spouses and friends aren't looking." She giggled to herself, a pleasant sound that made his wings poke at his shoulder blades.

"Let's go find a place to sit down and eat," Leah said, gathering up a stack of paper plates and handing them each one. "All the good shady spots are going to be taken, otherwise."

Xander did as he was told, serving himself random bits of food without paying any attention to what he was putting on his plate. It no longer mattered that he ate, but he knew it was a good thing that he would be eating alongside Summer. The human bonding rituals he had read about heavily emphasized eating together, putting it right up on the list with going through a traumatic experience. He didn't want their lunch to be traumatic, though, and he did his best not to sit too close to her on the blanket Leah spread over the grass.

The foursome tucked into their meal, with Leah and Holden giving occasional comments on the weather and the food. "Sue Reynolds brought the fried chicken again this year," Leah said, a drumstick in hand. "She always does an amazing job with it."

A group of young women in suits walked by, dressed inappropriately for a day in the park. One of them slowed as she glared at Summer. "I thought witches only came out at night," she said sharply.

Summer gave her a dazzling smile. "Sorry to disappoint you."

"You might as well tell me what dish you brought so I can be sure not to eat it. I'm allergic to eye of newt." The woman put a manicured hand on her hip and looked down her nose at Summer.

Though he didn't quite understand all the references, Xander easily recognized what was going on. He stood up, leaving his plate on the blanket, and stepped around so that he was between the hateful woman and Summer. "I think it's time you moved along and found something better to do."

"Oooh, looks like she's bewitched a man to take care of things for her," the woman replied, holding up her fingers and wiggling them in the air as though casting a spell. "Guess we'd better get going before she raises some zombies from the dead and sends them after us." She and the other women left, laughing loudly, and headed off to presumably harass someone else.

"You didn't have to do that," Summer said as he had a seat. Her face was turned down toward her food as she poked at her coleslaw with a fork.

"I don't mind." And he didn't. Granted, they weren't causing Summer any bodily harm, but he still couldn't stand the way they talked to her. "What's their problem, anyway?" He could see no reason for them to try to tear her down like that.

She shrugged. "It's the same as anyone else. They don't like me because I'm a witch. I'm used to it."

Xander bit his tongue against explaining that on his world, anyone who was capable of sorcery was highly revered. He didn't know how much of the truth about the dragons' past Holden had revealed to Leah, or in turn, how much she might have revealed to Summer. "They're grown women, and I take it their presence here means they're business owners. You would think they would be more mature than that."

"People rarely fall into the predefined categories that society has set for them." Summer was looking at him now, a spark of something almost like anger in her eyes. "You can't really expect them to do what they're supposed to."

"I can expect them to at least be respectful of others," Xander countered. He had been so sure of what he was doing when he had intervened, but Summer's reaction was suddenly making him feel less certain.

"But you can't enforce it. People are weird creatures. Now that Joanna thinks I'm bothered by her little antics, she'll probably start ranting about me on her blog again. I don't really care what anyone says about me, but she has the power to hurt my reputation and my business in this town."

Xander felt anger welling up inside his chest, but he wasn't sure why. It might have been anger at this Joanna woman for doing whatever it was she had done to Summer in the past, or it might have been as simple as his animalistic urge to protect her. Then again, it was equally likely to be frustration at the effort of carrying on an intelligent conversation while retaining his human form. "Clearly, I'm missing part of the puzzle."

"Joanna Cox works for the paper," Leah explained. "As a journalist, she can't just come right out and say what she thinks about Summer and her sister without good reason, but she can say whatever the hell she wants to on her personal blog. A lot of people in town follow her, so it's best to stay on her good side."

"That's no reason to cower down to her," Xander said, disturbed at the news that someone could control the citizens with her threats. "Maybe if people start standing up to her, she'll back down."

"Autumn already tried that." Summer looked sad now, the corners of her mouth turned down. It pulled at Xander's heart to see her that way, and it only made him all the more eager to find this woman again and give her a piece of his mind. "You haven't met my twin sister, but she's not the kind to back down from a fight. When Joanna started spreading lies about us on her blog, Autumn went after her. Unfortunately, people were more inclined to believe a journalist they trusted instead of a witch. We almost had to close the store. Finally, once Autumn backed off, so did Joanna."

"But—"

"Sometimes it's better to be happy than to be right," Summer said firmly. "It's not an argument I want to be involved in again. Joanna keeps to herself as long as we all just stay out of each other's way."

Xander ran the tip of his tongue against the roof of his mouth, trying to decide what to say. He wanted to argue with Summer and tell her that he knew best, that she belonged to him and she needed to follow his advice. But with the realization that he couldn't say those things to her came the understanding that the woman who was meant to be his mate was a *human*. How could he possibly tell her and make her understand? He would just look crazy.

Instead, he nodded curtly. "Very well."

The rest of their lunch carried on in spurts of stiff conversation and awkward silence, but the subjects of Joanna's treachery and Summer's witchcraft didn't come up again.

As Xander prepared to leave, he turned to Summer. This was his chance to tell her how he felt about her, or at least to ask her out on a date. But the way she looked up at him told him everything he needed to know.

"It was nice to meet you," he said before turning towards the car.

# 4

Summer tossed her hair over her shoulder and closed her eyes for a moment. She trusted her feet to find their way along the sidewalk even when she couldn't see it, and she counted on her spirit guides to keep her safe. It made the world seem a little off-kilter, a little different, and she liked it that way.

"Well, that was an interesting picnic," Leah said from her side.

Summer opened her eyes and glanced at her friend. They were walking back to their respective shops now that the event was over. "You've got that look in your eyes again."

"What look is that?" Leah asked innocently.

"You know. The one when you know something and you just can't wait to tell someone."

Leah shrugged and smiled. "I wouldn't say that I *know* something. But I've got a little bit of a hunch."

"Go ahead and spill it. I can tell you want to." Summer knew how frustrating it must have been for her psychic friend to sense things and not be able to just speak about them, so she always did her best to serve as a sounding board for her.

"Well..." Leah swung her hands at her sides and looked at Leah coyly. "I noticed a little bit of something between you and Xander."

Summer stopped in the middle of the sidewalk. Another group of people heading away from the park moved around them, flowing like water around a snag in a creek. "Are you serious?"

"Of course, I'm serious." Leah's smile faded. "Didn't you feel it?"

"Maybe, just a little, right at first. I mean, he's gorgeous. But that might be where it ends." There was no doubt that Holden's friend was attractive. She recalled his shock of black hair that he kept combed neatly, and those dark eyes that hovered somewhere between brown and green. His posture had been tall and confident, boasting wide shoulders and muscular arms. Then there was that charming smile, and in the bits of conversation they'd had, he seemed quite intelligent. The more she thought about it, the more she realized there was actually a lot to like about him. But something about him was so...different from her. She had felt the draw that Leah was talking about, but she didn't quite know how to put it into words.

"Are you sure?" Leah asked skeptically. "I picked up on some pretty distinct energy between the two of you."

"No, no." Summer started walking again, ready to open up the shop, get on with her day, and forget about the picnic and everything that had happened at the park. "You know I fully support your powers, Leah, but I think you must be wrong here. I can't imagine being with a guy like him."

"What do you mean?" They had reached the door of The Enchanted Elm, and Leah followed her inside. "I think Xander seems like a really nice guy."

Summer shrugged. "Maybe he is, but that doesn't mean he's the right kind of guy for *me*. You know how I am, Leah. I like to go for long walks in the woods, meditate, and write down all my dreams. Xander seems like he likes his world a lot more...concrete than that." She flipped over the sign on the door to let customers know they were open and flicked on the lights.

"Don't you think you're judging him before you know him? I mean, you only spent a short amount of time with him."

"That's true. But I think first impressions can tell you a lot about a person." Summer pressed the power button on the cash register, making sure it had plenty of receipt tape on the roll. Opening up the store had become such a habit for her that she normally never needed to think about it, but she was concentrating to keep herself focused. Mundane activities like those were far more pleasant than thinking about her awkward encounter with Xander.

"Okay, I'll give you that. I know the first few times I met Holden, I was picking up some pretty interesting vibes off him. It had completely messed me up on a psychic level until I understood what was going on, but it was clear that he wasn't just a normal guy. But I'm still going to challenge you. What were your first impressions of Xander this afternoon?"

Summer moved around the store, straightening the displays and adjusting boxes of incense. "Well, for instance, take the way he dresses. He looked like he was ready for a business meeting instead of a picnic. Even his pants were ironed."

Leah gave her a look. "And?"

"And it makes me think he's a little too uptight. Just look at how he handled that situation with Joanna. I didn't need his help. I know how to handle her, and I know that it's much easier to just play it off like she doesn't bother me. But Xander had known me for all of two minutes and he felt like he had the right to step in and defend me." Summer felt an unfamiliar sensation tightening her chest. When was the last time she had been angry?

"I think he was just trying to do the right thing." Leah leaned against the counter and folded her arms in front of her chest. "He didn't mean to offend you."

"No, maybe not," Summer admitted. "But it was still annoying. Now there's no telling what Joanna is going to say. And I meant it when I said I really don't care what she thinks of me, but if the business starts to suffer, then Autumn is going to be really disappointed." The store was incidental to her, a means for spreading her knowledge and helping when she could, but it was everything to Autumn. The last thing she wanted was to let her down.

"Don't worry about that. Joanna already had her fun dragging your names through the mud, and she's done it to me, too. Surely, she's got something else to occupy her time."

Summer grabbed an old rag from under the counter and dusted off a glass shelf that held stone eggs. "Let's hope you're right." Irritated at herself for not just casting a spell to keep the dust out of the shop in the first place, Summer tossed the rag back under the counter.

"Well, don't discount him just yet. I have a feeling he might surprise you. I trust Holden's opinion, if nothing else, and he wouldn't be friends with Xander if he was a bad guy."

"Maybe not, but that doesn't mean I'm interested in him." She couldn't quite explain her aversion to him. Xander hadn't done anything terrible, but he hadn't seemed to understand her position. Somehow, that had been enough.

Since there weren't any customers in the shop yet, Summer leaned against the counter next to Leah. She pressed her lips together, debating on asking the questions that had been floating through her mind ever since Leah and Holden had gotten together. "So, he's really a dragon, huh?" It was a lame start, but it was still a start.

"Yeah," Leah replied, her eyes sparkling at the subject. "It's crazy, isn't it? I mean, things hadn't worked out when I was with a regular guy. Victor could never understand what it was like to be a psychic. Holden might not be a psychic himself, but he definitely knows what it's like to not fit in with the rest of the crowd. He's used to being on his own and relying on only his closest friends, and I have to say I really like that about him."

"I guess that's what Naomi meant when she said there were others like her close at hand." Naomi had been a dragon shifter as well and a friend of theirs back in college. She had always been secretive about her past. Unfortunately, she had passed away in an accident five years ago, but Leah, Autumn and Summer were lucky enough to be able to speak with her when they held séances. Naomi had given them a cryptic message about Holden before they had understood he was also a dragon.

"She must have known somehow, but in a way, I'm glad she didn't tell me directly." Leah was smiling, her expression distant. "Being a psychic, I should know better than to expect messages to come to me outright. They're always shrouded in a little bit of mystery, but that's a good thing. It helps to keep life exciting."

"But it's got to be somewhat...difficult to live with a dragon, right?"

Leah paused for a moment before she turned to her friend. "Just ask me what it is you want to know, Summer; I don't mind. Holden knows that you're aware of what he is, and I think we both understand why someone might be curious about things."

Despite the open invitation, Summer still felt a little awkward. She was an open person herself, but she wasn't trying to live as two different creatures. And it really wasn't any of her business, even if Leah was one of her best friends. Still, this was the best chance she would get to ask. "Does he shift very often? I mean, is he usually a dragon or a human?"

"Most of the time, he stays in his human form. It's a good example for his son, Finn, since he'll be growing up on this world. I don't really mind when he does shift, and I know it lets out a certain amount of tension for him, but I think Holden and I are both more comfortable together when we're the same species."

Summer raised an eyebrow. There was no turning back now. "And in the bedroom?"

Leah laughed. "Completely human, I promise. Is that what's turning you off from Xander? I mean, he *is* a dragon, too, and that can be a lot to get used to."

"Of course not. I mean, I'm a witch. I'm not exactly the girl next door. And besides, Naomi was a dragon, too; she was one of the loveliest beings I've ever known."

It felt so uncomfortable not to know just what was happening with Xander, even though there really wasn't anything going on with him. She needed to find some time for herself to realign her chakras and forget about everything else.

But customers were starting to filter into the store, and it would have to wait.

"I'd stick around, but I've got some clients scheduled this afternoon. I'll see you soon." With that, Leah gave her friend a hug and left.

It was tourist season, and there were more customers in on a Saturday afternoon than The Enchanted Elm saw throughout most of the year. Summer did her best to keep up, taking incense out of the packages for people to smell, explaining the uses of different crystals, and pointing the way to books that might prove helpful for those seeking to learn more about their own latent powers.

As busy as she was, she couldn't stop thinking about Xander. She really had judged him too quickly, and that wasn't like her. Summer prided herself on being not just a free spirit, but a person with an open mind, someone who accepted all kinds of people and never made assumptions. So why had she done this to Xander? Was she really that upset that he had tried to defend her? She was an independent person and she didn't need his help, but she had been very ungrateful toward him. Leah had explained the situation, and Xander had backed off in the end. So, there must have been something else about him that was holding onto her mind.

"Excuse me," said an older woman who had come into the store. She had steely gray hair drawn back into a braid and bright blue eyes that belied her age. "I was looking for something that might help my granddaughter."

Summer smiled and took a deep breath. This was the sort of thing she was good at. She liked to help people, and as far as she was concerned, that was the real reason the store was open. It gave the public an open venue to come and talk to her or Autumn instead of tracking down a witch in the middle of the woods. "Gladly. What sort of trouble is she having?"

The woman frowned. "She's just started in a new school, and she's having an awful time getting along. She hasn't been able to make any real friends, yet, and the only thing she wants is to go back to her old school. She's so very sad and frustrated, and I hate to see her that way. I've tried talking to her and taking her out on the weekends to make her feel better, but it doesn't seem to be making any difference."

The woman's grief tugged at Summer's heart. At the same time, her mind was running a mile a minute as she tallied up all the different herbs, stones, and crystals that might help. "The best thing I could do for her is to make a talisman. She could wear it around her neck, and it would just look like a pretty pendant, but it would have elements to help heal her broken heart, build confidence, and make connections with others."

"You can really do that?" the woman whispered.

"I can. Of course, she'll need to understand what it is. If she thinks of it as nothing more than a necklace, it's not going to have nearly as much power. It will take me a little bit of time to put it together, but if you write down your name and number for me, I can call you when it's ready." Summer led her to the counter and handed her a piece of paper and a pen.

She scribbled quickly and gave it back. "Is there anything else I can do for her?"

"There is always *something* that can be done," Summer assured her. "You and I both know how fragile young girls can be. Keep working with her, and let her know you love her. In fact, take her one of these." Summer plucked a small pink stone from a nearby basket. "It's rose quartz, and it's the stone of unconditional love. Give it to her and tell her to put it in her pocket. Anytime she's feeling nervous, she can reach in her pocket and touch it, and she'll know you're always out there looking out for her."

Tears formed in the woman's eyes as she looked down at the stone.

She traced its smooth surfaces with her fingertip. "That's so sweet. I think she'll really appreciate that. How much do I owe you?"

Summer waved her hand. "Not a thing. Take it and let me know how things go. I'll call you as soon as I have the talisman ready, which should just be a couple of days."

The woman took a business card from the shelf next to the basket. "Thank you. I'm going to tell everyone I know about you and how wonderful you are." She practically flew out of the shop, eager to get back to her granddaughter.

Summer sighed with satisfaction, but she hoped that the woman didn't include the part about the stone being free when she told all her friends about her experience. Autumn would be pissed if she came back into town to find a line of customers out their door looking for free stuff.

There was already, however, a line at the counter. She hadn't been keeping track of time while she helped the woman, and she moved quickly to ring up her customers. As she did so, she realized that there might be a reason for Xander constantly coming to the front of her mind. Perhaps he needed help just as the grandmother did, and Summer would need to make a talisman of some kind for him. She couldn't pretend to know what he needed it for, and she wouldn't dare make it without him asking, but it made sense that he might need her help. After all, he was relatively new in this world, from what she understood about the dragons.

With the cash register caught up, she decided that she was correct. She didn't need to worry about what Leah saw as a spark between the two of them or what Xander's intentions had been when he'd jumped up to protect her from Joanna. The universe had thrust him into her life because he was going to need her in some way, and that was all the reason she needed.

## 5

---

"WELL, THAT WAS AWKWARD," HOLDEN SAID AS THEY DROVE AWAY FROM Beau's house, where they had just picked up the children.

"Thanks for being so delicate." Xander slouched in the passenger seat and rolled his eyes. "I should know about these things. I'm the one who's done all the research on this sort of stuff, so I should understand how to go about it. I knew that I should ask Summer about herself and try to get to know her, but it was next to impossible while I was fighting off a shift."

Holden put his hand in the air in half a shrug. "Tell me about it! I think I scared Leah half to death when I first met her. A guy tried to grab her at the bar, and I would have killed him for it. She saw that in me, and it was no wonder it took her a while to relax around me. But in the end, I think that's just the way it was meant to be."

"It worked out for you guys, anyway," Xander admitted. "But now I have to figure out how to make it work for *me*."

Holden took his eyes off the road for a minute to glance at him. "I take it that means you haven't given up yet."

"Do you think I should?"

"Absolutely not. If nothing else, you'll figure out that it was a false alarm and cross one more woman off your list. I have a feeling that's not the case, though. You've always been so put-together, and Summer is the first person who has managed to knock you off your high horse with nothing more than a look."

"I can't give up anyway." Xander looked to the backseat, where Nora was safely buckled into her car seat. She was the most beautiful thing he had ever seen, and he felt the same need to protect her as he did with Summer. "She deserves to have a mother, and the physical reaction I have to Summer tells me she's the one. At least, I *think* that's what it's telling me. Either that, or I'm allergic to her. For the first time in my life, I almost couldn't tell which form I was in."

"That's a familiar feeling," Holden replied with a grin. "So, what are you going to do?"

"Well, all the dating guides I've read have suggested things like bringing flowers and chocolates. I guess giving a gift is a way of apologizing."

"So, then you don't have to actually say you're sorry?" Holden rubbed the stubble on his chin. "I might have to remember that."

Xander shook his head. "I'm not sure it's all that effective. Humans don't seem to have hard and fast rules like we dragons do. Roses might work on one woman, but another woman might prefer daisies. I guess that's one of the questions I should have asked her as part of getting to know her, instead of just jumping up and thinking I could protect her from that vile woman."

Holden laughed. "She really got under your skin, didn't she?"

"I thought at first that she was just being nasty and calling Summer names, but then I realized that Summer really is a witch. I think you might have mentioned it to me, and then it clicked when she talked about the new age shop."

"Does it bother you? Her being a witch?"

Xander felt a lopsided grin tightening his cheek. "Honestly, I think it might even be a little bit sexy. I like the idea that she's not just some regular woman. I could find one of those anywhere. But a witch, well, that's different. Still, that other woman—Joanna whoever—has no right to belittle her like that." He curled his fist on the armrest, angry all over again. Joanna hadn't done Summer any physical harm, but the look in her eye said she wished she could have.

"Easy now, Knight in Shining Armor. I don't think Summer was too pleased with the way you stepped in. Maybe she's not looking for someone to be Prince Valiant."

"Who?"

"Something Leah showed me, an old comic strip. Anyway, that's not the point. Just tell me what you're going to do to win Summer's favor. I was purely lucky with Leah, but I don't think that's going to work for you."

"Thanks for the vote of confidence," Xander snorted. "I think I'll just have to show up, apologize, and ask her if we can start fresh. I don't know what I'll do if she rejects me again, though. I can't exactly kidnap her and fly off to a cave until she submits to my will." There were a few dragons back on Charok who had done similar deeds when they believed they had found their destined mates, but it wasn't a widely accepted practice. The females of the species were highly respected, which the dragons considered a mark of their high civilization. Xander had yet to determine just how well the human females were treated in comparison; the results seemed to be all over the board.

"I think you'll come up with something. Just be patient. Or introduce her to Nora and let her do all the work. She's better-looking than you, anyway."

Xander gave Holden a playful punch on the arm and began formulating his plan.

———

XANDER TOOK a deep breath as he walked up to Summer's door. It was a quaint little cottage, and not the sort of place that most humans lived in. Instead of apartments stacked on top of each other or houses crammed shoulder-to-shoulder, this place was practically in the middle of nowhere. He stood for a moment and just listened, taking in the sounds of the wind through the trees and the birds singing. He made a mental note to learn more about the different types of housing humans preferred and why, although he thought he understood already why someone would live there.

He cleared his throat as he knocked on the door, wanting to be prepared to speak. He had rehearsed in his head a thousand times what he would say, and he knew the words by heart.

But when Summer opened the door and looked at him with those big green eyes, everything changed. He still knew exactly what to say, but they were no longer the words that he had carefully prepared. They came from somewhere else inside him, and they demanded to come out. "Summer, I'm so sorry that I offended you earlier today at the park. It's not what I intended. I thought I was doing what was best, but I didn't take into consideration the way you felt about things. I hadn't even had the chance to know how you felt, and I never should have assumed." He held out the bouquet of flowers he had specially picked for her, a mix of wildflowers in numerous colors. "I hope you'll forgive me."

Summer blinked at him and glanced down at the flowers. "Xander, I...I don't quite know what to say. I never expected you to show up here." She paused a moment, tipping her head. "How did you know where I live, anyway?"

His face flushed, and he could feel the burning in his cheeks. "I asked Leah. She said it would be alright if I were to stop by."

She squinted one eye in a playful look of suspicion before finally nodding. "Well, I guess if she says it's alright, then it is. Come in." She opened the door further and stood back.

As soon as he stepped inside, Xander realized that he would have known it was her home even if he hadn't already known she'd lived there. There was such a sense of her about the place, and even though he didn't know her all that well, he could tell that she had made it very much her own. The furniture was a random collection of old pieces that had been reupholstered or repainted. Bright colors adorned the walls, from the paint to the light curtains that draped alongside the large windows. These were all open, letting a cool breeze flow through the place. A swath of beaded fabric set the living room off from the kitchen. It looked like the inside of a gypsy caravan if someone had taken off the wheels and parked it in the middle of the woods. "You have a beautiful place."

"Thank you," she said graciously, reaching down into a cabinet for a vase. Summer was wearing a long dress made of thin, purple fabric that showed off the gentle opalescence of the skin on her shoulders, and it draped gracefully around her body as she moved. She disappeared behind the curtain for a moment, and Xander could hear the sound of water as she filled the vase. When Summer returned, she set it on the coffee table and took the flowers from him. "You didn't have to do this, you know. I've already figured out what's going on between us."

"You have?" Xander couldn't hide the relief from his voice. If Summer already understood that they were meant to be together, then there was a big load off his shoulders in explaining it to her. It wasn't every day that he had to face the prospect of telling a witch that she belonged to him. "I'm glad to hear it."

She shook her head. "I'm ashamed of myself, really, that I didn't figure it out sooner. I'm a firm believer that people come into each other's lives for certain reasons. Although I never could have guessed just how important Leah would have been in my life back when we met in college, I know now that I couldn't have learned as much about myself as I did without her. She's been a vital part in my life."

"And us?" Xander watched as Summer arranged the flowers neatly in the vase. Her hands seem to move on their own, arranging and fluffing until the bouquet stood full and grand from the glass vase. She only had to breathe on them to make them bend to her will, and he wondered if there was some sort of magic at play. He didn't care. She could work all the magic she wanted, as long as he had the privilege of just standing there and watching her.

She turned to look at him over her shoulder, her eyes bright and sharp. "I wasn't sure at first. I think I was misreading the signs the universe sent to me, and maybe that was because I let Joanna get me frazzled. I haven't done that in a very long time." Summer straightened, moving across the room to sit in an overstuffed chair, upholstered in a thick fabric with tiny pink flowers. She gestured for him to have a seat as well.

Xander sat, barely resting on the edge of sofa's blue cushions. "It's interesting, isn't it, that we can feel so uncomfortable when we're near someone who's going to make such a difference? You would think it would be the opposite." He had never felt so strange in his life as he had that first moment he'd met Summer. There was a similar feeling taking over him in that moment, but it was different. His wings still throbbed, urging him to let them free, but it was a pleasant feeling. It was like being on the verge of orgasm, and yet being content to wait for it. He wondered if this was because it was just the two of them, and there was no one else around to be a potential competitor. He'd have to check with Holden and see what he knew later.

Summer nodded at his observation. She leaned against the back of the chair, her long hair tumbling down over her shoulders and gracing the curves of her breasts. Everything in the room seemed to compliment her, from the way the dark fabric in her dress brought out the boldness of her eyes to the delicate lilac scent that wafted through the air. "I agree, and I want you to know that I'm happy to help you."

"You...you are?" He wasn't disappointed to hear it, but it seemed like such an odd way to phrase things. Xander wanted Summer to desire him as much as he desired her, but she made it sound like she was just doing him a favor.

"Of course. People come to me all the time for such things," she replied with a gentle and knowing smile.

"They do?" Xander had a hard time imagining that random men approached her all the time asking her to be their mates. That didn't seem like the sort of thing most human women would like.

"Well, I do have a pretty good reputation around town. People don't always want to admit it, because they're embarrassed or ashamed. But it's what I do, isn't it? There's no reason to be afraid to ask for help every now and then."

Xander cleared his throat, doing his best to stay composed. His body was reacting more violently now, perhaps in reaction to his discomfort at what she was saying. It was time to just come clean about it all. "Summer, I'm not sure you and I are on the same page."

"Sure we are." She leaned forward in her seat, staring him straight in the eyes. He could see the tiny flecks of gold that danced around in the green seas of her irises. "You need a spell of some sort. You're looking for a talisman or an enchantment. You don't have to feel strange about it, Xander. Just tell me what kind of energies you're wanting to draw to yourself—or keep away, for that matter—and I'll be happy to make it happen."

Xander opened his mouth to reply, and then shut it again. This definitely wasn't what he wanted from her, not unless there was some sort of spell that would make her understand just how he felt. "I'm afraid that's not it at all."

She stared at him for a long moment, and the corners of her mouth turned down slightly. "Then I'm more out of touch with the universe than I imagined."

"Look, I'll save us both some time and just be direct about it. I think you know that I'm a dragon."

"Yes."

"And that my dragon brethren and I have come to Earth to find safe homes for the children of our queen, whom we rescued before they could be killed by the wizards and ogres."

"That's the gist of what I understand, yes."

He made sure to keep his gaze steadily on her. Based on what he'd read, humans often gave small signs when they were lying, like looking away from the other person. He didn't want Summer to have any reason to doubt him. "It's also our duty to make sure that these children have mothers, to make sure that they get all the care and nurturing that they need."

"If you're asking me for a love potion, that sort of thing is purely fictional—"

"No." He leaned forward, daring to take her hand. It was soft and delicate against his, her skin as smooth as silk. He never wanted to let it go. "I need *you*."

The shaking of Summer's head started out very subtly, almost invisible, but it gradually increased as she spoke. "That's not the kind of help I can give to you, Xander. I don't even know why you would ask me. I don't know much about children." Summer stood, moving across the room and standing near a buffet table covered in candles and stones. "It's all very flattering, but you can't just ask a random woman to be a mother to your child."

Somehow, her resistance made him even more determined to make her understand. He stood as well and stepped around the coffee table. He approached her slowly, not wanting to scare her off, but he didn't even want to let the distance of the room separate them. Not now that he had finally found her. "You're not random, Summer. Not at all. You and I are...meant to be together."

She stared up at him, looking curious and terrified simultaneously. "And how do you know that?"

"As a witch, do you believe in destiny? Fate?"

"Well, yes."

"Then could you also believe that for dragons, we have a special instinct that tells us when we meet the woman we're meant to be with? Summer, when I'm near you, I almost can't control myself." He had only ever shared his feelings about what it was like to be a dragon with the other men, but he would tell Summer anything and everything she wanted to hear if only it would make her understand. "My body can't decide if it wants to be human or dragon. There are primal parts of my brain that threaten to take over my consciousness, and I'm willing to do anything to be with you."

Her lower lip trembled slightly as she asked, "Should I be scared by that?"

"No," he assured her quickly, reaching out to delicately touch her arm with his fingertips. It wasn't enough, and he would never be able to touch her enough, but the sheer sensation of having his molecules touch hers was pure bliss, nevertheless. "Just know that I need you in my life. You're the only woman who has ever made me feel this way." He wanted to lean forward, bend his head and press his lips to hers. If his words couldn't get through to her, then maybe there was another way.

But she pressed a hand against his chest. It was small, but it was firm. "Xander, this is all very sweet. In fact, it's probably the nicest thing anyone has ever said to me, but you can't really think I would just accept it?"

His breath heaved in his chest with the urge to have her. She *had* to accept it. "Tell me what I need to do. I'll do it. Anything."

Summer moved around him, slipping out of his reach to stand near the door. "How do I know any of this is true? I don't mean to call you a liar, but you're saying that the universe is telling *you* we're meant to be together. So why isn't it telling *me*?"

This was something he hadn't thought about before. He'd never needed to, basing his future only on his reaction to her presence. Xander licked his lip. "I don't really know the answer to that. But I do know that Holden felt this same way when he met Leah, and I don't think either one of us can deny that the two of them are meant to be together."

"They're perfect together," Summer affirmed. "I don't think I've ever seen Leah so happy. But what's right for her isn't necessarily what's right for me. I think you're a good person, Xander, but I'm not ready to be in a long-term relationship. I still have so much that I want to do; things I need to do on my own. How can I just let someone step in on that?"

"Maybe I can make your work easier," he suggested. Xander didn't know if it was true or not, but he knew that he would try.

"You don't even know me," Summer countered. "How could we possibly be destined for each other?"

She was slipping away from him. He was going to lose her, and then what would he do? Spend the rest of his life wishing to relive the sensation of having her near? "You're right," he admitted. "I don't know you. But I want to. Couldn't we at least spend some time together, even just as friends? Give me time to understand who you are, and let yourself understand who I am. Not just as a dragon and not just as a man, and definitely not just as some crazy guy who insists that he's supposed to be with you." They both laughed a little at that, and it released some of the tension in Xander's chest. "I'm just asking for a chance."

Summer glanced at the flowers on the table and at the floor. She closed her eyes, her chest expanding as she took in a deep breath. Xander couldn't stop looking at her pink lips as she slowly let the air pass through them, and he felt the intensity of her stare when she opened her eyes once again. "There's nothing wrong with getting to know each other."

"Thank you." Not wanting to press his luck, Xander said goodbye and left. Beads of sweat stood out on his brow as he got back into his car, even though the hardest part of it was over now. He had told her. No, wait; that wasn't the hardest part at all. He had yet to *convince* her. Somehow, it almost seemed wrong to have to persuade a woman to see that she was his destiny, but it was the only option he had at the moment. He would have to take it and run with it. Xander pulled slowly out of the long, twisting driveway that led up to Summer's house, but he pressed the pedal to the floorboard once he was out on the highway.

## 6

ON MONDAY MORNING, SUMMER DRAGGED HERSELF OUT OF BED. THERE wasn't time for her morning walk, and she wasn't even sure she wanted to go. She snagged a pair of leggings and an oversized tank top from her closet, made a quick cup of coffee, and headed for town.

She showed up at the store early to unlock the door and turn on the lights, needing something to do besides sit around at home and think about what Xander had told her. While destiny was something she did wholeheartedly believe in, she wasn't sure that it extended to romantic relationships. Lots of people *thought* they were supposed to be together, only to wind up divorced later on down the road. Maybe people just didn't know what it really meant to be fated for each other.

But that didn't mean dragons didn't know.

Shaking off the notion, she picked up the phone and dialed Autumn's number. She had received a text from Autumn letting her know that she had landed safely, but she hadn't talked to her sister otherwise since Saturday morning. That was a long time to be without a twin, and she needed to hear Autumn's voice.

"Good morning," Summer chirped into the phone when her sister answered sleepily. "Don't tell me you're wasting your vacation in bed."

"What time is it?" Autumn asked grumpily. Some banging and clashing came through the phone.

"It's ten."

"Oh. Well, it would seem early to you if you'd been out all night partying, too."

"Trying to relive your college days? I hate to break it to you, but we're not twenty anymore." Not that Summer could really chastise her; she had stayed up late the past two nights just thinking. While she had started off cleaning the house or writing down ideas for new spells, she would then find herself just staring into space and thinking about Xander. It made for very restless sleep once she finally did go to bed, with his handsome face ever-present in her mind's eye, telling her that they were meant for each other. It was romantic in a way, the sort of thing that any normal woman would see in a movie and swoon over, wishing her real-life partner would say such things. But it was much more disconcerting when it happened in real life.

"You don't have to remind me," Autumn replied, bringing Summer back once again from her fantasies. "Marla doesn't seem to realize that we've gained another decade, though. She can still stay out and drink with the best of them. I was really glad to be living it up like that, at first. I wasn't thinking about the shop or any of my obligations, and I think I needed that. But I'm sure as hell paying for it now."

"It's good for you to unwind every now and then," Summer assured her as she busied herself with firing up the cash register and checking her list of things to do for the day. She had made the talisman for the woman's granddaughter, and she would need to call her later to let her know it was in. "You deserve this."

"I'm glad you think so. I feel bad about leaving you there to run the shop. Damn, I've got to find some water or something."

Summer smiled. "Don't feel bad. It's my store, too, and I'm happy to hold down the fort. Things were busy over the weekend, so you'll probably find a nice little chunk of change when you come back and pull the reports." At least, Summer hoped so. It had certainly felt busy while she was the only one there to run it, and she didn't want Autumn to have any excuse not to leave her again.

"I know this is going to be hard to believe, but I'm not sure I care about our profits right now. I'm just ready to get home and sleep in my own bed."

"When do you plan to come back?" Summer knew that Autumn had left her plane ticket open-ended with the pretense that she could come back early if Summer needed help with the store. Summer didn't take any offense to this, even though she knew she could run things just fine by herself. It was what made Autumn feel comfortable. But that also meant that a specific return date hadn't been discussed.

"Why? What's wrong?" Autumn suddenly sounded much more awake and alert.

"Nothing's *wrong*," Summer hedged. "It's just that things have been a little...strange around here."

"Strange how?"

Summer did her best to explain the picnic with Xander, the awkward situation with Joanna, and the bewildering conversation they'd had at her house.

"He actually told you that you're supposed to be together? As in, *destined*?"

Summer could close her eyes and relive the moment perfectly. "Yes. Just like that."

"You know, Summer, I love you. I think you're a wonderful person, but I think you can also be a bit gullible at times."

Pulling the phone away from her face to glare at it, Summer asked, "What's that supposed to mean?"

Autumn sighed. "You just try so hard to see the best in everyone. You like to think that the rest of the world is just as honest as you are, but that's not the case. Lots of guys will say things like that because they think it's what you want to hear."

"No, this is different." Why was she arguing *for* Xander? She had called Autumn in the hope of some form of reassurance, but this wasn't it. "I might not like conflict, but that doesn't mean I'm stupid."

"I never said you were stupid..."

"You implied it!" Summer's voice was loud in the store. Fortunately, no customers had come in yet.

"Listen, that's not what I meant to say. I just know that you tend to see your own goodness reflected back in other people."

"Then why is this guy upsetting me so much?" Summer demanded. Heat spread through her chest and stomach as she thought about every tiny irritation she had suffered since she'd met Xander. "Why does it bother me so much that he thinks we're supposed to be mates or whatever? It's a nice idea, I guess, but I'm not really ready for something like that. Why am I so disturbed at the idea that he just might be right?" As her own words echoed back to her, she realized the truth in them. That was exactly what was bothering her so much.

Autumn knew it, too. "Is it such a terrible thing to find someone who loves you and wants to be with you?"

"He can't possibly *love* me," Summer argued through gritted teeth. "He doesn't even know me. And even if he gets to know me, he's going to discover what I already know."

"And that is?"

"That we're two completely different people." It seemed so obvious to Summer, and it was frustrating that no one else seemed able to pick up on it. "He drives a luxury sedan and wears dress shirts and slacks. I'd be willing to bet that he has a specific schedule he follows every day and that he can't handle it when someone messes it up. I'm nothing like him, and he would be miserable with me. Wait, why are you laughing?" Summer tightened her grip on the phone. If it wasn't her twin on the other end, she would have hung up several minutes ago.

"Because you're being ridiculous. You keep going on about how he doesn't know you, but you don't really know him, either. Maybe he's not as uptight as you think he is. And who gives a shit what he wears? It's what he's got underneath his clothes that's going to matter in the bedroom."

It was just like Autumn to have sex at the forefront of her mind. "What about the way he interfered at the picnic? I don't need anyone to handle my business for me."

There was a pause on the other end. "You and I have always had each other's backs, right?"

"Of course." Summer wasn't sure where Autumn was going with this.

"And there are times when we've really needed to rely on each other, when we couldn't quite handle things on our own, right?"

"Yes."

"So, what's wrong with having someone else on your side? Just because he didn't handle it the way you wanted him to doesn't mean he's a bad guy. You should give him a chance, Summer. Just the way you're acting tells me that."

Summer felt as though her sister could look through time and space and see her standing there in the middle of the shop with her fingers raking through her hair, looking frazzled. "How's that?"

"You don't get like this. You're calm and quiet, letting the peace of the universe be your light. But right now, you're angry and loud. This guy has gotten under your skin, and that's got to mean something. I can't say if you're destined to be together or not, but you are at least destined to figure out what this man will mean to your life."

Summer felt weak and defeated. She had thought a conversation with her sister would replenish her energy and help her focus, but that hadn't been the case. And she still had an entire day of work ahead of her. "I guess Leah must think so, too," she admitted. "She's the one who told him where I live."

Autumn laughed. "Leave it up to the psychic! I've got to go, hun, but just think about what I said. I'll let you know when I'm on my way home, okay? Love you." She hung up with a click.

Puffing up her cheeks and blowing her breath out through her lips, Summer knew that her sister was probably right. But she didn't have to like it, and she didn't have to accept that there was any possibility of a relationship just yet. After all, the only thing she had agreed to do was to get to know Xander, and right now she had a store to run.

The bell over the door rang with perfect timing, admitting the first customer of the day. Summer plastered on a smile that she didn't feel and came around the counter. "Good morning. Is there something I can help you find?"

The young woman smiled shyly. "I'm just looking around at the moment, but thanks."

"Okay. Let me know if there's anything I can do for you." Summer was almost disappointed. If the customer had questions or wanted to know what a certain herb was for, then she would have an excuse to think about something other than Xander. Damn him for being so charismatic. The way he had come up to her, towering over her without making her feel trapped, explaining how desperate he was to have her...It had sent a certain sensation through her that she wouldn't have expected to feel for a man like him. Briefly, she wondered just what he looked like when he shifted...

"Excuse me." A customer stood in front of the counter, looking at her expectantly. It was an older woman with dyed hair, and she must have come in without Summer even noticing. "I heard you have herbal remedies here."

"What? Oh, yes. Of course. Right over here."

The flow of customers was steady that morning. The warm weather had made more people take time off from work, and they were choosing to spend that time coming in. Granted, Autumn and

Summer had recently renewed the spell of welcoming around the front door, but it had never worked quite as well as it had been that day.

She was just getting into the routine of things when an unexpected figure came through the door. He wore his usual attire that seemed just a tad too formal for everyday wear; that day, he chose charcoal slacks and a polo. He looked around the store with interest as he held a tiny girl on his hip.

"Let me know if you have any more questions," Summer said distractedly to a customer who had asked her about white sage smudge sticks. She threaded her way through the store until she stood in front of Xander, suddenly self-conscious about the way she had dressed that day. "What are you doing here?"

He smiled at her confidently. "I hadn't been in your store before, so Nora and I thought we would stop in."

"Oh. Um, okay." She shifted her weight uncomfortably on her feet. She'd never worried about what anyone thought about the store, other than the time that Joanna had harassed them on her blog.

"Is that alright? I thought it would be a nice step in getting to know you." His voice was so smooth; his eyes, so entrancing.

She swallowed. "Sure. Of course."

The little girl on his hip babbled nonsensically, calling Summer's attention to her. She was an absolute doll, with curly brown hair that rested like a halo around her head. Her chocolate eyes were innocent and curious, and she reached out to Summer with a pudgy hand.

"Well, hi there, sweetheart." Summer felt much more comfortable with the little girl than she did with Xander. She, at least, wasn't expecting anything from her. "How are you this morning?"

"This is my daughter, Nora," Xander said proudly.

Summer couldn't help but notice just how much he beamed when he spoke of her, and it sent a little thrill of electricity through her chest. She reached out to take the hand Nora offered to her, and the child gave her a very similar smile. Summer knew they weren't related biologically, but they might as well have been. "It's very nice to meet you."

Nora pointed eagerly at a nearby shelf, and Summer turned to see what she was interested in. "Oh, you like the stones? Come and see." Summer stepped over and picked one from the basket. It was a dark brown swirled with green, almost the same color as Xander's eyes. She put it in Nora's outstretched palm. "This one is called jade."

"Jay?" Nora asked.

Summer was tickled at the tot's attempt at the name. "Yes, you're a quick study, aren't you?"

"Careful with it," Xander warned his daughter as she examined the stone.

"She can't hurt it," Summer assured him. "In fact, she can keep it. Put it up on a shelf in her room. It attracts abundance and wellbeing."

Xander raised an eyebrow as well as the corners of his mouth. "That can't hurt. What do the other stones do?"

Easily diving into her area of expertise, Summer took more from the basket and explained what kind of energies they attracted. She paused as she thought about the pretty gems. "What's your birthstone?"

Xander gave her a blank look. "I'm afraid I don't know what that means."

"Oh, well there's a stone linked to every birth month. Garnet for January, amethyst for February, and so on." She had always enjoyed helping people find beautiful versions of their birthstones, and not the lab-created, fancy-cut ones they could find in a jewelry store.

He pursed his lips and scratched the back of his head with his free hand. "I don't know," he said quietly. "I don't have a birthday, in the normal sense of the word."

Summer instantly understood her mistake. Of course he didn't have a birthday. If they kept track of such things where he was from, then they undoubtedly used a different calendar than everyone on Earth did. "Of course. I'm sorry."

"That's alright." And she could tell that he meant it. "Nora does, though. She was hatched—I mean, born—in June. What birthstone does she have?"

"Ah. Come with me." She led them to a glass case on the other side of the shop floor, unlocked the door, and picked up a stone of dark purple. "Alexandrite. It brings joy and hope, and it's very rare. That's why I have to keep it locked up. One of the neatest things about this stone is that it looks purple because we're under incandescent lights, but when you go outside, it appears a greenish-blue. It's different depending on how you look at it."

"That seems very appropriate," Xander commented, admiring the stone. "How much is it?"

Summer's heart fluttered. She wanted to just give it to him. Nora was clearly fascinated by the stone, holding it tightly in her fist and examining it through her fingers. But this was an expensive item, and one that Summer would balk at being given away for free. Reluctantly, she showed him the price tag.

Xander nodded. "We'll take it."

"Miss? Miss! I've got a question for you about these essential oils over here."

Summer handed the stone to Xander and gently closed the cabinet. "Excuse me for just a second." She helped the woman, who wanted to know what kind of oil was best for keeping her sinuses clear. Then she had to dash across the store to help a different customer who knew she had seen a beautiful journal in there before and wanted to buy it for her niece's birthday, but she could no longer remember exactly what it looked like. A delivery driver arrived with a pallet full of boxes, and Summer had to make a pathway for his dolly so he could place it in the back room for her. There was no time to go through the boxes right then.

Several customers later, she finally returned to Xander. "I'm so sorry about all of that. I swear, we've been doing more business this week than we usually do, and of course it would happen when my sister is out of town."

And, of course, it would also happen when she had Xander standing there waiting for her. As much as she had tried to convince herself that the two of them shouldn't have anything to do with each other, she found herself wanting to get back to him and Nora far more than she wanted to help her customers.

"Don't apologize," he said gently. "You have a business to run, and I completely understand that. Besides, Nora and I have been very entertained looking at all the different candles."

As if to demonstrate, Nora reached out towards a pink candle, and then touched her nose. Her father did as he was asked, lifting the candle from the display and holding it up so she could smell it. She sniffed dutifully and then grinned.

Summer couldn't help but be enchanted. Nora was of the age when most children simply couldn't be controlled. "You know, I can't even count on all my fingers and toes the number of times someone has come in here with a child her age that was running wild. Touching everything, grabbing delicate items from the display cases, screaming. It's a delight to have someone like her in here." The connection she felt with Nora was a deep one that wrapped around her heart and squeezed gently.

The little girl reached out to Summer with both hands, opening and closing her fists.

"I think she wants you to hold her," Xander said with a knowing smile.

Summer wanted to scowl at him, but she simply couldn't. Instead, she held her arms out for Nora, who practically leaped to her. The child felt warm and soft against her, and Summer noticed the way her own body reacted. It seemed there was no greater privilege than having the baby close and feeling her little fingers and they reached out to gently caress Summer's earrings.

"Nay?" Nora asked.

"My name? I'm Summer, sweetie," she replied happily.

"I Nora," the girl replied matter-of-factly.

Giggling, Summer held her a little tighter. "Yes, I know. And it's a beautiful name. Do you like my store?"

Nora's eyes widened. "You?"

Summer didn't need to ask Xander for an interpretation. "Yes, this is my store. My sister and I own it. Do you like it?"

The child nodded so enthusiastically that her entire body bobbed in Summer's grip. "Pretty!"

Unfortunately, a short line of customers was once again forming at the counter. Summer turned to Xander, prepared to hand the child back, but then she had another idea. "Nora, would you like to come back here and help me with the cash register?"

Nora might or might not have known what she was talking about, but she nodded again.

"Okay, come on. We've got to go back here." Summer carried Nora back behind the counter. "Now, this lady wants to buy a pretty crystal. I'll type in the price, and then you push this big green button for me, okay?"

"Green!" Nora did as she was asked, clapping her hands with pride when she was done.

"Good job! Now we have to put it in a bag for her. Can you do that?" Summer reached under the counter for a small paper sack, flicking it open with one hand.

Nora very delicately picked up the crystal and set it gently down into the bottom of the bag.

"I think you're a natural at this." Summer swiped the customer's debit card and gave the woman her receipt, and then she had Nora help her with the next transaction. The young man was purchasing several items, so it was a little bit more challenging, but at least he paid with a debit card as well. That made it easier to do with one hand than if she had to count out cash.

She noticed the way Xander was watching them when she was done. The gentle, loving look on his face made her flush. "What?"

"Nothing. Nothing at all." But his face said otherwise. He had thoroughly enjoyed seeing the two of them together.

Summer couldn't even be mad about it or accuse him of using his daughter to get to her. Nora was an absolute delight, and no matter what qualms Summer had about Xander, she didn't regret getting to know the child. "Nora needs to help me ring up your purchase, now."

Xander stepped up to the counter with the alexandrite, as well as the pink candle that Nora seemed to love. "There's one extra thing I would like while I'm here."

"What's that?" Summer was distracted, watching as Nora gently bagged the items, giving the candle one extra sniff with her eyes closed.

"For you to go out to dinner with me."

Summer snapped her head up to look at him. Despite how well they had been getting along since he had shown up at the shop, she still hadn't been expecting that. And in her mind, she thought she would say no. After all, she had already explained to Xander that she wasn't interested in a relationship. But her mouth—and perhaps her heart—seemed to have other plans. "Alright, but only as friends so that we can continue to get to know each other. And only if you bring Nora. I think she's my new buddy."

"Works for me," Xander said with a grin. "What do you think, Nora? Do you want to go out to eat with Summer?"

The child responded with her usual enthusiasm, making her difficult to hold onto.

Xander took her back from Summer, the paper sack with his purchases in his other hand. "Does tonight work for you?"

She would have liked more time, but then again, Summer couldn't imagine what she would really do to prepare herself. Maybe it was best to just get it over with. "Yes, that'll be fine."

"Great. We'll pick you up at seven." He smiled again, and Summer swore she caught a quick wink from him as he turned to leave the store. Nora waved, shouting "bye-bye" enthusiastically over his shoulder.

Summer waved back, feeling a distinct emptiness in the store all of a sudden. One customer remained over by the book display, but The Enchanted Elm was otherwise empty. There were plenty of boxes in the back from the new inventory shipment that needed to be gone through and accounted for, but Summer didn't have the energy. She could go through the store and make sure the sale signs were all correct and straighten the displays that the customers had disturbed, but it didn't seem very exciting.

"There has got to be something seriously wrong with me," she murmured as she forced herself to head into the back room and open up the first box. It was filled with tarot decks. She would need to call Leah and let her know they had some new ones in, just in case she needed any, but it could wait. Summer slowly counted the decks and checked them off on the sheet, eager for the work day to end.

# 7

Xander stood in front of his bathroom mirror. He had read the articles in men's magazines. He had checked online dating blogs. He'd listened to podcasts from therapists. All the information was in his mind, but none of it seemed enough to prepare him for that night. He had changed his shirt twice and his pants once, and he was considering putting on different shoes. "Don't be such an idiot, Xander," he said to himself. "If she likes you, she likes you. It won't matter what shoes you wear."

But his body seemed to understand that he was going to be near her again soon. Their proximity in the shop had caused a different reaction than when he'd taken on the feral, defensive posture at the park or while at her house when he'd felt an unbearable, surging need. It had been a more pleasant experience earlier that day, with a warmth emanating through his body, keeping him in her shop as long as possible.

Perhaps Nora's presence had made a difference there as well, since he loved her so much. It had been the most beautiful sight in the world to see Nora in Summer's arms and the way the two of them clicked so easily. Summer knew all the right tasks to ask of Nora, never trying to get her to do more than she was capable of, and yet giving her just enough to keep her entertained. Nora, in turn, had taken instantly to Summer. Maybe she felt a similar yearning for her that Xander did, only in a motherly way.

Right then, however, his body seemed to itch all over. If ants had crawled up his pantlegs and spread out over his skin, Xander wouldn't have even noticed because he was already feeling so uncomfortable. It was like he was experiencing withdrawals from not being in Summer's presence, and he couldn't wait to get back to her to settle it all down again.

Tempted to shift and go for a quick flight before his date, Xander realized he didn't have time. He had said he would pick Summer up at seven, and he couldn't leave any chance of being late. Summer was already uncertain about him, and he didn't want to give her any cause to confirm those feelings.

Dressed and as ready as he was going to get, Xander turned to Nora. "It's time to get you ready for our big night, little one," he said gently as he picked her up and carried her to her room. He showed her the dresses hanging in the closet. "Which one do you think you want to wear tonight? There's the pink one? Or maybe purple?"

On Charok, the females of the species did most of the childrearing, at least at the beginning. It wasn't until dragonlets were old enough to start exploring and learning to hunt that the fathers truly became involved, other than providing food for their families. For this reason, Xander had wondered how well he and the other men would do with the eggs they had managed to save. But their only choices were to take the eggs along, or let them be destroyed or eaten by ogres, and so there hadn't been any room for argument.

He liked to think that he was doing well enough on his own. He knew how to bathe, feed, and clothe the child, and Nora seemed happy and healthy. She enjoyed playing with the other children—whom they had decided to call cousins—as well as spending time with her father figure. But now that Xander had seen the way Summer was with Nora, he knew that he wasn't enough. He was a good parent, but a child needed as many people to love and nurture her as possible. Summer would give Nora a different perspective on things, and that could only be good for her.

Xander patiently exchanged Nora's floral romper for the blue dress she had chosen from the closet. As soon as she had wiggled out of her casual clothes, she took off out of the room and down the hallway, giggling. Xander chased her down and brought her back, keeping her in check long enough to get the dress on. That was all the patience Nora had, apparently, because then she dashed off again. She cackled wildly when her father caught her.

"Alright, young lady," he said as he scooped her up into his arms. He wanted to sound stern, but it was impossible around her. Nora's laugh was infectious, and he was laughing himself as he brought her back to her bedroom to put matching barrettes in her hair. "We can't leave the house with your hair a mess," he commented. Nora always watched him with her big, dark eyes when he spoke, as though she was hanging on to every word.

"Hair?" she asked.

"Yes, hair. I've got to comb it out and put some pretty bows in it." It was the sort of thing a mother would do, normally, but as there wasn't one around, he knew it was up to him. He had seen numerous examples of single fathers here on Earth who let their children wear dirty, mismatched clothes and eat ice cream for lunch. Xander didn't claim to be perfect, but he was at least going to try.

Nora picked up one of the bows and held it out, pressing it against Xander's hair. "Daddy hair?"

He laughed. "Daddy already did his hair, but Daddy doesn't wear bows. Only Nora."

"Comb!" She snatched up the comb he had just set down and ran it through his hair, completely messing up everything he had already done. But the look on her face was so earnest. She was trying to help him in the same way that he was helping her. She might have only been a baby, but she understood that family took care of each other.

"Yes, comb." He finished doing her hair before he went back to his own room to undo her impromptu styling session.

They picked up Summer, arriving at her house five minutes before seven o'clock. "I hope we're not too early."

Summer emerged wearing a bright yellow dress, the hemline of which skimmed her sandaled feet. The bodice had a halter top that complimented her curves in all the right ways, and Xander made a conscious effort to keep his eyes on her face. Her hair flowed in golden waves down her back. Actually, everything about Summer seemed to flow, and that was one of the things he liked so much about her. She was soft and ethereal, like a wisp of wind or a ray of sunshine. She was everything the opposite of him, and she seemed to have come straight from the earth.

"Not at all," she replied with a smile as he held the passenger door for her. "I had just enough time to get home from the shop and get changed."

"You didn't have to do anything different," he commented. "You'd look beautiful in anything." Her outfit at The Enchanted Elm had been more casual, but it really didn't matter to him; she could wear a burlap sack and he would be happy. The thought made his bones ache, longing to transform into his dragon.

"Don't try to flatter me," she warned, but she was smiling. "This whole thing is just as friends, remember?"

"I do. Nora remembers, too."

Summer had already turned around in her seat to say hi to the little girl. "Hi, sweetheart. You look very pretty in your dress."

Nora daintily picked up the hem of her skirt in her fingers and made it dance across her lap. She grinned, Summer laughed, and Xander felt his chest tighten as he fought the urge to shift.

He headed into town, clamping his teeth together against the pain in his back at keeping his wings tucked away. As much as he wanted to be near Summer and to get to know her better, it was difficult to be only a few inches away from her and not be able to truly claim her as his. He wanted this to get easier, but he wasn't sure it would ever happen until he was able to convince Summer of the link between them. Until that time, he was stuck with muscles that were constantly trying to stretch, skin that itched to turn into scales, and the constant feeling that spikes were going to come thrusting through the back of his head.

"I appreciate you agreeing to come out with me this evening," he said quietly as he made his way through town. "I know that I threw you off with what I said, and I didn't mean to upset you. But I'm a firm believer in being honest, and it wouldn't be fair not to tell you."

She rubbed those luscious lips together. "Well, you're right about that. I would hate to start up any kind of relationship with you—friendship or otherwise—only to find out later that you hadn't been upfront with me. But since we're being honest, I have a hard time believing that we would work out. Even if we got to know each other more, we seem like very different types of people."

"Of course we are," he said with a mischievous grin, "you're a witch and I'm a dragon."

"That's not what I mean." But she laughed anyway. "I just don't think our personalities would really mesh."

"What's that thing people like to say? Opposites attract?"

"They often do," she said with a nod, "but that doesn't mean they're meant to be together or that they'll be able to stay together. I've seen so many people who try to make it work when they really don't have a leg to stand on. I don't think it's worth forcing things."

"I can see that." While of course Xander had never experienced anything like divorce or even a breakup firsthand, he knew that it was a very popular subject amongst humans. They wore their heartaches on their sleeves, often telling anyone who would listen about their troubles. It seemed odd to him, but he hoped he would never have to learn more about it through his own experience. "And I can also see how, to you, this would seem like we're forcing the subject. But I'm not going to rush you, Summer. As painful as it is for me, I don't want to make you uncomfortable."

"It's painful? You mean, physically?" She turned her wide, emerald eyes to meet his gaze. "I'm sorry. I had no idea."

She sounded so hurt at his pain, and it touched him. In a way, it almost made it more difficult for him than being near her had been in the first place. He hadn't necessarily been looking for her sympathy, but the fact that she could have any sort of feeling toward him was progress. Still, he didn't want her to feel bad. "Don't be sorry. You can't help it, and neither can I. It's just how my body works."

"What's it like...being a dragon?" Summer twisted a length of her wheaten hair around her finger as she spoke.

Xander lifted his fingertips off the steering wheel while he thought. He'd never had to explain it to anyone before. He had been that way his entire life, and it was just the way things were. On Charok, there had been no need to explain himself to anyone, because they were dragons as well. Earth, of course, was different. "It's not always easy," he admitted. "It took some time to learn how to keep myself in check, because it's instinctive to shift into a stronger form when it's necessary. If my emotions are heightened, then it makes sense for me to be a dragon instead of a human. It makes things easier to deal with." Sometimes that was because he was angry, and his reptilian form was far more intimidating. But other emotions were easier to handle in his other physique as well. Xander didn't know why, but he knew that's how it worked.

"I'm sure that's difficult."

"I manage to deal with it. But it would be nice if I had more opportunities to shift. It feels good—actually, great—at times, but I can't risk
being seen. I know what would happen to me if people found out what
I am, and I can't imagine what would happen to Nora."

Summer turned in her seat again and gave a soft sigh. "She's
asleep." She watched the little girl for a moment before she faced
forward again. "She's really special."

Xander smiled proudly; he couldn't argue. He pulled up in front of
the restaurant and let Summer out before going around the back to lift
Nora out of her seat, who woke at being handled and rubbed her eyes
sleepily. A hostess sat them at a booth near the back of the restaurant,
where they were out of the way of the staff and set off a bit from the
other diners. Xander had called ahead and reserved this table in
particular, not wanting to be on display for the townsfolk. They all
knew what Summer was, and it would only hurt her reputation more if
they happened to overhear what *he* was.

"Have you eaten here before?" he asked, glancing at the small
arrangement of choices on the kids' section of the menu. "The guys
and I like to come here occasionally. They have a nice selection of fine
food, but they still have simpler fare for the kids."

"I can't say that I have," she replied as she looked over the menu
herself. "I go to that vegan café down the street a lot, though."

Xander froze, realizing just how little he knew about Summer. "Are
you vegan?"

She waved off his concern. "No, I just really like some of the food.
They have an amazing Mediterranean salad that I'm crazy about."

The waitress came by to take their drink orders, and the trio went
ahead and ordered their meals as well. Nora was settled into her
booster seat, scribbling on a paper menu with the crayons the waitress
had given her. It seemed like a cozy setting, and Xander had managed
to calm his body down somewhat. He was with Summer amongst a
crowd, but no one was threatening them.

"I know we talked about it the other day at your house, but I want
you to know that I really am sorry if I offended you when you were
dealing with that Joanna character. I shouldn't have interfered, not
knowing the history between the two of you."

The waitress brought their drinks, and Summer took a sip of her
iced tea. "I shouldn't have reacted the way I did. You were just trying to

help, and I had no reason to get angry like that. In fact, I don't get mad very often; I'm a little surprised at myself that I did. I think I just wanted so badly not to have to deal with Joanna again, and I didn't want to risk losing the tenuous peace between us."

"Leah mentioned Joanna had written about you and your sister before. Has there been anything new on her blog?" Xander sincerely hoped not. He would have to blame himself entirely if the journalist had taken to slandering the sisters once again. Well, Joanna would clearly be at fault as well, but she didn't seem the kind of woman to take the blame.

"To be honest with you, I haven't looked." Summer fished her cell phone out of her oversized purse. "I've avoided her site for a while, and I didn't bother checking it once I knew she had quit her antics."

"I'm sorry. I shouldn't have brought it up." The idea of Joanna was making him uncomfortable. He didn't feel threatened by a human woman, but anyone who wanted to cause harm to Summer was an enemy. He could feel the great furnace in his chest, stoking up the flames and preparing for battle. Xander took a long drink of water.

"No, you've made me curious." She tapped away at her phone until she had the page pulled up. "Let's see. It looks like she did post about the SBA picnic."

Xander watched her face as she read, hoping it would remain neutral. But a frown soon turned down the corners of her mouth, and her slim eyebrows scrunched together slightly. "What is it?" Xander asked tentatively.

"Not much, but here. You can read it." Summer handed over the phone.

Quickly skimming the article, Xander mostly found boring information about what kind of food was at the picnic and what businesses were represented. There was a long paragraph about the formation of the Small Business Association and what it had done for the citizens. Towards the end, Joanna had written that members were so diverse that they even included the two witches who ran The Enchanted Elm. "Well, it's not directly bad, at least."

"No. I think she probably would have liked to do more, but something was holding her back. I couldn't say what, and I'm not sure there's a point in speculating, but I can handle one tiny little blurb about the fact that Autumn and I are witches. After all, we tell anyone who wants to know."

Xander was relieved that she was taking this so well. "So, you don't think it will affect business at all?"

Summer rolled her eyes up to the ceiling as she thought. "You know, I think it might have the opposite effect of what Joanna intended. Most people know about The Enchanted Elm, even if they haven't been there before. If they read her blog and find out that we're 'real witches,' we might have more customers coming to us for help than before."

It occurred to him that she had asked what life was like for him as a shifter, but he had not inquired much about her own background. Being in her shop wasn't the same thing as understanding what it meant to her. "Since you asked first, what's it like to be a witch?"

She seemed pleasantly surprised at this, and she sat back a little in the booth with a smile on her face. "Well, I've always been one. Our parents raised my sister and I this way, and we've never felt any resistance against it. There's a sense of peace that comes from it, and I don't think I would trade that for anything."

He had vivid memories still of the witches he had known back on Charok. Xander cleared his throat, trying to decide how to phrase his next question. "What kind of magic do you do?"

Their conversation was interrupted by Nora, who had wrinkled up her paper menu and dumped her crayons on the floor. She fussed at them in gibberish and wiggled in her seat, clearly unsettled by being left out of the discussion.

"It's alright, honey. Our food will come soon."

Nora looked at him, and if she were an adult, she would have shrugged him off. She was clearly displeased by being stuck in her booster seat, and coloring wasn't keeping her occupied any longer. Xander wished he had brought some small toys in her diaper bag, but he'd been in such a rush to get out of the house that he'd completely forgotten. "Hungry."

"Like I said, you'll get your chicken nuggets in just a few minutes. We have to be patient, remember?"

Most of the time, Xander could reason with his daughter and get through to her, but it just wasn't going to be enough today. She'd only had a short nap that afternoon, she was hungry, and she wasn't pleased. Nora gripped one of the crayons in her little fist, widened her eyes, gritted her teeth, and screeched.

"Nora, that's not how a young lady behaves."

But suddenly, Nora was a young lady no more. The thin skin around her eyes separated into small pieces, each of them flipping up on their ends before turning over to reveal the scales underneath. A thick tail with a pointy end sprouted from underneath the skirt of her dress, slapping at the back of the booth. Her face elongated and her arms thickened. Nora had completely shifted in the middle of the restaurant. She was no longer a frustrated toddler, but a small, dark emerald green dragon in a blue dress.

Xander froze, his mouth agape, as he took in the sight of his daughter. Very rarely had Nora shifted from her human form since she had hatched. It had happened maybe once or twice when she was very young, but that had been in the privacy of his own apartment. Now she had morphed out in public, and he wasn't sure what to do about it. "Holy shit! This isn't good."

Summer stood up, making Xander's stomach twist into knots. His relationship with her had already been a tenuous one, and now Nora had completely scared her off. She was going to leave him there with a reptilian child.

But when he looked up, he realized she had moved to stand right across the table from Nora, blocking the view from any other diners seeing her. "What do we need to do to get her to change back?" she whispered urgently. "I don't know how this works."

Sweat gathered in beads on Xander's forehead. "She's pissed, and she's having a reaction to it. This hasn't really happened before; not like this."

Summer nodded. "Alright, then." She squinted her eyes slightly as she made gentle swirling motions in the air with her fingers. It was subtle, but Xander could feel a change in the air like the crackling of electricity just before lightning struck. It pulled at his chest, or maybe that was just because he was afraid someone would notice Nora, but it was an interesting feeling. Summer looked over her shoulder, then pointed her finger at the table in front of Xander, and his fork stood up. It waddled on its tines over to Nora's place at the table, where it began dancing back and forth.

Nora watched it closely, her long scaly snout moving down toward the surface of the table to watch the hopping utensil. Her pupils, dark slits in a viridescent setting, expanded as she studied this new wonder. Finally, she reached forward with a clawed hand to snatch at it. The fork danced away, following the commands of Summer's finger. Nora squealed with delight and clapped her claws.

The fork continued its gyrations, leaping over the napkins and twirling around their cups. Slowly, Nora began to return to her human form. Her snout pushed in to create the little button nose that Xander was used to seeing. Her vertical pupils rounded, her fingers lost their claws, and the long tail disappeared under her dress.

Summer let the little girl catch the fork this time and sat down.

Xander looked at her with wonder. "I guess that tells me a little bit about how your magic works."

Just then, the waitress came to their table, balancing a large tray on her hand. "Sorry about the wait, but thanks for being so patient," she beamed as she set the plates down. "Is there anything else you need? Any sauces or seasonings?"

"No. No, thanks. I think we're fine for now." He really didn't know if they needed anything, but he just wanted the waitress to leave. Nora was fine at the moment, but there was no reason to push the issue.

"Okay! Well, you guys enjoy and just shout for me if you need anything." She picked up the tray and headed off across the floor, stopping to check on another table.

Xander eyed Nora as he broke her chicken nuggets into bite-sized pieces and handed her one of them. She gobbled it up and grinned at him as though nothing had happened. "That was a close call. I can't thank you enough. I'm not sure what I would have done if someone had seen her."

Summer smiled and shook her head. "It was my pleasure. I'll admit that I don't usually do those sorts of things outside the comfort of my own home, but I know how tough it is when people stare at you. I can pass as a regular person, but I don't think anyone would believe Nora was just wearing a Halloween costume."

He knew that he should have been the one to take action and help Nora calm down. It made him feel somewhat ashamed but also very excited that Summer had stepped up. It meant that she really did care for Nora as much as she seemed to. It warmed up that pit of flames inside him, but in a very pleasant way. "You could just as easily have walked away," Xander said quietly.

"I wouldn't have. I think you know that."

Xander did. Maybe he knew her better than either one of them had realized. "Yes, but I don't think you realize what an amazing woman you are."

She blushed. "It wasn't *that* amazing. Just a little parlor trick, really."

"That's not what I'm talking about—well, not just that, anyway. Your magic is impressive, and it's definitely something I'd like to learn more about. But the fact that you would do that for us says a lot as well."

"I don't mind at all, really. And don't go proclaiming me a hero. I didn't think I was really all that interested in children until Nora came along. She's so adorable; I can't help but want to spend time with her." Summer smiled at the little girl as she reached across the table to wipe a little piece of chicken off the corner of Nora's mouth. "Does she have a bib? I'd hate to see her ruin that pretty dress."

"Oh! Of course." Nora's transformation had left the after-effects of adrenaline coursing through his system, and he had completely forgotten. Xander whipped a bib out of the bag and fastened it around Nora's neck. "Don't forget to eat your mashed potatoes, Nora."

The tot shook her head emphatically. "No taters. Nuggies."

Xander pressed his lips together. If they were at home, and if circumstances were normal, he would have pressed the issue. After all, he was her father and it was his job to make sure she ate well-balanced meals. But considering the reaction Nora had just had when she'd gotten bored and tired, he was concerned. It dawned on him that his daughter's ability to shift could truly backfire on him as she got older and she could threaten to turn dragon if she didn't get her way. Xander had read that teenagers liked to rebel, which was not unlike the way things had been back on Charok. But there, no one would accept a dragon sitting at the table.

"Please?" he asked.

Nora pointedly put a bite of the chicken nugget in her mouth.

"You know, when I was younger, I would babysit my cousin sometimes," Summer said, one slim eyebrow raised in thought. "Nora is a bit older than he was at the time, but she might still enjoy this." Her fingers began moving again.

Xander glanced around the restaurant, making sure no one was looking their way and the waitress wasn't coming back to check on them. Somehow, Summer using her magic in public didn't make him quite as nervous as the potential for Nora to shift.

This time, the spoon lifted from the table and scooped up a bite of potatoes, swerving through the air in front of Nora. "Here comes the airplane!" Summer announced as she guided it with only the twitch of her finger toward the tot's mouth. "It's got cargo to deliver! Open wide!"

Fascinated, Nora did as she was told. She gobbled up the bite of white fluffy stuff and instantly began looking for more.

Xander couldn't help but laugh. He had never seen his daughter quite so happy with her food, even though she'd never been a particularly picky eater. She abandoned her chicken nuggets and eagerly ate every bit of her potatoes. When they were gone, she happily started in on her green beans herself.

"If I recall correctly, you told me just a few days ago that you don't really know anything about children. I think you underestimate yourself." Xander smiled lovingly across the table. He knew this was supposed to just be a dinner as friends, but there was no one more perfect in the world than Summer. She made his body burn, but even if he hadn't had that reaction to her, he would have been trying to find an excuse to proclaim her as the one. Never had he met a woman so gentle, sweet, and smart.

Summer dabbed at the corner of her mouth and set down her salad fork. "No, I really did mean it. I watched my cousin a couple of times, but I'm no expert. I think Nora just makes me want to try. I've never met a kid who grabbed at my heart so readily, and I have to commend you for that. I know it must be hard for you to raise her in such a strange world, one that's even difficult for the natives. But you've done a good job with her, and it really shows."

"Even when she turns into a different being at the dinner table?"

"Yes," Summer laughed. "Even then. I know children are far from perfect. You should have seen my sister and I when we were younger. We had a touch of natural magical talent about us even before we were officially taught, and of course the fact that we're twins just made things worse. We always knew what the other was thinking, and we could act on our plans without discussing them. We caused all sorts of trouble, and I'm sure my mother didn't appreciate it at all. But in the end, I'd like to think we turned out alright."

"I think so, too."

The waitress brought their check and Xander automatically took it.

Summer picked up her purse. "What's my share?"

"Zero dollars and zero cents," he replied as he attached his debit card to the little clip board. "This is on me."

Her face narrowed. "Xander, I thought we agreed that this was just as friends."

"And a guy can't buy his friend dinner?" he countered. He knew what she was getting at. Things had been changing slightly over the past few decades, according to his research, but the check wasn't normally split if a couple was out on a date. Still, he understood why Earth men always insisted on paying. The gesture made him feel as though he was taking care of Summer, and he didn't want that to be taken away from him.

"Not if he's doing it without honorable intentions."

The fire lit in his chest again, but it wasn't a pleasant one. He felt attacked, and his body was instantly ready to fight back. "I've had nothing less than honorable intentions with you, Summer. I'm not just trying to get you in the sack, here."

She shook her head and waved her hand in the air. "I don't mean it like that. I'm sorry, because I can see now how it came out. What I meant was that you agreed to go out to dinner as friends, but if you're picking up the check, then you clearly mean it as more than that. It's not fair to me, Xander."

"Alright then you can pick up the check the next time we go out." He grinned. He knew the game he was playing, even though he didn't want to be playing games with her. But Xander had to keep trying with her, whatever it took.

"Nice try. Xander, I thought things were going well between us, and I admit that I had a small spark of hope that you might be right. The idea of two people being destined for each other is incredibly romantic. But I'm still not sure I'm the right person." She looked sad as she spoke to him, as though she truly regretted what she was saying.

"But I *know* you are." He barely moved his lips as he said the words. His body was fighting him once again. It had relaxed a little as they had interacted over dinner and he was able to fool himself in believing that they were heading the right direction. But now that she was threatening to slip off into the night and never see him again, he wasn't sure he could move a muscle without instantly shifting. And it would be a lot more noticeable than when Nora had done it.

"And I need you to understand that *I* need to know that, too. It can't just be all about you, Xander. I know that you've dedicated your life to

Nora and to finding a mother for her, but you don't really want me to agree to such a thing if I don't know that I can be happy, do you?" She reached across the table and touched his hand, pleading for him to understand.

"No," he gritted out. The touch of her hand was almost more than he could bear. His body and his mind were in such conflict, and he felt like he might explode at any moment. "But don't you see what this would mean for you as well? I'm not just asking you to be my partner and Nora's mother. I'm promising that I will love and protect you from now until the end of time." He was sweating now, trying his damnedest to get the words out. If they had been at her house or his apartment, then it might have been different. He could have let his claws or his wings out to just release a little bit of the tension, and it would have made things so much easier. But not there. "And it's not just that. I would do anything for you, Summer. You are the one person on this planet—no, in the universe—that can make me feel this way. It's how I know that as terrible as the reasons were for us leaving Charok, we were meant to do so. You and Nora are absolutely everything to me."

Tears welled in Summer's eyes. "That's very sweet, Xander. It really is. I like you, but I don't know that I'm ready for something like that. I've tried to tell you, but it seems that what I need only comes secondary to what you say you need. I'm an open person, and that's why I was willing to give this a try, but I just need more time to think things through." She picked up her purse and stood up.

"Summer, please don't go. We can go somewhere private and talk this out. I know this is going to take some time to get used to, and I meant it when I said I would do anything you ask." He reached for her hand. Xander knew that it was dangerous for him to do so; the chemistry he could feel between the two of them was almost too much to bear.

She didn't pull her hand away from his, but she turned her sad green eyes on him. "Xander, all I'm asking of you right now is to please give me some space."

She waved goodbye to Nora and was gone in an instant.

# 8

SUMMER FELT NUMB AS SHE HAILED A CAB AND TOOK IT TO THE EDGE OF town. She had truly hoped that their dinner would go well, and for the most part, it had. Nora, despite her little reptilian fit, had absolutely enchanted her. Summer had felt the panic from Xander when she had shifted, and she wanted nothing more than to help. She didn't even mind using her powers in front of a man she hardly knew, because the time they'd spent together at The Enchanted Elm had made her feel as though she could be comfortable around him. He had been patient and kind, and those were qualities she looked for in any person.

She felt her heart was finally beginning to open itself to him, but the way he had acted right at the end of the meal had made her realize that she'd let her hope get ahead of her head. He was fun to talk to and spend time with, but Xander still wanted far more from her than she was ready to give.

"Right here is fine."

The cabbie pulled over as they reached the edge of town, where the houses had become more scattered and the lights of downtown were nothing more than a glow on the horizon. "You sure? This is the middle of nowhere."

"Yes, this is it. Thank you." She paid him, tipping generously as she always did, and got out. Summer was grateful that she wasn't one for high heels, or else the long walk to the end of her driveway would have been an uncomfortable one. As it was, she tried to use the time to realign her energies with the earth. Summer tipped her head up at the stars, studying the bits of flame in the sky, wondering just where out there the mysterious planet of Charok was located. She knew that she would never be able to see it, but that only made it harder to understand. Xander and his friends had traveled across the universe to find a safe haven where they could raise their children. How did it make any sense that she could be the one for him? If he had been able to stay on his home planet, would he eventually have found a female dragon who would have made him feel the same way he claimed to feel about Summer? There were so many things to think about.

A gentle breeze tugged at her hair as she entered her driveway. Trees lined it on both sides, which after sunset, made it a dark tunnel. Fortunately, she wasn't the kind of person who thought there were things to be afraid of in the dark, and she touched each tree as she made her way to the house, feeling the way the rough bark pulled at her fingertips. What would happen to Nora? Would Xander have to settle for a woman who wasn't his "destined mate," or would he simply remain a single dad for the rest of his life? Was it fair to leave him in the lurch like that when he really did need someone? And it wasn't that he was incapable as a father, but that Summer knew how hard it was on single parents in general. She'd had countless young women come into the store looking for herbs or potions for money, peace, and wellbeing. They were always stressed and worried. No one should have to go through that.

Reaching her door, Summer headed inside and grabbed a few things, putting them in a simple sack without bothering to turn on the lights. She didn't want to ruin her night vision, and she knew where everything was by memory, anyway. Stepping out her back door, she headed for a clearing in the woods that she had come to know well. Summer kept the leaf litter swept away on a regular basis, so she wasn't hindered as she drew a circle in the dirt on the forest floor. She stepped inside and called the four elements to assist her.

Summer turned to the east and threw her arms wide. "Welcome East, power of Air! Intuition, knowledge, and wisdom, come and send forth your inspiration, and be here now."

The south was next. "Welcome South, power of Fire! Energy, head, and flame, come and set forth your passion, and be here now."

Two steps to her left had her facing west. "Welcome West, power of

Water! Emotions, love, and courage, come and set forth your tranquility, and be here now."

The north was the last step in casting her circle so that the elemental guardians would watch over her ritual space. "Welcome North, power of Earth! Stability, structure, and growth, come and set forth your strength, and be here now."

A shiver made its way down her spine, but it wasn't one of fear or uncertainty. It was the thrill of magic in her system and a circle that had been cast well, despite the numerous distractions that were still running through her mind. Fortunately, Summer had done it so many times, it was old hat. The circle provided a safe space that kept her energies focused with it and kept negative elements out, and she could see the pale blue shimmer of power that radiated along the line she had drawn on the ground. At other times, if she was casting a specific spell, she might have any number of candles, stones, herbs, and other tools with her.

That night, though, she had no specific spells to ask of the universe; it was purely a meditation session. She would likely have been set off-kilter by the absence of her twin in the first place, but having Xander waltzing into her life had been enough to make her feel as though she had never come to know her spirit guides in the first place. She was torn and needed to center herself, control her thoughts, and seek guidance.

Summer reached into her bag, knowing each stone by the way it felt in her hand. The light from the stars barely penetrated through the trees, but she didn't need it. Sitting down in the center of the circle, Summer set a clear quartz in front of her for clarity of mind. Next to it, she placed a large amethyst for calming her thoughts, which were swirling like an ocean in a hurricane at the moment. On the other side of the crystal, Summer gently placed a lapis lazuli for awareness and truth. More than anything, she wanted to know just what she was supposed to do. Hopefully, her spiritual guides would support her.

Pulling a deep breath through her nose and letting it out slowly through her mouth, Summer let all the thoughts and worries she had been focused on come to the front of her mind. She tried not to formulate any words to go with them, concentrating on the visuals and the emotions behind them. The spirits didn't care how she phrased it, but more about what it meant to her.

She could easily see Xander's face, with those liquid eyes that were always soft when they turned to hers, and his dark hair that was a distinct contrast to hers. He invoked joy and intrigue. But also confusion. She couldn't deny that she felt a certain pull toward him that was growing stronger by the day. In fact, it was precisely because of that pull that she had let this whole thing bother her so much. If it wasn't there, Summer could just as easily have stopped thinking about him and moved on. It was he who created the most chaos within her that she'd ever experienced, and she didn't know if that meant his talk of fate and destiny was correct, or completely off-base.

Then there was Nora. With her dark curls and doe eyes, she induced the warm, sappy feelings that could be found in poetry and greeting cards. It made her want to learn more about her own surroundings so that she could teach that knowledge to the child. Even her little fit was endearing in its own way, and Summer sent waves of love radiating out into the universe.

Finally, even though it seemed narcissistic, Summer turned her thoughts on herself. She preferred not to put herself first, but in this particular situation, she felt that she had to. After all, accepting Xander's story would change the rest of her life. It would determine how she acted, what she said, and who she spent time with. It wasn't simply a friendship, but a lifelong and life-changing commitment. She mentally pushed out her heartache, her confusion, but also, her desire for a life of beauty and understanding.

The stones and her spirit guides began to do their work. Her tumultuous thoughts crashed and canceled each other out like waves as Summer concentrated on the way the Earth moved through the universe and the vibrations of the night sky around her. She inhaled peace and exhaled understanding. There were no direct words that came to her, but Summer knew that her guides had their hands on her shoulders. In a way, that was the only thing she really needed. She had someone on her side, and even though she knew she had Leah's support, it meant so much more to know that she also had it from the celestial beings who watched over her.

Achieving at least a serenity of mind, if not a decision, Summer slowly opened her eyes. The night was much brighter than when she had started. It was a trick of her eyes after having been plunged in darkness for so long, but the moon had also drawn higher and brighter in the sky. Its light pierced the leaves above her head and danced down in abstract shadows.

And just then, immediately before her on the dirt inside the circle, the shadows formed into the shape of a dragon.

It was at that point, Summer knew that Xander was right. She couldn't reach out with her hand and dash the symbol out of the dirt to deny it. The spirits had made it in their own time and in their own form, one that a simple human couldn't disturb.

All she needed was a little space to figure out how to move forward.

## 9

Xander hadn't slept much—in fact, he couldn't be sure that he had slept at all. The ceiling above his bed had been a series of still shots all night, with the shadows moving along in slow rotation to the movement of the moon.

The only thing he could think of was Summer. Things had been going so well, but they had changed so quickly. It was his fault. He shouldn't have reacted so angrily when she had called him out on treating the dinner as being more important than it was. He should have agreed with her, accepted his misstep, and moved on. But no, he'd had to keep shoving his agenda down her throat, regardless of what she wanted.

Morning came, but brought no revelations with it. He didn't know what he could do to fix things. Though he had no doubt that Summer would talk to him again if he tried—she was just that sort of person—he knew that he really did need to do what she had asked and give her some space.

Xander scrambled an egg for Nora and fried two for himself, serving them up with bacon strips and toast. He put her plate on her high chair and sat down at the kitchen table across from her. "We might as well eat up, little one. I don't have any other exciting adventures planned for us today. What do you want to do? Go to the park?"

Still in her pink footie pajamas, Nora picked up a piece of bacon between her thumb and forefinger and took a bite. "Some?" she asked.

"No, I don't need some. That's yours." Xander took a bite of his eggs but could barely taste them despite the seasonings he had adorned them with.

"Some!" Nora insisted. "Go see some!"

With an understanding that broke his heart, Xander felt his shoulders slump. "No, we can't go see Summer today. She's busy." He knew that at least this was mostly the truth. Summer likely had the shop to run, so that meant she was busy. But that wasn't why they couldn't go see her.

"Busy?" Nora asked.

"Yeah. She's got work to do. So, what are we going to do? Go to the park? Maybe go see some of your cousins?"

The little girl tore off another bite of bacon and nodded. "'Kay."

They dropped in at Beau's house later that morning. He answered the door in a white t-shirt, jeans, and bare feet. His dark blonde hair was combed back as usual. "You must be psychic or something; Elliot was just asking about Nora. We haven't seen you guys for a while." He opened the door to let them in.

Xander set Nora down so she could toddle across the living room floor to where Elliot was playing with a set of bulky plastic toy cars. "I know. I've been a little distracted." He did his best to keep the story of Summer as concise as possible while Beau led him into the kitchen and poured a cup of coffee for each of them.

Beau raised a flaxen eyebrow over his coffee cup. "So, you're saying that you know she's the one for you?"

"That seems to be the case." Xander easily recalled the turmoil she sent his body into every time she came near.

"I'm surprised you didn't tell me. That's a pretty big deal." Beau was the caretaker of the group, always concerned about everyone else's well-being. "What are you going to do about it?"

Xander swirled the dark liquid in his mug absently. "I don't really know. She doesn't seem interested in pursuing this whole thing. I can't force her to, and I know, at least for the time being, I need to let things cool down."

"That's probably a good idea. When you think about it, it's pretty crazy that we have to pair up with human women at all. They're different from female dragons in a lot of ways. I've had my doubts from the very beginning as to whether or not we could be successful at this."

Listening to the sound of the children playing, Xander had to disagree. "But we owe it to our children. I'm not saying we aren't good dads, but they need to have more than just us. Besides, we haven't been through the hard stuff like puberty here on Earth. They need someone who's going to really understand what it's like."

Beau said something in response, but Xander was no longer listening. His mind had shifted its attention to some strange vibration in the universe that was speaking only to him. He didn't quite understand what it was, but he felt the distinct bunching of the muscles in his back that meant his wings were threatening to come out once again. A buzzing settled in the pit of his stomach. "I—I think something's wrong."

Beau leaned in his chair to look at the children. "They're fine. They're just playing."

"No, not them," Xander replied impatiently. He tried to focus the energies that were coming to him, but he didn't understand them well enough. "It's something else."

"You say this woman is the one, right?" Beau narrowed his eyes.

"Yeah."

"Maybe it's her."

Xander had been thinking the same thing, even though it had seemed ridiculous in his own head. He shot out of his chair. "You mind if I leave Nora here for a little while?"

"She's always welcome." Beau followed him to the door. "Be careful. Let me know if you need anything."

With a kiss on Nora's forehead, Xander was off, headed for downtown. He couldn't get there fast enough, even though he didn't know why he was being drawn there in the first place. He only knew that he had to get to Summer and make sure she was alright.

When he pushed open the front door of The Enchanted Elm, he immediately noticed how quiet the place was. Instead of the steady stream of traffic he had seen the day before, there was only one customer in there, and she was on her way out the door.

Summer turned to the door with a smile upon hearing the bell ring, and her eyes widened as soon as her gaze landed on Xander. "Good morning. I can't say I expected to see you here today."

"I'm sorry." He charged up toward the counter. "I wanted to give you space; I know I've been coming on a little too strong. But I—I know this sounds crazy, but I just had this bad feeling, and I had to come in here to check on you."

"Are you sure that's not just an excuse to see me again?" She laughed as she turned away from him to restock a book on a shelf.

"I promise I'm not making excuses. I just wanted to be sure you're okay."

"I'm fine. Really." Pausing for a moment, she turned to face him again. "You know, I'm glad you stopped in. I've been doing a lot of thinking about things; about *us*. I value my independence, and I guess I've just been hesitant to give this a shot because I don't want it to get swallowed up."

Xander nodded. "I completely understand. I..." But he trailed off as the bell over the door rang again. A young man walked in wearing black jeans and a wifebeater that showed off his numerous tattoos. His boots pounded on the hardwood floor as he marched up to the counter. "We'll get back to this in a minute," Xander said.

He headed across the store floor and pretended to study a display of rune stones. He didn't intend to eavesdrop on Summer's conversation, but the demanding attitude with which the young man spoke caught his attention.

"Can I help you?" Summer asked.

"Yeah, I'm looking for a love potion."

"I could provide you with certain crystals that can enhance existing love or smooth out an argument."

"No, no. I want a love potion. I like this girl, but she won't talk to me. A buddy of mine said you could whip up a batch of something I could slip into her drink."

Summer's voice carried a trace of indignance, but Xander could tell she was trying to remain professional. "I'm afraid your friend is mistaken. There's nothing anyone can do to make someone fall in love with you. Love potions simply don't exist."

"I see how it is." The man nodded his head and tightened his jaw. "You gotta problem with me because of my tattoos? Or because you've heard I'm a troublemaker? Let me tell you something, lady, you're the only one who's a freak around here. Oh yeah, I've read about you online. I know you're out dancing naked with the devil in the moonlight. So, don't go acting all innocent."

Xander was eager to put the customer in his place, but Summer had made it clear that she didn't want any help from him. He would have to hold his tongue and let her deal with this.

"Get out of my store," she advised the man in a low voice. "I don't tolerate that sort of talk."

"I want the love potion, bitch! Quit being stubborn and fucking give it to me already."

"I've got nothing to give you!"

But he wasn't taking no for an answer. He leaned over the counter and grabbed Summer's hair, holding it firmly in his grip. "Give me the goddamn potion, you fucking freak! I know you can do it, so you'd better just give it to me now. And I'll take all the money in the cash register, too."

Just as Xander stepped out from behind the display and headed toward the counter, he saw the man pull a gun from the back of his pants. Xander's feet transformed even as he was moving them, shedding his human traits for his dragon ones. His spine lengthened and thickened, stretching forward and pushing his neck out into the space in front of his body. His skull cracked as his face shifted from round and flat to long and cylindrical, and he felt the heat of fire rage through his entire body. Wings tore through the back of his shirt and sent crystals and tiny glass figurines crashing to the floor. Xander reached out with clawed hands as the angry customer turned around to see what was going on.

"What the fuck?" he screamed, the gun waving wildly in the air. He let go of Summer's hair.

Xander knocked it aside easily, sending it into the same display of candles that he and Nora had been admiring recently, and several of them rolled to the floor. Snatching up the assailant by the back of the neck, Xander was once again at war with himself. While the urge to shift was no longer a concern, he knew even in his dragon form that he couldn't kill this man. He wanted to crush his head between his strong hands and watch as the blood flowed from his eye sockets, but Summer was just a few feet away, watching with her hand on her chest. She was a peaceful person, a loving person, and no matter what a rotten douchebag this guy was, she wouldn't want to see him murdered. Instead, Xander picked him up by the neck and pitched him across the room. He flew into a bookshelf, bringing it to the floor with a thud. Books cascaded down onto his head.

The customer dug himself out quickly, heading for the door on his hands and knees with blood running from his temple. But before he was able to leave, Summer raised her hands, joining both index fingers and pointing them at the menace's head. "You will have no memory of what you've seen here, and you will never return."

With a blank look in his beady eyes, the man fell into a trance. "I saw nothing. I will never return," he murmured. Summer nodded, and as she dropped her hands, the assailant's gaze resumed to normal. The bell dinged his exit as he scrambled onto the street.

Xander's breath heaved in his chest as he kept his fire contained. He took a deep breath and let his body slowly shift back. He adjusted his balance on his two feet as his tail narrowed and disappeared, and his wings folded into his shoulder blades with a decisive snap. He watched as his coppery scales turned back into smooth skin.

He glanced at Summer with his tongue between his teeth. "Are you okay?"

She nodded, but fear was still evident in her eyes. He didn't know if it was aimed at him, but it probably was. After all, a fully-grown dragon was a lot more intimidating than a baby one.

# 10

SUMMER HAD DIFFICULT CUSTOMERS BEFORE, BUT NEVER LIKE THAT ONE. She didn't know what she would have done, and there had been nothing more incredible than seeing the fierce form of Xander as a dragon charging forth to save her.

He turned to her, sadness in his eyes. "I promised to give you space, and all I did was come and wreck your shop."

Summer understood exactly what the spirits had been trying to tell her. She had fought so hard against Xander, but he truly was at the very center of her circle, no matter what her mind had been telling her. "You came here when I *needed* you to," she said, her cheeks warm and her chest even warmer. "Somehow, you just knew." She saw Xander as though through a soft light, and she could hardly take her eyes off him as she crunched across the floor toward the front door.

"You're not angry about the mess?" He gestured helplessly around him at the broken glass and the scattered stones.

Summer locked the door with a flick of her finger and stepped toward him. "Not at all. I'll just cast a spell to get things back in order." Smiling, Summer put her arms around his neck and pressed her lips to his. He was warm and firm, hard in all the right places as he wrapped his arms around her waist and pulled her close, deepening the kiss. She moaned a little at the pleasure.

It was then that she understood just what Xander had meant when he'd said they were destined to be together. She didn't need to be able to explain it or comprehend it. It didn't even matter how hard she had tried to resist it, because Xander was right. Her body surged toward his, demanding him. She didn't care about anything else, and she was determined to make him realize just how much he was beginning to mean to her, too.

Xander moved his mouth from her lips and trailed kisses down her jawline, still holding her tightly. His breath steamed along her skin as he made his way down to her collarbone, pulling aside the strap of her dress to kiss her shoulder.

"When you shifted," she admitted as she closed her eyes, "I could finally see every ounce of determination and passion in your eyes."

He laughed softly against her collarbone. "So, how did you like me when I was a dragon, anyway?"

Summer pulled his head up so that she could look him in eye. "I like you in any form you're in, Xander."

His mouth covered hers once more, and she melted underneath him. There was no shop to run, and there had been no dangerous customer. There was only Xander as the two of them tumbled to the floor. She pulled hastily at his belt buckle, desperate to get past his khakis and see what was waiting for her underneath. The giant copper dragon in her shop had been gorgeous, a striking figure that was both intimidating and awe-inspiring, but she knew the man would be just as thrilling. She wasn't disappointed when she revealed his hardness, ready for her, a dusting of fine dark hairs traveling up his rippling abdomen. Summer splayed her hands against his firm chest as he held himself over her, patiently waiting for whatever she desired, and her heart pounded in her chest.

She wasn't a virgin, but she might as well have been as Xander slowly peeled her dress down and shimmied it over her hips, exposing her naked skin. "You are even more stunning than I imagined," he breathed as his eyes roved ever downward. She could feel his gaze on her, blasting her like a laser with a heat that gathered and built between her legs.

Summer nearly cried out with the agony of wanting him, and he seemed to sense her pain. He bent his head to take her nipple into his mouth. Bolts of electricity shot through her body from the points where he touched her, combining with that heat and gathering into a tight ball in the very lowest reaches of her abdomen. "I want you," she whispered.

Xander smiled sweetly as he moved to her other breast. "I want you, too," he whispered back. "I *need* you."

He paid thorough attention to her nipple, leaving it cold when he removed his hot mouth from the pert bud and kissed a slow line down her quivering stomach. Summer obediently spread her legs as he brushed his lips against her delicate folds.

He pulled her thighs around his neck as he dove deeper, driving his tongue inside her as he explored her most delicate area. Summer shook around him as her muscles tightened. She tipped her head back against the floor and closed her eyes, focusing on that white sphere of heat and electricity that was her entire world at that moment. Xander wet his finger and slipped it inside her, leaving his tongue free to flick against her sensitive bundle of nerves. Every stroke of his tongue sent a spasm through her legs until she couldn't control herself any longer. Her fingers spread against the floor and her back arched as she came, crying out for more. Ripples of pleasure vibrated through her body like the waves from a drop of water on a still pond, and Summer embraced the chaos.

Xander showed no sign of stopping as long as she was pleased, but she couldn't take it any more. She had never been so turned on in her life, and it was almost more than her body could handle. "Xander, please. I can't. Oh, Goddess!" She rolled her head back as he sucked her into his mouth and got her going once again.

"What's the matter?" he asked gently, looking up at her with an evil gleam in his eye. "Don't you like it?" He slipped a second finger inside without waiting for her answer.

"Oh, you know I do," she gasped. "But I want to return the favor."

"I said I would do anything you want," he reminded her, "and I meant it. You just tell me."

"Stand up."

Xander did as he was told, standing so that he towered over her. Summer brought herself to her knees, coming face-to-face with his erection. She looked up at him, admiring his body from this new perspective, and pulled his member into her mouth. Slowly sinking her lips to his base, she flicked her tongue against the underside of his member and she pulled him back out. He was so hot and hard, and she couldn't believe she had fought so hard against something so pleasurable. She could have had Xander a week ago, and even that short of a time frame seemed like an eternity now that she knew what she was missing.

He reached out to steady himself on a nearby display cabinet as she sucked hard and then sank him in to the hilt, his head touching the back of her throat and her lips just barely around his root. "You have no idea how good that feels," he grunted, his fists balled at his sides.

"If it's anything like what you've done to me, then I know," she promised him. Summer brought up one hand to stroke his shaft, milking him tightly with her fingers. Xander's hips pulsed, and she could tell he was fighting to control himself. Knowing she had turned him on that much made that same white ball of flame in her core, but it could wait for a moment while she gave him everything she had. Summer sucked harder, working her tongue around his length and compressing her lips as she worked him.

Finally, Xander had reached his breaking point. He gave a roar as he pulled himself from her mouth and came down to the ground, mounting her. His lips covered hers as he plunged inside, and Summer wrapped her legs around his waist. She let him in because she wanted him, and because she needed him. They melded together into one, his hands tangled in her hair while hers traced the long muscles of his back. The two of them moved in unison, building, giving, and only taking because they were unable to help themselves. Summer felt the engorgement of Xander's cock inside her and the way her body responded, pulsing around him and pushing cries of passion from her lungs as she came once again, pulling him deeper into her body and never wanting to let go. Xander felt it, too, and he pulsed his hips harder and faster against hers, his bellow vibrating through the shop as he filled her up with everything he had.

Gasping and panting, they continued to hold on as they searched each other's eyes for what they already knew was there. Xander dropped a quick kiss on her forehead.

She smiled, feeling all the warmth and love of the universe around her. Most of it radiated off Xander, but in that moment, she had no doubt that he wasn't the only source. Her spirit guides had told her that he had a part to play in her life, and they were pleased that she had finally decided to listen.

# 11

XANDER THREADED HIS WAY THROUGH THE WOODS, WRAPPING HIS LONG, sleek body around trees as he pursued his prey. He wasn't all that far from civilization, not really, but he knew that he was safe there. Instead, he was the only predator as he chased the little ball of green scales that glimmered in the moonlight. "I'm going to get you!"

Nora giggled, a funny noise coming from a baby dragon, and scampered into a bush. She immediately peeked out again to make sure she was being pursued and laughed once more.

Pretending to pounce and miss, Xander grinned to himself as the little girl scampered away. She was happy there, and that was what really mattered to him. She had the freedom to shift when the time was right, exploring who she was; not just as a human, but as a dragon. He was raising her on Earth, but Xander didn't want Nora to forget where she had come from.

It didn't hurt that he got to enjoy the same freedoms. While nothing could compare to the tension he'd felt in his body when he realized he was fated to be Summer's mate, there were still days when he couldn't wait to shed his human form and become his true self for a little while. He enjoyed heading out to the remote forests, running through the trees, dodging shadows, and living like the wild creature he truly was at heart. There was nothing like spreading his wings and skimming over the tops of the leaves, feeling the moonlight on his wings.

As Xander thundered after Nora, she dodged behind a tree stump. He pretended not to see her as he slowed down. "Nora? Where are you? Come out, come out, wherever you are!" Xander felt his claws dig into the dirt and the leaves slither against his scales.

Nora giggled but didn't come out.

"I guess I'll just have to go home all alone, then," he said, making sure to sound dejected. "I guess I'm not a very good hunter."

That didn't get her, either, and her laugh tickled his spine. She was an amazing little girl, and he could almost imagine that he was back on Charok. There weren't any spiked mountains in the distance hiding sacred caverns, and the only other dragons there were the men and children he had come to think of as his brothers, nieces, and nephews, but he was happier than he had ever been.

Suddenly, a tiny yellow light began glowing on the ground near the tree Nora was hiding behind. It pulsed steadily like a young firefly and then zipped off about three feet away.

The little one gasped in interest, and Xander saw her small form come out from behind the stump to chase it. The glow skipped away again, just out of her grasp. Nora pounced on it but missed, the light slipping through her clawed fingers right as she attempted to close them. Xander followed at a distance, wanting to watch her, but not interested in disrupting her little game.

Finally, the luminescence danced right up to the back door of the little cottage that Xander and Nora now shared with Summer. The addition he had been building was a dark skeleton in the night, promising a future for the three of them where they could all be safe and happy. There was just enough room in the cottage as it was, but Xander was painfully aware of the fact that Nora had moved into Summer's library. For a short time, he had considered asking Summer to move in with him in his apartment, which was slightly larger, but he knew it would never work. His beautiful witch needed to be closer to nature, and it was easy to see that Nora did, too. The outdoor space they had together meant more than anything. Still, he knew they would be happiest in the long run if they each had plenty of room under the roof, and so he had begun the addition as soon as they had moved in.

The tiny bit of light floated up through the air and landed on the tip of Summer's finger, who was standing on the back porch. She waved her fingers and put out the glow before scooping down to pick up Nora. "I was wondering if the two of you were ever going to come in," she said gently as she snuggled the little dragon. "It's getting late. Bath time and then bed!"

Nora softened in Summer's arms, substituting her scales for skin and tucking her tail away. She smiled with human lips as she snuggled against her new mother's chest. "'Kay!"

Xander could have played outside all night, but Summer was right. He, too, shed his dragon features. His bones and spine shortened, his wings folded in and dissipated. His teeth lost their gleaming points, and the spikes on the back of his head laid down as hair. For the first time, he could honestly say that it felt just as good to be human as dragon, and he kissed Summer as he passed through the doorway.

Settling down on the couch with a book, Xander stared at the pages without reading them as he listened to the sounds of Summer giving Nora a bath: splashing, Summer's gentle laugh and Nora's pleasant half-English in return. If it had been up to him—truly up to him and not a product of providence—he couldn't have picked a better mother for Nora. The two of them got along so well that even he found himself thinking that Nora was their biological daughter at times. Nora put a special glow in Summer's eyes that hadn't been there before, and Summer gave the little girl the mother figure she needed in her life.

A few minutes later, Nora came bursting out of the short hallway in fresh pajamas and leaped into Xander's lap. "Night night, Dada! Night night!" Her hair was wet as she snuggled herself into his lap and looked at his book. "What you reading?"

He smiled as he watched her chubby finger pointing at the words. "It's just a book about construction. It tells me how to build a house, so that I can make you a new bedroom. And then we can paint it what-ever color you want." Although Xander found himself focusing less on human studies now that he had found his mate, he still craved knowl-edge. He had read about plumbing, wiring, and electrical work in between catching up on classic literature. Living with Summer had settled him into a comfortable routine of hard work and hard study that he found pleasing.

Scooping up Nora and laying the book inside, he brought her to her makeshift room and laid her in her crib, Summer at his side. They kissed their little girl on her cheeks, their smiles radiating warmth and love. "Sleep tight, little one."

Nora pointed at the mobile over her head, an antique that Summer had produced from the top of a closet. "Spin! Spin!"

Summer whirled her finger and the mobile followed suit. It twirled in the air over the crib, which was wonderous enough on its own, but each tiny creature that dangled from the fine wires came to life. Horses pawed invisible ground beneath their feet, bears threw their heads back in silent roars, and deer thundered through unknown prairies. It was a beautiful sight even to Xander, who had yet to grow tired of the things his partner could do. This was a trick that Summer had used on the first night Nora spent in the house to make her feel comfortable, and the little girl couldn't get enough of it.

"Goodnight, sweetheart. We'll see you in the morning."

As they softly closed the door, Xander grabbed Summer around the waist and pulled her into his arms. "I've been waiting all day to have some alone time with you," he growled softly as he nipped at her ear.

"Oh?" she asked as she laughed. "And just what do you plan to do with me?"

"Come into the bedroom and I'll show you." He picked her up as he kissed her, Summer's legs wrapping around his waist, and carried her to the bedroom. It would be like any other night between the two of them: a tangle of arms and legs as they explored and loved each other, each night bringing something new and different and exciting to confirm to both of them that there was no one else in the world they wanted to be with. They were destined for only each other.

———

# BEAU'S MATE

## DADDY DRAGON GUARDIANS

# 1

AUTUMN ABSENTMINDEDLY PLAYED WITH THE BUTTONS ON THE FRONT OF
her blazer as she scrolled through what were the very beginnings of
The Enchanted Elm's website. She and her twin sister, Summer, had
maintained a very simple web presence for their new age store since
they had first opened its doors, but she knew it was time to expand.
People weren't always interested in going to a physical store for their
needs, and the desire to shop online was an even bigger one in their
particular niche. Not everyone wanted their friends and neighbors to
know they had purchased a smudge stick to rid their home of
unwanted spirits or a crystal to enhance communication with their
partner.

"Do you think we should categorize the crystals by color, or by
use?" she mused to Summer, tapping her finger on the mouse.

Summer shrugged, her wavy blonde hair shimmering as it fell like
a waterfall around her shoulders. "I don't know. I'm sure either way
would be fine."

"And what about the candles? Do you think people are more interested in their colors or their scents? I mean, both are important."
Autumn hadn't realized just how many decisions there would be when
it came to this project. But it all had to be just right. She wasn't about to
launch the site until it was perfect.

Autumn finally looked away from the screen to find her sister standing on a ladder on the opposite side of the store. "What are you doing?" she demanded.

Summer gave her a look like she had gone crazy. "The same thing I do every year at this time. I'm hanging up the Halloween decorations." She turned to pin a cutout of a big, black cat to the wall.

"Don't you think there are more important things to be done around here? Look at this display, for instance." Autumn marched across the floor to an arrangement of essential oils. "Everything is in the wrong place! There's lavender where the lilac should be, and clove mixed in with the cinnamon."

Her twin shrugged once again. "That's what happens every time customers look at them. They smell every single one before they make their decision, if they even buy one at all, and they don't pay attention to the labels when they put them back."

"You sound bitter." Autumn's fingers moved quickly to arrange the tiny glass vials.

"Not at all. I'm just stating the facts. The same thing happens to all the other displays as well. It's just the way things are when you work in retail." Summer climbed down the ladder and moved it over a few feet, preparing to hang a tissue paper pumpkin from the ceiling.

"Maybe so, but I'd really appreciate it if you'd start taking your work around here more seriously. I didn't open this store just so you could slack off and pretend to have a job for the rest of your life." Autumn tucked a stray strand of her brick red hair behind her ear and marched around the counter to resume working on the website.

"Excuse me?" Summer stepped off the ladder and crossed the room to face her sister. "*We* opened this store, not you. And I put just as much effort into the place as you do."

"Oh, really? Then tell me why you've been late three times in the last two weeks, or why this floor never looks like it's been swept, or why you haven't written a single blog post for the new site yet. I'm doing everything, Summer, and it's not right." Autumn felt frustration well up through her pores like sweat. It was common those days, and she wasn't sure how to get rid of it.

"It's not nearly as bad as you think," Summer argued. "When I'm late, it's only by a few minutes. And I've got Nora and Xander at home, so there's a lot more I need to do in the mornings than there used to be."

"Why does Xander need you to do anything for him? And why

can't he just take care of Nora? She's his daughter, after all, and you have a business to run." Summer had found a man she felt to be the love of her life a few months ago, and the two of them had swiftly settled into coupledom. Xander and his daughter had not only moved into Summer's little house on the edge of the woods, but he had even built an addition onto the place. Autumn didn't know how she could stand having all of her time occupied by them, but Summer certainly seemed to be fine with it.

Summer blew a quick puff of air through her lips. "It doesn't work like that. Xander and I are a couple, and we do things together. I like to have breakfast with them in the mornings before I leave, and then Xander and I are usually making our plans for the evenings as well. And if Nora wants extra hugs and snuggles before I leave, then I'm not going to be the one to deny her." The blonde woman's face beamed at the thought of the little girl.

"You have plenty of time for that stuff without intruding on *my* schedule." Autumn didn't bother trying to keep the irritation out of her voice. They were sisters, and they were supposed to be partners. Autumn might know more about the business side of things, but she needed someone reliable and knowledgeable to work with her, someone who was good with people and who cared about The Enchanted Elm as much as she did. "Maybe I should just hire someone else."

Summer, who rarely fed into an argument, tipped her chin in the air. "Maybe you just need to get laid so you're not so freaking uptight."

"How dare you!" Before she had a chance to think about what she was doing, Autumn flicked her finger through the air. A miniature broom keychain whisked out of its display on the counter and smacked Summer in the arm.

"Hey!" Summer instantly responded in kind, sending a ballpoint pen whizzing across the counter. "We're not kids anymore. We don't have to fight like we used to!"

Autumn batted it away, aggravated that her sister would do such a thing when she was clearly the one in the wrong. "I'm just trying to get you to wake up and realize that you're putting all the weight of the store on me!" She sent a pack of organic ginger gum—one of the few 'ordinary' things she allowed in the store—toward Summer's cheek.

"You're the one who's all into business anyway!" Summer's green eyes snapped like fiery emeralds. "And I do a lot around here! But you've got to understand that there's more to life than just business. You need to open up your eyes and see the world around you, not just the profit and loss statements!" A tea candle hurtled through the air and bounced off her older sister's forehead.

Just as Autumn had levitated a much larger candle for retaliation, she realized that she was hearing more than the sound of small objects being telekinetically chucked through the store. It was coming from outside. "What the hell is that?"

"Are you just trying to distract me so I won't be ready? That might have worked on me when we were younger, but I'm watching you!"

"No, no. Sshh!" Autumn dropped the candle, holding her finger in the air now only to signal that she was listening. She could see movement through the front windows, but they were so crowded with displays of their merchandise, she couldn't quite tell what was happening. Autumn headed to the front door. "There's something going on."

"Well, at least it means you're paying attention to something besides your accounting books," Summer mumbled as she followed her sister.

"A protest?" Autumn marveled, taking in the large white signs being held in the air. "I didn't think people would get that upset over the new traffic light." She reached for the door handle.

Summer's hand was instantly on the back of hers. "I've got a bad feeling about this. Maybe we shouldn't go out there."

"Don't be such a chicken shit," Autumn said with a scowl. "I'm not afraid of a little protest."

But as she stepped out onto the sidewalk, the cool air blowing through the tight bun at the nape of her neck, she realized just how right her sister might have been. The area right in front of The Enchanted Elm was crowded with people, and their signs said things like *Go Back to Salem* and *The Only Good Witch is a Dead Witch*. Autumn put her hand at her chest, shocked that she would ever see such a thing.

"There she is!" An older man with wisps of gray hair across his balding head pointed at Autumn. He bore a sign that said *Purity and Pride*. "There's one of the witches right now!"

The others turned to face her, and Autumn had never felt so put on the spot in her entire life. She had already been angry, and this only increased her vexation. "What do you want?"

"For you to get out of town!" said a young woman with a thick braid of black hair. "You're a bad influence on our children, and we're tired of it!"

"I haven't done anything to your children," Autumn objected. In fact, people brought their kids into the store with them all the time, and that was why she was constantly cleaning grubby handprints off the front of the counter and finding inventory all over the store where it didn't belong.

"Then tell us why all of our children are pretending they're doing spells and dressing in long black robes? We don't want them to be under your evil influence any longer!" This cry came up from a young man near the street who held the biggest sign.

Autumn rolled her eyes. "Did you ever think about the fact that it's Halloween? Or that witches and wizards are really in right now? You can't blame me for popular culture!" She wanted to start throwing things all over again, but she knew it wouldn't help if people actually got to witness what she was capable of. No doubt, they were convinced she danced naked under the moonlight with Satan. No matter how modern the times got, there were always some who didn't update their beliefs about others. But if they actually saw her move things with her mind or could actually feel the weight of her spells when she cast them, they would be burning her at the stake in the town square before sundown.

"I don't care what time of year it is. We're going to shut this business down and run you out of our community!" This was the older gentleman again. As he raised his fist in the air, a rallying cry rose from the rest of the crowd.

"Well, good luck!" Autumn challenged. "There are only a few of you nutjobs out there; that's nothing compared to the number of our regular customers!" Her voice was nearly lost on the crowd as the fanatics waved their signs and continued to shout.

A piercing whistle broke the sound. Autumn looked off to her right to find the source of the noise, as did the rest of the crowd. A squad car pulled over to the curb and a police officer got out, a bored look on his face. She recognized him as Officer Carey. "Alright, alright. Move it along."

"We don't have to!" the older man said, his face turning red as he faced the cop. "We're American citizens, and we have the right to protest."

The officer nodded, his mouth a hard line. "That's right, Mr. Stone, but you *don't* have the right to block the sidewalk or the entrance to a building. I suggest you call it a day." He waved his arms gently through the air, shooing them out of the way.

Autumn stood there in the doorway and watched them go. Some got into their pickups and drove off with their tires squealing. Others made their way down alleys and side streets to their homes or vehicles, and a few went back to their businesses right there on the downtown strip. She curled her fist at her side, irritated that even her fellow shop owners could be so intolerant. "I appreciate that."

Officer Carey had stayed to supervise them as they left as well. He sighed and tucked his thumb into his belt, just accessible under his paunch of a stomach. "Don't thank me, Ms. Keller. I'm just doing my job. But keep in mind that they weren't wrong. They do have the right to protest, and if I know these types, they'll be back."

"Have they been staging other protests around town?" Autumn peered down the street one way and then the other, half-expecting some of them to come running back through to wave their signs one more time. "I have to admit they caught me off-guard."

The officer's lips pressed together even harder than usual. "Can't say that I've seen anything."

"Okay. Well, thanks anyway." Autumn retreated back into The Enchanted Elm, bumping into Summer. "Can you believe that? It's like the seventeenth century out there!"

Summer folded her arms. "I don't think there's much for me to disbelieve, since you wouldn't even let me out the door."

"It could have been dangerous." In fact, Autumn was considering locking the front door and closing up shop for the day, but then the zealots would only see it as them getting their way. "It's much safer inside."

"You do realize that I'm only younger than you by a few minutes, right?" Summer narrowed an eye.

"Don't start on me. I've got enough on my mind. This protest was the absolute last thing I needed. We already draw plenty of negative attention around town. That's part of the reason I wanted to get the online store up and running in the first place, but I'd hate to think we might eventually be running this place solely through the mail. Hey, where are you going?" Summer had disappeared into the back room even while she was talking to her.

"Hang on!" The blonde twin reemerged a moment later, carrying two steaming teacups in her hands. "I thought we could both use a little herbal remedy for stress. After all, Halloween is supposed to be a special time for us. We can't let those people ruin it."

Autumn bit her lip, casting a glance to the computer on the counter and wondering if sales had gone up for the month of October as they usually did. "That's true. I haven't quite decided if we should run a special on Ouija boards or authentic broomsticks."

"No, not like that." Summer shoved a hot teacup into her hands and slouched against the front counter. "I mean spiritually. With the veil between the worlds so thin, we're supposed to be focusing on renewing our own spiritual energy for the coming winter. Remember how much we used to love Samhain when we were kids? We looked forward to it all year. Now we're lucky if we remember to do anything about it."

"That's true," Autumn said with a nod. "I'm not sure when we traded in the leaves and flowers for black cats and pumpkins, either." She eyed the decorations that Summer had put up, realizing just how cheap and corny they looked. Only a witch with a green, warty face was needed to complete the set.

"We're subject to the commercialization of holidays just like anyone else. But I did get these." Summer leaned down into the box of decorations that hadn't been put up yet. "Nora and I spent some time out in the woods gathering all the prettiest leaves and flowers we could find. I know she doesn't really understand what it's all about yet, but it's so exciting to have her help me. I divvied them up between the house and the store."

"I should have done the same for my house." Autumn realized just how much the business had been taking over her life. For the past several years, she had been so focused on Halloween sales and the fact that people were aware of witches and ghosts all of a sudden that her own rituals had been quick affairs before she went to bed. There hadn't been time for meditation or even the baking of ritual cakes. "Maybe you're right. Maybe I need to get away from the store for a bit. I shouldn't have snapped at you."

"That's okay." Summer touched her sister gently on the arm. "You were probably getting stressed about this time of year without even thinking about it. This isn't the first time we've had people shouting at our storefront. Halloween comes around, and it reminds them that there just might be something out there other than their basic normal lives. They can't handle it."

"Maybe you're right." She was, but it didn't do anything to placate Autumn. There wasn't enough time in the day to get everything she wanted done with the store, and now the town had turned against them. And this protest hadn't been like the others. She had sensed far more anger and determination in those people than she had in previous years when they had a small handful of churchgoers watching the sky for broomsticks.

# 2

---

"Yep!" Julian threw down his pen and sat back with a satisfied look on his face. "That confirms it. According to my calculations, Zimryr should be taking place right around the Earth holiday of Halloween."

Beau Clark ran a hand through his golden hair, wondering if the festival of awakening would still be the same there on Earth. Back on Charok, the home planet that he and the other dragons had come from, they had glorious parties that lasted well into the night and often into the next day. He had enjoyed the holiday greatly back home, and he would miss the orange light of the festival fires against the craggy mountains. "So, what do we do?"

Holden picked up his son and looked into his blue eyes. "Well, we celebrate! We want to pass the tradition down to our children, don't we?"

Looking down at his own son, Elliot, who had crawled into his lap and refused to get down, even though the other children were all there at Holden's house as well. During the War of Storms, when the ogres and the wizards had teamed up to overrun the dragons' land, there had been little choice but to rescue the last eggs of their queen and run for it. A sympathetic wizard had provided the spell that landed them on Earth, but Beau had often questioned whether or not this had been a good idea. It wouldn't have been a good life for the little ones to constantly be on the run as the last of their kind had they remained on Charok, but it wasn't much easier to raise them on Earth. The fact that they spent most of their time in human form only helped to a certain degree. "I suppose so. But it won't be the same."

Xander looked up from his book. He was always reading, even when he was supposed to be holding a conversation. "No, but we can do our best. We can still prepare a big feast, get together, and celebrate life. From what I've read, this doesn't seem too dissimilar from what humans do on their holidays. It might be a nice way of blending dragon and human culture. That's what our kids will need to do anyway."

"True enough. I guess I just feel a little reminiscent of the old ways. That happens a lot, though. Sometimes I wake up in the middle of the night, and for a moment, I don't understand why I'm in a bedroom instead of a cave." Beau pressed his tongue against the inside of his cheek. It happened all the time, really, and he often wondered if Elliot had any idea that he no longer lived on the world he originated from.

"I'm home!" called a voice from the other end of the house. A moment later, a gorgeous woman with dark, curly hair appeared in the study. It was Leah, Holden's mate. She walked in, but staggered back into the doorway. "Wow, there's a lot of energy in here. What's going on?"

Holden rose from the leather sofa and crossed the room to plant a kiss on her lips. "I don't think you needed to use your psychic powers to figure that out."

Finn had been balancing himself against a play table, but he immediately dropped to his hands and knees to get across the room faster to see his adoptive mother. As soon as he reached her, he braced himself against her legs until he was upright again, reaching to get into her arms.

She instantly obliged, scooping him up and snuggling him close. For a moment, Beau felt a pang of jealousy at the tableau in the doorway: Holden with his arm around the woman he knew he was destined to be with, and she with their son in her arms. It was beautiful, and there were times he thought he might want the same thing for himself. But there were an awful lot of human women in the world to sift through, and Beau wasn't convinced he would ever find the one who made his scales tingle.

"We're trying to decide what to do for Zimryr," Holden explained. "Julian's just figured out that it falls right around Halloween."

Leah's face lit up, and she waved her free hand excitedly. "The festival of awakening that you told me about? How exciting! What kinds of things should we do?"

Holden shrugged. "Eating, spending time with friends and family. There's usually a lot of time outside under the stars with big bonfires burning, but that's not going to be very easy around here."

Leah pressed her lips together in thought. "What if we just had a big party here? We've got plenty of room. We could do a bonfire in the back as long as we clear it with the fire department, and we could serve food and cocktails inside." Her blue eyes sparkled with enthusiasm. "I know it's not an Earth holiday, but we could make sure we only invite our closest friends."

"Who, exactly, did you have in mind?" Xander asked hesitantly. "I'm not sure many people would be tolerant of coming to a party for dragons." Taking an almost scientific view of humans, Xander had been their resident expert—until Leah had come along—and by then, Xander was with a human woman as well. That gave them that much more knowledge about the world they now lived in.

"Well, all of us, of course. Summer and Autumn. David and Lisa Rochester from the print shop. They've never had a problem with the fact that I'm a psychic or that the twins are witches, and in fact they're actually enthusiastic about it. I have a few clients that are interested in anything paranormal and who would be thrilled to take part."

"I don't want this to just be some kind of a freak show to them," Julian countered. "It means a lot to us."

Leah shook her head firmly. "I don't want that, either, and it won't be that way. I'll only invite those that I completely trust."

"She can handle it," Holden affirmed.

"Great!" Leah set Finn down and clapped her hands. "I'll get started on planning! Is there anything specific that you'd like on the menu?"

Xander rubbed his stomach. "Not unless you can come up with freshly charred fraxen. I think that's what I miss the most about home."

Leah pursed her lips. "I have a feeling they'll be fresh out at the store. But we could always do some pork tenderloin on the smoker. I'll get started, and you let me know if you think of anything else. I'll be in my office!" She jetted off across the house.

"Well, you've got her excited," Holden remarked, watching his mate head down the hallway. "We haven't had a party here in a long time, and it's always just been us. I think she likes the fact that our little circle is growing. Personally, I'm just glad that we're not going to miss the festivities entirely. It won't be the same, but it should be a lot of fun."

"I'll watch the kids," Beau volunteered, running his fingers absentmindedly through Elliot's light brown locks. "You guys can drop them all off at my house so they won't be underfoot during the party."

"But then you would miss all the fun!" Julian protested, his wide eyes a little wider than usual.

Beau shrugged. "That's okay. They like me, and I like hanging out with them. It'll be a nice break from working on the house." While Julian's argument hadn't been completely wrong, Beau wasn't entirely certain he wanted to come to the party in the first place. It would only make him more homesick.

Holden crossed the room to tower over his friend, brushing back a lock of his dark hair. "Beau, you're always the one watching the kids."

"So?" Beau looked down at the children, who were all content to play quietly while their fathers talked. "I really don't mind."

"No, you're just avoiding the inevitable. When was the last time you went out on a date?"

Beau looked up at his friend to find Holden glaring sternly at him. "What's that got to do with anything?"

Holden sighed. "It's a party. There will be people here you've never met before. You'd be crazy not to take this opportunity."

Pulling in a deep breath, Beau remembered that he was in human form and couldn't spit a spiteful ball of fire at his friend at the moment. "I'm not that worried about it. Besides, take a look at it from a mathematical viewpoint. You and Xander both found mates right here in this city. What are the chances that my destined partner is right here as well? It seems astronomical to me." Not that he was interested in moving off to some other part of the world where he would be without his fellow dragons, but it was a good enough argument for the moment.

"You're being ridiculous. You never go out on dates. You don't try to meet new people. You always volunteer to watch the kids." Holden's fists clenched a little tighter with each statement, his frustration at his friend's stubbornness growing. "You can't keep holding out like this. It's not good for you."

"I'll watch the children," Julian volunteered.

Holden nodded his approval. "Sounds good."

Beau set Elliot gently on the rug and shot to his feet. "How is that any different? He hasn't found his mate yet, either!" He was really getting angry now, and he felt the underside of his skin begin to itch. If he shifted right there in the middle of Holden's study and broke a vase or two, then Holden had no one to blame but himself.

"We'll deal with him later. Besides, I happen to know that he went out on a date this past weekend. It might not have gone very well," he cast a knowing glance across the room, "but it was still a date. You're coming to the party."

"I can even do it right here in Holden's house, so that the children can at least take some part in the celebration," Julian offered with a smirk, clearly happy to have gotten away with something.

"Fine." Beau knew there was no point in continuing the argument. He enjoyed taking care of the little ones, and it gave him a certain sense of satisfaction to know that they were all clean and fed. Not that he felt the other dragons ever did a bad job, but he liked to see it for himself. Julian's suggestion of keeping them right there at Holden's house mooted Beau's argument before he could voice it. "But don't go thinking that just because it's a holiday celebration that I'm going to trip over my wings and fall in love with someone."

Holden sighed and shook his head. "I'm not asking any such thing. I'm just asking that you give the universe a chance. Xander and I both had some very intense experiences when we found our mates."

"And we're very fortunate that we have such a reaction to the presence of our true companions," Xander said. "Humans don't have that luxury; not really. They often think they're in love, but their minds and bodies can make them feel that way about any number of people. For us, it's just one." He smiled contentedly, no doubt thinking of Summer, the beautiful blonde woman he had met a few months ago.

"I see your happiness in love has made you forget how miserable and uncomfortable you were in the process," Beau pointed out. "You were in so much pain you could barely stand it."

"Are you afraid of a little pain?" Holden asked with a grin. "I thought you were tougher than that."

"Not my point."

"It'll be fine, and we'll all be miserable if we don't do something for Zimryr." Xander was smiling, his dark eyes soft. "I think our ancestors would be proud to know that we'll carry on what traditions we can in our new world."

Beau drove home an hour later. He'd wanted to leave as soon as the discussion about the upcoming party had ended, but he didn't want to make it look like he was being a poor sport. But it was late enough that he could easily make the excuse that he needed to get little Elliot to bed.

"I wish you could have seen the way our village looked at this time of year," he reminisced as he shampooed the little boy's hair in the bathtub. "There was a fire in front of every cave, and then once the ceremonial fires were lit, it was like even the sky could erupt in flames. It was so warm, a blessing for creatures like us, and we moved like we were born again. There would be dragons all over the sides of the mountains, roaring into the night."

"Rawr!" Elliot replied, curling his chubby little fingers around a plastic hippo like claws. "Rawr!"

Beau couldn't help but laugh. "Yes, just like that. I think you would have really liked it. I always did, even when I was young." He clearly remembered the way he felt on those sacred nights, like a new soul had crawled inside his body. He was wild and free, the very best version of himself that he had ever been, and his muscles moved with boundless energy. Beau secretly hoped he would get at least a little bit of that feeling at the party.

As he toweled off his son and dressed him in his pajamas, he thought about Holden's remark that he was avoiding the inevitable. Would he really ever find a woman to be his? A woman who would not only love him forever, but love Elliot like her own? That was the part that gave him the most pause. Whoever this mysterious woman was, she was nothing to Beau if she didn't want to take Elliot into her heart and treat him like her own.

"You know," he said as he pulled Elliot's arm through his sleeve, "I have to admit that your cousins seem to have benefited greatly from having mothers in their lives. Finn is crazy about Leah, and I've noticed he calls her Mama now instead of Lala. He loves her and she loves him right back." Beau took a comb from the shelf and gently ran it through Elliot's hair. "And then there's Nora. She runs through the woods with Summer, and I swear I see the dragon in her more and more every day. But in a good way, like she finally knows who she is."

Scooping up the little boy and carrying him across the hall, Beau set him gently on his toddler bed. Elliot had outgrown the crib a few months ago, when he had begun climbing over the rails at night and making his way across the hall to Beau's bedroom. Beau crouched down to lean over his son, almost not wanting to send him to bed just so he could hold him a little while longer. "You know, maybe I am avoiding finding my mate. I'm just worried I won't find the right one, and I don't want to let you down."

As though Elliot understood, he grabbed his father's thumb in his left hand and squeezed. With his right, he patted Beau's cheek. "Dada," he said with a smile.

"Yeah, you're right. It doesn't matter if I like it or not. I made a commitment to being your father, even if you were never mine biologically. I have to do things I'm uncomfortable with, and that just so happens to involve finding you a mother. I promise I'll do my best." He kissed Elliot on the forehead before standing up and flicking off the lights. The glow of the nightlight was a warm yellow throughout the room as he closed the door.

# 3

"I REALLY DON'T SEE WHY WE HAVE TO GO TO THIS THING." AUTUMN slumped against the back of the seat and crossed her arms in front of her chest.

Summer sighed behind the wheel. She usually didn't volunteer to drive, but they had argued enough over going to this party that she had insisted. "We've been over this. It would be so rude not to go. Leah has put a lot of work into it, and everyone is looking forward to the celebration."

"We're having our own Samhain, so why do we have to go to something that's Halloween and Zimryr and whatever else? We're going to get everything we need from our own ceremony." It wasn't that Autumn didn't enjoy parties, and back in her college days, she had been just as eager to drink the night away as anyone else. But there were more important things to do now. And the quiet festivities she had planned with her sister included summoning their friend Naomi, who had died several years ago. Autumn always looked forward to their seances.

"Samhain is going to be wonderful," Summer agreed as she turned off the main highway and onto the road that lead to Holden's house. "But so is this. At the very least, you should be happy to support Leah. And I don't want to hear an ounce of attitude out of you once we get out of this car. You can plaster a smile on your face, nod at the appropriate times, and pretend to be grateful for all of Leah's efforts."

"Yes, mother," Autumn retorted. In fact, she was certain she had heard very similar speeches from their mother in the past. "At least it's not a costume party. I would *not* want to be subjected to that sort of humiliation." She had settled instead for a simple black cocktail dress and low heels. Her tall stature meant that she rarely wore anything too high, not wanting to tower like an Amazon over the rest of her friends.

"What? You could have just painted your face green, worn your pointy hat, and brought your broom," Summer suggested with a smile. "It would be easy for Holden and his friends to dress up, too. They could just shift into their dragon form, and then we could have a fun game of guessing who was who." She giggled at the thought.

"You would have a distinct advantage there." Autumn had been supportive of Summer's new relationship with Xander. It didn't bother her that he was a dragon or that he had come from another world, and she certainly wasn't upset that being with Xander meant she had an instant family. Nora was an adorable little girl, one that Autumn was glad to call her niece. But she occasionally wondered just what it was like to be with a man like that, one who held just as much power as she did, if of a different kind.

"Not really." Summer tapped the wheel as she thought. "I mean, Xander and Nora shift when they go out to the woods together at night, but I try not to butt in too much on their time. He feels it's important for Nora to understand what it's like being in both forms, but it's certainly not something I can teach her."

"But you do see him shift sometimes, don't you?"

Summer smiled. "Yeah, but he's kind of private about it. You should see him, Autumn. He's got the most glorious copper scales. They're like burnished mirrors, a little bit darker towards his skin and lighter at the tips, such an exquisite color that I can't stop looking at it. And he's so big and strong. Oh, and the look in his eyes! There's something wild about him, but not so wild that I would ever be afraid he would hurt me. It's the complete opposite." Her face was soft as she reflected on her boyfriend's physique.

"You're such a romantic." Autumn rolled her eyes and turned to look out the window so she wouldn't have to see her sister's mushy side. Summer had always been a modern-day hippie, and most of the time, she found it nothing less than annoying.

"Don't say it like it's a bad thing." Summer slowed the vehicle as she pulled into Holden's driveway, which was already crowded with cars. "It's nice to be in love. And if someone ever cracks through that hard outer shell you wear all the time, then you might understand."

Autumn doubted it, but she didn't feel like arguing anymore. She just wanted to get this over with. She got out of the car and walked toward the front door, noting the purple lights shaped like bats that Leah had strung up around the doorway. It was the typical, cheesy, Halloween décor that most normal humans went for, and it didn't bode well for the rest of the party.

Leah threw open the door as they stepped up onto the porch, no doubt sensing the arrival of her guests. "Autumn! Summer! I'm so glad you made it! I think everyone else is already here. Come in." She held the heavy oak door wide and waved them in.

The grand, curving banister had been wrapped in vines of autumn leaves, their shades of gold, orange, and red reflected in various other fall decorations that had been scattered around the house. There was a cornucopia on a side table, a pumpkin scented candle, and a bundle of dried wheat hanging on the wall. So far, it all looked fairly normal and not too commercialized. Autumn nodded to herself. She could handle that.

Their hostess escorted them through the kitchen and out to a large sunroom on the back of the house. The walls and the ceiling were entirely made of glass, giving a lovely view of the night sky. Potted plants lined the walls, their leaves still green and lush despite the late season. More lights had been strung up in there, but Leah had held herself back and just used plain white lights that gave the area a charming glow. A long table in the center of the room groaned with food, and several other stations had been set up around the room.

"Bobbing for apples?" Autumn asked, trying to hold back her disgust as she eyed a large tub filled with red fruit. Summer had been right when she said to just nod and smile, but it was already proving to be difficult.

But Leah didn't seem to notice, or if she did, she didn't care. She nodded enthusiastically. "I thought it would be a nice idea to show off a few Halloween traditions here on Earth. I've tried to include a little bit of everything at this party."

"And what are these?" Autumn plucked an hors d'oeuvre from a tray on a table and popped it in her mouth.

Leah gave an uncomfortable shrug. "It's the closest I could come to replicating a recipe from Charok. It's charred meat, ground and rolled into a ball, covered in grain, and then fried. Obviously the meat is a little different than what they had on their planet, and Holden had to go with me to the store to find a grain that was closest. They're pretty good, really."

Autumn was just about to agree with her when she bit down on something hard. Extracting the item from her mouth, she held a small gold ring in between her thumb and finger. It shone in the white lights strung through the rafters. "Is this part of the recipe, too?"

"Just a centuries old Earth tradition," Leah said with a big smile. "Whoever gets the ring in their food is supposed to find their one true love that night. Good luck."

Ignoring her friend's winks, Autumn followed her out onto the back patio. This area was mostly illuminated by a large bonfire roaring in the backyard. Holden, Xander, and two other men stood near it, tossing something into the flames. "Typical men, playing with fire." But Autumn couldn't help but notice the outline of one of them, his strong legs and back limned by fire.

"Actually, it's part of what they do on Zimryr. They write down what they want to happen in the next year on a piece of paper and burn it. The idea is that the message will be carried in the smoke to the rest of the universe, helping them achieve their greatest desires."

"Hmm. Not too different from some of the things we do," Autumn said aside to Summer, recalling several spells that required a very similar practice. *Maybe this won't be such a bad party, after all,* she mused.

But her sister was caught up in watching Xander out near the fire, and she wasn't paying any attention to her anymore. Autumn did her best to mingle, saying hello to the Rochesters from the print shop and telling them she planned to put in an order with them soon, introducing herself to some of Leah's clients, and feeling sure that she had met a few of the other guests before, even though she couldn't quite remember their names.

"It's certainly a motley crew," she remarked to Leah when the hostess stepped inside to refill a pitcher of sangria. "You've got all sorts of folks here."

"Isn't it great?" Leah gushed. "I was so worried that we would just end up with people standing around looking bored, but I think almost every guest here has taken part in the ritual fire ceremony. It's pretty informal, which makes it easy to get into. Did you burn a wish yet?"

"Uh, no. Maybe later." While Autumn felt almost familiar with the practice, it wasn't the sort of thing she would have wanted to do in front of a crowd of strangers. In fact, she felt so uncomfortable that she wished she could dash out the front door, call a cab, and disappear for the night. "I'm feeling a little off."

"Are you sick?" Leah's brow creased with concern as she worked in the kitchen, ensuring that she had plenty of food and drinks for everyone.

"No. I just feel awkward."

"It's not that big of a crowd. And you deal with strangers every day. There's no need to be shy." Leah paused to lay a comforting hand on her friend's shoulder.

"It's not that I'm shy. It's just—" Autumn wasn't sure exactly how she would have completed that thought, but she didn't have a chance anyway. A deep voice was hollering Leah's name from outside.

"There you are!" Holden burst into the room. He was a strapping guy, and as he swept across the floor, he threw his arm around Leah's waist and pulled her tightly against him. He carried the energy of the party all on himself. "I've just started a game of Truth or Dare, and I didn't want you to miss it."

Leah laughed. "Truth or Dare? Really? Should we play Spin the Bottle afterwards?"

"I'm not familiar with that one. Xander explained Truth or Dare to us, though, and he says he's been dying to try it ever since he found out about it. You'll play, too, won't you Autumn?"

She opened her mouth to say she wouldn't, that she really had a lot to do and it was time she got home. But Leah answered for her.

"Of course, she will. We all will. Remember when we used to play that back in the day?" Leah's grin was so wide, it looked like her cheeks might burst.

Autumn, however, pressed her lips tightly together as she followed the couple back outside. She most certainly did remember those days. They had mostly been fun at the time, but she also distinctly remembered getting herself into a lot of trouble. Her skills as a witch were just beginning to develop, and she had cast quite a few poor spells because of dares. It had, however, helped her discover just what she was capable of.

Reluctantly, she joined Leah and the others in the circle of chairs that had been set up on the patio. Summer sat across the circle next to Xander, her arm looped through his as she gazed up at him with soft eyes. She was so ridiculously in love.

"Okay, let's get started!" Leah sat down to Autumn's right. "Lisa!"

The printshop owner groaned but she was grinning. "Truth."

"Have you ever gotten revenge on someone?"

Lisa exchanged a look with her husband and shrugged her shoulders, trying to control her lips as she grinned. She twisted her hands together. "Just this week, actually. Bill Harrington ordered a new set of sale signs for the grocery store and said he had to have them by Wednesday. I made them a day late because I saw he had put up one of those anti-witch flyers in his window."

The other guest whooped and cheered, but Autumn wasn't celebrating. "What? What flyers?"

Suddenly looking far more uncomfortable instead of just excited and nervous, Lisa turned her wide eyes to Autumn. "You haven't seen them? George Stone has been handing them out all over town, encouraging people to put them in the shop windows saying they won't serve witches. We didn't print them," she amended quickly. "They look like they were printed out on a home computer."

Autumn looked across the circle to her sister. "Did you know about these? We've got to get out there and rip them down!"

Summer closed her eyes and shook her head. "I heard about them earlier today. Don't worry about it for right now, Autumn. Let's just have fun."

But it was difficult to do any such thing when the same nuts who had been protesting outside her store earlier that week were now organizing the town against them. What would they do if things only continued to get worse? She didn't want to move.

Her attention turned back to the game when she heard Holden shout. "Dare!"

"Okay, but you asked for it," Xander warned. "Shift."

The crowd grew suddenly silent, and even Autumn was holding her breath.

"You don't have to do it," Leah reminded him. "It's just a game, after all."

But Holden shook off her concerns. He looked like he'd had plenty to drink, and he was truly enjoying himself. "No, that's okay. I'll do it."

He stood up from his chair and stepped outside the circle. Everyone watched, sitting on the edges of their seats, as he took a deep breath, closed his eyes, and clenched his fists. It happened so quickly that Autumn felt a single blink would make her miss the transformation. His wide, handsome face pushed forward into a long, scaly muzzle where smoke drifted from his nostrils. A row of spiky ridges erupted from his spine and jetted down onto a newly formed tail. He stood before the party guests on all fours, his brilliant crimson scales reflecting the firelight. Only his blue eyes carried some of the Holden she knew.

Everyone pulled in a collective breath, but then they burst into cheers and applause. Holden stretched his wings, dipped his head on its long neck down into a dragon's version of a bow, and then melted back down into his human form. The invitees continued to exclaim their praise for such a feat. Those who were nothing more than regular people were the most impressed, but everyone seemed pleased.

Once the chaos had died down, it was Holden's turn to challenge. "Beau, truth or dare."

The crowd faced a blonde man across the circle. Autumn knew he was a shifter like Holden was, but she hadn't officially met him. His pale hair was swept back, revealing a strong face and full lips. He had been quiet so far during the party, and now that it was his turn, he leaned forward with his elbows on his thighs. Autumn realized this was the same man she had admired near the fire. "Truth."

Holden, apparently feeling that he could still get something in on his fellow dragon, nodded. "Alright. Tell us what wish you sent up to the dragon spirits."

Beau looked shocked for a moment, his eyebrows raising. He pulled in a deep breath, and Autumn thought for a moment that he might refuse and take a dare instead. "To find a mother for Elliot and complete my family."

"I'm glad to hear it!" Holden stood up and crossed the circle to clap his brother on the back. "Your turn."

Autumn wondered to herself why this time of year seemed to focus so much on finding love. Was it because the dark winter months were coming, and nobody wanted to spend them alone? Or was it some innate biological urge so that babies would be born in the spring like other animals? She shook her head. Her mind was wandering to strange places that evening.

The corner of Beau's mouth tipped up, a handsome look on his face as he turned to Xander. "Truth or dare?"

Xander, who was the one who had been so interested in the game in the first place, replied, "Dare!"

"I dare you to eat a piece of celery." Beau nodded to one of the food tables.

He had been so animated only a moment ago, but his face instantly molded into one of disgust. "You're kidding me, right?"

"Nope." Beau shook his head. "You took the dare."

"Fine," Xander replied with a sigh. He went to the food table and picked up a green stick between his thumb and forefinger, barely wanting to even touch it. "God, and it's got cream cheese on it, too!"

The other dragons exploded in laughter, and even Leah had her fingers over her mouth as she giggled. "I'm sorry, Xander. I didn't know until I'd already made them that celery is basically the antithesis of anything dragons like."

"It's not your fault," he replied, glaring at Beau. But he gamely took a bite, chewing and swallowing as quickly as he could while everyone else laughed and wiped tears from their eyes.

Several more truths and dares were traded around the room without the game losing its energy, and Autumn suddenly found herself asked the question, "Truth or dare?" It had come from Summer, of course.

She didn't want to be there in the first place, but she wasn't about to be the one who ruined the party. "Dare."

Summer looked particularly devious. "I dare you to do that one thing you used to do when we were kids and we were bored."

"You don't mean...?"

Summer nodded. "I do."

"Alright." She felt ridiculous, but what Summer was asking wasn't nearly as personal as Holden turning into his dragon or Beau admitting his most secret desires. She danced her finger through the air, feeling the eyes of everyone else on her. Thinking of the way that George Stone and his followers in town thought of her, she wasn't sure she should be performing any kind of magic in front of others, even if they were supposed to be Leah's trusted friends. Still, she couldn't stop now. The carrots on the table stood up on end, dancing in a row. Several of the strange Charokian meatballs rolled off their platter and intermingled with the carrots, creating an intricate dance as they wound their way to the end of the table. This was a trick she had used often, but not for many years; it was what had helped Autumn realize that the magical gene she had hoped to inherit from her mother was alive and well inside her.

Summer clapped, starting a new wave of applause amongst the party guests. "I think you've gotten even better!"

Autumn waved off the flattery. It was a silly child's trick, and she felt heat in her cheeks as she realized everyone was staring at her. She dropped her finger, and the snacks fell where they were. The handsome blonde man on the other side of the circle was smiling at her, and she quickly looked away.

After several more rounds, Autumn felt she could finally get away with slipping out. Summer, enjoying spending the evening with Xander, didn't seem inclined to leave anytime soon, and Autumn didn't want to ruin her time. Truth or Dare was beginning to wind down, and she managed to excuse herself from the circle on the back patio. She bumped into Summer, who was just coming back out of the house with a plate in her hand.

"Where are you going?" her twin asked suspiciously.

"Home, preferably. Should I get a taxi, or are you planning to get a ride back with Xander?" He had come to the party early to help set up and to get Nora settled in with the others.

"I'll ride with him. Besides, it would take forever for a taxi to get all the way out here and then find the place. You sure you want to leave? It's still early."

"Not really." Autumn glanced at her watch. If she left right away, she could get home and be ready for bed in just over an hour. There would be just enough time to squeeze in about seven hours of sleep before getting up at her usual time. If she had things her way, she would wake up a little early and get some time in with the computer before she officially had to open the store.

As she made her way through the sun room and into the house, she stopped in her tracks when she saw a tiny boy standing in the hallway that led to the front door. He dragged a teddy bear by the leg and rubbed his eyes with his free hand. "Dada?"

It had been a weird night, and she had spent most of it feeling uncomfortable and irritated, but now she only felt warm and loving inside as she bent down to kneel in front of the little one. "You're looking for your daddy?" she asked gently. "I can help you."

Unable to help herself, she scooped the child into her arms. He was warm and soft, smelling of bath soap and sleep. Autumn suddenly realized just why Summer had taken such an attachment to Nora. There was something about a child this age that was simply irresistible. "Come on. You can show me who your daddy is."

Her desire to leave was instantly dissolved, relegated to the back of her mind as she stepped back through the sun room and outside. The boy in her arms, still clutching his teddy, pointed at the big blonde man Autumn had seen earlier. Her stomach lurched a little as she walked up to him, and she instantly chided herself for feeling nervous. He was just another person, and his son needed him. "Excuse me, Beau?"

He turned around, his eyes grazing across her face for a moment until he realized who was in her arms. "Elliot! What are you doing out of bed?" He immediately took the child into his own arms, not angry or upset that he had interrupted the party, and cuddled him close.

Autumn felt a distinct emptiness where the little one had been only a moment ago. "I found him in the hall, and he was asking for you."

Beau smiled down at Elliot. "Did you have a bad dream or something?"

But Elliot pointed at the bonfire. "Party!"

The big man laughed. "We already had the party, remember?" He turned to Autumn. "We let the kids have their own little version of Zimryr earlier in the evening. I guess he didn't quite get enough. Let's get you back to bed."

But Julian appeared, the worry on his face instantly turning to relief when he saw Elliot in his father's arms. "There you are! I was sitting there reading, and then all of a sudden, he was gone! I should have known, though. He was so excited about the party that he didn't want to go to sleep."

Beau gave his son more hugs and kisses before he let Julian take him back to bed. He watched them go through the house and down the hall before he turned back to Autumn, his eyes still warm. "Sorry, I hope he didn't interrupt your fun. The two of us are pretty close."

"I can see that." And she truly could. The bond between the two of them radiated such energy that it was impossible to miss, even if she wasn't a psychic like Leah. "He's adorable."

"Thank you. I don't think we've officially met. I'm Beau." He held out his hand.

Autumn took it, instantly feeling that same warmth she had seen in his eyes radiate up her arm and through her chest. She didn't know what it was, and she normally would have questioned anything that seemed like magic if she didn't understand it, but this man was sweeping her off her feet. "I'm Autumn. I'm Summer's twin."

Beau looked across the patio at Summer and then back at her. "Are you sure? The two of you don't seem to be anything alike."

"I'll take that as a compliment," Autumn replied with a surprisingly girlish giggle. "Don't get me wrong, I love my sister, but everyone always expects the two of us to think the same way and like the same things."

"I can understand that." Beau stepped aside to a table of pitchers and cups. He poured a drink and handed it to her before pouring one for himself. The cup looked small in his large hands. He looked completely comfortable in his body, showing no sign of having to live between two completely different forms. "I have a feeling everyone here imagines that Holden, Xander, Julian, and myself are all the same guys since we're all from the same planet. And then there's that whole part about us being dragons. But there's really quite a few differences between us."

Autumn took a sip of her drink. It was fizzy and tasted like nothing she'd had before, though she couldn't quite place it. It must have been another one of Leah's attempts to replicate Charokian holiday traditions. "Like what?"

Beau gestured around them at the grand house. "Take this place, for instance. It suits Holden well, but I don't think I'd like to rattle around in such a big house. Everyone needs a little space, but I like things to be a little bit more cozy."

"Makes sense to me." Autumn's house was huge compared to Summer's little cottage, but it was merely a guesthouse compared to the lavish mansion Holden had. "I bought my house because it has these great old wooden floors and little secret passages that go between some of the rooms. I feel like the spirits of those who lived there before are still there, and I just adore it."

"My place has some neat features, too, and I'm adding to it all the time."

"You do the work yourself?" If someone had asked her, Autumn wouldn't have said she found it attractive when a man knew how to use tools and build things with his hands, but for some reason the idea made her stomach jump around.

He nodded. "I do. I'm pretty passionate about it, really. The guys have suggested that I start doing it for a living, but I'm not sure. I don't want to ruin it with money."

Autumn started to agree with him simply because she found herself so entranced by this handsome blonde man, but she realized just before she answered that she didn't feel the same way. "It's pretty nice, actually. I love running The Enchanted Elm because it allows me to get involved in my craft without having to feel guilty about it. I never have to take off work to do the things I love because I'm already doing them. Really, it's the opposite. I almost didn't come tonight because I wanted to work."

"That would have been a shame." His eyes flicked to her lips and then back up again, just enough to let Autumn know he was feeling the same things she was. "What sort of work would you have done if you hadn't been suckered into strange food and party games?"

Without going into too much detail, she told him about her ideas for expanding to an online store and starting a blog. "As a matter of fact, I was just getting ready to go. It's too late to work on it tonight, but I've got to get up early and get back to the office."

"I'll walk you to the door."

Autumn felt extremely aware of every part of her body as she stepped alongside him. She could still feel those waves of heat rolling off his body, fighting off any bit of the autumn chill that was trying to settle in the air. It was a pleasant sensation, and she was wondering if it had anything to do with the fact that he was a dragon, but she didn't dare ask.

Now, with her hand on the doorknob, she looked up at Beau. Autumn always felt tall and distant from those around her, but this man completely changed that. If she had wanted to, she could have tucked herself right under his arm. It was a very tempting thought. "Well, it was nice to meet you."

"Maybe we could talk some more sometime? Over dinner perhaps?" His cobalt eyes burned into hers as he waited for her answer.

He was so charming he was even making her tongue tingle, and

Autumn pressed it firmly against her mouth for a moment to make sure it behaved itself. "Sure. That'd be nice."

It was difficult to drive home. It wasn't that she had a problem with driving or that her night vision was poor, but she couldn't stop thinking about Beau. To make things even worse, she couldn't stop thinking about Elliot, either. He and his father were equally appealing, in different ways. And the way Beau had looked at her as she had slipped out the door made her think that if the circumstances had been just right, he might have kissed her right then and there.

When she got home, her house seemed empty and quiet compared to the noise and vigor of the party at Holden and Leah's. She locked the door behind her and began getting ready for bed, wondering if she would even be able to sleep with thoughts of Beau spinning in her head. As she got undressed, she once again found the tiny gold ring that Leah had baked into the hors d'oeuvres, the one that was supposed to symbolize Autumn finding her true love. She delicately set it on the dresser, wondering just how much power had been put into the slim band of metal.

# 4

BEAU WALKED THROUGH THE LIVING ROOM AND TOWARD THE KITCHEN TO get a snack for Elliot.

"Just what do you think you're doing?" Holden asked from the couch, his dark eyebrows raised.

"Elliot always has a snack around this time. I don't want him to miss out just because I'm going out for the night." It had occurred to him just as he was getting ready to shave. It was no wonder he was always the one who volunteered to stay behind with the kids, because he never stopped worrying about them otherwise. Even having them right there at Holden's house during the Zimryr party had only comforted him a small amount.

"He's not going to miss out on anything," Holden argued. "Let me take care of it. You need to go put some pants on. I have a feeling the restaurant isn't going to let you in without them."

Beau looked down to see that Holden was right. He had ironed and put on a nice, button-down shirt and had spent far too long picking out a tie. He had even made sure his socks coordinated with the rest of his outfit, but he had left his freshly-pressed trousers lying on the bed and was standing there in his boxers. "Yeah, I'll get right on that."

When he was ready to go, he went back to the living room and glanced at the mantel clock. Even spending what time he had on his outfit, it was still far too early to leave. He paced in front of the large picture window that faced the street.

"You look like a caged animal," Holden remarked, looking far too relaxed from his position on the couch. "Are you alright?"

"Yeah. Mostly." He was a dragon. He was far stronger and more powerful than any human—and most of the animals—on the planet, yet his nerves were rattling against his bones.

"This is exactly why I've been trying to get you to go out more. It's too difficult to handle when you're not used to it." Holden leaned forward to give Finn and Elliot each another cracker, but he kept his eyes on Beau.

"I don't think that's it." Beau had been over and over it in his head, wondering if it was at all possible. "I think I would be nervous no matter what."

"Oh?" If possible, that eyebrow went a little higher.

Beau hesitated to tell Holden just what he had been thinking. If he was wrong, then he would look like a fool. But if he was right, then he would probably need the assistance of his fellow dragons just to keep himself a check. "Don't get excited, but there's a possibility that she just might be the one."

Holden was on his feet, his hands out in the air as he exclaimed. "Seriously? That's wonderful! Why didn't you say anything?"

"I don't know. I just kept questioning myself. I remember what you and Xander had both said when you met Leah and Summer, and about how being around them drove you absolutely crazy. I certainly felt something with Autumn, but I'm not sure it was completely the same."

"Tell me."

"It started when we were out at the bonfire behind your house and putting our requests into the fire. I wasn't kidding when I said I had written down that I wanted to find my mate. I felt a little silly about it, because I wasn't even sure if things would work the same way on Earth. But as I watched that paper curl up and turn to ash, it was like all of a sudden I felt something crawling under my skin. I can't be certain, but I think it was about the time that Autumn arrived."

Holden gestured for him to continue. "And then what happened?"

"Well, I kept looking at her, but she hadn't even so much as given me a glance. So I thought I was just wrong, or that maybe I'd gotten all caught up in the holiday. But then we started that game of Truth or Dare, and she finally looked across the room at me." He could still recall the way she had completely set him on fire with something as simple as a curious glance.

"Did she make you feel like you needed to shift right there on the spot? Like you couldn't hold your dragon side back anymore?"

And this was exactly what had made Beau wonder if he had been wrong. "No. I mean, not at first. I could definitely tell I was attracted to her, and it was a strong feeling, but it wasn't like that. It was just pleasant to be near her while we played and then later on when Autumn and I talked. And I have to say, she looked amazing as she came up to me with Elliot in her arms. It wasn't until she left that I thought I might lose it." Beau had watched her walk down the driveway and get in her car, gripping the doorframe to keep himself from running into the night and pulling her into his arms. He hated the idea that she might go out there into the world without him, that something might happen to her and he would be powerless to stop it. "I only had to wait a couple of days before our date, but it's almost been too much. I can't tell you how many times it occurred to me to just go to her. I wanted to go right down to her shop and demand that we go out right away."

Holden gave a small laugh. "I can understand. Don't be discouraged just because she didn't make you go completely insane right away. Xander didn't, or at least not as much as I did. From what I can tell, it seems to depend on the circumstances in which you meet."

"How's that?" Beau wasn't sure if he wanted Holden to confirm or deny for him that Autumn was the woman he was looking for. He knew he needed to find a mother for his son, and the idea that this beautiful redhead could be that woman was an intriguing one, but he wasn't certain he was ready to commit to such a thing.

"Well, think about it. When you met Autumn, there wasn't much competition in the room. You either knew the other people there, or you knew they were at least friends with Leah. Apart from maybe one or two of Leah's clients, there weren't any other single men. You didn't feel like the possibility of your relationship with her was threatened until she left." Holden sat back down, still smiling.

"What are you grinning about? This is miserable!" Beau paused and ran a hand over the windowsill, which he had replaced himself shortly after he had purchased the house. "I haven't been able to concentrate on any of the projects I have going on. I don't think I've touched a tool since I left the party."

"It's about damn time, that's all. Now don't worry about a thing while you're out. I've got the kids, and I'm going to take them back to my place. Leah and I will both be home all night, and I don't plan to see you again until morning." He grinned, picked up the diaper bag, and began loading the kids in the car.

———

A SHORT WHILE LATER, Beau was pulling out a chair at Le Papillon for Autumn. She looked absolutely stunning in black dress pants and a teal blouse that offset her dark auburn hair. "Have you been here before?"

"Once or twice," she admitted. "But I usually don't have much time for a place like this."

"Is the service particularly slow?" He glanced at the waiters, who seemed to be moving with quick efficiency throughout the dining floor.

"No, it's just that an expensive meal like this should be enjoyed. I'm usually grabbing a quick salad while I eat in the back room and work on my computer." Autumn gave him an apologetic look before perusing her menu.

"Sounds like you really are a lot different from your sister." Beau glanced at his own menu, but his brain was working too hard to focus on something as simple as food. He was controlling his tongue, hoping he didn't say anything stupid to Autumn. He was controlling his body, which was suddenly aware of the fact that there were so many other people in the upscale restaurant, any of which might be a threat to Autumn or to his relationship with her. And then there was the fact that every time he looked at her or even thought about her, his pants grew a little tighter.

Autumn snickered. "I take it you've spent some time with her?"

"Only a little. She and Xander stopped by my place a couple of weeks ago. I needed his help lifting some cabinetry. She's very laid back. I thought she would lay out in my garden all day." It wasn't that Beau had minded. The backyard was a beautiful place full of a variety of flowers, and someone ought to be enjoying it, but he had a hard time understanding how someone could waste so much time.

"That's Summer for you. She's the queen of chilling. I can't stand it myself. I want to feel like I'm using every minute to its maximum potential. If I'm waiting at the doctor's office or stuck in traffic, then I'm checking my email or looking into new inventory for the store. At the very least, I'm reading a book." She spoke firmly and with enthusiasm.

"I guess you and I are a lot alike. I can't relax if I know there's something that needs to be taken care of. If I'm not actively parenting Elliot, then I'm working on my house or designing plans for the next project. We've got a lot more downtime on this planet than we ever did while we were on Charok."

Their waiter came and they put in their orders, but Autumn instantly resumed the conversation. She put her arms on the table and leaned forward. "And what about the others? What do they think of the fact that you're constantly busy?"

Beau shrugged. It was something that did bother him sometimes, and he wasn't sure if it was the right thing to talk about on a first date, but she was asking after all. "It bothers them, especially Holden. He's always telling me to relax. But I guess I'm a bit of a control freak. I like watching the children because I know they're taken care of. I don't want to hire someone to fix up my house, because I want to make sure the job is done right. I've just always been the person who steps in and takes care of things."

When their food came, they digressed for a bit into idle chitchat about Autumn's plans for The Enchanted Elm, what the weather had been like, and how their food tasted, but the conversation never stopped. Beau found that the more time he spent with Autumn, the more he had to say. He wanted to tell her everything, from the type of nails he was using on his latest home improvement project to his hopes for finding a mother for Elliot. He resisted some of those urges, but as their plates grew empty, he knew he was running out of time. Beau would have to take Autumn home, and then he would have to give her back to the world. That was something he absolutely didn't want to do.

"Would you like dessert?" he asked spontaneously. "I hear they've got excellent chocolate mousse."

Autumn's green eyes grew wide with desire for the sweet, and Beau hoped that she would feel that way about him. "Oh, that's my favorite!"

But when Beau attempted to order them each a dish, the waiter informed them that they were out of luck. "I'm sorry, sir. We've run out this evening."

Beau's stomach dipped down into his shoes for a moment. It was too late to ask Autumn to go see a movie just to prolong their date, and he wasn't a fan of the human pastime anyway. He had a feeling Autumn would see it as being just as much of a waste of time and money as he did. But he realized he wasn't completely out of options just yet. "Why don't you come back to my place for dessert? I've got a few things at the house we can munch on."

Her thin eyebrows drew together, and she glanced down at the burgundy tablecloth. Maybe she didn't want to be out late because she wanted to get up early and work, and maybe she was just tired of spending time with him, but she was trying to think of an excuse not to accept. "Well, okay," she finally replied.

"Oh, uh, great. That's great! I'll just take care of the check and we can be on our way." Beau's body was in such turmoil that it barely allowed him to function as he fished out his debit card and paid for their meal. He felt as though he were comprised of numerous creatures all fighting for the same space, and no one was strong enough to come out the winner. It was a battle that felt endless, though he tried to stay as calm as possible on the surface as he walked Autumn out to his car.

After opening the door for her and getting her settled in the passenger seat, Beau walked around the back of the vehicle. He allowed himself a quick morph, just a shifting of the skin on his arms into scales and back again, to vent some of his excitement.

# 5

Autumn wasn't sure what she was thinking when she agreed to go back to Beau's place with him. She wasn't an easy woman, and it wasn't the sort of thing she typically did. When Autumn dated, she wanted to make it clear to any man she was with that he wasn't in charge of her and she would do as she wished.

But things seemed to be different with him. She actually *wanted* to go back to his place for dessert, and it was only her thought for the time of night that made her hesitate at all. There was a momentary pang of regret in the back of her mind for not getting the blog for The Enchanted Elm started yet, but she managed to brush it aside when they pulled into his driveway.

"It's lovely," she said as she looked up at the craftsman-style home. "It looks like it could have been designed by the same architect who came up with the plans for my house."

Beau nodded, his shoulders widening a little. "I've heard there are several like this in town. The realtor took me around to all sorts of modern places, thinking a single dad wouldn't be interested in a house that needed work. But I fell in love with it right away. The foundation and the general structure of it were very sound, so I knew I could do most of the repairs without any special equipment. Would you like a tour?"

"I'd love it." For some reason, Autumn couldn't wait to see the inside of the house. She couldn't remember the last time she had gotten excited about anything that didn't have to do with work. If she wasn't putting the final touches on a new spell, negotiating a bulk order of crystals, or figuring out the best price point for incense, then she wasn't interested. But, just as everything with Beau seemed to be, this was different.

He opened the heavy wooden door, a relic that hadn't been replaced or remodeled, and showed her into the living room. "This room was a wreck when I bought the place. I had to refinish the floor and repair numerous holes in the walls. The front window had to be completely replaced since it was leaking."

"Is the trim work original?" Autumn asked, admiring the golden glow of the wood.

"No. Someone had replaced it years ago with cheap stuff from the home improvement store. I made this myself."

She snapped her head around to look at him, expecting to find him laughing. "You're serious?"

He nodded like it was just an everyday thing to churn out quality work like this. "Yeah. I've got a router table in the garage. Here, I'll show you my latest project."

Heading down the hall, he waved her through a pocket door and into a small study. It was not as large and fancy as Holden's, but it still held that cozy air of a place that housed decades of books, learning, and decision-making. A pair of vintage armchairs sat by the fireplace, several books stacked on the table between them. On the other side of the room, the atmosphere of the place was interrupted by stacks of boards and several scattered tools.

"A few of the bookshelves suffered some water damage, probably from a former leak in the roof," he explained. "I'm working on replacing them all. It's been an interesting challenge to match the stain, but I think I've just about got it down."

Autumn couldn't help but notice several pieces of fancy trim work in here as well. "I have a rude question to ask you."

"Go right ahead." He didn't seem to be bothered by her statement, and she noticed that he had calmed down quite a bit since they had come back to his place. He had been pleasant at the restaurant, but there had been a certain air of tension about him that had somehow melted away.

"How do you know to do all this? From what little I've heard of it,

Charok was nothing but caves and rocks. I wouldn't have imagined that you had these kinds of tools and skills." She picked up a small hand tool that she couldn't identify, feeling completely mystified at his talents.

"That's a hand plane," he said. "Here, I can show you how to use it." Beau stood behind her and covered her hand with his where it rested on the large knob of the tool. "It takes off small layers of the wood, so you can shape and smooth it. It makes the best surface, it really makes the wood pop, and it makes a lot less dust than just sanding." Beau laid the plane down on a piece of wood and pushed it gently away from them, creating big curls of wood that looked like giant pencil shavings.

The heat of him at her back made Autumn tingle as though she had just cast an elaborate spell. His hand was hot and strong against hers, and he manipulated the wood easily. There was a certain amount of satisfaction from seeing the flat surface of the wood reveal itself, and she didn't mind that he took several more strokes of it this way.

"And to answer your real question, I did a lot of this at home. We did live in caves, but they were as elaborately decorated as any Earth homes. More of the work was done by hand instead of power tools, but they do make great shortcuts." His voice made his chest rumble against her back.

In answer, Autumn's stomach rumbled as well. Her face warmed as she blushed. She had hardly eaten a thing all day between being busy and knowing she would get a fancy meal at Le Papillon that night, and her dinner had apparently not lasted long. "Um, I think you said something about dessert?"

Beau's light laugh blew the hair away from her neck. He set down the plane and took her by the hand as he escorted her through the house to the kitchen.

Autumn knew she could find her way on her own if she needed to, but there was something fun about the way he pulled her along. It made her feel like a kid again.

"Don't mind the kitchen," Beau said apologetically as he waved her to a seat at an old laminate breakfast bar. "I've been tackling this place one room at a time, and the kitchen is going to be one of the most involved. Someone 'remodeled' it back in the seventies or so."

"I can see that." Cheap, premade cabinets clung to the wall in a depressingly dark stain. Most of the handles had come off the doors at some point, leaving little holes in the wood. The chipped countertops were a bright yellow that assaulted the eyes but matched the oddly patterned carpet on the floor.

Beau pulled out two plates and some forks and then opened the fridge. "You'd think I'd want to get this room done first, since I spend so much time in here, but I've been having a hard time deciding exactly what I want to do. I could keep the layout so I don't have to redo the plumbing, but I'd also like to rip it all out and start over so I can put the sink in front of the window and move the stove and fridge to a better spot."

Autumn frowned at the room. It really was awful. "I vote for the sink in front of the window. I didn't have much of a choice in my house. Someone had redone the kitchen just a year or two before I bought it. Not exactly to my taste, but nice stuff that I can live with."

"Here." Beau set a cheesecake on the counter in between the plates. "I just made this yesterday. Or I've got an Italian cream cake in here if you prefer." He pointed to the fridge and raised his eyebrows, looking like he was ready to display an entire buffet of desserts if it might please her.

"Wait a minute. You *made* that?"

"Yeah. What's wrong?" He slowly shut the fridge door, his body stiff.

Autumn blinked and shook her head. "There's nothing wrong with it. Not at all. It's just that if someone says they've made a cheesecake, it's usually one of those cheap ones from a box that's basically just cheesecake-flavored pudding. This is the real deal."

Beau served them each a piece, smiling at her from the other side of the breakfast bar. "Why do you look so surprised?"

"You clearly have no idea what men are like here on Earth, do you?" Autumn took a bite of the cheesecake. It was thick, rich, and creamy, just like it was supposed to be. Of course it was.

He tipped his head at her. "You can't tell me men don't bake. I don't watch a lot of TV, but I've seen plenty of cooking shows hosted by men."

"They might bake," she agreed. "And they might know how to do woodwork, or they might keep their house clean, or they might be great fathers, but they don't do all of it."

"Is there something wrong with someone who does?" he challenged.

"No. Not at all, it's just..." She trailed off and began laughing. "It's like you're from another planet or something."

Beau laughed as well. "Imagine that. I guess you don't want to hear that I like to cook as well."

Autumn pointed with her fork at the slice of cheesecake on her plate, which was quickly disappearing. "Is everything as good as *this*?"

"You'll have to come over and see for yourself sometime." His eyes were glasslike pools that pulled at her, his words an invitation and a challenge.

"I might," she said slowly, unable to look away. She could feel the distance closing between them, shortening slowly by millimeters, but she was powerless to stop it. "But I'm not sure I'm worthy of someone who's so perfect."

"And why not, when you're perfect, too?" His lips met hers, the warmth that had been teasing her since she first met him entering her body and filling her with the power of sunlight and fire. Beau was on her side of the counter now, having come around the edge of it, and her head tipped back in submission to his kiss.

They had been talking all evening, but now, there was no need to say a word. She allowed her hands to move of their own volition, spreading her fingers out across his wide chest, moving down to explore the hard muscles of his abdomen, and circling around to his back.

Beau's arms were around her, too, and they easily pulled her off the barstool and to her feet. His own hands explored her body, first cupping gently around the base of her skull before running down her arms and wrapping around her waist.

When he finally broke their lip lock, Autumn felt a distinct chill where he had been touching her, even though he still held her close.

Beau pressed his forehead to hers. "Autumn, I know we've only just met. But I had no idea there could be anybody on Earth like you. Say you'll stay with me tonight."

Every argument in her head instantly dissipated. Autumn always wanted to argue, she always wanted to say no, but she had no choice. "I will."

Pressing his lips to hers once more, Beau pulled away from her slowly before he picked her up by the waist and put her over his shoulder. Autumn sucked in a breath of surprise, but she found that she still couldn't argue. This man wanted her, and she wanted him just as much. There was something sexy about that, and her core tightened.

Beau's bedroom was just as marvelous as the rest of the house had been, or at least it seemed to be from what she could see in her current position. The hardwood floors held up a large bed piled with blankets and pillow in shades of gold and deep brown. Beau cast these aside to set her down on the mattress, allowing Autumn to see the exposed timber on the plaster ceiling.

To her surprise, he didn't just toss her down on the bed and ravage her. He laid her back gently, kissing her once again as he slowly undid the buttons of her blouse. The cool air in the house tickled at her bare skin, but the heat of Beau's body above her quickly won out. He cast aside the garment, letting it land as a puddle of silk on the floor.

Autumn wasn't about to let him have all the fun. He looked handsome in his nice clothes, but her deft fingers made quick work of his tie. It took effort not to simply rip his shirt off his body, instead releasing each button to reveal intricate Charokian tattoos and a dusting of pale hair across his chest. It led down to his abs, which were even more amazing to see now that there wasn't a layer of fabric in her way. His waist was trim and solid, and she couldn't stand the thought of his pants being around it any longer.

But Beau gave her pause as he reached around behind her to unsnap her bra, exposing her breasts and making her nipples stand alert. He bent his head to kiss one of them tenderly, gently flicking it with his tongue and sending sparks of electricity down through her body to create a fire between her legs. She ran her hands through his blonde hair, admiring the softness of it as she closed her eyes and let him have his way with her cleavage.

While his mouth worked, his hands were still busy. He unzipped her pants and had them off her in an instant, reminding Autumn of what she had been about to do a moment ago. She reached for his belt buckle, fiddling with the hard metal for only a moment before she had it undone. Her hands ran over his taught buttocks and down his hard thighs as she undressed him. He was hard and ready for her, the sight of his erection sending a tingle of longing through her.

"You have no idea how badly I've wanted you," Beau growled in her ear as his fingers slipped between her skin and the waistband of her panties, digging erotically in her flesh as he took them off. "From the moment we were in the same house, I knew I had to have you. The days between the party and tonight have been an eternity for me. I know that sounds crazy, but you're the most remarkable woman I've ever met and I want nothing but to be with you."

"No," Autumn argued as she pulled him down on top of her. His chest hair tickled her breasts pleasurably, the heat and weight of him above her was titillating. She spread her legs, feeling herself growing wetter by the moment. "It's not crazy at all."

He was gentle as he pushed his way inside her, his shoulders suddenly relaxing as though he was relieved to finally have his cock where it belonged. He moved his hips, exploring, probing. "Does that mean you've thought of me?"

Autumn could barely speak or breathe, but it was only because every ounce of her body was focused on the way it felt to be joined with his. "Yes. A lot. I've never met someone who could make me forget about the rest of the world." And he truly had. Autumn didn't care about work or about what time she got up in the morning. Everything she needed was right there in his bed.

"I know how you feel." Beau covered her mouth with his once again, their tongues twining in reflection of the way their bodies danced together.

As much as she was enjoying having him on top of her, Autumn wanted a better chance to explore his body. She touched her knee to his thigh, giving him a cue, and he rolled over until she was on top. Pushing herself up on her hands and bending her knees on either side of his hips, she rode him like she owned him. And as far as she was concerned at that moment, she did. That rugged, handsome face, that sexy body, that deep voice that made her stop just so she could hear it, it was all hers. Autumn pulsed on top of him, burying him deep inside her.

But Beau wasn't the only one who knew what he wanted. He took her hands in his and pulled her down so that her breasts were in his face. "I can't get enough of these," he moaned as he once again took her into his mouth, his tongue hot and wet on her tender flesh.

She let him have what he wanted, pushing her mounds gently into his face. Autumn knew she was still the one in charge, and she slammed her hips down as she felt the blossoming of an orgasm in her lower abdomen. As she reached her peak, she rode out the wave of pleasure, crying out in time to every climactic burst. Her body was alive in his hands.

Beau started to roll back over on top of her, but she put a hand on his shoulder to stop him. "I've got a different idea." Without letting his member slip out of her slick recesses, Autumn swung around on top of his hips so that she faced his feet. Bracing her hands on his legs, she continued her rodeo. Pulling her body up so that he was nearly out of her and then slamming back down again, Beau was at her mercy.

He proved it with his growl of pleasure as his hands massaged her backside, but Beau was still stronger than her. As he pummeled into her, he pushed her up until she was on her hands and knees and he was behind her. Autumn didn't complain, pleased that he was getting what he needed. She felt his member engorge, and it inspired in her yet another round of satisfaction. With a roar of victory and a final push, Beau reached the culmination of his efforts.

She lay next to him in bed, his strong arm around her and pulling her close as she rested her head on his chest. It was close and comfortable and she could feel sleep creeping in around the back of her eyes. "It's getting late."

"I can turn off the light if you're tired."

Autumn sat up and looked down at him, suddenly realizing just how caught in the moment she had been back in the kitchen. He looked tired but satisfied, a smile on his face and his eyes half-closed. "I'm sorry. I know I said I would stay, but I really can't. I've got things to do in the morning."

Beau's eyes snapped open at that. "So? Sleep here, and then you can go home in the morning."

"I'll sleep much better in my own bed, really." Autumn slipped off the mattress, surprised to find what a long way it was to the floor, and started picking up her clothes.

He was on his feet and pulling on his own pants, his hair flying as he moved. "You can't leave now. It's the middle of the night."

She looked over her shoulder at him, her eyes narrowed. "I'm a grown woman, I can handle it."

But Beau looked like a wild animal, standing there in front of her shirtless. He grabbed her by the shoulders, just firmly enough that she knew he didn't want to let go. "Autumn, it's not safe. I can't let you."

"You don't get to *let* me do anything. We had a nice date, and I had a lot of fun with you, but I'm going home." Autumn turned away from him to step into her shoes, and he let go of her. He didn't stand in her way when she headed for the bedroom door.

But he did follow her as she headed down the hall. "I'm sorry, Autumn. I shouldn't have said it like that. I'm just worried about you. And I know I appear to be human, but there's a lot more to me than that."

Autumn was at the front door now, having retrieved her purse from the side table. She turned to look at him, and she instantly knew that he was right. He was the perfect man, but he was also a dragon. She liked that he was the sort of man who covered every angle and didn't leave things undone, but there was a downside that came along with that. "Look, I get it. I really do. But I don't normally do this sort of thing. I'll be fine. I promise. I'll call you."

She headed out to her car and started the engine, realizing as the clock came up on the dashboard just how late it really was. She had stayed at his place until nearly one in the morning, far later than she had imagined any date being. There would be just enough time to grab a few hours of sleep before it was time to get up. It was going to take lot of caffeine to get through the work day, but it would be worth it.

As she drove home, she couldn't help but think about how sweet Beau was. He had almost gotten a little too overbearing there at the end, but he'd realized his mistake as soon as he'd made it. And, as he had pointed out, he wasn't just a regular guy. Well, Autumn wasn't exactly a regular girl, either.

Pulling up in her driveway and getting out of the car, Autumn's thoughts were so distracted by her hunky date to realize that she wasn't alone until it was too late. Someone grabbed her from behind, pinning her arms to her sides. Dark fabric came down over her head, and she could no longer see.

Autumn yanked her arms, struggling to free herself. A finger pointed in the right direction could be the difference between life and death. But whoever was doing this must have known that, because they held her fast. A hard object slammed into her head, and the darkness she saw became real.

# 6

SOMETHING POUNDED IN AUTUMN'S BRAIN, RATTLING AGAINST THE INSIDE of her skull and pushing at the back of her eyes. She moaned, wanting to go back to sleep instead of facing the pain, but her body wouldn't let her. Consciousness invaded her mind, making her aware not only of the agony in her head, but the ropes that bound her hands. She was upright instead of lying in bed, a hard chair beneath her. Autumn snapped her eyes open at the realization that something was very wrong, but she instantly shut them again to stop her stomach from lurching up her throat.

"She's awake!"

The voice was a familiar one, and Autumn forced her eyes to open more slowly this time. Her stomach still churned, but it was obvious that whatever was going on was something she would have to face. Her heart pounded as she took in the room lined in concrete blocks, which only made the hammering in her head worse.

"It's about time." This was a different voice, and as a figure pushed his way into the room, Autumn instantly knew who he was. It was George Stone, the older man who had led the protest in front of The Enchanted Elm just over a week ago. "Why do you have her face uncovered?" he demanded. "Who knows what she might do to us."

"She's not Medusa," replied the first voice. Autumn picked up her head to look at its owner, who sat slumped over in a wooden chair of his own. He, however, was not tied to it. "Besides, she looked like she wasn't able to breathe."

"Isn't that the point, Bill?" Mr. Stone countered. "We're wanting to rid our town of this vermin, after all."

Autumn realized he had spoken to Bill Harrington, the man who owned the grocery store. It was the same person Lisa Rochester had said put up one of George's witch-hating flyers in his window. He had a curly man perm that made him look like he had popped out of the seventies or eighties and squinty eyes that were bored and tired. "Okay, yeah, we don't want witches around here, but you never said anything about killing them. I thought we were just going to run them out of town."

Stone put his fist on his hip and gave Bill a glare. "And then what happens? She just flies back here on her broomstick and puts a curse on all of us. I thought you understood what you were in for. We're the descendants of witch hunters, after all, so start acting like it!"

Witch hunters? Seriously? Autumn wanted to ask Stone if his cheese had fallen completely off his cracker, but she was in no mood for quips. "Just let me go. I haven't done anything to anyone."

"The hell you haven't!" George was in her face now. "You and your kind have been a negative influence on generations of kids! There's no telling how many of them have fallen under your spell, and we're not going to rest until we know our town is clean! That's what the Purity and Pride Assembly is all about."

"The Purity and Pride Assembly?" Maybe it was just the ache in her head, but this man wasn't making any sense.

"Are you going to tell me you haven't heard of it?" George's wisps of gray hair had come lose during his rant, and he whisked them back with one hand. "We might have started out as a tiny group of people who met once a week after church, but we've expanded! I'm happy to say that there are several members who count the names of the greatest witch hunters in history as their ancestors, and now we have new blood joining us as well. Before you know it, we'll be driving your kind completely out of the country!"

"But I really haven't done anything," Autumn gasped. She hurt so badly, and it was hard to stay conscious. They must have hit her hard. By the way they talked, she wondered if they had Summer as well. She nearly opened her mouth to ask but thought better of it. If they hadn't gotten her—or better yet, if they hadn't thought of it—then it was best not to give them any ideas.

"Could you at least gag her?" George said to Bill. "I don't want her chanting any spells at us."

The grocer obliged, finding a strip of cloth and tying it around Autumn's face. She tried to spit it out, but the knot was too tight. The truth was that she could chant at them all day and it wouldn't make any difference. She needed the use of her fingers at the very least to manipulate the latent magic in the air, and the right herbs and crystals went a long way, too.

"Alright," Bill said with a sigh. "So what option are we going to go with?"

George sat down in one of the empty chairs in the room, leaning forward and rubbing his hands together. "Oh, let's do something particularly fun and burn her at the stake."

The entire time she had been growing up, Autumn had been warned of people who didn't understand their way of life. At one point in time when she was a teenager, she had been particularly interested in the history of people like her, and she had studied the Salem witch trials extensively. Never, though, had she imagined that they would be coming to life right before her eyes.

"I thought they hanged most of the witches," Bill said thoughtfully, rubbing his chin.

George made an exasperated noise. "That's not going to show people anything! They won't understand just how serious we are. No, I want everyone to see the black smoke rising off her body and know that there's one less predator in this town!" His voice grew louder as he spoke, echoing through the sparse room.

A knock came on the door. Bill stood up to admit two younger men who didn't look like they could be old enough to buy beer. "Good. You're here. You did a great job last night, and you ought to be around to enjoy this."

The taller one, with a bulging gut and wide shoulders, had piggy eyes buried in the flesh of his face. He grinned, losing the corners of his lips in his puffy cheeks. "Do we get to throw her in the lake and see if she sinks or swims?"

Yet another disgusted noise rose out of George. "Come on,

Matthew. Does anyone pay attention to what we're doing? Or listen at the meetings? Everyone knows how to swim these days, so that's not a test at all. In fact, we've got plenty of proof just in her daily actions. Why, she's got an entire store full of black magic. Have any of you been in there?"

The skinny young man who had walked in with Matthew slowly raised his hand. "I have."

"And what did she do to you, Josh?" George was on his feet again, bending down in front of the skinny boy and putting his arm around his shoulders.

His jaw worked in place for a moment, and he was even shaking a little. "She tried to get me to come to one of her devil worship services. Said there was a circle in the woods where she would dance naked in the moonlight for me and give me my deepest darkest desires." He glanced at Autumn and then shifted his eyes to the floor.

"I did not!" At least, that's what Autumn tried to scream. The gag made it come out as a muffled, unintelligible squeal.

"There, you see?" George straightened and threw his fist in the air, as though he had just won an argument that nobody was having with her. "This is exactly the kind of horrific person we need to get rid of. I've personally seen her sacrificing chickens on the front steps of her house, and she's always sneaking into people's yards to steal herbs or put spells on them."

Autumn protested again, but of course, it made no difference. They didn't care what she had to say, even if they could understand her. Their random conversations about the treatment of witches barely even made sense if they had been living back in the seventeenth century. She expected them to start talking about third nipples and the mark of the devil next.

Instead, Autumn tried to focus on getting herself free. She tried to look as though she were sitting still, her head hanging down, defeated, while she slowly worked at the bindings on her wrists. The ropes dug into her skin, and whoever had been in charge of that part of the abduction had not only bound her wrists, but had run coils of rope over her fingers as well. These men were obviously not all that intelligent, but they had done their homework. If she couldn't move her fingers, she had little chance of casting any spells that would get her out of there.

The men continued to argue and recount tales of persecutions from the "good old days," not caring that they were discussing her fate right in front of her as though they were deciding the best way to roast a tenderloin.

Autumn closed her eyes and focused her energies, hoping something would come to her soon.

"GO DOWN THE SLIDE! YOU CAN DO IT!" BEAU STOOD CLOSE BY WHILE
Elliot played on the small plastic slide in the kiddie section of the local
park. He had toddled over to the massive metal slide several times,
pointing eagerly to the top, but he wasn't anywhere close to being big
enough for that. Beau considered taking him down the slide on his lap,
but he wasn't completely sure it would hold him. Looking at it left him
with the distinct feeling that the legs would buckle and the entire
structure would topple.

In fact, that was the feeling he'd been having all morning. His
stomach was constantly jumping up into his chest as though he was
falling, and he couldn't seem to concentrate on anything he was doing.
As much as he wanted to brush the feelings aside, he knew the reason
for them.

It was Autumn. He'd nearly messed everything up the previous
night when he'd tried to get her to stay at his house. The flashing in
her green eyes as she argued told him that she wasn't the sort of
woman who wanted to be protected, and she certainly didn't take
orders from anyone but herself. He'd backed off and apologized,
knowing it was the right thing to do for their relationship.

But that didn't mean it was the right thing to do for her and for her
safety. They'd had an amazing night of lovemaking, the kind of scenes
that he never imagined would happen for him. He had thought of

nothing but having her in his arms from the moment he'd met her, and once he finally did, he knew he was home. That was enough for him to know that he needed to do everything in his power to protect her, even if she didn't appreciate it.

Beau had been kicking himself from the moment he let Autumn walk out that door. There was no telling what might happen to her out there. He knew that even though they weren't on Charok, there were still plenty of dangers in the world. Why had he let her go? He could have convinced her, or if it had come down to it, forced her to stay. Autumn wouldn't have liked him for it, but at least he would have known she was alright.

That morning, he couldn't say he felt that way. At breakfast, he had gotten himself so worked up about it that his wings had shot out of his back at the table, breaking the back off the chair and knocking several dishes off the sideboard. Elliot had laughed and clapped, but he wasn't the one who had to clean up the mess. Once the dining area was back to rights, Beau had dialed Autumn's cell phone, but he didn't get an answer.

Now, keeping a careful eye on Elliot as he peeked into a giant plastic playhouse, Beau grabbed his cell from his pocket and pulled up the number for The Enchanted Elm. Autumn wouldn't like being disturbed at work, and Xander would have advised him not to be calling her so soon after a date, but it would just be too bad. He had to hear her voice, even if she was using it to yell at him.

"Good morning and thank you for calling The Enchanted Elm," came a pleasant voice from over the line.

But it wasn't the one he wanted to hear. "Summer, this is Beau. Is Autumn there?"

She gave a little laugh. "I can't say she is. She must have had a good time with you last night if she's sleeping in this late. Autumn is never late for work, no matter what she's got going on."

That was exactly what he was afraid of. He'd kept her out past midnight, and they'd had an amazing time, but he knew Autumn well enough to know that nothing was going to keep her from work. "Okay. If you see her, let me know." He immediately hung up and dialed another number.

"I didn't expect to hear from you so early," Xander said when he picked up. "I imagined you and Autumn would be sharing a long, slow breakfast."

Apparently, everyone they knew had been invested in that first date. It might have been irritating had he the time to think about it. "No, she left last night. I think something happened to her."

Xander's teasing tone instantly changed to a hard one. "Why? What's going on?"

"I don't know." It was so hard to put it into words, but that was how everything with Autumn made him feel. He couldn't describe the way she affected him, even when she wasn't around. And he knew it should have been better now that he had been with her and knew she wanted to be with him again, but it was only worse. "I just have a sense of something happening. She left my house last night, and I instantly reacted. I was kind of an asshole about it, actually. I tried to tell myself it was just because I didn't want her to leave, but I think there's more to the story. Can you watch Elliot for me? I need to go look for her."

"Of course. You want me to come get him?"

"I'll swing by and drop him off. Your place is on the way to her house, anyway, and that's where I'm going to start." His plan was coming to him without any real thought, as though his instincts alone were formulating ideas.

"Sounds good. I'll get the other men rounded up to help."

"You can if you want, but I don't have time to wait. I've got to find her. And there's always a chance that I might be wrong."

Xander hesitated as though he wanted to argue, but he simply said, "Good luck."

"Okay, little buddy. It's time to go." Beau scooped Elliot up into his arms, taking at least a small amount of relief in knowing that he was alright. And he knew, despite some of the arguments he'd made as they were preparing for the party, that the other shifters were just as capable of taking care of the kids as he was.

"Play?" Elliot asked innocently, pointing over Beau's shoulder to the playground equipment he'd just had to leave.

"I'm sorry. I've got something I've got to go do." It was far more than he could explain to his son at this stage in his young life, but eventually he would have to. Elliot would probably someday know the feeling of finding a woman that he had no choice but to love.

"Venture?" Elliot asked.

Despite the grim outlook he had concerning Autumn, Beau had to smile as he put Elliot in the car and buckled him into his safety seat. He had been talking to Elliot about adventures, telling him stories at

night of the things he used to do back on Charok, and it was clear that
the tot had been listening.

"Yes, it'll be an adventure. But it's not one you can be a part of.
You'll get to go play with your cousin Nora, and I'll be back as soon as I
can. Okay?"

"Kay." Elliot sounded disappointed, but he had always been a very
sweet and compliant child. He didn't argue or throw a fit about being
taken away from the park or the fact that he couldn't go with his father.
Instead, he turned his pale blue eyes to the window and watched the
scenery pass.

———

IT WAS NEARLY afternoon by the time Beau finally arrived at Autumn's
house, which meant he had wasted far too much time worrying about
doing the right thing. Her car was in the driveway. As he leapt out of
the driver's seat and trotted up to the door, he carried a small hope that
he just might find her at home, dozing in bed and unwilling to start
the day after their tryst.

But from the moment he touched the door handle, he was certain
he would be disappointed. He didn't sense her energy at all. Still, he
knocked fervently for a moment before tucking in his shoulder and
ramming it against the wood. The door splintered around the lock,
and he stumbled into a large living room that wasn't too dissimilar
from his own.

"Autumn!" He raced into the kitchen before turning on his heel
and heading down the hall. He found the bathroom, her guest room,
and her bedroom, all empty. He ran back out into the main part of the
house and up a narrow set of stairs.

The open area at the top had windows facing in all directions.
There was very little furniture, but there were plenty of shelves laden
with books, crystals, and candles. On the wall opposite the door, a
large cabinet with glass doors held numerous small jars of herbs and
spices. A low, circular table in the center of the room served as an altar
table, a careful arrangement of talismans and candles on top of it. The
smell of incense was still thick in the air, but it was stale. Autumn
hadn't been there for quite some time.

"Shit." It was as he expected, but he had still hoped to find some
sign of her. Double-checking as he made his way to the front door, he

noticed he hadn't seen her cell phone, her keys, or her purse. Autumn hadn't even made it into the house last night.

Back outside, Beau forced himself to a stop. He closed his eyes and took in a deep breath, letting his body and the feral part of his mind take over. Energies and scents swirled around him, small hints as to Autumn's location slowly coalescing. She had been there, right there on the driveway next to her car. If he concentrated hard enough, he could just sense her energy. It smelled of sweat and fear, which brought out his instinct to guard her even more.

Following it like a trail, Beau left their vehicles in the driveway and headed out on foot in pursuit of his love. He moved like a wild animal on the hunt, so focused on finding his precious prey that he didn't bother paying any attention to other pedestrians on the sidewalk or even traffic as he crossed a street. His pace quickened as the signals from Autumn grew stronger and he knew he was on the right path, even though the energies that had emanated from her had shifted. They were calmer, and he no longer detected the distinct tang of fear. He could only hope that was a good sign.

But he knew, as he rounded a corner, that it wasn't. The abandoned house, set in a neighborhood of other small homes in various states of dilapidation, was ominous enough on its own. Dark windows gaped out at the bright and sunny day that surrounded it. Weeds stood as overgrown sentries in the front yard, clinging defensively to the weathered siding even as they slipped their tendrils in between the boards and slowly pushed them apart. A battered old car rested in the driveway, its rust spots indicating that it might have been there since the previous owners had deserted the house.

Beau knew better, though. As he walked slowly up behind the car and ran his hand along the shabby finish, he felt her spirit resonating from the torn interior. She had been in that car, and someone had transferred her from it to the house.

His back itched, his wings pushing insistently at the underside of his skin. This was a dangerous situation, and his body knew he was safer if he was in human form. But he had to at least wait until he was out of sight of any potential passersby.

Wading through the tall grass, Beau moved around the back of the house and up the rickety steps to the back porch. He had to dodge several holes, the black depths between the boards threatening to swallow him. Either the humans who had taken Autumn hadn't bothered to use the back door or they didn't think they needed to lock it, because it swung open easily on noisy hinges.

Beau paused, letting his eyes adjust to the darkness inside the home. Despite the fact that none of the windows had curtains, they only admitted a small amount of sunlight through the grime that coated them. If there was electricity in the house, it wasn't being used. Several remnants of furniture stood like dusty watchmen in the corners of the room, silently watching Beau as he made his way through the house. The floorboards creaked under his feet no matter how carefully he stepped. His skin rippled and pulsed, threatening to morph, but it wasn't any safer now that he was inside. Beau wasn't certain the floor would hold him. To make matters worse, he no longer had a definitive track of where Autumn was. Her energy was all over this place, filling it to the roof like a cloud of emerald that enticed and teased him.

The space he had entered seemed to be a dining room adjacent to an open kitchen, the doors on the cabinets hanging by their hinges like crooked teeth. Just as he made his way through to the next doorway, a noise behind him made him turn on his heel.

A man stood in a doorway on the other side of the dining room. He was older, a slim figure with tendrils of gray hair carefully combed over his balding head. He stood with his knees bent and his hands forward, like a cowboy in one of the Old West movies Xander had shown him. The gun in his hand was pointed directly at Beau. "Who are you?" the man demanded.

Beau hadn't thought to bring a gun or a knife. He wasn't used to the earthly idea of weapons, because he never needed them as a dragon. There had been rudimentary ones on Charok, but they were symbolic more than anything. Mere scraps of wood and metal didn't mean much when compared to impervious scales, fireballs or magic spells. "I'm looking for Autumn," he growled. "Where is she?"

"Oh, you mean the witch!" The man gestured wildly with his free hand. "I suppose you must have heard. As much as I've tried to tell the other members of the Assembly to keep their yappers shut, someone must have gotten too excited. We've got her, all right. Are you here to join us?"

Beau didn't know what he meant, and he didn't care. "I'm here to get her back."

"Revenge!" The older man's eyes were wild, like an animal who had finally pounced and caught a meal between its mighty paws. "I don't blame you a bit. Tell me what she did to you. I can log it as further proof against allowing her kind within the city limits."

Taking several steps toward the man, Beau clenched his jaw. "I don't think you understand. You have Autumn, and I'm here to take her back from you. Tell me where she is and get out of my way, and no one has to get hurt." He very much wanted to hurt this man, and anyone else who had been responsible for this, but that could wait until later if necessary.

But the man readjusted his grip on the pistol and stuck it out toward Beau's stomach. "Sounds to me like she's got you under her spell. I expect she's left an entire trail of men just like you in her wake. I know how she does it, too. She lures you in with sex, knowing it's a weakness, and then puts her hexes on you so you'll do her bidding. I can help you with that. We can exorcise the spirits she's put in you, and you'll be safe once again when you join us."

Feeling the fire raging in his chest, Beau took one more confident step forward. "You can stop with your crazy ranting. I'm not under any spell, and there's nothing for you to save me from. You'll be the one begging for help by the time I'm done with you." The skin on his forearms segmented and separated, each fragment standing on end for a moment before it flipped completely over to reveal the golden scales that waited underneath. The effect undulated up his arms to his chest as he reached out and smacked the man aside.

He hit the wall and collapsed to the floor. Beau stepped through the doorway the man had been guarding, finding that a set of shallow stairs led down to a basement. He couldn't stop his transformation now, despite the fact that it was going to make it harder for him to get through the house. His claws grated against the concrete steps like a knife on a whetstone as he descended, his newly germinated wings brushing against the walls. Smoke filtered up from his nostrils as his fire built inside him, ready to be used.

"Hey, what's going on up there, Mr. Stone? Mr. Harrington said you might need help," shouted a voice from below. A door at the end of the stairwell opened, revealing a stout young man with a jellylike face. His jaw was set, a determined look in his eyes, but all that melted away as he took in the sight of the monster coming down the stairs toward him. His hand fumbled for the door handle and he shot back through the doorway he had come through, slamming the door behind him. Even with the surface between them, Beau could hear his screams. "It's a monster! She must have summoned Satan himself! He's right there, with horns and claws and everything!"

"Calm down," commanded a firm voice. "It's probably just someone in a costume, coming down here to try to scare us. I know we have a lot of people who support us, but there are still plenty of people who don't believe in magic. You're getting yourself all worked up over nothing."

Beau couldn't help but smile. He had scared the holy living shit out of the kid, just as he deserved. It spurred him to move a little faster, bursting through the hollow lauan door and leaving it in shreds on the floor. It was cheap construction, the likes of which he would never have put in his own home, and it was barely fit to keep out a human, much less a dragon. He grinned as he rounded a corner, now following the sound of screaming and arguing. Autumn's energy was even thicker now.

He entered a large basement room, the walls and floor made of musty concrete. Water stood stagnant in one corner, unable to reach the clogged drain in the center of the floor. The joists of the floor overhead brushed against the spikes that lined Beau's spine, cleaning off cobwebs as he moved along on all fours.

Several men were gathered at the other end of the room. They had stopped and turned toward him at hearing the door break, and they watched him now with horror in their eyes.

"You see?" the rotund kid whimpered, pointing a finger. "It's Satan!"

"Don't be ridiculous!" This came from a tall man with curly hair and squinty eyes. "He doesn't look like Satan at all. He's not even red. This is something else, some other beast the witch has summoned from the depths of Hell." He reached into his shirt, taking out a cross on a chain. "Be gone, creature of the night! Your kind isn't welcome here."

Beau laughed, a deep, rolling noise as it keeled like thunder from his deep chest and his long neck. "Your little symbols have no effect on me. I'm here only for her. Where is she?" Every part of his body was tense and ready. He expected little fight from these men, but he was still wary of them. They were human, after all, a species that hadn't proven to be too kind to anything unlike it in the past.

"You can't have her!" the man shouted. Several others behind him nodded. There was the heavyset kid and another one that looked to be about his age, but they weren't the only ones. Whatever this Assembly was that the man upstairs had spoken of, it must have had a decent influence on the community. "She's evil, and we're going to cleanse the Earth."

Their words couldn't turn him back. "You're trying to keep me from my one and only goal. That's not a very smart move. I was under the impression that you humans enjoyed living." He raised one hand into the air, scraping his claws along the ceiling to demonstrate just how sharp they were.

The one who seemed to be in charge jumped forward, a knife in his hand. He thrust it through the air, missing Beau's face and attempting to sink it into the thick, muscular flesh of his shoulder. The gilt scales deflected the blade, offsetting the man's balance and making him tumble forward the floor.

Beau quickly planted his hand on the back of the man's neck, his long fingers clamping him to the floor. He felt how easily he could crush this zealot's skull. "I don't suggest you try that again. I'm not afraid of weak creatures like you."

The other men shuffled further into the corner, trying to get as far away from Beau as possible. That's when he realized the wall they were standing against held yet another door. The green vibrations he had followed there from Autumn's house told him she was in there. It was a sturdier structure than the one at the bottom of the stairs had been, but it was still one he could handle.

Just as he flung the curly-haired man out of his way and began advancing, a piercing pain shot through his tail. He roared and spun, finding that the old man from upstairs had recovered. Blood seeped from a wound on his shiny head, but that hadn't stopped him from burying a sharp knife into the flesh of Beau's appendage. It would have bounced off just as the other knife had, except that he had jabbed it up underneath the hard plates. He held on with the other hand as Beau yanked his tail from side to side in an animalistic urge to get the painful parasite off of him.

Encouraged by their leader's antics, the other men jumped to action. They pelted the dragon with anything they had on hand. Bullets zinged off his neck, one of them piercing the delicate skin between the long bones of his wings. They punched and pulled, stabbing with knives. They, too, had understood the right way to cut into a dragon, and blood welled up between the gold scales and turned them a brilliant crimson. Beau swiveled his head and bit hard into the flesh of one of the men, feeling the crunch of bone and the salty wash of blood in his mouth.

There were too many of them. Beau should have waited for help, or at least called the others when he knew where Autumn was. He had been able to follow the trail like a hound dog on a scent that led to her, but she was *his* mate. That same trail would be nearly invisible to the other shifters.

Beau roared his rage, the sound reverberating through the old house. His vision turning as red as the blood that mixed and soaked into the concrete beneath him. Letting go of his last vestiges of the human he was forced to be here on Earth, he unleashed his fire. It blasted through the flesh of his assailants, charring their skin as they screamed and let go. The scent of burning flesh filled the room. Several of the men still fought the demon they didn't understand, but Beau no longer cared. He still had one goal in mind, and he would use his dying breath to make it happen. He charged forward, shaking off the clinging hands of the humans. His head bent, he smashed through the final door.

Just as he had suspected, Autumn was there. Her body was limp, her eyes exhausted as she slowly looked up at him. That flavor of fear once again blossomed from her skin, making Beau angry all over again. He bashed one last human against the doorway with his tail as he entered the room, ripping at the ropes with his claws and yanking the gag off her head.

"Beau?" she whispered, her eyes glassy as she took in the long dragon muzzle and his pointed teeth. She reached out with a freshly freed hand and gently ran it down the delicate scales of his face.

He wanted to kiss her, to hold her in his arms and tell her she was far more beautiful than she could ever understand. He wanted to yell and rage at her for leaving him the night before, even when he had warned her that it wasn't safe and explained to her just how worried he had been. He wanted to ask her just who the hell those crazy guys were and what they thought they were doing with her, but all of that would have to wait for the time being.

Instead, Beau snatched up her shaking form in his forearms. He charged back through the door, blasting fire all around him as he went to keep any of the men who still had fight left in them from attacking.

He could take the wounds himself; his dragon form would allow him to heal quickly. But Autumn was a different case.

Kicking out to the side as one villain attempted to pull Autumn from his arms, he barreled through the basement and up the stairs. No scrap of the old house was safe from his assault of fire as he went, eager to burn the evil place off the face of the map.

Beau held onto Autumn tightly as he charged out the door and down the stairs, setting them aflame in his wake. He lifted off into the air, not caring who might see a large gold dragon flying through the neighborhood in the middle of the afternoon. He only knew that he had been right. Autumn was destined to be his, and it was his job to keep her safe. The fact that she was in his arms once again, however, didn't seem to satisfy his craving to be her guardian, and he feared there was more yet to come.

# 8

Autumn clung to the underside of the dragon, but there was no need. He had her tightly in his arms, and she knew she wouldn't fall. She buried her face against his scaly chest and closed her eyes, reveling in the safety of being away from those horrible men who had taken her.

She could feel the ground rising up beneath her as they descended, and she opened her eyes just in time to see that they had arrived in Beau's back yard. He set her gently on the grass before landing, and then he morphed quickly back into his human form. The gorgeous golden scales stood on end and flipped underneath his skin, a process that was odd and yet fascinating to watch. His thick limbs turned back into those of a human, and his wings sank into his back as his face flattened into the pleasant visage she was used to.

But he didn't give her time to stand there and admire him. "Let's get you inside." With one strong arm around her waist, he hurried her in the back door and pointed at the kitchen table. "Sit down. You must not have eaten anything since last night."

Still shaking from her experience, she sank into a chair. "I haven't. But I'm not sure I have an appetite right now." Her head was still reeling from everything she had been through, and even the fact that she was sitting there in Beau's kitchen didn't quite seem real. Autumn half-expected to wake up and find that she was still in that basement, bound and gagged.

"You need to eat anyway." He was working quickly, pulling containers out of the fridge and clattering them onto the counter. Beau dished several things out onto a plate and put it in the microwave. "That's too long for you to go without food, and you need to get your strength back."

She nodded feebly, wanting more than anything to just lie down and go to bed. "I want to go home."

"We can worry about that later." Beau set the plate of food in front of her, quickly placing a fork and napkin alongside it. "I'll get you some water." He moved like an athlete in a race, not someone who had just fought his way through a house full of crazies to save her.

"What about your wounds?" she asked, wishing her mind would clear and she wouldn't feel like her head was full of cotton. "When you burst into that room, you were bleeding all over."

Beau shrugged. "They happened while I was in dragon form, which means they heal very quickly. I'm fine."

"Are you sure?" She didn't think she would ever forget the way he had looked when he had saved her. He was glorious, gorgeous, and murderous. The color of his blood over his scales was hard to describe, like crimson syrup with the metallic elements shining through.

"Yes. It's different when I'm a human."

Autumn slowly lifted a forkful to her mouth, not paying much attention to what was on it at first. But the burst of flavors made her look down. "What is this?"

He set the glass of water down with a thump and looked at what she was pointing to. "Potatoes Romanoff."

"I assume you made this?" she said with a weak smile. He just had to continue proving how perfect he was.

But Beau didn't seem to be taking any pleasure in showing off his skills at the moment. "Of course. You stay here and eat. I've got to go in the other room and make a phone call."

She wanted to tell him he could just do that right there in the room with her, but she was too tired to worry about being polite. Autumn dutifully shoveled the food in her mouth. Beau had been right; she needed to eat. While she didn't feel ready to get up and go to work, she certainly felt better than she had when they had first gotten back to his house. By the time he came back in the room, she was polishing off the pile of green beans he had put on her plate next to the potato casserole. "Everything okay?"

Beau crossed the room to look out the back window. "It seems to be. I let the others know that I found you, and Xander is staying with Summer to make sure they don't go after her as well."

"Aren't they..." She didn't want to say it. She didn't like to think that someone had lost their life because of her.

"Dead?" Beau wasn't bothered by the word. "Yes, or at least as far as I know. But the older man spoke of some sort of organization, which leads me to believe there are more of them."

"The Purity and Pride Assembly," Autumn affirmed for him. "Yes, Mr. Stone told me all about it. It's just a group he started up because he doesn't think that anyone in Small Town America should have to put up with anybody who isn't a white Christian. I guess he managed to get enough people to go along with him, but I don't think they'll be coming after me again. I mean, they're not going to want to fight a dragon."

"Aren't they?" Beau challenged. "They went to extremes to make sure they could get rid of you, and now they just know there are other monsters out there that don't fit into their view of life. If anything, my presence is going to stir them up even more."

"So what do we do?" Autumn felt so helpless. "I can go home and start working on a protection spell."

"Right now, you're going to go take a shower and change into some fresh clothes. As long as you're done eating, that is."

Autumn looked down. Her teal blouse, which had looked so nice the night before, was torn and covered in dirt. She had lost one shoe, and her hair hung in limp tangles around her head. "I guess I can't argue with that." She slowly rose from the table.

Beau waved her into a large bathroom with a rounded corner shower and a big jacuzzi tub sunken into the floor. "Bath or shower, your choice."

"Just a shower is fine." Autumn suspected that if she allowed herself to sink into a tub of hot water, she could very well fall asleep and drown. Her limbs felt like rubber, and her mind had receded to the very back of her head.

"Go ahead and get started. There are fresh towels in the cabinet right there, and I'll find you something to wear."

As soon as the bathroom door closed behind him, Autumn

stripped. She threw her clothes in the trash can with a sigh; there was no point in saving them. Even if she had been able to mend the tears and clean out the dirt, she wouldn't want the memories that came along with them.

The shower head was a large one that rained down on her softly, and she took a long moment to luxuriate in the warm water before she bothered finding the soap. When she stepped out a few minutes later, Beau was sitting on the edge of the tub.

She jumped back, startled by his presence, but then grabbed a towel and wrapped it around her body. It wasn't as though he hadn't seen her naked before. "Worried that I can't handle a shower on my own?" she teased.

But his look was serious. "Autumn, I'm not letting you out of my sight until I'm sure these guys are taken care of."

"It's not that bad. Can I use this comb?" At his nod, she began gently raking through her hair, glancing over her shoulder at him in the mirror. "It's not as though the Assembly put on some grand heist. They just waited for me at my house and grabbed me. Now that we know they're out there, we're far more prepared."

"You shouldn't be so dismissive of this. They might be backwater eccentrics, but they're dangerous. If they had known I was coming to get you, they would have had much bigger weapons than a few knives and some pistols, and even those could kill you in an instant." He handed her a stack of clothing. "I tried to find what I could for you. We can go by your place in a day or two so you can get your things."

Autumn had turned around to take the clothing from him, but her hands slowed as she understood the meaning behind his words. Her eyes drifted up to look at his. They were still the same lapis eyes she had seen that night at the party, but they were also the same ones that had been embedded in his golden dragon face. They were angry and determined, and they burned with a fire that belied their color. "Beau, I'm not going to stop living my life just because there are some nutjobs out there. They win if I do."

"No, they win if you're dead. And I'm not going to let that happen."

Taking a deep breath, Autumn let it out slowly through her teeth. "Did it ever occur to you that maybe that's not up to you? I like you, Beau, and I think we might really have something here, but you don't get to just decide things without asking me."

"It's my responsibility to take care of you," he countered, rising from the edge of the tub. He would have been a formidable figure if she'd thought there was any chance that he might hurt her. "Nothing else matters."

"What about my happiness?" Why did this man have to be so enraging? "I don't want to get hurt, either, but there's a lot I can do to keep myself out of harm's way."

"Clearly, it's not enough!" Beau's voice rose, and his chest puffed out. "If that was the truth, then you never would have gotten kidnapped in the first place."

"Don't you *dare* blame me for this!" Autumn stepped forward so that she was only a few inches from him, even though he still towered a full head over her. She poked him in the chest with her finger. "Just because you want to come marching in like Billy Badass and save the damsel in distress doesn't give you any right to control my life. I should have known better than to be stupid enough to get involved with a dragon. So much freaking drama! Now get out of this bathroom and let me get dressed."

He opened his mouth to argue but then snapped it shut again. "Fine."

Autumn angrily ditched her towel and pulled on the clothes he had supplied. She muttered to herself as she worked, furious that he was being like this. Yes, she should have been more observant of her surroundings, but at that time, she'd had no reason to be. She was grateful that he had rescued her, but she didn't intend for her life to be ruled by anyone. Beau was just an overbearing, obnoxious dragon, and she didn't want to have anything more to do with him.

Pulling on her pants, Autumn blinked back a tear. She didn't like to cry, and she had long ago perfected the ability to hold in her emotions if there was even a chance of someone seeing that weakness in her. It almost spilled over onto her cheek, but she used her anger to shove the tears away. She had really liked Beau. For a moment there, she had even thought they might have a chance at something as wonderful as what Leah and Holden had seemed to have. But Holden wasn't the same as Beau, and Autumn definitely wasn't the same as Leah. She should have known better than to think she could just copycat their relationship or the one Summer had with Xander.

And maybe that was what made her angry most of all. She felt stupid. If there was anything she didn't like, it was feeling inferior. Most people who knew her would understand that a man needed brass balls if he was going to try to tell her what to do, but Beau just did it as though he had the authority. And he had her in a bad spot, too, since there really was a good chance that someone out there was still after her.

Autumn turned to the door, taking a moment to look at herself in the full-length mirror fixed to the back of it. Beau's sweats and t-shirt looked bulky and baggy on her, making her feel even more stupid. She gritted her teeth. This was all his fault. She would have to go find him and tell him so.

But Beau was waiting for her in the hall, leaning against the wall just outside the door.

"Really? Is this how it's going to be, Beau? Will I not even be able to take a shit without you standing outside?" She curled her fists at her sides, beyond angry now.

He closed his eyes for a moment, and Autumn thought he was trying to control his temper. Maybe he was better at it than she was. "I know you don't understand just how big of a deal this is, and that's why you're lashing out at me. But just trust me. Things will get better over time, and we've got the other shifters on our side for extra protection. You're angry right now because of what happened to you. You're not really angry at me."

"The hell I'm not!" Autumn swung back and slugged him in the arm, but he took the blow as though it was nothing more than a mosquito bite. "You're cruel, overbearing, and awful!"

"It's getting late. I have some things to do, but you need your rest. You can have the room at the end of the hall, since it's clear you don't have any interest in sleeping in my bed tonight."

"You're damn right I don't!"

"That's fine. I think you'll find that you have everything you need, but I'll be around if there's something I've missed."

His cool composure was only pissing her off more. Wasn't he the dragon? Wasn't he the one who was supposed to be flying off the handle? He had no right to act so calm and rational, as though she was just being a stubborn child and he was waiting out her attitude.

"Fine. Whatever." Autumn stormed down the hallway to the door he had indicated. For a guest room, it was large, but still cozy. It didn't look as though Beau had done as much work in there, if any at all, but it didn't need it. The original trim—not nearly as nice as the stuff Beau made himself—was still up around the doors and windows. Long curtains had been hung over the wide windows, and a double bed had been placed between them. The nightstand, dresser, and desk were all from the same matching set. Everything was simple, but elegant. "Right. Perfect. Just like he thinks she is."

Her body was tired; she couldn't deny that. She hadn't slept in the time she'd spent with the Assembly, and the warm shower and a belly full of good food were making her eyelids start to feel heavy. But Autumn couldn't rest yet. Her cell phone had been lost somewhere in the scuffle with those awful men, and it wasn't good enough that Beau said he had warned Xander to take care of Summer. She had to get out there and warn her sister personally, and then she needed to start on her protection spells.

"I'll be damned if I'm going to stand around and depend on a man to protect me," she whispered to herself as she pulled a jacket of Beau's from the closet and put it on. It was too big by a long shot, just as the rest of his clothes were, but it didn't matter. Once she got home, she could get herself back to rights. And in the meantime, at least no one would recognize her. Autumn opened the window and stepped out.

# 9

BEAU SMACKED HIS FIST INTO HIS OPEN HAND, STARING AT THE BEDROOM door that Autumn had just slammed behind her. He had done everything in his power for her, and he was determined to keep right on doing it, but she seemed just as determined to thwart his efforts. Didn't she understand that he was a caretaker? It was his role in life to make sure everyone else was out of harm's way. They had even talked about it during their dinner at Le Papillon, and he had gotten the impression that she had liked that about him. He thought this idea of finding his destined mate was supposed to be irresistible; easy, even. But somewhere along the line, that had gone wrong.

He moved through the house, checking that every window and door were secure. Beau wasn't in the habit of leaving anything unlocked, but it made him feel just a little bit better to know that every deadbolt and lock had been engaged. Pausing in the living room with his hand on the lock, Beau looked out across his front yard. He had never thought of it as anything but a patch of grass that he maintained, with a few flowers in the beds along the walkways. But at any moment, it could become a battlefield.

Turning away to continue his rounds, Beau mentally kicked himself. Maybe he had been wrong about Autumn. Maybe the way he felt about her was nothing more than lust. After all, he had committed himself during the Zimryr festival to finding his mate, and that might have made him choose to see her as the one, even if she wasn't.

Beau headed to the study and picked up the hand plane, the same one Autumn had held only the day before. He clearly remembered the way it had felt to wrap his body around hers as he had shown her how to use it. Her hands had been so soft underneath his, her curves so luscious. Though she was such a fiery, independent woman, her fingers had complied underneath his. If it had been a different situation, if there had been anyone else around to make him worry about whether or not she was his, then he would have gone absolutely mad with passion. Even now, knowing how angry she was, he could easily see himself back in that same position with his fingers curled down over hers. But if he had the chance to do it all over again, he would have turned Autumn around, gently taken the tool from her hand, and bent her over the large desk in the middle of the room. To have her in his arms again, pretending like none of the events of the day had happened, now that would have been perfection.

He set to work, smoothing the wood until it was as soft as Autumn under his fingertips. He could try to convince himself that she wasn't the one, but he would have been completely wrong. Just because they argued, it didn't mean they weren't going to work this out. She was a strong woman with a fierce wild side, and that was just the sort of thing they would both have to learn to live with. She would have to accept the fact that he was only doing what was best for her, and he would have to accept that she was her own person.

Beau set down the plane and picked up a sander, giving the wood a final once-over. The sander kicked up a small cloud of dust that he would be sweeping up later, but it would all be worth it once he applied a nice coat of stain, carefully matched to the rest of the wood in the room. A day later, when he gently brushed on the varnish that would make the grain of the wood the star of the show, he would know that every bit of work he had done would be worth it.

He silently wondered, as he wiped down the shelf with a tack rag, if his relationship with Autumn would be the same way. Would it be the sort of thing they had to work hard at, to forge out of a hard surface that had once been rough and wild? Would they be able to plane out all the rough edges, scraping them away one by one with the sheer force of their hands to reveal the true beauty underneath? He paused in his work, glancing toward the door, thinking perhaps he had heard her come down the hall. But there was nobody in the study but him.

No, he had simply hoped that she had come to him, and it was then that Beau understood. He could question it all he wanted to, but his body had told him the truth. So had that look in Autumn's eyes when he'd found her in the basement, and the way she had gently run her fingers down his scaly cheek. Nobody had ever touched him like that. The sex had been amazing, but it was that raw moment that had meant more to him than anything. Autumn might fight him, but she wanted the same things he did.

Beau ran his fingers through his hair and started working again. He would give her time to cool off, he'd decided. She was probably going to need a lot of that in the time they would spend together. He entertained himself with fantasies of their future lovemaking and their future fights. She could yell and rage at him, but at the end of the day, they would fall back into bed together and make up. He would kiss those full, smirking lips of hers and watch as she slowly closed her emerald eyes to get lost in the moment. He would pull her away from her desk when she had insisted on working all day without a break and bring her to the bedroom, stripping her of her business clothes and exposing the true woman he knew was underneath them. They would go to bed at night with their bodies tucked into each other, his arm and leg around her and pulling her close, breathing in the scent of her hair like a lullaby. In the morning, he would wake her with the scent of a homecooked meal, and he wouldn't let her go to work without enjoying it first.

He almost called Xander or Holden to see if they'd heard or seen anything, but he pulled his hand away from his pocket without removing his phone. If something had happened, they would have let him know. His time was better spent elsewhere.

Tossing the rag aside, Beau charged out of the study. He would make it up to her. He would tell Autumn just how wrong he had been, even though he knew he would have made the same choices all over again. He would tell her just how cute she looked in his clothes before he pulled them back off of that gorgeous body of hers, and they would make the bed shake with their lovemaking. His body had heard his thoughts, and he felt the prickle of scales on the back of his neck as excitement took over. Beau wondered if he would ever get used to having her around, but it was alright if he didn't. That jumping feeling in his stomach and the constant urge to shift were things he would gladly put up with if it meant he had her under his roof.

"Autumn," he called as he reached for the doorknob. "I want to talk to you. I'm sorry for what I—" His words faded away, his mouth still open to speak them, as he opened the door and took in the scene before him. He had come in the room while Autumn was in the shower, making sure the sheets were fresh and the windows were locked. He had even turned down the bed and quickly wiped a thin layer of dust from the dresser. He would have let her stay there for as long as she'd liked until she was ready to return to his bed.

But where he had expected to see her head on the pillow, there was nothing but the clean bedding he had arranged for her. The closet door was open. A gentle breeze brushed the curtains aside, revealing that the window had been left open. Beau rushed across the room, clinging to the window sill as he stuck his head out into the yard. "Autumn!" he shouted into the night as various scenarios ran through his mind. Had someone managed to get in and abduct her once again? Or had she been brazen enough to leave on her own?

He swung over the sill and landed easily in the yard on his feet, taking in the shadowy trees and the lush grass. There was no sign of her. Instead, he had only her scent and that same spiritual energy of hers that he had followed the first time. It didn't reek of fear this time, but of a single-minded resolution.

He shot through the yard, over the row of bushes along the front of it, and down the sidewalk. His feet pounded underneath him as he ran, his hair blowing back and his fists pumping. When he found her, he was going to tell her just how stubborn she was, but not until he had pulled her into his arms and kissed her thoroughly.

Turning out onto the main street, Beau realized he knew where she was headed not only because he could sense her but because he knew her. She would be out to protect her sister. Even though she had been grateful for his rescue, she hadn't seemed satisfied with leaving it at that. She had wanted to leave right away to start a protection spell. That meant she could have been heading out to Summer's place to make sure she was alright, but it was a long walk out past the city limits to the wooded area where Summer and Xander resided. No, it would have made more sense for her to go straight to her house where she could get her supplies and start her enchantment. He dodged through yards, finding his own shortcuts, until he arrived in front of Autumn's house.

To his dismay, there was no sign of her there. The door still stood open where he had left it, unable to close it completely after he had broken the latch. The lights were all off. Most of all, he couldn't sense any of her energy there. His hands dropped to his sides helplessly. If she had gone all the way to Summer's house, it might take all night to find her.

A scream ricocheted off the siding. Beau turned, searching in the darkness for the source. His heart pounded in his ears, nearly drowning out the sound. He charged forth once again, this time away from Autumn's house. The screaming, now joined by the sounds of a scuffle, led him to an alley a block away. He immediately turned into the dark corridor, unintimidated by the lack of light. He might have been in his human form, but his vision was still far sharper than any other two-legged creatures around.

Autumn's scream reached his ears again, but he could tell now that it wasn't one of panic. It was a cry of anger, fury, and power as she swiped her fingers through the air. The muscles of her arms stood out in relief as she swept them from side to side. A trash can lifted from the gravel surface of the alley and shot through the air, clocking a man in the head and sending him reeling. He staggered but didn't fall. Another man was already unconscious on the ground, his head bleeding and a scrap of steel pipe lying next to him.

Beau ran up to stand beside her, but he didn't feel the need to shift. There was only one adversary, and he could handle this. "Get back," he growled.

"No." Autumn's fingers moved with a surprising dexterity as she twirled them. The steel pipe that had taken down the first man rose into the air and swiped at the backs of her foe's knees, sending him sprawling forward. "I can handle this."

"But you don't have to," Beau argued, curling his fists. "Don't you see, Autumn? You don't have to do any of this alone."

She had just enough time to glare at him from the side of her eye. "And neither do you, but you insist. You think you're the only one who knows best." The pipe thumped the man on the back of the head.

"And maybe I do, considering that you've gotten attacked again." Beau felt the sharp but satisfying pain of his claws extending from his fingertips. He was eager to get involved in the fight himself. "If you had stayed safely at my house, this wouldn't have happened."

"And if you had just let me go to my place on my own, or even offered to drive me over there if you were so concerned, then I would have been able to put that protection spell together and this still wouldn't have happened. So stop trying to act like I'm just being wild and reckless." The man she was fighting managed to get to his hands and knees, but Autumn gave him a final whack that rendered him unconscious.

Beau tried to put his arm around her waist as she turned toward the mouth of the alley, but she pushed him away. "Don't you dare! I'm not happy with you right now."

"Fine." He reminded himself that he had been planning on apologizing to her anyway. Maybe he should just leave well enough alone. "But I'm still not going to leave you. You're stuck with me, Autumn. I'll take you back to your house, and you can do what you need, but don't try to send me away."

There was fire in her eyes as they stepped back out onto the street, and her jaw was tight, but she didn't argue. "Just don't get in my way."

Beau pressed his tongue against the inside of his cheek, keeping it still so that he didn't say what he was really thinking. His entire being was concentrated on her. Autumn took up his entire world other than Elliot, and he had to find a way to make her understand that. Maybe then she would calm down a little bit. Maybe.

Just as they reached her house, Beau had the distinct feeling that something was wrong. It was the same feeling he'd had when he had carried her home in his arms after getting her out of that basement, but it was much stronger. The danger was more immediate. "Autumn, wait."

"No." She charged up the walkway to her front door. "I thought you said you wouldn't try to stop me."

She wasn't going to listen to reason, but that was the problem. Autumn wasn't feeling the same things in the air that he was. He stormed forward, wrapping his arms around her and pulling her into the safety of his embrace as they tumbled down onto the grass and rolled. A sharp pain stabbed into his shoulder, just above the sensitive scar where his wings would have been rooted if he had been in dragon form.

"What the hell?" Autumn screamed, trying to fight him off. But then she saw that they weren't alone.

Beau struggled to his feet, fighting the assailant hand to hand. His fist landed with a crunch on the man's jaw.

"You might have killed George Stone," the man gasped as he swung out at Beau, "but the Pride and Purity Assembly lives on in me."

"Yeah, and probably in those assholes I disabled in the alley," Autumn said sarcastically.

Pounding into him with his fists, Beau fought with every ounce of strength and energy his human body possessed. His shoulder burned, and he felt the hot trickle of blood down his back, but that would have to be addressed later. At that moment, he had more pressing concerns than a flesh wound. He sent one final punch through the air that turned the man's head on his neck. He collapsed onto the grass but recovered quickly, scrambling off down the street.

"There," Beau panted, watching him run. He wanted to hunt him down, but that would mean leaving Autumn. "Now, let's get going."

She pursed her lips as she took his arm and led him to her front door. "The only place you're going is inside so I can treat that wound."

"It'll be fine," he insisted. "We can grab what you need and get back to my place. It's more secure."

Autumn gave him a level look, one that brooked no argument. "You've been working all this time to take care of me, Beau. The least you can do is let me return the favor."

They went in the house, and Autumn turned to shove the door shut. She cast her fingers through the air, moving a heavy chair in front of the door to safeguard it since the lock was broken. "Come on." She waved to the stairs, insisting that he go up first.

"I'm not going to fall," he said stubbornly, refusing to put his foot on the first step. It didn't seem right not to let her go ahead. Even if he was injured, he was still a gentleman.

She raised an eyebrow. "Then how am I going to look at that tight ass of yours?"

He laughed and shook his head, complying. They were in the same room he had discovered when he had broken in there the day before. It seemed to come to life at her presence. He could smell the different oils in the candles, the incense, and even the various herbs from their place in the cabinet. Every surface reflected her energy back at her, and he understood why she spent her time up there.

"Sit." Autumn pointed to a cushion on the floor near the altar table. "And take off your shirt."

She moved deftly through the room as she selected ingredients from the shelves and cabinets, which she mixed thoroughly in a small jar before she moved around behind him.

"Oh, that's cold!" The sensation had been a surprise, since he had seen her light a candle and let some of the wax drip into her mixture.

"It's just peroxide," she said with a laugh. "I'm a big fan of natural medicine, but there's nothing better for cleaning out a wound than a little bit of old-fashioned first aid. It's not too deep."

Her fingers were delicate but efficient as she cleaned out the wound. The warmth he had been expecting finally came as she dabbed her remedy onto the cut. A feeling of relaxation and healing seeped instantly through his body, and he closed his eyes in relief. "That feels amazing."

"You're not the only one who can take care of someone."

The tension between them in that moment was heavy. "I'm sorry," Beau finally said, slicing through it with his words. "I wasn't listening to you. I should have paid more attention to what was important to you, but I was only focused on keeping you safe. I wasn't trying to be a control freak, I was just worried about you."

"I think we both made some mistakes," she admitted. Her breath was a wisp on the back of his neck. "I lost my temper. Summer tells me I do that all the time, and I'm starting to think she's right. If I had just stayed calm and talked to you maturely, then I like to think we could have worked something out."

Beau turned to face her, expecting to feel pain in his shoulder, but was surprised to find that it was hardly more than a tingle. "And what about now? Do you still think we can work it out?" She was so gorgeous, kneeling there behind him with wax and herbs on the tips of her fingers. She still wore his clothes, and her hair was tousled gracefully around her face.

She smiled. "I'd certainly like to think so."

He turned completely then, pulling her toward him by the hips until he could wrap his arms around her completely. "Me, too." He pressed his lips to hers, closing his eyes to tune himself into the one woman he couldn't live without. She didn't fight him off or argue. They would probably argue again at some point down the road, but that was alright. Everything was alright.

Beau ran his fingers across the small of her back, tracing them slowly upward to the base of her neck. He pulled away from her just enough that he could move his hand back down and around her ribs, bracing his hand over her breast.

She broke their kiss but not the embrace, pressing her lips near his ear. "Not here," she whispered. "Downstairs."

Unable to resist the chance for it, Beau stood and lifted her off the floor. He carried her back downstairs as quickly as his feet would allow, turning down the hall. He knew now where her bedroom was, though he had only cared about it before because he had been hoping to find her in it. Things were different now.

Beau let go of her legs but kept his arms tightly around her waist, letting her slide slowly down the front of his body as he set her down. He kissed her again, her palms on his chest, his hands scraping against the flesh of her buttocks, never wanting the moment to end. "I need you, Autumn. We're both stubborn, self-sufficient people, but I can't deny that I need you in my life."

She brought her fingers up to lay them on either side of his jaw, kissing him purposefully. "I need you, too. And I can take care of you just as well as you can take care of me."

Their hands worked quickly to remove each other's clothes, which was easy work for him since she still wore his baggy t-shirt and sweatpants. He tossed them aside and pulled her naked body against his. As much as he desired to be inside her, simply being close to her was almost just as rewarding. Her breasts pressed against his chest, and he couldn't seem to touch enough of her at once.

Her legs seemed to slip out from underneath her as she slowly knelt down in front of him, making him suck in his breath as she wrapped her lips around his member. Her mouth was hot and wet, and she pulled him in deep enough that his head touched the back of her throat. Beau pulled back instinctively, afraid that he had hurt her, but she only sucked him in again. Hard. He felt his balls pull up against his body with excitement as he ran his fingers through her hair. Yes, she certainly could take care of him.

It was all he could do not to pound his hips against her. It felt so good, and it was obvious that she was putting all her effort into pleasing him. But Beau wasn't about to let that happen without her getting pleasure as well. He lifted her to her feet and brought her to the bed, laying her down gently on the bed and kissing her deeply. He moved down her throat to her breasts, giving each one the attention it deserved before gliding down the soft flesh of her stomach to taste the treasure waiting for him between her legs.

Autumn's fists clenched at the sheets as he worked, flicking his tongue slowly over every surface and then burying it inside her. He wrapped his hands around her buttocks, pulling her in close so he could get as deep as possible. She bent her knees and wriggled against the mattress, her breath escaping her lungs as gasps.

Unable to resist, Beau slowly slid a finger into her wetness while he suckled at her clit, taking delight in the way she moved against him. It turned him on to know she was enjoying herself, and he felt his dick grow even harder.

Autumn cried out, a stuttered gasp that let him know he had done his job. He couldn't wait any longer, and he moved up the bed to bury himself deep inside her. She clutched at his shoulders, careful to avoid his wound, as though she needed him inside her just as badly as he needed to be there.

Still under the spell of his tongue, her core welcomed him with warm ripples that pulled him even deeper inside her. Beau pulsed against her, sinking to the hilt before pulling out again. He was so engorged he was dizzy, but that only enhanced the effect. Every part of his body was focused on his bond with her, and he gave a cry of triumph as he finally gave her all of him.

As he lay there next to her, brushing her hair back from her face, he wondered why they had ever argued about anything.

# 10

"Zoo?"

"Yes, honey. Just as soon as we have everything ready." Autumn rushed around the house, trying to make sure that she hadn't forgotten anything. She had spent most of the previous afternoon back at her place completing the online store for The Enchanted Elm, and she now regretted that she hadn't had more time to prepare for the trip. But it seemed to work out for her and Beau if they lived their domestic lives at his place and she saved her own house for work. She had everything she needed there, including her privacy, but she still had a place and a pair of open arms to come home to. It was one of many compromises they had made, and like the others, it seemed to please them both.

Beau charged into the room, his hair freshly combed. "It might be a little chilly. Did you get Elliot's sweater?"

"Right here." Autumn held it up for a moment and then set it on the chair by the door. "But I didn't pack our lunch yet." She was looking forward to sharing a picnic with Elliot on the grassy expanse at the center of the zoo.

"I did that last night," Beau replied, dodging into the kitchen to fetch the cooler. "I hope you like turkey and Swiss."

"You know I do." She dropped a kiss on his lips as she passed him to head down the hallway for the sunscreen. When she came back to the living room, she scooped Elliot up off the floor. He had been excited about the trip to the zoo ever since they'd told him they were going, and she knew he would enjoy it even more since his cousins would all be there. But he had waited patiently while his father and his new mother got everything prepared, occasionally asking them about animals he had in his plastic toy zoo.

"You're such a good little boy," she said as she snuggled her nose into the softness of his neck. He smelled of baby shampoo from the bath Beau had given him the night before. He was such an attentive father, and it was obvious that Elliot only benefited from it. The child never seemed scared or insecure, always confident that his father would be standing right behind him.

"Ata," Elliot replied with a smile, unable to say Autumn's name just yet.

"Oh, I didn't get his extra outfit packed yet," Beau said. "I was waiting until the last load of laundry was done."

"Already took care of it," Autumn assured him. "Go put on your shoes and we'll be ready to go."

"You're amazing."

She watched Beau leave the room, admiring his backside as he went. He was a strong, wonderful man, and he did a lot to take care of her. He hadn't stopped his work on the house, and yet he always seemed to find time to cook or throw in a load of laundry. She was lucky to have him, and she knew it.

"You know," she whispered to Elliot, "I never thought I could love someone as much as I love the two of you. I really like taking care of you and your daddy."

A pair of strong arms suddenly wrapped around the both of them, and Beau pulled them in close. "We can all take care of each other now."

———

# JULIAN'S MATE

## DADDY DRAGON GUARDIANS

# PROLOGUE

Naomi rested her long, graceful neck on Julian's shoulder and admired the way the sun sparkled off his deep emerald scales, bringing out flecks of gold and purple. "They said there's nothing they can do," she said softly.

Julian's head moved swiftly, and he moved her off his shoulder so he could look into her eyes. "That can't be true. The mages know how to heal everything. Have they consulted with the witches as well?"

She was already tired. Naomi didn't know what this illness was, but it was slowly consuming her body. She could hardly sleep at night from the pain; during the day, she had so little energy, she was barely able to hunt for food. It was only because Julian insisted on bringing her fresh meat that she hadn't starved to death. And then, of course, there had been the long climb to the top of Mount Taendru to visit the mages. It had taken the last of her spirit just to get there, and then they had given her the worst news she could have imagined.

"They have," Naomi affirmed. "But they've tried everything they know. Ervol even said he's seen this sort of thing before, but it's so rare, they don't have a name for it."

"There's got to be something." Julian was up now, pacing so quickly, he stirred up the thick red dirt under his clawed feet. They had come to their secret meeting place, a clearing in the woods on the far side of the mountains. It was where they had talked for hours into the night, made love, and made plans for their future together. But this time, there was no excitement or romance in their rendezvous.

"Not from them." She had known it would come to this, but still she didn't want to tell him. How could she get him to understand what a desperate position she was in? The life she was living wasn't one that was worth holding onto, and the risk just might be worth it. Still, it was impossible to explain.

Julian, sensing that she had more to say, stopped pacing and turned a malachite eye to her. "What do you mean?"

Turning away to study the deep foliage that was such a contrast to the crimson rocky mountains that surrounded their settlement on Charok, Naomi searched for the right words. She only had one chance to do this right. If not, Julian might become angry with her or even try to stop her. She didn't want either one to happen, because she wanted to leave on good terms. "There is one thing that hasn't been tried yet, but it's not something the mages can do. It means that I'll have to go away."

"Okay." Julian's scaly lips tightened as he tried to remain patient. "You mean to gather a mineral in a distant mountain range or a plant that grows in a different set of woods?"

"No." She turned to look him in the eye now, knowing that he deserved it. He had been so good to her. "I'm going away permanently. I won't be back, ever."

"Naomi, you can't—"

"Don't try to stop me, Julian. You've got to promise me that you won't ask me any more about it or try to find out what I'm doing. And you can't follow me. You just can't." A tear leaked from the corner of her eye, though she thought she was all out of them.

"Whatever it is, just tell me! I can go with you. I can help in some way. But you can't just disappear and ask me never to wonder what happened!" His fists curled in the dirt, sending a red cloud into the air.

He was getting angry, and her instinct was to yell and rage right back at him. If she had been in good health, she might have done just that. Naomi had never been afraid to express her opinion around him, and it was one of the reasons that the two of them worked so well together. But she had no energy to argue, and there wasn't even time for it. She would have to leave soon. "If you love me, then you'll do what I'm asking," she pleaded, her words nearly carried away on the breeze they were so soft. "Please, Julian."

There was fire in his eyes, and he looked as though he was about to argue once again, but he took a deep breath instead. "When is this all supposed to happen?"

"As soon as possible."

"I don't even get to have one last night with you?"

A second tear followed the first one, and it absorbed quickly in the warm ground. "No. I'm afraid not."

"And you're certain I can't come with you?" His voice was pleading now, desperate. "There's nothing that says I have to stay here. I won't be missed."

He would be, but Naomi knew she couldn't convince him of that. "Come with me back to the mountains, but beyond there, I have to continue alone." Even this was a compromise on her part. Naomi knew she could have told him to stay in that clearing for hours, and then there would be very little chance he would see where she was heading, but at least she would still be giving him something. Besides, she wasn't certain she could make it all the way back on her own.

They spoke very little as they journeyed. There was nothing much to say. Every now and then, Julian let his wing bump gently against hers, as though he was reminding her that he was still there. It would have been easier for them to fly, but that would have taken far more out of her than what she had.

When they stood once again on the rocky ledges of the mountains, she turned to him. "I have to go now. But I want you to know that I love you, Julian. I feel as though I've loved you my entire life, and I'm sorry that I won't get to spend the rest of it with you."

"I love you, too." He curled his neck around hers, letting his wings come forward to embrace both of their bodies. It wasn't the sort of thing they would have done a few weeks ago, before Naomi grew ill. The two of them had been determined to keep their relationship a secret as long as they could, unwilling to spoil it with the prying eyes and nosy wonderings of the other dragons. But it didn't matter now. Let them see, if anyone was around.

"I know you say you aren't coming back," Julian whispered, "but I'm going to wait for you anyway."

"No, don't do that," Naomi protested. "You deserve a chance to move on, to be happy."

He gave her a small smile, the barest upturn of one corner of his mouth. "I think we both know that can't happen. But thank you anyway."

Naomi turned and headed down the mountain path, veering to the left halfway down to travel north. Without looking back, she knew Julian was watching her. He stood on the top of the mountain, waiting to see if she would turn around and tell him she had changed her mind. But Naomi knew she couldn't change her mind. She would only die, and that wasn't going to help either one of them.

It was a long journey, and a hot one. Naomi had to stop and rest at shorter and shorter intervals, barely catching her breath before it was time to move on again. Her feet ached, and by the time she reached the bush of purple flowers that marked the hidden path, her wingtips were dragging on the ground. Her neck slung low, parallel to the ground, and she turned toward the woods once again.

The little hut was right where she had left it before, and Varhan swung open the door before he reached it. "Sit, sit!" he commanded as he came rushing out. "I can see that the journey has taken its toll."

"You could say that," Naomi whispered. She took no comfort from the shade of the trees or the padding of leaf litter underneath her. "I didn't think I would make it at all."

The wizard was at her side, his pale, fleshy fingers gently moving across her scales. "It's gotten quite bad, hasn't it?"

She tried to nod but only managed to slightly roll her head in the dead leaves on the ground.

"You're certain you understand how all of this works?" Varhan asked. "You have to be completely committed to the idea, or there's a chance that it may not work at all."

"I know what you said, that the energies are different in this other place. That I'll be healed simply by being there. What did you say it was called again?"

"Earth," Varhan replied. "It's an odd sort of place, but most of the creatures there are in human form, just like myself--or you, if you're so inclined. Do any of your people prefer to go around on two legs instead of four?"

"Not very often. Only when we have to, or if we go to the Great Court. You can fit a lot more dragons into a small space that way. But personally, I like my scales." Now that she thought about it, she might have had an easier time getting to the wizard's hut if she had shifted.

But that took energy as well, and there was no telling if she could accomplish it anymore.

Varhan gave a soft laugh and ducked through the door of his hut. Naomi could hear him inside, rattling bottles and moving things around. "That's one of the reasons I've always found dragons to be so fascinating. In your own way, you can be even more stubborn than wizards."

"Is that why there's always someone arguing over land in the Great Basin?" Naomi wheezed. "Because everyone is too stubborn to compromise?"

The wizard shrugged as he emerged from his home, a roll of his shoulders under his tattered brown robe. He was by far the most humble wizard Naomi had ever met, and the only one who would condescend to talk to her. "That might be a large part of it, indeed. I hate to say it, but I wouldn't be surprised if our people ended up going to war. And over something so silly." He shook his head as he dipped a brush into a small clay jar and began painting a cool substance over her body, starting at the spine and working his way down. "The idea makes me sad. I think we have a lot to learn from each other."

"You're right." Naomi closed her eyes, enjoying the sensation of the salve. She didn't know what it was, but its cooling effect was glorious. It had seemed that her fire was constantly building up inside her since she'd fallen ill, but she couldn't seem to muster the desire to dispense of it. "And I don't even want to know what Julian or anyone else would think if they realized I had come to a wizard for help."

"Don't you worry about Julian. He'll be fine."

She swiveled her head to look at him, immediately setting her chin back on the ground after the effort. Still, she could see his round face and his dark hair. He was much younger than any of the other wizards she had seen. Maybe that was why he didn't carry the same biases as the others. "You know Julian?"

"I know a lot more than you might think." Varhan stretched up on his tiptoes to reach the long bones of her wings with his brush. "I've lived out here a long time, and I come out to talk to anyone who comes by. I've never been bold enough to march right into your town and make my presence known, but I've still managed to gather quite a bit of information."

Naomi was silent for a while as she watched him finish with the silvery substance. It made her blue scales, normally shiny, a matte grey color. "Do you really think this will work?"

Varhan took one last stroke of his paintbrush down her tail and returned to her head. He kneeled down in front of her, his grey eyes looking calmly into hers. "I do. I've studied long and hard. There are numerous factors at work here, but I think I can manipulate them in all the right ways to get you to Earth. But I need you to understand that this isn't as simple as transporting a being from one place to another. It pulls on the strings of the universe, changing and manipulating things in ways that even I wouldn't have imagined during my studies under Master Knexon. In other words, I'm changing your entire life as well as the lives of others."

"Am I putting anyone in danger? I'd rather die here than know I had blood on my claws."

"No, no." Varhan stood and went inside his hut once again, coming back out with a burlap sack. He began removing stones from it one by one, setting them in a large circle around the dragon. "I know most wizards aren't too concerned with who gets caught up in their spells, but I'm different. This whole thing is different." He paused, resting his fingers against his mouth for a moment as though unsure of how to proceed. "Naomi, I have studied the way the universe pulls at each of us as individuals, and I can tell you that this spell is going to have lasting effects. But they're going to be good ones. It's on Earth that you'll meet your true love."

Her heart rose in her chest, out of fear instead of hope. She had already met her mate, and he was there, on Charok. "But—"

"And your presence will ensure that three others meet the ones they're truly meant to be with, though they might not meet them otherwise. So take heart in knowing that not only are you saving yourself, but you're giving one of the greatest gifts to others as well."

This all sounded too good to be true, and Naomi didn't like the idea of not knowing for certain what was happening. "Varhan, I—"

"Hush," the wizard whispered. He turned an ear to the treetops, lifting his eyes to the sky for a moment. "We have to finish this quickly, or the opportunity will be missed. This application will protect you during the transition, but it only lasts so long." He placed the last of the stones around Naomi and began chanting. It was a language she didn't understand, but she knew this was no time to question him. Varhan moved around her, his hands waving quickly as he manipulated the very air around them. Soon enough, Naomi could see sparks flying from his fingers as he worked.

She gave one last thought to Julian. How she wished she could have told him what was happening, but she barely even understood it herself. This sickness, this disease that even the mages couldn't cure, was only going to resolve if she left the planet itself. And to make things even more shameful, it required the help of a wizard. The other dragons would never have let her go if they had known, and that was why she had not even told Julian the entire truth. If someone discovered what had happened, she didn't want him to be part of it.

Her scales tingled as the leaves on the forest floor began to swirl around her. The light from Varhan's fingers had now become streaks instead of sparks, and they joined the whirlwind. The ground trembled beneath her, but she no longer had the energy to be afraid as it dissipated. The wizard's chanting had either stopped or been lost in the sound of the wind, but either way, it didn't look like the spell needed him anymore. The dirt and leaves separated completely beneath Naomi, revealing a blackness deeper than anything she had seen before.

She felt one last tear leak from her eye as she fell through.

# 1

JULIAN AWOKE, PULLING IN A GASPING BREATH AS HE SAT UP IN BED. HE panted for a moment as he studied his surroundings, taking in the deep brown walls, hardwood floors, and framed abstract paintings on the walls. He knew he should recognize it all, but the dream world he had just come from stopped him at first. As Julian woke fully and his hands touched the soft blankets spread over him, he was once again hit with the hard reality of where he was. Earth.

He sank back onto the pillow with a sigh, closing his eyes to help retrieve whatever fragments of his dream he might still be able to recover before they were lost to the light of day. It wasn't the first time he had dreamed of Naomi, not since she had left him back on Charok and not since he and the other shifters had arrived on Earth almost a year ago. She visited him often, her cerulean scales and the delicate shift of her slitted eyes so clear in his mind that she could have been standing right in front of him. The visions were so realistic that at times he could reach out and touch her, feeling the thin skin that stretched between the bones of her wings.

And in those dreams, she was healthy. They always took place when she and Julian first met and fell in love, spending all of their time together in that hidden meadow in the woods where nobody else could see them. Julian knew that there was no real reason to keep their relationship a secret. Most of the dragons didn't have the same sort of

odd sensibilities that Earthlings did about who their friends and
family decided to be with. But it was fun, nonetheless, and they never
had a chance to come out and declare their love publicly before she'd
had to go.

So many times, Julian had wondered what had happened to her.
Had she died on some craggy mountaintop on her way to this mysterious promise of health? Or had she been able to find what she needed
and started a new life? It didn't really matter, since the War of Storms
broke out only a few years later and killed every dragon on Charok. If
she hadn't died from her illness, then she had surely died from the
spell cast by the evil Tazarre.

Rolling over, Julian stretched and checked the time on the alarm
clock. It wasn't even set to go off for another half an hour, but that was
nothing unusual. He found that he had never been able to sleep as
deeply in a soft bed as he had on the hard floor of a cave, and lately,
the problem had only been getting worse. That was just as well,
because he had plenty of studying to do before Kaylee awoke.

Slipping quietly past his daughter's bedroom and to the kitchen,
Julian retrieved a mug from the cabinet and poured a large serving of
coffee. While he hadn't found pleasure in everything that was involved
in being a human on Earth, the black drink and the automated coffee
pot were two things that he took great comfort in. He carried his cup to
the library and sank down into a leather chair, putting his feet up on
the matching ottoman.

Retrieving a Book of Shadows he had borrowed from Autumn,
Julian stared at the cover for a moment, his mind slipping back to how
he and his friends had gotten to Earth in the first place. Life had been
good back on Charok, when they were free dragons living peacefully
amongst the mountains. But no peace could last forever, and when the
ogres started a war against the dragons over who had the right to use
the Andrullian Lake, Julian wasn't certain it was worth fighting over.
But the wizards, who had been disputing the land in the Great Basin,
soon joined the fight. That was when he knew it was all over.

It was Tazarre, the leader of the wizards, who had come up with
the spell that would kill all of dragonkind. He was confident enough to
announce his plan for all species to hear, making even the ogres
tremble before him. Julian had been studying a few spells himself, but
it had never been anything more than a hobby. He didn't have
anywhere close to enough knowledge to do anything about it. Even

now, he could remember that day so clearly in his mind that the library disappeared around him, replaced by the woods on the far side of the mountains.

"*VARHAN!*" *Julian trudged through the woods, not willing to risk flying. He would be seen instantly and taken down. From the horror stories he had been told, he would be tortured for several days before they finally killed him. Instead, he had opted for his bipedal form, feeling it was the safest bet. "Varhan, are you home?"*

*To his relief, the little wizard came rushing out of his hut. His eyes were wild, his hair standing out from his head as though he had slept upside down. "Julian! What are you doing here, my friend? It's a death sentence for you, surely!"*

*"Yes, but you and I both know that I have death looming over my head, anyway. I've watched everyone around me die, slowly poisoned by the black magic that Tazarre has injected into every rock and blade of grass. There are so many carcasses on the mountainsides that we can't keep up with them." His eyes blurred, making the wizard little more than a pale, shadowy form. "I need your help, desperately."*

*"And what about the others?" Varhan looked behind Julian expectantly.*

*Julian's shoulders sagged a little, feeling shame for not trusting the wizard completely. "Yes, they're here with me, too. How did you know?" He had told his friends to stay behind until he knew whether or not it was safe for them to come. Julian had known Varhan for quite some time, visiting him at his little hut and learning everything he could about spells and magic. But he hadn't known if there would be other wizards around. What if they had discovered Varhan's sympathies for dragons and had set a trap?*

*"That's alright. I knew they would be. I've been expecting you for a few days now. Tell them to come. We'll have to hurry."*

*Julian gave a whistle to the others. "What do you have planned?"*

*Varhan's lips pressed together, and he shifted his feet in the leaves. "Something I've been working on for a very long time. I'll be sending you someplace safe."*

*"But rumor has it that the entire planet is affected," Julian argued.*

*"I know. I know." Varhan stepped inside his hut, leaving the door open as he talked. "You won't be on Charok anymore."*

*"There's something you should know." By this time, Holden, Beau, and*

*Xander had come up behind him, each carrying a heavy load. "We're not alone."*

*The wizard stepped back through the doorway, a small clay pot in his hand. He stirred the contents vigorously with a brush, but he stopped as soon as he saw what the other men carried. Stepping forward, Varhan laid a delicate finger on the silvery surface of the oblong item in Holden's arms. "Is that what I think it is?"*

*Holden gave the wizard a dirty look, but he held his head high as he answered. "The last four eggs of our queen, who now lies dead in her throne room. As far as we know, they're still viable."*

*Julian watched Varhan with a ball of despair in his throat. "Do you think you can help us? All of us?"*

*The man nodded slowly, and then more forcefully. "Yes. Yes, I can. This is perfect, actually. It's even better than I had anticipated. You'll all need to shift, though, and do it now. We don't have time to be shy about such things. If we don't get you out of here soon, there won't be anything I can do for you."*

*The dragons did as they were told, taking on the shapes they had been born with. It was usually a pleasurable experience, one that Julian looked forward to after he had spent some time as a man, but at the moment, he just wanted to get it over with. "Varhan," he said when he was finished, "you sound as though you knew this was coming."*

*"I did, but there's no time to really explain it. Just know that you're going where you're destined to be. Remember that, if nothing else. Now come here." The wizard reached up with the brush and began painting a sticky substance over Julian. "This will protect you in your journey. There should be enough for the eggs, as well."*

EVEN NOW, Julian could still remember the way that bristly brush had felt against his scales. It had burned off completely by the time they had arrived on Earth, and so he could only assume it had done its job.

With a sigh and a shake of his head, Julian opened the Book of Shadows and found where he had left off the evening before. He had come no closer to finding a way to return to Charok, no matter how many books he read. Xander had a library filled with books about humans and life on Earth, but Julian's collection consisted almost purely of books about spells, hexes, voodoo, and otherworldly experiences. It might take forever, but he still held out hope they could return to Charok with their children and that perhaps some of the dragons there would have been spared.

Kaylee awoke half an hour later when Julian was deep into a section about protection spells. "Da-deeee!" she called from her room.

Julian eagerly set the book down and hopped to his feet, trotting down the hall to retrieve his baby girl. She might not have been his by blood, but bringing her across the universe in the form of an egg was enough of a bond for him. With her olive tones and brilliant green eyes, she looked every bit as though he had fathered her.

"Good morning, sweet thing," he cooed as he lifted her out of her crib and hugged her. "Did you have any good dreams?"

She grinned at him and wrapped her arms around his neck. "Doughnuts?" she asked.

Julian had to laugh. He'd made the mistake of letting her experience the sweet breakfast treat two weeks ago, and she hadn't stopped talking about them since. "No, I think we'll go with scrambled eggs and some toast, instead. Then we'll go see your Uncle Holden for a little bit."

"Otay!"

An hour later, they pulled up in front of the massive house Holden had chosen as they each settled into their new life on Earth. On the outskirts of town, it was the sort of place that was apparently very impressive to most humans. Though he couldn't be certain, Julian imagined Holden had picked it out because the roofline reminded him of the mountains back on Charok.

"You're just in time," Holden said as he flung open the front door. "Leah has just left for work, and Finn has already been asking what we're going to do today. I'm sure he'd love to play with Kaylee for a bit."

"I thought about taking her to the park, but it looks like it's going to rain." Julian stepped into the foyer and set down his diaper bag. "Besides, I wanted to talk to you, and it isn't the sort of thing I would want the other parents at the park to hear."

"Oh?" Holden led the way down the hall to Finn's bedroom, where his little boy was stacking up wooden blocks until they were as tall as he was. He clapped and grinned when he saw his cousin.

Julian set Kaylee down, watching with satisfaction as she crawled over to play. He'd been putting off this conversation for a while, content to wait things out as long as he could, but there wasn't much choice but to bring it all out in the open now. "Do you remember, when Varhan was sending us here, that he said we were going where we were destined to be?"

"Of course, I do." Holden leaned against the doorway and folded his arms in front of his wide chest. "I have to admit I wasn't very certain about him when you first said there was a wizard who might help us. After all, I had seen what Tazarre and the others had done. But there was something about the way Varhan spoke, like he knew far more than we did. It's what let me know we were doing the right thing."

Looking down at Kaylee, who had picked up a block and was turning it over to examine each side of it, he nodded. "And I think in many ways, we did. We saved the children from a doomed fate."

Holden scratched his chin. "I have to admit that I was worried at first. If we were meant to be here, then in my mind, that implied we would find our mates here as well. But I knew we had to, for the children's sake, and I can see now that Varhan really was right. Xander, Beau, and myself are all taken care of. Now I just have to find a way to get you out of the house."

"That's exactly what I wanted to talk to you about. I've made a few efforts, as you know, hoping that you were right. But there's more to the equation that you don't know, and I don't think I will find my mate here." He should have brought it up a long time ago, but it never seemed like the right time.

"What are you talking about?"

With a sigh, Julian tried to make as short of a story as possible about Naomi. "I already met my mate, back on Charok."

Holden raised an eyebrow. "You never told me that."

"We didn't tell anyone. We didn't want the pressure of going through formal ceremonies, and it was exciting to have our little trysts. But she got sick and she left in search of some cure she wouldn't tell me about. She's dead now, just like all the others." He thought it would make him feel better to tell Holden, but the weight of the telling was heavy on his shoulders like iron. Somehow it didn't make things any better to admit out loud that he would never see her again.

His friend stood for a long time, his lips slightly pursed as he studied the floor. "I see," he finally said.

"I thought you should know because you've always been the one encouraging us and giving us hope of having a real family here on Earth. I have Kaylee, and I have you guys. Now I have Summer,

Autumn, and Leah as well. But it's never going to be more than that."
He had taken comfort in knowing that he wasn't the only dragon on
Earth. Having the children around made a difference, and so did
knowing that his friends were happy with their mates. Some days that
was enough, and some days it wasn't. Right then, after yet another
vivid dream about Naomi, it wasn't.

Holden's thick hand clapped him on the shoulder. "You don't know
that."

Julian snapped his eyes up. "Did you not hear what I just told you?
I already found my fated mate. I felt the fire burning inside me
anytime we were apart. I even tried to take on a human form around
her, just to prove to myself that I couldn't keep it for more than a few
minutes before I had to shift back. I had her, and now she's gone."
Frustration and anger built up in his chest all over again, and he
wished he could shift right at that moment just to vent it all out in a
massive ball of flame.

"I heard you," Holden assured him calmly. He never got bent out of
shape, not unless someone was threatening his woman or his child.
"But I'm not entirely convinced."

"Are you seriously going to tell me I don't know how to tell when
I've found the one? I might have been a bit younger when it happened,
but I wasn't stupid. It's a fairly unmistakable feeling." He wouldn't fight
Holden, not over something so stupid, but the urge was definitely
there.

Holden gave a light laugh. "I'm not saying that at all. Calm down. I
was just thinking about the fact that none of us were very confident we
would find our mates, but three out of the four of us have. Maybe your
first love is gone, and I hate the thought of that, but it doesn't mean
that you're completely out of luck."

"I think you've been on Earth too long and you've forgotten that
we're not actually human." Julian knew perfectly well that humans all
*thought* they had one special person out there waiting for them, but in
reality, they fell in love over and over again.

"Just listen, okay? I've thought about this a lot, even though I
know that Leah is the one person I'm supposed to be with. But we're
not talking about dragons being with dragons. We're talking about
dragons being with humans, and maybe that's different. Maybe we're
not restricted to just one person. Maybe there's more than one who
could make us happy. It's impossible to say, and I hoped that none of

us would ever need to find out, but I guess you'll be our experiment."

"Gee, thanks." Julian was pretty sure Holden had been spending too much time with Xander, making anthropological theories that they had no real way of proving. "I feel so honored."

"I just don't want to see you go through your life with no one at your side. I know it's made a big difference for me, and I'd like to think that it will for you, too. I know you've got to be heartbroken, but don't let that affect the rest of your life. Consider that it will affect Kaylee, too."

"Oh, I have." Julian had weighed the consequences either way. It would be good for his daughter to have a mother in her life. She loved the other women, but it would be different if she had someone to call her own. But if Julian didn't pick the right woman—something that could easily happen since he wouldn't feel the same sort of wild emotions that happened when a dragon met his true love—it could also cause great devastation for Kaylee. What if they didn't get along and the woman he chose left? Then his daughter would be worse off than she had been in the first place. He did his best to communicate these concerns to Holden.

"Don't give up just yet," he advised. "I know I haven't given up on you."

## 2

AUTUMN'S HOUSE WAS QUIET, BUT IT WAS CLEAR TO THE THREE WOMEN who sat on the floor around a candle that they weren't completely alone. They had cast their circle and called to the spirit guides, hoping to make a good connection with Naomi.

Feeling a distinct sensation of being watched, Autumn slowly opened her eyes. The image of the blue dragon that hovered in the air above the flame was faint this time. In fact, she could see Leah's solemn face right though it. But the dragon was there, nonetheless.

"Naomi! We've been trying so hard to reach you. We've had several seances lately with no success. I was beginning to worry about whether or not you were still there." She hadn't yet figured out exactly where 'there' was, but the spirit realm in which their friend now existed seemed to be one with a thick veil around it.

"I'm here," Naomi said faintly, "but it takes a lot of energy to keep the door between the worlds open. And I'm not always alone."

"Are you in danger?" Leah asked, her blue eyes desperate.

The dragon's head rolled on her long neck. "Yes and no."

"What does that mean?" Summer's long blonde hair fell forward over her shoulders as she leaned toward the apparition. "Please, Naomi. We've been so worried about you."

Naomi watched them, turning slowly to look at them each in turn. "I'll be fine."

And in an instant, she was gone.

Autumn, feeling the weight and pressure of their circle suddenly broken, lay back on the floor and spread her arms wide. "Do you think we'll ever get to talk to her for more than a few minutes? I thought I had a decent technique down, but I'm starting to question myself."

"Don't go getting yourself a 9-to-5 job just yet," Leah advised, rubbing her hands down her face. "It's exhausting for all of us. I would have hoped that knowing her as we did would make this easier. Maybe it has something to do with the fact that she's in dragon form all the time in the spirit realm."

"At least she seems to be." Autumn had been thinking about this a lot ever since they had started their seances to try to reach Naomi. "I swear it's like she isn't either one at first, not until we call to her. It makes me wonder if there's some other shape she can take, or if we're just interpreting her as being a dragon because that's how our minds understand her."

"That's an interesting proposition." Summer, Autumn's twin, bent over her stretched legs like a ballet dancer warming up for a show. "We only saw her transition into dragon form, what, once?"

Autumn nodded. "She was always so private about it." The three of them had met Naomi back in college, back when they were still trying to figure out who they were and where they belonged in society. Leah was a psychic, and the twins were witches, which made it difficult to get along with their peers sometimes. Naomi had been a perfect addition to the group.

"For a long time, I wondered if she was telling us the truth about being a dragon," Summer admitted. "Not that I ever thought she was doing it to be dishonest, but like that was just her excuse for not being the same as everyone else. Naomi was so quiet and reserved, like she was uncomfortable being on Earth, even."

"And I guess we all understand that a lot more now." Autumn had talked with her boyfriend about this quite a bit since they'd gotten together a few months ago. He, like the others, was a dragon shifter from Charok. Summer had paired up with Xander, and Leah had been the first one of them to discover that there were still dragons on Earth when she started dating Holden.

"Isn't it ironic," Leah mused, "that a dragon had been a part of our lives for several years, and then we all ended up with dragons? Naomi had said she was the only one, and I guess she would have been at that time since Holden and the others weren't here yet. But I had never considered the possibility that more of them might come. Or that they might be so hot." She grinned.

Autumn had to agree. "I just wish we could talk to her longer about where she is. I'd love to find a way to get her back. If she had come across the universe once already, then it doesn't seem so unlikely that we might be able to free her from the spirit realm as well."

The three women were silent for a moment, remembering, until Summer spoke. "I remember so clearly the day she died," she said quietly, her wide eyes still trained on the candle flame even though they all knew the séance was over. "At that point, we knew for certain that she was a dragon, and it seemed so unreal that she could die from something like a car accident. That was the part that hit me the most, that even though none of us are just normal humans, we're still very mortal."

Autumn closed her eyes and was instantly transported to the hospital. She'd received a phone call, but that part had been blotted from her memory. Instead, what she recalled most was bursting into the emergency room, the smell of antiseptic whacking her in the face and trying to shove her back outside into the fresh air where she belonged. But she surged forward instead, trying to keep her voice steady as she asked the woman at the desk about her friend.

The surgeons were busy working on her, but even that hadn't given Autumn hope. What was the anatomy and physiology of a dragon shifter like? Would the normal procedures and medications even work on her? Or would they be able to save her, only to have the government swoop in and keep her for experiments once they realized she was different?

In the end, none of that had mattered. Naomi had died on the table, and none of the doctors acted as though anything strange had happened.

"She was a good friend," Autumn said with a sigh. "I feel like I'm being a bad one since I can't bring her back."

"Stop that." Leah stood and crossed the room to a low table, pouring herself a glass of wine. "I want Naomi back just as much as you do, but I don't think most people expect to be brought back from the dead. We're doing what we can, and it's not like we've given up yet."

But the truth was that Autumn had considered it. She'd tried every spell she could think of, and nothing had worked. There was very little in her spell books that she hadn't thoroughly examined and tested. Even if she did somehow manage to open a portal between their two worlds and drag Naomi back, what about her physical body? There were so many complications, and it didn't give her much hope for the future.

"The truth is stranger than fiction." Summer had muttered the words so quietly, Autumn wasn't sure she had heard her correctly.

"What?"

Summer rose and followed Leah's example, pouring herself a generous glass of Merlot before returning to her cushion on the floor. The candlelight danced in her golden hair as she took a slow sip and then tipped her head back. "I've been watching a lot of movies lately. It's not the kind of thing I normally like to do, and I'd be fine with not even owning a TV, but Xander really likes them. He says they tell him a lot about what it means to be human, because people take all the things they want from life and make them into movies."

"Are you sure that's your first glass?" Autumn challenged. "I thought we were talking about Naomi."

Her sister gave her a sassy look. "It is, and we are. Just be patient for a minute. Xander's big thing right now is scary movies. We have to wait until Nora is in bed, because we don't want to scare her, and then we cuddle up on the couch. A lot of them are ones that I saw as a kid, but I notice so much more about them now than I ever did. And you should hear some of the questions Xander asks me! If he watched nothing but horror movies, he would think humans were complete idiots."

"The point, Summer?" Autumn knew she shouldn't be impatient with her, but she also knew that she had done more research on this than anyone else in the group had. If she didn't know how to bring Naomi back, then she doubted anyone else would. And some dumb movie wasn't going to help them, since they were living in the real world.

"The point is that I've seen numerous movies where someone gets sucked into a ghost world of some sort, and then they *send someone in* to retrieve them. It's not about casting the right spell or anything, it's more of a physical solution." Her face was alight as she explained, as though she had just come up with a Nobel Prize-worthy theory.

"It's a friggin' movie, Summer, not real life. The people who write those movies have no idea what magic is really like." And it was for that exact reason Autumn didn't usually bother watching movies like that. She didn't mind a romantic comedy or even a drama, but it annoyed her to no end when people pretended to know something about magic.

Her sister sighed. "I know they don't. Or at least, as far as we know they don't. But there might be some logic to the scenario."

"Right now, the only thing we're able to do is open up a window for us to look through and talk to Naomi. That's it. There's nothing like a room for a person," Autumn argued.

"It's an interesting theory, though," Leah volunteered. "And it might not be exactly what we're looking for, but I think it's worth exploring. I was hoping we could get at least enough of a connection that I could establish a psychic link with her. Maybe that way, I could get a good understanding of exactly what's going on with her. But so far, that hasn't worked. We've got to keep our minds open to any option."

"Yeah, I guess you're right." Autumn followed suit with the others and poured her own drink. It was a good wine, one that Leah had picked up on the way over. She never went cheap on things now that her psychic business and her books were doing so well. "I'm just so frustrated because I've spent a lot of time on this. I consider it my goal in life at this point, and I haven't made any progress."

"It's a process of elimination, at least," Summer offered. "I wonder if maybe the guys can help us."

This was something that had occurred to Autumn already, especially when Julian had asked to borrow some spell books from her. "I wish I could say that they can, but I don't think it's possible. Julian likes to study spell books, and even did when he still lived on Charok. But it's more of a scholarly knowledge than applied. Even *he* doesn't know much about the spell that brought them to Earth. It happened so quickly, and he's spent months trying to figure out how to replicate it, but to no avail."

"Surely that's different from what we're talking about," Leah mused. "In some way, at least. It's probably still worth talking to him about it."

"I'll do that next time I see him."

When the other women had gone home and it was time for Autumn to go back to the place she shared with Beau, she hesitated. This house was now completely dedicated to her spiritual needs. She had Beau and Elliot at her new home, and she was able to dedicate this space to meditation, storing herbs, and working new spells. She and the other women had a private, sacred place for seances and spell-work. It was a wonderful sort of freedom, and Beau never demanded that she be home early or stop what she was doing simply because he wanted to be with her. He respected that she needed her privacy and her alone time, especially when it came to focusing in on what she truly was: a witch. But all the space and time and materials in the world didn't seem to be enough to bring Naomi back.

She couldn't help but feel that there was something she was miss-ing, something she should have seen a long time ago. She reached out to Naomi in her mind, knowing that she couldn't possibly even say hello without the help of the others, but determined to do it anyway. There was nothing there for her. With a sigh, Autumn picked the cush-ions up off the floor, grabbed her purse and locked the door on the way out.

## 3

A week later, Autumn had managed to shrug off the heavy weight of her mostly unsuccessful séance. It would be another month before they would try again, since they would only drain themselves of all their energy if they attempted contact too often. Instead, Leah was across the street doing psychic readings and Autumn and Summer were back at work at The Enchanted Elm.

Running a new age store in a small town was often a challenge, but it was one that Autumn enjoyed. She had dealt with other business owners who didn't appreciate a couple of witches running a shop next door, and she had handled the religious fanatics who didn't accept the Keller sisters as part of the community. That was in addition to the ordinary challenge of finding just the right profit margin to keep the money coming in without driving the customers away. And with her business degree, that was just the sort of thing Autumn was good at.

Taking care of her customers and running a successful business was just what she was thinking about when the bell over the front door rang. Autumn was bent over the counter, deciding whether or not to buy a sponsorship in the program for the high school spring play. She glanced up at the man, ready with her usual spiel of offering to help if he needed anything, but she could tell by the confused look on his face that he was going to need assistance right away.

"Good morning. What can I help you find?"

The man was young, probably in his early twenties, and his eyes were the same cool grey as the clouds that had been hanging over the town all morning, threatening with a rain shower, but never actually coming through on it. He glanced at Autumn as he approached the counter, but quickly averted his eyes to the floor as he rubbed his face.

"Well, um, I don't know if you'll have what I'm looking for..."

"Even if I don't, I can probably find it for you. We do special orders all the time." Usually, customers at The Enchanted Elm knew little enough about magic that they were able to walk in and buy whatever caught their eye. But there were still a few folks who wanted a specific scent of incense or candle or who felt their cousin in Ohio would prefer a teal dreamcatcher instead of a purple one. Sometimes, Autumn or Summer would need to order a particular crystal they knew was needed to heal a client.

"Well, it's sort of strange. I don't think it has anything to do with Wicca." He had reached the counter now, and he shifted his weight from foot to foot.

"That doesn't matter," Autumn assured him, growing more curious by the moment as to just what this man was searching for. "We supply all sorts of belief systems with no discrimination."

He nodded, finally looking up at her again. "Okay, here's the thing. I saw a show recently about shamanism, and I thought it might really help me. I spent several years on drugs, and I've been trying to get my life back together. I'm clean, I've got a job, and I've even got a girl-friend, but I just feel like there's a part of me missing. The guy on TV was talking about soul retrieval, and that it's a way to find the pieces of yourself that you don't have access to. Like maybe I could use a shamanic ritual to gain access to the parts of my brain that I cut off with all the drugs, you know?" He talked faster and faster as he went on, and a few beads of sweat popped out on his forehead. "I'm sorry. I don't know why I'm telling you all this."

But Autumn understood exactly why, even if he didn't. "Because you want to be healed, and it's a scary process that you can't always do alone. I understand. I've heard of soul retrieval, though I admit I don't have any experience with it. What particular supplies do you need?"

"A drum, apparently. Or at least, that's one way to get started. The sound of the drum beating puts you in a sort of trance, where you can access other parts of yourself or the world or something. I don't under-stand all of it yet."

"Let me see." Autumn began looking through their inventory to see if they had anything that would work. "Are you having someone beat the drum for you, or are you doing it yourself?"

"My therapist says he'll do it with me. It's new to both of us, but he was really excited when I brought the idea to him. He says he has lots of patients who are going through the same stuff I am, so if this is successful, he might even start doing it on a regular basis."

Autumn desperately wanted to ask him the name of his therapist and if he was there in town. Any time she found someone who was open-minded like that, she liked to take note. "That's wonderful. It's always good to have someone navigating for you when you're on a spiritual journey. I don't have anything in stock at the moment that will be quite right for you, but I can order something. Here." She turned the screen around to show him. "My supplier has these drum sets in stock, and if you like one of them, I can have it here within a couple of days."

His eyes widened at he bent to look at the screen. "Yeah! That's just like what the guy on TV was using. I'll take one of the cheaper sets. I don't want to spend a lot of money until I know if it works or not."

"Completely understandable." Autumn rang up the transaction and put in the order, requesting a couple of extra sets to put in the shop's inventory as well. If this guy wanted drums, then someone else might, too. She gave him a copy of the receipt. "I'll give you a call as soon as it comes in. If you don't mind sharing, I'd love to know how this goes for you. Feel free to stop in and tell me about it."

He smiled, looking more positive than he had since he'd first walked in. "Thanks. I'll do that."

When he had left and the store was quiet once again, Autumn turned back to the form for the school play. She knew that buying a small place in the back of the program wouldn't actually bring in any new business, but she liked the idea of supporting the drama club and being a part of the community. But even as she wrote out a check, she found that she wasn't all that interested in advertising and marketing anymore.

Her mind returned again and again to the young man's request for shamanic drums. Maybe it was time to expand her own horizons. She clicked open her browser and began her research.

———

"LOOK, I know it's different than everything we've done before, but that's exactly why I want to try it." Autumn had gathered her friends in her house, feeling hopeful and tentative. The sun shone through the big windows on the back of the house as they shared a Saturday morning brunch and mimosas. She'd done weeks' worth of research without saying anything, wanting to make sure she had all the information before she brought it to the others.

"It *is* different," Summer acknowledged, a small smile playing on her lips, "but only in a few ways. It seems more like a cousin of what we do on a regular basis. We'll still call in the directions and cast a circle." She sat in the breakfast nook with her knees pulled up to her chest.

Autumn herself was dressed and ready for the day in a pale lavender top and khakis. She considered it her weekend casual look, even though it was far more formal than what either of the other women were wearing. "Yes, but someone will need to go into a trance instead of casting a spell. I know I dismissed the idea you had about going in to retrieve Naomi like they do in the movies, but I can see now that there is some legitimate theory behind it. We're not physically tying a rope around your waist and shoving you through a portal, but it's sort of the psychic equivalent." As she was discovering more and more about shamanic rituals, Autumn had realized that the scenes her sister had described were simply fun, cinematic ways of showing something that was done on a fairly regular basis in certain communities.

"And what about her physical body?" Leah asked. She stood from the table and stepped to the breakfast bar to mix herself another mimosa. "We know that our world doesn't support spirits on their own for very long."

"I've thought about that, too. I had to do a lot of digging, but I found a spell that we can use in conjunction with the ritual. It should create a new body for her, and Naomi's spirit will still dictate what it looks like. It calls for very basic ingredients, since everything in the universe is made of the same stuff anyway." She pulled a piece of paper out of a folder and set it in the middle of the table. "Basically dirt, plants, and stones. The spell wouldn't be anything on its own, but if we're successful in bringing Naomi back, then I think it will work."

"And I suppose you plan on being the one who goes into the trance?" Summer asked.

"I thought I would be a good candidate," Autumn affirmed. "I'm the one who's been doing the studying, so it makes sense."

"That's only because you left us out of it up until this point." Summer's words were pointed, but her look was gentle. "But that's alright. I'm down for this whenever you're ready."

"Same here," Leah said with a smile. "I'll even beat the drums for you."

———

THEIR ENTHUSIASM WOULDN'T HOLD them long, and as soon as the moon was right, the women were upstairs in Autumn's house, standing in a circle in the center of the room. The windows, one facing each direction, were open all the way to let in the fresh spring air and the sound of the gentle rain that had begun falling just as the sun went down.

They had called in the directions and cast their circle, and Autumn felt the familiar tingle of a safe ceremony fall on her shoulders. There was no better feeling than knowing she was about to explore something new and exciting in the spirit realm. Her heart leaped in her throat as she turned to face the other women, excited for this to begin.

"Every ritual is different, depending on who is performing it and what the intentions are. For now, we'll rely on the drum beats to induce the trance. If I can bring Naomi back, then Summer, I'll need you to perform the spell for her body."

Her sister nodded, the excitement equal in her eyes. She adjusted her fingers on the hand carved drumsticks she held. "Sounds good."

Summer and Leah began beating. They had been practicing together for the last couple of days, making sure that they could create a rhythm that was easy to keep going for long periods of time and worked on being in sync with each other. It was a simple set of four beats, louder at the beginning and growing slightly softer toward the end.

Autumn tipped her head back and closed her eyes, watching the way the candle threw light and shadow at her eyelids. She began her normal mediation routine, consciously relaxing each part of her body beginning at the top of her head and working her way slowly down to her toes. There was no concern about keeping track of time or worrying about how long this entire ritual might take. It could last all night, and they would continue it on into the next day if they had to. There were numerous accounts of shamanic rituals that lasted for hours or even days, with the resulting exhaustion only enhancing the results.

With her body loose and feeling light, Autumn turned her focus to her breathing. She concentrated on filling every corner of her lungs with air, inflating them to their fullest potential before she expelled every atom.

Just as she was about to focus on a mantra, Autumn heard an odd sound to her left. She dismissed it and brought her mind back to her breath, not wanting to lose the progress she had already made. It was going to be a long and perhaps difficult journey to get into a trance and open up the window between the realms in order to fetch Naomi.

But the sound came again, and she couldn't help but open her eyes. The candle was the only source of light in the room, but it was too bright. Autumn squinted, thinking it was just because she had been closing her eyes for so long, but she soon realized that it was burning brighter and hotter than it normally did.

Summer moaned again, that same noise that had brought Autumn out of her meditative state in the first place. Her head was tipped back on her shoulders so that she faced the ceiling, but her eyes were rolled so far back in her head that only the whites were visible. It was as though she was bending her body backwards to look behind herself. Despite this, her hands kept moving rhythmically on the drums.

Concern grew in Autumn's mind, and as she looked across the circle to Leah, she saw that same worry reflected in her eyes. This wasn't the plan. But what if Summer had already achieved the trance? It might not be safe to pull her out of it. There was no good or clear choice but to continue.

Autumn closed her eyes and focused on her breathing once again, but instead of looking to achieve the trance state herself, she channeled all her energy to her sister. She could feel it flowing through her veins now, like bright blue streaks of lightning, and she pushed every bit of it to Summer.

It was enough. Her sister's moans turned to odd gurgling noises, and her head began to sway so that her hair danced across the floor behind her. Still, her hands kept the rhythm, and for the first time since they were kids, Autumn felt a genuine fear of what they were doing. She was confident in her practice and in her knowledge, but they were stepping into new territory. It was one thing to put herself at risk, but it was something completely different to do that to her sister.

*Don't stop it.* Autumn heard the voice clear as a bell in her head, and she snapped her eyes across the circle to meet Leah's.

Autumn herself wasn't a psychic, and it had been a long time since the three of them had attempted to communicate telepathically, but she did her best. *Is she alright?*

*I can't see anything, but she's okay.*

The message was cryptic to Autumn at first, but she took this to mean that although Leah couldn't see into Summer's mind and interpret exactly what was happening, she didn't detect any danger. That would have to be good enough for the moment. It was killing her not to know all the details, but she didn't seem to have a choice. The drums had called to Summer.

Summer's noises grew more intense and more frequent now, and they quickly built up to a scream that deafened Autumn's ears. She was writhing now, her shoulders moving at odd angles and her spine undulating like a piece of grass in the breeze.

Autumn no longer bothered with closing her eyes. She needed to know what was happening, and she spoke aloud to Leah this time. "What's going on?"

"I don't know, exactly." There were tears in Leah's eyes. "I've tried to see through her eyes, but it's not working. It might if I touch her, but I don't want to risk it. Wherever she's at, though, I don't think she's here." Leah reached out with tentative fingers, spreading them out near Summer but keeping just a few inches of space. "I'm pretty sure she's not alone."

With a spike of adrenaline pushing at her heart, Autumn couldn't take her eyes off of Summer. "Does that mean she has Naomi?" Her fingers itched to begin the next spell. This was going to take a lot out of all of them by the time it was over, but for the moment, she had more energy than she knew what to do with. Not for the first time, she wished she had more of a coven to help her.

"I don't know," Leah replied honestly. "We'll have to wait and see."

Summer's spasms carried on for several more minutes until the candle's light burned so brightly that the pillar of wax exploded. Droplets of hot wax cascaded through the room, but somehow, the flame was still alight. Just above it, the air congealed and swirled, as though Autumn was looking at the room through a puddle. The swirling intensified, growing faster until a rupture formed in the center. A brilliant blue dragon writhed inside it, mirroring Summer.

Acting quickly, Autumn checked that the dish of fresh earth was placed directly next to the candle. Some wax had gotten in it, but there was nothing to be done about that now. She dug her hands down into the dirt as she chanted the words she had committed to memory, asking her spirit guides to form a new vessel for her friend. "Take this earth, as it is the mother of all of us, and build a new body that it might contain a spirit. Take these stones, as they are the bones of all of us, and create new bones that might hold her upright. Take these plants, as they are the nourishment of all of us, and nourish her new home."

The vision of the blue dragon writhed and coiled around itself. It was small, as though they were seeing it from a distance, but Autumn knew it could only be Naomi. "Just keep doing what you're doing, Summer," she whispered. "I'll have it all ready for you when you get back." The energy that she had been giving to her sister she now pushed down into the bowl.

As the vortex opened wider, the dirt, stones, and plants in the bowl rose up into the air, the particles scattering out into a wide sphere. Naomi's form emerged into the room, limp and lifeless as though she were floating on an invisible sea. Her body was brilliantly blue, the same color as Autumn's energy, but where a speck of dirt stuck to her, she became a deeper shade. More and more of the pieces flew to her, clinging to her for a moment before sinking in and leaving a deep cerulean shadow in their wake until she looked like she was freckled with the depths of the ocean. Soon enough, she was entirely the color of lapis lazuli.

In one swift moment, the flame went out. Naomi fell to the floor with a hard thud, and the vortex slammed shut.

# 4

---

JULIAN STOOD AT THE BACK OF THE BIG ROOM IN THE LIBRARY, WILLING his mind to stay focused on the story. It was just some children's book about a young elephant who didn't feel that he fit in his own skin. It probably wasn't all that poignant to most of the kids who sat and looked at the pictures as the old woman read it to them, though he knew it could be a good lesson for Kaylee. She had two different skins to learn to love, after all.

But his mind had been covered by a cloud all day, and as he thought about it, even last night. He hadn't been able to get to sleep for several hours. Every time he closed his eyes, he could think of nothing but Charok and the numerous events that had happened there. None of the memories that came to mind were good ones. He was haunted by visions of Naomi, ill and dragging herself across the mountains, or the dead bodies of all his comrades as they lay in the red dirt. In the morning, after several cups of coffee, he'd thought he was finally ready to start his day. He'd chased the heavy feeling from his eyelids and he was determined to make sure Kaylee enjoyed their day together. But even something as simple as taking his daughter to story time at the library seemed difficult, and he felt restless as he waited for the book to be over.

"Which one is yours?" whispered a voice next to him.

"Hmm?" Julian turned to see a young woman smiling up at him.

She had blonde hair that bounced around her shoulders and big brown eyes. She looked like she was dressed to go to the bar instead of the library. "Oh, the one in the front with the pink shirt." He pointed at Kaylee, where she sat raptly watching the storyteller.

"She's an absolute doll!" The woman had deep dimples when she smiled. "Mine is over there in the purple. Maybe we should get them together to play sometime, and you and I can have coffee."

There was nothing wrong with her suggestion. After his discussion with Holden, he had started to think that perhaps his friend was right. Just because he had known Naomi back on Charok didn't mean that he couldn't find someone to be with here. But thinking it was a possibility was an entirely different thing than acting on it. This woman next to him was attractive, and it was clear that she knew what life with kids was like. She might be a perfectly good candidate for any other guy, but the idea made his skin itch so badly, he wanted to scratch it off. "Um, I've got a lot going on right now. I don't think I'll have the time."

She pouted, shrugged, and turned her attention back to the story.

Julian tried to do the same, but his mind wouldn't shut off. He could see Naomi on the inside of his eyelids every time he blinked, and his entire body seemed to vibrate with the need to find her. She was gone. She was dead. No matter how hard he looked, he would never see her again. But his blood was boiling in his veins as though she were right in the next room, waiting for him to come to her.

Unable to stand it any longer, he carefully picked his way through the crowd of children on the floor and scooped Kaylee into his arms.

"Story!" she wailed.

"Sshh. Let's not ruin it for everyone else." Julian trotted out of the library as quickly as possible, avoiding the curious stares of the other parents. He'd already made a scene, and it was only going to get worse. Kaylee loved story time. He tried to explain as he trotted across the damp parking lot and opened the car door. "I'm sorry, sweetie. I really am. But I've got an emergency."

She looked up at him with damp eyes as he buckled her in. "Story?" One large tear clung to her eyelashes.

It broke his heart, but he knew as a father that there were going to be many more of those tears in the future. He got behind the wheel. "I'm sorry. We'll come again next week, and maybe we can check out the book the librarian was reading. I know you don't understand right now, but if everything works out, then you will someday."

Julian fired up the engine and dialed Holden before he was even out of the lot. "Are you available to watch Kaylee today?" he asked without preamble.

"Sure," the deep voice replied. "But are you okay? You sound like you're upset."

Julian tightened his jaw, knowing there was no good way to explain. "Yeah, I'm okay. Essentially. I've just got something I've got to take care of."

"Sounds to me like you've got a woman. I don't think I've heard that much urgency in your voice since we arrived on Earth," he laughed.

Grateful that he had Holden on his headset so Kaylee couldn't hear, Julian was tempted to argue. Naomi wasn't just a woman. She was far more than that. She was also *dead*. But he could practically hear her calling to him, sending her need for him out through the universe. He didn't know what he would need to do to find her, but he would do whatever it took. "Something like that."

"Well, bring the kiddo on over and take your time. Leah was out late last night, so Finn and I were just going to do some baking while she slept."

Kaylee's tears dried as soon as she realized she was going to get to play with her cousin. Julian dropped her off as quickly as he could, ready to focus on these strange urges that were taking over his body and figure out just what the hell he was going to do about them.

But Holden stopped him on the front steps. "Julian, whatever is going on, just know that we've all been through it."

Julian knew what he meant. There was a certain rage that took over a male dragon when he found his mate, and it made life very difficult for a little while. "I know. I'm not sure if this is that or something else. I'll keep you posted. And thanks." He took off, knowing his daughter was in good hands.

Back behind the wheel of his car, Julian started driving. He didn't really know where he was going, and he paid no attention to speed limits. Allowing his body to take over and trying not to think about it too much, he wound his way back into town and down side streets. He was getting closer, and when his bones shook against one another, he stomped the brake. Julian looked up.

He had seen this house before. Hell, he'd even been inside it for a

New Year's Eve party. It was Autumn's house, but her car wasn't in the driveway as he pulled up. "This is weird," Julian muttered to himself. He knew Autumn because of Beau, and he had borrowed a few books from her, but he couldn't say that they had been particularly close. He got out and looked up at the front of the place, wondering what the hell was going on. There was no good reason for him to be at her house. And he knew there was really no good reason for what he was about to do. But he tucked his shoulder and prepared to break down the front door.

# 5

NAOMI COULD SEE THE EXHAUSTION ON THEIR FACES. "YOU SHOULD GO and rest. I know you're all as tired as I am, at least." She had slipped back into her human form as soon as she realized she was back on Earth, glad to finally shed the mantle of her dragon physique. Most shifters preferred to be their scaled selves, but for the moment, it seemed easier to be a human. That form didn't require as much energy to sustain.

"I'm worried about leaving you," Autumn said as she leaned over the bed. "You've been away for so long, and we've never done these spells before." She had explained briefly what they had done to get her back to Earth, talking of drums and shamans and other things Naomi didn't have the presence of mind to even try to understand.

"The Otherworld," Naomi whispered. It was what she had come to call the place where she had gone after she died. Humans had concepts of heaven and hell and places like that, but Naomi knew this was definitely not either one of those.

"Tell us about it," Summer said gently. "If you feel up to it, anyway. We've been so worried about you."

"It was difficult," Naomi admitted. "There were good beings there, ones made entirely of light. They were warm and kind in their own way, but they couldn't always talk to me. And there were other creatures there, too. Dark ones. I did my best to keep away from them, but I could tell they were very strong."

"Did they want to hurt you?"

How could she explain something that took place in a completely different realm? Even the thoughts inside Naomi's head had been different, as though the language of her mind had been changed. "I don't really know. It was a very lonely place, I can tell you that. No matter how many other spirits were around, none of them were ones that I knew. There were a lot of them around when you pulled me back, though. I think the other beings there could sense the rift you created, and they wanted to see what was happening."

"Can't blame them there," Autumn remarked. "It sounds like it might be a holding place of sorts, for spirits who don't belong anywhere else. Like purgatory, if you will."

Naomi nodded, but the action hurt her head. "That would make sense. I'm glad to be back, but my body is so heavy. I'm not sure it was a good idea." It wasn't just her body that made her feel that way. It was something else, something her befuddled mind couldn't quite grasp.

"You're just not used to it yet." Leah smiled down at her. "You've been nothing but a spirit for several years now. You don't even know what gravity is anymore."

"I felt it." Naomi was only growing more and more tired, but it had been so long since she'd truly been able to talk to her friends. "When you would reach out to me, it was like a tiny hole had erupted in front of my face. It pulled at me, like Earth was calling me back, but I could never do anything about it. I put my energy into that window, but it didn't always seem to help."

"I'm sorry. That must have been very frustrating for you." Summer gently rubbed her arm.

"No, it's okay. It was good to know that you were still thinking of me, at the very least. I had no way of knowing how long I'd been there, because there was no such thing as time, but it felt like an eternity." There were no nights or days, just endless drifting. As heavy as her new body was, weighed down from the soil it had been formed from, she didn't miss the Otherworld.

"Listen, you really need to get some sleep. We all do." Autumn's eyes drooped a little at the corners. "We're all going to go home and give you some peace and quiet so you can get some good rest. We'll come back later this evening and have some dinner. Does that sound good?"

Naomi nodded. The others had offered her food shortly after she had come back, but her stomach was still churning from her transition. "Yes. It's been so long since I've actually slept. I'm not sure I even remember what it's like."

"Trust me. You'll enjoy it." They said their goodbyes and left the room, closing the door behind them.

Naomi could hear them chattering with each other as they made their way through the house and out the door. She stared up at the timber frame ceiling, trying to wrap her mind around the fact that she was back on Earth. It had been forever. As nice as it was to be back again, she wondered what it would have been like if the women could have brought her back to Charok. Was Julian still there? Did he still think of her? He had occupied her thoughts a lot since she had awoken, but she hadn't bothered to say anything about him to her friends. It's not as though they would know anything about him, and no matter how powerful their magic was, they couldn't reunite her with her true love on a distant planet.

Eventually, her eyes began to close. Light leaked in through the curtains, but she didn't care that it was still daytime. Just the fact that she was away from all the confusion of the Otherworld made her feel more comfortable than she had in a long time. She wondered if she would dream.

Just as she was about to doze off, she heard a noise. Her eyes flipped open and her hands reached out at her sides, but she had no weapons at hand. Maybe time had passed more quickly than she had realized, and Autumn and the others had already returned. But the slow and careful footsteps were made by only one person; that much she was sure of.

Her heart pounding in her chest, she slipped out of bed. Autumn had lent her an old t-shirt and a pair of shorts, and they didn't seem like enough to protect her from whatever was coming. She realized that if she stayed where she was, she would be trapped like an animal. Naomi wasn't strong enough to climb out through a window, and her best chance was to make it to another door before the intruder found her.

Peeking out the bedroom door, she saw nothing. Naomi dashed across the hall and through an open door. She found herself in another bedroom—one that seemed to have been used for storage, judging by the stack of boxes in the corner—but there still weren't any outside doors there. With little option, she crawled under the bed and scooted all the way to the back near the legs of the headboard.

The footsteps had turned down the hallway and paused. Naomi held her breath, willing the stranger to give up and go away. But the bedroom door creaked open. She could easily see his feet as he stood in the doorway, probably surveying the room, trying to figure out where she was.

She held back a scream as he slowly stepped toward the bed. There was no other place to go. Whoever this was, he would get to her before she ever made it out of the room. Her friends had done so much work to bring her back, and now she would be gone again.

The interloper crossed the hardwood floor and stopped again at the edge of the bed. He knelt down, and when he peeked underneath the bed skirt, she could no longer hold back her scream.

"Naomi?"

# 6

JULIAN KNEW HE SHOULDN'T HAVE BROKEN DOWN AUTUMN'S FRONT door. He could have just tried to call her, or even Beau. But the desperation that flooded his body was impossible to ignore, and he didn't have time to explain or ask permission. And now that he crouched there in an unused guest bedroom, seeing Naomi underneath the bed, he knew it had been worth it.

She had stopped screaming, and he reached a hand out to help her up. "It's okay. It's just me. But how are you here?" He wondered for a moment if he had gone crazy and he was just hallucinating. Or maybe it was just someone who *looked* like Naomi. But his body told him otherwise.

"How are *you* here?" Naomi was still the same as she had always been. There was no mistaking those brilliant blue eyes and her dark, straight hair. Even a little disheveled and shaken, it was absolutely her. The touch of her hand was like fire against his skin, and as he pulled her to her feet, he could feel his wings burst through the skin of his back.

She responded in kind, her almond eyes elongating even further as her face stretched to a muzzle and her hair turned to a cascade of spikes along the curve of her skull. He watched with fascination as her wings unfurled, taking up half the space in the room. They were the most beautiful shade of blue he had ever seen, and she was an even more magnificent dragon than he had remembered.

Julian had been so fascinated with Naomi's transformation that he had barely noticed his own. The sensation was nothing compared to the way this woman made him feel and the animalistic urges she had been inspiring in him even before he had truly known that she was here on this planet. As unreal as it had seemed, his instincts were right. She really was back.

She studied him, her clawed hands reaching out to run down the smooth scales on his cheek. "It's you. It really is you. He said I would find you here. I didn't believe him, and it took so long that I thought he must have been wrong." Her voice was quiet, musing.

"Who?" None of this made sense. Just seeing her at all was confusing enough.

"Varhan. He's a wizard who helped me get to Earth. That's what I was doing when I left. He said the energies here would heal me. I couldn't tell you because I knew what it meant to have associations with one of his kind. Even if you understood, I didn't want anyone to blame you."

It had been so long since he had heard that name spoken aloud that for a moment, Julian didn't know who she meant. But a vision of the little round man in the middle of the woods soon came leaping to his mind. "Varhan. Varhan!? But I knew him. I worked with him all the time, even before you and I started seeing each other. I never would have been upset about that. It's because of Varhan that I'm here, along with three of my friends."

She smiled, a beautiful look on a dragon, and she reached out to touch his face once more. "He said that the spell to bring me here would change the lives of others. I suppose he meant you and your friends from Charok."

As suddenly as his heart had lifted at the sight of her, it fell like a stone into his stomach and all the fire in his chest quickly extinguished. She couldn't possibly know about Tazarre and the spell of poison, or the fact that all the other dragons on Charok were now dead, and he'd have to be the one to tell her. "Possibly. But right now, I just want to know how you got here."

Naomi nodded and looked up at him. "I lived here as a human for several years after Varhan sent me. The spell worked, and I felt much better. But it was lonely, especially because I was the only dragon here.

Eventually, I made friends; I suppose you'll meet them when they come back. But five years ago, I was killed in a car accident and my soul was sent to another realm, a place unlike any I've been to before. But my friends hold special gifts and were able to use their powers to bring me back. Actually, I've only returned to Earth a few hours ago."

"I know your friends," he whispered. "There's so much that I have to tell you. It's going to take a long time of just sitting and being together." How could he explain that all the dragons on Charok had been purged and that he and the other men, along with the eggs they had snatched, had been the only survivors? It was more than she should have to hear about right now, but eventually, he would also be able to explain that her friends and his friends were all very well acquainted.

"That sounds wonderful." Naomi butted her head up underneath his chin. "For right now, just let me know that you still love me as much as you did when we knew each other before."

"Absolutely." He closed his eyes as he leaned toward her, her scales where he touched her smoothing out to soft skin. The waterfall of her hair showered across the back of his hand as he cupped the back of her neck, and he felt all the tension that had been building up in his body immediately dissipate as his lips met hers. He wanted to melt into her and become part of her, never having to give her up again.

Instinctively, his hands wrapped around her waist and lifted her up, pulling her close as he deepened their kiss. The raging instincts that had brought him to the house were now a craving in his veins, and he was finally getting to satisfy that craving after all these years. His fingers drifted underneath the hem of her t-shirt and up the smooth planes of her back.

Naomi's arms had wrapped around his waist, but she leaned back in his grasp to lift her shirt over her head. She hadn't been wearing a bra, which made sense since she had been wanting to sleep, and she revealed to him the pearlescent mounds of flesh that he needed so badly.

Julian laid her down on the bed. His mouth drifted down the hollow of her neck, slowly tracing the curves there, until he made his way to those gorgeous breasts. They were soft and sweet in his mouth, her nipples growing hard as his tongue flicked across them. Naomi groaned pleasurably and ran her fingers through his hair, pressing him harder into her.

This was so much more than Julian had imagined, even in his

wildest fantasies. He had been so certain that he would never see Naomi again, yet he had allowed himself to envision what it would be like if he had. Now, having her right there in his arms and in his mouth, he wasn't sure he would be able to contain himself long enough to enjoy it.

"Oh, Julian," she breathed. "I've missed you so much."

"I've missed you, too." He was nuzzling her neck again. There was no square inch of her body that he didn't want to explore. "The other dragons I'm here with paired off with their mates, but I knew I could never do the same thing. There was only one woman in the universe for me." As he nipped her earlobes, his hands drifted down her long, lean body to the waistband of her shorts. Naomi arched her back as he pushed them away, making it an easy task. Her simple cotton panties came next.

Julian sat back on his knees to admire his mate. She was glorious in her nakedness. Her tumble of straight hair was dark against her snowy skin, the rosy buds of her nipples like delicate flowers on a teacup. Her waist tucked in underneath her ribs before the spread of her hips. Julian moved down toward the end of the bed, eager to explore the new frontier he had just discovered.

He ran his hands down her thighs as he gently pushed them aside, bending to kiss the delicate folds. She gasped and pulled away at first, but as his hands gently cupped her buttocks, she relaxed and spread her legs a little bit wider. He investigated her thoroughly, thrilled with the way she squealed and bucked underneath him.

"I want you," he heard her whisper. "Please, Julian. It's been so long."

These were the words he wanted to hear, and he instantly rose to his knees and maneuvered himself on top of her. She took him in with her body and with her soul as she wrapped her arms and legs around him and he sank down into her depths, the heat of her core blazing against him. He wanted to just stay like that forever, but his body had other plans. His hips moved, and hers easily picked up the rhythm. Their mouths and tongues entwined, and they were like one creature caught in a spiraling moment of ecstasy.

He felt her breathing come more rapidly as she undulated around him, suddenly even wetter and hotter than she had been before. He moaned into her mouth as he came, the years of loneliness and frustration exploding out of him as stars danced around the edges of his vision.

Afterwards, he lay next to her on his side, the back of his finger grazing against her cheek as she smiled up at him. "I know it's you. You're right here next to me, and you're the exact same person I've been dreaming about all these years. But even making love to you doesn't seem like enough to make it real. I'm afraid I'm going to wake up and find out that this has all just been an amazing dream." Julian didn't even want to fall asleep for fear that he would have to come back to reality eventually.

"I understand." She reached up to touch his hair. "I've spent far too many years wondering where you were, and if you were even alive."

With those words, Julian realized it was time to tell her all the things she hadn't been around to see. "Listen, I need to share some things with you. I don't even want to, but it's not fair to leave you in the dark." Doing his best to give her a full account without focusing on too much detail, Julian told her of the War of Storms and how the wizards had jumped in with the ogres to fight against the dragons. He explained the spell that Tazarre had cast and why they could never go back to Charok. With a mix of hope and worry in his chest, he explained how he had come to be the foster father of Kaylee, how the other men had children of their own, and how her own friends' fates were intertwined with the dragons'.

By the time he was done, her pillow was soaked with tears. "I'm sorry that I've upset you, Naomi. I know it's a lot to take in, but you needed to know."

She nodded and wiped at her eyes. "I knew about some of this— vaguely. While in the Otherworld, I sensed that many of the dragons on Charok had been destroyed, and there was a group of dragons who had escaped to Earth, but I didn't know the entire story. And I didn't know that you were one of the dragon refugees." She took a deep breath and raised her eyes to the ceiling, blinking away her tears. "At least I have you, and that's more than I've had in a very long time. And I suppose, from what you're telling me, I'll have a daughter as well."

As much love as Julian had found in Kaylee and Naomi individually, it was nothing compared to what he felt at the idea of having them all together as a family. "Yes. You will. And I can't wait for you to meet her."

Naomi looked as though she was about to respond with something equally mushy, but the look in her eyes suddenly changed, hard and aware, her irises like blue stones.

"Julian. You have to get out of here."

"What? No. I'm not leaving you. Not for anything."

But she was off the bed and yanking her clothes back on, standing still as she listened. "You are. And now. There's no time to mess around."

Getting dressed himself, Julian reached out to her. "Naomi, it's been a long day. I think maybe you just need a little bit of rest."

She slapped his hand away. "No. You need to go. Now. It's for your own safety."

"But if there's some sort of danger, then I should stay." Julian, however, sensed nothing of the kind.

"Okay, okay." Julian finished dressing, wondering what he had done wrong. But it was clear that Naomi wasn't in the mood to answer such questions. He would give her time. That was probably what she needed more than anything. "I'll leave for a bit, but I'll be back in a few hours, Naomi. I need you to know that. I love you." He desperately wanted to kiss her, but the sharp look in her eye stayed him. He left, feeling a heavier weight on his shoulders than he had felt in a long time. He did his best to rig the door shut so it would still be safe while he was gone and exited through the back of the house.

## 7

SHE DIDN'T WANT TO SEND HIM AWAY, BUT IF THERE WAS ANYTHING SHE had learned while she was in the Otherworld, it was to trust her instincts. Making love to Julian had temporarily blinded her to the potential dangers that surrounded them, and she had let herself believe that she was safe now that she was back in the physical realm of Earth.

But something was wrong with that notion. She couldn't tell Julian what it was; those instincts were still in that indecipherable language of the Otherworld. It didn't matter. She only knew there was trouble there, and she had to get him out of the way.

Now, completely alone once again, she stood still in the middle of the room. She heard nothing. Naomi shook her head and drew in a deep breath. Maybe she had imagined it all, her mind unwilling to let go of the images that had danced before her eyes the entire time she had been gone. Being caught in that ether was like one long hallucination where nothing made sense, and she couldn't expect herself to come away from it undamaged.

Naomi made a silent promise to herself to call for Julian later—if she could even remember how to do that—and apologize to him. For now, she needed that nap she had been unable to get earlier. Padding back across the hall, she lay down, closed her eyes, and let her mind wander. Its first instinct was to think of Otherworld. She didn't know what the actual name for it was, only that it wasn't the same as any place she knew and loved. She felt the light and shadow that mingled there, a palpable substance around her that felt like swimming in a murky ocean.

Mixed with these images were ones of her and Julian back on Charok. These were the visions that gave her hope. She remembered how it felt to leap off the top of the mountains and let her body fall through the hot air until it was almost too late to snap her wings open. Julian had been right at her side during that daring stunt, the tips of his emerald wings just barely touching hers. It was a habit he had of always letting her know that he was right there. She hadn't needed him back then the way she did now. Naomi had been a young, confident dragon who—as of yet—had no reason to worry about life or what the future would bring. But still she had felt a certain sort of comfort in knowing she had such a sweet, steady love at her side. She let herself fall into the vision just as she had fallen in real life, with a wild sense of abandon.

But the back of her mind continued to fight her, and she was yanked back to consciousness. This time, she knew exactly what was going on. "I know you're there," she said to the air around her. The day was beginning to fade, sending long shadows across the floor, but there was another shadow in the room that she couldn't see. "I can sense you."

The response was there, but it wasn't an audible one. It was more like a deep rumble in the back of her mind, almost a laugh.

"You came through the portal with me." Her voice echoed in the empty house as she prowled down the hallway to the living room, certain she would find this other spirit soon. Its vibration was a familiar one that she had sensed in the Otherworld, but it hadn't been given a physical body in the same way that she had. Naomi wondered how it had survived, but that was a question for another time.

Another rumble sounded and she noticed a movement out of the corner of her eye, but as soon as she turned, it was gone.

"Leave here!" she commanded. "You don't belong. You're not from this place."

There was another flicker out of the corner of her eye, but this time she was careful not to look at it straight on. She followed it through the house, unsure of how to get through to this thing or even figure out exactly what it was. It moved faster as she pursued it, slipping through the pane of glass in the picture window at the front of the house and scuttling off into the growing darkness.

Giving up and tired beyond any sense of worry, Naomi went back to bed. This time, she actually fell asleep.

# 8

SHE HAD SENT HIM AWAY, BUT JULIAN FOUND THAT HE COULDN'T STAY away for very long. He needed Naomi in the same way that he needed air or food, but perhaps even more desperately. She was like his very lifeblood, and knowing that she was once again on the same planet as he was meant that he simply couldn't live without her.

After picking up Kaylee, he drove back to Autumn's house and pulled up in the drive right behind Autumn's car. The three women were just getting out.

"What are you doing here?" Summer asked with a smile. "We've got some amazing news for you and the other guys."

"I know." Julian hated to ruin the surprise, and he could see why they would be so happy to tell them that there finally was another dragon on Earth, but it was what it was. "I've already seen her."

"You have?" Autumn folded her arms in front of her chest, looking offended. "How?"

He did his best to explain, feeling a flush burn at his cheeks as he did so. Julian wasn't really in the habit of announcing his feelings aloud, and then there was admitting that he had broken into Autumn's house without her permission. "We're linked from our time on Charok, you see. I knew as soon as she came back. I mean, I didn't understand it, but I still knew. I could sense her presence, which I haven't been able to do in a long time."

Autumn gave a nod, Leah smiled, and Summer was jumping up and down and clapping her hands. "Julian! That's so exciting! I had no idea! Honestly, I didn't even think about her as a potential mate for you. I was just to happy to have her back."

He blushed a little harder. "So am I. And I can't thank you three enough for what you've done. But she doesn't seem to be quite the same. She was absolutely terrified when I found her."

"Most women would be if a man broke down the front door and charged into the house." She frowned at the splinters she noticed on the front step. "I wonder how many times I'm going to have to replace this thing."

He cringed. "Yeah...sorry about that. I'll pay for the repairs needed. But I have a feeling it wasn't my grand entrance that scared her." He could see her point, but in his mind, there was something deeper. "It was different. She got past it, and we managed to...spend some time together. But then it was like a switch was flipped, and she went right back into that defensive mode. She wouldn't even let me stay with her, insisting that it was for my own safety. It didn't make any sense, but I'm very worried about her." If what Naomi had told him was true and the three women had been her friends before she had died, then perhaps they knew her even better than he did.

Autumn reached out and touched his arm. "She's had a pretty crazy day, and even the last few years have been rough for her. Naomi probably just needs some time to adjust. I thought she seemed a little confused, myself. She mentioned something about there being shadowy creatures in the Otherworld, so that's bound to have affected her. Maybe there's something you can do to help reacquaint her with what normal life is like here."

"I've got Kaylee in the car, and I thought about picking up Naomi and bringing her back to my place for dinner. Just something nice and quiet. I don't think she's ready for a restaurant just yet." He would have loved to take her out to a fancy, romantic place with just the two of them, but for the moment, it would be simpler to go home and throw a few steaks in a cast iron skillet.

Leah smiled at him as she carried a duffel bag around Autumn's car and handed it to Julian. "That sounds like a lovely welcome-home dinner. She's also going to need a chance to go shopping for clothes, but us girls can help her with that. For the moment, I've picked up a few essentials and grabbed several outfits from my closet. Go ahead and take it with you."

He took the bag and realized just what all of this meant. He actually had Naomi back. It wasn't even going to be the same as it had been on Charok, because they wouldn't be sneaking off for secret dates. She would be living with him, or at least he hoped so. That wasn't even something they'd had a chance to discuss. There was so much to be addressed still.

When he made his way into the house, Naomi was just waking up. She still looked worn out, but she gave him a sleepy nod when he asked her to come back to his place for dinner. His heart jumped with excitement as he opened the back door of the car. "Naomi, I'd like you to meet Kaylee."

The light that had faded from Naomi's eyes was suddenly alight again. She instantly dropped to her knees and reached out to delicately touch Kaylee's hand. "Hi there, sweetheart. I've heard so much about you."

Kaylee grinned, her green eyes taking in every aspect of Naomi's face. "Pretty!"

"Why, thank you. I think you're very pretty, too. I hope that you and I can be good friends someday. Your daddy has asked me to come back to your place to have dinner. Would that be alright with you?"

The little girl nodded, reaching out with one tiny hand to gently touch Naomi's hair. It was a beautiful sight, and one that Julian had never thought he would get to see. Maybe things weren't going to be too difficult after all.

His love was quiet on the drive over, her body stiff in the passenger seat and her eyes watching everything carefully as they passed. At first, Julian speculated that she was just getting used to the sight of Earth again, but as they approached the other side of town, he realized there was something more to it. It was as if she were watching for someone. He opened his mouth to ask her about it and then quickly shut it again. Naomi would tell him when she was ready.

Arriving at his house, Julian's stomach crunched in on itself. He had no reason to really be nervous. Naomi probably wouldn't care too much about what his place looked like, and he knew there was plenty of room for both of them. It was a modern affair, very unlike Holden's big mansion or Beau's craftsman-style bungalow, but he had chosen it with the thought of a future family in mind. And if she didn't like the color of the walls or the floor, then he would gladly change it for her.

Still, there was something nerve-racking about the whole idea. It was as though he was a little bird and had built a nest just for her, but if she didn't like it enough, she might not stay. "I'll give you a tour first, so you know where everything is. I want you to be comfortable here. Then I'll start cooking."

Naomi nodded, and she looked in each room as he showed it to her, but she didn't seem all that interested. It wasn't until they reached Kaylee's room, right across the hall from his, that her eyes lit up again. "What a beautiful room you have, Kaylee," she said with genuine awe. "You must have a lot of fun in here."

The little girl wriggled in Julian's arms, and he obligingly set her down. She toddled to her toy box and pulled out a doll, holding it in the air proudly as she brought it back to show Naomi.

"That's a very nice doll. Is she your favorite?"

At this prompt, Kaylee went to her bed and yanked down an old ratty teddy bear. Julian had bought it for her as soon as she had hatched, and it showed evidence of all the love she had given it.

Despite its appearance, Naomi readily took the teddy bear, gave it a hug, and handed it back to Kaylee. "It's absolutely lovely."

"Play?"

"Maybe in a little bit," Julian answered. "I've got to go cook dinner. You go ahead and play." He took Naomi by the waist and escorted her to the kitchen.

"You're smiling an awful lot," she noted.

He was glad to see the warm look in her eyes. It drifted in and out, and he had his concerns that she didn't really want to be there with him or that she was somehow disappointed in him, but then she would look at him like that again. "How can I not smile? You're here. I never thought I would see you again, and here you are in the flesh."

"Well, new flesh." Naomi looked down at her body. "It was a spell Autumn performed, since my original body had died. It felt strange at first, but I'm getting used to it."

"I think it feels quite nice." Julian waggled his eyebrows suggestively before turning to get the steak out of the fridge. "I had no idea you were so good with children."

"What do you mean?" Naomi took a seat at the breakfast bar where she could watch him make his preparations.

Julian shrugged and pulled a pan down from the rack. "You just seem to take so naturally to talking to Kaylee, like it's easier than having a conversation with another adult. I'm not complaining, I just think it's interesting."

Naomi looked down at the counter top. "I guess there's just less pressure. Seeing you again makes me happier than I can even explain, but it's also hard. There's so much explaining to do. I know there will be things to decide, and I'm not sure I'm ready to make any decisions. With Kaylee, there isn't any of that."

"She seems to like you," Julian noted. He knew they were all still in their honeymoon period, but at least they were off to a good start. "And as far as decisions, don't feel like you have to make up your mind about anything right away. We all understand that things have been difficult for you. I'm hopeful that you'll live here, but you can have all the time in the world to think about it." If he had it his way, he would have her under his roof and in his bed from there on out, but he didn't want to chase her off.

Her cheeks flushed. "I hadn't even thought about where I would live yet. Isn't that silly?"

"No. I think that just means you know you have plenty of friends here, and lots of options. I'm sure Autumn would be glad to let you stay at her place, as would any of the others." *But your rightful place is here with me.* He wouldn't say it out loud, but she knew he felt it.

Their conversation seemed to stagnate for a bit. Julian occupied himself with warming up the pan, tossing a salad, and browning dinner rolls in the oven. This wasn't anything like their experiences together back on Charok, and they had each spent their time on Earth separately. This was a situation unlike any he had been in before, so he tried to keep the conversation going by catching her up on everything that had happened since he had arrived.

"I'd really like for you to meet the other guys. You won't have much choice anyway, since they've all paired off with your friends, but I think you'll really like them."

"Oh!"

"What is it?" Julian turned to see Naomi staring off into the distance, but she looked surprised more than scared this time.

Her gaze slowly drifted to him and focused, bringing her mostly back to the present moment. "When Varhan sent me here, he said I would be changing the lives of others as well. He said three others would meet the ones they were meant to be with, and that I would be changing their lives for the better, even while I saved my own. Maybe he actually meant Autumn, Summer, and Leah."

Julian set down the pair of tongs he had just flipped the steak with. "That's interesting. That means he would have to have known that he would send the rest of us to Earth as well. Could it somehow have been all part of the same spell?" He had tried so hard to figure out just what Varhan had done to send them to Earth, but he hadn't known that Naomi was already there. Was that the part he was missing? Did it matter, since he knew they would never go back to Charok again?

"I always had a feeling that Varhan knew much more than he was willing to tell. He seemed so wise for his age, and the things he spoke of weren't typical to the ways of wizards. Granted, he was the only one I knew well."

Reaching across the counter, Julian wrapped his hand over hers. Naomi's fingers were long and cool, and they made the slightest movement upward to touch his. "I guess it doesn't matter, since we're all here now." He turned back to the stove, feeling a sense of peace and comfort that Earth had never afforded him before. It would be a process to get to know Naomi again, and to understand what she was like there as opposed to how she had been on Charok. It could even prove to be a difficult adjustment. But he loved her just the same, and they would get through it, no matter what.

## 9

JULIAN LOOKED SO COMFORTABLE THERE IN HIS KITCHEN, COOKING AND talking as though this was something they did together all the time. It was nice, but in a way, it only made her feel more uncertain about their future together. He was confident that everything would be alright; he exuded it like cologne.

But she wasn't as certain.

Earth wasn't quite the same as she had remembered it. Naomi had never felt as though she completely belonged there, but she had never felt such a sense of impending danger before. Now, it was like she could do nothing but look over her shoulder. Julian had noticed, she was sure. How could he not after she had thrown him out of Autumn's house? But he hadn't brought it up, and she was content to let the subject go for the time being.

There at Julian's, she knew she should have no reason to be scared. She pulled in a deep breath and focused on the sound of his voice, if not the words. Naomi felt that she needed something to keep her rooted there; something that would keep her from feeling as though she might float away if she didn't hold on just right.

"You should have seen Beau change a diaper for the first time. He was sure he could do it without any issues, but it didn't go so well for him." Julian laughed as he plated up a steak and turned around. His smile instantly faded. "What's wrong?"

Naomi's spine felt stiff. The apparition was back again. She hadn't seen it, but she could feel it. It lurked somewhere nearby, so close and yet so hard to see. Was it in her mind? Had she been seeing things? Reality was impossible for her to grasp right now. "It's here."

"What?" Julian's green eyes, which looked so much like Kaylee's, searched the room. "I don't see anything."

Her breathing was ragged now, as though the air had become too thick for her lungs. "I don't really know. I think something came through with me when Summer pulled me over from the Otherworld."

"What *kind* of something?"

"Something evil. Julian, it was in Autumn's house earlier today, and now it's here. You and Kaylee have got to leave!" With a sudden realization that nearly knocked her off her stool, Naomi remembered that she wasn't completely helpless in this situation. There had been long periods of doing nothing in the Otherworld, but she had also learned a few tricks to keep the shadow creatures at bay. She wasn't certain if they would even work there on Earth, but maybe she could try them.

"Now, hold on. I'm not going to leave this time, no matter what you say." Julian flicked off the stove with an angry gesture. "If there's some sort of danger here, then we're in it together."

"But you don't understand!" Naomi was on her feet now, a sense of panic expanding in her chest like a balloon. "Whatever this is, I brought it here. It's my fault, and I need to take care of it."

Julian came around the counter and took her by the shoulders, his eyes intense as he stared into hers. "You were alone for a long time. I get it. I know it's going to be hard for you to get used to it, but you *aren't* alone here. You've got me. You've got Autumn, Summer and Leah. Even though you haven't met them yet, you also have Holden, Beau and Xander. We're all here for you and for each other. If there's something going on, then we'll get everyone together and figure out how to handle it."

"I...I don't know if we can." The sense of dread that had been tingling against her spine was now a crushing pressure. Naomi turned to face it.

There was a small triangle of a shadow in the far corner of the dining room. To ordinary eyes, it probably seemed like an innocent enough space where the light from the fixture in the center of the room couldn't quite get past the china cabinet. But to Naomi, she knew it was more. As if she were willing it to life, the shadow began to take on a new shape. It bulged in the center, pushing upward and out into the light. It grew larger, the top of it forming into a head with wide shoulders. Soon enough, it reached all the way to the ceiling, a shadow so dark, it absorbed the light that attempted to bounce off it.

Naomi caught her breath as she took in the long, pointed horns that curled down on either side of its face and its slitted eyes. They were barely distinguishable from the rest of the form, only a slightly different hue of murkiness from the rest of him. He had less of a form as the shadow reached the floor, as though he had wrapped himself in a cloak of darkness.

"You see it now, don't you?" She pressed her back against the breakfast bar, putting her arm out to keep Julian from getting any closer to the creature.

But Julian showed no signs of seeing anything. "Naomi, we're completely alone. There's nothing here."

That deep rumble she had heard in Autumn's house was now a deafening thunder in her ears. "He's been here too long, and he no longer knows how to see things that aren't in physical forms."

"Who are you?" Naomi demanded. She had to get to the bottom of this.

"Who is who?" Julian sounded desperate.

The demon moved forward, sending a blast of cold air through the room. "I am the reason that there are no more of your kind on Charok. And I will be the reason that there are no more of your kind on Earth." His voice was heavy and low, like the sound of an avalanche.

"What do you mean?" But Naomi thought she already understood what he meant, she just hoped she was wrong.

"I am Tazarre!" the creature roared. "I paid the ultimate sacrifice when I cast the spell that killed all the dragons on Charok, and now I'm here to finish the job."

Tears streamed down her face, but Naomi barely felt them. How could this have happened?

"Naomi? What's going on?" Julian was at her side, his thumb wiping a tear from her jaw. "Whatever it is, we'll get everyone together and figure it out."

"No!" She shoved him away. That was exactly what Tazarre wanted. If all the dragons were together in one room, and with the bonus of a couple of witches and a psychic, then it would be a walk in the park for this evil wizard to finish what he had started on the other side of the universe.

"You knew I was there," it growled. "You could sense me the entire time we were in the Otherworld. You should have done something about it then. But you were a weakling, just as you are now. Just as all your friends are. It will be simple enough."

No. It couldn't have been him; surely, she would have known if there was something that terrible with her. Everything in the Otherworld was jumbled and nonsensical, and it was nearly impossible to straighten it out and force it into the organization that Earth life demanded. And now that this thing was there and even Julian couldn't see it, she wasn't sure exactly how she was going to fight it off.

"Naomi? Please talk to me. Tell me what's happening."

"You're only going to think I'm crazy," she whispered. Naomi moved slowly away from Julian, testing the beast. It followed her with its eyes, barely even noticing that Julian was still in the room. She headed for the sliding glass door just off the back of the house, never turning away from Tazarre as she grasped the handle and pushed it open.

"Where do you think you're going, little dragon? My fingers have been itching to wrap around your throat ever since I came to the Otherworld." It glided forward on its shadowy, imperceptible feet.

"Then why didn't you do it then?" she challenged. "You were there. You know how it was. You could have killed me several times over." More than once, Naomi had seen figures of light fall to those of shadow. It was a distant, abstract thing, but still she had known what was happening. Such events sent a shiver of fear that made its rounds through all the innocents in the ether. Naomi stepped out onto the back porch, the warm air wrapping around her like a thick, suffocating blanket.

Tazarre laughed as he slid along in her wake. "You already know the answer to that. If I had taken you then, I never would have had the chance to come here with you. I bided my time, waiting until the very last moment to attach myself to you as you went sliding back to Earth. Tell me, do your friends know what you've done for them?"

"Naomi!" Julian still stood by the breakfast bar, a desperate look on his face.

For a moment, she was terrified that he would try to follow her. The demon stood between the two dragons, his dark form taking up the entire doorway out onto the porch. She didn't want to know what would happen if Julian got too close to Tazarre. "Just stay there, Julian."

"I don't know why you're trying so hard to protect your little friend," the demon grumbled. "I'll come back and get him when I'm ready. But right now, my mouth is watering for you. I want to have your bones crunching between my teeth and your blood running down my throat." Tazarre was out of the house now, the two of them standing in the back yard.

If anyone was watching from their windows, they would see nothing more than Naomi slowly walking backwards down the path that led from the covered back porch to the main area of the backyard. They might wonder who she was, never having seen her at Julian's house before. They might even wonder why she was walking back-wards instead of looking where she was going, especially in the dark, but they wouldn't see that she was trying to evade a demon. Even Naomi had a difficult time seeing him in the dim light. Julian insisted that Naomi wasn't alone anymore, but he was so wrong.

Part of her wanted to just fall to the ground in tears and give up. She had suffered for so long, constantly evading the darkness in the Otherworld and wondering if her presence there would ever end. It had, but she was no closer to being okay.

The other part of her, however, knew that she couldn't do that. She was responsible for Tazarre being there. She was the one who had endangered her friends and other dragons. At the very least, she could lead the phantom away from them. "If you want me, then come and get me."

Naomi finally turned her back to Tazarre. She felt the spread of her wings as her feet flew forward, lifting off the ground before she managed to complete her shift. Her partially-human body was heavy and awkward, and the absence of a tail threatened to send her head-first back to the ground. But her legs grew shorter and thicker, her toes curling into claws. She felt the extension of her spine as her tail regen-erated, swiftly compensating for the fact that she was already in the air. By the time she turned to look at the demon, she was not just turning her head, but snaking it around on her long, elegant neck.

Unwilling to let his victim get away so easily, Tazarre did exactly what she hoped he would do. Great dark wings expanded from behind him, filling up the yard as their feathered tips reached into the sky. He ascended with ease as he flew after her, a single wing stroke sending him rocketing through the air.

Naomi hadn't flown in a long time, not since before she had gotten ill on Charok. Earth had healed her body, as Varhan had promised, but now she could only hope that the new body she had been given would keep up with her demands. She faced forward once again, stretching her neck and tail and tucking her legs beneath her as her wings forcefully pumped through the air. "I'll sacrifice myself if it keeps him away from the others," she whispered to herself.

# 10

---

It didn't take long for the others to arrive. There had been no question as to where they would meet or just how urgent the matter was. Holden had heard the panic in Julian's voice, and now all the dragons and their mates were sitting in his dining room. It was well past bedtime for the children now, but they were all playing amicably in Kaylee's room. The steak dinner Julian had cooked had grown cold on the counter.

He did his best to explain what had happened. "I just stood there like an idiot, watching her fly off over the neighborhood. I didn't know what else to do. She was so insistent that there was something in the room with us, and she was even talking to it. By the time she left, I don't even know if she could hear my voice anymore." The others were sitting, but he paced the floor in front of the breakfast bar. He couldn't sit still as long as he knew Naomi was out there, possibly in danger—or possibly going insane.

"It's okay," Holden assured him. "We'll find her, and we'll figure this out."

"You said this was a demon?" Autumn asked, her eyes sharp. "Did she give it a name or say anything else about it?"

"Just that it had followed her here from the Otherworld." Julian wondered how things could have gone so wrong so quickly.

"Oh, no." The whispered voice had come from Summer, who had

suddenly gone several shades paler. "I should have said something last night."

Autumn leaned across the table. "What?" she snapped.

Summer floundered, her hands moving through the air and her lips trying to find the words. "I never expected to be the one to go into the trance. We had all agreed it would be Autumn. But then I found myself just sliding down into that other world, like a hole had opened up in the bottom of my brain and I had no choice. I didn't mind, because as long as we got Naomi back, that was the only thing that really mattered. The drums were serving as a line to bring me back when I was ready."

"That all sounds pretty normal from what I recall reading," Autumn replied.

"Okay." Summer pulled in a deep breath and let it out slowly. "It was like I dove down into the Otherworld. Everything was thick and blurry, and there were shadows and light, just like if I was swimming in a pond with a bunch of shade trees over it. Naomi was like this brilliant burst of light, but there was darkness all around her. As soon as I grabbed her hand—or whatever you would call the equivalent of a hand in a place like that, since nothing has any real form—I felt something cold and icy against my spine. I just assumed it was a part of being there, and I didn't think about it at all. Not until we'd had some time to recover. I was going to ask Naomi about it when we got back to Autumn's house, but then we found out about her and Julian and everything just went from there. I figured there would be time later, once we were all rested."

"Don't blame yourself." Leah sat next to Holden, her face lined with concern. "None of us really knew what we were getting into when we brought her back. It was one big experiment."

Autumn was on her feet now. "There's no need for blame," she agreed. "There's only time right now for action. We brought this thing into the world with a shamanic ritual, right?"

"Right," the other two women chimed in.

"Then maybe there's a chance that we can send him back with one." Her eyes were alight, and she was making a slow circle around the table as she thought. "Clearly, the trance that Summer went into was a powerful one."

"But dragging her back down into the Otherworld could be

dangerous," Xander protested, his fist curled against the wooden surface of the table. "What if we lose her?"

"You won't," Summer promised. "Now that I've done it once, I know more about what to expect. I'll be in complete control."

"The rest of us aren't completely useless, either," Beau volunteered. "We've got plenty of firepower to attack him with. There's just the matter of finding him."

"I don't think that will be a problem." Ever since she had left, Julian had been resisting the urge to go flying off into the night sky afterward. It was only Kaylee that kept him from such a foolish errand, and he was grateful. It would be much better if he had his friends at his back. "I can find her."

Leah cleared her throat. "I took the liberty of calling the Rochesters on the way over here, just in case. They said they can come right over to watch the kids if we need them." The couple ran the local print shop and had always been sympathetic to both Leah and her psychic powers and the twins with their new age shop. They had met the dragons at a party last year, and they were now the closest 'normal' friends of the group.

Julian looked into the eyes of each of his friends and saw the same determination he felt in his heart reflected back at him. "It looks like we do."

———

THE SKY WAS BEGINNING to lighten. It would soon be morning, and people would be getting up out of bed and getting ready for work. Somewhere, out on the edge of town, someone might be stretching as she got out of bed, pausing by the window to admire the sunrise. She might be surprised to see four dragons go whizzing by her window, the early light reflecting off their scales. That would be a surprise enough, but it would surely be even more of a shock to see that three of those dragons had riders.

"How come we've never done this before?" Autumn shouted over the wind to the gold dragon between her legs. "This is amazing!"

"Silly me. I thought I was giving you enough of a ride as it was," Beau retorted.

"Get a room, you two," Leah said with a giggle. She was perched on top of Holden, his red scales brilliant in the sun. But she looked as though she was enjoying this as well. After all, there wasn't much they could do until they actually found Naomi.

Summer was on Xander's back, her hands running slowly down his copper hide as though she was sending him messages through her fingers. Her head was tipped back and her blonde hair streamed out behind her. With her eyes shut, she looked as though she was already slipping into the shamanic trance they were all relying on. She had one of the drums strapped over her back.

Julian, flying solo at the head of the group, felt a bolt of loneliness in his heart. He'd had Naomi back, and now she was gone once again. The rest of the crew seemed confident in their ability to find her and save her from this beast that had followed her to Earth, but the only thing Julian really knew was that he couldn't survive without her once again. It would break his heart beyond the point of bearing.

He spread his wings wide, letting the wind lift him higher as they zoomed past the city limits and the trees underneath them began to thicken. Now that he was back in dragon form, he knew he had a better chance of finding her. Every sense was trained on her, listening for her heartbeat or the sound of her lungs, his nostrils flaring as they sought her scent, his very blood coursing only for her. If this was what the others had felt when they'd met their mates, then he almost felt sorry for them.

"Are we at least headed in the right direction?" Xander asked. They had made their best guess based on the orientation of Naomi's escape and the fact that she seemed to want to keep away from all the rest of them. It would be just as difficult to find her in a rural area as it would be to find her somewhere in town, unfortunately.

"I think so," Julian replied. He had been wondering if the faint clues of her scent that he'd caught had just been his imagination, but she was growing more solid in his mind as they left town. He closed his eyes, listening for her with every sense he had and letting his body do the work. He felt himself drift slightly east, and he didn't fight it. The others followed suit.

As the rural homes on smaller plots of land grew into large farms and then dwindled into forest preserve, Julian felt the raw beast inside him suddenly come to life. His claws itched to dig into flesh, and he desperately wanted to burn down anything that got in his way. "She's close."

Swooping down in a dangerous nosedive, Julian picked up on her scent. It was heady, making him feel drunk, and he had to get to her as fast as possible. Once he did, he only wanted to scoop her up and take off with her, carrying her to some far-off place where they wouldn't need to worry about anything. But there was no such place on Earth right now, and they had work to do.

He landed with a thunk in front of a bluff. The rounded rocks created a sheer face tangled with vines and weeds. At one time, this edifice may have looked out over a lake or river that had long ago been lost. Julian headed forward even before he heard the others landing behind him. "Naomi!" he roared. "I know you're in there. You can't hide from me, and I want to help you."

A long blue muzzle poked out from the dark entrance of a cave. This side of the bluffs was still in shadow, the sun not yet high enough to reach down into the valley it formed. "Go away, Julian. You don't belong here."

He turned around. Holden caught his eye and nodded, urging him forward with a tip of his narrow head on his long neck.

"I do," Julian affirmed, still coming closer. He didn't think the cave could be very deep. If it was, Naomi probably already would have buried herself in it. "We're here to help you."

She thrust her head out all the way now, the deep blue stones of her eyes hard. "I left to keep you safe," Naomi yelled. "That thing is following me, and I'm the reason it's here. Now go away before it comes back and finds you all right here where it wants you."

Julian couldn't say he was unafraid of death, but at that moment, he would have gladly died at Naomi's side. "No one should have to fight their demons alone, and neither do you. I'm not going anywhere."

"Julian—"

"Don't bother trying to argue with me." He was at the mouth of the cave now, and he could just see the outline of her body in the darkness. "I love you, Naomi. You can't run from this thing forever, and you can't defeat it by yourself."

"But you don't understand," she insisted. "This isn't just some evil creature. This... this is Tazarre."

"What?" Julian's head snapped back slightly on his neck. That name wasn't one he had ever expected to hear again. "Surely, you don't mean—"

"I do. He told me that he was the one responsible for poisoning all the dragons on Charok. He was killed in the process, and that's how he ended up in the Otherworld. But he's here now, and the only thing he wants is to finish the job. I don't care if he kills me; I've already died. But I can't let him kill you, too."

The confidence he had been feeling drained from his system. Julian gestured with a wing for the others to join them, and he told them Naomi's news. "This is even worse than we imagined."

"It doesn't have to be," Autumn said stubbornly. "Knowing a thing's name actually makes it easier to take down, not harder. We just can't let ourselves be affected by that knowledge."

"That's easier said than done, for those of us who were there," Beau replied. "Tazarre is a thing of nightmares. We haven't even told the children about him."

"And with a little bit of luck, you won't have to." Summer, who always looked so peaceful and pleasant, jutted out her chin as she whipped the drum from her back and looked at the dragon in the cave. "Naomi, tell us where to find this thing."

"I don't know for certain, but I'm sure it will be back." Her wings shuddered against each other. "He's powerful, so much more than you probably imagine."

As if on cue, a darkness blotted out what little sunshine they had. It slowly slipped down the rockface, so massive that Julian had to take a step back to see the entire thing. It was no wonder Naomi had acted the way she had when the demon had shown up in his dining room; Tazarre was a terrifying sight. He'd been only a shadow to Naomi back then—and invisible to Julian—but now, he somehow had a depth to him that seemed infinite. As his massive form slowly descended down the bluff, the very oxygen seemed to be sucked from the air. "I can see him now."

"I see it, too," Holden gasped.

Tazarre bellowed a laugh like a collision of planets. "I've grown stronger. I'm getting used to this planet, and I think it suits me. Maybe once I'm done slaying your lot, I'll stay here and see what I can accomplish with the humans. I have a feeling they're a weak species."

An odd noise struck Julian's ears, and he realized that Summer had started drumming. She sat on the ground at the mouth of the cave with her eyes closed and her hands moving rhythmically. Her eyes were closed, which was probably a good precaution.

Leah, who had been standing just behind Holden's wings, ran to her side with her own drum and joined in.

Tazarre watched them for a moment before he let out another roaring laugh. "Just as I suspected! Not only weak, but ignorant, too! At least the dragons on Charok had put up a bit of a fight and made things a little more fun." Two long shapes detached from the shadow and became arms with ghastly hands. They waved through the air, red sparks flying from their newly-formed fingertips.

"I don't think we have time to stand around and wait for the trance to start!" Beau shot into the air, puffing out his chest before unleashing a massive fireball. It struck the evil wizard and gave him only a moment's pause before he resumed his efforts.

Julian lifted himself on his wings. Holden was at the monster's face, filling it with a blasting heat, so Julian swung around behind. He pushed his body forward and his wings back, reached out into the air with his claws as he descended onto the back of Tazarre's head. He felt flesh under his grasp, but not like any other flesh he had encountered. It was cold and almost spongy, and the small amount of blood that spurted out of it was just as black as the rest of his body. Tazarre shook his horned head and sent Julian careening toward the cliff face.

Catching himself just in time, Julian rode the wind current up into the air and turned to look down. This was going to be a long and difficult fight.

## 11

Naomi shot forth from the cave, charging with her full strength. The men were in the air, but that gave her the perfect opportunity to fight from the ground. She tucked her head, slicked back her wings, and launched herself forward with every muscle in her legs and back. Slamming into Tazarre was like hitting the rock wall behind him, and it rang through her head and sent her reeling.

Naomi stumbled backwards and turned away from the demon to gather herself. Why did Julian have to show up? She was the one who had brought this thing into the world with her, and she was trying to protect him. Didn't he understand that? And bringing the other dragons along meant that Tazarre had them all together in one space, with a few bonus humans he could kill right along with them.

Summer and Leah were still beating away on their drums. Summer had a look of peace on her face, but Leah's brow was furrowed in concentration. Naomi recognized the sounds they were making; these were the same drums that had thundered through her soul as Summer was bringing her back from the Otherworld. She suddenly understood what they were trying to do, but she didn't think it was going to work.

She wound around then to Autumn, who stood just behind Leah and Summer with her hands out and her fingers spread. "He's too strong, and there are too many distractions. You'll never be able to drag him back there, and if you do, he'll keep Summer with him. We have to stop this and find something else to try."

Autumn kept her pose, but she nodded her head toward the other dragons. They were buzzing around the beast's head, blasting and tearing at him. The sun now filled the valley, making their metallic scales shine. They looked like robotic dragons, a wondrous sight if it were only under other circumstances. "They're giving him some pretty major distractions, and I'm sending my power to Summer to help her get into her trance. We'll get this done, Naomi. I know we will."

Naomi opened her mouth to protest, but she took a step back and realized what a magnificent scene she had before her. It didn't matter that she had ordered Julian to go away or that she had told her friends their efforts were useless. They were there for her, not just to protect their own lives, but to let her know she wasn't standing alone. Julian, in all his viridescent glory, was fighting for her just as he said he would. He was a gentle man, but he was a fierce warrior.

Still, red energy crackled between Tazarre's fingers. It grew, coalescing into a ball of electricity that steadily grew bigger and brighter. It was a horrifying image, but it brought the memory of a different one to the forefront of Naomi's mind.

*She couldn't tell how long she had been in the Otherworld, because every second seemed like an eternity. Things moved differently there, including time. Her body was an unformed thing, floating in the murky world of ether that surrounded her. She was vaguely aware of the others, who came and went as orbs of lightness or darkness.*

*These, at least, were easy to distinguish. There were numerous shades of light beings, some brilliantly white and others a gentle glow, but the dark ones were nothing but the absolute absence of light. They hung on the fringes, waiting until they had the right opportunity. They gnashed at the light creatures with their teeth and broke them down, using them for fuel. Sometimes, when they had a particularly large or powerful adversary, they actually worked in teams. It was a horrifying thing to see the dark beings converge, but their cooperation only ever lasted for a short amount of time. Once their prey had been taken down, they turned to target each other.*

*Naomi had managed to stay out of the way at first, but it was only a matter of time before one of the shadow creatures noticed her. She could hear its thoughts as it approached, feel the hunger it had for her energy. It floated closer and closer, and she knew what fate she would meet. She'd seen it happen hundreds of times already, and now she would be the power that kept some evil creature alive. Naomi pulled all her energy inwards, terrified of what was about to happen, and when the being formed a gaping hole with which to eat her, a brilliant white beam of light shot it backwards.*

*Naomi looked, sure that she had been mistaken, but the black being was in full retreat.*

*After that, she did her best to pay attention to the energy she emitted. It had come because she was scared, but over time, she learned to focus it and use it. The dark ones stayed away; perhaps they heard of her power. The light ones gathered around her, and so her time in the Otherworld was slightly better than it had been before. But even the 'good' creatures were still only near her because they wanted what she had.*

REALIZING THAT HER PHYSICAL BODY, dragon or not, wasn't enough to maim Tazarre, Naomi sprang into the sky. She swooped between the other dragons, careful to avoid their swiftly beating wings. The others were building fire in their chests, filling up the special cavities within their reptilian bodies with the hottest flames they could generate, but Naomi was filing hers with something else. She pulled in all the energy, frustration and fear that this creature had caused. She added to it the pain and loneliness of being stuck in the Otherworld.

On top of that, she piled the sorrow of knowing that everyone back on Charok was gone.

As she swept into the fight, she balled it together and fired. The blast blew her backwards, her wings folding in front of her face. She could barely see, and she sped back with such velocity, she couldn't get her wings around to lift her weight.

Naomi fell toward the ground, watching in slow motion as a massive wall of white and blue raced through the sky toward the demon, spreading out like fireworks and cascading down over his head. Tazarre paid it little attention at first, instead knocking Xander aside as he tried to dig his teeth into the evil wizard's wrist. But where the dazzling sparks fell onto his obsidian hide, they burned down into his skin, sizzling away at his flesh and sending small plumes of smoke into the air. Tazarre writhed with the sudden shock of the pain, and the sphere of red that had been building between his fingers suddenly dissipated.

It was good. It was what she had hoped for. But still she couldn't gain control of her wings. She fell like a stone.

Until she was suddenly hurtling up again, strong arms around her middle. "I don't know what that was," Julian said from just behind her ear, "but I sure as hell hope you can do it again!"

"I can't," she gasped, suddenly realizing just how taxing that burst of light had been. "I can't do it again. I don't even know if I can stand up."

Julian set her down gently on the ground. His claws clicked gently against her cheeks as he looked into her eyes, making sure she was alright. "You'll be fine. You have to be. We all have to be."

She watched him soar back into the air, her heart breaking all over again. What use was she if she was only good for one shot?

A cool hand, a human one, touched her shoulder. It was Autumn. "He's right. We must keep fighting, no matter what. Tell me how you did that."

"I don't really know. It was just something I used to do when I was in the Otherworld. I wasn't even sure if it would work here. And it took everything out of me." Her muscles felt as though they had turned to liquid.

Autumn's green eyes glittered. "If you can get yourself in the air and focus on what you need to do, I'll take care of the rest."

"But don't you need to help them?" Naomi looked over Autumn's shoulder to Summer and Leah, who still drummed away. The beats filled the air, though she had hardly noticed them while she had showered her light onto Tazarre. Summer's eyes were closed, but she didn't look as though she was in any sort of trance.

"I'll figure it out. I'm not sure how much good I'm doing her right now anyway, since she's still in our world. What we do know is that whatever you did seemed to work, and we need to expand on that. Just go, and don't worry about a thing." Autumn trotted back to the other two women, a bounce in her step.

Naomi knew she was right. Summoning the last of her strength, she pushed herself back into the air. Julian gave her a glance over his shoulder, clearly worried about her, but since she was in the air, he continued to fight. Naomi stayed a little back from the fray, trying to focus her mind once again. She felt some of that white energy building, but it wasn't nearly as much as she'd had before. Apparently, her first blast had left her with little to commit.

Just as she was about to give up and start fighting with her claws, she felt something crackle in her veins. It was a blue light this time, one that she didn't recognize as being her own. It vibrated through her blood and out into her muscles, building a shield around the cavity in her chest. With a grin, Naomi understood what was happening. Autumn was sending her energy to Naomi, just as she had promised.

Naomi closed her eyes for a moment, trying to summon that ball of light again. But it was hard to do with her friends being knocked around by the demon. Even more distracting was the thrilling sensation of Autumn's power in her own body. It was good to know she had friends, but it was almost too much excitement for her to bear.

A voice sounded inside her head. *Concentrate. You can do this, Naomi.*

It was Leah, reaching out with her mind and communicating with her. Naomi still heard the drums on the ground below, so at least she knew they hadn't given up their own plans just to help her. *I can't. I'm not angry anymore. I'm not even scared. I don't understand it.*

A tickle went through her mind that could have been a laugh. *It's because we're all here. That's okay. Use it. Use the knowledge that you're not alone. Pull your energy from us.*

*I don't know if it will work!* A volley of hatred and violence would probably be far more effective than one of love and joy.

*Try it anyway, Naomi. It's at least worth a shot.*

Naomi pulled in a deep breath and centered herself. She hovered in the air, relying on the other dragons to keep Tazarre distracted enough that he wouldn't go after her specifically. She expanded her chest as she pulled in all the love she had felt for Julian back on Charok. The friendship and fun she had found on Earth mixed with it easily, and it continued to grow as she concentrated on the intensity her relationship with Julian had taken on. The final topping was the new fondness she was just beginning to find for Kaylee, a sweet little girl who needed a mother and a friend, someone whom she barely knew but wanted to spend a lot of time with.

The energy crackled up through her throat and out her mouth almost without her own will. It burned in a pleasurable way as it sparked over her tongue, casting a light so bright and so white that it made even the sun seem dull.

Tazarre looked up, scowling at the new attack. He'd been building his energy once again, and he raised his hands over his head to keep the glittery orbs of light from landing on him. He spread his hands, creating a scarlet net with which to catch Naomi's light.

Her heart sank as she watched the first few sparks land on his net and stick. Tazarre laughed, and Naomi understood his intention. He would catch it all and throw it right back at them. Naomi had not only brought the demon there, but she had created the blast that would be the downfall of all of them.

But the sparks that had accrued on the net suddenly broke through, sending a deluge of Naomi's blast right down into Tazarre's face. They sank in like napalm, burning away at his dark flesh. The smell of old ashes spread through the air, and the demon screamed. It was a horrifying sound, one that could be heard all over the valley, but it was a shriek that heartened Naomi and her friends.

While the evil creature writhed, Naomi snuck a look back at Summer. She drummed away, but her head was tipped back. Her eyes had rolled back in her head so that only the whites were visible. Naomi didn't know much of anything about what they were doing, but this must have been the same sort of trance that had brought her and Tazarre back from the Otherworld.

Newly inspired, Naomi gathered and sent another blast at Tazarre. It didn't have as much energy behind it; Autumn and Leah were concentrating on Summer now. But she could do everything in her power to keep him weakened. They had helped her, and she would do the same for them.

"No!" Tazarre screamed. "You won't send me back! You're too weak!"

But as Naomi circled around the back of his head to blast away, she saw that Autumn had lit a candle and set it between the drums. The flame was unusually big for just a small pillar candle, and the tip of it was beginning to spark.

She didn't know how to send her energy to the others as they had done for her. She had only ever been alone, but she whispered a prayer of hope and love on the breeze and hoped that it would reach their ears. In the meantime, she sent another explosion down on the back of Tazarre's head and watched as Julian and the others sent their fire blasting after it. The flames and the white spheres touched, detonating like a bomb and blasting a hole several feet wide in the evil wizard's shoulder.

The sparks over the candle flame had now turned into a small, swirling vortex. Naomi felt a bolt of fear run through her as she saw what was on the other side. It looked like nothing more than swirling colors, dark and light, indefinite and abstract. But she knew the hell of being in that place, a purgatory that no one should have to suffer—no one but Tazarre.

The bottom of the demon draped against the ground like a shadowy robe, but a corner of it suddenly picked up as though blown by an unseen wind. It tapered and pulled toward the vortex, slowly getting sucked in.

"You think you can defeat me? I'll take you all with me, and then I'll pick your bones out from between my teeth as I eat you one by one!" Tazarre reached out toward Beau, trying to slap him out of the air. The gold dragon dodged to the side just in time.

But no matter how strong he thought he was, Tazarre was no match for what the women had done. Naomi's firepower had weakened him, and although his fingertips still crackled with crimson, he was slowly being pulled into the vortex. His arms fell to his sides and melded with the rest of his body, rendered useless. His great horns, which had looked so intimidating when he had first appeared in Julian's dining room, melted down into the sides of his head. His eyes, slits of red that had thirsted for her blood, sagged into his cheeks.

Summer and Leah pounded harder and faster on the drums. The vortex picked up speed, pulling Tazarre in. His shadowy form dragged along the ground as he struggled against it, but the force was too strong for him to resist. His blackness now filled the circle over the flame. Summer's body writhed, her hair dragging in the dirt. Autumn kept her hands out in the air near the vortex, protecting her sister from going in, too.

One last moan spilled from Tazarre's lips as his body was pulled into the Otherworld, and the vortex slammed shut.

Xander morphed as he landed, running up on two legs to his mate. "Summer! Are you alright?"

She opened her eyes and gave him a beatific smile. "Of course."

A wingtip touched Naomi's and she turned to see Julian at her side; he looked tired, but victorious.

"Let's go home."

## 12

---

IT WAS A BEAUTIFUL MORNING AS THEY MADE THEIR WAY OUT OF THE forest and back to town. The sun was completely up now, and it illuminated all the beauty of the countryside below them. Naomi felt tears burn in her eyes as she surveyed the scene.

"What's the matter?" Julian, as always, was at her side, gliding beautifully through the air. "We did it, Naomi. We not only defeated him, but we got our revenge for what he did to all the other dragons back on Charok. We made sure that Earth is safe for the children. What's there to be sad about?"

She shook her head and touched her wing to his. "I'm not sad, I'm happy. I had forgotten how beautiful Earth was. Being here, and having everyone back, it's just too much."

"I guess you'll just have to get used to it," he said with a grin. He lengthened his body and flapped his wings, rocketing through the air toward home.

The others weren't far behind them when they landed in the backyard and shifted back to their human forms, and they all rushed inside to relieve the Rochesters of their babysitting duty. It had been late when the kids had finally gone to bed, and most of them were still asleep.

"Let's make sure we get together and have a big party," Autumn said as she walked in the back door. "But let's do it after we've all had some sleep and a hot meal."

"And a shower," Summer added with a wink. Her blonde locks were caked with dust from her trance, staining the ends of them a light brown.

When they had scooped up their sleeping children and headed off to their own homes and the Rochesters had been thanked a thousand times over, Naomi and Julian were left standing alone in the living room. Julian had checked on Kaylee, who was still fast asleep in her crib with her teddy cuddled at her side.

Naomi stood uncomfortably near the coffee table, not sure what to do with herself. She had been so happy on their journey back from the battle site, but now what? Everyone else would resume their normal lives, but she didn't even know what a normal life was.

"You were incredible out there," Julian said as he came back from the hallway. He took both of her hands in his. "How did you do that?"

"It's something I had to learn while I was in the Otherworld. I didn't even know for sure if it would work here. If it hadn't been for Autumn and Leah's help, I don't think I could have done it more than once." She tried to shove the memory of it out of her mind. It made her weary just to think about the process.

"It certainly did work. I don't think we ever could have defeated him otherwise. Summer may have pulled him through the portal, but I don't think she could have done that if you hadn't weakened him like you had. And the way that your fire mixed with ours? I don't think I've ever seen anything so beautiful!" They had been awake all night and fought all morning, but Julian was somehow still full of energy. He had let go of her as he spoke, pacing the floor and gesturing wildly with his hands.

Naomi couldn't help but admire him. He was so full of life, and that was one of the things she had always liked about him. Even when he was reading and studying, he did it with an air of enthusiasm that was contagious. It was just that energy, though, that made her wonder how he had managed to stay single all this time.

"Julian, I want you to know that I never expected you to wait for me, especially not for so long. I never thought I would even see you again." The words came straight from her heart and out her mouth, and she couldn't stop them. It was something that had weighed heavily on her mind since he had found her in Autumn's house, and it almost made her feel as though she didn't deserve him.

Julian paused, his hand in his hair. He turned wild eyes to her as his hand dropped to his sides, and he came around the coffee table. "Of course I waited for you. But don't make it sound like I did something heroic. I didn't even really know that I was waiting for you, because I thought you were dead. And I guess you were, at least part of the time. I just couldn't see being with anyone else."

"I understand." She looked down at where their hands were once again holding each other, their fingers intertwined. When she had met the other women and gone to parties with them, there had been plenty of men who had hit on her. She was flattered in a way, but none of them had the same sincerity in their eyes that Julian did. "I guess I'm still just trying to understand how we're lucky enough to be together again."

"Naomi, I love you. I'm so glad I get to hold you in my arms again, even if we had to cross the universe to do it. You mean more to me than you'll ever know, and I want to be with you for the rest of our lives. That is, if you want to be with me?" His eyes were soft, a liquid green with flecks of gold that swirled in his irises.

Her heart swelled, and that brilliant white light that had been her weapon was also her love as it swirled in her chest. She needed Julian, and it completed her soul to know that he needed her as well. "Of course I do."

Their lips met, and Naomi felt herself melting into him. She opened her mouth to let him in, reveling in the feeling of his tongue against hers. Her arms were around him, instantly pulling at the hem of his shirt. She needed him desperately. It didn't matter how tired she was or that they had just defeated a horrific wizard in the form of a demon, Naomi would never be able to rest until she had her man.

Julian seemed to feel the same way, and even as he held her and kissed her, he began walking toward his bedroom. No, *their* bedroom. As he reached the door, he scooped her up off the floor and carried her over the threshold. Julian flung the door shut with his foot and headed for the bed.

Naomi barely registered the California king-sized bed or the high thread count sheets as he set her down. Her mind was set on something else. She felt the cool air against her as he pulled off her clothing and ran his hands down her skin. It felt so good, but she needed more.

Whipping Julian's shirt over his head, she flung it aside and reached for his belt buckle. She quickly revealed his member, hard and ready for her. Naomi sank down off the mattress and to her knees.

He had done so much to please her when they had met before, and now it was her turn. She took his length into her mouth, growing warmer at the moan that escaped from his lips. Her hands explored the hard muscles of his thighs, his narrow hips, and the curve of his buttocks as she sucked at him, eventually coming around to circle her fingers at his base.

"Oh, my god, Naomi!" His hands were in her hair, gathering it into a rough ponytail at the back of her head so he could see. "You don't have to do that."

"Yes, I do," she insisted, taking a break from her work only long enough to argue with him. "I want to."

He tipped his head back as she pulled him in again, sucking his head all the way to the back of her throat. "As long as it's turning you on as much as it does me."

"Mmhm." She refused to let him go this time, and he understood what she meant. Naomi let her left hand slide down between her own legs, touching the firm bud of her clit. Julian had no idea how much it turned her on to do this for him, and she felt a tingle of excitement race upward from her core to her nipples.

Julian's hips pulsed gently, encouraging her. "I don't think I can do this much longer. I need you."

She sucked harder.

"Naomi, please. This feels too good."

She let him go, and he pulled her to her feet just so they could tumble down onto the bed together. They lay facing each other, kissing, exploring, touching. But Naomi wanted more, and she climbed on top of him.

He smiled in surprise. "It certainly seems like you know what you want."

"I do." She spread her legs and pierced herself on him, gasping at his girth as he filled her up. His hands cupped her buttocks as she slid back and forth on him. He was so hard, and she pushed her hips as far down as they would go, grinding against him.

Julian pulled her down so that their lips touched. She moaned into him, unable to control the waves of pleasure that suddenly undulated through her. He was hot and hard, and her walls pulsed against him.

She tried to pull back as he moaned his satisfaction, wanting the freedom of movement to give him the utmost enjoyment out of this. He was the most magnificent man she would ever meet, and she wanted him to know just how much she appreciated him. But he had other ideas, and he kept his hands cupped over the back of her skull so that he could continue to kiss her. Just as his cock was buried in her, he buried his tongue in her mouth. Their hips bucked and pulsed, clamoring against each other as they found their climax. Naomi's scream was only stifled by their kiss and she felt his circumference grow in response.

But to her surprise, Julian wasn't done with her just yet. He rolled her over so that he was on top, sinking his shaft just a little bit further inside under his weight. Their bodies were glued together, and she surged around him once again. He plowed her into the mattress, the headboard bumping against the wall. Naomi squealed as the spasms racked her body once again, making her twitch down to her toes. Julian finally broke their kiss and buried his face into her neck as he came with a roar.

Julian held her in his arms, their legs tangled together as he pulled the blankets over their naked bodies. She rested her head against his chest, feeling completely satisfied and yet knowing that she wanted him even more than she had before. She would never get enough of him, and that was just the way it should be.

# 13

EPILOGUE

JULIAN SMILED AS HE LANDED IN THE BACK YARD, TURNING TO WATCH Kaylee. She was just getting used to her wings, since he had spent a lot of time encouraging her to remain in human form. But he had someone to help him in the sky now, and the three of them loved taking evening flights. Kaylee was always impatient for the sun to go down, bouncing in joy as she waited for the right time. And she always slept very well at night afterwards.

The little dragon spread her wings and tipped them upward, trying to slow herself down. She was coming in too steep, which was usually her problem. Naomi was right at her side, touching the tip of her wing to the little girl's. "Keep flapping, dear. You need a little more lift!"

Kaylee obediently swooped back up as she slowed down, landing lightly in her father's arms. She screamed her excitement. "Again! Again!"

"No, sweetie. It's about time for bed. You need to get your rest so we can go again tomorrow. And maybe we can go even further." He watched as Kaylee shifted back to her human form in his arms, her wings tucking into her back and folding away. Her scales each stood on end and flipped over, rippling down to soft skin.

"Yes, it's definitely time for bed," Naomi agreed. Her wingtips touched the ground as she walked toward the back door, and she shifted more slowly than usual.

"Are you alright?" Julian had noticed that she'd been tired a lot lately. He had chalked it up to the fact that she was still getting used to being on Earth, plus the fact that they had a little one to run after all day. Kaylee was energetic, and she could be a lot to keep up with.

She shrugged, now completely back to a form that was acceptable by society, should any of their neighbors happen to look out the window and see her profile in the porchlight. "I'll be fine. I didn't sleep very well last night, so I think I'll turn in early."

Julian nodded. "You go ahead and get ready for bed. I'll give Kaylee her cup of milk and her bath." He didn't mind being the one 'stuck' with bedtime duty. He enjoyed the quiet moments with his daughter, when he could wash her hair and talk to her about the events of the day. She was getting bigger all the time, constantly learning new words and showing him new things she could do. He didn't want to miss out on any of it.

When he had her all clean and dressed in her pj's, he carried her to bed. She could walk very well on her own now, but there was nothing better than snuggles from a freshly-bathed child. He sat in the rocking chair and pulled a book from the shelf. "How about this one? We haven't read it in a while."

Kaylee nodded her agreement, and he began reading about a little puppy who couldn't seem to stay out of trouble. Julian flipped the pages slowly, knowing that she needed to get to sleep, but was unable to resist this wonderful, special time with her.

His reading was interrupted by a thump against the wall. "Naomi? Are you alright?"

"I'm fine!" came the muffled reply.

Julian read two more pages before he heard a crash. He gathered Kaylee from his lap and set her in her crib before dashing out of the room and across the hall. "Naomi!" But when he grabbed the bedroom doorknob, it was locked. "Let me in!"

"Hang on!" There was more crashing and a gasp that sounded pained.

"What's going on in there?" The dark fantasies that occupied Julian's mind were a scary thing. Had another demon shown up, one they didn't know about? Was there some other enemy, perhaps a neighbor who had seen them in dragon form?

"Just a sec!"

The next few seconds were painfully silent, and then Julian heard the click of the lock. He rushed in to see Naomi standing demurely at the end of the bed, a smile playing on her lips. Several books had been knocked off a nearby shelf, and a porcelain lamp lay broken on the floor. "What happened? Are you alright?"

"I am," she nodded. "It turns out we don't have quite enough space to shift indoors."

He felt completely stupefied as he looked at her. "But why would you do that? We just spent over an hour with Kaylee as dragons."

Naomi looked down at the floor for a moment before lifting her eyes to meet his. "There are some things I just can't do as a human."

"Like what?" he asked slowly. "Naomi, you're really starting to make me worry."

She reached out and took his hand, leading him around the bed and pointed to the floor. On a pile of blankets lay a shimmering silver egg. Julian stared at it for a long moment, his brain refusing to acknowledge what he was seeing. "Is that...?"

Naomi beamed at him. "Yes. Now I know why I'd been so tired and why I hadn't been able to sleep. I'd never gone through this before, so I had no idea what to expect. But as I was about to change for bed, I had this overwhelming sensation to shift. I couldn't stop it."

Julian knelt down to touch the smooth shell. It was just like the egg Kaylee had come out of, but larger and more robust. And it was his. Truly his, and Naomi's as well. He felt a tear trickle down his cheek. "It's absolutely beautiful." He stood and pulled her into his arms, kissing her.

"So, you're happy?" she asked when they finally broke apart.

"More than you could ever know." He didn't even know quite how to put it into words, but they were going to have a child together. Another dragon would soon be hatched on Earth. Not only would they be expanding their family, but extending a race nearly brought to extinction by genocide. Only time would tell if future generations would keep the line going, but at least for now, they had one more soul to love.

Julian squeezed her hands and let go. "I think we've got a sleepy little girl in the next room who would love to see this." He slipped back across the hallway.

Kaylee was standing in her crib, leaning on the rail. She watched her father come in the room with wide, curious eyes. "Story?"

"We'll finish in a minute, I promise. But first, I've got something exciting to show you." He picked her up and took her back to the master bedroom, smiling at Naomi as he did so. "Look right over there. You're going to be a big sister!"

She pointed one chubby finger at the shape on the floor. "Egg?"

"Yes, sweetie." Naomi took Kaylee now, wrapping her in a big hug. "We're going to have a baby."

Kaylee clapped her hands. "Baby! Baby!"

Julian held his mate and his daughter, staring down at the silver egg that would bring their family and friends incredible joy. He had left so much behind on Charok, but there on Earth, he had found so much more.

———

# DRAGON'S ROYAL GUARD

SHIFTERS BETWEEN WORLDS

# 1

KAYLEE TURNER SHIFTED UNCOMFORTABLY IN HER NARROW SEAT. Usually, she saw these international flights as the perfect time for reading and research. While other passengers complained of boredom, air sickness and cramped conditions, Kaylee was content to lose herself in a good book or an essay from her field of study.

But that wasn't the case today.

Turning and pressing her forehead against the cool glass of the window, Kaylee studied the land formations below. She'd found that every country—and every state, even—looked a little different. She'd been on so many flights, she'd started to recognize them from the air, even before the captain would announce where they were in a thick accent over the speaker. This time, she was heading into Zimbabwe, which meant she wouldn't get to see much of it from the air. The airport was on the western edge of the country, and the site she'd be visiting was much further east.

Even so, she scanned the hot, dry earth below her. Deep inside, Kaylee sensed she was looking for something. She'd always felt that way, and she would continue her pursuit when she landed and traveled across the country in a vehicle. Her search had been constant for most of her life, though she never quite knew what she was looking for.

That was what had inspired her career—that and her love for books and languages, which her father helped foster ever since she was a baby. Kaylee was always reading, and not always in her first language. She had a gift for words, one that she couldn't explain any more than her yearning for finding that missing something. She took in everything below her, longing to feel some sort of connection to it. She'd been born on this planet. She'd been a part of it for her entire life, yet she never felt that way. The disconnection left her with an unsettled feeling in the pit of her stomach.

―――

"I TRUST YOU HAD GOOD TRAVELS?" Dr. Morrick clasped her hand in both of his, his fingers warm and worn as he greeted her near the entrance of the Great Zimbabwe. Releasing her, he pushed his dark glasses up on his nose and ran a hand over his slick, gray hair. His pale, skinny legs stuck out of his baggy khaki shorts, and his matching safari shirt was soaked with sweat.

"It gave me the chance to get a lot of work done," she admitted with a smile. Kaylee had always liked Dr. Morrick. He'd been one of her first archeology professors, and his enthusiasm had helped her find her own passion.

He tipped his head to the side and frowned a little. "Are you all right? You're not unwell, are you? I've heard the airplane food is quite terrible these days."

"No, I'm fine. I'm just a little tired." Kaylee scrunched her toes inside her boots, wishing she could take them off and rest her bare feet against the hot soil beneath her. The sun baked them where they stood, and it was clearly making Dr. Morrick uncomfortable. Beads of sweat rolled down the sides of his rounded cheeks, no matter how quickly he swiped them away with a handkerchief. To Kaylee, it was a glorious heat that sank through her skin and down to her bones, something she would carry with her once she got back on a plane in a few days. She would miss it when she returned to the chilly weather back home.

Dr. Morrick smiled. "That can be fixed. I've set you up in one of the nicest hotels in the area. No sleeping out on the ground for the best translator in the world!"

Kaylee flushed as she followed him down a dirt pathway. It had been carved by thousands of feet, traveling amongst the crumbling stone walls that had once housed numerous people. While some parts of the ruins were remarkably preserved due to the masterful masons who had once built them, there were others that had been reduced to nothing but piles of perfectly shaped granite bricks. "You don't have to say that just because I'm right here."

"I don't *have* to say anything; that's true. But I don't think either one of us can deny that you're at the forefront of our industry. People talk about you, my dear."

"I'm not sure it's always in a good way." The curving walls of the Great Enclosure rose up in front of them, and Kaylee felt an immediate appreciation for the site. It spoke of ancient people, lost religions and stories that spanned centuries. Archeologists would never truly know everything about the Great Zimbabwe, a monument so stunning that an entire country was named after it, but it was still a lot of fun to guess.

Dr. Morrick reverently touched the stone walls that framed a doorway. "Don't take any of that to heart. They're just intimidated by you. Some of them have studied for decades and yet they can't decode the way you can. They don't think that a young woman such as yourself should be able to hold so much genius in her brain. Sexist, I know, but old ways die hard."

"Or they die without a single explanation of *why*." Kaylee had read everything she could get her hands on about this ancient site as soon as she'd received the request from Dr. Morrick to come out there. She'd been excited both to work with her mentor and to see a new place, but as soon as she'd begun packing her bag, she started to realize the reality of it. She could handle the rigors of airport security, even when it involved flying to a different country. She could handle living out of a small suitcase for a week. She could even handle the inevitable change in diet.

But she knew the worst of it was yet to come.

"Perhaps you can help uncover a few of her secrets," Dr. Morrick replied hopefully. He led her into a circular stone wall and past several other structures, all built of the same stone. They reached another doorway, and upon entering it, descended down a set of stairs that had been freshly uncovered from the earth. "As I said in my email, we've only just recently uncovered this new chamber. It's been quite exciting for us, as I'm sure you can imagine. These new technologies that keep popping up are hard to keep up with, yet they're always giving us new information about old sites. I love it. Anyway, we've found a tablet we'd like you to interpret for us."

"Has anyone else had a go at it?" The steps beneath her were still slick with the dirt that had been covering them for centuries, but Kaylee confidently made her way down them. She glanced up from her footsteps to see that a vast underground cavern had been dug out of the dirt. LED lights on strands had been set up at intervals, run by a generator that grumbled to itself somewhere above them. Several other rooms extended off the one they were in with more glowing lights emanating from them.

He paused at the bottom of the stairs and turned to her, a look of concern in his houndlike eyes. "Well, Dr. Atwood is here."

Kaylee's heart, which had been fluttering somewhere between excitement and anticipation, now dropped into a solid state of dread. She knew how Dr. Atwood felt about her, but then again, he'd made no attempt to hide it. She raised one eyebrow. "And did he have any success?"

Dr. Morrick's mouth was a hard line. "Not exactly, although he claims he'll have all the answers very shortly. I should tell you he was rather offended that I called anyone else in on this project. You know how he is, always thinking he's the end-all, be-all of any given situation. I never would've brought him on except that his connections with the local university helped me get the permission to dig here in the first place. Besides, I know you have a lot going on while you finish up your degree. Tell me, were you able to make sufficient arrangements with your professors?"

That had been the very first thing Kaylee had done when she'd received Dr. Morrick's invitation, and her teachers had been happy to accommodate her. Knowing where she was going and why had only made it easier. "Of course. I'll have a few things to catch up on once I get back, but it shouldn't be an issue."

"Good, good. Then let's get started." Dr. Morrick strode confidently across the dirt floor and through a doorway. While the first room at the bottom of the stairs had been fairly nondescript, this one was most definitely a library of some sort. The wall across from the doorway was covered in ancient scripts that had been preserved by centuries underground and away from the elements. A u-shaped assemblage of stone seemed to form a seating area in the center of the room, and shelves had been carved into the other walls. Each of these held thick sheaves of primitive paper, ancient wooden boxes, and stacks of stone tablets.

"It's beautiful," Kaylee breathed, immediately intrigued by the amount of knowledge they might find there. Even if these writings were nothing more than diaries or recipes, they would certainly give the scientists some definitive insight into the lives of the people who'd once occupied these spaces.

"I thought so, too," Dr. Morrick said proudly, his chin rising slightly. "I assure you, the other rooms here are wonderful, but none are as fascinating as this one. Oh, where are my manners? I believe you know Dr. Parkinson?"

A slender older woman with graying blonde hair stood up from where she'd been crouched on the floor, gently flicking dirt away from a small statue with a paintbrush. She extended her hand and smiled warmly. "So nice to see you again, Miss Turner."

"And you know I never leave the country without my partner in crime, Dr. Davison." Morrick gestured to a man who turned away from the stone shelves to approach them, a fine coat of dust clinging to his salt and pepper beard.

"No need to be so formal, Douglas. Call me Jonathan. I've heard so much about you that I'm starting to think Dr. Morrick here is thinking about adopting you." He shook her hand as well.

Kaylee felt a little better. Maybe she didn't need to dread this trip at all if there were such good people there. "I've heard quite a bit about you, too."

"Only good stories, I hope?" Jonathan raised a furry gray eyebrow at his partner.

"Mostly," Kaylee replied with a smile.

"Oh, she's here." This voice came from the doorway, and Kaylee turned to see a rather rotund man filling it. His dark hair had been slicked back and held in place with either gel, sweat, or a mixture of the two. Overdressed for the occasion, he'd eschewed the traditional garb of khakis and shorts for a dark suit. He made a disgusted face as he swept a bit of dust off the sleeve of his jacket.

"Dr. Atwood, this is Kaylee Turner. I've asked her to give us a little help with the tablet." Morrick forced a smile onto his face.

The grimace on Atwood's face increased, making him look like he'd caught a whiff of some old cheese as his eyes raked over Kaylee. "Yes, I know of her." He advanced into the room with purposeful steps as though he owned the place until he stood directly in front of Kaylee. He didn't offer to shake her hand. "You might as well fly right on back to your little college town and hang out on the quad, my dear. There's nothing here for you to do."

Morrick cleared his throat. "There's plenty for her to do, Atwood. You know as well as I do that she's a true genius when it comes to this. Besides that, I'm the one in charge of this dig."

Atwood narrowed his eyes at the doctor, his chins wobbling slightly. "Do you really want to claim that? When you've brought in an impostor like her? We all know that she doesn't really translate anything on her own. She's got someone in the wings who does it for her, someone who's happy to give her the credit. This child hasn't been around long enough to know *anything* about what we're doing here." His voice increased in volume as he prattled on, his face slowly reddening.

"Sounds to me like you're a little jealous," Jonathan cut in. "You've had the first stab at it, but it's time to step back and let the professionals handle this. Come here, Miss Turner. I'll show you what we're dealing with." He took Kaylee by the elbow and turned her away from Dr. Atwood. "Don't mind him," he whispered as they headed to the far corner of the room. "He never likes anyone who he thinks might show him up."

"It's okay. I'm used to it." Unfortunately, Atwood wasn't the first person who'd treated her like that. She'd been called in on several other digs and either openly ostracized or whispered about behind her back. If they only knew the truth, there would be a lot more scientists who felt that way about her.

"As you can see," Jonathan said, "there's quite a lot in this old room for us to go through. Most of it is pretty mundane, and we haven't had too much of an issue with the interpretations. But this tablet was set aside in a small stone box with a few other artifacts. We're not yet sure what any of it means. Usually, we can get some idea simply from the context of where an item is found, but we're a bit mystified."

He gestured at what was indeed a small stone box. Like the shelves on the walls, it had been carved out of the structure of the room itself. A carefully fitted lid had been lifted and set aside, revealing the contents.

"What makes it even more of a mystery is that we don't know what language it's in," Dr. Morrick added from over her shoulder. "It doesn't appear to be the same as what we see in the rest of the documents here."

Kaylee was heavily aware that Dr. Atwood was watching her, but she was slipping into her professional mode. She knew what her job was, and she was excited to do it. There was a special, peaceful feeling that came over her when she was presented with a new item to translate. It drowned out the rest of the world, and it gave her a sense of purpose. She quickly pulled her pack off her lap and removed a flashlight from it, shining it down on the tablet. A small smile crept across her face. She knew exactly what it said.

But she also knew how the world worked. She couldn't just turn around and reveal an exact translation of an ancient tablet written in an unknown language. Instead, she handed her light to Dr. Morrick. "Hold that just there for me, please." Kaylee removed a camera from her bag.

"What are you doing?" Dr. Atwood bellowed from behind her. "Nobody is allowed to take any evidence from this site until the work is completed!"

Kaylee ignored him and quickly began firing away, taking as many images as she felt were necessary. She knew what the tablet said, but there was nothing wrong with documenting it thoroughly.

"Considering this is the only price she requires and that I trust her, I say it's all right," Dr. Morrick argued. "Besides, you can't expect her to just camp out here for weeks while she translates it."

Putting her camera away, Kaylee nodded at the professor. "I think that's all I need. I'll contact you as soon as I'm done."

"Good, good. Then come with me. There are a few other things I'd like to show you while you're here." Dr. Morrick led her back up the stairs and out into the fresh air. They wound their way around several walls until they were on the opposite end of the Great Enclosure from the fresh discovery. "I truly am sorry about that. I knew he'd be a pain in the ass, but I didn't think it would be that bad."

"It's fine," Kaylee assured him. "He can gripe all he wants to, but it won't stop me from my work."

He pressed his lips together and dipped his head, looking up at her curiously. "So, you *can* read it?"

Kaylee had long wondered if Dr. Morrick knew her secret. She'd never told him, but she'd worked with him more than anyone else. As tempted as she was to just reveal the whole thing, Kaylee knew it was best to just pretend that everything was normal. "I'm sure I can."

## 2

---

ARCHARD LAY BACK ON THE ROCKY SURFACE OF THE MOUNTAIN, absorbing the last bit of heat from the day before the chill of the night completely took over. He propped his head on his hands as he stared up at the sky, watching the slow whirl of the stars overheard. It was barely noticeable, the kind of thing he'd never been patient enough to watch for when he was a child, but now he easily tracked each of the stars he was so familiar with move through their nocturnal dance. "It's almost time for Zimryr."

"So?" Callan asked from off to his left. "It's not like it means anything."

Archard sat up, his back stiff from being in his human form for too long. He spent much of his time in his scales, but it was easier to communicate when he was among the remains of his clan and they were all walking on two legs. Nobody could lash out and slice a throat with one swipe of a claw, and their teeth and tongues were more precise when they spoke. It was the way things had been for centuries or more, and at least some of their old habits still remained. "It could mean something if we wanted it to."

Callan shoved his dark blonde curls back off his forehead. The fire-light reflected the mischief that always lived in his eyes. "Why would we? Archard, you know as well as I do that all the old ways are dead. We should move on and find our own way to live."

But the mere idea made Archard's blood boil inside him, and he felt the ripple of scales threatening a shift on his back. "So we just forget? After everything that's happened, after everything that our people have gone through, we just decide that none of that matters anymore?" Cousin or not, Archard was tempted to challenge Callan. He deserved it many times over.

"Look, just because you still think you have some sort of sacred duty doesn't mean the rest of us have to be subjected to all the boring ceremonies and stuff."

"Excuse me, but I very much do have a sacred duty! And you would as well if you'd actually bother to follow it. Your family has been time-keepers for more generations than you can even count, but you're never the one watching the stars or noting the shift in the sunrise and sunset." Archard was on his knees now, furious that Callan should challenge the legacy that had been in his family for so long.

"All right, boys!" Lucia stood up and stepped around the campfire they'd built in their midst, holding her hands out to stop her son and her nephew from arguing any further. "I don't see much point in having the exact same argument every single year. If Archard wants to celebrate then he's most certainly welcome to. Personally, I'd be happy to join him."

Callan snorted his disgust and got to his feet. "Whatever. I'm done with all of this." He turned and stalked off down the mountain towards the woods, his form slowly shifting into a larger, more agile one as he disappeared into the shadows.

"He'll be fun in the morning." This came from Kieran, who had been lounging on one elbow and watching the altercation with amusement in his dark eyes.

"Don't mind him. I'd hoped he would find his way in the world, but maybe it'll just take a little more time." Lucia settled herself onto the rock next to Archard and laid a cool hand on his shoulder, bidding him to calm down. Her long brown hair had streaks of gray in it now, her thin face a little more drawn than it used to be. "I think it's very admirable that you still want to keep the old ways. Life has changed so much since the War of Storms."

"I know," Archard sighed. Or at least, he knew what had been told to him. He'd been so young when the war between the dragons and the ogres had broken out that he didn't remember any of it, except for the general idea that it happened. Things hadn't looked too bleak until the wizards had decided to join forces with the ogres, and it was the spell cast by the evil Tazarre that had wiped out the vast majority of the dragons. The Great Curse had backfired, however, taking many of the ogres and wizards as well.

"I remember what it used to be like," Lucia said with a smile. She turned her head to look up at the mountain behind them, toward the ancient caves where their ancestors had once dwelled. "There were so many fires that they lit up the night, burning with such a pleasant warmth that even the oldest dragons felt young again. We sent our wishes for the coming years up into the flames, dispersing into the universe."

Archard was quiet for a moment, delving into the back of his mind for the few faint memories he had of the holiday as a child. "I've been spending a lot of time in the royal caves," he finally admitted.

"I know," Lucia replied quietly. "We all know, but I think I might be the only one who understands why."

"Hey, give me a little credit," Kieran argued. "I like to think I perform my duties here as best as I can. There's just not much of a border left to guard anymore." He looked off into the dark distance as though he longed for someone to come charging in upon their secret little spot, someone to challenge him and make him rise up to the occupation that had been in his family for time immemorial.

Archard knew that feeling. His father and grandfather had been royal guards. It was what Archard was destined to be, but it was impossible now that there were no royals left to guard. The Queen had been killed by The Great Curse, and the King had died fighting the wizards. Even with the rulers gone, Archard still felt that innate pull inside him, demanding that he do something to fulfill his destiny. "Have you ever taken the time to read the walls inside the royal caves?"

"Those old stories? Don't let Callan hear you mention those. You'll just piss him off all over again." Kieran threw a small stick in the fire and watched it burn.

"Go on," Lucia encouraged.

Archard could see the intrigue in her eyes. She understood. She kept up with her job as timekeeper, even though it didn't really matter anymore. "As I said, I've been spending a lot of time in the royal caves. I'm no linguist, and I haven't been able to understand all of it. I probably don't even understand most of it, if I'm honest, but I can't seem to stop trying. Even though it's written in our own language, it doesn't all make sense. What gets me most of all is what seems like a prophecy."

Kieran sat up. "You're trampling on dangerous ground now. I haven't ventured up to Mount Taendru, not knowing if the ogres are living at the base of it, but I hear there are still a few prophets in the world. They won't like you butting in on their job."

"I'm not butting in on anything, and if they want to come on over here and look at it themselves, then they're more than welcome. If the clans start fighting with each other, then we really are worse off than we were during the War." Archard knew that Kieran liked to play devil's advocate simply for argument's sake, but he wasn't in the mood to debate this. "Anyway, there's this one wall that indicates a return of the Awakened One."

"Ah, yes. I've heard of this. A descendant of royalty, if I recall correctly, but who isn't from here." Lucia's dark eyes were bright.

Archard nodded enthusiastically. Day-to-day life didn't intrigue him much, especially not compared to the potential for what else might be waiting for him out in the universe. "I don't really know what that means. It doesn't make a lot of sense, but I can't help but wonder if there are other dragons out there." He looked to the sky again, wondering where they would come from. There were so few of their own kind left on Charok, and he knew he wasn't the only one that felt the loneliness of it. They were sociable creatures, ones who needed their duties, their clans, and their mates. With only his aunt and his cousins around him, Archard knew there was a lot he was missing.

"I wish I had the answers for you." Lucia stretched and leaned a little closer to the fire. "I admit the idea is compelling, but I'm afraid I also have to say it's far-fetched. If ever there was a time when we needed someone to come and help us, it would've been decades ago. During the War or even right after, we could've used some back up. I'd like to think they're coming, Archard, but I don't think it's very likely."

He knew she was just being practical. That was how Lucia was. Archard liked to think he was practical most of the time, but he couldn't deny the deep swirl of emotions that lived inside him. It was like the universe was tugging at him, demanding something of him, and yet he didn't know what it was or what he should do about it. Archard hadn't told anyone, not even Lucia, about this. It was ridiculous, a reflection of the old ways, of the ancient rhythms of the dragons on Charok, of the way things no longer were.

He knew what he would be asking for during Zimryr.

## 3

KAYLEE GUIDED THE CAR DOWN THE NARROW COUNTRY ROADS THAT LED to her parents' home, irritated by the constant cold drizzle that clung to the windshield. She still remembered the smaller home they'd occupied when she was young, but shortly after her little brother had been born, the Turners had decided to find a much bigger place out in the country. The old mansion was near her Uncle Holden's place, which had been convenient when she wanted to spend time with her cousins or when her parents needed a babysitter. In truth, Kaylee suspected her father had chosen that particular house solely based on the massive library it held.

And that was exactly where she found him. Julian sat near the fire, his feet propped up on an ottoman with a book spread open on his lap. He'd fallen asleep, and his head tipped back against the chair as he snored softly.

Kaylee smiled at him. He spent more time sleeping in the library than his own bed, since he was always studying well into the night. As excited as she was about the trip she'd just returned from, she didn't want to wake him. Instead, she tiptoed forward and gently laid the photographs on her father's lap before turning back to the door.

"You didn't think you could sneak up on the old man, did you?"

Kaylee laughed as she turned toward the fire once again. Her father smiled at her, his green eyes bright against his olive skin. His hair was beginning to show his age around the temples, but he wore it well. "I'm home!"

"I can see that!" Julian set his book aside but kept the pictures in his hand as he got to his feet and wrapped his daughter in a hug. "And it looks as though you've been busy."

"Not as busy as I would've liked. The Great Zimbabwe was a beautiful place, and Dr. Morrick got to show me around a little, but my reception was a little less welcoming when it came to Dr. Atwood."

Julian's excited smile faded. "You can't let people like him get to you."

"I know, and I really try not to. But it's difficult when I know there are people like him out there. Atwood probably tells everyone who'll listen just what he thinks about me. He's going to damage my reputation before I even get a chance to build one."

Her father's arm tightened around her shoulders. "Trust me, my dear. You've already built yourself a reputation, and it's only a good one. Atwood just doesn't understand your natural gift, and it's best that he doesn't."

"I wish *I* understood it," she mumbled.

"You're using it to help people; what's more to understand than that?" He flipped through the pictures, an approving look on his face. "Fascinating. And I assume you have them translated already."

"Of course." Kaylee reached in her back pocket and handed him a piece of paper. "It gave me some interesting things to think about."

"Such as?"

Heavy footsteps indicated they weren't alone, and a brawny young man soon came striding into the room. "I thought I heard you come in!" He crossed the room in only a few steps and whisked Kaylee off her feet in a bear hug.

"Stop it, Jake! Put me down!" Kaylee squealed as her little brother swung her in the air. "You're going to make me throw up!"

"That's the goal, isn't it?" Jake set her on her feet easily. Born of a silver egg, Jake had been a weak and sickly baby. Their parents had worried that he wouldn't make it, or that he would have health issues for the rest of his life. Fortunately, he'd managed to outgrow his childhood illness and had turned into a startlingly strong young man. "Remember when I used to hold you by your feet every time you threatened to tell on me?"

"How could I forget?" Kaylee chided with a smile.

Julian just shook his head in amusement, used to the antics of his children.

Jake grew a little more serious, his dark brow creasing. "Did I hear you say you're having problems with someone? Cause you know I'm more than happy to crack some skulls."

Kaylee sighed and laid a staying hand on her brother's bulky arm. He might have been her junior by a couple years, but Jake had always been very protective of her. In high school, most boys who were interested in her were immediately turned off when they saw Jake lurking in the wings, pounding his fist into his palm. It was sweet, but she didn't mind getting a little distance from him once she'd started college. "It's not necessary, and it wouldn't be a fair fight anyway. I can handle this."

"If you're sure," he replied dubiously. "You don't even have to say I'm your brother. Just say I'm your bodyguard or something."

"I swear, you were born looking for trouble." Kaylee's mother, Naomi, floated into the room. It was easy to see the resemblance between mother and son with her catlike blue eyes and dark hair, even if her build was a much slighter one. "Kaylee, I'm so glad you're back home! I heard there are some nasty snow storms coming in, and I was afraid your flight would get caught up in them."

"Snow coming?" Julian looked hopefully out the window. "That sounds perfect! Good weather for studying by the fire."

"As if you don't do that all the time, anyway," his wife reminded him with a loving smile. "Kaylee, what did you find on this expedition?"

Her parents had been so supportive of her interest in archeology, and it made her appreciate them all the more. She knew there was still something out there, something she needed to find, but at least when she was tired of searching, she had a comfortable little spot in the world. "Something that really got me thinking, actually. This tablet is different from all the other ones they found beneath the Great Zimbabwe. It speaks of a shaman that lived among them, a man who came from another world and knew more than they could possibly imagine. He served them for a very long time, what sounds like it was far longer than a normal lifespan for these people, and they believed he had mystical powers."

"Interesting..." Julian rubbed his jawline as he looked over the photos, scrunching his eyes at the foreign words. "I'm certainly glad *you* can read it, considering it's nothing more than chicken scratch to me. What language is it?"

"I really don't know," Kaylee admitted. When it came to translating, it hadn't ever mattered what language it was. She could simply read it, and while her gift let her in on secret knowledge that the rest of the world wasn't privy to, this facet of it was a bit frustrating. "I'll have to spend a little time with it to make sure I have a decent translation matrix to give to Dr. Morrick, but I thought it might really help you with your work."

Julian looked at her curiously, as did her brother and mother. "You know I appreciate any ancient artifacts, but I don't see how this particular one is relevant."

Kaylee took a deep breath, hoping that saying the words out loud wouldn't make them seem silly. They'd made perfect sense inside her head as she'd thought about it on the plane and on the drive back home, but she had yet to determine if her theory was a sound one.

Julian and Naomi had both come from the planet Charok, a place that, at one point, had been populated with dragons. Her father had regaled her with the tales of the craggy red mountains, the deep quiet forests, and the more primitive yet satisfying way of life they'd lived while there. When war and an evil spell had threatened their way of life, it had only been due to the help of a kindly and compassionate wizard that a handful of dragons had escaped to Earth. Julian had been one of them, along with Kaylee when she was just an egg. Naomi had joined him later. Though Julian and the other dragons had adapted to life on Earth fairly well, Julian had never stopped looking for a way to go back to Charok and see if any dragons remained.

"Okay, bear with me here. The account on this tablet isn't an unusual one. There are stories from all over the world of people who have uncanny powers or who seem to come from somewhere else. Most of the time, we don't have any real explanation for this. Some say they're aliens of some sort, and I've seen scientists claim that these powerful people were born with some sort of defect that allowed them to access more of their brains than typical humans. I don't have any real answers, either, but it made me think: What if Varhan came to Earth as well?"

The mention of the rogue wizard who had sent Julian to Earth made her father pause for a moment, but then he shook his head. "I don't think it would be possible. He was able to send us, but I don't see how he could've been able to send himself. The spell was very precise, and I think he would need someone to perform it on him. I can tell you there weren't any other wizards on Charok like him, and nobody else would've been sympathetic to his cause."

"Besides that, Varhan said he was sending us here because we were destined to be here," Naomi added. "He never mentioned that he had a calling on Earth as well."

"Maybe not," Kaylee admitted, some of the hope draining from her heart. "But I don't think it's entirely outside the realm of possibility. If it were, then you would've stopped looking for a way back there yourself. And what does it hurt if we look for him?"

Julian nodded slowly, a smile spreading across his face once again. "I suppose that's true. I wouldn't mind seeing my old friend again, and I'd love for him to meet you kids. I think he'd be thrilled to see that we fulfilled our destiny here."

Jake looked doubtful. "Wouldn't he have let you know he was here?"

Kaylee shrugged. "Maybe, but this is a big planet full of people. We haven't exactly charged out into the world and announced ourselves as dragons. How would he know where to find us?"

"That's true." Julian was pacing back and forth in front of the fire. "I have to admit that I'm so used to digging through ancient scrolls that I'm not sure how to find someone in the modern age myself. I think I'll need your help with that, Kaylee."

"You've got it," she said with a grin. "I wouldn't miss out on this for the world."

Naomi gave a light laugh. "You two were always thick as thieves when you had a project to work on. Come on, Jake. Let's leave them to it. You can help me make dinner, as long as you promise not to eat it all before it hits the table."

Eager to get to work, Kaylee pulled her laptop out of her bag. She needed to unpack, do laundry, and catch up on her school work, but nothing was more important than the work she had in front of her. "Where do you think we should start? Would he have used his real name?"

But Julian didn't answer, and when she looked up, he was leaning against the mantel, gazing into the fire.

"What's wrong?"

"Hmm? Oh, sorry. This has just really got me thinking. You know, at one time, I had some hope that Varhan was around, but I quickly dismissed it. It just didn't seem likely to me. But now I can't help but wonder if I've actually fulfilled my destiny on Earth at all."

"What do you mean?" It disturbed Kaylee to think that she might've upset her father. They'd always been so close.

"When I first came to Earth with you, I felt the need to go back to Charok. I didn't quite understand it at the time, but it was because I didn't have someone to spend my life with. There weren't any other female dragons here, and I didn't feel that there were any humans who could possibly be right for me, especially after Naomi and I were already mates back on Charok. She was so ill and had to leave if she wanted to have any possibility of surviving, as you know, so I thought I'd never see her again. But once she arrived here on Earth, all of that changed—yet I still keep looking for a way to go back. Am I betraying what Varhan thought my purpose was? Do I need to just let it go and be satisfied?" He pounded his fist gently against the mantel, making a picture frame jump slightly.

"I don't think there's anything wrong with exploring the possibilities," Kaylee countered. "And maybe you had more than one destiny. It's something I think about a lot, honestly."

"It's because you're a dragon," Julian explained quietly. "We don't always know exactly what it is that leads us, but it's like we have a tie to the stars and they pull us around like wagons until we get it all figured out. That's how Naomi and I knew we were right for each other. It's how I knew I was doing the right thing by coming to Earth. And it's how I know there are great things in your future, even though I can't possibly know what they are." He smiled at his daughter. "Now, let's see what we can find."

––––––––

KAYLEE GOT SO LOST in her work, she nearly forgot she had a dinner date with her cousins that night. She left her father to his studies—because she knew he wouldn't set the work down whether she stayed or not—and headed out to their favorite restaurant. Tranquility wasn't like most other establishments, where the sounds of other diners drowned out the conversation from just across the table. Instead, low walls separated each of the tables, like private booths with cushy, leather seating. The soothing background music played just loudly enough to make the diners feel as though they wouldn't be overheard, but it wasn't so loud that they had to shout. The plush carpet, dark walls, and ambient lighting made Kaylee feel more as though she'd walked into a cave versus a restaurant.

The maître d' escorted her to a table in the back corner, where her cohorts were already waiting for her. Finn, Nora and Elliot were raised by the other dragons who'd come from Charok at the same time Kaylee's father had. They'd grown up closely and saw themselves as cousins.

Kaylee settled in next to Nora, who instantly wrapped an arm around her and squeezed. "I'm so glad you're back!"

"I was only gone for a week," Kaylee protested with a smile. "It wasn't really enough time, honestly."

"Maybe not," Finn replied from across the table. He raised his glass, his big blue eyes glowing in the dim light, "but we're still glad to see you. It's just not the same when we're not all here together."

"Exactly," Elliot agreed. "Who else can I complain about my parents to that will actually understand? As a matter of fact, my dad will be thrilled to know you're home. He worries about you when you leave the country like that."

Her Uncle Beau had always taken on the role of caretaker of the group, often even fussing over his own generation because he was always concerned that everyone was taken care of. "Please tell him it's very sweet of him," Kaylee replied.

"I don't want to hear any complaints about your parents," Finn said, running a hand through his shaggy blond hair. "It's almost time for Zimryr, and you know how nutty my mom and dad get over that." His father, Kaylee's Uncle Holden, always insisted on having the cere-mony at his place. He wanted everyone to be there, no excuses, because he felt it was important. Like the others of his generation, he thought the old ways of Charok still had to be observed.

Nora sighed in sympathy. "Yes, but you know they're going to drag us all into it as well. I was happy to just go toast marshmallows over a big bonfire, but now that we're all older, they really want a lot more from us. I can eat until I'm stuffed, and I can even send my desires for the next year up into the universe if I have to, but I don't think I can possibly listen to them drone on and on about how things used to be back in their day." She rolled her eyes and picked at her napkin.

"I don't know," Kaylee replied. "I mean, it's not like they're asking all that much of us. What's one evening to spend with them? It's a great time for everyone to get together, if nothing else."

"I think you're getting to be just as bad as they are," Elliot said with an affectionate smile. "Does this mean your dad is any closer to finding a way back to Charok?"

She shook her head, deciding right then not to tell them about her and Julian's plan to find Varhan. They wouldn't really want to know, anyway. Though she'd grown up with these people and felt more at home with them than anyone else in the world besides her immediate family, Kaylee knew she still didn't quite fit in. She didn't think the same way they did. They loved her and accepted her, and they even knew what she could do with languages, but there was still a certain amount of distance between them. "No, I don't think so. It's just a hobby at this point."

"Good, because I can't even imagine how much my dad would be driving me up the wall if we actually could go there." Finn reached into the center of the table, where a waiter had just set down a large appetizer sampler. "He'd be all over me until I agreed to go back."

"But aren't you at least a little bit curious about what it would be like?" Kaylee asked. "I mean, we've lived on Earth our entire lives, but we actually *know* there's more out there. Everyone else can just speculate, but we *know*." In her heart, she couldn't quite even confirm which planet she felt she needed to live on. But she knew there was something demanding that she explore, that she push past her boundaries, that she find the one thing that nobody else knew about. She would be the first one to volunteer if they found a way to go to Charok.

"What we know is that a terrible spell eliminated most of our kind," Nora commented, snagging up a French fry and dipping it in a thick, cheesy sauce. "Who's to say the place isn't completely decimated? What could be there for us now? I mean, my parents are here. You guys are here."

Kaylee slumped against the soft back of the seat, trying to find a way to explain. There were no words that quite described the tug on her heartstrings, not even when she was trying to understand it herself. How could she make anyone else fathom what she felt? "I guess I'm just curious."

"There's nothing wrong with that." Elliot picked up a tiny tortilla bowl filled with guacamole and topped with shrimp. "Think about it like all those who emigrated to America way back when. I know this girl from school who's of Irish descent. Even though her family's been fully American for generations, she's dead set on going back to see what she considers her homeland. She's never set foot on it, but she thinks she belongs there."

"Yes, exactly like that!" Kaylee exclaimed, nearly jumping out of her seat.

"Exactly like that, but," Elliot put up a finger to stall her thinking process, "the majority of humans are perfectly happy just living as Americans and enjoying what they have here. They don't have to go back to the motherland to feel fulfilled."

Kaylee couldn't argue with that logic, but at least Elliot had given her something to relate to. There were too many questions that were unanswered. What had really happened to the dragons on Charok? Had anyone else escaped the Great Curse? What were things like there now?

She hoped that, someday, she would get to find out.

# 4

SIX MONTHS LATER

"ARE YOU READY FOR THIS?"

Kaylee looked to her father, who was practically trotting up the steep mountain trail like a child, despite the heavy pack on his back. He'd been impatient during the long flight to New Zealand, shifting uncomfortably in his seat and complaining under his breath that it would've been much easier to use his own wings. Now that they were getting close, though, he was filled with a new excitement and energy.

"I'm as ready as I'm ever going to get," she replied. It had been a long and grueling search, looking for any information they could find about mysterious travelers, suspected aliens, shamanic people with supernatural powers, or simply strangers who had gained notice while passing through town. Kaylee knew it was only through her father's relentless drive and arduous work that they were on this trail right now, and she hoped it was the right one. She didn't want to see the disappointment in his face if it wasn't.

"It should be just around the bend here, if what the man down in the village told us is correct," Julian puffed.

Kaylee reached out a hand, stopping him on the trail. "Dad, you know there's a possibility that this won't be Varhan, right? I mean, we can be fairly certain that whoever does live here is a little different from the rest of the local community, but it doesn't mean he's a wizard from another planet. It's a big risk." She couldn't help but focus on the practical side of things in this situation; she needed to in order to keep herself in check.

"Kaylee, I know exactly what you're doing, and I appreciate it. But there's absolutely nothing you can do to make me any less excited about this. I'm sure that he's here. And it's not because of our hours of research, and it's not even because the poor man at that restaurant where we stopped for lunch is afraid to come up the mountain. It's because no matter what we find here, it'll be something new. Not only that, but it's an adventure that I got to go on with my daughter. Nothing could be better than that."

"I only hope I'm that enthusiastic when I'm your age. Come on, then. Let's see what we can find."

The trail grew even more narrow and a little steeper as it clung to the mountainside, the cliff face falling away beneath them until it ended in a pristine blue lake. Kaylee tried not to look at it as they forged ahead, concentrating only on the task at hand.

"There it is, just like he said." Julian pointed as the trail turned into the mountain, revealing a tiny home snug against the rock. It wasn't much more than a shack, but plants and flowers grew all around it, nearly blending it in with the landscape.

"Okay. Let's do this." Kaylee stood half a step behind her father as they approached the door, her stomach jumping up and giving her heart a high-five every few seconds. She had to admit to herself she was just as excited as Julian was. But she knew the likelihood of finding a friendly wizard from a distant planet was a very slim one, and she had to remind herself that they were probably just disturbing some old hermit who would much rather be left alone.

But as soon as the door swung open, Kaylee knew that wasn't true. She'd had never before laid eyes on the round face, the friendly gray eyes, or the steely hair that receded from a wide forehead. But she immediately knew they'd found the right person, without even asking.

Julian stared for a long moment before he finally swallowed. "Varhan? Is it really you?"

"As I live and breathe!" The stout man just inside the door enveloped Julian in a hard hug. "I'm excited and yet terrified to see you here!"

"Terrified? But why?" Julian looked completely flabbergasted, a state Kaylee had never seen before. He'd always been so calm, collected, and sophisticated. This had thrown him for quite the loop.

"Well, the last time I saw you, there was an evil wizard about to ruin the world. I hope you're not coming to me now for the same reason." Varhan raised a thin eyebrow.

Julian laughed. "No, nothing of the kind—at least, not as far as I know. Oh, I'm sorry; where are my manners? This is my daughter, Kaylee."

Varhan turned to her, and as soon as their eyes met, Kaylee felt a distinct peace settle over her. The minor inconveniences she'd noticed on the trip—aching shoulders from carrying her luggage, a patch of skin on her ankle that always itched, a slightly upset stomach from the foreign food—all seemed to completely disappear.

"It's, um, very nice to meet you." Kaylee held out one shaking hand.

The wizard grasped it, his fingers warm and dry. "And you. My goodness. I never would've thought."

"Thought what?"

*You're really something, my child. So much more than I ever realized you'd grow up to be.*

Kaylee didn't understand what his mind was transmitting to hers. *I'm not really anything but a student.*

*A student of the universe, perhaps.* Varhan smiled benevolently. *There are great things in store for you, indeed. I can tell, and I think you can, too.*

"Are you two all right?" Julian asked, his head swiveling from one to the other. "What's going on here?"

Varhan let go of her hand and waved them into his home, chuckling to himself. It was a tiny house, consisting of only one room that served as kitchen, bedroom, and living area all in the one. The back wall was nothing more than the side of the mountain itself, and the floor was simply clean-swept rock. It was dark and cozy inside, if a bit cluttered. "I'm sorry, Julian; that was quite rude of me. But I haven't been able to talk to anyone that way in a very long time. Kaylee is quite gifted." He gestured to two crude wooden chairs near a low fire.

Kaylee was grateful for them, because it was at that moment she'd fully realized they'd been talking without using their voices at all. The experience had left her drained, but not necessarily in a bad way. She sank down onto the chair, taking comfort in the solidity of it beneath her. "Did that really just happen?"

The wizard busied himself with putting a kettle of water on to heat. "Oh, indeed. Sit down, Julian, and stop staring at me like that. You look like you've seen a ghost. I know this little hovel isn't much, but I haven't had company in at least five years or so."

Julian sat, but he still looked stunned. "I'm afraid I don't quite know what's going on here."

"Neither do I," Kaylee admitted, but she certainly wanted to know. Everything was just happening so quickly.

"Kaylee is a star child," Varhan explained as he rooted through a nearby cabinet, speaking as though they weren't talking about anything more important than the weather. "Or at least, that's the human term for it. Not quite accurate, but it's the best I can do."

"What does that mean?" Kaylee breathed.

He turned to her with yet another smile as he set two mugs on the little table near their chairs and crumbled some leaves into each one. "You have a connection to the universe, one that very few people have. I can't exactly explain the science of it to you, but you're very special indeed."

"How do you know this?" Julian demanded. He suddenly didn't seem as excited to see his old friend again.

"Because I'm one, too," Varhan explained simply, brushing his hands on his raggedy robes and retrieving the kettle. "It's how I knew I was doing the right thing by sending you to Earth, and how I knew to perform the spell in the first place. As a matter of fact, that's how I was able to send myself to Earth as well. That part was a little trickier, mind you. But clearly, I made it happen!" He chuckled as he filled each mug with water.

"I'm *very* confused," Kaylee admitted weakly.

Varhan slammed the kettle down onto the table, causing the mugs to slosh dangerously. He gave a hard look to Julian. "Doesn't she know?"

"Know what?" Kaylee demanded.

"Of course she knows," Julian argued, his face coloring deeply. "I've told her all about how you sent her and I over here when she was just an egg to avoid the War. I've had to raise her to be as human as possible in this world, but I've never hidden Charok from her."

The wizard's eyes narrowed as he stared at the dragon. "I see."

"Well, I don't!" Kaylee would've stood up if she didn't think the effort would knock her right back down again. "There's been very little that's made sense to me since I walked through this door!"

Varhan picked up one of the mugs and placed it in her hand. "Drink this. You'll feel much better."

"What is it?" she asked suspiciously. She'd been so happy to come here with Julian, but her life was suddenly being turned on its head.

"Chamomile." Varhan pulled up a low stool and parked it on the other side of the table where he could face his guests. "You should drink, too, Julian. I grew it myself."

Kaylee sipped her tea, surprised to find that the flavor was much stronger than the commercial stuff they had back home. She forced a deep breath in and out of her lungs. "Maybe we should start at the beginning. Why was I able to do that?" Now that it was over, the idea of telepathy seemed discomforting. But when it had happened, she had barely even noticed it.

"Star children often recognize each other, and usually they can communicate in ways the outside world can't even fathom. Think of it like a gift. I imagine it's not the only one you have?" Varhan's voice was calm and patient.

"For languages," Kaylee admitted. "At least when it comes to reading them. I can translate almost anything."

Varhan nodded. "Fascinating. Anything else?"

She shook her head. "Not that I'm aware of. Where did all this come from? Why can I do this?"

"As I said, I don't really know. Perhaps your heritage?" He looked to Julian.

Her father cleared his throat. "Not that I know of. This is going to take some time to get used to, so perhaps we should get back around to why we're really here. Varhan, we hoped you'd come back to the States with us."

"And leave my glorious castle?" He gestured at the tiny hut and laughed. "I'm just kidding. You know I've always lived minimally. It doesn't matter to me where I live. But why would you want me to come back with you?"

Julian seemed to have recovered somewhat. Perhaps it was the tea. He set his mug down and leaned forward, bracing his elbows on his knees. "I want your help. I've been trying to find a way to get back to Charok for the last twenty years. If there's anyone who can do it, I know you can."

Varhan chuckled again. "If that's so, then why did you wait so long to find me?"

"I didn't know you were here. And I could ask you the same thing. You knew I was on Earth, because you sent me yourself. Couldn't you have just come to the same place?"

The wizard tipped his head from one side to the other, a smile playing on his lips. "It doesn't always work that way. In any case, it wasn't my role. I'm not sure it was yours, either. But Kaylee is a different matter." He turned to her, his eyes alight. "You're a completely different matter."

"Once again, I have to ask what that means." She was growing impatient with these constant riddles and partial truths. She still didn't quite understand what a star child was, and yet according to this man, she was supposedly one.

"I mean that we're not all sitting here because of me, and we're not all sitting here because of your father. We're sitting here because of *you*." He touched the tip of his finger to her nose.

Kaylee scowled at him. "Okay, I admit this was my idea."

"No, no. It's much more than that. But I don't have all the answers, and I wouldn't even try to give them to you. If I were you, I would worry more about understanding the questions than finding the answers."

"But what about *your* answer?" Julian pressed. "Will you come back with us?"

Varhan looked from Julian to Kaylee and back again. "Let me just pack my things."

# 5

SIX MONTHS LATER

KAYLEE BREATHED IN THE STIFF NIGHT AIR, SENSING THE ENERGY THAT crackled through it. They had been working so hard for so long, and she wasn't sure she'd hardly slept at all over the last few months. Between school and this, her life was completely taken up. She didn't really mind, though. She knew they were working toward something big.

"I think we're ready," Varhan said, his voice a mix of joy and anticipation. "The stars are all aligned correctly, at least as far as I can tell. I've spent far too much time studying the constellations on Charok, and I've had a lot to catch up on."

"Seems to me that you've done very well." Julian clapped his old friend on the back. "You've come here and done a lot more in a short time than I've been able to accomplish in twenty years or more. I can't tell you how excited I am about this."

The wizard leaned on the railing that surrounded the balcony along the back side of the house. "Don't get too excited. Remember what I said: this is only a glimpse into the old world. If all goes right, we'll be able to see what things are like on Charok. I can't guarantee that we'll be able to talk to anyone—provided anyone is still there, of course—or even that it will work."

"Varhan, you're too hard on yourself. You were the one who got us all here in the first place." Julian's grin took up his entire face. It was a welcome look, considering how tired he'd seemed lately.

The wizard's grip tightened on the railing. "Still, I'm concerned."

"But we've been over everything about a million times!" Kaylee enthused. She could feel how close they were to making this happen. Even though it wasn't exactly a portal to Charok, it was something so much bigger than they were. She needed this. She knew it had something to do with the way she'd felt her entire life, and ever since she'd started working with Varhan and Julian, she'd no longer felt as though she was searching for something that could never be found. She'd long dismissed the 'star child' talk as crazy, old man nonsense, but she knew they were finally working toward something. "We've mapped all the stars and traced the energy between them. We've gone over the spell so much that I'm pretty sure I've been saying it in my sleep. We have all the ingredients we need. What more can we possibly do?"

Varhan sighed and took one of her hands between his. He was like an uncle to her already, and his kind gaze meant the world to her. "My dear child, I can't tell you how proud I am that you have such talent. I only wish that I knew as much as you when I was your age. But you have to understand that magic works differently here on Earth. Your scientists say that physics is the same on any planet, but that's not so with magic. I can't predict what kind of side effects there might be. I couldn't forgive myself if one of you got hurt."

"We both know the risks," Kaylee assured him with a glance at her father, who nodded his assent. "We're doing this. We've got to."

The small smile that cross Varhan's lips was enough to let her know that he wanted this, too. "I guess I'm just used to being the only one involved. It's been wonderful having research partners, though, especially ones like the two of you. But there's one more thing that's been weighing heavily on my mind."

"Go on," Julian encouraged.

"Let's say everything goes according to plan, and we can see what Charok is like now. There's a good chance we'll see nothing but wilderness and ruins, but what happens if you see there is still life there? Dragons, even? You know we won't be able to bring them over here, at least not yet. I have no reason to believe that the spell that brought you here would work in reverse to send you back."

Julian tipped his head back to the stars. "I know, but it would be something else for us to work on. And it would give me a lot of hope.

All these years, I've been devastated to know that I made it out alive when so many others perished. I have my loved ones, and I'm very grateful for that, but I'm far too lucky. I'd like to think there are still others out there like us who managed to survive."

"Well, there's only one way to find out."

The three of them went back inside and to the library. They'd debated for the last several weeks on the best location for the performance of the spell. While they didn't want anything to happen to the library if something should go wrong, it had quite a bit of open floor space to give them room to move about. All of their research was close at hand, as well. The idea of doing it outside had been kicked around some, but there was too much risk that they might be seen. It would only take one person who happened to be flying a drone overhead or going for a late-night walk on the trail through the woods and they would be found out.

"All right. Here we go." Kaylee began shoving furniture up against the walls, requiring her father's help to lift the heavy leather sofa and the coffee table. The area rug was easily rolled up and placed on the back of the couch, and Julian retrieved a broom to sweep the floor beneath it clean. They'd already traced a large circle on the wooden floor, taking care to make it as perfect as possible.

"I know we all know this very well, but I'm going to check our work as we go along." Varhan picked up the ballpoint pen and notebook he'd been writing with. He'd been fascinated with the modern writing tools, and while he often commented that an old-fashioned quill was more stimulating, he liked the fact that he almost never an out of ink. "First, the salt."

Kaylee fetched the canister of salt from a nearby shelf. She now knew that it would absorb extra psychic energy that didn't belong there, serving as a bit of protection for them. She carefully sprinkled it all along the circumference of the circle on the floor.

"Next, the citrine."

Since her aunts ran a New Age store, it had been easy to find the crushed citrine that aided in communication. The stone glittered beautifully in her hands as she spread it over the salt.

"The silver bowl."

Julian handed this to Kaylee. It was already filled with celery seeds and coltsfoot, and she set it in the very center of the circle. Her father then handed her three smooth stones, their black surfaces marked with brilliant splotches of white. Kaylee had fallen in love with the snowflake obsidian as soon as her father had brought it home, and she placed them at equal intervals around the silver bowl.

"I think we're ready to go." Kaylee stepped out of the circle to pick up a box of matches.

"No, no. I want you to say it. I'll light the herbs," Varhan insisted.

Kaylee paused, one foot inside the circle and the other outside. "But you're the wizard. You're the one who knows how to do these things."

He smiled and bobbed his head. "In the past, yes. But there's no doubt that among the three of us, you're the one who's gifted with words. They roll off your tongue like they were made for you, and it would be a shame to let one of us old geezers stumble over them."

"Well, all right." She took the notebook from Varhan and stood near the silver bowl. Her eyes drifted down to the words on the page, written carefully in the wizard's Charokian script. She didn't need to read them. She knew exactly what they said, and in her heart, she knew what they meant. Most of it couldn't quite be translated to English, but the general idea was one of reaching out to the past and over distance to reunite two things that belonged together. It thrilled her heart to think she might soon be seeing the place where she'd come from.

"Julian, you know your role?" Varhan asked.

He stepped inside the circle, and the three of them crouched down so that their toes were between the obsidian stones. He laid a hand on each of their shoulders. "Yes, but I'm still not sure I'm the right one for the job. I mean, my sister-in-law is a psychic. It seems to me that she would be far better at stabilizing the two of you."

"You keep saying that, but I keep telling you that she wouldn't. She only knows what's here on Earth, and it's much better if we're all natives of the land we're trying to reach." Varhan braced the match in his hand against the outside of the box. "Are we ready?"

The other two nodded, and he struck the match. The small flame fizzled brightly, and Varhan made sure the stick had completely caught before dropping it into the dried herbs. They blazed up, and Kaylee knew it was time.

She closed her eyes and recited the words in a language far more suited to dragon tongues than human ones. It sounded like nothing more than a series of clicks and growls with a few vowels thrown in, but the meaning was clear. Kaylee let the words take over her mind as she felt the warmth of the flame on her face and the steadiness of her father's hand on her shoulder. Though she couldn't see him, she knew Varhan was tracing delicate patterns in the air with a tiny wand made from an ancient tree that had grown near his home in New Zealand. She lost herself in the tranquility of it all, her lips moving on their own, and she felt that she could drift off to sleep right where she was.

It was only when she heard the gasp from Julian that she opened her eyes again. Her lids were heavy, but she forced them back wide when she saw that the floor beneath them had completely disappeared. They were hovering over a red mountain, the boulders and precipitous cliffs clear beneath their feet. The vision wobbled slightly, as though they were on a tall tower that wasn't quite balanced, leaning out over the forest at the base of the mountain and then floating to the other side of it completely.

"That's it," Julian choked. "That's Mount Rokalo, where the royal caves are."

Kaylee didn't recognize any of it, but she craned her neck in an attempt to see it all more clearly. She'd never seen anything as beautiful as the contrast between the ruddy stone and the deep emerald of the trees that surrounded it. The mountain itself looked as though it belonged in the desert, yet the forest was thick and deep.

"Yes." Varhan's voice trembled. "It's working! Oh, praise be to all the spirits that watch us from above!" He clapped his hands gently.

"Can we see anywhere else?" Kaylee asked, desperate to find out more about this place.

"I'll try." Varhan rubbed his hands together and pressed them to the floor. The circle of vision beneath them started to shift slightly.

Movement caught Kaylee's eye just on the outer edge of it. "Wait. What's that?"

Julian sucked in his breath. "It can't be."

But Kaylee knew. She had already known as soon as she had seen it —or rather, *them*. A small flight of dragons careened though the air near the summit of the mountain, their scales glistening in the sunlight. "Varhan, is there any chance that what we're seeing is taking place at a different time? I mean, this is happening right now, right?"

The wizard swallowed audibly before replying. "As far as I can tell, yes."

"Incredible," Julian whispered.

Kaylee felt as though she could float there above Charok all day, but the universe had other plans. The herbs in the silver bowl had burned down to a slow smolder, but the celery seeds began popping from the heat. Ash tumbled over the side of the shallow container. Kaylee instinctively took a slight step back, still squatting near the center of the circle, but it wasn't enough. The obsidian stones that surrounded the bowl began cracking and splitting, sending shards of black stone into the air.

"Something's going wrong," Varhan said. "Get back, quickly!"

The three of them scrambled out of the circle. The vision beneath them had changed completely, a white, swirling mist obscuring the beautiful scenery that'd been there only a moment ago. Kaylee's heart thundered in her chest. "What do we do to stop it?"

"There are a few things I can try, but I'm not sure," Varhan admitted, large beads of sweat forming on his forehead. "The spell was designed to only last for a few minutes. It should just wear itself out and stop, but I'm not sure what's happening here. I'll get my book."

Kaylee had never felt so helpless as she watched the mist change. It turned from white to red to a deep blue, and it began spinning so fast that it formed a vortex at the center. To her surprise, the bowl and the remnants of the stones fell right into it. A rising wind was now flowing through the room, rifling the open books on the tables and whipping her hair around her face. "I think we need to get out of here!"

"Not yet!" Varhan shouted over the noise. "I can't just leave it! I don't know how far it will go!"

Kaylee looked to her father, who nodded grimly. She understood. While she was no wizard, an out-of-control spell could be a very dangerous thing.

The door to the library flew open, but not because of the wind. Jake filled the doorway, his eyes wild as he took in the scene. Naomi was just behind him, clinging to his arm. "What the hell is going on in here?"

Nobody took the time to explain. It was too much to put into words when a whirlpool of air and magic and who-knew-what-else had opened up at their feet. Instead, Varhan moved around the circle to Kaylee's side and handed her his spell book.

Kaylee took the ancient journal in her hands, feeling its cracked leather cover and smelling the stale paper. The wizard poked his finger over her arm at a spell. "Read it! Out loud!"

"Shouldn't you be doing this?" she yelled, trying to hand the book back. The wind rushed loudly in her ears.

"No time for modesty!" he insisted. "Read! And don't stop until I say so!"

Kaylee could hardly hear her own voice over the gale that tormented the room, but she did as she was told. The verses he'd indicated were written in the same odd writing as the original spell, but the words were different. Kaylee paid little attention to them as she let them flow from her lips.

As soon as she was done, Varhan shook her elbow. "Keep going!"

The vision at her feet that had become a real thing so quickly terrified her, so she allowed herself to get lost in the words. Her tongue brushed the roof of her mouth and slid across the backs of her teeth as she spoke. She didn't stop the spell even to breathe in, reciting the words with every movement of her lungs. She closed her eyes. Varhan's hand on her shoulder kept her rooted as she spoke, and soon enough, she felt her father on the other side.

A gasp from her mother made her open her eyes again. The mist now looked as solid as water, and it spun so fast, it made her stomach churn. The downdraft in the center had now lifted upward, and a dragon came shooting out of it. The beast nearly hit the high ceiling before he caught himself on one of the heavy wooden timbers. Three more came after it.

Varhan bent forward and touched the portal with the tip of his wand, and in an instant, it froze back into the hard, wooden floor that it had been originally.

## 6

ARCHARD SHOVED THE REST OF HIS CLAN BEHIND HIM AND SPREAD HIS wings, feeling a ball of fire building in his chest. It had been a normal day on Charok when the sky had opened up and sucked them through a long, winding passage full of light that made his stomach turn. Now, he had no idea where he was or why, but he knew he didn't belong there.

"Who are you, and what do you want with us?" he demanded.

A man stepped forward, holding his palms out and grinning from ear to ear. "I can't tell you how happy we are to see you!"

This fool was clearly of no consequence, but some sort of magic had happened to bring them there. Archard craned his neck toward the little old man on the other side of the room, who was trying to dislodge a stick from the floor. "You! You're a wizard! Are you all wizards?" It was the first conclusion he'd come to, considering this confined, stifling place they were in. Only a wizard would put them in a place like this.

The smiling man flicked his arm, shifting his hand into a clawed one for a moment. "We're dragons, just like you are. Well, Varhan *is* a wizard, but I promise he's on your side."

"Get out of the way!" This came from Callan, who slid his dark brown reptilian form around from behind Archard. He approached the strangers, quickly morphing into his two-legged self and reaching out his hand just as his claws and scales transformed into fingers and nails. "I apologize for my cousin's behavior. We just haven't seen any other dragons in a long time."

"Callan..." Archard warned. What he said was true, but just because they were dealing with fellow dragons didn't mean they were safe.

"It's quite understandable. My name is Julian." The man shook Callan's hand. "This is Varhan, my daughter Kaylee, my wife Naomi, and my son Jacob."

Archard's eyes glanced around the room at each person Julian introduced, but they swung immediately back to the one named Kaylee. With her deep brown hair and brilliant emerald eyes, she greatly resembled her father. Unlike him, though, she looked slightly horrified. Archard focused on her dark pink lips and felt his scales ripple. Perhaps she was a wizard, as well, because he felt as though she'd put a spell on him.

"It's very nice to meet you," Callan enthused.

Now Lucia came forward. She touched Archard reassuringly with her wing before shifting into her human form as well. "I think you'll set our minds at ease if you could explain what's happened."

Archard didn't like the idea of his clan putting themselves at risk like this. They didn't know these people, and the four of them were all they had left. Still, he wanted to hear their side of the story.

Varhan gave a final yank at his wand, and the flames inside Archard prepared to leap forward, lest he put another spell on them. But the wood snapped, and the wizard hit the floor with a hard thump. He examined the splintered stump in his hand. "Ah, damn."

This was enough to break the tension in the room for many of them, but Archard wasn't ready to put his guard down just yet.

"Easy there, big boy," Kieran whispered from his side. His silver scales had melted into warm skin and a shaggy beard, and his dark eyes looked into Archard's with sympathy. "There's not enough room in here for all your rage."

"Fine." It took a lot of effort and several deep breaths, but Archard folded his wings into his back. The strong reptilian legs stretched while his neck shortened, and he shook his head as his face took on the shape of his human configuration. He ran a thick hand through the dark hair that replaced the spikes on the back of his head and suddenly felt self-conscious as he noticed that Kaylee was still watching him.

"This is a little difficult, because I'm not entirely sure myself of what's happened," Julian explained. "You see, we came from Charok two decades ago, just as Tazarre cast his spell. Varhan helped us. My son was born here, and I brought my daughter here while she was still growing in her egg. We were simply trying to see what things were like over there, but something went wrong with the spell."

"I warned you there would be some side effects we couldn't predict," Varhan grumbled as he got to his feet with Kaylee's assistance, dusting off his robe. "While I can't explain what went wrong, I did the best I could do to fix it. I used another spell I'd been considering, but I wasn't sure what it would do. Apparently, it brought you all here."

"But where *is* here?" Archard demanded.

"Earth," Kaylee answered, and her voice pierced straight into Archard's heart.

She was too beautiful, and he'd never seen anyone quite like her. He wanted to shift back, and the skin on the back of his neck flipped over into scales. He gritted his teeth against each other to regain control. Clearly, if she was part of whatever spell that had brought them there, then she had some sort of power. So why did he feel the need to dart across the room and separate her from the rest of these strangers?

"As far as we can calculate, our planet is on the opposite side of the galaxy from Charok," Varhan said gently. "It's a long way unless you have the right spell."

"You're saying that you escaped before the Great Curse?" Archard asked. "You abandoned us while everyone was dying? You ran off to another planet and *left* us?" He couldn't quite wrap his mind around this foreign planet they were supposedly on, but the idea left a distinct sense of disgust at the base of his spine.

"I promise you, I had a very good reason for going. I've spent my entire life since then wishing there was something I could've done to save everyone. But there was very little time," Julian explained.

"And my resources were limited, unfortunately," Varhan added.

Lucia nodded. "I think we can understand that," she said in her calm and diplomatic voice. "And I think there's much more for all of us to talk about. But I have to admit that this spell and the idea of being on a different planet has left me feeling rather overwhelmed. This is going to take some time."

"Of course!" The woman named Naomi jumped forward. She was, as far as Archard could understand, Kaylee's mother, but the two women looked nothing like each other. "Perhaps we should start with giving you a tour of our home. It's big enough, and I think we can find accommodations for all of you."

Archard took a solid step forward. "What I'd prefer is for you to send us back," he asserted. "We never asked to come here."

Julian glanced at the wizard, who rolled his shoulders uncertainly. "Ah, you see, that might not be a very simple thing."

Archard's blood thundered in his ears. It was a very human reaction, and one that he didn't prefer to experience. It was easier to handle these situations as a dragon, and his body certainly wanted to be back in that physique, but there simply wasn't enough space in this room for them all to shift back. "Are you telling me we're stuck here?"

The corners of Varhan's mouth stretched down toward his wobbly jaw. "I'm afraid so, at least for now. But I promise you I'll get working on it right away!" he added quickly.

"I know it's hard to understand right now, but you should really give Earth a try," Julian said. "There were several other dragons who came through with me, and we've all adjusted very well. It's quite a pleasant place once you get used to it."

Archard wasn't so sure. He didn't want to come here, and as far as he was concerned, he wasn't going to stay any longer than he had to. "I want to go back as soon as possible. I can't just leave my entire world behind."

"I know it's difficult right now, but be patient. It'll be all right." Julian led the way out of the room, the rest of the dragons following him.

Archard brought up the end, seething inside. It was easy for Julian to tell him to be patient. He'd come to this place of his own volition. But Archard had duties back on Charok, ones that he couldn't just abandon. Nobody there would understand that, though, not even his own family. He stepped out into a hallway, which made him even more uncomfortable than the library had.

"For what it's worth, this really wasn't what we intended."

He whirled to find Kaylee at his shoulder. Standing right next to her like that, he could see that she was only a few inches shorter than him. Her dark curls tumbled around her shoulders, and she still looked as breathless as she had when they arrived. He studied her face, feeling as though he'd seen her somewhere before. "I'm not sure it matters."

"Suit yourself, but I just want you to know that we meant no harm. I'm looking forward to finding out more about your world. Well, technically it's my world, too. Just not in the same way." They followed the others down the hall, and Julian could be heard at the front of the line giving a grand tour of the place.

"It's not your world at all," Archard insisted. "I can see already that you live completely different lives than we do on Charok. I can barely even tell that you're a dragon." He hadn't realized it until he'd said it out loud. Dragons always knew each other, even if they'd never met before. It was an instant knowledge that reached their brains, and though he didn't know the science behind it, he knew it to be true. Kaylee was more human than dragon, yet there was something else inside her as well.

She tipped her head up ever so slightly, her eyes narrowing. "There aren't many opportunities to shift in this world. We live among humans who don't know about us, and we'd like to keep it that way."

"Are you seriously telling me that I can't even be who I am here? That I can't fly and hunt and do...everything else dragons do?" He'd gotten too close to her, his body only a few inches away from hers, and his mind had turned in the wrong direction. Archard should be concerned with his freedom and his future, yet he was suddenly much more interested in grabbing Kaylee and dragging her off through one of the numerous doorways around them so they could be alone. It was a strange feeling, and one he knew he shouldn't be having.

"There's a lot you can do," she replied patiently, obviously having no idea what he was really thinking. She glanced down the hall, where the rest of the party was turning off into a large room and leaving them behind. "It's just that over the years, a lot of us have gotten out of the habit. Bad things could happen if we're discovered, so we have to be discreet. But it's not so bad, really."

"That's easy for you to say," Archard snarled. Now that the rest of them were out of earshot, he was having a harder time controlling his body. The most difficult part was that he wasn't even sure what he wanted to do. Part of him wanted to keep this beautiful woman safe from anything that might harm her, and the idea that they were surrounded by humans who wanted to do just that made his blood boil.

The other part of him knew that someone was going to have to step in and make sure Kaylee was safe from *him*. The longer he stood here near her, watching the way the shades of green shifted in her intelligent eyes and studying the warmth and tone of her skin, the more he wanted to wrap his arms around her waist and crush her against his body. Even the way her mouth moved when she spoke, like the words only existed because she allowed them to, was hypnotizing. If they were somewhere else and in a different situation, he might not have bothered to control himself at all.

Kaylee crossed her arms and raised one eyebrow, her lips tightening. "Fine. If you want to be grumpy and negative about this, then that's your problem."

"What?" He'd gotten so caught up in the energy that crackled between them that he'd nearly forgotten everything he'd said.

"I know this can't be easy on you," she replied, her voice impatient. "I can't pretend to know exactly what you're going through, but I'm doing my best. You won't even let me be nice, so maybe I should just stop trying." Kaylee brushed past him and stormed down the hall to join the rest of the group.

Archard watched her go, any argument dying on his lips. Earth was going to be quite a challenge.

KAYLEE'S BODY ACHED. SHE WAS SO TIRED THAT HER EYELIDS threatened to close as she helped her mother clean up the kitchen, but she knew she wasn't going to sleep anytime soon. The evening's events had been far too exciting.

After Julian had shown the new dragons around the house and assured them numerous times that they were welcome to stay, Naomi had prepared a large dinner and Jake had added the extra leaves in the dining table. It was like the family reunion that Kaylee had never realized she'd longed for. Lucia made polite conversation, always thanking their hosts and commenting on how delicious the food was. Callan was fascinated with the new world and asked questions about everything, which kept the conversation going long into the night. Kieran was quiet, but his eyes were wise and it was obvious to Kaylee that he observed everything going on around him. Every now and then, he'd cracked a dry joke that was funny, no matter what planet they were on. Archard had been another matter, but she tried to ignore him as best she could.

Naomi took a dirty plate out of her hand and smiled. "You look dead on your feet."

"Something like that," Kaylee admitted. "I just can't stop thinking about it all. This wasn't supposed to happen, but I can't say I'm unhappy that it did."

Her mother put an arm around her shoulders. "Sometimes accidents give us the most wonderful gifts. Mind you, I plan to have a stern talking-to with your father and Varhan. If that spell had gone differently, you might've been seriously hurt."

"Oh, Mom. I'm fine. I just can't believe this happened." Her cheeks were already tired from smiling so much, but she couldn't stop herself. It was thrilling, and it meant so much for their future. She knew even without asking that her father would be eager to start on the next step, whatever that may be.

"Neither can I, but I suppose I shouldn't be surprised. Stranger things have happened." Naomi smiled gently to herself as she rinsed the plate and put it in the dishwasher.

"Like what?" As she moved through the kitchen, Kaylee realized just how strange of a thing this probably would have been for the new dragons in their home. From what Julian had told her of Charok, they didn't have modern conveniences like dishwashers or refrigerators. It was a much more primitive society, though civilized.

"Oh, I don't know. I think your father and Varhan are waiting for you in the library. You'd better go, or they'll start talking without you."

Kaylee dried her hands on a towel and left the kitchen. As she headed for the library, she tipped her head up toward the ceiling. In the extra bedrooms upstairs, her parents had made room for each of the new dragons. Julian had apologized numerous times for the strange sleeping conditions, since none of them were used to sleeping in beds in a house, but they all seemed to accept the hospitality well enough. Even Archard didn't say much, simply closing the door behind him.

As her mother said, Julian and Varhan were in the library. The remnants of the salt, citrine and ashes had been swept from the floor. The rug was back in place, as was the furniture. Except for a few pieces of paper that'd been blown around the room and the piece of Varhan's wand that still stuck out of the floor, it was like nothing had ever happened there.

But the looks on the men's faces were enough to remind her that it most certainly had. "The two of you are absolutely amazing," Julian enthused, straightening a vase on a shelf. He was too excited to sit down, and he busied himself throughout the room. "More dragons! Who would've thought we'd not only find them, but bring them back here?"

Kaylee sat down heavily, the leather couch cool on her back. "Yeah, it's pretty heavy stuff."

Varhan rubbed a hand over his forehead. "We should be getting to sleep soon. We have a lot of work ahead of us."

"Agreed. I want to try the spell again as soon as possible." Julian tapped a finger against the silver bowl, the inside of it tarnished from the burning herbs it held earlier.

The wizard let out a low laugh. "No, my friend. That's not going to happen anytime soon. We need to recover, for one thing. You're excited right now, but when you wake up in the morning, you'll realize just how much the magic has drained you. And I think you're also forgetting that the spell went wrong. It was all purely accidental, and even if we tried, I couldn't guarantee that we'd replicate it."

The smile faded only slightly from Julian's face. "Even so, we have an excellent starting point. With a little bit of time and research, I imagine we can bring more dragons over within a week or two. Lucia said there were other clans still on Charok, ones that managed to survive the War and the Great Curse. We can't just leave them there."

Kaylee cleared her throat. She didn't want to argue with either one of them, but this was her opportunity to express the concerns she'd been having all evening. "Don't you think we should be working on sending them back instead?"

"What do you mean?" Julian almost looked offended, but Varhan's eyes twinkled at her.

"Well, they didn't want to be here in the first place." Archard's words were still fresh in her mind. "We know that at least one of them wants to go back, and I think it's only fair that we try to accomplish that."

Varhan leaned forward, bracing his elbows on his knees. He looked particularly old, his face lined with worry, and Kaylee realized she had no idea how old he was. "It's a noble thought, and one that I'm glad to hear you're having. The problem is that I don't know how to send them back. If I did, then I could've just sent Julian there like he'd always wanted."

"I did want that," her father admitted, biting his lower lip and shaking his head. "But I'm not so sure now. I mean, there's a lot more opportunity for us here. We don't even have to live in caves or hunt for food. They're much better off, and we can help them."

An uncomfortable feeling squirmed inside Kaylee's stomach. "But

I'm not sure we did the right thing. I know it wasn't on purpose, but it's not fair for us to just assume they want to be on Earth because *we* think it's better. They might miss their home. Hell, I've never lived there and I feel like I miss it."

Julian put his hands up in the air. "Fair enough. You're right. I'll talk to them some more tomorrow. But like Varhan said, we don't know how to send them back. Not yet. In the meantime, they'll have the chance to see what Earth is really like and make their decision from there."

"What about the others?" Varhan asked. "Have you told them?"

"I called Holden and explained things. He thought I was playing a joke on him at first. We both agreed that we should take things slowly. We'll give it some time before we bring everyone else over. They seem a bit overwhelmed as it is, except for Callan. I've no doubt he'll be staying."

"It's Archard that I'm concerned about," Kaylee said quietly. "He seemed very unhappy about being here; angry, even. I don't know that he'll be able to keep this all a secret." She'd tried not to think about him, especially after their encounter in the hall, but Archard had been on the forefront of her mind ever since the new dragons had arrived. She couldn't deny her first thought: that she'd never seen such a gorgeous being in her life. His dark hair was swept back against his head, and he kept it a bit shorter than Callan did. Paired with those jet blue eyes, a strong jaw, and wide shoulders, he was like something out of a movie. Even his hostility hadn't completely turned her off at first. He gave her a strange feeling in the pit of her stomach, like her own skin was suffocating her. The way Archard watched her made her feel like she was the only person in the room, and Kaylee had yet to decide if that was a good or bad thing.

"Don't worry about him. He's just an angry young man who's been pulled away from everything he knows. Some of it is his age, and he'll get past it. Give him time. And for the rest of us, Varhan is right. We need some sleep ourselves. Good night, Kaylee. I'm very proud of you." Julian kissed her on the forehead and opened the door to the library.

———

DESPITE VARHAN'S promise that their spellwork would leave them exhausted, Kaylee couldn't sleep. She'd changed into her most comfortable pajamas, but the soft fabric kept twisting around her body as she tossed under the covers. She stripped them off and tried sleeping naked, but it was no better. As long as her mind was racing, her body wasn't going to rest.

With a grunt of frustration, she flung the covers back and got dressed. She was just wasting her time, and that was something she couldn't stand. If her brain insisted on being awake, then she was going to put it to good use. In her bare feet, she crept downstairs to the library.

Kaylee wasn't surprised to see a line of light under the door. She sighed and shook her head. Her father had sent her off to bed, but he probably hadn't even tried to get any sleep himself and opted instead to stay up and do exactly what she was going to do. Kaylee didn't know nearly as much about spells as her father and Varhan did, but she could still do her best.

She opened the door, prepared to find her father on the chair in front of the fireplace. But the dark figure in the room was none other than Archard. He stood in front of a large window on the wall opposite the door, his long arms stretching out to brace against the trim work. He looked over his shoulder when he heard her enter.

Kaylee softly closed the door behind her, not wanting to wake the rest of the house. "What are you doing up? I thought you went to sleep hours ago." It had thrown her completely to find him there, and a bolt of adrenaline now made a heady mix with her blood.

"No. I went to the room your parents said I could use, but I haven't slept at all. I don't think I'll ever be able to, not under a roof like this. I'm used to being out in the open."

She wrung her fingers together, unsure of what to say. "I suppose you could ask if you could camp out in the yard tomorrow."

He whirled around, a strand of hair coming down to hang in his face. His fists were curled at his sides as he advanced toward her. "That's just the problem! I shouldn't have to ask permission for something like that! I'm practically being held prisoner here!"

"Keep your voice down!" she snapped, irritated. "You're not a prisoner. I guess you can do whatever the hell you want to. It's just courtesy to talk to the owner of the house, especially considering that the outside world doesn't know who you really are!"

"Keep your own voice down, then, if you care so much." His sapphire eyes blazed. "And that doesn't exactly make it any better.

Even if you and your family aren't trying to contain me, your society is. I never wanted to be here, Kaylee."

It was the first time she'd heard him say her name out loud, and the sound made a vibration that rippled through her bones and caught in her throat. "I know that," she choked, realizing that every cell of her body seemed to be aware of every part of his. If she closed her eyes, she'd still know exactly where he was and how he stood. "And I explained it was an accident."

"Accident or not, it was irresponsible of you to try such a thing. I have duties on Charok that are far more important than your experimental magic." He tightened his fist and turned away once again.

Kaylee worked her tongue in her mouth, trying to find the right words. She'd never had a hard time with that before. She'd always been quick with her tongue, even before she knew about her gift. Archard made her feel there were no sufficient words, no matter what she was trying to say. "I understand. I can't really argue with that. But the fact is that we don't have a way to send you back, at least not yet." She cringed inwardly, waiting for another violent reaction from him.

Instead, he just shook his head and turned toward the window. "Of course not."

In that moment, Kaylee realized that their spell hadn't gone completely wrong. They'd created a window to Charok because they wanted to learn about its current state. Now, they could not only learn about it, but get firsthand accounts of it. "Could you tell me about it?"

"Charok? Why would I do that?" His hand rubbed over the back of his neck and remained there, his biceps firm in the dim light of the lamps.

"I just want to know. I've always wanted to know. I've never felt like I really belonged here on Earth, and I have to admit I wanted to go to Charok just as badly as my father did. Don't punish me for this, Archard. It's not something I ever would've done on purpose."

He pulled in a deep breath that Kaylee was sure would fuel some sort of retort, but he let it out again without speaking. After a long moment of silence, he said, "It's nothing like this place, at least as far as I understand. My clan and I stay in the foothills of the mountains, where we're close enough to the forest to hunt fraxen and gather vegetables, but where we can retreat to the safety of the caves when we need to."

"You don't live in the caves? I'm sorry. I'm just going off of what my father told me." She dared to take a step forward. His back was still turned to her, but she knew he heard her soft footstep against the floor. Dragons had excellent hearing.

"Not for a long time. So many of our people died there, and it feels almost haunted. It was easier to start new lives for ourselves, at least as much as we could. There are some of us who still try to fulfill the roles our families have served in for generations, but others have ventured away from that. Callan, I'm sure, will be happy to see how your kind live."

"My kind?" The phrase seemed almost offensive. "We're the *same* kind, Archard. We're not really that different." Why did she care? She'd told herself earlier in the night, when he'd been so stubbornly angry outside the library, that she wasn't going to waste her time on him. But she very much wanted him to understand her and even accept her, as far-fetched of an idea as that seemed to be.

"Physically, maybe, but that's about it. Our lives are completely different. We've spent a long time wondering just how many of us still existed and why all this happened to us." A heavy sigh rippled through his shoulders. "I always had a feeling something big was going to happen, like there was something out there waiting for me. I didn't think it was going to be this."

Kaylee understood that feeling, and she took a few more steps and tentatively reached out her hand. She touched his shoulder. In the split second that her fingertips grazed his shirt, she felt a bolt of electricity shoot through her hand and up her arm. It was no mere static electricity, and she immediately yanked her hand back.

Archard spun around, but he only looked at her with curiosity.

She cleared her throat, the air between them tense. "I really am sorry. I want you to know that. And since it's my fault you're stuck here for now, why don't you let me give you a little tour?"

"I've seen the house," he growled.

She almost laughed. "No, I mean of our city. Come with me tomorrow and see what a day is like for us here. I'll take you out of the house. I can't guarantee it'll make you feel better about being here, but it's worth a shot." Kaylee looked up at him hopefully, unable to avoid studying his handsome features. He was rugged and strong, and a shadow of a beard had cropped up along his jaw since he'd arrived.

"All right," he finally said. "I guess I might as well try, since there's no telling how long I'll be staying here."

"You'll have to stay in your human form," she warned him.

He gave her a serious look. "Yes, I understand that."

Her body wanted to surge toward his. Kaylee had never been the kind to throw herself at a man, no matter how attractive or mysterious he was. It shouldn't have made any difference that Archard was a dragon or that he'd come from a world she'd always been desperate to understand. Maybe that wasn't even why she felt this way about him, but either way, she knew it was dangerous. At least while they were out tomorrow, they'd be in public. "All right. We'll leave after breakfast. In the meantime, try to get some sleep." She turned and left the library as quickly as she could without running.

Back in her bedroom, Kaylee felt as though she couldn't catch her breath. She leaned against the door, energy and excitement running through her body likes balls of fire. "So much for sleeping," she whispered.

# 8

---

ARCHARD AWOKE FEELING STIFF AND CANTANKEROUS. HE'D MANAGED TO get a little sleep after opening the window and pushing his bed up against it, allowing a stiff breeze to blow into the room. It wasn't nearly the same as his favorite spot on the side of the mountains on Charok, but it was the best he could do for the moment.

As he got dressed and the scent of hot food beckoned him down to the kitchen, Archard realized what a fool he'd been for accepting Kaylee's offer. He shouldn't be around her at all, not with the way she made him feel. He needed to keep his distance from her before he did something he regretted.

But when he entered the kitchen, he knew he couldn't back out. Kaylee was already there, dressed for the day. She sat at the table with a mug of something hot on the table in front of her, her head braced on her hand as she wrote in a notebook. Archard stopped in the doorway and stared for a long moment, examining the way a few stray curls gently caressed the back of her neck.

"Good morning!" Naomi enthused from her position near the stove as she scooped strips of hot, sizzling meat out of a pan. "I didn't expect you up so early, not after a long night like that. I'm afraid I don't have everything quite ready yet."

Archard took a deep breath, reminding himself to be polite. Despite his feelings about Julian and the wizard, this female dragon had been very welcoming. "That's all right. Don't feel rushed because of me."

Kaylee got out of her seat and came across the room. "We don't need an entire buffet, Mom. Whatever you've got is fine." She grabbed one of the strips of meat and handed it to Archard. "It's bacon, and it's delicious."

Seeing that she was getting another one for herself, Archard tried it. The salty, smoky flavor was surprisingly pleasant, and it made the back of his mouth water for more. "This doesn't taste anything like fraxen."

"It's pig. There are several different cuts of meat we get from them, actually, and almost all of it is amazing."

Naomi gestured toward the paper Kaylee still held in her free hand. "What are you working on?"

"Oh." Kaylee tucked it into her back pocket. "I'm taking Archard around to see a few things today. I was trying to make a list of the best places to go."

Archard felt incredibly uncomfortable at the way Naomi's slanted eyes studied her daughter and then him. "I don't want to burden you. I'm sure you have other things to do, and I'm tired anyway."

"Here. Drink this." She poured him a cup of something hot and shoved it at him.

He did as he was told. The drink was bitter but flavorful, and he couldn't decide quite how he felt about it. "What is it?"

Kaylee laughed at the faces he made. "Coffee, and pretty much everyone on the planet drinks it. It'll perk you up, if nothing else. Now shove a few biscuits down your throat and let's go."

"You seem to be in quite the hurry to leave," Archard remarked when he followed her out of the house ten minutes later. The fluffy hunk of bread Naomi offered had been almost as good as the bacon, and it sat comfortably in his stomach. Though he wouldn't have admitted it to anyone, he was eager to taste more Earth food.

Kaylee had led him into a large room that, while it was attached to the house, didn't seem to quite be part of it. The walls weren't finished the same way, and it was much colder. The large metal contraptions that filled it gave off an unpleasant smell. She leaned against a red one. "I wanted to get out before everyone else got up and asked a lot of questions."

As much as she angered him sometimes, Archard found himself

amused. "You don't want anyone to know that we left together?"

"It's not that," she said with a roll of her eyes. "I just don't want everyone in my business. I stayed at home when I started college because I still had work to do with my father. And I'm gone a lot, so it made sense. But I'm kind of tired of everyone knowing every move I make."

"College?" Archard knew they were speaking the same language, but there were so many terms he had yet to learn.

"Let's just put that on the list of things to explain. For right now, let's go." She turned around and pulled a lever on the red metal thing, making part of it pop open. Kaylee started to get in when she noticed him standing there like an idiot. "I'm sorry. I'm not thinking. Here." She led him around to the other side, popped it open again, and pointed at the odd chair inside.

Archard got in, wondering if he'd made the right move. He had no idea what this thing was, although Kaylee seemed perfectly comfortable getting inside it. A large door opened up in front of them as the device roared to life around him, growling quietly to itself.

"It's a car," Kaylee laughed, her cheeks reddening prettily. "I'm sorry. I'm so sorry. I've never met anyone who didn't know what a car was before. I should've warned you. It's just a machine that helps us get around." She pushed several levers and the car slowly glided outside.

Digging his fingernails into the upholstery underneath him, Archard tried not to let himself react too much. His instincts told him to find a way out of this thing immediately. "Wouldn't it just be easier for everyone to fly?"

"You've got to remember that all the people on this planet are humans. They don't have wings. A few of them have some other abilities. I've got an aunt that's psychic and two others who are witches, but those are rare occurrences. There's no magic here. People had to create inventions to help them along in life."

Archard wasn't sure that he'd ever thought of shifting as magic. It was just something he and everyone he knew could do. "What about wizards? Are there any here besides Varhan?" He watched curiously as a stripe of gray ground slid away beneath the car and joined in with other, similar creations.

Kaylee shook her head as she confidently operated the vehicle. "Nope. All of that is make believe as far as most humans are concerned. They like to write stories about it, but they don't actually think it's real."

His stomach rolled uncomfortably. Archard didn't like the out-of-control feeling the car gave him, and even being near Kaylee wasn't enough of a distraction. "I don't like this thing."

She looked at him with concern. "We'll be at our first stop in just a few minutes, I promise."

Soon enough, she pulled up in front of a large brick building and showed him how to open the door to the car. He was grateful to get his feet back on the ground again, and he tipped his head back to look at the structure. "This house is even bigger than yours."

"This isn't a house," she explained. "It's a library. It's a place where people come to borrow books and to learn. I thought it would be a good place to start, because if you're here for a while, you can come learn, too. I spent a lot of time here as a kid."

"It's for children?"

"Part of it is, but not all of it. The biggest rule is that you have to be quiet, okay?"

Feeling stupid yet intrigued, Archard followed her inside. A musty but pleasant smell attacked his nostrils, and his lips parted at the sight of so many books. "This is incredible."

She smiled proudly. "I've always thought so. My dad said you had books on Charok, but they weren't very common."

He shook his head. "I've only seen a few of them in my lifetime. Well, other than the ones in your home. I thought that was a huge collection, but clearly I was wrong."

"There are a lot here, but we also have something called computers. That's going to take a much longer time to explain, though. Anyway, you can find almost anything you want to learn about. The encyclopedias can be a nice way to find out a little about a lot of things." She showed him a beautiful set of heavy books that had numerous topics in them. They carried a few to a table and laid them out.

Archard had never been as studious as his Aunt Lucia, but he still felt as though he could stay in this big, quiet building all day. There were other people around, and he'd expected to attract attention, but most of them had their heads bent toward books or were searching for something on a shelf. "We don't have anything like this on Charok. What books we do have are stored in a cave specifically for archiving,

but most of our stories and histories are written directly on the walls."
He marveled as he slid his finger over the glossy pages.

Eventually, he looked up to see Kaylee watching him. "You're ready
to go?"

"I didn't say that."

"No, but..." Archard trailed off as he realized she was right. She
hadn't said a word. She hadn't even so much as tapped her finger
impatiently on the table or let out a heavy sigh. He just knew that she
was ready to move on to something else, but he didn't want to say it.
That would sound crazy. "I'm sorry. I guess I just got the idea that there
was more you wanted to show me."

"You're not wrong," she said with a smile. "We'll put these back. I
only hope you like the next place as well as this one."

Archard didn't truly want to leave the library behind, but he was
eager to see what else Kaylee had to show him. He was also pleased to
find that it wasn't as difficult being around her today. She made him
uncomfortable, but not in such an infuriating way. It was an odd thing
regardless, but at least it was more pleasant.

When she pulled to a stop this time, there were numerous other
cars around them. "This is the mall. It's where people come to shop for
things like clothes or gifts. There are going to be a lot more people
here, but since it's such a common place to go, I thought we should get
it out of the way. And we might want to get you something else to
wear."

Archard looked down at his woolen shirt and trousers. "What's
wrong with what I'm wearing?"

"There's nothing really wrong with it," she replied quickly. "It's just
that you'll really stand out if you aren't dressed like everyone else."

Though he didn't like anyone to think he was impressed by Earth
structures, he was quite shocked to see the large, open space around
him. "Your builders must be very talented."

She smiled. "I guess you're right. I don't really think about it much,
because I've grown up in these kinds of places. But it's pretty neat."

He saw that she'd been right about the number of people there,
and none of them were dressed quite like him. They also weren't as
polite as the ones at the library had been, staring at him openly. "How
do you know they aren't wizards?"

"What?"

"You said everyone is human, but how do you know? They look the same as us when we're in human form. There could be dozens of wizards here."

Kaylee looked around, her eyes slightly alarmed for a moment, but then she shrugged it off. "I just know. It's how things work here, and I've spent a lot of my time studying humans. It's actually what I plan to do for a living when I'm done with school."

He looked down at her as she walked along next to him, wondering how such a beautiful dragon could get so caught up in these human affairs. It didn't make sense, but then again, nothing made much sense to him right then.

She took him into various places she called stores, and he could hardly keep up with all the new words she defined and human habits she explained. It was all fascinating until she made him try on clothes.

"But I'm going to look ridiculous in this," he argued, holding the flimsy shirt between his thumb and forefinger. "And why are the pants so heavy?"

She pressed her lips together, suppressing a laugh. "They're called jeans, and they're great once you get used to them. You go in there, close the door, and put them on. I'll be sitting right here, and you have to come out and show me."

"Why?"

Kaylee giggled. "It's just how things are done. Besides, you don't know how they're supposed to fit, so you need my opinion. Just do it."

Archard felt a flush of embarrassment heat his cheeks as he went into the little room she indicated. He told himself he had no choice but to play along, but when he stood in front of her a few minutes later, he wished he'd refused.

Her eyes raked over his body openly, and he couldn't tell if she smiled because she was pleased or amused. "The jeans look good, but I don't think the orange shirt is your color. Try this one on instead." She handed him a very similar garment in a dark blue.

Archard cursed himself under his breath. He was making a complete fool of himself. If his cousins ever got wind of this, they'd give him hell until he died.

But Kaylee's reaction when he came out of the dressing room this time was a different one. Her eyebrows arched, and her mouth turned into a little knot. She stood up and adjusted the collar of the shirt. "This is much better," she said quietly, her hand lingering against his chest.

"I'm not sure you're right," he replied, matching her volume. "I feel silly, parading around in front of you like this."

"No." Her eyes focused on the two buttons just below his collar. "It's just what people do."

The electricity between them practically crackled in the air. "And what do they do after this?" He knew very much what he would like to do.

Kaylee cleared her throat and took a step back. "You go put your own clothes back on so I can pay for these. Then we'll go get some lunch."

———

THERE WERE restaurants in the mall, but after picking out a soft pink sweater that Kaylee insisted would look lovely on Lucia, they went to a different, smaller building. It was on the other side of the city, and though it was crowded, it didn't feel nearly as strange as the mall had.

Kaylee took a long drink of tea. "I'm sorry. I know this has been a lot to take in, and I'm sure it doesn't even all make sense. I'm doing my best."

"It's fine," he assured her. "To be honest, it's been a lot more fun than I thought it would be. It's certainly given me a lot to think about. For the moment, I'm more than happy to see what this tastes like. What did you call it again?" He pointed at the slab of meat between two pieces of bread that a young woman had just placed in front of him.

"A hamburger. It's a very common American food."

"And these?" There were little golden sticks on the plate next to it.

"Fries. Try them with some ketchup." Kaylee picked up a red bottle from the center of the table and tried to squeeze something out of it onto his plate, but only a few drops came out. She frowned. "Hang on. I'll get some more. Try the burger, though."

She got up and headed toward the counter, where a large woman poked at buttons on a machine. Just as she was coming back toward the table, though, two young men came barreling through the aisle of the diner. They were pushing one another, and one of them slammed right into Kaylee. The bottle flew into the air as Kaylee hit the floor.

Archard was on his feet in a moment, sailing past another customer and grabbing the man by the collar of his shirt. His voice came out in a roar as his knuckles tightened, and he let go with one hand to pull his arm back.

It was only the grip of Kaylee's fingers on his arm that stopped him. "Archard! Let him go!"

"But he hurt you..." Archard kept his gaze directly in the man's eyes, the instinct to draw blood having completely taken over him.

She pulled at him again. "He's just a kid! Now set him down!"

Archard tipped his head as he studied his victim. The man was almost as tall as he was, but the more he looked, he could see what Kaylee meant. He still wanted to pound him thoroughly, but Kaylee's words seemed to have even more authority than his gut reaction. Archard set the other man on his feet and turned to Kaylee, who pulled him back toward their table and told him to sit.

"What the hell is wrong with you?" she whispered angrily from her side of the table.

"I don't understand. He hurt you."

Her eyebrows knotted. "They were just a couple of kids horsing around; it was an accident."

Now that his adrenaline had subsided slightly, Archard could see what she meant. There was no malicious intent, but Archard had reacted as though there had been. "I'm sorry. I...just wanted to be sure you were safe."

"I don't know how exactly how things work where you're from, but we try to be a little more civilized here." She'd retrieved the bottle of ketchup, and she shoved it at him crossly. "I'm perfectly safe. If someone is actually threatening my life, then you're more than welcome to intervene. But really, you went too far."

"I'm sorry," he repeated. It was the only thing he could think of to say. What he knew, though, was that he'd overreacted in a way that even he couldn't understand. He'd felt this need to protect her ever since he'd first met her, and he'd instinctively acted on that the second he'd thought she was in danger. She didn't belong to him. There was no reason he should feel that way. But he did.

She sighed. "It's okay. Really. I can't expect you to come out into the world for half a day and understand it all. No harm was done, and if anything, that kid will probably watch where he's going for the next few days. Let's eat."

The waitress came by to initiate an exchange of paper with Kaylee that Archard didn't quite understand, and before she left the table, she turned to him with a smile. "Okay, I've been wondering ever since you got here, so I have to ask. Where are you from? I've never heard that accent before."

Archard watched her closely, still not quite convinced that there weren't wizards among the humans. "Accent?"

"Yeah, the way you talk. It's strange."

Kaylee reached across the table and touched his hand, giving him a meaningful look. "He's from...uh...Iceland."

The waitress gave her a doubtful look. "Really?"

"Yeah. Here. Keep the change." Kaylee handed her some green paper and sent her away.

"I don't speak strangely," Archard said, watching the woman retreat. "If anything, she does."

Kaylee's hand was still on his, and she patted his knuckles before pulling it back. "You do sound a little different than most people around here. We should just be grateful we can both understand each other. Maybe we should go home. I think this has been enough for one day."

Archard was enjoying his time with her, but he thought she was probably right. It'd been fascinating to see how the Earthlings lived, but it'd also been disorienting and exhausting. He didn't think he could ever belong here on this planet, but at least he'd learned something. Archard laughed to himself.

"What?"

"What?" She'd caught him off-guard, lost in his thoughts.

"You were laughing at something." Kaylee opened the door to the diner, making the little bells that hung on the door jingle.

"I was just thinking that if I ever make it back home and tell someone what I've seen here, they probably won't believe me. It's so different that I never could've even imagined it."

"If you stay long enough, then maybe you can come with me on one of my trips. I see a lot of different cultures, ways of life and religions. While some people live like what you've seen today, it's not like that everywhere on our planet."

As they walked to the car, Archard noticed one of the waitresses out in the parking lot. She was leaning against a car and talking to a male, swirling her hair around her finger. He leaned in and kissed her, and in a moment they were just a tangle of limbs and clothing.

"I guess humans aren't very discreet with their mating," Archard remarked as he got into Kaylee's car, thumbing over his shoulder at the lustful couple.

She smiled at him again. It was the same smile she'd given him numerous times that day, amused, but something more. "They're not mating, necessarily."

"What do you mean?" Once Archard's parents were gone and it was up to his aunt to raise him, she'd told him how dragons found their mates. It wasn't a matter of picking and choosing, but of finding the one you were fated to be with. He couldn't imagine acting that way with someone who wasn't his mate.

"Well, they're probably just dating." She put the key in the ignition but didn't turn it, sitting back against the seat. "You remember how you tried on those clothes?"

Archard nodded. "Of course."

"People do that to make sure they fit and that they're comfortable before they take them home. It's kind of like that with finding a spouse. They're trying each other out."

He glanced at the couple again, who hadn't ceased their display. "By sticking their tongues down each other's throats in a parking lot?"

Kaylee's laugh was like bells, and so different from how serious she could be. "No. Well, that's part of it sometimes. But they go on dates and hang out."

"Dates?" He saw the look of weariness on her face. "I'm sorry. I've asked too many questions."

"No, no. I told you I would take you out so you'd understand, and that's what I'm going to do. I just never realized how hard it is to explain things I've understood my whole life. A date is basically just a chance for two people to spend time together; to get to know each other. They might go out to eat, or go shopping, or see a movie. It can be almost anything, really."

Archard thought about that for a moment, suddenly realizing that he was even more confused about Earth life than he thought. Though they were out in public, he felt like being in this vehicle separated the two of them from the rest of the world. There was no room at all to shift in here, but once again, he felt that white-hot need underneath his skin as he looked into her eyes. "Is *this* a date?"

"What? Oh, this?" She waggled her finger back and forth, pointing at him and then herself, laughing uncomfortably. "No, of course not."

"But you said a date was when two people went out and did things together to get to know each other. We've certainly done that. If this isn't a date, then how do you know?"

"Well, ah..."

A crimson flush bloomed over her cheeks and her breath came in short bursts, causing her chest to move in an alluring way that Archard had to fight to keep from staring at. It was a cool day, but the heat between them was unmistakable. He knew what it was. He'd tried to deny it from the moment he'd met her, but keeping the truth a secret wouldn't change reality. Still, the last thing he wanted was to scare her away. "Kaylee?"

She turned her head to him, her eyes looking into his and then drifting down to his mouth. She was irresistibly stunning, full of life and desire. But as quickly as the moment had happened, she ended it by turning away and starting the car. "I guess you just know."

The corner of Archard's mouth tipped up slightly as he turned to look out his own window in order to give Kaylee a little privacy. Yes, he certainly did know. It was crazy and it didn't make a lot of sense, but he knew. Now he just had to wait for her to understand. He only hoped he could be that patient, since it was clear that Kaylee was just as stubborn as any other dragon he'd ever met.

Their conversation turned to daily matters as she headed out of town and into the more rural area where her house was located. They discussed what the weather was like there, and Kaylee spent a full five minutes talking about breakfast foods. Archard paid some attention, but most of his focus was on the way her soft lips moved around the words she spoke.

They came in the door from the garage to find the kitchen empty and a note on the table. Kaylee read it out loud. "We went to Holden's place for lunch. Feel free to join us if you'd like. Love, Mom."

Archard's body reacted to the knowledge that they were alone. Kaylee stood with her back to him, and there was nothing he wanted more than to gently brush the stray curls from the back of her neck and kiss the warm skin there as he wrapped his arm around her waist, holding her just tightly enough to keep her close. In his mind's eye, he envisioned her turning around in his embrace to kiss him fully. The thought made his wings threaten to burst from his back at any moment.

Kaylee turned to him, but not with the idea of kissing him evident in her eyes. "I can take you over there if you'd like, but I have some things I really ought to be doing. I've got classes tomorrow, and I haven't prepared for them." She'd told him of her education, and while Archard didn't understand why she'd be so interested in studying humans, he knew it was important to her.

"No, that's all right. I'll meet them some other time, and you do what you need. But I do want to thank you for what you did today." Archard's eyes refused to look anywhere but at her. He'd seen amazing things on his flights back on Charok, from steep waterfalls to high mountains, sometimes bathed in the glow of sunrise or the brilliance of midday, but none of them compared to her. He felt he could survey the bridge of her nose for hours and still not think he'd taken in the sight of her enough.

"Of course. I had a good time." She tucked a strand of her hair behind her ear as she set the note back on the table. "It was neat to get a different perspective on things I've been taking for granted my entire life."

His body moved closer to hers, though Archard wasn't aware of moving his feet. "I'll just need to find a way to pay you back."

Those viridescent eyes traced down his face to his lips again. She'd tried to brush him off, just as he'd tried to do, but Archard knew she understood. The magnetism between the two of them was undeniable. The only thing he didn't know was if her body was reacting the same way his was. If he let himself go for just a fraction of a second, there would be a dragon standing there in the Turners' kitchen.

They were inches apart, even closer than they'd been outside the dressing room at the mall.

"Pay me back for what?"

Archard swallowed. "For your time, for the things you bought for me. For the meal."

"I was happy to do it," she said breathlessly.

"I want to," he insisted. "More than you know." Slowly, he brought up his hand to delicately graze his fingers along her elbow.

It was only a millimeter that separated them now, though it felt like a mile. "Then I suppose I shouldn't stop you."

His lips met hers, and Archard was tempted to pull back instantly. Her lips were soft and giving, her body warm, and her perfume surrounded him in a subtle cloud, but the violent frenzy happening just under the surface of his skin was unbearable. His arms shook as they threatened to shift, yet he wrapped them around her waist and deepened the kiss. Sparks of electricity streaked through his body, starting at any point where he made contact with her and making it all the more difficult to retain his form. Scales rippled down his back where her hands touched him, and a growl threatened to rise from the deepest pit of his lungs.

Kaylee pulled back slowly, melting away from his body just as easily as she had come to it. Archard felt an icy chill on his skin where she'd touched him, his very cells pining for her immediately. He grinned at her.

"What?" she asked, looking embarrassed.

He reached up slowly to touch her face, where a faint line of shimmering green scales had erupted along her cheek bones. Archard grazed his thumbs over them, causing them to undulate in response to his caress. "You're the most exquisite creature I've ever seen."

She glanced down at the floor. "Um, I really should get going. You sure you don't want me to take you over to my uncle's place?"

"No, don't worry about it. I can entertain myself." He stood in the kitchen, exhaling deeply as he watched her go. She glanced over her shoulder at him as she passed through the doorway, and it was almost enough to make him lose control completely.

When she was gone, he wrapped his fingers around the back of a kitchen chair until his knuckles turned white and closed his eyes. Archard tried to think of boring, mundane things that would keep him in check, at least until he could find the time and space to shift.

"I'd like to know just what you think you're doing."

Archard opened his eyes to see Jake leaning against the doorway that led to the basement stairs. The bulk of his shoulders was accentuated by the way he folded his arms in front of his chest, and his eyes were hard. His t-shirt was soaked with sweat, and he had a towel flung over his shoulder.

"Standing here." Archard still wanted to shift, but for a completely different reason now.

"You know that's not what I mean."

"I thought everyone was at Holden's house." While it'd been tempting to meet Kaylee's extended family, Archard had put his body through enough that day.

"I stayed behind to get in a workout, and it's a good thing I did. I saw you kiss my sister."

"What business is that of yours?" He kept his hands wrapped

around the chair where they couldn't do much harm. Jake was bigger than he was, but not by much. It would be one hell of a fight, but one that Archard doubted Kaylee or the others would appreciate. She'd made it very clear that she didn't want him to pummel someone on her account. Things would only be worse if it was her own brother.

Jake crossed the kitchen until he stood on the other side of the table. "Don't try me. I've spent my entire life protecting her."

"Is that so?" Archard raised one eyebrow, appraising this Earth dragon once again. He was strong in human form, but did that translate to his reptilian constitution? "It seems to me that she knows how to take care of herself pretty well."

"I'm sure it does seem that way. Kaylee is just as headstrong as the rest of us are. But she has no idea just what I've done behind the scenes to keep her safe. There have been any number of guys who come along, thinking she's nothing but a hot piece of ass, and I've kept them all at bay. I'm not going to let you slime all over her just because you're one of us."

This made Archard wonder just how well Kaylee knew the human mating process. He'd never asked if she'd been on the dates she described to him, or if she'd enjoyed the companionship of a human male. The idea made him angry, but only because he didn't want to share her with anyone. "I think that decision is up to her, not you."

Jake shook his head. "She can think that, but I know the truth. I love my sister, but she doesn't always know what's good for her. Besides, from what little I know of you, you're not the kind of guy she needs to be hanging around with."

"Is that so?" Archard came around the table, his teeth sharpening in his mouth. Being Kaylee's brother didn't give Jake the authority to keep the two of them apart, especially considering what Archard knew about their relationship. He was meant to be with her, but he couldn't expect some Earthling to understand. "And who's going to stop me?"

Jake took the slightest step backward. "I'm not going to fight you, but only because I know Kaylee wouldn't want me to. You can consider this your warning and be thankful for it." He turned and stomped back down to the basement.

Archard took a few deep breaths before heading up to his room. He was going to have to get out of this house on his own, and soon.

## 9

THE NEXT MORNING, KAYLEE COULDN'T SHAKE THE EVENTS OF THE DAY before. She had plenty going on at school, from meetings with her professors to classes and a study session in the library, but none of it seemed important. All she wanted was to be with Archard again.

She settled down into one of the private study rooms at the back of the university library and opened her books, but her mind wandered once again back to Archard. Showing him life on Earth had been a much more complicated thing than she'd imagined, but it'd also been very satisfying. He'd really made her see things from a different viewpoint, and she'd enjoyed seeing the way his eyes lit up with understanding. Kaylee had underestimated how difficult it was to describe and explain things that were so run-of-the-mill for her. She'd never met anyone who hadn't been in a car before. Even Varhan had a little experience by the time she and Julian had found him.

And that kiss... Kaylee had focused mostly on her studies so far, but that didn't mean there hadn't been a few exchanges behind the bleachers in high school or an occasional coffee date once she'd started college. But up until recently, there hadn't been any dragons on Earth besides her cousins. Spending time with a man had always been nice, but it was nothing when compared to spending time with Archard.

"Earth to Kaylee! Come in, Kaylee!" Nicole plopped her books down on the table and giggled when Kaylee jumped in her seat. "You were a million miles away."

Kaylee smiled. "Sorry. I was just thinking."

"About what? Wait, I think I know that look on your face." Nicole pushed her glasses up with one finger. "You've found yourself a man."

Nicole had been Kaylee's best friend since high school, when the two of them discovered they both had a love for archeology. It'd started in their social studies class freshman year, and while Nicole was leaning more toward becoming a history teacher, their friendship hadn't waned.

"Why do you say that?" Kaylee asked, once again reliving the tender yet arduous way Archard had kissed her. He'd set her body on fire in a way she'd never experienced before.

"Oh, come on! I can see it written all over your face! You're not thinking about ancient languages, you're thinking about the one universal language that everyone knows." Nicole giggled at her own joke.

"Stop it!" Kaylee could feel the heat in her cheeks, something that was becoming a permanent state of affairs these days.

"You might as well just tell me now." One blonde eyebrow arched over Nicole's tortoiseshell glasses. "I'll find out eventually. Is it that cute guy down at the coffee shop?"

"No. He's cool, but he's not my type. You know, *you* should ask him out. It's been a while since you've had a date." Kaylee flipped through her notes just so she had something to do with her hands.

Nicole shook her finger in the air. "Don't change the subject! We're talking about *you*. If not coffee guy, then who? Oh, maybe someone you met on your most recent trip? Do I have to tell Dr. Morrick he needs to keep a closer eye on you?"

Kaylee smiled. It was useless to pretend she didn't have something more on her mind than her classes, and there was no way she could tell Nicole the truth. Even her best friend had no idea who she really was. But she'd been in Colombia only a couple of weeks earlier, and a man from a foreign country who Nicole would never have a chance of meeting was just as good an excuse as any. "Okay, you got me. I met a guy on my trip. But it's sort of a long-distance thing, and I doubt it'll work out."

Long distance to be sure, if Archard went back to Charok at some point.

"I knew it!" Nicole clapped her hands softly and bounced in her seat. "You've never been good at keeping secrets, you know."

"Yeah, I know." Except for the biggest secret of her life, and it would have to remain that way. "I just didn't want to say anything because I'm really not sure where it's going." Once again, she could feel the way his hand had traced up her spine to the back of her neck, cradling her skull as he'd kissed her. It'd been delicate and yet commanding, and Kaylee's body reacted at the mere memory of it.

"Does he feel the same way about you?" Nicole pressed.

Kaylee shrugged and thought about the way Archard looked at her, like he hungered for her. That was a thrill, but was it anything more than lust? She knew he made her feel things—new, strange things—but maybe that was simply because he was another dragon. "I don't know yet. I guess only time will tell."

"I'm not sure about that." Nicole pulled a can of soda out of the side pocket of her book bag and cracked it open. "I'm starting to think we women should just put ourselves out there and say how we feel, you know? Tell the guy you like him and you want to be with him, and if he can't handle that right away, then he's not worth keeping."

"That's all perfectly well and good for some situations, but I don't think all guys are like that. Some guys are a little more old-fashioned, and I think they like to feel that they're in control." She'd seen the gentle, sophisticated side of Archard, but it was very clear to Kaylee that an animal lurked under the surface.

"Then it's up to you to make him see the other side of things," Nicole countered. "Hell, if you like him enough, you should fly right back to wherever it is he's from and tell him so!"

Kaylee smiled at her friend. She made it all sound so easy, but things were much more complicated than that. If she could just hop on a commercial flight to Charok, that would be one thing.

Their conversation eventually turned to their studies and their upcoming tests, but thoughts of Charok still bubbled under the surface. Kaylee had always wanted to go, and she hadn't realized just how badly she wanted to be there until she'd seen that vision of it just before Archard and his family had accidentally been brought to Earth.

Absentmindedly, she made notes for her upcoming test and once again wondered if there was a way to get there. If there was, then she might take the biggest trip of her lifetime.

—————

THAT EVENING AFTER DINNER, when she was back at home and things seemed quiet, Kaylee found Varhan in his room. Despite the numerous books in her father's library, the wizard had turned his room into a study of his own. Books and scrolls lined the walls, and a box of more books peeked out from under the bed. He sat in a rocking chair in the corner, carefully sanding down a stick of wood into a new wand.

He glanced up at her as she knocked on the doorway. "Good evening, Kaylee. What can I do for you?"

She clenched her fingers together. "Do you mind if we talk for a moment? In private?"

Varhan set his would-be wand down on a nearby table and heaved his weight from the chair. He ushered her into the room and closed the door softly behind her. "Of course. Is everything all right?"

"Yes, it's just that I don't want anyone else to know about this." Speaking with the wizard had never made her nervous before. He'd instantly been like an old relative, even though she'd only met him a year ago.

"Mmhmm." The wizard squinted at her. "Better let it out and tell me, then."

Kaylee took a deep breath. If she wanted to, she could've opened her mind and let Varhan right inside instead of trying to explain what she wanted. English words simply weren't adequate for some things. But the two of them had spent several weeks learning how to stay out of each other's thoughts to afford them some privacy, and there were some things on her mind that didn't need to be brought to the surface. "I want to know what it would take to go to Charok."

Varhan watched her for a long time, his deep stare making her uncomfortable. "Does this have anything to do with Archard?"

Her stomach knotted as though someone had sewn strings through it and yanked on them. "Why do you ask?"

He gave a soft laugh. "First of all, because I know he was the first one to demand he be sent back home. Second, because you'd already brought that idea to your father and me on his behalf. But also because I may be old, but I'm not oblivious. You've spent more time with him than with any of the other new dragons."

The heat in her skin had nothing to do with the warmth of the room. "I have been, but this is about me. I've always been curious about Charok, and seeing it the other day only piqued that. I need to know more about where I've come from. I want to see it firsthand, not just in a vision." He was right that she'd initially brought up the idea because it was what Archard wanted, but she'd come to understand that there was much more to it. She needed to do this to satisfy her own curiosity.

Varhan lowered himself into the rocker once more, and his sand-paper made quiet rasps against the wood. "You think there's something more for you than what you've found here on Earth."

"Well, yes, I guess that's true." Archard's arrival had distracted her from her initial mission, but Kaylee knew she had to pursue this. "We both know it's possible to create a portal between the worlds. You did it when you sent my father and the others to Earth, and we did it when we brought these new dragons through."

Holding the wand out to study the grain in the firelight for a moment, Varhan began sanding once again. "The first time was on purpose, and I knew it was the right thing to do. I'd done my studies, and it was like it all mapped itself out in front of me. I knew I needed a special potion to help them get through safely without burning up. I knew I had the right spell. Though I'd never tried it before, there was no doubt in my mind I was doing the right thing. I could see the path clearly in front of me, and I knew in my very soul that your father and the others would not only be safe here, but that they were *destined* to be here. It's a very distinct feeling, and one that I'm certain only came to me because of my gift."

"Yes, I know that feeling well. Anytime I'm working with languages, it's like I have a purpose in life. There are lots of other things that I might question, but I have no doubts about myself when I'm doing that." She was so glad there was someone else in the world who understood it.

"And then bringing Archard and the others here, you know that was purely accidental. It could've gone very poorly, both for them and for us, and we're lucky we've all survived it. I thought I made it quite clear when we talked the other night that sending someone back to Charok is a very big knot to untangle, and probably an impossible one." He turned the wand to check the other side of it, then flicked it expertly between his fingers.

"I know, I know. But this is something I really have to do. It might be hard, but if people have come from Charok to Earth in two different ways, then that only give me hope that we have a chance to go the opposite way." Her father had been looking for the right spell to do that for many years, but Kaylee knew they couldn't give up just yet.

The wizard set his work down once again and dusted his fingers on his robes. "That's a very positive outlook you have there, but I have to say it's not very practical. If there were a way to do this safely, then your father and I would've found it already."

"Safely?" She'd latched onto the word as soon as it'd come out of his mouth. "So there is a way?"

"No, no. I never said that." He picked up the wand again and began sanding furiously.

"Yeah, you pretty much did. Varhan, if there's possibly a way to go there, then I've got to try." With the obstinate look on his face, she knew it was time to throw caution to the wind. "I was horrified when we brought those dragons through, but I've since found a connection with Archard that I never even knew was possible. At first, I thought maybe he was what I'd been waiting for my entire life. But then I realized there's still so much work out there for me. I was talking to a friend of mine at school today, and it made me think about all the places I've been and all the places I have yet to go. Why stop at archeological sites here on Earth? Why stop with humans? Archard told me about the archives they have on Charok. I've got to go see them. I *know* there's something there for me." She pointed her finger into her palm as though pointing to some place on a map.

Varhan sighed. "Kaylee, I admire your determination. I understand it, and I sympathize. But I have yet to even understand the cosmic implication of our spell the other day. What if we find a way to send you to Charok and it affects someone else's fate?"

"Nobody else has to go with me," she argued. "Not unless they want to."

The wizard leaned forward and looked at her with pity in his eyes. "It's not as simple as that. You have a gift for seeing and understanding languages, but my gift is for seeing and understanding destinies. Like any other magical work, I find that it's much harder here on Earth than it was on Charok. I do my best, and sometimes I have moments of clarity, but it's just not the same. I'm not comfortable with diving into a spell I'm not certain about. I had my doubts about our vision spell, and that should've been enough to stop me. Now, I'm concerned that I've done something very wrong indeed."

"I don't think that could be." Kaylee wanted to cry at seeing the sadness in the old man's face. "It's all been very strange, but knowing there are more dragons in the universe has completely changed my life. So has Archard. I don't quite understand how yet, but I know I'll never be the same again." She wouldn't dare go so far as to say she loved him or that they were going to have the romance of a lifetime. She'd seen enough of life on Earth to understand that what Julian and Naomi had together wasn't normal for most people. But she knew she'd changed.

"Kaylee, listen to me very carefully." Varhan took both of her hands in his and held them tightly as he looked up at her. "I love you as though you were my own daughter, and I'm begging you not to pursue this. It isn't safe, and you could wind up as stardust. I promise you that I'll work on it, and I'm sure your father will as well. But this is bigger than any of us, and I couldn't live with myself if something happened to you."

"So be it, then," she said softly, but she knew it was a promise she'd have to break.

## 10

ARCHARD KNOCKED SOFTLY ON THE DOOR.

"Come in," Lucia said pleasantly.

As he'd suspected, all of them had already gathered in her room. Lucia sat in a chair in front of a dressing table, while Callan and Kieran lounged on a small sofa beneath a large window. The Turners had given Lucia a rather grand room with a sitting area, and the delicate styling of the furniture seemed to suit her taste. Sitting there in front of the mirror, she looked as though she belonged. The thought gave Archard pause in regard to what he'd gone there to talk to them about.

"Well, well, well. I'm surprised you're not out on the town with your little Earth girl," Callan remarked. He held one of the devices that so many of the people here seemed to think necessary—a cell phone, Archard thought it was called—and he barely looked up at his cousin.

"You missed quite the meal with Holden and Leah," Kieran said, elbowing Callan. "Put that thing down. You've been starting at it for a full day."

"Hey, if Archard gets to learn about this world in his way, then let me learn in mine. You wouldn't believe everything they have on here. These shows are like stories that people act out, but you can watch them whenever you want to. You can even skip through the boring parts. And you can contact people on here or play games. It's amazing."

"I think it's addicting," Lucia admonished gently. "Have a seat, Archard. We've barely seen you since you arrived."

"That's because he's following Julian's daughter around like a hungry beast," Callan said without looking up. "Why should he want to be around us?"

Kieran stroked his beard. "You're just jealous that some woman didn't want to show *you* around."

"Really, boys. You can be such children sometimes." Lucia stood and once again motioned for Archard to sit in a large armchair next to the sofa. "I can tell there's something on your mind. What is it?"

Archard studied his aunt's face. She was many years older than him, yet her skin had remained as smooth and tight as ever. It was only the wisdom in her eyes that truly revealed her years. Archard felt as though he'd aged quite a bit in the last few days. His body was heavy and cumbersome, and his mind was constantly flooded with ideas and worries. He'd always been restless, but this was different. "I'm glad you're all here together, because this is relevant to all of us. I came to see if any of you are interested in going home."

"That's an interesting way to put it," Lucia said with a small smile. "Perhaps you should tell us what *you* want."

"To go back, obviously."

"What about your woman?" Kieran's question didn't have the mischief behind it that Callan's words always did. Archard could tell it was an honest question.

Archard sighed. "I don't think I can say she's my woman. And while I can't deny that I enjoy spending time with her, I know that I have duties back on Charok." He'd been thinking about it a lot, and he'd had time to considering that he'd been avoiding Kaylee since their day out together. It wasn't because of Jake, but because he wasn't sure he could control himself. The kiss they'd shared had left him in a state of inner turmoil. If he'd been back on Charok, he could've gotten some release from a long flight, some hunting, or even some meditation and reflection in the caves. It just wasn't like that here.

There was pity in Lucia's eyes. "Archard, I'm not sure you're thinking straight."

He let out a deep breath and stood, feeling too antsy to sit any longer. "I've been wondering that myself. Maybe it's the air here; I don't know. But I know I can't stay."

His aunt glanced at the others, and Callan actually set the phone down. "Right after we arrived, the wizard explained that he probably couldn't send us back. Even if he can, it's clearly not something that's going to happen right away."

"That doesn't really answer my question."

She glanced at the other two once again. "I can only speak for myself. Personally, although there are a few certain things I miss about Charok, this world is fascinating. I've spent quite a bit of time with Naomi, learning about how they cook. I love the clothing, especially that sweater that you and Kaylee got for me."

"I have to agree," Kieran said with a nod. "It's comfortable here, like we've suddenly landed in the lap of luxury. I know you feel that you should be on Charok guarding the caves, but I think it's time we all admit that our old jobs there aren't relevant anymore. What little is left of our society isn't the same as it was years ago. I'm not sure there's a point in holding onto the past."

Callan glanced at the phone again, but he put it on a side table when his mother cleared her throat. "You couldn't get me to go back to Charok for anything. I've only seen a fraction of this place, and I like it. I can do whatever I want here, and there are so many people."

"Humans," Archard reminded him. "They're not like us."

"Who says they have to be?" his cousin argued. "It's not like we've grown up in a big community full of dragons. We've only had each other. There's a lot to explore here. Oh, and have you had some of their beer? It's amazing." He grinned and ran a hand through his hair.

"There might be a time when we're ready to go back, but I don't think this is it," Lucia said. "This is our chance to find new lives for ourselves. That's not something I ever thought I'd say, but it's true. Please don't be offended if we don't agree with you."

"No, of course not." Archard knew he could be difficult, but he'd never demand that they agree with his every whim. "Just understand that I can't be happy here."

"Not even with that pretty little thing on your arm?" Callan challenged.

Even Kieran watched him carefully for his answer.

"Kaylee is a nice distraction, but I can't just leave behind every-thing I've ever known." She'd affected him in ways he hadn't even known were possible, but even the most gorgeous woman in the universe shouldn't let him forget his sacred duties. "I just thought I'd check with you first."

Before they had a chance to argue with him any longer, Archard headed downstairs to the library. He didn't have to live very long in this house to know he'd find Julian and Varhan there, and as soon as he opened the door, he found he was right. The two of them sat at a long table with their heads bent. Books and papers were scattered all around them, and they looked up in surprise when they heard the door open.

"Archard, come in," Julian said with his usual friendly smile. "How are you today?"

"I'm not well, but I'm hoping you can fix that." Archard shut the door behind him and studied the two men. They didn't look particularly powerful.

"Are you sick? Or injured?" Varhan asked with genuine concern.

"Nothing like that. I need to go back to Charok. Now."

The two men shared a long look, and then Varhan sat back with a heavy sigh. "May I ask why?"

This riled Archard even more than his obstinate cousin had. "Does that matter?"

"It might," he hedged. "What you're asking isn't very simple."

Archard clenched his fists at his sides. Now that he'd made up his mind, he was ready to get this underway. "I never expected it to be. But I have things I need to do at home, things I doubt either of you would understand. I didn't ask to be brought here, and I'm ready to leave."

Julian looked like he wanted to say something, and Archard had a feeling it had to do with Kaylee. The time they'd spent together hadn't escaped anyone's notice. But he cleared his throat and set down the pen he'd been holding. "To be honest with you, Varhan and I have been talking about this a lot. You made it clear the very beginning that you wanted to leave. We knew it would only be a matter of time before you'd come to us."

"And?" Archard didn't have the time or the patience for this.

"It's possible to go to Charok, and we believe we know how to do it." Julian paused, waiting for an encouraging nod from his friend. "I had the basics of it down, and then Varhan helped me improve upon it. The problem is that it's a very complicated spell, more than either of us are comfortable with. It's also quite likely to kill you."

Archard stared at them for a long moment. This wasn't the answer he'd been hoping for. "I'm willing to take the risk."

Varhan braced his hands on the table as he stood. He crossed the room to one of the numerous bookshelves that lined the wall, removed several volumes from it, and slid aside a secret panel. "You must understand the only reason I'm about to show you this is because I know you aren't capable of performing the spell yourself. That's not an insult, but simply the truth. I do, however, want you to understand this isn't as simple as waving a wand and sending you away."

From the compartment behind the shelf, he retrieved a tattered, leather-bound book. Archard was fairly certain he'd seen it before, perhaps right when they'd arrived. The wizard immediately turned to a page near the back and handed it over.

Archard studied the scribbling on the page. He understood most of the words, since they were written in the traditional language used on Charok, but he had to admit he didn't quite know what it all meant or how it worked. "I guess you're right. I don't understand. But can't you just send me there, the same way you sent Julian and yourself to Earth?"

Varhan tapped the page with a thick finger. "Magic is like a completely different animal here on Earth than it is on Charok. The person performing the spell will also be sent through the portal it creates."

Archard's jawline tightened. Why did everything have to be so complicated? Why couldn't he have just lived his life out on Charok without ever knowing about these other dragons or the possibility of other worlds? He'd never have met Kaylee, but maybe that would've made things easier. He knew he'd have to leave her behind. "Can you teach me?" he ground out hoarsely, feeling like a fool for asking a wizard for help.

Varhan tucked the book back into its hiding spot. "I can do my best, but I'm afraid there are no guarantees with any of this. And if you truly want to do this, you'll have to make two promises."

Asking for help was bad enough, but now he had to make oaths? It was humiliating, but the tug that Charok exerted on him even from somewhere else in the universe was a strong one. "Very well."

"First, you can't tell anyone about this. And by that, I mean that you can't say you're learning the spell, what your plans are, or even that you know where my spell book is hidden. I can see you're a particularly obdurate man, and I knew you'd never just accept my word. But this type of knowledge is very dangerous, and I don't want anyone else in this household to get their hands on it." There was a certain fire in Varhan's eyes that Archard hadn't expected out of the otherwise calm man.

"I can do that."

"The other thing I'd like you to do is spend some time here on Earth. You've got plenty of it, considering you can't just snap your fingers and leave. But I want you to make sure this is what you want. It's not a decision to be made quickly or lightly."

Archard nodded slowly. He'd already made the choice, and knowing more about the spell wasn't going to make him change his mind. He understood Varhan's reasons, and he would play along if he had to. His life was nothing if he wasn't the royal guard he was born to be, even if no one else in this house seemed to understand that. Archard would do what he had to in order to get Varhan's help.

"Fair enough. Thank you." He left the library, but as soon as he stepped into the hall, he felt the distinct sensation that someone had just been there. He paused for a long moment, listening for footsteps or shallow breath in case someone was still hiding nearby.

Instead, he heard the two older men in the library continuing their conversation. "I'm worried about him," Julian said. "The others seem much more relaxed, and I think with some time, they could come to think of Earth as their home. I'm not sure the same is true for him."

"That's not the only thing you should be worried about." There was a warning tone in Varhan's voice. "He's been spending time with Kaylee."

"They had a day out while she showed him around. It's not like they're getting married."

The wizard's reply was merely a snort.

"What?"

"Archard is a very determined young man. There's something about him I can't quite put my finger on, but he strikes me as the sort of person who can accomplish anything he sets his mind to."

The sound of a chair scraping the floor leaked through the door, and Archard envisioned Julian rising to pace the room. The soft creaking of the floorboards enhanced that image. "Isn't that a good thing? Kaylee's not very different, really."

"That's just the problem," Varhan replied. "Julian, you have no idea just how powerful your daughter has the potential to be if she sets her mind to it. Her gift for languages could very well translate to a gift for spells. They're all about using the right words and the intent behind them, after all. It makes me wish I hadn't shown Archard that spell."

A long pause made Archard move closer to the door in case he missed something.

"And then there's the other thing."

"Which you should've told her about a long time ago," Varhan insisted. "You can't keep her in the dark forever."

"You think Kaylee could perform the spell?"

"She could," Varhan admitted, "and I know she'd jump at the chance. She came to me and asked me specifically, saying she wanted to go herself. I don't know if Archard was influencing that, but we can't let her go. No matter how capable she is, the force of being thrown back to Charok could still kill her."

"Damn. Then we just have to hope we really can trust Archard not to tell her, no matter what's going on between the two of them."

Archard ground his teeth together in frustration. They didn't trust him enough to explain Kaylee's powers to him, yet they hoped he would keep his promise. He wanted to burst back through the door and tell them what fools they were, that he would do absolutely anything—even die himself—if it meant keeping her safe.

Instead, he turned and moved quietly down the hall. He resolved to bide his time, learn the spell, and leave.

# 11

KAYLEE DOVE INTO HER BEDROOM AND TURNED THE KNOB AS SHE CLOSED the door, hoping to avoid any telltale signs that she hadn't been in there all afternoon. She felt as though she could finally breathe again, and she threw herself on her bed, gasping.

She hadn't meant to spy on the three men in the library. Her intention had simply been to retrieve an old file from one of her digs the previous year so she could use it as a reference in a paper she was working on. But when she'd heard Archard's voice resonating through the wooden door, she'd stopped in her tracks.

Staring up at the ceiling, she tried to reconcile her heart with her head. It made perfect sense that Archard should want to go back to his home world. But couldn't he also want to stay with her? The time they'd shared and the kiss that had practically made her heart explode meant something to her. Did it mean anything to him?

And then there was Varhan's betrayal. He'd only admitted to Kaylee that there was a way back to Charok after she'd practically dragged it out of him, but he'd also been quite clear that she wasn't to attempt it. Why should Archard be any different? Why should he be allowed not only to see the spell, but to learn it? Why should her father and Varhan put his needs above hers?

Exasperated, Kaylee launched off her bed and crossed the room to the window. She slid the glass and then the screen aside, letting in the cool October air. It was almost time for Zimryr once again, and there was no doubt in her mind the holiday would be a much different one than all those she'd experienced before. Her life was already changing faster than she was able to keep track of.

She needed time and space to think, and her room wasn't going to do it for her. Kaylee lifted first one foot and then the other until she perched on the windowsill, hoping her body still remembered how to do this. With a shake of her head, she felt the vertebrae in her neck grow and multiply as her spine stretched. Her legs grew thicker and heavier, and a tingling sensation crept along her arms as her skin split into pale green scales. Her hair hardened and shortened until the back of her head bore only spikes. She was forced to go ahead and jump out the window as her wings sprang from her back, and she spread them to catch herself as she soared into the night.

Kaylee turned and headed out toward the back of the property, where the area only grew more rural and she was less likely to be seen. It was a black, moonless night, but as her eyes adjusted, she began to see the trees and farms below her. She tossed her head in the wind, feeling the fall air cool the heat that naturally radiated from within. This was exactly what she needed. How long had it been since she'd let herself go?

With a smile curving her reptilian lips, Kaylee tucked her wings at her sides and did a barrel roll through the air, tumbling toward the Earth until she once again caught herself. The worries that plagued her disappeared for a while as she remembered this other body she'd been hiding away for so long, and she whipped her tail to explore its length.

But as she caught an updraft and swooped into a circle, Kaylee suddenly sensed that she wasn't alone. She paused in the air, looking. She hadn't seen anything specific, just a dark shape that blotted out the stars overhead. If it'd been one of her cousins, he or she would have called out to her. Her mother or father would've done the same. Detecting nothing, she decided to continue in the direction she'd been going only to find her path blocked.

"You're quite magnificent when you don't think anyone's watching."

Kaylee couldn't see the form in front of her as much as she could sense he was there, but she recognized Archard's voice. She flew backwards a few feet, squinting her eyes in the dim light to find the details of his dark, charcoal-colored body. "What are you doing out here?"

"I could ask you the same thing," he challenged.

"Fair enough. I came out here to think."

Archard flew in a slow and lazy circle around her, his dark body absorbing the starlight. He was barely more than a silhouette, with a few scales coming into relief every now and then. "I had similar reasons. What did you need to think about?"

Perhaps it was the kiss or the gentle way he spoke to her. Kaylee couldn't explain it, but being near him made her a different person. She'd hidden secrets from numerous people all her life—even those she was close to—yet she couldn't do the same around him. "I'm going to Charok."

He paused, his wings moving just barely enough to keep him in the air. "What do you mean?" His voice had changed from curious to harsh.

"I heard your discussion in the library."

"Kaylee..."

"Don't talk to me like that! I'm not a child, and you have no right to scold me for eavesdropping. It was purely an accident, but I'm glad it happened." She darted off into the night, further from her home.

Archard followed her, keeping up with her easily. "Is that your excuse for everything? That it's an accident?"

She knew he was referring to the spell that'd brought him and his family there, and she felt a dagger of anger in her heart. "It was, whether you believe me or not. But if Varhan is going to help you get back to Charok, then I'm going, too."

He dodged around her, his body gliding through the air until he stopped short directly in front of her. She tried to go to the left and then the right, but he blocked her any way she turned. "Kaylee, you can't. It's too dangerous."

Kaylee bolted upwards, but she hadn't spent enough time in her dragon form. Archard was right at her side. "I can if I want to," she finally retorted when it was clear she wasn't going to lose him anytime soon. Her wings were growing tired, and she glided down toward a clearing in the woods.

They touched down, Kaylee less gracefully than Archard. The ground was hard, but she refused to let out the grunt of pain that built in her lungs. For a moment, she considered shifting back to her human form, but she didn't want him to have more of an advantage over her than he already did.

He advanced toward her, his eyes sparkling with anger. "You don't understand. You could die."

"I don't care." As she said the words, she realized how true they were. "This is something I have to do. I can't explain it in any rational way, but I *know* I have to go to Charok. I've spent so much of my life searching for something, and it's very hard to find when you don't even know what it is. Varhan says it's because I'm a star child, but I think there's more to it than that. I'm supposed to go to Charok."

Archard touched her shoulder with one clawed hand. "I can't let you. Besides, you don't even know where the spell is."

She let out a puff of steam and backed away from him, turning her back. "You forget that I've spent my entire life here. I've explored every nook and cranny of that house, and I know all the secret hidey-holes. Trust me, I can find it."

"There's more. You don't understand."

Kaylee whirled back around to face him. "Then make me understand."

He advanced slowly, his eyes locking with hers. Even in dragon form, she wasn't immune to him. Kaylee's heart thundered while her blood carried sparks of excitement through her body until she was painfully aware of every move he made.

"I don't think I can make you understand," he finally said, his voice a soft contrast to the sharpness of his white teeth, "but I'm asking you to trust me. You can't go."

She pulled away, fighting against this spell he'd cast on her. "I thought you would be on my side. You said you wanted to go, too."

"I *am* on your side, but you simply can't go! I won't allow it." Archard's voice roared into the night, waking the daytime birds in the nearby trees and sending them fluttering off to a quieter place.

"What did you just say to me?" This unexpected, overprotective behavior was ridiculous. "Just because we had a little moment together doesn't give you any right to boss me around, Archard."

A dragon's sigh sounds more like a hiss, and Archard's held a hint of regret. "Yes. Fine. You're right. Just please, please promise me you won't do anything foolish."

Kaylee shook her head, trying to understand how she'd ever

thought there was something between the two of them. She could never have true feelings for someone so controlling. "I don't have to promise you anything." Kaylee shot up into the night sky and away from the clearing as fast as she could.

And Archard didn't follow.

## 12

IT'D BEEN A FEW WEEKS SINCE KAYLEE HAD SPOKEN SO BITTERLY TOWARD him in that clearing in the woods. She'd said nothing in the meantime about going back to Charok, and he was beginning to think she'd finally given up on the idea. He'd hated that he couldn't tell her the truth about why she couldn't go, but Julian and Varhan had been right in keeping the spell a secret from her.

Unfortunately, she had also given up on him. By the time Archard came down for breakfast, Kaylee had always come and gone before him. On the rare occasions when she hadn't beat him to the kitchen, she kept her distance as she poured her coffee and grabbed a bagel. She refused to even look at him. Archard had tried to make casual conversation with her, knowing better than to bring up the subject of Charok, but even his subtle "Good morning" or "How's the weather?" wasn't good enough for her. This seemed to make Jake pretty happy, considering the smug look he always wore on his face. No doubt, he thought the distance between them was his own doing.

After a dinner that wasn't any different from the rest, with Kaylee sitting as far away from him as possible and making excuses to leave the table after only a few minutes, Archard paced irritably in his room. The soft knock at the door made him hopeful, but it was only Kieran.

He strode in, looking concerned. "Are you all right?"

"No better or worse than I've ever been since we got here," Archard grumbled. He gestured toward the desk chair.

Kieran sat, his gaze still focused on Archard. "I'm not sure that's true. You seemed to be doing quite well for a couple of days shortly after we got here, and then your attitude went downhill again."

Archard glared at him, but he knew he was right. "There's been a lot on my mind."

"Still wanting to go back to Charok?"

He couldn't reveal the truth about the spell, not if he was going to keep his promise to Varhan, but it was no secret that he wanted to leave. "I don't belong here."

"I think you could if you wanted to. Just listen." Kieran put up a hand to stop Archard from arguing with him. "I know you feel obligated to your family's legacy, but there's nothing left to guard."

"If that's true, then why do I feel such a need to go back there? Why do I feel like I've left my post and something bad is going to happen if I don't take it up again?" Archard brought his hands together, weaving his fingers and squeezing until his knuckles whitened. "I'm so torn. I know I have to go back, but..."

"But?" Kieran pressed.

Archard groaned. "You can't tell Callan what I'm about to tell you."

"All right."

"You know how Lucia told us about what it was like for a dragon to find his mate? That there would be this indescribable feeling that comes over us; something we can't resist or deny? Something that pushes us even harder than the occupations handed down to us have?"

He bobbed his head. "Of course."

"I think I felt that with Kaylee. At first, it was kind of an anger, but then it turned into something else. I'm not the same person when I'm with her, but then again, maybe I'm the person I've always been meant to be. I want to shift, and I want to protect her from any dangers that might befall her. Hell, I even want to protect her from herself. I can feel the pull of my duties on Charok, but I feel the pull that Kaylee has on me as well."

Kieran laughed softly. "I haven't felt it myself, so I don't suppose I can say, but it certainly sounds like you've found the one you're destined to be with."

Archard pounded his fist into his thigh. "Then why does she hate me so much?"

"I don't think she hates you at all. I've seen the way she looks at you when you're not watching. She's probably going through the same thing you are, and the two of you need to just sit down and talk about it. Or, you know, find some other way to show how you feel about each other." His grin lifted his beard.

Archard gave him a playful punch on the arm, but he knew his cousin was probably right. "Fine, then. But if she tears me into pieces and leaves my charred remains on the lawn, then it's your fault," he laughed.

Leaving his room, Archard went to find Kaylee. The library was empty, and her car was still in the garage. He headed back upstairs and down to the end of the hall, but just as he raised his fist to knock on her bedroom door, it swung open.

She stared at him, surprised, and then tried to shut the door again.

Archard easily stopped her with a booted foot on the threshold. "I know you've been shutting me out, Kaylee, and now you're doing it literally. I just want to talk."

"I can't talk right now." She stared down at his foot, her mouth pursed.

It was then that Archard noticed she was hiding something behind her back. "What do you have?"

Her eyes widened, and she scooted a little further behind the door. "Nothing."

Archard knew better. Kaylee couldn't hold the door for long, and he pushed his way inside. She backed away from him, still holding her hand behind her back. He advanced across the room, hoping he was wrong, but there was only one way to find out. Archard grabbed her in both arms.

Kaylee pushed at his chest with her free hand, but it was no use. His hand closed on the book behind her back. He kept his left arm around her while he looked at it, his breath stopping in his lungs. It was Varhan's spell book.

"I'm putting this back where it belongs. You shouldn't have it." With a little regret, he let go of her. He was angry, but he still liked the way she felt in his arms.

She glared at him. "Fine, but it doesn't matter. I've taken it quite a few times already. I just put it back when I'm done with it and Varhan never knows the difference."

"He's going to now," Archard promised. "I should've told him right away about your plan, but I hoped you'd let it go."

"Tell him all you want, because I already know everything I need to know. I've got all the ingredients and I have the spell memorized. I'm going to Charok, Archard."

"No, you're not," he insisted. "This spell could kill you."

"Then it's worth the risk. Stop trying to get in my way; you're no different than anyone else here. You think you know what's best, but you have no idea what's going on inside me. It's like there's a string on my heart, and it's yanking on me constantly."

Archard took a deep breath and set the spell book down on her dresser. She couldn't take it again without him seeing it. He walked slowly toward her, knowing she was likely to dodge around him and try to run away again, and he stopped when they were face to face. Archard desperately wanted to reach out and touch her face, to brush back her hair with his fingers, to wrap his arms around her waist and pull her tightly against him once again. But he kept his arms firmly at his side. "I do understand that. I know that feeling more than you could ever imagine. That same sort of string is pulling me in two different directions, and I don't know which one to follow."

She tipped her chin up at him, and he swore he could see hope in her eyes. Did she know she was one of the forces that pulled at him so hard?

Archard hated himself for what he was about to say. He was about to go against everything Julian and Varhan asked of him. He was about to let Kaylee put herself in danger. But if she insisted on going, then at least he knew he could make sure that both the strings tugging on him were finally pulling in the same direction. He had to go home, but he had to protect Kaylee. "I'm going with you."

She blinked. "What?"

"If you insist on going, then I'm going with you," he replied. "And before you argue with me, just remember that you've never been to Charok before. You'll need someone there to keep you out of trouble."

Those were the wrong words, and he knew it as soon as he saw her eyebrows draw down. "I don't need you," she said bitterly.

"You do." He felt like such a jackass, but there was a truth inside him that refused to be ignored any longer. "If you want to do this, then you very much need me. You need me to keep you safe on Charok, and you also need me to keep this a secret from your father."

Her countenance turned to a scowl, but she nodded. "Fine. We're leaving tonight."

## 13

KAYLEE FELL, AND THE WORST THING ABOUT IT WAS THAT SHE COULDN'T see how far she had yet to go. Cold wind rushed past her ears, and her body tumbled in the wormhole she'd created with that spell. Her stomach had revolted as soon as the portal opened, and she'd been almost surprised to see that she'd pulled it off so easily. But it wasn't over until they were standing on Charok, and there was no choice but to jump in.

Archard was falling somewhere near her, but she couldn't open her eyes to find him. The wind and the light were too much, and they made her eyes water so badly, she couldn't see. It was easier to keep them shut.

The ground came out of nowhere, and she slammed into it before she saw it. Every molecule of oxygen left her lungs, and she lay gasping on the hard surface for a long minute.

"Kaylee? Are you okay?" Archard's chiseled face loomed over her, and her body began working again.

She nodded instead of answering aloud, and she let him help her up. "Did we make it?" she finally gasped. Kaylee didn't recognize the forest they stood in, but it could have been a grove of trees anywhere on Earth. She slowly picked up the backpack she'd brought along, grateful it'd made it through the trip.

Archard nodded. "I believe so. Either that, or it's someplace that looks a lot like Charok." He smiled at her, a look that transformed his face from its usual solemnity. "We did it!"

Kaylee sagged against a nearby tree. "I'm not feeling so great after that..." She slid to the leafy ground.

"That's understandable. I haven't studied any of these spells as much as you have, but Varhan told me the transition could make me sick—if it didn't kill me, that is."

"I think I just need some water and I'll be fine."

Archard glanced around uncertainly before nodding. "I think I know where we are, and there should be a stream not too far from here. You think you can walk?"

"Not right now. Why don't you go see if it's there, just to be sure, and then I'll get up."

He held out his arms. "I can carry you."

"No!" She cleared her throat. "No, thank you. I'm sure the spell wasn't easy on you, either. Just see if you can find it and we'll go from there." Kaylee waited until he'd disappeared over a small ridge before jumping to her feet. She didn't know what direction she was headed in or exactly what she was headed for, she only knew she had to get away from him. Archard would be pissed when he came back and found her gone, but he'd get over it.

Her stomach lurched once again, still upset about the long journey to Charok, but she could deal with that. She barreled through the woods, surprised at how little undergrowth she encountered. She considered shifting, but the tight trees would restrict her. It was best to stay human for now.

Heavy footsteps crashed in the leaves behind her, sending a shiver of fear up Kaylee's spine. Archard must've realized what she'd done, and he was after her. She pushed her legs harder, wishing she'd being doing more jogging, but it wasn't enough. The steps were drawing closer. She could see the edge of the woods up ahead, where the sunlight shone in a brilliant sheet, but she was too late. A hand wrapped firmly around her middle and yanked her off her feet.

But it wasn't Archard's. The thick limb was covered in lumpy green skin, and it pulled her back with a reckless force that her fellow dragon never would've used on her. It flung her through the air and pinned her to a tree, her feet suspended above the ground. The repulsive green face that pressed itself near hers matched the arm. The beast stared at her with dark beady eyes, sniffed her with its crooked nose, and snarled with a mouth full of sharp teeth. "What are you?" it demanded in a deep, rolling voice.

Kaylee couldn't answer if she wanted to, considering the thing was holding her by the neck. She scraped at his wrist and tried to pry his fingers back, but her efforts were futile. The world was beginning to darken around her, and once she passed out, she'd have no defenses left at all.

But a black form barreled into the side of the green beast, knocking it away and leaving Kaylee to fall to the ground. Her instincts told her to run while she could, but her body had been tapped. Between the spell, the run, and the encounter with that horrific green beast, she was barely conscious.

She watched through half-lidded eyes as the two creatures battled each other. Her captor went down with a few blows from the newcomer, slinking off into the woods and yelling over its shoulder. It was only as the victor approached her that she realized it was Archard.

Without a word, he scooped her into his strong arms and stalked off through the woods. She didn't fight him at first, knowing she didn't have the strength. After a few minutes, she coughed and told him to put her down, but he only held her tighter.

It wasn't until they'd reached a clearing where the ground was hard rock that he finally put her on her feet, but he held one clawed hand at her back to make sure she was steady. "Stay here," he grumbled.

Kaylee wasn't in the mood to argue. She looked around, noting that they were on the edge of the woods and getting into the foothills of a mountain range. Judging by the red rocks that surrounded her, this had to be part of the same mountain chain she'd seen in the vision just before Archard and the others had come through. Just behind her, the boulders and bluffs formed a small, unoccupied cave.

Archard returned with his arms full of wood. He arranged it just in front of the mouth of the cave, took a step back, and spewed a line of fire at the pile. It erupted into flames, and it was only as the warmth reached Kaylee that she realized just how cold she'd been. Archard didn't look at her as he slunk back into the woods.

She parked herself near the fire, leaning against the stone behind her and realizing how much of an idiot she'd been. They were lucky to survive the trip from Earth, something that her father and Varhan would be happy to hear if they ever saw her again, but there were so many other bad decisions she'd made besides running off to another world.

When Archard returned again, he'd shifted back into his human form. Kaylee glanced at the fish he set down near the fire and the pile of berries he emptied from one of his pockets, but she studied his face with much more interest than she had in the food. Her stomach rumbled, but she'd angered him. In the short time they'd known each other, she'd pissed him off plenty of times and he'd done the same to her. But this seemed completely different.

"I'm sorry," she finally admitted, her words sounding strange after such a long silence. "And thank you. I'm sure you saved my life back there—from whatever that thing was."

Archard had been wrapping the fish in leaves and setting them at the base of the fire where several hot coals had formed. He looked up at her, his jaw still hard. "It was an ogre. You have no idea how dangerous it can be here."

"Clearly," she retorted. "I really am sorry, Archard. For everything. I haven't exactly been fair to you. I'm not sure I've been fair to anyone else, either. I've been selfish. You said you didn't want me to come here because the spell might kill me. I knew I could make it, and I didn't think past that for one second."

"It's all right." His gaze was focused on the fire again, and he kept his hands busy by pulling tiny stems off the berries.

The distance between them was so great that they might as well have been worlds apart, with one of them still on Earth. It irritated her that he'd been right all along. "No, really. It's not."

"For what it's worth, I'm sorry, too."

This surprised her, and though Archard didn't look at her, she continued to watch him. "For what?"

He shrugged. "Everything. I should've trusted that you knew what you were doing with the spell instead of treating you like an impudent child. And maybe there's some other stuff, too." He looked almost sad as he poked experimentally at the fish.

Kaylee sighed. She'd been such an idiot. "You were dragged out of the only life you'd ever known, and then I put my problems ahead of yours."

"If we're both apologizing, does that mean we're both forgiven?" he asked.

She smiled. "I hope so."

"Sounds good to me. It's getting dark, but the fish should be ready soon."

Kaylee looked up at the stars that were beginning to peer down at them. "It's strange. It was the middle of the night when we left Earth."

"I don't think the days are the same length," Archard replied. "Varhan said something about it, and it seemed right to me."

Eventually, Archard removed the wrapped fish from the fire and handed one to her. "The leaves are from the wyssandra tree. They have a lot of water in them, so they don't burn in the fire, and they add some flavor. Mind the bones, unless you feel like shifting."

Kaylee took them gratefully, realizing that she had just as much to learn about his world as he did about hers. "And the berries?"

His eyes met hers over the fire, and he smiled a little. "They're not my first choice, but I got what I could on such short notice."

They were tart and didn't hold much flavor otherwise, but Kaylee was still grateful for them. The meat of the fish peeled away from the bones easily, and it'd been cooked to perfection. "I didn't realize you knew how to cook."

"Just because I live in a more primitive world than yours doesn't mean we eat raw meat off the hoof. I'm fairly certain all dragons prefer their meals thoroughly cooked."

Kaylee finished off her fish and licked her fingers. "I never thought about it before, but thank you."

They sat in companionable silence for a long time, watching the flames lick at the logs. Kaylee had a million thoughts racing through her head as she wondered if they would encounter any other dragons, if they were safe from the ogre, and what they would do next. But she also remembered how tiring it was to educate someone on your entire life all at once, and she kept her mouth shut.

Archard broke the silence instead. "Do you remember, back at your house, when I told you there were two forces pulling me in different directions?"

"Of course." It had been a moment of clarity for Kaylee, and she'd been surprised to find that he felt the same way.

"One of those forces was demanding that I return here. I think you understood that part."

"Yes."

He stood and came around the fire until he sat next to her, his eyes blazing into hers. "The other force that pulled me was you."

"Me?" Being in such close proximity to him was difficult enough, but hearing him talk that way was hard to handle. Her body craved him in a way she'd never felt about anyone before, and she longed to taste his lips again. She realized she was staring at them, and she whipped her eyes back up to his.

"I don't know how much your parents have told you about our kind, and...finding our mates?" Archard looked almost shy as he asked the question.

"They told me how things worked here, when there were still a lot of dragons left. But I guess they probably didn't think they would happen on Earth, because the only other ones of our kind were my relatives." She licked her lips and looked away. It was hard to say these things out loud, but she knew she needed to. "It's different with you."

"How different?" he pressed.

Kaylee smiled coyly at him. "Maybe you should tell me first."

His eyes were blazing orbs as he tipped her chin toward him with the gentlest of touches. "Being near you is almost unbearable. You make me angrier than I've ever been in my life, and if you ask my aunt, that's pretty damn angry. But in the next instant, you make me so happy that I can't remember any part of my life that doesn't have you in it. You make me want to shift, and I don't know if it's because that's my natural form or because I think it will impress you, but it's very hard to control. It's like both sides of me are fighting, and they don't realize they're on the same side. There's a lot I don't know, but the one thing I understand is this deep compulsion to protect you. I want to stand between you and anything that might hurt you or make you unhappy. I'm sure I don't have to tell you how hard that is when one thing could do both." His hand grazed down the side of her jaw, his thumb brushing her earlobe.

Kaylee's insides imploded, her body reacting to his words. "That's very sweet of you."

"It's not sweet," he argued. "If you knew what I want to do you, you wouldn't think I'm sweet at all."

She kissed him then, grabbing him by the shoulders and pulling him toward her. It'd been on her mind since that first, intense kiss they'd shared in her kitchen, and there was no better time than now to live it all over again. Kaylee closed her eyes and let herself dive in, immersing herself in the bond that had formed so instantly between them. She needed him, and for so much more than protection on Charok.

Archard responded, his lips demanding but soft as he grabbed her by the waist and pulled her onto his lap. His thumbs explored her hips before his hands wrapped around her back and slipped up her shirt. She arched forward, encouraging him to continue. He fumbled with the snaps on her bra for only a moment before releasing them, and when his warm hands embraced her breasts, she thought she was in heaven.

"Archard," she whispered as she finally broke the kiss. "I really do need you."

That was all it took for him. He pulled her shirt up over her head and set it aside. She did the same for him, sucking in her breath as she took in the width of his bare chest and the dark curls covering it. His abs were solid and tantalizing, and she wanted to see the rest of him. She'd seen the power he held in the reptilian version of himself, but she was pleased to find that he had that same power in human form. He was so much bigger and stronger than she was. With those bulky arms, he could snap her in half. But Kaylee knew he never would, and she reached for the button of his pants.

The two of them were soon naked in the firelight, the heat of their desire for each other keeping them far warmer than the fire. Archard laid her back against the cool rock, covering his body with hers as he resumed their kiss once again. His lips trailed down along her neck as his fingers stroked and explored her body.

Kaylee reached between his legs and found that he was hard and ready for her. She wanted to spend all night like this, but knowing what he had waiting for her made her impatient. She wrapped her leg around his waist and pulled.

Archard accommodated her. Neither one of them had to ask if the other was sure, because their hearts and souls had already bonded in a way that their minds and bodies couldn't truly fight. He pierced her gently and started to pull back when she gasped, but she kept him in place with a tug of her leg.

He smiled as he moved his hips against hers, caressing her neck and shoulders with his lips, gathering her hair in his hands. Kaylee's body picked up his rhythm, and the two of them moved as only those who are destined to be together can. She knew what he meant when he'd said what it was like to be around her; that it made him fight against himself. She realized she'd been feeling the same way, even if her dragon side wasn't as strong as his. Now that they were melding together, she felt a peace come over her, like she was finally able to rest.

*He* was the other half of her she'd been looking for.

She'd known she needed to come to Charok, but it was because they needed this place for the two of them to finally understand they were soul mates.

Most of her body was relaxed, but she felt a spasm starting deep inside her. Kaylee tightened her core, encouraging it, and the ripples began building to waves. Archard sensed it, his own body responding as he became even more engorged, and he continued to bury himself within her. Kaylee grasped at his shoulders and his back, trying to keep him as close as possible as she pressed herself against him. Her breath shortened until she was panting, and when her entire body seemed to shatter into stardust, she never wanted it to end. Archard's soft moans in her ear were enough to keep her going until they were both done, and still Kaylee hated to be separated from him in any way.

They lay next to each other, their arms entwined as they caught their breath.

"I'm glad we came here," Kaylee said softly.

"Me, too."

# 14

---

ARCHARD SPRANG UP FROM THE GROUND THE NEXT MORNING AS SOON AS the sun began peeking over the horizon. He hadn't felt this good in weeks. He knew part of it was because he was back home, but it was also because of Kaylee. They'd both fought so hard against themselves and each other, but spending the night together was exactly what he'd needed. His muscles felt alive and vibrant, and he had so much energy, he almost didn't know what to do with it.

Kaylee was still asleep, her chestnut hair a cloud around her head and her face peaceful. He could've stood there and watched her until she woke, but his stomach rumbled to remind him he had important things to do. He scrounged up a quick breakfast for them, and she awoke to the smell of roasting meat.

Her sleepy eyes looked happy as she stretched and stood. "I never thought I would be comfortable sleeping on a rock," she commented with a yawn. "In fact, I don't think I've ever slept so well in my life."

Archard smiled. "I know. The bed at your house was comfortable, but in a different way. Now eat up. We've got a big day ahead of us."

"We do?" she asked with a blink.

"Absolutely. We're going to the royal caves. There's a lot I want to show you while we're here, but I want to start there."

"Whatever you say."

Three hours later, when they'd made love once again after breakfast and then taken a long hike up the mountain, Archard stopped in front of a massive cave. "I never thought I'd see this place again. I spent so much of my life here."

Kaylee peered into the darkness inside before retrieving a flashlight from her bag. "How come?"

Archard realized he'd never actually told her much at all about his life on Charok. She only knew that he lived there. "My family has had the honor of being royal guards for as long as anyone can remember. There aren't any members of the royal line left, but I still feel an obligation to learn about this place and make sure it's safe. I guess that seems silly, but I can't help it."

She shook her head. "It doesn't sound silly to me at all. I understand. I don't have the same kind of attachment to the archeological digs that I go on, but I still want to see everything from them preserved. It's something I really love about my job."

The cave floor was smooth and hard. The winds had only brought a few dry leaves inside, but it appeared to have otherwise remained untouched in the time he'd been gone. "Look at the walls. You have your libraries on Earth, but this is like ours—well, one of them. There are other caves as well, but this one carries everything about the royal family. I've spent so much time looking at these walls, I think I practically have them memorized."

"They're beautiful," Kaylee said as she leaned forward to examine them. "You told me about this, but I couldn't have imagined the detail and the color."

Archard saw the cave drawings with a new appreciation. She was right. Even though they were drawn on rough rock walls and with limited tools, they were just as impressive as the paintings he'd seen back on Earth. The main difference was how much these meant to him, since they were all about the people he'd spent his life wanting to protect. It left a hole inside him to know that he'd been born too late and had missed the last of the great Kings and Queens. "Can you read them?"

"Yes." She touched the wall, careful not to put her fingers on the delicate writings. "This section speaks of the birth of a child. It's so loving; so tender."

"Some of the birth announcements are a little more boastful than that, but the royals seemed to love their children as more than just the continuation of their line." He pointed to another section on the other side of the wall. "There are tales of war, peace, and everything in between. They continue the further you go into the cave, and it goes on for miles." He realized as he spoke that he'd brought the perfect person back to Charok with him. "It's this part that I've always wondered about the most. Maybe you can help."

"I'll do my best. What is it?" She traced her flashlight over the wall to the section he indicated.

Archard sighed as he once again studied one of the most recent writings. It was still as old as he was, but so many of the scribes had been eliminated by the Great Curse. "The prophets wrote it here as the War broke out. I asked Lucia about it, and she always just brushed it off as nonsense."

"The Awakened One shall return when the time is ripe," Kaylee read easily. "You shall know her by the mark of the Queen."

"I always hoped that meant there were would be more dragons who would come back here, maybe even with the Awakened One. I don't know where they'd be coming from, and I can't say what it means to be an 'Awakened One,' but it gave me some hope." At that time, though, it'd been because he hoped to find his mate. He'd found her now.

"And the mark of the Queen?"

He gestured to the underside of his chin with three fingers. "Three scales, right in a row, and completely clear. It's a trait that was passed only through the sovereign bloodline."

Kaylee had turned pale. "Surely, someone else could have that birthmark, right?"

"No. It was passed down through the female line, so it always stayed in the family. Lucia saw it on the Queen herself before she died. Why?"

But Kaylee didn't answer. She stepped away from the script and headed for the opening to the cave, her flashlight making a circle of light next to her on the floor.

Archard glanced at the wall again before following. When he caught up to her, she was sitting on a small boulder just outside the cave entrance, bending forward and clutching at her stomach. "Are you still stick? Or maybe those berries didn't sit right with you. You're not used to eating them."

"It's not that."

Archard's forehead wrinkled in frustration. Things had been so wonderful only a few minutes ago. "Then please, just tell me what it is. We already know what happens when we don't talk, and I'd rather we fix this now." They were fated to be together, and they could get through anything. He knew it.

"I'll have to show you." Kaylee took off her backpack and laid it on the ground next to her. Her shoulders shuddered as her wings erupted, and her nose and mouth elongated to the beautiful form of the shimmering green dragon he'd found in the night back on Earth. His hunger for her grew once again to see her in this form, but her eyes remained sad as she turned to look at him. Instead of saying anything, she tipped up her chin and showed him the three crystal clear scales that resided on the soft spot at the top of her throat.

He understood now why she had to show him. "I didn't see them before, because it was dark," he mused. "Kaylee, this is incredible! You're...the Awakened One?" Joy surged through him.

But Kaylee dashed it away as she melted back down to her human form and tears rolled down her cheeks. "It's news to me, too. I knew there was something strange about my birth. My father only told me that my mother had died here on Charok. I always knew Naomi was my stepmother, but she's been around since I was a toddler. I didn't think about it all that much."

"I don't understand," Archard said softly, lowering himself to the ground in front of her so he could look up into her face. "The Queen's been gone since The Great Curse, and you said you were born on Earth."

She nodded. "Yes, and there are words hidden in the pictures that go along with that script you showed me. Several of the Queen's eggs were taken away from this place after she died, but the prophets didn't know where they'd gone. That's why they hoped at least one of the dragons born of those eggs would survive and return. According to this," she gestured angrily at her neck, "I was the one."

He took her hand, and when she tried to jerk it away from him, she only pulled harder. "I know that must be hard for you, but it doesn't mean that things are any different. You still have your father and your mother, and you said you always knew you weren't hers biologically."

Kaylee slowly pulled away from him, crying harder. "What it *does* mean is that you only feel what you feel for me because you're a royal guard."

"Don't say that."

"But it's true! You said yourself that you have an obligation to protect those of the royal family. You think the way you feel about me has to do with love, but it's not like that." She stood up, grabbed her bag, and stalked down the mountain.

Archard watched her go, the pit in his stomach deeper than the deepest gorge on Charok. His job was to protect the family, not to get romantically involved with them. What could he do?

# 15

KAYLEE SWIPED THE TEARS AWAY FROM HER EYES, BUT MORE CONTINUED to come, blurring the path in front of her. Archard had insisted on walking up the mountain so she could see all the details of the place he loved. It would've been easier for her to fly off, but she didn't know where she was going anyway. There was no place there that was special to her. There might have been a reason for her to come, but the truth she'd discovered hadn't resolved that disconnected feeling she'd had all her life. If anything, it was worse. She knew now that her parents had lied to her, and the one person she thought she belonged with was only driven by a moral obligation passed down from his family.

She heard him behind her, and this time she knew for certain that he wasn't an ogre. Archard called after her as he clambered down the steep slope. "Kaylee, wait! We should talk about this!"

"I don't want to talk!" she shouted back, and the effort only made her cry harder. Why hadn't her father told her the truth about her royal lineage? There was no chance that she would love Naomi any less.

"Just stop, please!"

But she charged on ahead and regretted it only a moment later when the ground disappeared from under her feet. She flung her arms out to catch herself, but her fingers met with only dirt and sand. She was too terrified to even scream for help. The slanted ground beneath her was loose and unforgiving, and as the tears cleared from her eyes, she saw that it ended in a sharp precipice. Kaylee was heading for a cliff, and there was nothing she could do to stop it. This was it. She'd risked everything to perform that spell and come here, and now she was going to fall and kill herself.

But the black figure of Archard appeared once again to pluck her out of danger's grasp. His claws wrapped around her just as the ground disappeared completely. He brought her back to level ground, all the way up near the royal caves, and let her down roughly. "What the hell do you think you're doing?"

"Killing myself, apparently," she retorted, embarrassed that she'd once again put herself in physical danger. "I couldn't see where I was going."

He huffed as he circled around her. "Even so, you could've shifted. That would've saved you from the ogre, and it would've saved you from that damn cliff." His scaled lips stretched back slightly in a draconic smile. "I think you've spent too much time among humans."

If he was trying to be cute, Kaylee wasn't up for it. "Yeah? Then why do you keep helping me, if you think so little of me?"

Archard tilted his spikey head, watching her closely. "I suppose it's my job, isn't it?"

"Great, so that's what this is? I really am nothing more than a job to you? How romantic." She turned away from him, but that only put her facing the royal cave again. There was no good place to turn.

"Hey! I never said that."

"You don't have to, and neither do I. We both know it's the truth. And it makes perfect sense, really. You've lived your whole life waiting for the royals to come back, so of course it would seem like something more than that when we finally did meet. Archard, there are so many implications here that I can't even keep track of them all." She felt betrayed on so many levels, even by herself. She'd been a fool not to see that there was a much bigger picture, and she hadn't bothered to step back and try to see it until now.

"I can't seem to change your mind," he finally said quietly. "But at the very least, I'll still perform my duties." He remained in dragon form as he lit a fire just inside the entrance to the royal cave and flew off to find them a meal. By the time it was done and he'd implored her to at least eat a little bit, the sky was beginning to grow dark. "We'll sleep in here," he said, gesturing to the place that had started all the trouble. "It's going to be cold tonight."

"Isn't there someplace better?" She didn't want to spend the night near those ancient murals that told of her family history.

"Not close by. Come on."

She threw bitter daggers when she finally turned to look at him once again. "I don't want to sleep anywhere near you."

His tongue flicked over his sharp teeth. "Suit yourself, but I suggest you at least shift. You'll stay warmer than you will in that." He nodded at her human body as though it were merely a garment and talked into the cave.

Kaylee rubbed her shoulders, knowing he was right about the weather. She'd been plenty warm the night before, but that had been in the safe confines of his arms. He was probably right about shifting, too, but the last thing she wanted to do was take the form of her ancestors. She headed inside after him, settling down on the complete opposite side of the grotto from the dark dragon and wrapping her jacket tightly around her. It was going to be a long night.

## 16

In the morning, Kaylee slipped out just before daybreak. She'd hardly slept at all, and there was no point in continuing to try. When she was out of earshot of the cave, she pulled her binder from her backpack. She'd not only taken careful notes when studying Varhan's spell book, but had also taken numerous pictures and printed them out to copy the pages. It was going to be difficult to find all the different ingredients she needed, especially since she wasn't familiar with the lay of the land and only had the wizard's scribbled drawings to show what they looked like, but she would do her best.

She didn't get far before she heard Archard calling for her. He appeared over the edge of the ridge above her, his pale skin gleaming in the sharp sunlight, bringing his dark hair to more of a contrast. He descended quickly after her, and she could see anger combined with something else in his face. "I'm glad you're okay. You know how dangerous this place is."

Kaylee stopped her walk to turn to him. "You don't have to guard me, Archard. Forget about your job and leave me alone. I'm going back to Earth."

"You can't do that," he responded automatically. "I mean, you showed me that spell, and so did Varhan. It's not as difficult as the one that got us here, but it's not exactly simple."

She glowered at him, pissed that he would once again question her. It had nothing to do with her supposed position as a member of the royal family, but she had a feeling he would treat her like she was incompetent no matter who she was. "I can, and I will."

"Kaylee..." He put a hand on her arm.

She stepped back. "There's nothing left here for me. I wish I'd never come."

"So what are you going to do instead?" he challenged. "You can't just run away from everything."

"Why not?" Kaylee threw her arms in the air. "I've spent my whole life running towards it all; I just didn't quite know what direction to run in. Now I can go home, confront my parents about lying to me, and then go off to live my own life somewhere away from other shifters. I don't want to see my parents or any of the rest of them. I don't want to see you and your family, either. It'll only remind me of what a sham my life has been." She felt tears pricking at her eyelids once again, which only pissed her off more.

"You don't mean that," Archard said quietly.

"I do, and you should be happy. You won't need to worry about your job anymore, at least not when it comes to protecting me. You can stay here and guard your musty old caves, but you won't have to save me from ogres or catch me before my stupid ass falls over the edge of a cliff." She turned away, determined to continue her descent and find the necessary herbs.

He wouldn't let her. His hand latched firmly onto her hips and yanked her back until he held her against his body. His voice was low in her ear. "I understand. It's got to be so difficult for you. I've always known what I was meant to do, and it isn't fair that your own truth should be hidden for so long. But you can't just give up on all of it."

"Archard, I don't belong anywhere. It's not something I'm still waiting to find out; I know it. It's time for me to go." She pushed away from him, and he let her go. Her skin was cold where it missed his warmth.

"At least let me come with you."

She paused, considering it. None of this was really his fault, but being near him caused her such pain now. "No. I don't want you to feel any obligation toward me. We'll go our separate ways."

She felt the hole in her heart grow bigger as his footsteps retreated.

## 17

ARCHARD WOULD'VE KICKED HIMSELF ALL THE WAY UP THE MOUNTAIN IF he thought it would've helped. Why did he have to open his mouth and say such stupid things? Why didn't he just take her in his arms, kiss her the way she deserved to be kissed, and remind her that they were *meant* to be together? No, instead he had to crack jokes about how it was his job to be with her, and that wasn't something any woman wanted to hear.

But as he neared the royal cave again, he knew exactly why. It was because he had his own doubts as soon as she'd revealed her true heritage. How was he to know if the way he felt about her was because she was his fated, or the person he was supposed to protect? How could he distinguish the two, when he knew he would want to protect his mate just as badly as he would want to protect someone of the sovereign family?

He stepped inside the cave and picked up a torch. He'd made them what felt like ages ago now, always keeping a supply on hand for when he wanted to explore the caves. It was easy enough to light, and he passed the prophecy as quickly as he could before descending into the darkness. Archard slowed as he examined portraits of ancient Queens and Kings. They were always shown as dragons, though any official hearings and courts were always held in human form. Many more bodies could fit into a room when they walked on two legs, and it tended to keep things more civilized. At least, that was how it'd been told to him. Archard had never been there for any of it, and he knew for certain that he would never be now.

Continuing on, the torchlight flickered over the lengthy description of a war that lasted for nearly a decade between two rival factions of dragons who had long since reconciled. Then there was a piece about a Queen who bore so many children, she could hardly keep track of their names. Several ribald comments had been scrawled in at some point in time, doubtless long after the Queen in question had died.

Archard headed in even deeper. He didn't know what he was looking for, but Kaylee's words echoed in his mind. She said she didn't belong there; that there was nothing left for her on Charok. It made him wonder what could possibly be left for him. He had the caves, but he knew that no one would return to them the way the prophecy predicted. Kaylee had already come, as an heir to the Queen, but she had turned around and left him, too. Was there much point in him protecting this territory any longer? He didn't even have his family there now.

As he studied a detailed picture of royal guards marching along the bottom of the cave wall, each roaring their wrath for anyone who dared to assault the Queen behind them, he felt like a complete failure. How did the generations before him perform such an impossible task? Were all royals so stubborn? The Queen in the painting was a similar color to Kaylee, a pale green. Her face was proud, yet beautiful. Perhaps Kaylee was just like anyone else of her line. It was her determination, after all, that drove her to always be looking for something more to life. When she let go of that, she was fun and carefree. She had flaws, certainly, but those flaws were part of what he liked about her so much.

No, *loved*. She'd mentioned that word, even though they hadn't said it to each other. Archard knew they didn't have to. He did love her. But how could he love someone when he was supposed to be her servant?

Archard continued to advance into the mountain, finding the older paintings that didn't have nearly as much care and detail as the newer ones. Instead of being sectioned off, with each piece carrying a central theme, it was more like the graffiti Kaylee had explained to him on Earth. Random pictures and words were recorded wherever the owner felt like putting them. He'd dismissed them as old and worthless, but he was seeing them with new eyes now.

A fat dragon lay on its back, picking bones out of its teeth, and another one was stuck forever between its two forms as it tried to fly off a cliff with the legs of a man still dangling beneath it. But at least someone had been serious at one point, because a poem was scrawled off to the left.

> *None is safe from the spell we call love.*
> *It haunts him, no matter where he hides.*
> *And if, by chance, he happens to escape,*
> *Then in his heart only misery will abide.*

ARCHARD STARED AT THE WORDS. He'd seen them before, but they'd never meant much to him. He never imagined that he would be one to turn away from true love. But did the poet know the dilemma of loving someone who wasn't meant for him? Did he have any idea what it was like for a man to fall in love with the woman who could be his Queen? Judging by the careful script and the small drawing of a dragon laying with his wings spread around him like a wet blanket, he probably did.

Hell with it. He could be completely wrong, but Archard didn't care anymore. He couldn't just give up and let this go. He might not be able to perform the duties of his forefathers, but he'd be damned if he'd let himself be a weak man. Turning back toward the entrance, he ran until his two feet on the packed sand turned to four, the tips of his wings brushing the roof of the cave. The torch fell and fizzled against the rock wall, and he burst from the cave and into the air.

Kaylee was nowhere on the mountainside. He'd spent far too long poking around in the cave, and there was no telling where she'd gone to get the ingredients for her spell. In his duress, Archard couldn't even remember what they were. He closed his eyes and spread his wings wide, letting his instincts tell him where to go. He caught an air current that pulled him down to the foothills and over the woods. *Damn. She could be anywhere amongst the thick trees, and so could the ogres.* He should've told her that it wasn't safe; that at the very least, she could stay on the mountain with him until she was ready to leave.

But a flash of movement caught his eyes. She was there, by the stream. He crashed through the treetops and splashed down into the creek, shaking the cold water from his foot as he shifted back to the form she was more familiar with. Her eyes were red and puffy, and by the way she held her mouth, he knew she was going to send him away again.

"Kaylee, you've got to listen to me. I love you. I don't care if I'm supposed to be a royal guard."

"But that's what you've always wanted," she started to argue.

"No! I don't care about any of that, not in the same way that I did before. It's a legacy, and it's one that I'm proud of, but life isn't the same as it was for the dragons who lived here a generation ago. It's time that I accepted that. And that even if things hadn't changed and the Great Curse had never been cast, I still wouldn't care. I'm supposed to be with you, Kaylee, and I'm going to be, royal guard or not." He let it all out in one breath, fearing that if he stopped for even one moment, she would find a way to change his mind once again. "You told me to go away, and I listened to you because I wanted to make you happy. But I'm not ever going to go away again, because that's not what makes *me* happy."

Her face reddened a little more, and then she fell into his arms. Her sobs racked her back and shoulders, and Archard simply held her.

She wiped her eyes on the backs of her hands and finally looked up at him, still beautiful despite the tears. "I've made so many wrong decisions, and I can't seem to make the right one. Things are cloudy when I'm around you, but they're even worse when you're gone. I love you, too, but I don't know what we're going to do."

"It doesn't matter," he assured her. "We can be here on Charok or on Earth. You can be a Queen or an archeologist. I can be a royal guard or find something else to occupy my time. I just know that I want to be with you, and I don't care what any being from any time or any planet has to say about it. We just have to love each other."

"You're right," she said, tears and laughter mixing in her throat. "You're absolutely right."

After contemplating the choice for a time, both dragons knew they'd be much happier on Earth, but decided to spend one last day on Charok together. The following day, they'd recite the spell that would send them back to Earth forever.

# 18

Kaylee looked in the mirror, shocked at the transformation. She was used to the version of herself that was ready for an expedition, with her hair barely tamed by an elastic band, a clean face, and practical clothing. But when Lucia and Naomi stepped back and finally let her see herself, it was like a completely different person stood there.

"I don't know how I didn't see it before," Lucia remarked, her eyes sparkling. "You look like a Queen."

Kaylee blushed. "No, I don't."

"Yes, you do," Naomi argued, straightening the short train of the brilliant white dress. "You always have, even when you've tried to hide it. I think we've got you all ready physically, but how are you? Are you ready for this?"

Leave it to her mother to be focused on how she felt. That was one of the many things she loved about Naomi. "More ready than I thought I could be. Everyone always says they're so nervous, but I'm really not." She hadn't been nervous about any of it, not when she went to pick out a gown, not when they settled on a venue, and not even as the day approached.

Naomi winked. "That just means you've found the right one."

A knock sounded on the door. Naomi cracked it open to make sure the groom wasn't trying to sneak a peek at the bride, and then she held it wide to admit Julian.

"If you ladies don't mind, I'd like to have a word with my daughter."

Naomi, Lucia and the bridesmaids cleared the room, adjusting their shoes and giggling. Kaylee looked to her father expectantly.

Julian kissed her cheek. "You look beautiful."

"Thank you." She ran her hands down over her dress. "I hope Archard likes it. I know he thinks this whole ceremony is a little over-the-top and too human, but he's humored me so far. I can't help that all these Earth traditions rubbed off on me."

Her father sat down in one of the numerous chairs in the bride's dressing room. "You don't have anything to worry about, dear. I'm pretty certain Archard would do anything for you. I mean, he did travel to another planet and back for you."

She shook her head and smiled. "I'm glad you approve. It's all happened so fast, but I'm so happy. I love him so much."

"I know you do. Listen, I know we don't have a whole lot of time before the wedding starts, but I just wanted to make sure you're okay. This whole thing about your lineage was a lot to take in, and—"

"Dad, don't. We've been over this." Julian had explained that he and his friends had each taken the last of the Queen's eggs and crossed over to Earth to keep them safe with Varhan's help. Once they'd come to Earth and the eggs had hatched, they'd each raised their drag-onlings as their own children.

"I know we have, but it's bothered me so much. You were so upset when you got back. I'd been horrified once I realized you'd left, and then I thought I was going to lose you for good because I hadn't told you the truth. I only did it because I thought it would be best. I didn't think we'd ever really have a chance to go back to Charok, and I wanted you to have the most normal life possible."

She smiled at the old dragon. "Thanks to you, I'll never be normal. And I wouldn't want it any other way. There is one thing I've been curious about, though."

He watched her expectantly. "What's that?"

"Do you think my heritage has anything to do with my gift for languages? Was the Queen that way?" It was something she'd thought about off and on ever since she'd first seen and understood that prophecy in the royal cave.

"I don't suppose we'll ever know. It could be that, or it could be simply that you were born with bit more brains than the rest of us. Is there anything else?"

"No." And she meant it. Kaylee had spent plenty of time thinking about her true mother and where she belonged in the world, and she would think about it plenty in the future. But for now, she was happy to set it aside. "Not today."

"Very well." He took her hand. "Let's get you down that aisle."

———

THE WEDDING WAS JUST as beautiful as she'd hoped, and perhaps even more so. Kaylee felt like a glowing haze had descended over her eyes, showing everything in its best light as she and Archard exchanged their vows. The peach and lavender roses she carried and that had stood proudly in centerpieces on white tablecloths were breathtaking. Her maid of honor, Nora, and her bridesmaids were the epitome of style and grace. Her parents and honorary uncles were noble and distinguished. Even her brother was on his best behavior, and since Kaylee had found out about his threat to Archard, she was watching him closely.

Most of all, her new husband was the same strong, caring soul she'd come to know better over the last six months.

Only her feet ached from being on them so much, and she kicked her shoes off under the table as they finally sat down to eat. "You look hot in a tux. I'll have to find ways to get you in one more often."

Archard raked his eyes down to her dress and back up again. "You look incredible, but I think you look best wearing nothing at all." The deep blue of his eyes was a sea of mischief, but it was one she could swim in for all of eternity.

She touched his thigh suggestively. "Keep talking like that and we're going to have to cut the party short."

"Is that a challenge? Now that the champagne has been uncorked, I don't think anyone's paying much attention to us."

Archard grabbed her hand and rose from his chair, bringing her with him as he made an escape from the grandiose hotel ballroom. He slipped into the stairwell across the hall and pushed her up against the wall. "I've been dying to get a hold of you all day. I haven't seen you since last night, and I don't think I ever want to be away from you that long again." He kissed her deeply, his fingers exploring her body through the soft material of her gown.

"I'd tell you that you'll get your wish, but you might not. Dr. Morrick has invited me to another dig. I leave in two months." She kissed him back, delighting in that warm, strong body. She hadn't been able to get enough of him, even knowing they would be permanently bound for the rest of their lives. He'd been so completely right when he'd come after her on Charok. It wasn't simply his duty to be with her, it was their destiny to be together.

Her husband squinted one eye while he calculated the dates in his head. "Sounds to me like it'll just be an extension of our honeymoon."

"I haven't even told you where it is yet," Kaylee laughed, wiggling her fingers under the jacket of his tux and absorbing the heat that came through his shirt.

"I don't care," Archard replied. "It could be an island, the mountains, or the desert," he continued, kissing her after he listed each location. "I'll explore the world with you if you want, as long as you're willing to take me with you."

Her heart melted for the millionth time. He had a way of doing that to her. "Sounds wonderful."

"For now, though, let's see if we can sneak up to the room and back down again before anyone notices." Archard swept her up into his arms and trotted up the stairs to their hotel room.

She knew many languages, and now she knew the language of love.

———

# ROYAL DRAGON'S PROTECTOR

SHIFTERS BETWEEN WORLDS

# PROLOGUE

THE CASTLE HAD BEEN BUILT OF THE SAME RED SANDSTONE THAT MADE up the mountains of Charok. It rose like a bloody fortress in the light of the setting sun, its battlements bristling with cannons and spears. Guards stalked every wall and stairwell, their beady eyes alert and their weapons at the ready. A traveler appeared on the narrow road that led up to the castle, coming from the south. Red dust clung to his robe, and though he'd worn his boots through long ago, he hurried, knowing his life depended on it.

The disciples came from all directions, joining the first traveler as they returned from various parts, scurrying to report what they'd seen on the battlefield back to their master. They hustled up the mountainside, which had been cleared of the evil dragons who'd once inhabited it long ago, and in between two long, sharp-toothed skulls on posts on either side of the barbican. The followers glanced up at them, knowing they represented the further triumph that was to come.

Servants rushed about the stone enclosure, lighting the torches all along the walls and inside the keep. The great wizard Tazarre had ordered that the castle be kept alight at all hours of the night, to serve as a reminder both for both friend and foe that he was in residence. The flames danced against the stone, hot and dry as the wizards made their way between them to the innermost chamber of the castle.

"It's about time you came," Tazarre boomed into the hot room as the door opened and admitted the wizards. "You're supposed to be among the most powerful sorcerers on this planet, yet you can't even tell time."

Murmurs of apology rippled through the assembled men as they gathered in the room, eyeing their master with sideways glances. One man had dared to look Tazarre straight in the eye a month ago, and not a soul had heard from him since. He was a menacing figure with slitted eyes and dark robes that fell to the floor. The two horns that curled down from his forehead and pointed inward near his chin were a more recent addition. Some claimed they'd been a result of a spell gone wrong, while others believed he'd created them on purpose. But no one had dared to ask Tazarre himself.

"Go on," he growled. "I don't have all night. I have plenty more work to do." A massive stack of parchment sat on the corner of the slab of stone that served as a desk, the wrinkled edges suggesting it had already been scribbled on vigorously. A fresh stack sat on the opposite corner, awaiting his words. He shoved aside the sheet he'd been working on but continued to hold his quill, the brilliant feather said to have come from a phoenix he'd sacrificed earlier in the year.

An elderly man hobbled forward, leaning heavily on a twisted wooden cane. "Your spell is taking a firm hold in the region of the southern woodlands," he reported in a shaking voice. "I personally saw at least a dozen dragons, their bodies twisted in pain as they took their last breaths. Your spell is very strong, my lord."

"And how do I know I can trust you?" Tazarre turned on the man, leaning forward to squint his dark eyes at the speaker. "All you ever give are vague reports, news that doesn't sound any different than what everyone else has to tell me. For all I know, you're on *their* side."

"No, lord, no! I never!" The poor wizard shook and trembled, but not from his age or feeble body. "I swear, I've done all in my power to fight them."

"Guards!" Tazarre roared, his voice thundering through the keep as two broad men in armor came marching in through a side door. He flung his finger at the old man. "Take him away for interrogation. I have reason to believe we might have a traitor among us."

"Please, sir." His cane dropped to the floor as the guards grabbed him by the elbows, and he pressed his hands together as he plead for his life. "I've been nothing but a loyal servant. I wouldn't even speak to someone who wasn't. You must believe me!"

"No, I mustn't," Tazarre replied in a low growl. "I know what's happening. Some of you think you're stronger than I am; more proficient. You think you know a better way to defeat the dragons and their ilk. But I know far more about the danger of these beasts than any of you possibly could!" He snatched up the sheet of parchment he'd been working on and held it triumphantly over his head. "I've received messages from the spirits that walk in the Otherworld! They know the truth, and they chose to give it to me. Listen to my words, or perish in ignorance!"

Tazarre's disciples fell to their knees, pressing their foreheads to the hard floor as the old man was dragged away. His screams echoed in the hall, but no one dared to step to his aid or argue for him. To go against Tazarre was death, and not a pleasant one.

"I hear there are some amongst our ranks who don't believe the dragons are truly the enemy. To them, I say death is the only answer! Only *I* have talked to the lords of the Otherworld, and only *I* know the truth. It's my job to pass it along to you, to help you, and yet so many of you choose not to believe my words."

"We believe you, great one! We believe you!"

But Tazarre only shook his head. "You say you do, but I believe your minds are still contaminated with false truths. You must hear it again, to preserve it in your mind, so you can tell your children and your children's children!"

"Yes, lord."

"Long ago, Charok was peaceful. The wizards had made their homes here. They carried out their work from day to day, using only enough magic so that they might live comfortably. They had a peaceful contract with the neighboring ogres, and they planned to live forever in prosperity on this wild and bountiful land." Tazarre intoned the tale like a story in a book, although he didn't need to read from any of the pages on his desk to know the words. The other mages had heard it a thousand times, and yet they listened raptly.

"One day," the great wizard continued, "the dragons arrived. No one truly knows from whence they came, but they must have come from the darkest, most evil place in the universe! They scorched our crops, burned our homes to ashes, and ate our children. Late at night, you could hear the crunching of young bones in the dragons' teeth. Mothers wept at their heartache, fathers fought bravely, and yet the dragons continued their destruction."

"Soon enough, they had overrun the land. They were *everywhere*. Our way of life was not only disturbed, but threatened. We were about to become extinct until the lords of the Otherworld spoke to me. They told me there was a way to save my people, and all I had to do was learn their ways. I spent many dark days in meditation, learning and understanding; memorizing. It is only because of these wise spirits that the tides have turned in the battle. They have called on me to be your savior, and I shall be so!" He strung out the last syllable, calling it out from the depths of his lungs.

A rattling cry arose from the small assemblage. Some of them even wept.

"What else can you tell me about the battlefields?" the evil wizard pressed. "Something more specific, I hope."

A slim wizard with piercing yellow eyes sidled forward, a confident smile creeping across his face. He knew when the time was right to put himself in the good graces of his master, and this was certainly one of them. Tazarre was looking for someone loyal, faithful, and willing to carry on his mission, no matter what happened, and this subservient mage knew he was the one. "My liege, your experiments with the poisonous Great Curse are indeed a success. I visited the northeastern region, where the mountains begin to grow cold. We know there are very few dragons there to begin with, but that, of course, makes it the perfect place to experiment. We wouldn't want the main populace to get word of it and ruin the surprise." He smiled wickedly as he tapped the tips of his long fingers together.

"And?"

"And they're dropping like enormous flies. I must admit I found one who hadn't fallen to the spell. I believe he hadn't been in the area when it was cast and only returned to find his relatives slowly suffering. I slayed him myself."

The great horned head nodded slowly. "Good. If only we could have the pleasure of taking them one by one. But their numbers are too great. They've infested this planet, and it's our job to eradicate them. The Great Curse is the only way, but there is something you'll need to know."

The wails of the man who'd been taken by the guards had died away, and the remaining wizards leaned forward slightly to hear their master's words. Things had been coming to a head in the war against the dragons, and the tension in the atmosphere had been palpable for months.

"I have finished my calculations on the final spell, and they confirm that it will completely decimate our enemies."

A resounding battle cry went up amongst the wizards. They'd seen so many of their own perish since this battle had begun, and a guaranteed victory was just what they needed to continue on.

"However," he silenced their cheers with one long, pointed finger in the air, "it will come at a great price: my life. This spell will require such power that I will no longer be able to stay in this body. I'm more than willing to pay that price, considering what it will do for the rest of you."

Another round of shouts and applause echoed through the keep as several of the wizards once again dropped to their knees, this time in gratitude. The yellow-eyed disciple felt particularly thankful. He'd lost everything to this war, and their master was willing to sacrifice himself in order to see it come to an end. They couldn't have found a better leader if they'd tried.

"I only ask for a few small favors in return."

"Anything, my lord," the wizards chanted as one.

Tazarre held up his finger once again. "First, that you continue to fight as you have, even though you know I'll be ending it all soon. I want the dragons decimated and for the wizards to rise to the top on our good name. I don't want anyone to have reason to think we gave up simply because of a particularly powerful spell. I don't think this is too much to ask."

"Very well, my lord."

He nodded, a twisted smile coming across his face. It was an ancient visage, one that'd seen centuries go by; one that'd been through more than all the other wizards combined. The puckered, weathered skin around his mouth had become stiff and hard; his eyes squinting from years of searching for all the answers. He held up another finger. "The second is that you continue in my name, no matter what happens. I know this will work, and we will win. But inevitably, there will surely be some clever dragon who thinks he has escaped my clutches. I won't stand for that, and neither should you. Just because the war is over doesn't mean you can retire to a peaceful life. We must carry out our mission until we die!" His roar filled the chamber, ricocheting in the wizards' ears, causing them to fall back slightly.

A sorcerer with long, black hair dared to look up for half a second before returning his gaze to the floor. "We thank you, liege, for everything you've done for us. You are truly a most powerful and benevolent master."

Tazarre laughed, a deep tone that made the stone walls vibrate around them. "It's a good thing you think so. Things are about to change on Charok. Mark my words."

# 1

TWENTY-FIVE YEARS LATER

"WHAT ARE WE LOOKING FOR TODAY?"

Nora Mitchell tipped her face toward the sun, which shone down brightly onto the path from the gravel parking lot and into the woods. It was a gorgeous day with just enough light to shoot by, and the late hour meant most of the other visitors to the national park would have already left for the evening. Perfect conditions for a video. "Whatever we can find. I'm not too picky today."

Holly adjusted the camera bag on her shoulder, swiping a strand of coal-black hair from her face. "Really? Most days, you have some sort of agenda. Are you feeling all right?"

Nora laughed. "I'm fine. I just don't feel like having a schedule or a set purpose today. I've hit a thousand subscribers on my channel, which is something I never thought would happen just by tromping around the woods to identify plants. We can think of this as something along the lines of a celebratory post."

It'd been just over a year since Nora had started her YouTube channel, Seeds of Knowledge. She didn't expect anyone to really watch her videos unless they were as fascinated by botany as she was, and she figured that was going to be a pretty small audience. But a few shares managed to get her posts in front of the right people, and she'd received emails from teachers all over the country who were showing her videos in their classrooms and thanking her for actually sharing something educational on the internet in an entertaining way.

"What, no top ten?" Holly asked.

Nora shrugged. "I thought about it, but I don't think I've really got enough material yet. That video we did in the parking lot of the Grocery Giant was a good one, though. Even I was surprised at how many different plants we were able to identify there."

"No, how many plants *you* were able to identify. We both know I'm just here for my mad cinematography skills." Holly flashed a bright smile. She'd earned a degree in film and photography, much to her parents' displeasure.

"Hey, works for me. Especially since you do it for free!" Nora and Holly had met in the library two years ago while studying for finals. It'd been one of those chance encounters that you just can't replicate in life, when two people who seemingly have nothing in common suddenly click.

"Not completely free," Holly reminded her. "You still owe me a coffee at Java Jump later on. I have a lot of work ahead of me tonight."

"Looks like we're not the only ones," Nora replied in a low voice. She pointed further down the trail, where a woman was walking toward them. She carried a pair of sandals in her hand, digging her bare feet into the soil. Her wild, dark blonde curls stood in a cloud around her head, with a few leaves and twigs buried in her locks. "Good evening, Aurora."

"Hmph," the other woman replied. She'd looked perfectly happy a minute ago, but now that she'd seen them, her shoulders hunched into a distinct sulk. "Come out here to ruin the peace, I guess, huh?"

Nora smiled and shook her head. Aurora looked like she could be a super model, with beautifully arched eyebrows and generous pink lips, but her attitude didn't make her very easy to be around. "You should know by now that I care just as much about this land as you do."

Aurora held up a bag of trash. Some of the packages were faded and covered in dirt, suggesting it'd been out there for quite some time. "Then maybe you should make one of your videos about *this* shit," she grumbled, marching on down the trail past them.

Holly waited until she was out of earshot before leaning over and whispering, "What do you think she does out here all the time? It looks like she's been sleeping on the ground."

"I wouldn't doubt it. She's not supposed to, since there are designated campsites, but those would probably be too close to other people for her taste. I don't think she's hurting anything, though." Nora glanced over her shoulder to where Aurora was disappearing around a curve of the trail. She couldn't help but like the grumpy-natured girl, even if she didn't quite understand her. At the very least, they shared a love for the living world. One of these days, she'd convince Aurora that she wasn't the enemy.

"No, probably not. I feel for anyone she actually catches in the act of littering. There's no telling what she'd do."

"Yeah. I've run into her so many times out here that I guess I've just gotten used to her." Nora's thoughts turned away from the strange woman of the woods and back to their original mission. "Oh, look over there!"

"Hey, now! Don't get too excited, girl; I don't even have the camera ready yet." Holly pulled the bag off her shoulder and removed the video camera, quickly setting it up to shoot. "Okay, you're good to go."

"Hey there, plant nerds!" Nora beamed into the lens. "My friend Holly and I are just out for a walk today to see what we can find. If you watch this channel regularly, you know we're out in these woods a lot. You might not expect us to find anything we haven't seen before, but that's one of the things that's so fascinating about nature. It's constantly changing, and you can walk down the same path dozens of times and still find something new to look at. Today, we've been lucky enough to stumble across ginseng!" She waved at Holly to zoom in on the little plant. "Since it's fall, ginseng is particularly easy to identify due to these little red berries. Other than being just a cool-looking little plant, ginseng has been well-known in herbalist circles for its numerous healing powers. These haven't been proven in clinical trials, but it still makes this a very in-demand plant." Nora felt the usual rush of energy she felt when sharing her knowledge with the world, even if it was only a very small part of the world. She sometimes impressed herself with how much information she could regurgitate on the fly. By the time she'd explained how difficult it was to find wild ginseng due to over-harvesting and how to prevent it, they'd already shot at least ten minutes of footage.

She was just about to wrap things up when she heard a resounding crash off in the woods. Nora was used to hearing things out there; birds were always chattering away or dropping seeds out of trees. A daring rabbit might shoot across their path. Squirrels were the worst, sounding remarkably like humans when they bounded along the forest floor. But this was something much bigger. And heavier.

Nora paused in her lecture about ginseng and looked at Holly. "Did you hear that?"

Her friend was glancing around, but still held the camera steady. "Yep, but I don't see anything."

No matter, they weren't going to stop filming just for a falling tree limb. Nora looked back into the camera. "There you have it, folks. We just might have heard big foot himself!"

They cut and Holly grinned. "I don't think you got your celebratory vid, Nora. This is a good one on its own."

"I think you're right, but that's okay. It just means we're ahead of schedule. I can post the ginseng one this weekend, and maybe while we're out here, we can find something else for next weekend. Oh, and I also wanted to talk to you about ideas for fall. I want something really good for Halloween."

"That's almost two months away."

"Yeah, but I'm excited. I've always loved autumn. It's such a wonderful time to be outside, and the colors are so gorgeous. The only bad part is that I have to spend all winter in the lab instead of outdoors, and it's going to be difficult to come up with enough to shoot to keep the channel going all winter long." They headed on down the path, Nora's eyes constantly sweeping from side to side, watching for anything else that might be of interest to her viewers.

"I'm sure you'll come up with something. You had some good ones last year with the identification videos and lab equipment. Maybe we can even do some shots through the microscope." Holly had shouldered her bag, but she kept her camera at the ready, just in case.

"That could be cool." Nora scanned the trees, noting that a few of the leaves had begun to turn slightly. Full fall colors would be taking over before they knew it. "I hope Ted and I get a chance to go to a pumpkin patch or something like that. There's just something romantic about this time of year." Her mind filled with thoughts of hayrides, pumpkin spice lattes, and hand-knit scarves.

"Speaking of Ted..." Holly trailed off, her steps slowing.

"What is it?" Nora knew Holly well enough to know something was wrong. She paused on the pathway, her intrigue with the plants and trees around them brought to a sudden halt.

Holly sighed. "I don't know how to tell you this. I don't want you to be upset with me, but I think we both agree we should always be honest with each other."

This only made Nora more nervous, and she wasn't a particularly anxious person. "Just spit it out. Whatever it is, I'm probably imagining it to be much worse than it actually is. I won't be mad; I promise."

"Okay." Holly took a deep breath. "You brought up Ted. I know you've been pretty happy with him over the last few months, but there's something about him I just don't like."

Now, thoughts of her video were completely gone. She and Ted had been dating since February, when they'd commiserated in the graduate's lounge over all the lovey-dovey Valentine's Day crap plastered everywhere and how it rubbed singledom in the faces of the unattached. They'd decided to go out that night on a whim, just as friends to keep each other company, but things had taken off like a rocket from there. Soon, they were spending all their time together. Ted had been awarded a teaching position only a few months later, and that kept him very busy, but he always managed to at least give her a call in the evening to wish her goodnight.

"You've never said anything before. What's not to like?"

Holly looked at the ground and ran a hand over her ponytail. "It's nothing specific, I guess. I just don't always feel like he's really being... honest with you. Like when he texted you last week and said he was going to bed early, but then he was active on Facebook an hour later."

Nora shrugged it off. "Like I said, he probably just couldn't sleep. Or he just didn't feel like being on the phone."

"If the latter were the case, then he should've just told you. You're a big girl, and I'm sure you could've handled it if your boyfriend didn't feel like chatting." Holly made a face, clearly not buying any of Nora's excuses.

"Is there anything else?" Nora thought of Ted, with his big, brown puppy eyes and wild, dark hair. He was a typical academic, opting for sweaters, khakis, and nice shoes. He'd majored in English, and he'd turned the spare room in his apartment into a small library, complete with leather-bound books and comfortable furniture. Ted was like an old-fashioned gentleman, the type of guy who didn't exist anymore. It was hard to believe there could be anything about him that Holly wouldn't like.

"It's not anything specific, which is why it's taken me so long to say anything," her friend admitted. "I just don't feel like he's as committed to the relationship as you are."

Unfortunately, this was the sort of sentiment that echoed some of Nora's own concerns. She'd never believed that he was anything other than the refined, polite guy she'd come to know, but there had been a certain amount of distance growing between them lately. He still went through all the motions of opening doors and pulling out chairs, but he wasn't really present, it seemed. Nora was usually the one calling and making plans, and she was the first one to go in for a kiss or to express some mushy sentiment. Not that she minded being a strong woman and taking the lead, but it didn't feel completely genuine. "I'll have to keep that in mind."

"Oh, don't make that face! Now you've made me feel bad!" Holly whined, frowning.

"What face?"

"Like you're all sad and miserable!"

Nora rubbed her cheeks and plastered on a smile. "Is this better? Really, though, I'm just disappointed. You're not wrong, and it's made me wonder what I should do about our relationship. And I'm definitely not mad, by the way. It takes a good friend to be honest about stuff like that." She wrapped her arm around Holly's shoulders and gave her a tight side hug. "Thank you."

They did a little more filming, but they were soon losing light. "I think we'll have to call this a night. I should be available again in a couple of days if you want to do more. I'm going to be pretty busy with work for a bit, though."

"Your freelance work keeping you busy?" Nora asked as they headed back toward the trail.

"Very! I've surprised my parents and even myself with how many jobs I'm getting. In fact, that's what I need to be working on right now. I'll let you get me that cup of coffee another time."

When they reached the parking lot, Holly took off toward her house while Nora headed to the university. She needed to check on a few things before she left for the evening. She took her position as a lab assistant very seriously, and she wanted the place to be perfect before she left for the night.

The side doors to McKnelly Hall would have been locked at least an hour ago, but the main entrance was still open. She slipped through the giant door, holding the handle so it wouldn't slam shut behind her and send a roaring echo through the hall. It was quiet and peaceful in there at night, when all the students and most of the teachers had gone home for the day. Nora was a social person, and she loved talking to people, but she loved feeling like she had the whole building to herself. It gave her a spark of excitement in the pit of her stomach as she trotted up the stairs toward the lab.

The second-floor hall, with its vaulted ceilings, solid wood doors, and ancient flooring, made her feel like she was part of something much bigger than herself. Nora smiled as she made her way to the end, but her smile faded when she saw a familiar security guard come around the corner.

Kieran was a burly man, probably bigger than anyone she knew. He carried his muscular frame with ease, and it fit nicely under his uniform. With startling dark-blue eyes and a rare but warm smile that occasionally emerged from his beard, he was the kind of guy most women would turn their heads at. Kieran was quiet and he only worked evenings, so most of the other staff didn't really get the chance to know him. Nora didn't know him all that well herself, but she knew his secret.

He was heading in her direction and there wasn't anything she could do to avoid him. Nora had met Kieran briefly at her cousin Kaylee's wedding. She'd been busy as a bridesmaid, which kept her from spending too much time with the other guests, and she'd suddenly been crushed by a panic attack that'd sent her home early that evening.

She offered Kieran a small smile and a whispered "Hi" as she rushed past him. His eyes, deep blue sapphires that burned brightly, even in the dim light of the hall, followed her closely. Kieran gave her a grunt of acknowledgement as he moved on.

Nora took a deep breath, letting it out slowly through pursed lips to calm her thundering heart. Her insides were twisting and writhing, demanding that she recognize both Kieran's true identity as well as her own. For some reason, it was much easier to think about him being a dragon than it was for her to acknowledge the same fact about herself.

Chiding herself for being so immature, Nora made it to the lab and shut the door behind her before she even flicked on the lights. When she did, the fluorescent bulbs cast a cold illumination over the black-topped tables. It was a comforting and familiar setting; a place where she'd spent a lot of time both learning and teaching. She'd carefully tended to the rack of plants over near the window and curated the shelf of books on the opposite end of the room. Along with her cozy apartment, it was one of her safe havens.

But as she set her bag down and went about watering the plants, she didn't exactly feel pleasant and restful. She'd avoided Kieran as much as possible since he'd gotten a job at the university, but the fact that he patrolled the building she worked in made that difficult. Every time she saw him, especially if she was anywhere near him, her inner dragon went crazy. The watering can shook in her hands as she fought the urge to shift; to let her wings freely emerge from her back as her teeth sharpened into glistening points.

Finished with the plants, Nora wiped down the lab tables and did her best to focus on her life here on Earth. She might've been born on a distant planet named Charok, where dragons had once thrived, but she'd been carried away to Earth while she was still technically an egg. She had no connection to her reptilian ancestry besides the family she knew and loved, and they were all living as humans here on Earth as well. She'd done her best to focus on the life she had and not the life her father dreamed of, and most of the time, it wasn't difficult.

But the new clan of dragons who'd recently come through a portal created by her cousin, Kaylee, her uncle and a kindly wizard named Varhan, had changed everything. These dragons had been living their life *as dragons* on Charok, and they were still trying to adjust to life on Earth. This included Kieran, his aunt, and two of his cousins. Nora felt they were kind people, but their presence had dug up old dirt that she didn't want to deal with.

She pulled in another deep breath, dropped the paper towels in the trash can, and stepped over to look out the window. The university grounds were well-lit at night; old buildings surrounded a beautiful quad with a bell tower. It was the kind of college they'd portray on TV; the kind that'd made her want to continue her education when she was younger. She had gotten her love of plants from her mother, and that hadn't hurt, either.

She focused on the few figures still moving along on the sidewalks below. They were likely concerned about their own worries, like if they were going to have a date for the weekend or what their parents would say when they found out they'd dropped out of one of their classes. They didn't need to fret over what would happen if they *shifted into a freaking dragon* in front of someone. They didn't need to keep the beast inside them at bay, suppressing it as much as possible, hoping that someday, it would quit trying to rear its ugly head altogether.

Why did Kieran have to do this to her? They'd barely even talked. If Ted had any idea—not only of who she was but of what the security guard's presence did to her—he'd be furious for sure. Nora speculated her reaction had something to do with his more recent connection to their mutual home world. She wondered how much time he spent in dragon form and how tenuously he was hanging on to his human form. It wasn't fair that simply being near him made her own instincts take the reins.

Nora felt a shiver of energy go down her spine as she forced herself to ignore Kieran. It was late and she needed to get home, knowing she had an early morning planned.

# 2

Kieran forced his legs to keep moving, increasing the distance between himself and Nora. They'd run into each other numerous times since he'd started working at the university a couple of months ago, and he felt he should've been used to it by now. After all, he spent plenty of time with his fellow dragons, and none of them incited this riot inside him. He curled his toes inside his boots until it was painful and concentrated on the itchy fabric of his uniform, anything to distract his body from the desire to change shape. He was a dragon, but right now, he had to be a man. Just a man, and nothing else.

When Kieran had come to Earth, it'd been a complete accident. He'd never meant to get drawn through that portal, and at first, he hadn't even intended to stay. But Aunt Lucia had reminded them all that they had a chance to start over in a place where they didn't need to fear being hunted. Sure, they had to keep their true identities a secret, but there were other dragons there. They had a chance to be whomever they wanted.

Kieran paused to check if a door was locked before continuing on. The first few weeks on Earth had been interesting, but he'd quickly gotten bored after that. Nora's family had encouraged the newcomers to get jobs and do their best to fit in, and Kieran had found his position made him feel as though he were fulfilling his ancestral duties as a border guard. The university was quiet and austere at night, and some of the buildings reminded him of the refined caves the dragons had lived in many years ago back on Charok.

Heading down the stairs and wondering if he would see Nora again before he left, Kieran did his best to keep himself focused on his job. He ran a few students out of the break room, ensured the side doors were locked, and did a quick check on the surveillance cameras. He patrolled the small parking lot closest to the building, checking for up-to-date permit stickers on the few cars that remained and made sure they were faculty, not students. The fall air was crisp and clear, and he sucked it in as though he needed it to live. He tipped his head up to study the emerging stars, still in unfamiliar patterns he hadn't yet gotten used to.

Kieran turned to look up at the window where Nora's lab looked over the parking lot and out to the quad and noticed the lights were off. She'd gone home. He hated the way she was constantly on his mind; it made him feel like a stalker, even though he knew he would never do anything to hurt her. What was it about this woman that drove him so crazy? Did she have any idea what was happening to him every time she so much as walked by?

He stomped back inside and down to the basement to while away the next couple hours of his shift in the security room, watching over the security footage and checking the log books. He turned to a clip-board near the door that held the schedule for the next few days and saw that he'd been switched to a different building for the next night to help cover someone on vacation. Good. Then he'd have all the excuses in the world to avoid Nora.

When it was time to leave, he called Archard as he clocked out. "Hey. I didn't wake you, did I?"

"Not at all," his cousin replied. "I was doing some work, and I didn't even realize what time it was." Back when they'd lived on Charok together, Archard had constantly visited the abandoned royal caves and studied the ancient narratives and prophecies written on the walls. Now that he'd married Kaylee, a literary archeologist, he had even more fuel for the fire that'd already been burning inside him. He was composing an anthology of various myths, and from what Kieran had heard, he was becoming quite the writer. "What's up?"

"I just got off work, and I thought I'd see if you wanted to hang out. There's a good special running at The Cellar." It'd been strange living in this new world where he wasn't constantly surrounded by family.

On his home planet, they were practically unavoidable. It'd been a nice consolation, considering so many of their numbers had been slashed by the Great Curse, and for Kieran, it'd just always been a way of life. Things were different now, with everyone living on their own and only seeing each other when they had free time.

"Sure. I could use a break anyway."

The two men met up twenty minutes later. The bar wasn't far from the university, but it wasn't one that was usually frequented by students. The high price of drinks combined with the muted atmosphere meant that professionals and faculty were there more often. It was a basement place, with a bright neon arrow that pointed down a set of concrete stairs just off the sidewalk. The exposed brick walls, antique oak bar, and wooden floors made it feel almost homey. Kieran ordered a round of beer for both of them as they settled at a beaten table in the back corner. He'd come to like the drink, even though it was far less potent than the home brew they used to make. The carbonation was a pleasant texture on his tongue. "How are things coming on the book?"

Archard's deep blue eyes sparkled in the dim light, and Kieran knew he was in for a long lecture now. "It's amazing. You should see all the different scrolls Kaylee has translated, and she's only been doing this for a few years. There's so much information, and the different myths and stories she's collected from around the world aren't all that much different from the ones that used to be told back home."

"And she's not interested in putting these stories together herself?" Kieran took a sip of his beer and looked around the room. It was relatively busy for a weeknight, but he could tell they were the only two dragons in there. No one could quite explain it, but there was something about that inner beast that always let him know when another was around. It was like that for all of them. It just happened to react a little more strongly when he was around Nora.

"The literal translations are all she's truly interested in. For her, it's more of an academic thing. She found me writing up my own version of one of the stories and told me I should keep going. She thinks it'll help bring new light and interest to these tales. Personally, I want to use this as a jumping-off point for some of our own histories. I'll have to market it as fiction, but I'm all right with that."

"Have you told Lucia that?" Having lost their own parents to the curse, both Kieran and Archard thought of their aunt as a mother figure. She was always graceful, dignified, and understanding.

Archard gave a short laugh. "She thinks it's a great idea! It's a good way of blending life on Charok with life on Earth, and no one will be the wiser. Here, I brought you the first few stories to read." He reached into his pocket and presented a small plastic object on a keychain.

Kieran held it up and frowned. "What am I supposed to do with this trinket?" he asked impatiently.

"It's a flash drive. You just plug it into your computer and you can read the file. It's really easy."

"Easy for you to say. You've had a lot more experience with this stuff than I have." Kieran accepted the flash drive and tucked it in the pocket of his jacket, but he wasn't sure he would ever actually get around to reading the stories. It sounded like a lot more work than just opening a book.

"No, I haven't," Archard argued. "You're just stubborn, and you don't like electronics because you don't take the time to understand them."

"That's not—"

"Don't get offended," Archard interrupted, stopping him from jumping to his own defense. "It's not like we grew up with these things the way the Earth dragons did. And they didn't grow up having to harvest their own food and build their own shelters. We each have our own advantages."

"If you say so," Kieran grumbled. It was true that he wasn't crazy about all the screens that humans seemed so fascinated with. He'd learned to use the equipment for work, but it was simple and he had practice from using it every day. In his off time, it seemed like he was getting introduced to a new device every day. "Have you talked to Callan lately?"

Archard grinned. "If you were on social media, you'd know that he's working at a cell phone repair shop downtown. Unlike you, he's taken quite the liking to all these gadgets."

"And he can have them," Kieran grumbled. "I'm glad he's found something he likes so much."

"What about you? Is your job going well?"

Kieran bobbed his head. "Better than I could've expected, actually. I took it because it was open and they wanted to hire me. Whoever it is that Julian hires to forge paperwork is damn good, because there wasn't a single question as to my identity. I thought it would just be something to do and get a little money. But I really like it, there's not any stress at all, and from what I understand, it pays well compared to other positions I'd be qualified for."

"Then why do you look so disturbed?" Archard leaned across the table, squinting his eyes and looking solemnly at his cousin. "Don't get me wrong; I don't mind stepping out for a drink every now and then just because. But I can tell you've got a lot more on your mind than small talk about my work and your lack of interest in modern conveniences."

Kieran sighed. He and Archard had known each other their entire lives. They were cousins and best friends, and while they lived on Charok, they had relied on each other for survival. If there was anyone he could say this to, it was Archard. Yet Kieran still felt a deep sense of dread over broaching the subject. He'd never encountered anything like this before.

"Come on. Out with it." Archard flashed him a brilliant white smile. "I can tell you're in your own head about this, just like you always are. It'll be a lot easier for me to help if you just tell me."

Another sigh from Kieran. "I wanted to ask you about Nora."

"Nora? What about her?"

"Well, I see her all the time at the university. She and I work in the same building." He paused, the words sticking in his throat.

"Isn't that a good thing?" Archard pressed. "You have someone there that you know."

"Yes, but I get this horrible feeling inside whenever we're near each other. Like there's this writhing, angry snake living in my soul. It's not just nerves, either, so don't smile at me like that. This is something else; something closer to wanting to shift. But it's not quite that, either. I'm sorry; I don't really know how to explain."

Archard put his elbows on the table and laced his fingers, tapping his thumbs against his chin. "What do you think it is?"

Kieran was at a loss, but he was saved by the waitress coming around and bringing them each another beer. She made some sort of small talk, but he didn't pay much attention.

Archard raised a dark eyebrow. "You must be more distracted by this than I thought."

"Why do you say that?"

"That waitress was flirting with you. I'm no expert in human behavior, but I can tell when a girl smiles and bats her eyelashes at you like that, it means she's interested." He gestured with his head toward the waitress, who had moved back off behind the bar.

"I don't care. It's nice, I guess, but I don't have any time for that."

"Right. Back to your problem. What do you think it means?"

Kieran sipped the foam from the top of his mug. "I'm worried it's some sort of omen, and something bad will happen to her. I get such a strange feeling when she's around, and it can't be good."

"It's possible," Archard agreed, fiddling with a napkin on the table. He folded it a few times before he looked up and grinned. "Or maybe she's your fated."

"C'mon, man. I'm serious." Kieran wanted a definitive answer, but he should've known better than to think Archard could give him one. He wasn't there when Kieran passed Nora in the hall, and he couldn't feel that squirmy, sick feeling that took over his body.

Archard shrugged. "I am serious, in a way. You know what Lucia told us about finding our fated mates. It's a little different for everyone, and there's no guidebook for it. But it certainly seems like a possibility. Something to think about, anyway." He took a long pull of his drink. "You could just talk to her, you know."

"And say what? That either she's in danger or I'm allergic to her?" Kieran couldn't imagine how that conversation would go. Nora seemed nice enough when he saw her chatting with one of her colleagues in the hallway. She appeared to have a kind, bubbly personality that people found infectious, since they were always smiling at her. But she definitely wasn't like that when she was near him.

"She's not really that hard to talk to," Archard advised. "It took me a minute to get used to the dragons who were already here. Even the older ones who'd lived on Charok, like Julian and Holden, didn't seem to really be the same as us. But really, we're all dragons. It's something we've got in common that no one else on this planet can say for themselves. It's a starting point. And you don't have to actually say anything about what's going on, not right at first."

"You make it sound really easy, but I can tell she doesn't want to have anything to do with me." Kieran shook his head and sighed once again. "That shouldn't bother me. There are plenty of people on campus who don't know who I am and don't even look my way when I walk by. I'm just part of the furniture to them, and I'm fine with that.

Most days, I even kind of like it. But she clamps up and skitters by like a fraxen trying not to be eaten."

Archard laughed at the comparison. "You're a big guy, but I'm sure she could handle herself."

"Yeah." Kieran frowned at the bottom of his mug, surprised to find it empty once again. This stuff went down too easily.

"You could do a lot worse, you know."

Kieran looked up. "What?"

"You could do a lot worse than Nora. I don't know her all that well, but she seems nice. And she's pretty. Maybe you should just go for it."

"You're not much help, you know that?"

A different waitress brought their drinks this time, one who simply plunked them down on the table and swept away the empties without a word. It was a bit rude, but it was easier to deal with when nothing was expected of him. Kieran watched her march back to the bar to continue her job and wondered if he'd ever really get used to life on Earth.

"Have you dated at all since we've been here?" Archard asked, interrupting his thoughts.

Kieran let out a grunt of a laugh. "No way. I haven't had the time or the desire to. A year ago, if you would have asked me if I'd like to be on a different world where there are women everywhere, I would've been dying to go. But it's different when it actually happens, and people live in a way so unlike what you're used to. I've gotten used to things like the fact that the plants outside my window are for decoration and not a source of food, but I would much rather spread my wings and fly to work than get behind the wheel of a car."

On this, at least, it was easier for Archard to sympathize. He swiped a hand through his dark hair and then let it fall to the table with a thump. "I know. There was plenty of room at Julian's house, but Kaylee and I rented that little place on Madison Street when we got married because we thought we wanted our privacy. It's not really all that private when you live right in the middle of town and your neighbor's house is only a couple yards away. I don't know what I was thinking."

"I do," Kieran said with a grin. "You'd have done anything Kaylee asked just as long as you knew she was yours. I don't think I've ever seen someone so smitten."

"You could be the same way if you just let it happen."

"Shut up."

"At any rate, I've told Kaylee I'd like to move out to the country when our lease is up. It doesn't have to be a huge place, but I don't want to feel like I have to go out to Julian's house every time I want to stretch my wings. I know we're all more than welcome, and Julian and Naomi always seem happy to have the company, but still."

They finished their beers and each headed home, Archard back to Kaylee and their ancient texts and Kieran back to his own place. It wasn't far from campus, but just far enough that college kids weren't having wild parties at all hours of the night. That was one aspect of human life that he'd learned well: the offspring didn't bother growing up until they were well into their adult years. Kieran suspected this had something to do with the fact their lives weren't threatened on a weekly basis by ogres and wizards and they could find all the food they needed in grocery stores. His own childhood hadn't been that easy.

He headed up the stairs to his apartment. Normally, he was pretty happy there. The building was a quiet one and the rooms were spacious. The tall ceilings had exposed beams that made it seem a little less modern, despite the stark white drywall and the beige carpeting. It couldn't compare to sleeping out under the stars or in a cave, but it kept the rain off his back.

Taking off his uniform shirt and making sure the blinds were drawn, Kieran took a deep breath. As he let it go, he also let his wings free. They unfurled slowly from his back, stretching their leathery expanse from his shoulder blades until the tips nearly touched the ceiling. He moved them gently, knowing from experience that these massive appendages didn't fit so well in this apartment. He'd already broken a lamp or two the first few times he attempted this. It was at least a little bit of release, but it was nothing compared to soaring through the sky without any worry about who saw him.

Tucking his wings away, he headed to bed with thoughts of Nora still echoing in his mind. He played out scenes that he knew would never happen, ones where he actually stopped her in the hall and had a conversation with her, and even one where he asked her out to dinner. This last one, as he envisioned her smiling up at him, made his inner dragon start going crazy again. He cursed at himself as he rolled over and tried to go to sleep.

# 3

"YOU'RE HERE LATE, MISS MITCHELL."

"Hmm?" Nora looked up from her desk to find Dr. Ward standing in the doorway of the lab. She glanced at the clock and saw it was well past dinner time. "Oh, wow; I didn't even realize. I got so caught up in getting things ready for tomorrow."

Dr. Ward smiled as he came to look over her shoulder at what she was doing. A kindly professor with a true passion for botany, he nodded approvingly as he adjusted his thick glasses on his nose. "What have you got planned?"

Nora beamed as she spread out the worksheets she'd just printed off. "First, I thought we'd start with some identification. I've got a great handout that'll help them recognize at least most of the local plants. We can get them outside and walk over to Thompson Woods, so they can see what it's like to work in the field. For actual lab time, I found a great observation experiment where we freeze plants with liquid nitrogen, examining the cells under a microscope before and after so they understand why some plants get all slimy and gross when they've been frozen. If we have time, I'd like to do something with gravitropism, as well." It was only supposed to be an afternoon, but Nora wanted to make sure these kids didn't have a bunch of extra time to sit around and get bored or cause trouble. If she could, she'd have planned an entire day for them.

Dr. Ward looked through the sheets. "It all sounds wonderful. I know it's the kind of field trip I'd have enjoyed at that age. Most junior high students don't get a chance to come out to a university lab. They might not think much of it on its own merit, but I think they'll have a great time with you."

"With me?" She scooted her chair back a little to see him better. "I thought this was something you wanted to do."

He smiled. "I want to be around and maybe talk to them a little. I definitely want to see them in action here. But there's no doubt in my mind that these kids are going to connect much more with you than with some old codger like myself. They want someone young, dynamic, and passionate, and I'm just an old fuddy-duddy."

"Don't say that." He was certainly much older than her, with silver hair that he wore just a bit too long, but he was nowhere near being put out to pasture.

"Hey, it's not like I'm upset about it. I'm just happy to know we're giving these kids a head start and maybe igniting something in them they wouldn't know about if they didn't get the chance to come here. Besides, it's clear you've done all the work on getting things set up. You should get to be a big part of it. And if any of them have seen your videos, they won't be paying attention to anything else anyway."

Her face flushed. "You've seen those?" She'd never really talked about them much while she was at work unless Holly happened to come by the lab to show her the latest edit. Nora was proud of them on a personal level, but video on the internet just wasn't the kind of thing to brag about to university professors.

"I have, and I'm impressed. You shouldn't be locked up in a lab all day. You should be out there talking to people, teaching them. If a position comes open in this department, then I hope you go for it. I'll be ready to write you a letter of recommendation anytime you need it."

Nora was flattered; honored, even. She'd come to respect Dr. Ward in the years that she'd been a student, and now he was practically inviting her up to his level. "Thank you. I really appreciate it."

"Good. Now you'd better finish up and get out of here. I'm sure everything will run smoothly tomorrow, and you won't change that by staring at your experiment sheets any longer. It's dark out. I can walk you to your car." There weren't many people like Dr. Ward left in the world. He genuinely cared about her, and he came from a generation when men watched out for women.

She gathered up her papers and stacked them neatly on the end of a lab table, ready to go when the students would arrive the following day. "That's okay; I'll be fine. I have a few stops I need to make, anyway. Have a good night!"

"Oh, before I forget..."

Nora turned around expectantly.

"There's a new lab assistant starting in a couple of days. She's going to be working downstairs, but I think it would be good if you could spend a week or two with her showing her the ropes. She's transferring from Michigan."

"I can do that," she replied with a smile. It was just another chance to network with someone with a mind for science. Since lab life could be lonely, it would be fun to have a buddy around for a while. "Sounds like fun."

"Great. I always know I can count on you, Nora."

Nora left the lab feeling happy. She was truly looking forward to spending time with a younger crowd the next day. Dr. Ward was right; some of them might've already seen her videos and would be eager to talk to her. It wasn't fame or popularity that she cared about, but the idea that she was actually making an impact with her work. Her original plans hadn't included teaching, since she was more interested in learning and experimenting than anything else, but the professor's words gave her something else to think about.

She trotted down the stairs and left a note for Dr. Burke to remind her of the session with the junior high students. The professor had said she wanted to help, but she was notoriously forgetful. Then she slipped out through the front doors of McKnelly Hall and out into the parking lot. The sun was just sinking, casting an orange glow over the campus. The warmth of the day radiated from the brick buildings and the sidewalks, but the cold of autumn was creeping in on a night breeze. Goosebumps stood at attention on her arms as she walked quickly to her car, thinking it was probably a good night for a bowl of soup.

Nora glanced over at Neilson, the building that housed most of the English department. That included Ted's office, and ever since they'd started dating, it'd become a habit for her to admire the massive brick structure whenever she happened to be nearby. It wasn't that she stood there and waited to see if he'd be coming out anytime soon, and she wasn't even completely sure she could see his office window from where she stood in the parking lot near McKnelly, but it was simply the fact she knew he was in there. It made her happy to know she was dating someone who was also eager to pass his knowledge on to future generations, and Ted was genuinely good at what he did. He hadn't been teaching for long, but his lectures were already known on campus for being lively and entertaining as well as educational.

Her feet started carrying her in that direction before she'd consciously decided what to do. But she needed to see Ted, and his car was in the lot near the hall, so she knew he was still around. She could just check in with him for a minute and maybe make herself feel a little better.

Holly's words had been rattling around in her brain and mixing with her own, making her wonder what kind of future their relationship had. On the surface, at least, they seemed like a compatible pair. While Nora didn't necessarily want to spend an entire weekend reading Shakespeare and Ted wasn't all that interested in cross-pollination or plant genetics, they were both smart, independent people. They worked on the same campus and both loved coffee.

How far did that sort of thing go, when it came to being with someone? Nora wasn't sure. She'd dated plenty, but nothing had really ever been long term. She knew other women her age who'd already been engaged a time or two. Her cousin Kaylee was already married, a thought that was still hard for Nora to wrap her head around. She liked Ted a lot, but they definitely weren't ready to walk down the aisle together.

She stepped into Neilson Hall, noting that it was even quieter than McKnelly. Whatever professors still remained for the day were probably quietly reading over their students' papers and heavily marking them in red pen or pondering the symbolism in the poetry they'd just read. She missed the hum of a centrifuge or the quiet clinking of beakers.

Nora smiled to herself as she imagined the surprised look on Ted's face when he saw her. They didn't have any plans for that evening. They were both always so busy, and they'd learned early on to respect each other's schedules. It was too stressful when they tried to cram in dates they didn't have time for. But just a quick hello couldn't hurt either of them.

She paused outside his door. Ted was reciting poetry, something by Burns maybe, and it made her smile all over again. He was a romantic at heart, and it was nice to think that even sitting alone in his office, he enjoyed the sound of the words. But when she heard a giggle in response, her heart froze in her chest. Nora pressed her ear closer to the door.

"Oh, Teddy, you're such a sweetheart. Tell me more."

It was impossible to mistake the exchange for anything other than it was. Nora's hearing was excellent, something she could attribute to her heritage, but at that moment, she wished she was deaf. Her hand hovered near the doorknob as she debated what to do.

Ted was spouting more verse, his voice muffled. The giggles came again. Those weren't the laughs of a student who suddenly found inspiration or magically understood centuries-old poetry that hadn't made sense to her before. This was something else; something unbelievable.

Feeling numb and cold, Nora started to turn away. She didn't want to see this. She didn't want to think this could possibly be happening. She and Ted were happy together. Holly wasn't sure they were meant to be, but there would always be someone around to doubt a relationship, no matter who she was with. If he hadn't been happy with her, he hadn't given her any indication. Her doubts and fears were a writhing ball of energy in her stomach that she didn't know what to do with.

She took another step away. Nora could run down the hall and out the door, and Ted would never have known she was there. But then what? She'd have to wait around for him to finally say something? For him to admit that he'd had someone else in his office? Or confront him the next day, scream and rage at him about how she'd heard everything? Would Ted even admit to it, or would he spout some lie and try to convince her she'd been mistaken? A few weeks earlier, she wouldn't have had any doubt in her mind as to his loyalty. Things were different now.

Nora turned back to the door. If she went home, she'd spend the rest of the night wondering exactly what was going on in that office. It would only take a quick second, and then it would all be over with. Like ripping off a Band-Aid.

She laid her hand on the knob once again, cold and hard beneath her hand. With one quick movement, she turned it and flicked the door open, not giving the occupants any time to react. Ted was in his chair behind his desk. That was normal enough, but the TA sitting on his lap wasn't. Her legs were straddled across his hips, her arms around his neck. Ted's hands gripped her backside, and he lifted his head from where he'd been nuzzling her neck to give a dirty look to whomever had interrupted. But his face changed from one of anger to horror as he realized just who had opened the office door. "Nora!"

The TA, a girl with bouncy blonde hair and a very tight sweater, turned around. She waggled her fingers in the air as she got off Ted's lap and straightened her clothing. "Hi! I'm Jessica."

"I know who you are," Nora growled, her right hand gripping the doorway as though she were holding onto it for dear life. It was one thing to believe you knew what was happening, but it was an entirely different matter to see it for yourself. "We've met before. Several times."

Ted's cheeks colored as he ground his teeth together. "Jessica, this is Nora. My girlfriend."

"Your girlfriend? Oh, shit." She pressed her fingers to her mouth, where her bright red lipstick had become slightly smudged. "I'm so sorry. I—I had no idea." She gathered up her things in rush, trotted out of the office and disappeared down the hallway.

Ted ran a hand through his already messy hair as he looked up at Nora. "What are you doing here?"

"Really? Don't you think I should be asking you that?"

He stood up and came around the desk, putting his hand on the door to close it behind her. "It's not what it looks like. We can talk about this."

Nora put her hand out to stop the door from swinging shut. "I have a feeling it's exactly what it looks like, and I don't think we have a whole lot to talk about. We're *done*, Ted."

His shoulders sagged, and he gave her those puppy dog eyes. "C'mon, Nora. I know you're angry, and you have every right to be. But at least give me a chance to explain myself before you go."

Once again, she was faced with either finding out the truth or letting her imagination come up with it on her own. In a way, it was better to know. He'd been caught, so there was no point in him lying about what happened. "Fine. But make it quick. I have other things to do."

"Right." He shut the door quietly, keeping his hand on the knob as he took a few breaths. "I'm sorry, Nora. I didn't mean for any of this to happen."

"I'm sure she just accidentally fell on top of you, and you mistak-

enly grabbed her ass and kissed her neck, and it was a complete coincidence that you were baiting her with all your stupid poetry. I was
dumb enough to think I was special when you whispered verses in my
ear, but now I know it's nothing more than your usual schtick." Her
chest heaved as tears hovered behind her eyes, a burning threat. Nora
clenched her teeth, determined to stay strong. He couldn't see how
much this was getting to her.

"I just got carried away, is all. We spent a lot of time together, and it
was really nice to have someone else so interested in the same things. I
know she doesn't seem all that bright, but she's really got a head for
literature and stories." He gestured helplessly at the door, as though
Jessica was still standing on the other side of it.

"Yep. We can just blame English. It couldn't possibly be your fault,
especially considering that she didn't even seem to understand that I'm
your *girlfriend*. What kind of lies have you told her? That we broke up?
That you just weren't happy with me and you needed someone who
truly understood you?" She was rambling now, saying anything that
came across her mind, but she realized that she was saying these
things because she could easily see him concocting a lie like that.

"I don't think either one of us have really been happy, Nora."

"Then why wouldn't you just talk to me about it?" Was she in the
wrong for not expressing her doubts to him? She'd barely been able to
admit them to Holly, or even to herself.

"Maybe because I knew you'd fly off the handle." He made a frustrated flap of his hand toward her, demonstrating her anger as his
justification for everything.

"I'm allowed to be mad when I find my boyfriend screwing around
on me," she pointed out.

He shrugged. "Okay, fine. But what about all the other times?
You're not exactly easy to get along with. You get so wrapped up in
your little projects and videos that you don't even keep track of the
time. You get cranky when anyone disturbs you from your work, and
the only things you ever talk about are your stupid fucking plants."

Nora couldn't believe this. He was trying to make this all her fault.
She knew she wasn't a perfect person. She wasn't even human, for
god's sake. "I can't recall a single time when I didn't drop what I was
doing to come hang out with you when your schedule cleared unless I
was in class. And if there's anyone here who refuses to be disturbed, it's
you. You're the one who got all pissed off when I dared to text you

during your time in the library, simply because I forgot that was where you were." She could see all the signs now, all the little indicators that made Holly wonder if he was really the right man for her. Nora kicked herself for not understanding earlier and saving herself the trouble. "If this is how things are, then fine. We'll go our separate ways, and you don't ever have to see me again."

She turned to open the door.

He slammed his hand against the wood. When he turned to her, there was fire in his eyes. "Listen, Nora. You can't tell anyone about this."

"Excuse me?" She'd felt so many emotions in just the last minute, but his words were sparking pure hatred. "I come over here after work just to say hi and see what's going on in your world because I thought we meant something to each other. I find you fucking around with that skank, and you have the nerve to tell me I'm not allowed to say anything about it? You're one hell of a piece of work, Ted."

He was standing between her and the door now, and he put his hand out in an effort to keep her calm. "Would you just settle down? It's really not that big of a deal. I just don't want it to get out and ruin my career. You were all excited for me when I got this job, and I don't want you to ruin it."

"Of course, I was excited!" she spat. "I cared about you. I wanted the best for you. But apparently, the only thing you're concerned with his how many different girls on campus you can screw at the same time!" The beast inside her had awakened once again. It was angry, a whirling mass of flame that wanted to come out and show Ted just what she thought of his antics. For the first time in her life, she found herself with a strong desire to torch someone. "It's not up to me to ruin your job, Ted. You did that yourself."

"What does that mean? You're going to go running to the dean? I never should've dated you, Nora. I knew what a little suck up you were, and now you're proving me right."

"Fuck you. I'll go sing it from the mountaintops if I want to. Not being able to keep your dick in your pants is just as much my business as it is yours." Now that he was trying so hard to stop her, Nora wanted to make up flyers and post them all over campus just so every single person would know what a piece of shit he was.

"No, you're not. And I'm not letting you leave until you promise you're going to keep your mouth shut." There was a darkness in his eyes she'd never seen before, one that disturbed her on an instinctive level.

She backed away from him, but that meant she was getting further away from the door. "You can't threaten me, Ted."

"I'll do whatever I have to."

Nora didn't like this. Ted had always seemed like a great guy, the kind who wouldn't lift a finger to harm someone. He'd never even gotten into bar fights. But there he was, essentially keeping her prisoner in his office until she agreed to do what he said. "I'm leaving now." She headed straight for him and reached for the doorknob.

He grabbed her wrist and shoved her backwards. Nora cried out, shocked at the pain he'd caused by wrenching her arm backwards. He pushed harder, and she lost her balance. Nora crashed into the desk, sending several books falling to the floor. A ceramic pencil cup smashed on the linoleum.

Ted was standing over her now, still holding onto her wrist and snarled at her as he tried to grab her other hand.

The door opened just then, slamming backwards against the wall. Nora couldn't tell what was happening, but Ted was suddenly jerked to his feet. Kieran, massive and angry, held him by the throat against the wall. "Give me one good reason not to snap your neck right now."

Ted squeaked in fear, his airway cut off by Kieran's hand. He grabbed desperately at the security guard's fingers, but his efforts were futile. He might have been stronger than Nora in her human form, but he didn't compare to Kieran.

"What the hell do you think you're doing to her?"

Nora struggled to absorb what was happening as she staggered to her feet. She shoved her confusion aside when she noticed a line of silver scales erupting on Kieran's arm. As horrible as this business with Ted was, the very last thing she wanted was for someone to realize there were dragons on Earth. It would mean the exposure of her entire family; of everyone she loved. Though she didn't know Kieran and his cousins all that well, it would mean horrible things for all of them. She couldn't let that happen, no matter what kind of terrible things Ted wanted to do to her.

She laid her hand on Kieran's arm, surprised at the hardness of the muscle underneath. A bolt of electricity shot through her system. "Just let him go. He's not worth it."

Kieran didn't move for a long moment, keeping his fingers

wrapped around the man's throat. She could see the dragon inside him, barely controlled, and it called out to her own. Their instinctive urges blended with only the barest touch. She quickly pulled her hand back and Kieran let go.

Ted slid to the floor, collapsing in a pathetic heap. He gasped for air as he put his own hands protectively around his neck. "You're a crazy bastard," he gulped. "And you're a fucking bitch."

Kieran started to reach for him once again, but Ted scrambled backwards. "Are you going to leave her alone? Because if I hear of you laying a hand on her again, next time, I won't stop."

"I'm done. I'm done." He glared at Nora but said nothing else as they turned for the door.

Nora walked just behind Kieran as they left, unable to tear her eyes away from him. She didn't understand. How had he known what was going on? What was he even doing in the building? It was tempting to turn around and take a last glance at Ted, to see just how miserable he was, but it didn't really matter anymore. That chapter of her life had ended. She followed Kieran out into the hallway and closed the door gently behind her.

**4**

---

KIERAN'S BODY WAS WARRING WITH ITSELF. IT WOULD'VE BEEN SO EASY to crush that little pissant's skull and show him what he could've really done. Since he'd come to Earth, there hadn't been any situations when he needed to defend himself or anyone else like that, but seeing that man standing over Nora had been the closest he'd ever come to revealing himself.

They were gaining their distance from the incident as they slowly walked down the hallway toward the front doors, but his inner dragon showed no sign of calming. It'd be much easier if he wasn't near Nora, but that wasn't going to happen. He couldn't leave her now.

"You want to file a report on him?" Kieran finally asked, keeping his voice low. It was too quiet in the building, and even a whisper felt like a scream.

His words seemed to startle her slightly, and she gave a minuscule jump before glancing up at him and then away again. "No," she finally answered. "I think it's probably best if we don't. I'll have other issues to report on him, but he didn't actually hurt me."

"You're sure? I can take you over to the infirmary and have them check you out. They'll be able to tell if you should go to the hospital or anything. That might make a difference on whether or not we document this." Kieran's mind was spinning through all the red tape that revolved around a disturbance like this, or at least what would be involved if it was anyone other than Nora. This wasn't the same as just breaking up a couple of kids fighting out behind a building. Technically, there was a ton of paperwork he'd need to fill out, but he was willing to let it go if she didn't want to make a big deal out of it.

"No, I'm sure." She looked at her wrist and then let it fall again. "He surprised me more than anything. I've never seen him act like that."

Kieran swallowed. Archard hadn't been wrong when he'd said that Kieran could do worse than Nora. Her thick, curly hair flowed in dark waves down her back. He'd seen it tied up in a bun or a ponytail, and sometimes she wore it in a long braid when she was leaving the lab. She wore it down that night, and it was difficult to resist putting his hands through it. He knew she had big brown eyes and a wide smile, but she kept her face turned away.

"Do you want to talk about what happened back there?" He felt the ripple of scales on the back of his neck as he once again envisioned his hand around that man's throat. Damn, this was going to be hard.

She sighed. "Probably not right now. I think I'm just ready to go home."

"I'll walk you to your car." He didn't really want to let her out of his sight. If one person had already attacked her, then there was no telling what else might happen. But he couldn't exactly make her stay there on campus with him.

"You don't have to do that."

"It's my job, isn't it?"

Nora nodded. "I guess that's true. Do you like it? I know it must be very different than...where you're from."

He allowed himself a small smile. He'd gotten used to talking about himself like a man from another planet, and he didn't worry a whole lot about who overheard him. It seemed to Kieran that most humans were so wrapped in either themselves or their cell phones, they weren't paying any attention to what went on around them. They'd talked about Charok and their true identities out in public plenty of times. As long as they didn't stand up and announce it, no one cared.

"It is different," he acknowledged. "But in many ways, it's much better. I still have my family here, but I actually feel like I'm doing something. All of our ways and traditions on Charok had pretty much been eliminated after the Great Curse. My parents and grandparents had all been border guards, and I still felt that same pull to fulfill my duty. This isn't exactly the same, but it's close enough."

"I'm glad." They'd come out the front doors now, and Kaylee tipped her head up slightly to look at the stars. Kieran got a glimpse of her face. Even in the dim light, he could see the tension around her eyes and the start of a frown that threatened to tug at the corners of her mouth. Her hair had turned a deep coal black in the night. "I think about you guys a lot and how hard it must be for you. I was lucky enough to come here before I was technically even born, so in a lot of ways, I'm just like anyone else walking around on this planet."

"Well, except for that one thing," he said with a smile.

She rewarded him with a smile in return and a look that lasted longer than a microsecond. "Yes, there's that."

"You know, you could've used that tonight." He hadn't thought about it at first; he was simply acting on his instincts to help her. But once it was all over with and they'd left the office, he'd realized Nora could've shifted and taken care of him quite easily.

"Maybe, but it's been a really long time since I've, um, changed. And then Ted would've told everyone he knew. It would've been a mess."

"Either that, or everyone would just think he was crazy for talking about the angry dragon lady who beat him up in his own office."

Her laugh sent a shiver of pleasure down his spine, and he knew there were a few more small scales running down his back now. He didn't bother trying to hide them; no one could see them under his uniform anyway.

"I can just see the headlines now. 'College Teacher Confined to Mental Hospital.' I guess it's the least of what he deserves." They'd reached her car, and she fished around in her bag for a minute. "Shit. I must've left my keys in the lab. I'm sorry."

"Don't be sorry. We'll go get them, and then we'll come back." Kieran turned toward McKnelly, grateful for the few extra minutes with her. This was the most conversation they'd ever had, and his body was finally starting to quiet down a bit. He knew it wouldn't cooperate fully, and he'd have a hard time getting himself to settle down in human form when he got back to his apartment later that night, but he was willing to accept that.

"How did you find us, anyway?" There was just enough room for the two of them on the sidewalk that led to the science building, and her arm brushed his slightly. "I thought you only worked in my building."

*So much for getting myself together.* "Normally, yes. But Carl's on vacation tonight, and they sent me to Neilson to cover for him. Beyond that, I could hear the two of you arguing from quite a ways away." His naturally excellent hearing, thanks to his dragon genetics, was part of what made him a good security guard.

"Of course. I should've thought of that. I guess that means you heard what it was all about." As they approached the building, the glow from the yellow lampposts illuminated the flush of her cheeks. "That's so humiliating."

"I don't think I heard all of it," he quickly amended. "And it's none of my business." Truthfully, he wanted to know everything. He wanted to know exactly why that asshole would cheat on someone like her, and why he thought he should be able to get away with it. Even more, he wanted to know what made him think it was all right to attack her like that.

She fell into silence as they walked into McKnelly. She put her hand behind her to stop the door from slamming, something Kieran always did but rarely saw anyone else do. He wondered if it was a dragon thing, left over from centuries of living in cave life where a noise like that could echo on forever.

"So, how long have you been working here?" Kieran hadn't meant to embarrass her, and it seemed easier to talk about anything other than the reason they were walking together that night.

"About a year. I started while I was still a student, and I just couldn't leave. I love it." A different flush colored her cheeks now, one of pride. "I know plants are pretty boring to most people, but they've always fascinated me. My mom has always been really into nature, and from the time I was little, she taught me to love and appreciate it. I don't think there was ever a single room in our house that didn't have a live plant in it. In fact, I know there wasn't, because it was often my job to water them. I never really looked at it like a chore, though. I was just excited to see how they would change from day to day."

"It sounds like you found your calling very early in life." He wondered if it had anything to do with her biological parents and what their roles had been back on Charok. But Kieran had been told all about how Nora and her cousins had been smuggled off of their home world just before the Great Curse was cast. Their parents had perished, and this didn't seem like a good time to bring that up.

"I really did. I remember being in high school, and even once I'd started college, there were so many other kids who just had no idea what they wanted to do with the rest of their lives. I know I've got a place here, and I feel like I can make a difference in the plant world. Dr. Ward has some fascinating experiments he's working on, and he's always keeping me involved. I just love it." She opened the door to the lab, turned on the lights, and quickly found her keys on the desk. "Sorry about that."

"You really don't have to be."

They fell into silence as they headed back out to the parking lot. Kieran tried to think of something to say, just to keep their conversation going. Archard had advised him to just talk to her, and for the most part, it was proving to be much easier than he'd imagined. He didn't have to tell her about what happened to him when he was anywhere near her; they could just talk. It was too bad it had all gotten started from such a terrible event, but it was even more terrible that it was about to end now.

An odd noise from the campus woods distracted him from trying to come up with the right words. "Did you hear that?"

"Hmm?"

"Sounded like there was something in the trees." He strode along beside her, his protective instincts kicking in even harder. It definitely wasn't Ted, who was likely still nursing his wounds on the other side of the quad.

"You know how those campus squirrels are. I've heard they'll come right up to students eating outside and take their sandwiches out of their hands."

Kieran grunted his concurrence, but he wasn't convinced it was merely a squirrel. It sounded much bigger than that. As far as he knew, there was nothing in those woods that could hurt them, and he knew he could defend them regardless, but still.

"I should thank you," Nora said, turning around to face him when they reached her little blue Nissan. Her eyes shone in the pale light. "What you did back there, it was…" She trailed off and looked down at her hands.

"I was more than happy to." He forcefully kept his eyes off her lips, even though he desperately wanted to pull her body close and kiss her.

"And I should thank you for stopping me. I was about to lose control back there."

She gave a shy shrug. "I guess we've got to look out for each other. I've gotta get going. I'll talk to you later."

Kieran stepped up onto the sidewalk and watched her back out of the parking space and drive out of the lot. He continued to watch as she pulled out onto the main road on campus, and he tracked her tail-lights until she was out on the highway. He hoped that when she'd said she'd talk to him later, she actually meant it.

## 5

"Nora, this is Allison, the new lab assistant I was telling you about."

"It's great to meet you!" Nora set her pen down and reached out to shake the new girl's hand. "I think you'll love it here."

"I'm sure you're right." Allison was pretty in her own way, even if her jaw was a bit angular. She wore her deep red hair in a wavy ponytail at the nape of her neck, and she looked like she was seeing a lab for the first time as she looked around. "There's so much equipment in here. I don't think we had all this where I was working before." She had a strange accent that Nora couldn't quite place, but the university attracted people from all over the world.

"Oh, don't worry about that," Dr. Ward soothed. "Nora here knows this lab like the back of her hand, and she's the perfect person to show you the ropes. She'll have you up to speed in no time. I understand you'll be working for Dr. Burke?"

Allison nodded and twitched her fingers against her blouse. "I just came up from her office."

"Good, good. Did she send you to the bursar's office to get your paychecks sorted out?"

The new assistant suddenly looked utterly confused. "Um, no?"

"That's all right. Nora will show you around a bit more, and then she can take you down there. It's kind of in an odd place."

Allison looked relieved. "Thank you so much. Everyone is so nice here."

"We do our best," Mr. Ward beamed. "I'll leave you ladies to it."

When the professor had left, Allison turned to Nora. "I'm really sorry you got stuck with me. I'm sure you have more important things to do."

"Oh, no; I don't mind at all. I practically live here anyway, so it's always nice to see a new face."

Truthfully, it couldn't have been better timing. Nora really had been looking forward to meeting Allison, but it was even better now that she was so determined not to focus on her own life. The previous night with Ted—and then Kieran—had been almost too much to handle. She'd gone home, thinking she was so exhausted, she could just drop into bed. But she couldn't sleep, no matter what she tried. When she got up, figuring she might as well get some work done, her brain refused to focus on anything beside the events of the evening. It hadn't been any better that morning, and she felt she was running strictly on caffeine.

The lab tour took much longer than Nora had expected. Allison asked a ton of questions, and for someone who'd supposedly worked in a lab at a different university, she didn't seem to know much about the equipment or procedures. Granted, she'd come from a smaller school that probably didn't have as many instruments as they did there, but it made Nora worry about how well she'd work out. At the very least, Nora would need to give her a lot of training.

"I think that about sums it up," Nora said. "The only thing we haven't really covered are the plants, but I think the ones in Dr. Burke's lab are on a different schedule than ours up here. Oh, and we still need to get you to the bursar's office."

"Dr. Ward made it sound like I should've already done that. I feel so stupid." Allison tucked a stray strand of hair behind her ear and looked at the ground.

Nora closed the door to the lab and led the way toward the stairs. She looked around to make sure no one else was within earshot. "Here's what you need to know about Dr. Burke. She's a great professor, but she has a horrible memory. She might tell you on Tuesday that she's taking Wednesday off work, but then she'll go ahead and show up anyway. It can make things a little difficult sometimes, but the rest of us have just learned to deal with it. She really is a great person, even if she can't remember anyone's name or what day of the week it is."

"That's good to know," Allison said with a shy smile. "This place is just so big, I feel like I won't ever get used to it."

"Sure you will." Nora opened the door and they headed across the quad to the administrative building. The first classes of the day were just beginning, and students headed back and forth at a dizzying pace across the sidewalks to get to their seats on time. Nora spent so much time there in the off hours, she often forgot just how busy it could be during the day. "I completely understand it being a bit intimidating, though. My parents sent me to a really small high school because they thought it would be a good experience for me. In a lot of ways, they were right, but our classrooms were closets compared to what we've got here. I was pretty scared at first, but you'll find that everyone is so nice here, it doesn't matter. You'll get used to where everything is and how it all works, and you'll be an old pro before you know it."

"Thanks. I just need the same kind of confidence you have. I saw some of your videos. It's obvious you really know what you're doing."

Nora turned to her in surprise. "You have?"

"Yeah. You're building quite a name for yourself out there. A quick Google search pulled your channel up right away."

"No way; that's awesome!" Nora had gotten a little behind on her posting. She was supposed to have put up the video about the ginseng the previous night, but obviously, that hadn't gotten done. Feeling a shiver of unease, she pulled her mind away from that whole scene and firmly rooted herself in the present moment. "You know, sometimes I need help with those. My friend Holly does most of the filming, but she's not always available. Maybe you and I could work together sometime."

Her pale brown eyes flickered with delight. "Really? That would be amazing! I've never gotten to do anything like that before."

Now that she'd said it, Nora wasn't quite sure what had made her invite someone she hardly knew into a part of her life that was so important. She hadn't even asked Allison if she had experience with a camera. But there was something about her that Nora just liked instantly, and she knew she was going to enjoy the next couple of weeks getting to know her. The busier she was, the less time she would have to think about how Ted had betrayed her, how Kieran had rushed in to her aid, and how her dragon seemed to be suddenly awake after being content to be asleep for so long.

As she headed into one of the administrative buildings, Nora realized that was a lot of what bothered her so much. She'd learned to shift back and forth easily as a child. She used to go on flights in the woods with her parents, when they knew they were safe from prying eyes. But as she'd gotten older, she hadn't been interested. Nora knew it had disappointed her father, but she'd been more interested in hanging out with her friends and fitting in than focusing on something she could never really be. She would never see Charok, and she was content to remain in human form as much as possible. That hadn't been a problem.

Until Kieran had come to work at McKnelly Hall. It was then that her instincts started taking over, pushing all her logic aside and reminding her of who she really was. It was only with him that she felt any real semblance of being a dragon. The evidence of that was in the fact she hadn't even attempted to shift when Ted had threatened her. Kieran was right; she could've easily shifted, or even partially. It would've only taken a quick swipe of a claw to lacerate his throat. Hell, if he'd seen her wings or what her teeth really looked like, Ted probably would've run for his life and never come back. But she'd remained utterly human until the security guard showed up and reminded her that she was something more.

"Are you all right?"

Nora shook her head, realizing she'd been miles away. "I'm sorry. I've just had a lot on my mind lately." She felt like a fool for diving into her own problems when she was supposed to be making someone else feel comfortable and welcome. "Um, so what made you come to the area? Do you have family here?"

Allison shook her head sadly. "No, not here. Not anywhere, actually. My parents died when I was really young, so I just bounced around in the system for a while until I aged out. I've been on my own ever since."

Nora's heart reached out to her. She'd always known that Xander and Summer weren't her biological parents, but it hadn't bothered her. Xander was a dragon just like her. Summer was a kindly witch who ran a new age shop with her sister, Autumn. The two of them had never treated Nora like she was anything less than their very own little girl, showering her with love and affection constantly.

It was only when Nora's cousin Kaylee had found a way back to Charok several months ago that she'd discovered they were actually the descendants of the last dragon queen. She died in the first wave of the Great Curse, leaving her eggs in the royal caves. Her father and her uncles had each taken one and smuggled it to Earth with the help of Varhan, a wizard who was on their side. They committed themselves to raising the eggs as their own and giving them the best life. It only made Nora feel slightly different now that she knew her real mother had been a queen. After all, she'd never known that mysterious dragon.

Still, she couldn't exactly sympathize with Allison by revealing the truth. "I'm so sorry to hear that. My parents died when I was a baby, but I was fortunate enough to be adopted when I was really young. I don't even remember anyone before them." She turned down the next hall.

"You really are lucky, then. There's a lot I don't remember, but I do know there was a terrible war. A lot of people died, and not just my parents. I have to consider myself fortunate that I got out, even if I didn't have as nice of an upbringing as you did." Allison's eyes were moist, and she ran the tip of her tongue along the edge of her teeth nervously.

Nora felt horrible. She'd just met this poor girl, and now she was digging up a painful past. "Here we are. You just need a few forms and then you should be good to go."

The clerk at the bursar's office checked Allison's identification, handed over the forms, and instructed her to have them back as soon as possible to avoid any delay in the dispersal of her payments. Nora stuck with her, feeling guilty about leaving her alone. Allison was probably perfectly capable of being alone if she'd made it through all of that as a child, but still.

"If there's anything you want to know about the town or the campus, just ask me," Nora offered as they made their way back out of the admin building. "I've lived here my whole life, so it's all old hat to me."

"That's so nice of you, Nora. I've got a decent little apartment, but you know how it is when you change towns and jobs. Everything just happens so fast, and I don't feel like I even have time to sit down and grab a cup of coffee." Allison's eyes danced watching the students walk past them as they emerged back out on the quad.

"There's a great place just down the street. They make an amazing cappuccino, but even their hot chocolate is excellent. We can meet up after work if you'd like. I still have a few things to do in the lab."

Allison's face seemed to completely transform with excitement. "Thank you! I'd love that!"

But just as she was about to finalize their plans and confirm what time Allison would be getting off, Nora remembered what day it was. "Wait. I can't. I've already got plans to go out with my cousins tonight."

"Oh, you do? That's nice." A strange look passed over Allison's face, one Nora took to be jealousy.

She shouldn't have said anything about her big family. Of course, Allison wouldn't have any cause to be jealous if she realized just what a strange family it was. But it was too late now. "Yeah. There are four of us, and we always try to get together about once a week or so. We all have a lot going on, and it's not easy to schedule sometimes, but we make it happen."

Allison laid a hand on her arm, creating a zing of static electricity from the tip of her finger onto Nora's arm. "You're so lucky, Nora. You have no idea."

Feeling guilty, Nora made sure Allison found the way back to her own lab and showed her how to get started sterilizing the test tubes so they'd be ready for the experiment Dr. Burke had planned for her students that afternoon. She then headed back upstairs to her own lab, feeling like she had a reason to feel guilty, no matter what direction she looked.

———

WHEN SHE STEPPED into Tranquility later that evening, Nora felt the familiar ease of being around her closest friends. Kaylee arrived right after her, and the guys were already waiting in the same booth they always reserved for these dinners. The restaurant was a quiet one with a plush atmosphere and snooty waiters. The food cost a lot more than it should have, but there was just something about the place that made them keep coming back. Nora thought it was probably the fact that it was their hangout, not an eatery their parents favored.

"I've been dying for a good meal," Elliot grumbled as he slapped his menu on the table. "I don't even care what they bring me. I'll eat it."

"You've always been so refined," Nora teased him affectionately.

"Seriously. If I had any idea I'd spend so much time locked up in a library reading boring law books, I might've decided to go for a different degree. Or maybe I wouldn't have gone to college at all. I could be traveling or something."

"Because your parents would approve of that," Kaylee remarked. "They'd shit a brick wall if they thought you were going to do anything below your maximum potential."

"No kidding."

"How's married life treating you, Kaylee? Does your new husband still let you run off to the other side of the world at the drop of a hat?" Finn directed the conversation away from Elliot, who looked rather frustrated.

"*Let* me?" Kaylee asked with a smile. "That's not how it works at all. And actually, he likes to go with me. As a matter of fact, we're headed to Egypt next month. He's never been, of course, and he's already packing."

"You two spend a lot of time together. Aren't you tired of him yet?" Elliot asked with a grin.

Kaylee shook her head. "Not a bit. He's amazing. I didn't think I'd find someone I'd be willing to marry for at least another ten years, and I definitely didn't think it would be someone I'm so compatible with. He's incredible." Her face took on a happy glow as she spoke of Archard.

"What about you, Nora? I haven't seen any of your videos lately." Finn signaled a waiter, who told them he'd be with them in just a moment.

Nora looked down at the table, studying the grain of the wood. If there was anyone she could be honest with, it was her cousins—well, technically, they were her siblings, but they'd been calling each other cousins for so long, they preferred to see it that way. They were the people she'd known the longest, and they were her best friends. They understood who she was on a level that no one except their parents could. Still, some things were just hard to say. "I've had some shitty things happen lately, and I haven't had a lot of time for anything else."

The waiter chose that moment to swiftly approach their table and offer to take their orders. "We'll start with the appetizer sampler," Kaylee told him without even turning her head to look at him. "What's going on?"

Nora had been so wrapped up in what'd happened with Kieran

that she hadn't had much time to grieve over her relationship with Ted. She sagged her shoulders and took a deep breath, reminding herself that she didn't have to cry about it now. She could do that later when no one could see her. "I caught Ted cheating on me with his TA."

Kaylee's arms flew around Nora's shoulders instantly. "Oh, honey. I'm so sorry."

"Want me to kick his ass?" Elliot asked, his brows knitting together in anger.

Finn patted her hand. "We could always find some way to ruin him financially, if you'd like. Or blackmail is always fun."

Nora had to smile, knowing she had so many people who had her back. "No, I don't think any of that is necessary. He's already gotten a little bit of his just desserts." She went through the story of Ted attacking her as quickly as possible. It enraged them, and she could feel their energy colliding in the air.

"You've got to be shitting me," Kaylee hissed. "He's dead."

"No, really; it's not necessary. Kieran happened to be working in that building that night, and he came bursting through the door. Before I could even say anything, he had Ted pinned to the wall by his throat." She didn't know if she wanted to laugh or cry about it. "I think Ted pissed his pants, and Kieran threatened him never to come near me again."

"Wow." Elliot and Finn looked at each other. "I don't think I expected to hear that."

"I didn't expect to see it," Kaylee admitted. "He and I haven't really talked to each other much. We pass in the hall every now and then, but that's about it. To make matters even worse, he nearly shifted. I had to step in and stop him before he did something stupid."

Kaylee still had an arm around her cousin. "That could've been bad, but it was still cool of him to step in."

"Yeah, I guess."

"What do you mean, you guess?"

"I'm worried that he went too far."

"Let me tell you something about them," Elliot said, referencing the dragons who'd most recently come to Earth from Charok. "They're not like us. They didn't grow up here, and they still have a lot to learn about how things work on this planet. I've spent some time with Callan, and he's still pretty wild. It's like trying to domesticate a feral cat. I say you're lucky he didn't kill Ted. Not that I would've blamed him."

Kaylee pressed her lips together. "I have to say I agree. I obviously know Archard better than any of the others. I know he's had to suppress a lot of his instincts just to make his life here work. I help him with that on a regular basis. I do still think it was sweet of Kieran to step in. You needed his help, and he was there for his fellow dragon."

"Right." But Nora didn't feel any better about the situation. She couldn't explain what made her so uneasy about it, other than the fact that her body went absolutely nuts when she was around him. There she was, sitting in a cushy restaurant booth with three other dragons, and yet there was no reaction like that. The words to explain those feelings to them were right on the tip of her tongue, threatening to come out, but she sipped her Moscow mule instead. Her life was slowly turning upside down, and she was still getting used to it.

# 6

KIERAN HAD STOPPED TRYING TO KEEP TRACK OF HOW LITTLE SLEEP HE was getting. It wasn't as though it was helping him get any rest, and he had work to do. Unfortunately, with so little happening on campus, his work wasn't enough to keep him occupied. His mind constantly flashed back to being in Ted's office. He saw the fear on Nora's face as if she were still right in front of him. He had to wonder if she'd been afraid of Ted, or of him.

He knocked on his supervisor's door and entered at the gruff invitation that followed. Chief Jenkins was sitting at his desk, his feet propped up on the battered metal surface. He glanced up over his wireframes and his newspaper to see who'd intruded on his quiet time. "What can I do for you, son?" An older man on the verge of retirement, he spoke to everyone as though they were his children.

"I was looking over the schedule for next week, and you've put me in the wrong building." Kieran put his copy down on the desk.

Jenkins folded his newspaper and set it to the side, letting his feet drop to the floor as he sat up. "Let's see here." He adjusted his glasses on his nose and looked at the schedule. "No, that's correct. I bumped you up to the recreation center."

"I'd like to stay at McKnelly."

The chief looked up at him. "Why? You're off probation, and I think you're ready for a more challenging area. That's how you get promotions, you know. Besides, I think you'll scare the living shit out of these kids who like to goof around in the bowling alley after they've had too much to drink. You probably won't have to do anything but show up."

Kieran steeled his jaw, trying to find the best way to put this. Anyone else was probably interested in promotions and such, but not him. "With all due respect, I'd much rather stay in the science building."

"And again, I ask why." Jenkins took his glasses off and rubbed his hand over his face.

He couldn't tell his boss he wanted to stay at McKnelly because one of his fellow dragons worked there and he felt a desperate need to protect her. He couldn't explain that he'd nearly clobbered one of the teachers to death and was afraid Ted would come back and exact his revenge on Nora. He'd get fired if he explained he planned to make sure she got safely in her car every night to go home, no matter what he had to do. "There are a few people there I have my eye on."

"Really? I don't think we've ever had much trouble there. The science nerds pretty much keep to themselves."

"I know. It's just a hunch I'm going on; something I want to make sure doesn't turn into anything bigger." He hadn't filed a report on Ted, just as Nora had asked. If someone figured it out, or if another staff member happened to see any of it and turned him in, he'd be kicked off campus permanently. Everything he was doing now was walking a fine line.

"All right. If it makes you happy, then who am I to interfere? I'm sure Mac will be happy to take the rec center instead. Just don't come whining to me when you don't get to move up the ladder."

"I won't, sir."

"And when I retire in six months, I don't want you telling my replacement that I stiffed you. In fact, I'm going to put it in your record that you requested to stay at McKnelly. I'll keep my ass covered even when I'm not here anymore." He picked up a pen to show he was serious.

"Of course, sir."

Jenkins sighed. "I have to tell you, Kieran, you're the strangest security guard I've ever had here. I like you, and you're good. You always show up to work on time, and you never try to leave early. Hell, I don't think you've even called in for a sick day. I've never gotten a complaint about you, and trust me, people around here are plenty happy to rat out a security guard who doesn't walk the line. But I just don't understand you."

Kieran didn't know what to say. "I appreciate you doing this for me."

This made the chief laugh. "Of course you do, because you're never anything but polite. It's fine, Kieran. Just go and enjoy your science building. I'm going to refill my coffee."

Heading back out into the main security office, Kieran felt relieved. The idea of switching buildings was simply impossible right now. For a moment, he wondered what Nora would say if she had any idea what he'd done. He wasn't trying to obsess over her, but he wanted to keep her safe. There wasn't anyone else on campus who could do that the same way he could.

At least Jenkins was willing to let him stay where he wanted for the time being. There was no telling what might happen when he'd retire and someone else would step in, but he would face that when the time came. He had the threat of Ted to deal with, but he'd seen something else the previous day that'd made him even more uncomfortable.

As he walked out of the office and down the hall, he was stopped by a female student with long blonde hair. She paused with one hip cocked and her chest out, barely covered by the tiny belly shirt she wore. "Hey, do you think you could help me with my car?"

Kieran was fairly certain he'd seen her around campus before, but he didn't know what her name was. He felt like being alone, but he was technically on duty. Otherwise, he'd have referred her back to the office. "What's wrong?"

She batted her eyelashes and smiled. "I locked my keys inside it. God, I'm such an idiot."

"Just a moment." Kieran ducked back into the office to grab a few tools they kept there for just this sort of occasion. It happened all the time with busy students and forgetful professors. He was no mechanic, but he'd learned how to do this pretty well. "Lead the way."

The girl trotted ahead of him out to the parking lot, stopping next to a sleek little sports car. She leaned against it. "Here it is!"

Kieran didn't know a whole lot about vehicles. They didn't have them back on Charok, nor did they need them, so he didn't see much value in them other than to blend in with society. But he had a feeling this was the kind of car a college student couldn't afford on her own.

Still, he stepped up and pulled the handle on the driver's side. The door didn't budge.

"I was in such a hurry trying to get to my classes this morning," she cooed. "I didn't even realize what I'd done until later."

He grunted an answer as he started to unroll the small case of tools, but on a hunch, he went around to the other side of the vehicle. One quick flick of the handle and the passenger door popped open. "There you go." He didn't dare try crawling in to retrieve the keys from the ignition; the car was too small.

"Oh, look at that!" she gushed as she rushed around to join him. "You're so smart! What do I owe you?"

He rolled the tool case back up and shoved it in his pocket. "Nothing."

"I'm sure there's something I could do to pay you back." She sidled up close to him, batting her eyelashes and shoving her chest out again.

"No. It's fine, really. Have a good day." Kieran turned and walked away.

Helping the girl in the parking lot had put him on the wrong side of campus. He could go around the outer perimeter on the designated sidewalks, but it was much easier to take a shortcut through the library.

He liked this place, with its maze of shelves and tons of old books. It was the most cave-like area on campus, and its quiet solitude only increased that effect. He inhaled deeply, feeling the breath reach all the way to the base of his lungs before slowly letting it out.

It caught in his throat when he saw a glimpse of familiar chestnut hair disappearing behind one of the stacks. He paused, trying to decide what he should do. Technically, his shift was about to start. He needed to get over to McKnelly, check on the security cameras, and start his rounds. But as far as Kieran was concerned, right now, his real job was to make sure Nora was safe. If he had any doubts, his dragon didn't. The writhing inside him had begun once again. He followed her, turning between two tall shelves of books.

She was standing with her back to him as she plucked a volume from the shelf. Nora flipped quickly to the part of the book she wanted, running her finger down the page and nodding to herself as she skimmed it. Turning without looking up, she headed back toward the circulation desk. It wasn't until she nearly ran into Kieran that she looked up. "Oh!" Her gasp resounded through the big library, and she clamped her hand over her mouth. "You scared the crap out of me," she hissed.

"I'm sorry. I was coming through here and saw you, and there's something I want to talk to you about."

For reasons Kieran couldn't explain, she seemed irritated by his very presence. Nora practically pressed herself against the shelf as she squeezed past him. "I'm kind of busy."

"It'll only take a minute." His spine threatened to stretch and expand, one of the first steps necessary to accommodate his other form. Kieran clenched his shoulder blades against it.

Nora charged toward the circulation desk, quickly checking the book out. Kieran hung back, waiting for her, wondering if anyone else noticed what was happening. The way she was acting made him even more uncomfortable than usual. Was she embarrassed by him?

He waited until they'd exited the library through a different set of doors before he tried talking to her again. "I noticed you hanging out with the new lab assistant."

She stopped in her tracks and glared up at him, her eyes fiery. "What? You're following me now?"

Kieran pressed his tongue against the roof of his mouth. In a sense, he was. But it'd been a complete accident that he'd seen her with the new girl. "I have a bad feeling about her."

"Seriously?" Nora angrily shoved the library book in her bag and continued her march toward the front of the building. "She's perfectly nice. Even if she isn't, I don't see what it has to do with you."

He didn't like that reaction in her. "I've tried to convince myself of the same thing, but it doesn't seem to be working." Kieran wasn't about to go into detail and explain how different things were now. He'd just been a normal dragon when he lived on Charok, and even though things had been a little unsettled once he moved to Earth, he could handle it. It was like something had crawled under his skin over the last couple of weeks and he couldn't shake it. The new lab assistant didn't make anything better. There was a certain smell about her that reminded Kieran of much harder times in his life.

"Find a way to make it work," she snarled. They were outside now, and the sun made rainbow highlights in her hair that Kieran couldn't stop looking at.

"Look, it's just that after all that happened with Ted, I want—"

She whirled on him, standing directly in front of him on the sidewalk. Her small frame was minute compared to his, with her head coming barely to his shoulders. She couldn't physically stop him, but she had a power over him like no one else did. "I don't want to talk about Ted. I wish none of that had ever happened. I don't need you to come to my rescue."

"Clearly, you did." He was getting angry now, but not at her. Maybe at the universe or himself, and definitely at Ted, but not at Nora. "I hate to think of what would've happened if I hadn't been there."

"So you come to my rescue once and you suddenly think I'm a helpless damsel in distress? Kieran, this is ridiculous. You're being way too overprotective, and I don't understand why you think you have any right to be protective over me at all." She looked fierce, and Kieran swore she was fighting against shifting herself.

He also swore he could feel the echo of her heartbeat thundering in his own chest. The two of them might not agree, but their dragons were a different matter. She could yell at him all she wanted, but he still knew the truth. "No? You want to deny that you and I are the same?"

She opened her mouth to continue arguing and then snapped it shut again as she angrily swiped a tear away from the corner of her eye. "Yeah, okay. There's that. And I'll even admit that I'm grateful you were there. But that doesn't give you any right to just decide you're in charge of me."

"You're right, and I'm sorry." He glanced at a student walking by, wondering what she thought of this exchange. Kieran lowered his voice. "It's just that...I..."

"What?"

He'd never had trouble saying what was on his mind. Back on Charok, Kieran had been content to be quiet when the mood dictated it, letting Archard and Callan argue until it was finally time to step in, but he never let his opinion go unheard if he felt it was something that needed to be said. Nora made everything different. "I think what I'm really trying to say is that I'd like to take you out to dinner sometime."

Nora gaped up at him. Kieran could see the emotions flitting through her eyes, one after another. She flapped her hand helplessly in the air, tearing up again as she finally found words. "No. I—I can't."

"Okay." He hadn't even realized he was going to ask. It'd just come out, and Kieran had a feeling that was his dragon again.

"It's just that I've tried so hard to live a normal life, despite my weird parents and my even weirder lineage. It's been a constant struggle, knowing I've got this secret that I can't talk about. I want to be as far away from all that as possible. It's only been harder since you guys came here from Charok, and now it's even more complicated." She was gesturing wildly with her hands as she spoke.

Kieran took each of her wrists gently, feeling the delicate bones inside. She didn't resist him, relaxing slightly, and Kieran felt his own nerves calm down a bit. "Nora, it's okay. You don't have to explain. You don't have to have a reason. I just wanted to see." Slowly, regretfully, he let go, knowing he would probably never get a chance to touch her like that again. It'd been such a small thing, and yet it'd felt so good. He'd just have to be content in knowing that he tried. Kieran moved past her and continued on down the sidewalk. They were both heading for the same building, but that was all right. He would keep his distance.

"Kieran, wait."

He paused, his feet heavy as the concrete he was standing on. He almost didn't turn around, afraid of what she might have to say. There was no point in hoping that things would change. Nora had told him how she felt, and at least now he knew.

But he turned anyway, sensing her standing there behind him, reaching out to him. She was only reaching with her mind, not her hand, but that was enough.

"I'm sorry."

He blinked. His skin threatened to transform, shattering into a million tiny pieces.

"Is that invitation still open?"

Kieran looked at her, with the sun illuminating her skin. She looked so perfect, and yet she could make him feel so strange. There was nothing on this planet harder to understand than the way he felt about her.

**7**

---

NORA'S STOMACH TWISTED AS SHE PULLED ON A DIFFERENT OUTFIT AND checked it in the mirror. "I don't know what's wrong with me. It's not like it matters what I wear."

Holly lounged on Nora's bed, eating a bag of chips and flipping through a photography magazine. "Why wouldn't it matter? You're going out on a date. It always matters."

"You're not helping," Nora replied, giving her friend a withering look. "It shouldn't matter because it isn't as though he hasn't seen me looking completely terrible. I have my bad days, and I've shown up at the lab in ratty jeans and a t-shirt before. Hell, he's probably also seen me in my lab coat and goggles. Super sexy."

"It matters because it's a date. It's different. If you don't show up looking nice, then he'll think you don't care. It's not just a matter of how you look, but what you're trying to communicate." Holly flipped the magazine shut and sat up, swinging her legs over the edge of the purple comforter.

"Did they teach you all that in photography school?" Nora reached into her jewelry box and retrieved a silver necklace. The resin pendant contained a tiny bundle of perfectly preserved forget-me-not flowers which matched her blue dress nicely.

Holly shrugged. "In a way, yeah. There are some much deeper

classes in the curriculum than you'd expect. So, are you excited?" She gave her friend a mischievous grin.

"I don't know *what* I am." Nora ran a hand down her arm. She could feel her body trying to change, and she wasn't even near Kieran yet. Several times, she'd been tempted to tell Holly who she was just so she would have someone else who could understand. But no normal human could ever really understand, and she didn't want to risk chasing her off.

"Then why did you say yes?" Holly pressed. "You said he's friends with one of your cousins or something, right? And you see him all the time at work. So at least he's not a complete stranger."

Nora sighed. "I think that's part of the problem. He really does seem like a nice guy. It just really got me unsettled, seeing him choke out Ted like that."

"Girl, you're crazy. Ted deserved it, and they just don't make men like that anymore. It's pretty romantic, when you think about it." She tossed the bag of chips in the trash can.

"Yes, Ted deserved it. But it's also my fault Ted got hurt. I knew something was happening in that office, and I never should've stuck my nose in there to see what it was really all about. Hearing that TA giggle like that was all the proof I really needed."

"Whoa, hey. Don't you dare go beating yourself up over that!" Holly stood up and took Nora by the shoulders. "Ted was the one messing around on you. Ted was the one who wouldn't let you leave. Ted was the one who tried to hurt you. From everything you've told me, all Kieran did was step in and stop him from taking things a step further. He could've put him in the hospital if he wanted to. I've seen him around campus."

"I didn't know you'd noticed." Nora turned back to her jewelry box to find a pair of earrings.

Holly snorted. "He's kind of hard to miss. The guy's huge! And muscly. And handsome. And apparently, ready to protect you from anything that might be a threat."

"Okay, okay. That's all true."

"You're damn right it is. Now you make sure you enjoy yourself tonight, and I don't mean for his sake. I mean because you've been really tense lately, and that's not like you. I want my happy, carefree friend back. So have a few drinks or whatever and don't worry about everything else."

"I'll do my best," Nora promised with a smile. "And thanks for coming by to help me get dressed. You're awesome."

"That I am," Holly winked. "Now go get your shoes on. I'm heading home to do some photo editing, so think of me while you're out getting wined and dined."

---

NORA AND KIERAN had decided on a lunch date instead of dinner, since it worked with their schedules better. He picked her up at her apartment and drove them out to a little café on the edge of town. "You look really nice."

"Thank you. So do you." Ever since he'd started working at the university, she hadn't seen him in anything other than his security guard uniform. In a dark green polo and well-fitting jeans with his hair carefully combed back, he almost seemed like a different person. For a second, she could forget he was the same man who'd been ready to shift into a dragon and kill Ted with one hand.

"Have you ever been here before?" He read over the menu quickly.

"I think once or twice, a long time ago. It's got a nice view of the lake." She pointed out the window to where the water and sky formed a nice backdrop between the large trees that grew on the property.

"That's why I chose it, actually. There was only one large body of water near where I lived on Charok, but that was part of the land we were fighting over. It didn't have very good memories, and of course, we lost that battle." He glanced out the window, squinting slightly against the brilliant sun.

Nora felt for him, but she was more concerned about their privacy at the moment. "Aren't you afraid someone's going to hear you? They'll think you're an alien or something."

"Well, I am, really. So are you."

She shook her head. This had already started out awkwardly, just like any date, but now it was taking a turn for the worse. "I don't really want to talk about that. The whole idea makes me uncomfortable, especially knowing what Kaylee discovered."

"About who your mother was? There's nothing to be ashamed of. The queen was unquestionably revered by every single dragon alive. She was wise and caring, and all of dragonkind that was left mourned her when she was gone." Kieran turned over his menu and cleared his throat. "I mean, that's what I've always heard."

"It's strange to think you have so much more of a connection with Charok than I do, and yet we're only a few years apart in age. Do you miss it?"

He set the menu down and folded his hands on top of it. "In a lot of ways, no. I don't miss the hard work required every day just to survive. I don't miss wondering if there were ogres nearby, waiting to pounce on me or someone I cared about. I don't miss accidentally stumbling on skeletons out in the woods while I was out hunting. I do miss the peace and quiet, and the ability to just be myself. I could shift at any time, whether it was because it was the most convenient form to be in, or simply because I wanted to."

"I'm so sorry you had to go through all of that. You know, if we had any idea there were still dragons living on Charok, and if Varhan and Uncle Julian had been able to figure out a way back sooner—"

Kieran laid a hand on the back of hers, quieting her. "You don't need to apologize or make up for it. I'm happy I got to stay there for as long as I did, and now I get to experience something else. I wish you'd gotten a chance to see what it's like. I think you'd really be surprised by how pleasant it is."

"Kaylee told me, after she and Archard had come back. Out of all of us cousins, she was the one who wanted to go the most. She was always much more curious about where we'd come from than the rest of us were." She easily remembered the way her cousin had described it, with impressive red mountains surrounded by lush forests. Kaylee had spoken enthusiastically about every detail. It was almost enough to make Nora jealous, except for the parts about getting captured briefly by an ogre and almost falling off the side of a cliff.

"Maybe you'll get a chance someday."

"Oh, I don't know about that. Uncle Julian is fairly certain there's no safe way to reopen the portal between here and Charok. He and Varhan are still trying to figure out what kind of consequences there might be for bringing you guys over here in the first place, accidental as it was." She took a sip of her tea and laughed a little. "It must've been terrifying to just get sucked through a wormhole and dropped on a planet like this, considering how wild Charok is."

He gave her a warm smile, one that made her feel a ripple of heat down to her toes. "It was definitely disconcerting, but I think the rest of us took it much better than Archard did. Your uncle gave us a very warm welcome, and we were almost immediately invited to be part of his household. I have a feeling I could've lived there as long as I wanted and he wouldn't have objected."

"That's probably true. Julian is pretty social, despite all the time he spends buried in his books." Their sandwiches came, and they fell into a companionable silence for a while. Nora found that she was growing more comfortable around him. He was huge, and so far, he was the only dragon that had ever frightened her before, but Holly was right. He'd confronted Ted to defend her, and there weren't a lot of guys willing to do that sort of thing. At the very least, this could be a new friendship.

"I owe you an apology," she said as she finished the first half of her sandwich.

"For what?" Kieran looked up sharply as though she'd just said she was on fire.

"For the way I treated you after…what you did for me. I don't know why I'm having such a hard time with it."

His eyes held hers. "Can I be honest with you?"

"That's the way I prefer things, generally."

"I completely understand why you're having a hard time with it. I told you I overheard part of your argument with him, and that's true. It was enough to let me know that you cared about him. You were angry with him, but we can't just turn off our feelings because we're angry. He hurt you, but that didn't make it any easier to see him hurt."

Nora played with the frilly toothpick that had been holding her sandwich together. "Yeah. I guess you're right."

"While I'm not sorry about what I did, I *am* sorry if it hurt or disturbed you in any way. I know I'm not like you and your cousins."

That last statement sent a pang of guilt through her chest. "I never meant to make you feel that way."

"You didn't have to. It's the truth. We're all the same, but I think we'd be crazy if we didn't acknowledge there are some pretty major differences."

After their meal, Kieran asked her if she'd like to go outside to walk along the lake. "Or we could see a movie, or whatever you'd like to do."

"A walk outside would be wonderful. I've spent way too much time cooped up in the lab. Dr. Ward is a very hands-on type of teacher who wants his students to really understand the concepts and applications in real life, so there's a lot of work anyway. Now that I'm also training Allison, it feels like I have a second job."

As they headed around the building toward the beach area, Kieran stiffened slightly at the mention of Nora's new coworker, but didn't say anything.

Nora took notice of the slight shift in his energy. She hadn't wanted to talk to him about it before, but the space between them was growing less tense. Now was as good of a time as any. "What did you mean when you said you had a bad feeling about Allison?"

He paused, standing just out of reach of the water where it lapped at the rocky sand. It was too late in the season for anyone to be laying out for a tan or building rough sandcastles. He watched a lone fisherman out in the middle of the lake. "You seemed upset by that. I don't want to make you angry."

Nora poked at a rock with the toe of her boot. "I overreacted before. I just had a lot to think about, and it was something extra I couldn't handle at the time. But you don't have to treat me with kid gloves. I'd much rather know what you think and find a way to explain it than to wonder."

In a very gentlemanly fashion, he offered her his elbow and escorted her toward the path that led away from the beach area and wound around the lake. "That's just it. I don't have anything specific to tell you. It's just a bad feeling, like she's not who she says she is. Like she's hiding something."

"I don't think she'd be able to work at the university without proof of her identity," Nora pointed out.

Kieran nodded. "Yes, but I work there. We both know there are some very good forgers out there, or else none of us would be able to live and work here in peace."

"All right. That's a good point. But it doesn't mean Allison is doing anything wrong." She liked the way her arm felt tucked inside his. Nora meant it when she'd told him she didn't want to be the damsel in distress. Her parents had raised her to be independent and strong, and she didn't want to feel she had to rely on any man to be all right. But there was also something nice about knowing a man like him cared about her and was on her side. "I don't think you could expect anyone who's been through what she has to fit in perfectly, at least not at first."

"You know, I think there's one big difference between the dragons who've been here for a long time and those of us who haven't."

"What's that?" She wasn't sure she wanted to know. She could sense the subject of Allison had reignited the tension between them, but at least they were able to talk about it without arguing—or rather, without her flying off the handle simply because he was trying to warn her.

"Don't take offense at this, but I don't think you rely on your instincts the same way I do. When I overheard your argument with Ted, I was almost on the complete opposite end of the building. The fact that I'm a dragon means I have certain abilities regular humans don't have, and I don't try to turn them off. It doesn't always work out, which is why you saw me starting to shift that night, but for the most part, I think it gives me a distinct advantage. I can't exactly put my finger on what I don't like about Allison, but I know that my guard instantly went up when I saw her."

Nora didn't want to believe him. He hadn't really met Allison or talked to her, and it wasn't fair to solely judge someone based on intuition. But that didn't mean he was completely wrong. "I used my hearing that night, too, but not until I was right outside his door. If I'd been more attuned to it, maybe I would've known he was cheating on me earlier."

"A blessing or a curse, depending on how you want to look at it." He looked down at her hand and then back out across the water. "It's beautiful out here."

She resisted the urge to lean her cheek against the bulk of his arm. It was so close, and so tempting. Nora wished she could explain why she'd felt so strange around him before, with her insides churning and her body arguing with herself, and yet she was completely fine now. Comfortable, even. She let her gaze slide down to the ground and she stopped in her tracks.

Kieran's muscles tensed, turning to heated marble under her hand. "What's wrong?"

"Nothing at all. Look, it's a chicory plant." She let go of him to bend down and examine the weedy little bush. It was covered in delicate little flowers a shade of violet blue, like the sky just after the sun went down. "I've been keeping my eyes open for one for a while. I'm not surprised I haven't found any on campus. They yank anything they think is a weed, but I haven't been able to find it in the national forest, either."

He knelt next to her. "What's so special about it?"

"A lot, really. Both the leaves and flowers can be eaten. They're just a little bitter, but they're great when mixed into a salad. The root can be toasted and boiled and made into a coffee substitute. Not as good as coffee, mind you, but better than nothing. Here." She pulled her cell phone out of her purse and handed it to him. "Help me do a quick video?"

The device looked minute in his massive hands. "I don't know. I'm not really good with this stuff yet."

She came around to his side and pointed to the screen. "Just push that button when I say. Keep it steady on me. Anything else, I can edit out later."

What was going to be a quick video about chicory turned into something much more. As Nora finished talking about the whimsical little plant, she noticed a small cluster of dandelion nearby. It was in the same family as chicory and was quite edible as well. Kieran patiently followed her to some clover and some wood sorrel next.

She got so caught up in what she was doing, she hardly realized how much the daylight had faded. It was too dark to shoot, which seemed to be a common problem for her. "All right, folks. It looks like that's all we can fit in for tonight. We'll see you next time!"

Kieran pushed the button to stop shooting and handed the phone back to her. "You're really into this stuff."

"Yeah, thanks for being so patient with me." She took the phone and flicked through the video, wondering just how much of it she'd have to edit out due to poor lighting. There was no way Ted ever would've followed her around the lake like that, just quietly filming and waiting for her to do her thing. "I really appreciate you doing this for me. I know it's a lot to ask."

She looked up to see Kieran watching her. The sun made a brilliant display on the few clouds in the sky as it sank behind the lake, and it cast a fire in his eyes that gave her pause. The more she looked, the more Nora realized the fire wasn't coming from the sun at all, but from inside him. His eyes flicked to her mouth, and her body surged towards his.

Their bodies were like magnets as they came together. Kieran bent his head to kiss her, and Nora readily tipped her head back to accept him. She sank into his strong arms, feeling safe and comfortable and more like herself than she could ever remember being. The dragon inside her swirled pleasantly, very much alive but no longer fighting against her human form.

Kieran's hand slid down her waist to her hip, pulling her even tighter against him. When he broke their kiss, he kept his forehead pressed against hers. "Fly with me."

"Hmm?" She tried to ask him what he meant, but her mouth wasn't yet ready to form words. She liked the way he felt against her, the heat and strength of him, the barely tamed wildness about him.

"It's almost dark, and no one will see. Let's fly over the lake." His words were a low rumble in her ear.

Nora started to say no, but it was only because she didn't want to let go of him yet. But he was right. No one would see. They had wandered far from the restaurant, and the last rays of light were fading quickly. It was more rural out there than anywhere else near the town, and even the lone fishing boat had docked for the night. She bit her lip and smiled in anticipation. "All right."

She stepped back regretfully and took a deep breath. "It's been so long, I'm not sure I can even do this anymore."

"Sure you can."

For reasons she couldn't quite explain, Nora really wanted to do this for him. He'd touched a part inside of her that no one else had ever accessed, and she wanted to further this thing they shared. She relaxed her shoulders and let the air out of her lungs, feeling her spine stretch. It was an odd feeling to let her wings and tail go, but deeply satisfying to feel her claws finally extend from her hands and feet. A tickling ripple waved out over her skin as it split and turned, revealing the deep emerald scales she'd been hiding for so long. She hardly realized she'd closed her eyes until she opened them again to see that Kieran was finishing his transformation.

He was huge in human form, but it wasn't much different for him now. She didn't need much light to see the massive silver dragon that now stood before her, his wings gleaming in the new starlight as he stretched them. An array of metallic spikes extended from the back of his head and matched the ridge of hard plates that marched down his spine and gave Nora an excited thrill in the pit of her stomach.

Kieran took a step toward her, craning his head down on his long neck so that he was only inches away. "You look gorgeous like that."

"You're not so bad yourself." A smile was a unique experience as a dragon. Her lips stretched back across the smooth cones of her teeth, and a joyous sensation sparked down the sides of her neck. "Are we really going to do this?"

"Let's go." Kieran shot into the air with the skill of a dragon who wasn't completely out of practice.

Nora went after him, finding that her wings had suffered from disuse. She tipped to the right slightly as she swept out over the lake, trying to keep up with him. He was quick and nimble, but he had quite a bit of size to compensate for. Nora swept up to his side and laughed into the wind.

Kieran's wing tip extended out as he glided over the water's surface. He touched it to hers, a small and yet intimate gesture on such a sensitive bit of skin. Nora felt another shiver of electricity and didn't want it to end. She tipped slightly to slide her wing just under the edge of his.

They rolled and swept over the lake, and Nora couldn't remember ever feeling so free. This body was the most comfortable thing she'd ever put on, and yet she'd been denying it to herself the entire time. It was even better to share this experience with a man like Kieran, who didn't seem to be enjoying it any less just because he was used to it.

With both of them in their natural forms, Nora could no longer deny the attraction between the two of them. It was though a cord attached their souls, and no matter where he was around her, she could sense him as she sensed her own skin. With the wind through her scales and the roll of her spine, Nora was a completely different person.

When they finally came in for a landing under a thick grove of trees along the far shoreline, they fell into each other's arms as they shifted back in human form. Her lips demanded his as they clung to each other, and the entire world faded away except for what they shared.

# 8

KIERAN'S MIND WAS FULL OF HIS MEMORIES WITH NORA. SO MUCH, HE could barely concentrate on work. He didn't care if someone parked in the wrong spot or stayed too late in the lounge when he needed to lock the doors. He was hardly paying any attention to the time, anyway.

Their date had been nice enough on its own. Kieran had almost expected her to show up half-heartedly, only having accepted an outing with him because she felt some sort of obligation to. But she'd smiled as she got in his car, and she'd worn that gorgeous blue dress that definitely wasn't the sort of thing she normally wore to the lab. Kieran didn't know much about human dating, but he did know enough to recognize that things with Nora were going well. He enjoyed something as simple as going out for a sandwich, and even though he'd figured he'd do the traditional thing of asking her to a movie, their walk around the lake had proven to be much more fruitful.

His dragon shivered pleasantly as he recalled that flight. There hadn't been nearly enough chances for him to shift since he'd come to Earth, and certainly none of them had happened alongside a stunning female. Nora had been absolutely glorious in her reptilian form. She'd taken his breath away, and for a moment, Kieran hadn't been certain he'd be able to fly in her presence. There was something about her that simply debilitated him, but in the most gratifying way possible.

By most standards, their outing had been innocent. After their flight and another long, deep kiss, they'd lain in each other's arms and watched the stars swirl slowly through the branches of the trees above them. What Kieran had suspected he knew now to be true. He was meant to be with Nora. There was nothing like having her there in his arms, talking quietly about the nighttime plants around him or the exhilaration of the flight they'd taken. They hadn't done anything more than kiss and hold each other, yet he never wanted to let her go. He couldn't wait to see her again.

But there was something else pressing on his mind that he couldn't let go of, either. He had an appointment he had to keep; one that he'd made without bringing up to Nora and one that he doubted she would approve of. When he got off work the next night, he drove out to the edge of town where Julian's massive house sat on a large plot of acreage.

Varhan himself opened the door to let him in before Kieran even had a chance to knock. "Come to the library. Julian's already there. I haven't been able to pull him away from his books since you called."

"Have you told anyone else?" Kieran asked nervously. The dragons who'd helped bring Kieran and his family here from Charok—albeit accidentally—were kind, but they were also Nora's family. It would take very little effort for news of this to get back to Nora, and he didn't want her to hear about it from anyone but him.

"No. I don't want to scare anyone unless there's good reason to." Varhan opened the heavy wooden door to the library and waved Kieran in.

Julian sat near the hearth, a low fire crackling away and keeping the room comfortably warm. He sprang out of his chair as soon as he saw Kieran. "Come in, come in. Have a seat. I don't think I've slept at all since you called."

Kieran slowly lowered himself into an overstuffed chair. He'd stayed in this home for the first few months or so after he'd come to Earth, and normally, he'd be comfortable there. He'd even gotten used to Varhan, despite the fact he was a wizard. But the subject matter at hand rested like a ball of snakes in his stomach. "I'm sorry. I hope I'm completely wrong about this."

"There's something to be said for instincts, no matter how strange they seem. Please, tell us anything you know."

Kieran rubbed his nose. "I don't really *know* any of this to be true."

"That's fine," Varhan said gently, his gray eyes focusing Kieran. "Just tell us."

He sighed. "All right. You know I've been working at the university for a few months. Everything is pretty normal there. The only other dragon on campus is Nora, and everyone else is undeniably human. I can just tell, you know?"

"Of course." Julian nodded. He did know, because there was that deep sense of familiarity dragons always recognized in each other.

"Earlier this week, a new lab assistant started working in the same building where Nora works, and that's usually the one I'm posted to as well. I haven't met Allison personally, but she gave me a disturbing feeling as soon as I saw her." Kieran shifted in his seat unsure of whether or not he should go on. Reporting all this to Julian and Varhan meant revealing some information about himself, as well. "At first, I thought it was just me. I've been having some...rather protective feelings toward Nora."

Julian raised a dark eyebrow, and the hint of a smile played at the corner of his mouth. "Really?"

"Um, yes. Maybe even that has something to do with this Allison as well."

Varhan's eyes were sparkling, and he exchanged a look with Julian. "That's certainly possible. Go on."

Kieran cleared his throat. "Anyway, I couldn't just leave it alone. I wanted to know more. I tried to get close to her without being too obvious, but that's difficult when she's in the lab. Security guards don't normally go in there. But I happened to catch her on her way out the door, and I held it open for her. The most horrific stench came off her as she went by, and this wasn't the normal stink of unwashed humans. It was a smell I remembered very clearly from when I lived on Charok."

The two older men were on the very edges of their seats now. "Charok, you say?" Varhan asked.

"Yes." Kieran remembered it distinctly. He'd been very young when the wizards were overrunning the dragons, and his aunt had taken him and his cousins far into the woods to survive. Still, that had been after the wizards had come through his part of the dragons' settlement, the funk of rotting flesh sweeping up from the hems of their robes. It was the kind of scent memory that he'd never thought of until it came up once again. "A wizard, but not one like you, Varhan."

Varhan pressed his lips together and his skin turned a shade paler. "I've been worried about things like this. I wonder what we really did when we opened that portal to Charok, or when Kaylee opened up another one to get there and back. We know so little about this magic." His eyes were distant, and he was talking to himself more than anyone else.

"He's been picking up on magical signatures he doesn't recognize," Julian explained with a concerned look at the wizard. "It's not an entirely unusual thing. There are, after all, creatures native to Earth who have their own magical powers, and it's a simple process to figure it out. But there have been several he'd found that we can't narrow down, and it's been sitting uncomfortably on our shoulders. I haven't even told Kaylee, because we don't want to scare anyone unless we think there's a real reason."

"I'll be right back." Varhan stood and hurried out of the room, closing the door behind him.

Kieran didn't like how disturbed the wizard was. "Do you have any idea what it might be?"

Julian nodded solemnly. "There's a possibility—nothing we know, mind you, but just a theory—that something else might've come through one of the portals besides dragons. Without actually recreating one of those portals, we don't know for sure, but it's too dangerous to even try. If we're right, we'd only be inviting more of these creatures to Earth. We've compromised it enough as it is."

His inner dragon was disturbed by this information, and it fought angrily against Kieran's human form. But he'd let it loose out by the lake, and that was going to have to be enough for a while. Kieran wasn't about to shift right there in the middle of Julian's library and ruin the place, especially not after the man had done so much for him. "That means I need to get to Nora. She could be in danger."

"Hold on. If we're right, then it's not as though she or anyone else is in more danger right now than they were a day ago or even a week ago. It's been months since those portals have been open."

"That's true." But it didn't make Kieran feel any better. If Allison was anything else other than what she claimed to be, then he didn't want her near Nora. "I should've known."

"You couldn't have, Kieran. And neither did I. It's only because we're lucky enough to have Varhan here that we've got any clue as to what could be happening. He'd gone into town to the library and he said the magical signature just slammed into him, like a wave of electrical energy. I've honestly never seen him so shaken. Even when he transported me and my brothers to Earth with our eggs and the wizards were practically breathing down our necks, he was pretty calm. He'll be back in a second, but until then, do you want to talk about Nora?"

Kieran's muscles stiffened, and he clenched the arm of the chair. "What do you mean?"

Julian smiled. "It's all right. We don't have to. But you know I'm always here for you, whatever you might need. I know your life has changed a lot, and I know I'm at least partially to blame for that. I've come to think of you and your cousins as merely an extension of my family. Lucia is over here at least once a week, and she and my wife, Naomi, have really bonded. I guess I'm just saying that I'm glad to have you here."

"Thank you." Kieran didn't know what else to say, but he was glad to know he wasn't alone.

The library door opened, and Varhan slipped inside. A sheen of sweat covered his wide forehead, and he held a battered book in his hand. The leather cover had been scuffed around the edges and gouged across the front. "I'm sorry to have left so suddenly. I wanted to get some of my notes."

"I thought you kept all your books in here." Kieran had seen the wizard in Julian's library numerous times, poring through his scrolls and books.

Varhan bobbed his head. "I did, at first. But then I realized it might be smarter to spread them out a little, just in case something happens."

Kieran didn't bother asking him what that something might be. He wasn't sure he wanted to know.

"I kept a bit of a diary, I guess you could call it, when I was still on Charok. Wizards are trained to do a lot of writing so that we might keep track of our magical progress, but I tend to keep a log of just about everything. When the wizards united under the evil great Tazarre, I wrote more than ever." He set the volume down on the coffee table and sat in front of it, staring at the battered book. "The funny thing is, I don't even need to open it to know what's inside. I remember every word I scrawled in there, and many of them were under great duress."

He pulled in a deep breath before he continued. "Things were already getting a little unsettled in our world, and when the majority of wizards united under Tazarre, it calmed down a lot. We finally had a leader. But he didn't show his true side, at first. He was very charming, and he could make anyone believe he was the most powerful wizard who ever existed. It was very much like politics are here, where people say what the voters want to hear until they get the position they want. Anyway, he soon started recruiting disciples into his inner circle. Their meetings were private, and the wizards were under strict rules not to divulge what was happening there, but I was invited to one of them."

Kieran held his breath as he listened. He'd come to trust Varhan, far more than he ever thought he'd trust a wizard. He'd never thought of how things must've been for anyone but the dragons, because that was what he'd lived through. But now, he could easily envision what it must've been like for Varhan, no doubt trembling under his robes, to go to Tazarre's castle where he'd been summoned.

"I didn't really want to go. I already had my doubts about Tazarre's ability to lead, even though there was no denying we needed some sort of structure. Still, you can't turn down an order. I heard all sorts of horrible things the wizards wanted to do, and of course, most of the actions they wanted to take were against the dragons. I had no choice but to go along with them and agree. I was outnumbered by a long shot, and there were some sorcerers there far more powerful than I. Now, I feel horrible about sitting down and listening, smiling and nodding at all the appropriate places, when I should've stood up and argued against them."

"That wouldn't have done you any good," Julian reminded his friend gently. "They would have killed you on the spot, and then you never would've been around to help the rest of us."

"That's true enough, I suppose, but I'm afraid it doesn't make me feel much better. I wrote extensively in that book as I tried to decide what to do. Every tiny detail I heard went in there. Most of it was about how Tazarre knew he wouldn't survive the casting of the Great Curse. He wanted his disciples, as they were, to continue on in his name. That's why the dragons continued to be hunted, even after the Great Curse was cast."

"Tell me, do you think one of these disciples could be here on Earth looking for dragons?" Kieran's stomach had turned to soup. He didn't like hearing his suspicions confirmed, and it meant he needed to get to Nora, no matter what.

"It's a possibility we have to keep in mind, but I don't know anything for certain." Varhan licked his lips. "One thing I do know is that there were reports running through the wizard communities saying someone had seen the royal eggs being carried off from the caves."

"I saw him myself, I believe," Julian volunteered. "It wasn't an easy task getting to such a prominent place without being seen, but we thought we were doing well. At one point, I swore someone was watching us from the woods as we came down out of the mountains. I saw a pair of yellow eyes. By the time I raised the alarm, they were gone. Someone knows the Queen's eggs were taken from the cave, and depending on how far he followed us, he could have potentially seen us carrying them through Varhan's portal as well."

Kieran didn't need Julian to continue his narrative to know what that meant. There was a possibility that the same person who'd seen Julian and his friends take the eggs also knew they'd been taken away from Charok. This was bad. "What do we do about it?" Kieran thought a good solution might be ripping Allison's head from her shoulders, but if she truly was a wizard, she might have information they needed.

"If you can, just be patient for now. What you've told us gives us a more definitive direction in our research. Don't engage her until we know what we're up against. We'll contact you as soon as we have something."

It wasn't the answer Kieran wanted. Really, they'd only confirmed his fears. He bid them goodnight and headed out the door, his shoulders feeling even heavier than they had earlier in the day.

Kieran drove back into town, wishing he was on the wing instead of behind the wheel. This metal thing around him wasn't a convenient way of getting around so much as it was a cage. He slid the windows down and tuned his instincts to the night air around him. It was late enough that Nora wouldn't have been on campus anymore, but it was a good place to start. It seemed he was driving aimlessly, but he knew he was getting closer. Scales undulated down his back and on his legs as he got closer, his dragon getting harder and harder to keep quiet. She wasn't far.

He pulled into the parking lot of a taqueria. The scent of grilled meat and vegetables filtered out the building, increasing in intensity every time someone opened a door, but Kieran sensed something else in the air. Nora. She was there. And so was Allison.

Getting out of the car, Kieran leaned against the warm hood and watched. A nearby tree blocked the glow of the streetlamp from reaching him, keeping him hidden in the dark. The restaurant was a busy one. It wasn't the sort of place to have a knock-down, drag-out fight with someone who might have been a wizard. Julian and Varhan hadn't wanted him to do that, anyway. He had to trust them, even though he desperately wanted to act and make sure Nora was safe.

A few minutes later, the front door swung open. Three women stepped out, laughing and talking to each other as though they'd been friends their entire life. The first was Holly, whom Kieran had seen with Nora numerous times. Next came Allison, the stench of her thick in the air as she whispered and giggled.

Nora was last. Even from a distance, Kieran felt an instant surge inside his body toward her. Her laughter rang out through the night, calling to him. His dragon remembered the way it felt to extend his wings and fly out over the lake with her, the deep connection they made and how much he didn't want to let go of it. He studied her beautiful hair, bouncing around her shoulders as she came down the steps at the front of the restaurant, and the bright sparkle in her eyes as she laughed with her friends.

Except one of those women really wasn't her friend, and she had no idea.

Kieran watched as Holly and Allison went to their own vehicles off to the left. Nora headed toward his right, where her car was parked several rows closer to the building than his own. She unlocked and opened the door before completely freezing for a second. Kieran's skin tingled as he watched her slowly turn and look straight at him. He knew no one could really see him, and yet he felt her gaze penetrating the darkness and burning against him.

Nora marched through the rows of cars until she stood right in front of him, waves of anger preceding her. "What are you doing out here?"

"We need to talk."

"You're damn right we do! You were just going to let me get in my car without saying a word. If there's something you need, you could've sent me a text, or called, or even come into the damn restaurant. I don't like the way this looks, Kieran." She was absolutely sexy, even when stark raving mad at him. A strawberry patch of color had risen in her cheeks, and she moved with a ferocious grace that he knew came from the dragon side of her.

"Yes, you're right. But for the moment, I just needed to be sure you were safe. We can't really talk about it here, anyway." He glanced up to see the car Allison had gotten into was exiting on the other side of the parking lot. The major risk was gone, but this still wasn't the sort of thing to discuss out in the open.

"Oh, but we're going to," Nora warned. "I want to know why you're here and what you think you need to protect me from. Right now."

His shoulders sagged. She was incredible, but could also be incredibly difficult at times. Kieran wanted to reach out and put his hands on her hips, pulling her close and keeping her safe from the world, but that was only going to piss her off more. "I don't want to go into any details, but I have good reason to believe danger is very close by. Someone isn't who they say they are, and—"

"Don't you dare tell me this is about Allison again." She stepped forward, their bodies only inches away, but it wasn't the same kind of closeness he was craving from her. Nora's voice was low and threatening as she looked up into his face. "I've already told you I didn't want to hear about that, and then I was stupid enough to think we could get past it."

"Are you going to tell me you didn't have a good time?" he challenged. He knew she had. There was no mistaking it, not with the way she'd nestled into his embrace when they'd lain on the lake shore together under the stars. That night, they'd become so much closer in both their forms; close enough that he'd known for sure they were meant to be together. He nearly told her that, the words clinging thickly to the back of his tongue, but he couldn't quite launch them forward into the air.

"It doesn't matter if this is how you're going to be. God, dragons are no different than humans, apparently!" She retreated a few steps, folding her arms in front of her chest. The tree didn't hide her now as it did him, the patchy light from the streetlamp falling across her face.

"What's that supposed to mean?" There was something deep inside him that didn't like being compared to a human. Plenty of them were decent enough people, but he wasn't one of them and neither was Nora.

"Just because you're a man, you think you have to come sweeping in to protect me constantly. I guess I need to remind you that I've been on this planet a long time, and I've been able to take care of myself. I don't need your help or your paranoid concerns about danger."

"It's not paranoia. I know what I'm talking about, Nora, and you've got to listen to me." He reached out for her, desperate for her to hear him out. "Let's just go someplace private and—"

"No!" She took another step back, her face fierce as she jerked her elbow out of his reach. "I'm not going anywhere with you. I don't want to see you, and I don't want to talk to you. Just get the hell away from me."

"Nora." He followed her as she stalked back to her car. "At least let me make sure you get back to your place safely."

She whirled on him. "What, so you can sit outside and watch my windows? I don't think so, Kieran. Maybe *you're* the person I need to be protected from. I don't want to hear from you again; whatever was happening between us is over." Her words bit through the air and straight to his heart.

She had no idea what she did to him as she stormed off, got in her car, and drove away. Kieran felt part of himself die, and he didn't know what he could possibly do about it. There was a very real danger in the area, but she wouldn't listen. Even if she didn't want to be around him, at the very least, he wanted to keep her safe. But she hadn't been wrong with that last statement. If he'd followed her home, he'd prob-ably have stayed right outside until morning or even longer, sacrificing whatever sleep and comfort he needed to just to know she was all right. All he could do now was go home.

# 9

Nora tapped her pen against the black lab table irritably. She'd hardly gotten any sleep the night before, something that was becoming a more common occurrence for her. There was always a bounty of cheap coffee around, but she'd had too much of it. Her veins shook from the overdose of caffeine, and her mind churned with anger.

"Nora? You okay?"

She blinked and looked up to find Allison standing in front of her, a concerned look on her pale face. "Yeah, why?"

"You look like you're about to murder someone." Allison sat down on the opposite side of the lab table. "I just came up to see if you could help me figure out what I need to do to get an experiment ready for Dr. Burke, but I'll just figure it out."

"No, no. I can help." She reached for the paper Allison had brought with her. "Let me see what she's got going on today."

"Did you have too much to drink last night?" her friend asked. "Those margaritas were pretty strong, and I know we were all feeling pretty good when we left."

"It's not that." The pounding in her brain would've been more pleasant if she could explain it away with a hangover, but Nora really hadn't had much to drink at all. She was always careful about those things if she knew she'd be driving home later. "It's Kieran."

"Oh, that's your boyfriend, right?"

Nora sighed. "I wouldn't call him that. Definitely not now, and maybe not before, either. We were just getting to know each other. I knew he had some flaws; we all do. But I thought it was something we could work through because we have so many other things in common. After last night, I think it's just impossible."

Allison took the lab sheet out of Nora's hands and set it aside. "Let's talk about it. You can get it all off your chest, and you'll probably feel way better."

Checking the clock on the wall, Nora decided they had time. Dr. Burke's class wouldn't start for another hour or so, and she'd already done most of her own work for the day after coming in early. Nora liked to be busy, and that was even more important when she was agitated. "When we left the restaurant last night, I found Kieran at the back of the parking lot, watching me."

"That sounds super creepy. Does he think you're cheating on him or something?"

"No." While the invitation to talk about her relationship troubles was nice, there were so many factors that Allison just couldn't know about. Nora liked her on a lot of levels, but this was more complicated than basic human stuff. "He's just really overprotective. I don't know exactly why he was there except that he thought I was in some sort of danger. Like I can't walk through a parking lot by myself. It just makes me so angry that he thinks he can march around like some big body guard and keep me in a bubble. I told him I didn't want to see him again." They had been her own words, and yet somehow, they still hurt so badly.

Allison nodded. "How long have you guys been dating?"

"Hardly any time at all, really. We already knew each other before, but not well. It's just been something that's developed over the last week or two." That strange, magnetic pull had increased significantly when he'd saved her from Ted, and their date at the lake had confirmed it in her mind. But his antics at the restaurant the night before had changed everything.

"Men are terrible," Allison said with a roll of her eyes. "If he's going to be that much of an asshole that quickly, then maybe it's a good thing you got rid of him. You don't need that in your life. Oh, I know!" Her eyes brightened as she leaned forward. "You should get revenge."

"Revenge?" This was unexpected. Allison had seemed so sweet, innocent, and lonely, and now she was calling for revenge on something that amounted to a conflict of personalities. "Don't get me wrong; I'm angry with him. But I don't think that's necessary. I mean, he works on campus, so I'm still going to have to see him every now and then." That thought bothered her the most. If it'd been so hard to pass him in the hallway before, it was only going to get worse.

"All the more reason to take action!" Allison enthused. "Embarrass him, or tell some sort of secret that'll get him fired. You probably know a lot about him if you guys had been spending time together. Did he tell you anything dark and deep, something that would make his boss wonder if he's actually qualified to work here?"

"I do know a lot about him," Nora conceded, "but he doesn't deserve that. I think he's a nice guy at heart; we just don't get along." Tears burned the backs of her eyes at that thought, because she was both sad and angry. It wasn't fair. Kieran was wonderful on so many levels, and no human man would ever understand what she truly was. But she couldn't live with someone constantly trying to squash her under his thumb. She'd grown up so free and self-sufficient; she couldn't imagine being fettered by Kieran's instincts like that.

"Aw, don't get upset. It'll be okay." Allison reached across the table and patted Nora's hand. "You've still got me and Holly. She's wonderful. And then you said you've got a big family, right?"

"Yeah." She had to smile at that. She would always have someone around who understood her. The time with Kieran had made her appreciate her heritage a bit more, and maybe she could use this opportunity to bond with them. "That's true. It's not like I have any real reason to be lonely."

"Of course not. Tell me about them."

"Who?"

"Your family, silly," Allison laughed. "I'd love to know what it's like to be a part of that."

"It's crazy, honestly. I know we're all related, and we're so much alike in more ways than I can count, but our differences make for some really interesting get-togethers. My parents and all my aunts and uncles tend to be kind of old-fashioned, and the rest of us are always trying to pull away from their traditions. But in the end, we still love each other."

"What kind of traditions do you have? I never really got to experience anything like that. I went through so many foster homes I lost count, and every single one was a bit different."

Her already painful heart hurt a little more in sympathy for Allison, but she couldn't explain the Charokian holiday, Zimryr, or how her father had brought her over from Charok. Her mother being a witch didn't exactly make things simple, either. "It's kind of complicated. They do a lot of things from before they ever came to this country."

"I understand. Do you guys get together very often? I know Dr. Burke said she almost never sees her family. Seems like that would be a waste if you had so many people around you to love you." She fiddled with the corner of the lab sheet, looking dreamy.

"I definitely make sure I see my cousins on a regular basis, which I think I'd already mentioned to you. Getting everyone together is a little more complicated, working around everyone's schedules and such. I'd say it's a little more random, unless there's a holiday or something." Nora's family had fallen into a similar routine as many of the humans around them. They didn't have much of a reason to celebrate the same holidays as Earthlings, but they still often ended up off work on those days and would at least gather for a meal.

"It sounds just wonderful. Do you guys go out or do you all go to someone's house? It seems like it'd be hard to fit a bunch of people all in one home."

"Not really. Two of my uncles have pretty big places. We're usually either at my Uncle Holden's or my Uncle Julian's."

"Oh, yeah? Where do they live?"

Discussing her own family had been a nice distraction from all the business about Kieran, and Nora could understand why an orphan like Allison would be interested, but she didn't want to talk about herself anymore. They'd already spent too much work time wallowing in her misery, and no matter what was happening in her personal life, she needed to keep up with her job. "I think we need to get Dr. Burke's lab set up. C'mon. I'll help you."

Once again, she threw herself into her work as she checked off all the instruments on the lab sheet and made sure each station was fully stocked with supplies. Nora was hardly even paying attention to Allison, so focused on getting the job done that she wasn't really training her at all. She just needed something to center on besides her personal life.

Even so, thoughts of Kieran constantly loomed. Every time a figure went past the lab door, she glanced up in anticipation of seeing him there, even though she hadn't seen him at McKnelly that day. Why did he have to be such a stubborn dragon? And if they weren't going to work out, then why couldn't she just let it go? Sure, they'd had an amazing night. There was definitely a very heavy attraction between them, something that went beyond the physical. But that didn't mean they were good for each other, and it didn't have to be this hard.

"You sure you're gonna be all right?" Allison asked when Nora finally turned to leave Dr. Burke's lab. "We can meet up for coffee or something this afternoon if you'd like."

The pit of Nora's stomach felt like a ball of lead, spinning faster and faster on its axis. She didn't know if she was nervous or upset or what, but she didn't like it. "Thanks. I'll keep that in mind. Right now I think I just want to be alone."

# 10

---

AUNT LUCIA'S HOUSE WAS ALWAYS SO WARM AND INVITING. DESPITE THE looming autumn weather that was growing cooler by the day, it felt like spring when Kieran stepped into her living room. That might've been because of the dozens of live plants she kept all over the house or the gentle chirping of the little bird in a massive cage in the corner. Or maybe it was because his aunt had always made him feel like home, no matter where they were.

"Oh, Kieran! I'm so glad you're here. It seems as though I've hardly seen you over the last few months, and you sounded so upset over the phone." Lucia put her cool hands on his cheeks and smiled, her dark eyes affectionate. Her thin face had earned a new wrinkle or two, and she'd changed her hair, but she was still the most familiar thing in Kieran's life. "I knew it had to be something bad if you actually wanted to see me."

"Why do you say that?" Kieran sat on the white couch and watched as Lucia ran through her routine of checking all the clocks in the room. Just as he fulfilled his ancestral role of border guard by working at the university, she satisfied her calling as a timekeeper by collecting clocks. Julian had told her she could easily get a job at a clock shop or a position as a personal assistant, but she'd chosen to retire instead.

Lucia turned away from an old cuckoo clock to smile at him. "All you boys are so busy now. You don't really need me anymore. Archard is enjoying married life, and Callan is doing the complete opposite. You have your work, which I know is important to you. Don't get me wrong; I understand. But I spent so much time protecting you as I raised you, and then the four of us were all the family we had. Sometimes I miss that time we spent together."

"I'm sorry. I didn't even realize." Kieran felt guilty for not thinking about what she might need and made a mental note to visit more often.

"Don't apologize, not at all. I'll admit I'm very much enjoying my 'retirement,' I guess you'd call it. Naomi has become a very close friend of mine, and I'm getting to know her sisters-in-law as well. They've taken me in as one of their own, and I had no idea how pleasant it was to have other women around me. I'm very lucky to be here." She sat down across from him and poured tea from a silver pot she'd placed on the coffee table, handing a cup to him. "Now, tell me what's the matter."

The teacup was minute in Kieran's hand, and he felt he could break it if he so much as sneezed. "It's Nora."

"Xander and Summer's daughter? The one that works at the university with you?"

"That's the one." He took a small sip of tea and set the cup down to tell his tale. Lucia listened attentively as he explained the way he felt around her, his involvement in her argument with Ted, and the less intimate details of their date. As much as he hated to, Kieran also explained what happened at the Mexican restaurant. "She's so angry with me, but I'm just trying to keep her safe. She won't even let me tell her about the danger. If there's truly a wizard in our midst, then we can't just ignore that."

Lucia's narrow lips tightened, whitening around the edges. "That's a problem, indeed."

"The worst part is that I don't even care what happens with Allison. I just want things to be right with Nora again." It was true, even though he knew it was wrong. Kieran should be focused on the bigger picture, but he couldn't get Nora off his mind. He stared at the tiny slosh of tea left in the cup, frustrated.

"Kieran, do you think the two of you are fated?" Lucia asked quietly.

"Yes," he admitted, looking up. "Or at least I did. But I'd think two people who are meant to be together shouldn't have this many problems. When things are good, they're amazing, and then they change in an instant."

Lucia leaned across the table and rested her fingertips on his arm. "Kieran, dear, relationships aren't always easy. It doesn't matter what planet you're on, and it doesn't even matter if you're fated. You both have to work at it. Be patient with her. She's probably suffering the same way you are, and the two of you will find yourselves on common ground once again."

"I hope you're right. I also hope it doesn't wait until we're battling her new friend. I think if I had some way to prove to her that she was in danger, then she might listen. But I think by the time I have the evidence I need, it'll be too late." His shoulder muscles tensed just thinking of Nora being in danger. If she were a mere human, he could do something completely bullheaded like grab her in his arms and fly away to some remote island. She wouldn't be able to stop him. She would probably also hate him for the rest of her life.

"Maybe there is." Lucia rose and went to a side table, picking up her cell phone. "Strange little devices. I didn't think I needed one at all, but Callan insisted I get one. He said it was for emergencies, but really I think he just wanted to send me these strange little pictures when he gets bored."

"I don't want Callan involved in this, or anyone else for that matter. Julian and Varhan didn't want the other dragons to know about the possibility of a wizard just yet."

"That's all right. It's Varhan I'm talking to right now." She smiled as she pecked away at the touchscreen.

Kieran paused, watching her to see if this was a joke. "Are we talking about the same person?"

"Of course." Lucia tapped the screen again and nodded, putting it in her purse. "It's all set. We're going over there right now."

"But I've already talked to them about this. They said they'd let me know when they found something." Kieran got off the couch, confused.

"Your dear old auntie has a few tricks up her sleeve. I made a simple suggestion based on some things I learned on Charok, and he's working it all up right now. I'll drive, since I need the practice. By the time we get over there, he should have it all done. Come on." She led the way through the kitchen to her garage.

"You're not making any sense. I always thought Callan was the annoying one, but maybe he gets it from you." Still, he stomped after her.

Lucia gave him a pat on the cheek and a mysterious smile. "I love you, Kieran, but you're always so focused on the bigger picture, you forget to acknowledge the details. Sometimes it's a good thing, but right now, it's not helping you. Do you remember those little stones I used to hang in the trees when you were a dragonling?"

"Of course. You said they had a protective magic to them, and no one could see us as long as we were inside that ring of stones." Kieran clearly remembered this from his childhood. Lucia had used the tiny rocks less and less as the boys got older, but when he was young and afraid, they'd been a comfort.

She got behind the wheel and adjusted her mirrors, sitting primly and properly in the seat. "They did have a magic to them, but not in the way I explained it to you. There was nothing I could do to keep someone from finding us, but those stones were supposed to help break a spell cast by a wizard. If nothing else, I thought they might give me little bit of notice if someone was coming."

Her car was much smaller than his own, and as Kieran struggled to fit his hulking frame comfortably in the car, he wished he'd just offered to follow her in his own vehicle. "I don't see how any of this is going to help. We're not on Charok, and I'd guess they don't have the same types of stones here as we did back then."

Lucia pulled out onto the road and zoomed into traffic smoothly. "That's somewhat true. There are many things we had back there that we don't have here. But I just happened to have a few things on me as we came through the portal. The real point here is that we might be able to help you determine whether or not Nora is truly at risk. Then you'll know what you should do, or at least have a better idea."

"All right."

They drove on in silence for a while, Kieran brooding about Nora and Lucia simply looking pleased to be out of the house. When they arrived at Julian and Naomi's, it was once again Varhan who met them at the door. "Come in! Lucia, I have to tell you you're a complete genius! I immediately found the stone you told me about."

"I hope you understand why I left it here," she said genially. "You seemed so eager to help us when we came to Earth, but I'd been wearing that pendant for so many years. I hated to just put it away or get rid of it, and at first, I didn't know who to trust. I'd forgotten I'd hidden it under the floorboard until I spoke to Kieran."

"What?" Kieran looked from one to the other, feeling completely lost.

She laid her hand on his arm. "I kept one of those stones and made it into a necklace. It made me feel better, if nothing else. When we were pulled through the portal to Earth, I wasn't sure what to do with it. At that time, I didn't yet know if Varhan and the others could be trusted. I found a loose floorboard near the door of my bedroom, and I tucked the stone under there. It was almost like keeping them tied to the trees just like we used to do. Of course, it turns out I didn't really need it, but now you do. That's just as good."

Varhan pulled a very plain-looking rock from his pocket, tied to a coarse string. He grinned as he watched it spin in the air. "I was trying to make something from scratch, but this is so much better! It required only a small modification, a quick spell far easier than what I thought I was going to have to do. It should work like a charm, literally!" He beamed at the newcomers, obviously very proud of his work.

"What exactly is it going to do?" Kieran asked skeptically.

The wizard held it out toward him, insisting that he take it. "The stone's energy interferes with most magic. I had to be a bit careful with it myself, to be honest with you. Wear it around your neck. In most cases, it'll disable the spells of any person standing within a few feet of you."

"Is that why the stone was able to be carried through the portal, then?" Kieran asked. "Because you weren't standing near us when we were caught up in it?"

"Precisely, my boy."

"I see. So, if I get close enough to Allison, I'll be protected if she is, in fact, a wizard and tries to cast a spell." He accepted the talisman, feeling the vibrations of it against his palm.

"That's the idea."

The little gray rock looked so innocent, but Kieran was afraid of the real damage it would do. "I have a feeling Nora isn't going to be very happy about this. She wanted me to leave her and Allison alone, but I'll have to get close to them to test this out." He closed his palm around it, feeling torn. He'd already upset Nora enough as it was, but in order to keep her safe, he needed to know if his intuition was right.

"Kieran, you come from a very long line of border guards. It's in your blood to protect, to make sure those around you are safe. It's not reasonable to expect you to just toss that aside and deny your heritage. We don't work like that. Nora is already upset with you, so if this turns out to be a bust, then you've lost nothing. If Allison truly is a threat, then she'll find a way to forgive you."

"I hope so." The stone was cool in his heated hand. It was so small, yet it held the power to completely change his life.

"I know so, dear. And what would happen if you didn't do anything?"

He knew he didn't really need to answer. Lucia was just trying to get him to think, like she always did. If there was no threat, and he did nothing, then Nora would simply fade from his life. If she was in danger and he did nothing to save her, then he would never forgive himself. It was a risk he needed to take.

"YOU READY?"

Nora waited patiently as Allison fiddled with the camera. She knew no one would be as good as Holly, but since her bestie had been booked for a photo session, she had to make do. The video with Kieran had come out remarkably well, but Nora didn't like the way she radiated light and energy every time she looked at the camera during that session. It made her realize just how much she felt for him—no, how much she used to feel. There was nothing between them anymore. There couldn't be.

"Okay, I think I've got it. Go."

"Hey everyone! I hope you've been taking advantage of all this beautiful weather and getting outside. I've gotten a lot of feedback on one of my previous identification videos as well as the most recent one about chicory. I'm so grateful to all my viewers, and I want to keep you happy, so I'm proud to announce that today's video will be all about identifying dangerous plants. And, for the rest of you, there will be an upcoming video about edible plants! I'm super excited about both of these, and I hope you are, too."

Nora took a few careful steps off the trail and knelt next to a tiny plant, waiting for Allison to get the camera safely onto the tripod. It seemed like a good precaution to make sure she had good footage for the steady shots, since her helper was inexperienced. "We're going to start with a rather infamous plant. I know most of you probably already know exactly what this is, but a quick review never hurt anyone. Poison ivy is very common, and you may even find it in your back yard. The rash from these suckers is terrible, although there are some people who seem to be resistant. If you've had the rash before, you definitely know what I'm talking about!" She lost herself in her work once again as she described the plant and where it liked to grow. In this segment of the national forest that butted up behind the university, there were plenty of examples of it. Nora told her viewers not only how to identify it, but how to keep themselves safe from it when walking in the woods. She also allowed herself a little bit of time to gush about how gorgeous the leaves were in the fall, when they took on the same stunning colors as the leaves of deciduous trees. "Now, let's head a little further down the path and see if we can find some poison oak."

Allison followed along behind her. "Do you want me to keep recording this part?"

"Yeah, just keep it rolling. I can edit out anything unusable, and I'd rather we not miss anything that might happen. One time when I was out here with Holly, we stumbled on a flock of crazy wild turkeys. It wasn't plant-related, but it was fun, and that video got a lot of views."

"Doesn't seem like you'd come across much of anything out here. We're in the middle of nowhere."

Nora thought she detected a bit of nervousness in Allison's voice. With her back to her friend, she smiled. "We are in a way, but we're still on the trails that Department of Natural Resources has established. I guess I've come to like being out here all alone. But don't worry. We're perfectly safe."

She had to wonder if she really was. Nora knew what she could do if she shifted, even though she almost never chose to do so. She didn't worry about carrying any kind of protection with her when she went in the woods either, and maybe for most young women, that would've been a mistake. If nothing else, her time with Kieran had reminded her that there was much more she was capable of if the need arose.

"Oh, here we go." She once again stepped off the trail, turning to smile at the camera as she pointed to some poison oak. "I knew we'd find some pretty quickly, but that's exactly why it's so important to be able to identify it. These plants are prolific, and it's dangerous to cut them down or burn them. The best thing you can do is make sure you know what it looks like so you can avoid it."

"Hey, what's that?" Allison turned to look down the trail behind them.

Nora was about to tell her not to worry about forest noises and focus on the camera, which was currently pointing up into the trees. But she picked up a large form heading toward them down the trail, and the video was no longer her priority. Nora got to her feet, feeling a flush of anger in her face despite the cool morning. "What are you doing here?"

Kieran was heading quickly down the path toward them, his gaze focused on her, but shifting occasionally to Allison. "I need to talk to you."

"Um..." Allison still held the camera uncertainly. "What do you want me to do? Do I keep rolling?"

"No. Just set it on the tripod, and we can finish up the video in a minute." Nora stepped back onto the path, her hands on her hips. It'd been a beautiful morning, and she'd been looking forward to slipping back into the normal routine of her life. She needed her time, yet there was Kieran to suffocate her all over again. "How the hell did you even know how to find me?" The only people who knew she was there were Holly and Allison.

Kieran's sapphire eyes burned into hers. "I have my ways." He stepped to the side as though he were trying to get to Allison.

Nora quickly shot out her hand and put it on his chest, surprised by the stab of electricity that shot into her palm as soon as she touched his skin. It shivered through her body, touching all the most sensitive points, before it finally dissipated. She knew exactly what he meant when he said he had his ways of finding her. Kieran hadn't needed to interrogate Holly or stalk Nora to find out where she went. It was probably the same way he'd found her at the Mexican restaurant that night, and it was the same way Nora knew when he was anywhere nearby at the university. They could sense each other, and she should've realized he was coming long before he appeared. She pulled her hand away just as quickly as she'd reached out with it. This wasn't the time to think about all that. "I told you I don't want to see you or talk to you. You should just go away and mind your own business."

"You *are* my business," he argued, energy and tension rolling off his massive form. "I know you think I'm being ridiculous, but you'll understand it all soon enough. I just need to speak with you alone for a moment."

Nora could swear he was about to shift right then and there. She didn't see any telltale scales or fangs, but they were on their way. Her own dragon reacted, twisting inside her, demanding to be let out. "Whatever you have to say to me, you can say in front of Allison." It would only piss him off more, but she was all right with that. He needed to be pissed off. He needed to understand just how frustrating he was. It was vindictive and petty, but Nora was beyond caring.

"All right. If that's the way you want it, then that's how it'll be. But just remember that this is exactly what you asked me to do." Kieran glared at Allison again, who was standing just behind Nora on the path. "I know you don't believe me, but there's a good chance you're in danger. Maybe all of us." He paused.

In that moment, Nora almost stopped him. She could see in his eyes that he was about to say something that would reveal their secret. It wasn't easy for him, even only having been on Earth for a few months. Nora knew the right thing to do was probably to agree to talk to him, to bring him further down the trail where they could be alone. But that only increased the chances of his charms working on her once again, making her think they could be something more than what they were.

Kieran licked his lips. "Your friend here isn't who she says she is."

There it was. He was avoiding what he really wanted to say, she could tell, but he was still involving Allison. "Seriously? You're going to accuse her of this again?"

"Wait, what's this all about?" Allison asked, looking from Nora to Kieran and back again. "What do I have to do with any of this?"

Nora didn't answer her. That explanation could wait until later. She kept her focus on Kieran. "What do you want? Do I have to go raid the administrative building and show you her birth certificate? You think just because she's new around here that she's a problem? You're so paranoid, Kieran. You're letting your instincts take over instead of just being a logical...person." She stumbled a little on that last word, almost saying "human" instead. But he definitely wasn't that, and neither was she.

"I'm not paranoid, and I'm not the only one who thinks this is a big deal. I've talked to Lucia, and Julian, and Varhan. They agree with me."

The muscles in her neck tightened as Nora clamped her lips

together and let a steamy breath out through her nose that threatened to be fire. "You've been talking to everyone else but me about this?"

"What choice did you leave me, Nora? You wouldn't listen. You still won't, but ignoring the danger doesn't make it go away. I can even prove it to you if you'll just give me a chance."

"Um, I don't know exactly what's going on here, but I don't want to get in the middle of whatever you want to call this." Allison gestured helplessly between the two. "I can just head back to the car, Nora, and you can meet me there whenever you're ready."

"Absolutely not!" Nora took a step toward her friend and wrapped her arm around Allison's. "Kieran's being an idiot, and it has nothing to do with you. Let's go finish our video. I'm done here." She turned and marched back toward the camera with the intent to snatch it up and head deeper into the forest.

"I can't let you go." Kieran grabbed her from behind, easily picking her up off her feet.

"Hey!" Nora felt his massive hands on her waist. Startled, she let go of Allison to fend off Kieran, but there was little she could do. He was so much stronger than she was.

Kieran set her down behind him and reached down his shirt. He whisked out something that looked like a rock on a string, holding it out in front of him toward Allison as she charged at him.

Nora pummeled his back with her fists. "What the hell are you doing, you crazy bastard?" But she could see exactly what was happening, even though it didn't make sense. Allison stood there on the trail, or rather, not Allison. Her image flickered like an old movie, the lab assistant she knew replaced for a moment by something altogether different.

It was like something out of a nightmare. The creature was dressed just as Allison was, in jeans and a t-shirt, but it definitely wasn't her. Its hunched back and claw-like fingers were humanoid, but its bulging yellow eyes were something different. The hair on its head was long and stringy, missing in massive clumps. The next second, it was back to looking like Allison again.

"What the fuck...?" Nora stopped her ineffective pounding of Kieran and took a step back.

Allison didn't seem aware of what was happening at first until Kieran thrust the amulet toward her once again. She cringed back, hissing. Her form flickered again, happening so quickly, Nora couldn't quite believe her eyes.

"I know what you are," Kieran growled.

Nora froze, rooted to the spot, watching in horror as the repulsive fiend shapeshifted back to Allison's form and began to attack Kieran.

# 12

Kieran had all the proof he needed. The image had been a quick one, gone as soon as it'd come, but it was enough to confirm the truth about Allison. He hoped Nora had seen it, but they could discuss things later. It was time for action.

He dropped the amulet as he unleashed his reptilian form, his tail lashing against a nearby tree. Kieran had never been so happy to let his fangs and claws come forward, knowing they'd be useful. His wings were too big to function as well as they should've under the branches, but he barely noticed the leaves brushing against him. His entire focus was on destroying Allison, or whatever the wizard's name actually was.

The wizard scrambled backwards, and for a moment, Kieran thought this was going to be easy. He was far bigger and faster, and it would only take one crunch of his jaws to snap his neck in half. Saliva dripped from his razor-sharp teeth as he lunged forward.

But the wizard turned and clapped his hands together. He drew them apart slowly, sending a wave through the air that pushed Kieran back with a surprising force. "That's one thing you dragons have yet to learn," the wizard teased. "You rely on nothing but your strength. But maybe that's because you don't have any brains to use anyway!" He cackled at his own humor before forcing another wave through the air.

Kieran pinned his wings against his body as a ball of fire built up easily in his chest, the warmth of it pleasant as he let it fly forward.

The flames engulfed the wizard for a moment before they took on a spherical shape and then receded; he was using a shield.

The wizard took a bold step forward before slashing the air with his fingers and sending a ball of energy right back at the dragon. "You're pathetic! You've gotten so caught up in how to fit in on Earth that you couldn't even come right out and tell her who I was! This is why the dragons have fallen, and why they deserved it! Tazarre shall live on forever through *me!*"

Kieran felt a shiver down his back at the mention of the evil wizard who'd cast the Great Curse, killing the majority of the dragons on Charok. It was a name of nightmares, a name he'd grown up trying to avoid. The wizard's magic bounced off his tough hide and into the woods, sending a small plume of smoke up from some dry leaves on the ground. "I'll kill you, but first, I'll hold you down and pull each of your appendages off one by one. You'll regret ever coming here!" Kieran slashed out with his claws, the sharp points easily splitting the papery skin of the wizard.

"Who are you?" Nora shouted from behind him. "Why are you here?"

Kieran didn't care if the wizard answered or not. He was clearly not Allison and clearly no friend to Nora, and that was all that mattered to him. His original thoughts of holding the wizard hostage to ask him questions were no longer valid. This thing would die, and he would be the one to kill it.

"I am Rhebin, disciple of Tazarre!" The wizard's fingers seemed to be permanently disfigured into a clawed shape, and now Kieran could see why. He held his hands together, the air between them crackling until he built up another ball of energy. This one was much larger, and it swirled with every color of the rainbow.

Kieran steadied himself on the path, bracing himself for the pain. It could hurt, and that was fine. He would get past it and kill the gruesome imp. But when the blast came, it was almost more than he could stand. Every nerve in his body was on fire, yet his muscles were as cold and stiff as ice. He stood motionless on the path, no part of his body cooperating with him. Panic enveloped his chest as Kieran realized what kind of trouble he was in. Not only was he doomed, but that meant Nora would be as well.

Rhebin stepped forward, closing the cap between himself and the silver dragon until he could look Kieran directly in the eye. "You tried to keep her safe, but in the end, you should've known there was nothing you could do. We've killed almost all the dragons on Charok, and now it's my turn to make sure all the dragons on Earth die as well."

"How did you even find us?" Nora's voice, coming from behind Kieran, made him cringe. He wanted to shout at her to run, to get the hell out of there and find help, but he couldn't move. The wizard's magic was strong, and the stone amulet was gone.

The wizard answered her question, but his yellow eyes continued to look straight into Kieran's. "You can thank this dear friend of yours for that. I saw the royal eggs as they were smuggled off the planet all those years ago. There was little I could do at the time, being a young wizard and not having yet built up the skills necessary for such a task. I made it my life's work to hunt down each and every imperial descendent and destroy them in Tazarre's name; to carry on the legacy he worked so hard to build."

"He's nothing but a murderer!" Nora yelled.

Rhebin ignored her. "I thought for the longest time that I'd never be able to complete my quest, as I had no way off of Charok. But one day, when I spotted *this* dragon and his family on Charok, just as I prepared to slay them in the night, a portal to Earth opened and sucked them up, and I was transported along with them." He spoke now to Kieran directly, his yellow eyes only an inch from Kieran's. He was confident his spell would hold firm as he spoke in a hissing whisper. "Now, not only do I have your family to slay, but you've led me to the imperials as well. What luck! Does that make you proud, wretched beast? To know it was your arrival here that sealed her fate? I'll tear her to pieces right in front of you, and then I'll track down the others. You think your silly little rock can stop me, but I'm far more powerful here on Earth than I ever thought I could be. I'll pluck every scale from her hide as you watch, and you'll both know the same ending will be coming for the others."

Kieran fought desperately, but he could only fight from the inside of his body. His jaws were clamped together, useless if they couldn't snatch the sniveling wizard by the throat. He'd dug his claws into the earth below him, and even the greatest effort couldn't make them twitch. His wings weren't even disturbed by the breeze that filtered around them. He was as useless as a statue, and he cried out inside for the fate that awaited Nora.

But a sudden crash sounded behind him. The wizard was knocked aside as a blur of green shouldered into him. The spell was broken as Nora appeared, fully shifted and glorious in her dragon form, wearing the amulet around her neck. She had Rhebin pinned to the ground, her claws digging into his wrists. Hot black blood oozed around them and soaked into the ground. "Let's see you try your little tricks now," she snarled.

Her sudden attack had broken Rhebin's spell over Kieran. A strange buzzing still hummed just beneath his scales, but it was nothing compared to being frozen in place like that. "Stand back, Nora. I'll take care of this."

But she didn't even seem to hear him. Her wings were spread behind her, a canopy of shade, and her emerald scales twitched with anger. "I thought I didn't want to have anything to do with being a dragon. I thought it was something to hide, something to be ashamed of. You think you've come here to defeat me, but you've only strengthened me. You've made a fool of me, and I'll never let that happen again. Enjoy your last breath, you hideous thing. In the name of the throne, I will destroy you."

A thundering noise rose on the path behind him. Kieran whirled to find a fleet of dragons racing down the pathway toward them. Their hides shimmered in the patches of sunlight. He recognized the amethyst of Lucia and the deep charcoal of Archard as they sped toward him. Julian's dark green scales so perfectly matched his daughter's, they could've been the same dragon. The autumn forest nearly camouflaged Callan, his coppery scales flecked with olive. Varhan was the only misfit, remaining in the only form that came naturally to him and that was far less repulsive than the wizard trapped under Nora's feet.

"It's all right, Nora. Everyone's here now," he shouted to her. Kieran was relieved to know they weren't alone, but it didn't stop that same protective urge that'd been haunting him. He had to keep her safe. He had to keep her out of harm's way.

But Nora was in her own world now. "When you get to the Underworld, you can give Tazarre a personal message from me: We dragons will *always* reign supreme. While you rot for all of eternity." She let go of his wrist and swiftly sliced a claw through his throat before he could summon another spell.

The putrid stench of his blood permeated the air, even out in the open. Nora left his corpse and wiped her claws in the dirt, the rest of the dragons watching in shock. She kept her eyes on the ground as she stumbled back to Kieran, melting back into her human form as she fell into his arms.

Kieran folded her into his embrace, allowing himself to morph as well. The danger was past. Rhebin was dead. It'd all happened so quickly that he hardly knew what to think about it. "Are you okay?" he whispered hoarsely.

"You saved me once," she mumbled, her face buried in his chest. When she looked up at him, tears streamed down her cheeks. "I thought maybe I could return the favor." She pressed her forehead into him once again and sobbed.

# 13

---

Nora hurriedly finished her work, eager to get out of the lab. There was plenty to do now that the new lab assistant had mysteriously disappeared. The police had been all over the university, trying to figure out what'd happened to Allison after Dr. Burke had reported her missing. But the pandemonium had died down quickly once they'd realized all her identifying documentation had been forged, and several other employees told Nora just how lucky she was that nothing bad had happened to her after all the time she'd spent with Allison.

As she left McKnelly Hall, Nora smiled into the stiff wind that greeted her. Winter was firmly coming in to take its hold. The grass was covered in frost every morning, and even the brilliant sunshine during the day couldn't quite drive away the chill in the air. But she didn't mind. She was letting her inner dragon come out to play a little more often, and she found that it kept her quite warm.

"Do you need an escort to your car?" asked a gruff voice from behind her.

Nora whirled, not surprised to see Kieran in his uniform standing there on the sidewalk. He'd always been a handsome man, but she now found herself even more attracted him. She enjoyed tracing her eyes over his muscular form. The security guard attire wasn't flattering for most men, but with wide shoulders and tight abs like Kieran had, it wasn't half bad. He'd trimmed his beard back slightly, looking a little less wild than he had before, but she still knew the untamed beast within him. "I guess that would be all right."

He arched a thick brow at her. "Hey, now that your YouTube channel is so popular, you might need a little extra protection from the masses, anyway." Allison—or rather, Rhebin—hadn't properly turned off the camera while recording the last session, so her flickering transformation was caught on video. After the fact, Nora decided to play it off as merely special effects, knowing the video could go viral—and it had. In a matter of hours, she'd hit a million subscribers, and the comments wouldn't stop flowing in.

Kieran fell in step beside her, slipping his hand warmly around hers. Nora smiled. Things had become so much easier between the two of them in the past week now that they could live normal lives—or at least, as normal as was possible for people like them. Their relationship still had a new feeling about it that sent a thrill of excitement through her when she heard his voice or saw him down the hall.

"Are we still on for tonight?" he asked as they reached her car.

"Of course." The entire world revolved around them when they were together, and Nora relished the feeling of freedom she had in knowing the dragon inside her was so happy. Her two forms had never fit so well together, and it was a relief to know she could be her true self and be proud of it. "I think I can still pencil you in."

She could sense that Kieran wanted to kiss her or pull her into his arms, but they'd both agreed that would have to wait. They still had their jobs at the university, and if they didn't restrict themselves to being professional while on campus, there was no telling what would happen. Nora wasn't all that concerned about being reprimanded by the administration for fraternizing with other employees. It was more a fear of getting so distracted from her work with Kieran around that she'd never get anything done at all.

"Good. I'll pick you up at seven."

She sighed happily as she got in her car and turned the key in the ignition. That would give her just enough time to wind down a little from work and get ready. It would also give her time to rehearse all the things she still needed to say to Kieran, all the things that had refused to come out before. Nora knew they'd have to be completely honest with each other if they were going to make this work, and she didn't doubt that Kieran would tell her anything that crossed his mind. He was more direct like that, and he was closer to his true form than she was.

Back at home, Nora showered and put on her bathrobe. She laid out a dark green belted cashmere sweater and a pair of skinny jeans, leaving them on the bed while she put on her makeup and did her hair. It was nice to have a reason to get dressed up a bit instead of just bumming around the lab all day, and it was even nicer to know she was doing it for Kieran.

Her mind was still reeling with all the things she wanted to say. Her thoughts were jumbled and full of emotions, and she knew if she dared to say them out loud to Kieran, they would just come out as a mess of tears and nonsense. Still in her robe, Nora went into the living room and sat at her desk, clearing away a pile of books to make some space. She found a notebook and a good pen and started writing. The words didn't have to be neat or clear, she just had to get them out. She filled up several pages, her eyes blurring over every now and then as she wrestled with herself.

Nora couldn't be sure if it would help or not until she saw Kieran, but it seemed like a good start. She tore the pages out of the book, held them at arm's length over the kitchen sink, and sent a fine stream of fire straight into the center of them. They fell in a pile of bright ashes, and Nora watched with interest as her words vanished.

———

"ARE we heading back to that little café we went to before?" Nora asked an hour later as they headed out of town.

"Sort of, but not exactly." He smiled from the driver's seat. "I enjoyed our time at the lake, but it turns out the café is closed for the winter months. I have a slightly different idea in mind."

When they pulled into the parking lot, he produced a small cooler and a tote bag from the back seat. "I thought we could just have our own meal."

Intrigued, Nora followed him as they headed down the path to the lake. Her arm in his, she looked out over the choppy water and thought about how much things had changed. Just a few weeks ago, she thought that change was a bad thing. She'd been so content to just live her life as though there weren't any dragons in the world and that she'd come from a perfectly normal family. The way things were leaning, she felt they were tipping toward certain disaster. She'd been so wrong.

They walked for a long time, slow and leisurely, until they reached the same shore where they'd lain together on the night of their previous date, holding each other under the stars after their flight. Kieran set down the bag and basket and took her hand. "Would you think it'd be too boring if I asked you to go on another flight with me? I know that's what we ended up doing last time, but I had so much fun."

Nora grinned. There were so many moments she'd been reliving in her mind from the past few weeks, but that one had been one of her favorites. "I was hoping you would say that, actually. But do you think it's dark enough?" She could accept who she was, but the rest of the world never would. They still had to be careful.

He nodded down the path the way they'd come. "The parking lot is completely empty. The restaurant is closed. It's pretty damn cold out here for anyone who doesn't have a natural fire in their chest. I think we'll be all right."

Instead of answering, Nora took a step backward. She let her wings fly out from her back like an umbrella, snapping in the breeze. Kieran responded with his own shift, his glorious human body lengthening and stretching as silver scales replaced his wings. She still hadn't gotten over how huge he was in this form, and she loved it.

They swept out over the lake. Nora dipped the tip of her wing in the icy water experimentally, feeling a whole new rush of exhilaration. She'd been really missing out by denying herself all these years, and now she couldn't get enough of it. She loved the long, lean lines of her body, the way her scales glistened in the slanted rays of the sun, and the floating feeling of the air under her wings. She felt she could fly forever.

And it was even better to have Kieran by her side. Despite his larger size, he was just as nimble in the air as she was, if not more so. He was so comfortable on the wing that it was hard to remember he walked around on two feet most of the time. He swiveled his head on his long neck to look at her, a proud and loving look in his eyes.

Nora only let herself think for a moment of what they must look like if someone could see them from below. Some might think they were horrid alien creatures, or monsters hell-bent on consuming human flesh, but she knew the truth.

After a while, Kieran turned back toward the shore. Nora followed him, ready for a rest and some time to talk. They'd spoken little while they were in the air, but only because it was more difficult over the sound of the wind in their ears. They came in for a soft landing under the trees, spreading their wings until their feet gently touched the cool earth. Nora almost hated to shift back, but she knew she'd get more chances to explore her reptilian side now that she had Kieran back in her life. She pushed her shoulders back as her wings folded and melded into her skin, and a cool shiver ran down her back as her scales flipped over and joined, creating smooth skin. It was an odd sensation to feel her fangs and claws recede into normal teeth and nails, almost a little painful even, but she could handle it.

Kieran had already finished his transition, and he watched her with interest.

"What?" she asked, suddenly feeling self-conscious in this body she was so used to. "I can't help it if you're faster at this than I am."

"I'm not complaining," he said softly, "just enjoying."

Kieran unfolded a large blanket from the tote bag, and then set out cold fried chicken, sandwiches, potato salad, and an array of fresh fruits. "It's nothing special, but I had to make something that was easy to transport. I even got on the internet and looked up what people usually do for picnics."

"You *made* all this?" Nora kneeled on the blanket, her mouth watering at the display of food. "That's amazing."

"Why? I had to cook all the time back on Charok. We didn't have restaurants or frozen meals. Every meal was a picnic back home." He blushed, a touch of color just above his beard.

"I'm sorry. I didn't mean to sound so surprised. I guess I still forget sometimes that we've come from such different backgrounds. But lots of guys on Earth don't know much about cooking, to be honest. I'm not much better myself. I wouldn't dare make my own fried chicken when I could just go to a drive-thru place." She picked up a drumstick and bit into it, savoring the delicious morsel. The outside was crispy and flavorful, while the inside was juicy.

Kieran held up his own drumstick. "Turns out the internet is also really good for recipes."

They ate on the shoreline, the water lapping noisily at the water and the sun moving toward the horizon. Nora knew she couldn't have planned a better date herself, and she was suddenly so grateful for having Kieran in her life that it nearly made her cry. She finished off her potato salad, took a drink of iced tea from one of the bottles he'd brought, and took a deep breath as she recalled everything she'd written in that notebook at her apartment. "There's something I'd like to say."

He looked at her expectantly. "What is it?"

Nora looked away. In her fantasy, she could just let it all out while she looked him right in the eye. It was much harder in real life, though.

"Kieran, I want to thank you. I'd been trying to so hard to avoid acknowledging who I really am, and you've made me realize that my true self and my heritage are things I should be proud of. I am different from almost everyone else on this planet, but that doesn't have to be a bad thing."

"Of course not." He reached out and touched the side of her face, holding it like a precious treasure. "But you don't have to thank me for that. I never set out to change you or make you think differently."

"It still happened because of you. And I also owe you an apology, because I was so damn stubborn about the whole thing that I was rude to you. Sometimes, I don't know why you still want to have anything to do with me, but then there's the other thing." It was one thing to thank him or even to say she was sorry. The last part was the hardest, even though it was the most truthful.

"Go on," he encouraged.

"I think we're supposed to be together. Not just in the way that people say that because they're happy together, but fated. I've heard the old tales about how dragons feel when they find their mates, and for the longest time, I just thought it was old-world bullshit. But now that I'm with you, I completely understand; I get it. It's like you bring out a part of me I didn't even know existed."

Kieran's hand was on the back of her head and his lips pressed against her mouth before she could blink. He caressed her face, indulging himself in her as though he'd never get another chance. "Oh, Nora. I've felt it, too, but I didn't want to scare you off. You don't know how happy it makes me to know you feel the same way."

Her arms were around him now, exploring his body, touching every muscle. She couldn't get enough of him, and as she felt his hands reaching for her clothing, she did the same. Nora didn't even care that they were out by the lake instead of the privacy of one of their own homes. Kieran made her a bolder person, someone who did what needed to be done and didn't care about what anyone thought.

With a sweep of his arm, Kieran cleared the dishes from the blanket and laid her down. With his body above hers and his member hard and ready for her, he took a moment to run his hands gently down the entire length of her body. "You're exquisite." He dropped a kiss on her collar bone, moving slowly down to her breast. He lingered there for a moment before continuing to her stomach. "I think I could spend all day looking at you, no matter what form you're in."

Nora giggled at his touch, pleased and incredibly turned on. "You're not so bad yourself, you know."

His fingers made paths of pleasure down her thighs. "I don't even know where I want to start. I just know that I want to be with you forever."

Reveling in the figure of him over her, strong and powerful yet incredibly sweet, with the dark hair across his chest trailing down to entice her eyes toward his hard abs and what lay further below, she pulled him down towards her. "We've got all the time in the world."

"That's not fair." Kieran slid inside her, gasping at the sensation. "You feel too good, and there's so much more I want to do. Both to you and with you."

Nora closed her eyes and tipped her head back, moving her hips to match the slow rhythm of his. She knew what he meant. They fit together like puzzle pieces, as though they were quite literally made to go together. She didn't speak for a bit, just wanting to lose herself the same way she lost herself in her work. This was what she'd needed, what she'd been waiting for without even knowing it, and yet she knew there would be so many more moments like this. His body, hot and solid against hers, his words delicate in her ears, and their hearts entwined so deeply that even when they were apart physically, she knew she'd still be tied to him.

She felt her body pulsating from the inside, both her dragon and its human counterpart tipping toward ultimate rapture. Her breath came short as her muscles tightened. "I love you, Kieran."

He roared as she came, emptying himself into her with such rigor, he nearly collapsed on top of her when he was done. He caught his breath before whispering in her ear. "I love you, too."

They lay together in the cool night air, the sun having disappeared behind the lake without their knowledge, and Nora snuggled into her mate's chest, knowing she was right where she belonged.

They could've been on any world at that moment and it wouldn't have mattered.

As long as they were together.

———

# ROYAL DRAGON DADDY

SHIFTERS BETWEEN WORLDS

# 1

FINN STUFFED HIS HANDS IN HIS POCKETS AS HE WALKED DOWN THE street, feeling good. It was a beautiful night, with the warm air cooled every now and then by a humid breeze. It would've been nice if he could have shifted into his dragon form and flown to get to the restaurant a little faster, his wings lifted by the thick air, but he was perfectly content in his human form. He spent most of his time like that anyway, something his father would never understand.

But a human form was necessary for living on this planet, dealing with its people, and earning a living. His reptilian heritage was a wonderful thing, and it'd given him a solid family of good people, but it wasn't the sum of who he was.

Finn pushed open the door to Tranquility, his face breaking out into a smile as soon as he saw his cousins in their booth in the far corner. It was a tradition for them to meet on a regular basis, just the four of them, and catch up. He'd been afraid the custom would die off once Kaylee got married, or that Nora would suddenly no longer have time once she'd gotten together with Kieran, but so far, that didn't seem to be the case. They were all right there where they belonged, just like always.

"There you are!" Nora stood from her seat and wrapped him in a hug. Her brown eyes shone as she pulled back and grinned at him. "I was starting to wonder if you were still coming."

"Wouldn't miss it for the world." Finn slid in next to Elliot, pleased to see they'd already ordered him a Coke. "I just got a little hung up at work, but I can't say that I minded."

Kaylee raised an eyebrow. "This job must really be something, considering how much time you've been spending at the office. I haven't even heard you complain about how little partying you get to do."

"There isn't much time for that," Finn said, feeling his cheeks heat up. He'd had his college days of carousing and staying out late at night. There'd been plenty of flings and hangovers and nights he didn't quite remember, but getting hired at Anderson Environmental had changed his life completely. "The job's great. I like knowing that we're making a difference in the world."

"What's your latest project?" Elliot asked. "I think you said something about packaging?"

Finn smiled and nodded. "We're always working on packaging. It's one of the biggest problems around the world. It's unbelievable just how much plastic is floating around out there. If you get online and start looking up some videos and pictures, you'll be shocked."

Nora tipped her head to the side thoughtfully. "It's the kind of thing no one would've had to worry about on Charok. People were civilized without being so wasteful and materialistic."

"That's something I've thought about a lot," Finn replied honestly, taking a sip of his drink. His father, Holden, had come to Earth after the War of Storms had started between the dragons and wizards over twenty years earlier on their home planet. Holden's three friends came along, too, hoping to escape the Great Curse laid down by the evil wizard, Tazarre. Each of these dragons had gathered the last of their slain queen's royal eggs before fleeing in an attempt to preserve the future of their kind. Those four eggs had become Finn and his "cousins," they were raised to know each other as, although they hadn't found out about their royal lineage until fairly recently.

"Anyway, what's really happening is that my boss is about to give me a promotion," he said with a grin. He'd thought about holding back the information until he knew for certain, but it was difficult to keep any secrets from his cousins. He was closer to them than anyone else in the world. "He pulled me into his office and told me he's got his eye on me for business development officer once the guy in the current position retires."

The others let up a whoop of congratulations, and Elliot nudged him with his elbow. "Look at you, all grown up. I thought you'd stay young and dumb forever."

"Looks who's talking," Finn joked. "I know I shouldn't let myself get too excited about the position. There's no guarantee he's going to give it to me."

"Do you think he'd actually say anything to you about it if he didn't already have you pegged for it?" Kaylee asked, brushing her dark hair behind her shoulder with her hand. She'd recently come back from another one of her expeditions, exploring archeological sites for evidence of ancient languages. It must've been some place sunny based on her deep tan.

"I don't know. Mr. Anderson is an old hippie. He's one of those guys who just sort of speaks his mind and doesn't worry about what the consequences might be. Some of that is how he's gotten so far in business, because he never holds back. But I think it means he could also change his mind if he thought someone was better, and he wouldn't worry too much about the fact he'd practically promised it to me. Still, just knowing he thinks I'm right for the position is one hell of a compliment."

"Don't be so naïve," Elliot said, signaling the waiter so they could order their appetizers. "You want this job, and you should fight for it. Ask him if there's anything you can do to seal the deal. Let him know you're willing to go after it."

Finn nodded, knowing his cousin was probably right. He was lucky to be able to work for such a great company, and it would be a shame to let someone else step up and take the position out from under him just because they were more vocal. "I'll see what I can do."

"With a job like that, you're not going to have much time for dating," Nora said, smiling. "You boys are falling seriously behind in the relationship department, you know. Kaylee and I can't be the only ones keeping the older generation happy."

"You can start talking about that once you start having babies," Elliot said, pointing a finger at the ladies. "On the other hand, don't do that. Then our parents will go nuts, and we'll never hear the end of it. I know I'm not interested in any real relationships right now. I've got too much going on with finishing up school, and the last thing I need is some woman begging me for a diamond and babies."

Finn had to agree, at least in part. "Can you imagine all the

Charokian wisdom they'll be trying to impart once they think there's another generation coming? It'll be unbearable. It's terrible enough as it is." Finn appreciated and understood that his father wanted to pass on the knowledge of Charok. After all, there were only a handful of dragons here on Earth, and they couldn't exactly talk to the natives about their ancestral home. But he also understood the importance of blending in with the other humans here and living a fulfilling life.

As he thought about the future of his fellow dragons, Finn's phone rang. He pulled it out from his pocket, ready to dismiss the call and worry about it later, but it was Mandy. He hadn't heard from her in months. "Excuse me, guys. I've gotta take this."

Finn stepped out of the restaurant, trying not to sound to breathless as he answered. He and Mandy hadn't lasted long, but he'd enjoyed their time together. She'd been fun and exciting, never doing the same thing twice.

Definitely not the kind of girl his parents would be happy about, but still.

"Hey, Mandy. How's it going?"

"Finn... we need to talk."

He stiffened at the tone of her voice. "Is everything all right? I can meet you somewhere—"

"There's no easy way to say this, so I'm just going to get right to the point. I'm pregnant and the baby's yours. I'm actually about to give birth, but I'm going to give the baby up for adoption, okay? I wasn't going to tell you because I didn't think you'd want to be bothered, and I figured it would just be easier for both of us to pretend it didn't happen. But my mother won't leave me alone about telling you, so now I am."

Finn's breath caught in his throat, his mind whirling with a million thoughts. *Pregnant? Since when? Why hadn't she told me before? How could she think of giving up our child for adoption?* But anger suddenly overtook all the worries and questions, and he felt a familiar heat expanding in his chest. "No, that's not okay. That's not okay at all, and don't you dare give my child away!"

"What do you expect me to do, Finn?" Mandy asked, exhaustion and impatience clear in her voice. "I can't go backpacking across Europe with a *baby*. And what do you think this is going to do for my music career? You can't make me keep it. I'm not ready for this."

The heat was spreading from his chest to the rest of his body. Finn couldn't remember the last time he'd shifted, but it was suddenly difficult to keep his body in check. He felt a familiar itching on the underside of his skin as his scales threatened to break free.

He wasn't ready for this, either. A child? Already? "Where are you?"

Mandy sighed heavily. "I'm at my apartment."

"Good. Stay right there. I'll be there as soon as I can."

"Finn, you don't have to—"

"Yes, I do. I'll be right there."

As he pulled the phone away from his ear, he could hear Mandy grumbling. "Shit. Thanks a lot, Mom."

Finn stalked back into the restaurant, the light-hearted, free feeling he'd been experiencing earlier replaced by a heavy weight on his shoulders. This was bad enough as it was, but there were implications Mandy didn't understand. The girl didn't know who he really was, or *what* he really was.

Or that the baby she was about to deliver would be half dragon.

The others could read his face as soon as he reappeared at their table. "What's wrong?" Kaylee asked, dropping her French fry back onto the plate.

He leaned on the heavy wooden surface, not sure if he could hold himself up any longer.

"I'm about to be a father."

## 2

---

*Humans are disgusting creatures.* Aurora sneered at yet another piece of trash alongside the trail as she bent down to pick it up. Even the ones who claimed to care for the environment were usually doing just as much to damage it as they were to save it. Maybe they couldn't be blamed for not being able to see the life all around them and just how important it was, but that didn't upgrade their status in her mind.

She lifted her head, listening to calls of the birds around her in the forest. Someone was coming. Aurora smiled. They weren't supposed to be there, and she would make them understand soon enough. She slipped off the trail and melted into the woods.

"Right up this way, Mack," said a gruff voice. "You should see the amount of timber in here. It's crazy that no one's ever been able to log it before now."

Aurora peered through the undergrowth, seeing a hairy man in a t-shirt and jeans pointing to the trees around them. His companion, a skinny guy with his hair pulled back in a man bun, looked nervous.

"I don't know if we should be here..." he hedged.

The hairy man snorted. "You think I care? The old lady that owns this property wouldn't know anyone was here even if we marched right up to her house and knocked on the front door. She's deaf, and she's stubborn as hell. But the boss says we'll get this land one way or another."

"What about what Jones said? The way the birds were acting and how he kept getting lost even when he knew what direction he was going. It's like the place is haunted or something." The slender man looked over his shoulder.

"Stop blathering about that shit. There's nothing here that's going to hurt you, unless you're afraid of squirrels."

Aurora could barely suppress the giggle that rose in her throat. These men were so cocky and so naïve, and it was almost too fun to mess with them. But she knew exactly what they meant to do with this property. They were going to tear it apart, slashing the trees down for profit and clear the land to build factories. The old woman who owned the property was indeed deaf and stubborn, but she wasn't going to give up.

Fortunately for her, neither was Aurora. She set her hand against the trunk of a nearby tree, closing her eyes for a moment to send a message. She felt it ripple through the bark and into the pith, sinking down into the roots. The trees were packed so closely there that communicating with any of them was easy. A touch on one tree could touch the roots of a thousand others.

Right on cue, a gnarled root from a nearby birch inched out of the ground, right in front of the skinny man's foot. It caught the toe of his boot and sent him pitching forward with a pathetic little scream.

"Watch where you're going!" the burly man snarled as he hauled him up by the back of his shirt. "You're so used to sitting behind a desk that you can't even walk an easy trail!"

Dusting dead leaves from his clothes, the slim man didn't seem convinced. He looked behind him again as they continued their walk, and Aurora noticed he was watching the trail as he stepped forward.

The two men were talking again, discussing business plans of some sort. Aurora didn't pay much attention, since she knew they'd never get to carry out those plans anyway. She touched the tree once more, this time sending the message upwards. The branches of the tree shivered and waved, its leaves chattering against each other as it communicated with its fellow. Their branches took up the same movement, creating their own breeze that sounded ominous to anyone who thought they were simply heading down the trail on a nice spring day.

It picked up into a howling wind that drove the birds from the branches, having understood what was going on themselves. They dove down from the sky, whizzing down the path and just barely missing the men as they helped create a tunnel of wings and wind.

"What the..." mused the hairy man.

The skinny one didn't stop to think about it. He flailed his arms around his head as he screamed, turning around and running back the way they'd come. Soon enough, the other was on his tail, and the men were gone.

The forest returned to its normal peaceful state, the birds chirping happily to each other about their accomplishment while the trees sighed down to their roots. The loudest voice was that of Aurora, laughing. These weren't the first humans she'd driven from this acreage. She doubted they'd be the last, but it didn't get any less entertaining as she continued her work.

It was getting late, and she needed to head home. Aurora would speak to the woman who owned the property another time. She was one human she could stand, but she still didn't want to expose the truth any more than necessary.

Aurora slipped through the trees and brushes, away from the property she was trying so hard to protect and toward the deeper parts of the forest. People didn't go back there, not even to camp or have impromptu picnics. If they did happen to stumble upon this spot, they would see nothing but lush, emerald vegetation.

For Aurora, it was home. She dug her bare toes into the earth as she waved her hands before her, parting the thick leaves and exposing her true destination. A butterfly flitted against her cheek as she entered the fae realm, and Aurora instantly felt at home. The area wasn't much different from what the Earth forest had looked like numerous years ago, before the humans had invaded and driven the wildlife back. Animals, birds, and insects were just as at home there as the fae were, filling the air with their music as they greeted Aurora and welcomed her home.

She crossed a small wooden bridge over the creek, stopping to say hello to fish who swam underneath it. These conversations took no real words. As a fae princess, she could speak to any of the plants and animals there with only a thought. It was so instinctive at this point, she hardly had to think about it at all, and having real conversations out loud was often a more difficult task. She dipped her head to acknowledge a fat catfish who swam lazily near the bridge, but she paused as she picked up what he was trying to tell her.

Aurora unfurled her wings, the wispy appendages cool against her back. It hurt to keep them hidden for long periods of time, but that was a necessary sacrifice when moving among the humans. She let them lift her from the ground as she sped toward the castle. The trip was a short one, but along the way, she felt the other animals whispering similar concerns to her.

Aurora's heart clenched with concern when she lowered herself to the ground in front of the stone edifice that was the heart of the fae realm. She'd grown up there, played in the shadow of the walls and watched the flowers push up around its base. For so many years, she'd been content to languish in her own kingdom, carrying out only the smallest amount of work that was required of her. It wasn't until her father had taken her into the human world that she'd realized what her true calling was, and she'd been determined to save the animal and plant life there from the constant destruction the humans inflicted.

Now, she feared, it might be her own world she needed to save.

Her feet pattered on the cool stones as she raced down the hall to the throne room. The roof was open to the sky, the sun shining down on the lush tapestries that covered the walls. It was an opulent room that allowed as much nature to come flooding in as possible, with rambling vines flowing over the walls and down to the floor, where they wrapped around the legs of the throne.

Her father sat there, his face pinched and tired. He was an ample man, a simple robe covering his wide chest and the slight belly that hung down over his lap. The wreath of leaves in his hair that had always added to the sparkle in his eyes seemed much heavier for him today, his shoulders slumping and his head tipped toward the floor. Several of his attendants had flocked around them, their wings fluttering in agitation and lifting them an inch or two from the floor on occasion. They parted as they saw Aurora, touching their slim fingers to their lips and glancing nervously at the king.

"What is it?" She didn't bother with any of the courtly formalities the rest of the fae would need to observe. This wasn't her father's office to her, nor was it really even the seat of the kingdom. It was her home, and her father was obviously worried about something. She hadn't seen him look so serious since her mother had passed on into the next realm.

King Oren brushed his hand through the air, dismissing his

courtiers. "There's nothing we can do about any of this right now. Go to your homes, be with your children and your spouses, and be safe. I advise you to keep to yourselves for now. Don't even come back to the castle unless I call for you. It's not worth the risk."

The attendants whisked off as they were told, a few of them laying a hand on Aurora's shoulder as they passed or giving her sympathetic glances. She didn't even know what that was for, and it made her worry all the more. "What's happened? I wasn't gone all that long." She knew trouble was brewing. She had picked that up easily enough from the animals, but they hadn't been able to give her specifics.

"Come, my dear. I want to speak to you in private." He hefted his weight from his throne, stepped down from the dais, and moved through an arched doorway.

They were already alone, even in the court room, but Oren had never preferred to have intimate conversations there. It was a place for the running of the kingdom, not for reprimanding his free-spirited daughter or imparting bad news.

The king's private chamber was similar to the throne room, still with the open ceiling and wide windows that allowed nature in. But the chairs around the heavy table were much simpler than the opulent furnishings of the throne room, the tapestries less imposing. "Have a seat, Aurora."

"I don't want to sit," she said stubbornly, curling her hands into fists. "Just tell me already! I don't want all the waiting and protocol."

Oren sighed as he lowered his bulk into the chair and looked up at her with his deep brown eyes. "I'm afraid the wizards are not turning out to be a very good ally."

"What do you mean?" Aurora sat now, taking the seat directly across from him. "They've been mending the thinning area in our protective veil that's along our border with Earth. Their magic is strong, and without it, we might be seen. We'd become a spectacle for the humans to profit from."

The enchanted veil that had been thriving for so long around their realm, keeping it safe from prying eyes, was no longer as easy to sustain as it had once been. The humans didn't realize it, of course, but as they were diminishing the natural resources of their planet, they were also diminishing its innate magic. There were also far fewer fae who knew the old ways, and both of these factors meant an irregularity in the stratum around their domain was a difficult thing to repair.

"Yes, they certainly have been. I just didn't realize it would come at such a price." Oren folded his fingers on the table, leaning forward as though he could no longer hold his own weight.

"What price? They just harvested a few herbs. We can't really begrudge them that." She was starting to wonder if her father was getting too old to deal with these sorts of things. Not that she wanted to take over the throne for herself anytime soon; that would be at least another century away.

"Oh, they did take the herbs. I directed them to the right place myself, and I was fool enough to think I didn't need to monitor them more closely. But now..." He shook his head, his face falling.

Aurora reached across the table and touched her fingers to the back of her father's gnarled hand. "Father, just tell me."

"They've been taking our people, using the fae magic to enforce their own. They grab them out of the fields and shoot them out of the sky, shackling them in spellbound iron to make them bend to their will." He moaned as he brought his hands up to cover his face, his fingers shaking.

Aurora was on her feet once again. "Why haven't you stopped them? Why haven't our people stood up to fight? I know it's not normally our way, but we can't just let this happen!" She was indignant with rage, furious that something like this could possibly happen.

Oren brought one hand down to the collar of his robe and pulled it aside, exposing a thick iron chain that banded his neck. The links of the iron shimmered with enchantment, which was responsible for depleting one's stores of magic and sending it to the wizards.

"Oh, no..." she breathed. Aurora longed to reach out and yank the metal from her father's neck, but she knew it was impossible. Iron caused the fae great pain, making it a very effective way of controlling them. Aurora knew this, as all fae did, but she didn't remember ever having to deal with it in her lifetime.

"Yes. They've got me as well, and because of its enchantment, no amount of our magic seems capable of removing it. If I don't cooperate and let them do what they want, they'll vaporize the veil around my kingdom. Our kind will be left completely exposed and helpless."

Aurora breathed out and felt as though she couldn't breathe back in again, drained by the idea of the wizards running their kingdom by force. "But what is it they want, exactly?" she asked.

"They believe there are dragons on Earth, and they want them. I don't know the nature of their dispute with the dragons, but the wizards seem determined to find a way to locate them and take them down. I told them over and over that I don't know anything about such creatures. There's so little natural magic left on that planet that it doesn't even seem likely to me." Oren shook his head sadly, reaching down to his side to stroke his hand against a strand of ivy.

"Oh." Aurora did know there were dragons, or at least she'd had very confident suspicions. She often ran into a woman in the woods near the university, one who acted as though she cared very much for the local plant life. It was a good start, but it wasn't really enough to convince Aurora that this woman was trustworthy. But one night, she swore she'd seen Nora and the man she often brought with her flying just over the treetops, their leathery wings skimming the leaves.

She cleared her throat, suddenly feeling guilty for not explaining what she'd seen to her father. It had surprised her, but she hadn't been threatened by the idea of dragons in their midst. "I might be able to help."

"No, dear. There's nothing you can do. Your magic is very strong, but we're nothing compared to these wizards. They're powerful, angry, and determined. Until some miracle from Goddess comes along, we're stuck."

"Just trust me. I might have an idea." She licked her lips, trying to decide just how to tell him what she had seen. "I think—"

"No!" King Oren had almost never raised his voice at his daughter, but his look was suddenly stern. "I order you to refrain from taking any action against the wizards. They'll destroy you, and I've already lost so much. I won't hear another word about it."

Aurora put her chin in the air, keeping her eyes cool. "Very well, then. As you wish." She slowly turned and left the room, feeling as though she were abandoning her father. There was no good reason for her not to help, nor for their people not to rise against the wizards. Even if it was a futile effort, they should try.

If the king refused to do anything about it, Aurora decided she would have to.

## 3
---

FINN STRAIGHTENED HIS TIE, HOPING HE HADN'T OVERDRESSED. MR. Anderson might wear a suit to work one day, but the next, he could just as likely be found in a wrinkled shirt and khaki shorts. He was an odd mix of bohemian and businessman, which made him both fun to work for and impossible to please.

Raising his fist, Finn knocked on the door. His stomach clenched, and he chided himself for it. There was no reason to be nervous. Mr. Anderson was just another person, and he wasn't going to bite Finn's head off. Probably.

"Come in!" called a friendly voice from the other side of the door.

Finn poked his head in the room, his fingers still on the handle. "I was curious if you had a free minute. I'd like to talk to you."

Mr. Anderson looked up from the laptop on his desk, his furry eyebrows raised with curiosity. He'd worn his hair loose, and it fell in silvery waves over the collar of a button-up shirt with a disturbingly loud print. There weren't any papers scattered over the bamboo surface of his desk as one might've expected in a typical executive's office. "Come in, come in. I think I'll go cross-eyed if I look at any more of these reports, anyway."

"Thanks." Finn closed the door behind him and took a seat in the chair in front of Mr. Anderson's desk. It'd been made by one of their sister companies, and Finn knew it was fashioned out of recycled and sustainable materials. It also cost a fortune, but that was the challenge of environmentally-friendly products. "I wanted to make sure you got my most recent report." He immediately felt like an idiot as soon as he said it, considering his boss had just been complaining about reports.

"Oh, yes. The garbage bags. It's a fabulous idea, Finn. The kind of thing we're really looking for. We need products that people can easily apply to their everyday lives. I won't forgive myself for letting those other guys beat us to biodegradable drinking straws, but we can catch them up." He smiled with enthusiasm, leaning back in his chair and folding his hands over his paunch. "I also happened to see, when I was going over the review from human resources, that you've added a child onto your health insurance package. Congratulations, my boy! I had no idea you were a family man."

Finn felt several beads of sweat pop out on his forehead and hoped Mr. Anderson didn't notice. "Oh, yes. Well, I'm just glad the company offers such good health coverage."

Mr. Anderson tipped forward and rested his elbows on his desk. "You didn't come in here to talk about reports or health coverage, did you? Why don't you just tell me what's on your mind. I can handle it." He opened the top drawer of his desk and removed a ball, then turned slightly and began bouncing it repeatedly against the wall.

Finn's eyes followed the path of that ball as it bounced against the floor and the wall and then smacked back into his boss's palm. "Well, in a way I did. You see, now that I have a little one at home, my job is even more important to me. I want to make sure I can provide Phoenix with everything he could possibly need, and I'm still very interested in taking the business development officer position when Mitch retires. I know we already talked about it a little, but I was curious if there's anything I can do to help secure myself for the job." He felt a hard knot in his throat as he wondered if this was really a good idea, after all. Elliot had encouraged him to go hard after what he wanted, but Finn had been forced to set some of that aside once Phoenix had been born. It was only now that he had a little more space to think that he'd decided to go for it.

*Bounce, bounce, smack. Bounce, bounce, smack.* Mr. Anderson closed his fingers around the ball and looked up at the ceiling thoughtfully. "You know, at one point in my life, I never imagined I'd be in charge of people's futures. I didn't realize that by building a company that would fulfill my own dreams, I'd also be building or even breaking the dreams of those around me. It's an interesting position I'm in, and it's not without its burdens." He replaced the ball in the drawer. "Fortunately, I think this is one of those times when I get to make everyone's dreams come true. Mitch is getting what he needs by retiring early and becoming a travel writer. I'm getting what I want by moving a promising young person into the position. And, if all goes well, you'll be getting the job you want." He smiled, his thin lips spreading against his generous cheeks.

"If all goes well?" Everything else Mr. Anderson had said made Finn feel confident about his chances, but that phrase didn't sound like a good omen.

"Well, you know, sometimes things happen. I don't have complete control over it all, but you're definitely the man in the lead. And if you're interested in solidifying that, I do have a special project I think you'd be perfect for."

Finn leaned forward in his seat. "I'm listening."

"We're desperately trying to acquire some land just to the south of here, not too far from the university. It's privately owned property, and our scientists believe it could be vital to the local ecology due to the number of endangered plant species that live on it. Anderson Environmental needs to build its image not just as a manufacturer, but as a conservation-minded entity. I want to acquire this property in order to protect it, and we've been trying to convince the woman who owns it to sell."

"I see." Finn could handle that.

Mr. Anderson held up a finger. "Hold on, it's not a simple as dropping by for tea and walking out with a sales contract. Every time I send men onto that property, they come running back here with... ghost stories. Some of them are even sustaining injuries—albeit minor—and they believe the place is haunted."

Finn couldn't stop that snort that erupted from his lips. "That's kind of ridiculous."

"Of course it is. But you're a sturdy young man, and I think you can handle it. Go see what's happening on that property, and see if you can convince the owner to sell. I'll have Cindy give you all the details."

"I'm on it. Thank you, sir." Finn stood up, shook his hand, and left, confident he'd have a new office by the end of the year.

———

"REALLY?" Nora asked as they tromped deeper into the woods. "Wow, that's wonderful, Finn! If you need me to take you suit shopping... actually, no. Just ask Kaylee to do that." She grinned over her shoulder at him.

"Yeah, I'm pretty excited. And the best thing is, this guy has no idea he's sending a dragon into some haunted woods. I don't think a little whistling wind is going to scare me." He laughed at the idea, anxious to come back from his visit with the property owner unscathed. The other men wouldn't be able to believe it.

"And what about Phoenix?" Nora asked, stopping to examine the whorled leaves on a tiny plant pushing through the detritus on the forest floor. "How's he doing?"

She didn't look at him as she asked the question, and Finn thought he knew why. The little boy he was now parenting was still an awkward subject for the dragons. No one had rejected the child, and Finn's parents had been thrilled to have a grandson despite the circumstances, but Finn felt that no one had quite gotten used to the idea of him as a father. "He's doing well, I guess. I mean, he seems happy, and he eats. I just don't know much about doing this. My dad insists that it all comes naturally, but he's also the one who invited me to move back into their house for a while to make it easier."

"Are you going to?" She pulled an expensive-looking camera out of her bag and snapped a photo of a white flower bud.

"No," he replied immediately. "I can't lie; this is the hardest thing I've ever done. I never know if I'm really making the right decisions or not. I'm glad Mandy signed away all her rights to him so I don't have to deal with that, but it also doesn't seem fair that the entire burden is on me."

"So move in with your parents for a while. I could easily see Leah and Holden jumping right in to help."

"That's exactly the problem. I don't want them standing around, watching me with him, and thinking I'm doing it all wrong." Nothing had shaken his confidence quite like this child, nothing more than a warm bundle in a receiving blanket when Mandy had handed him over. He was just grateful Phoenix had been born in human form. None of them could have predicted exactly how that would work out with a baby that was half human and half shifter.

Nora turned to look him in the eye now. "They don't think that. None of us think that. You're in a tough position, and that's okay. We're lucky to have so many people around us who are willing to help. As a matter of fact, I think having Phoenix around has even put some ideas into Kieran's head." Nora's shifter boyfriend was a mountain of a man who'd accidentally been transported to Earth from Charok about a year ago, along with a few other remaining dragons.

"That's just because he doesn't have one yet. I love Phoenix, but I'm tired. And it's nice to be able to get out here for adult conversation." He concentrated on the warm sun on his shoulders and the sound of the breeze through the trees.

"I just appreciate you coming out here with me today. The weather was too gorgeous to pass up, but my video assistant friend Holly had stuff to do with her family and Kieran had to work. I just hope... oh." Her shoulders slumped visibly as she looked down the path.

"What is it?"

Nora turned and pulled him close to talk quietly. "It's Aurora. She hangs out here all the time, and she drives me crazy. She thinks no one cares about the environment but her, and she has the worst attitude. I can't seem to bring myself to just blow her off, though, so I'm sorry that I'll have to introduce you."

Finn shook his head. "Doesn't bother me." He looked up the trail again, and this time he could see who Nora was talking about. A tall, curvy woman was advancing down the path toward them. Her dark blonde hair hung in a million long ringlets past her shoulders, some of them wildly bobbing in the breeze. With slim, arched eyebrows and eyes the color of coffee, he couldn't stop gaping at her.

"Hi," Aurora said with a smile. "Getting any good shots today?"

Nora fiddled with her camera for a moment, clearly taken aback. "Um, yeah. I mean, I've done some stills for my website so far. We're getting ready to start rolling video shortly."

"That's great. It's a perfect day for it. Who's your friend?"

Those deep brown eyes slid to Finn, and he no longer felt as though he were in charge of his own body, feeling the uncontrollable urge to shift into his reptilian form. Nora had warned him that this woman was rude, but maybe he hadn't heard her correctly.

He reached out his hand. "I'm Finn, Nora's cousin."

"Aurora." Her fingers were long and cool against his own, and they lingered for just an instant against his skin. The spark of electric fire that traveled up his arm, across his chest, and spread out over his body was unexpected, but incredibly arousing. It rippled under the surface of his skin, reminding him just how easily it could split into a million dragon scales. He swallowed, restraining the urge to shift with every cell of his body.

"It's nice to meet you. I don't think I've seen you out here before." Her smile dimpled her cheeks just slightly. With dramatic features like hers, the woman looked like she could have just walked off a Paris runway.

"Um, no. I'm usually at work, or..." He trailed off, uncertain of how to continue. He glanced down at the ground, noticing the beautiful woman was barefoot. It might've been weird if anyone else did it, but with her, it just seemed natural.

"Oh, where do you work?" Aurora seemed genuinely interested, leaning forward slightly.

Finn could no longer see anything around them. He didn't notice Nora looking confused and slightly huffy, just off to his left. He'd completely forgotten he was the one holding the video camera. The sun, the birds and the breeze had all disappeared. "Anderson Environmental. We specialize in making everyday products that are eco-friendly."

At this, her pink lips turned, intrigued. "That's exciting. I'm a big advocate for the environment, myself. That's why I spend so much time out here. I feel I need to be as close to nature as possible in order to truly understand it." She held his eyes with her own like magnets.

"That's great." Finn felt himself longing to touch her hand again, but of course there was no longer a reason to shake it. He simply wanted to feel the way her skin rubbed against his, even on the most microscopic level. "I wanted to work for a company that really meant something to me, but still allowed me to have a career. I couldn't have gotten luckier. And now I'm getting to help acquire some land for preservation in the name of the business. It's just over that way." He pointed, hoping he was getting the direction right. His brain had gone completely fuzzy.

"Finn? Are you going to answer that?" Nora, with her dark brows drawn together, was pointing at his pants pocket where his cell phone was chirping madly.

"Oh!" He yanked it out, hoping to silence it, but it was his mother calling. "I'm sorry. I've got to take this. It might be about my son. It was nice to meet you, though." Jolted out of his strange reverie, Finn turned and headed down the path a few paces. He felt as though he'd been yanked out of a warm bed and into a cold winter morning, his body suddenly denied of something incredibly pleasant, something he didn't want to be without. He slammed his eyes shut and pressed his cell close to his ear, concentrating on what Leah had to say with all his effort. A vision of Aurora remained in front of his vision as though she were there, no matter where he looked.

When he finished his phone call and turned back, Aurora was gone. He was much more disappointed than he would've imagined.

"Everything okay?" Nora asked.

"Yeah. Mom was just telling me Phoenix is almost out of diapers." He'd been able to take off on paternity leave for a couple of weeks, and his mother Leah had been watching Phoenix while he worked since then. She was absolutely crazy about the baby, but Finn knew he'd need to find a daycare once his son got a little older. It wasn't fair to expect Leah to spend all her time caring for the little one.

"Gotcha." Nora was staring off down the path, frowning. "That was so weird. Aurora is usually the worst person to be around. I've never seen her being friendly, much less interested in what someone has to say."

Finn felt a distinct empty spot where the woman had been only a moment ago. She'd come out of the foliage as though she'd been made of it to stand solidly in front of him, and then she was gone again, disappearing like a wisp of smoke he couldn't catch. Finn hadn't thought about women much at all since he'd become a father. There simply wasn't time for that. But she had reawakened something inside him. "She seemed nice to me," he shrugged.

Nora snorted. "If you say so. It was flat-out weird, as far as I'm concerned, because she's never nice. She usually spends all her time complaining about how terrible people are. Maybe she's high or something. But anyway, I think I know what I'm going to do for my video today. You ready to start shooting?"

"Oh, sure." He fiddled with the video camera, barely listening to Nora's directions.

His mind was still focused on the mysterious Aurora.

## 4

HIS JEEP BUMPED AND RATTLED DOWN THE OLD DIRT ROAD. FINN SLOWED to navigate the deep ruts that had been carved by unchecked rain and never repaired. He hadn't met the owner of the property yet, but Mr. Anderson had described her as an older woman who lived alone. He had to wonder how someone could stand to live so far out there, where emergency crews probably couldn't navigate or even find the right road. He'd only found it himself because Anderson Environmental had taken aerial photos with a drone to check out the property.

The woods finally parted before him, revealing a tiny log cabin in a clearing. It was like something out of a fairy tale—or maybe a horror movie. Wind chimes sang merrily to themselves where they hung from the covered porch, and vivid spring flowers ran wild along the foundation. A small barn off the left housed a skinny horse, several chicken fluttering at its hooves.

The road simply ended at the edge of the clearing without any real indication of a driveway or where he should park. Finn paused, not wanting to run over some prized flower or another and offend the owner before he even had a chance to speak with her. He finally pulled his Jeep in next to an old farm truck, carefully dodging a patch of mud as he got out and walked up to the house.

The door opened as he set his foot on the bottom porch step, revealing a scrawny old woman in a floral print dress. Her hair was a bubble of tight curls around her head, and her eyes looked huge through her glasses. "Can I help you?" she asked.

"Well, maybe. Are you Cecilia Alberts?" Finn smiled as he came up onto the porch but hung back a little, not wanting to scare her off. If she lived out here all by herself, she might not react well to a strange young man getting too close. Finn wondered if Mr. Anderson had ever thought to send a woman out there instead. "My name is Finn Reid, and I work for Anderson Environmental. I'd like to talk to you about purchasing your property."

The woman looked him up and down, her eyes squinting slightly as she studied him. She then opened the door wider. "Come on in. I've got a kettle on."

Finn stepped into the cabin behind her. The place seemed to be almost entirely one room, with a doorway off to the side that must have led to a bedroom. The woman had gone to the right into an open kitchen, where she was already pouring two cups of tea.

"You have a lovely home," he said as he noted the numerous quilts and afghans. The bright colors contrasted with the exposed wood walls to create a homey feel that he liked. He'd never had a grandmother, really, and he could suddenly see what he'd been missing.

"Thank you. I'd like to keep it that way." There was a hint of anger in her voice now as she carried the delicate cups to a worn oak table between the kitchen area and the living room. "Do you prefer sugar or honey?"

"Oh, neither one. Thank you." He sat, surprised by how comfortable the hard, wooden chair was beneath him. In fact, everything about this place was comfortable. He felt incredibly distant from the rest of the world, as though he'd found the last isolated place. Even the thought of heading back down that rutted, bumpy road when he was done there no longer bothered him.

He'd left his laptop and the few papers he'd printed out—Anderson Environmental frowned on using any unnecessary paper—in his car, hoping to keep this first visit as casual as possible. They were ready if he needed them, though. "How long have you lived here, Mrs. Alberts?"

She carefully dropped a sugar cube into her tea cup, stirring the dark liquid with a tiny spoon and watching the sugar dissolve before she snapped her eyes up to look at him. She was ancient, but there was still a spark of vitality in those eyes. "Just cut the crap, kid. I'm going to tell you right now that I'm not interested in selling."

Finn widened his eyes in surprise and then regained his composure. She might be saying that, but she wouldn't have invited him in if she was truly against selling. Would she? Mrs. Alberts could've just slammed the door in his face, but maybe she was lonely. "I can understand why you wouldn't. It's a beautiful property, and I doubt there's anything else quite like it around. In fact, I know there isn't. But it also must be a lot for you to maintain, and we're willing to give you a good price." He'd planned to wait until the timing was right to talk about money, but it was clear she wanted to get down to the nitty gritty.

"Oh, sure. Of course you'd pay good money. Why, just think about how much profit you'd make by the time you cut down all these beautiful trees and sold them off for overpriced furniture. And then you'd probably do something else stupid like bottling up all the creek water. Once you've cleared it all out and chased away the wildlife, it'll be the perfect place to build a factory." She glared at him over her teacup as she brought it to her lips.

"That's not what we want to do at all. I don't know what anyone else might've told you, but Anderson Environmental is interested in acquiring this property so we can preserve it. There are native species here that can't be found anywhere else, and it's one of the largest contiguous pieces of land in the county. Mrs. Alberts—"

"Call me Cecilia," she barked, setting her cup back down with a dangerous rattle. "You seem nice enough, much nicer than the other suits they've sent out here. In fact, I can tell there's something a bit different about you. You're not like most people, are you?" She raised one grizzled eyebrow in a challenge.

Finn's mouth worked silently for a moment as he tried to decipher what she was really telling him. Did she somehow know he was a dragon? Were there people who could tell? His mother was a psychic, and his aunts were witches. There was certainly a possibility that someone else out there had a notion that dragons were living on Earth. But no, he brushed off the notion as being ridiculous. She was just trying to intimidate him, and he couldn't let a woman half his size scare him out of getting this new promotion. "No, I'm not," he replied confidently. "I happen to think that's rather a good thing. But no matter who I am, I think you're crazy not to sell. The amount of money the company is prepared to offer you—"

"What's a bunch of money to me?" she demanded, slamming her wrinkled fist on the tabletop and making the tea set jump. "This land has been paid off for years. I can pay my land taxes with the loose change out of my old truck. I grow most of my own food, and I hardly have any bills. What good is a bunch of cold cash sitting in the bank when I can be surrounded by the beauty and tranquility I have here?"

He didn't know how to answer that. This woman was clever; he had to give her that. "It can't be easy to keep up with this place, though. And you're out here all alone, where you can't get access to emergency medical care. It could be dangerous for you."

"Hmph. Don't try to talk to me like you have any concern for me." She rose from the table and headed for the door. "Come with me."

Finn walked obediently after her out the door, down the porch steps, and around the back of the house to a narrow trail that threaded through the woods. A rabbit raced off into the underbrush, and he heard the crash of a deer in the distance. Cecilia said nothing as she shuffled down the path in her orthopedic shoes, and Finn wasn't sure he should say anything, either.

He pressed his tongue against the back of his teeth and wondered how he was going to get this done. Mr. Anderson hadn't told him his new position was riding on this project, but Finn knew it was important. Becoming the new business development officer would mean working some longer hours at first, but it would also mean he could afford the best daycare in the city. Maybe even a personal nanny, so Phoenix would have the comfort of being at home. His heart swelled as he thought of his child, with his fringe of gold hair and his bright blue eyes. Finn's parents had shown him a picture of himself at about that age, and the two were indistinguishable. He wanted everything for that sweet baby, even though he didn't know exactly how to give it to him.

The path dipped downward suddenly, and Finn feared for Cecilia's footing, but she made her way down like an old mountain goat until they stood on the rocky shore of a vast pond. He'd seen it as a big blue splotch in the aerial photos, but it was nothing compared to standing next to it. A cool breeze stirred the waters as bird dipped and swooped over it. The emerald green of the forest surrounding it was simply surreal.

"There are spirits here, Finn Reid of Anderson Environmental. This place isn't just a piece of land for me to sell off like I own it and all

the life on it. People tend to think that way, and that's a problem. I'd
like to think a young man like you who supposedly works for an eco-
friendly company would understand that, but you're still all about the
money. And you're naïve enough to think this land will go on being the
way it is once a corporation gets its hands on it." She shook her head as
she stared out over the water. "I'm going to sit here for a while, but I
want you to walk back down that path to the house. Listen to the trees,
to the birds, to everything here, and you tell me what you think."

"I hate to just leave you out here..."

She turned to him, her fists on her bony hips. "But you're going to.
Goodbye." She settled herself on a rickety little bench, defiance
obvious in the set of her shoulders.

Finn did as he was told, despite his qualms about it. Was this what
Cecilia had done every time someone came out to ask her about
selling the property? It was a strange experience, but it certainly wasn't
the kind of thing to make him think it was haunted. He hadn't been
injured, and it didn't seem likely there was anything there that could
hurt him, even in human form.

He was formulating his plan for his next visit—because he knew
he couldn't simply give up—when the wind picked up. It rattled
through the branches overhead and carried the scent of wildflowers to
his nose. He lifted his head to appreciate it when he noticed the path
in front of him was completely blocked with trees.

Finn turned in a slow circle, wondering how he could've gotten
himself lost. He didn't remember seeing any forks in the path. Maybe
he'd missed something? He headed back the way he came, looking for
another turn off, but soon enough, he could see the lake through the
trees once again. "What the hell?" He could go back to the lake and ask
Cecilia for directions, but she'd like that too much.

He stomped back off down the trail, moving slowly, knowing he
must've missed something. It irritated him on a deep level, considering
he was usually so good at these kinds of things. His innate dragon
senses allowed him to experience more of the world than most
humans did, and he never had a hard time getting his bearings. If most
men didn't stop to ask for directions because they were too proud,
dragons didn't stop and ask because they simply didn't need to. He felt
a fire growing inside him, burning in his chest and sparking energy out
to his fingertips. Finn glanced at his hands to make sure he hadn't
extended his claws. His body was threatening to shift, and he rolled his

shoulders in an attempt to calm it. He wasn't the kind of guy to turn into a beast just because he was angry or frustrated. *There's something strange going on in these woods...*

The path was blocked once again, and this time, it seemed as though a different tree had grown up in the middle of the trail. He stepped closer, wondering if maybe it was just a bend in the track that was creating an optical illusion. No. He paused, suddenly feeling as though he wasn't alone. The spot between his shoulder blades, right where his wings threatened to sprout forward, stung as though someone had shot him.

"What are you doing here?"

He spun around, his claws and wings barely controlled, ready to spring free. But the beautiful woman leaning against an oak tree was a familiar vision, with her blonde curls catching in the rough bark. His breath caught in his chest, and when he spoke, it came out strangled. "Aurora?"

She smiled, but he could still see the confusion in her eyes. "Did you get lost?"

He gestured helplessly, now embarrassed as well as frustrated. "Apparently."

Aurora stood up straight and walked toward him, her eyes focused on his. Her gaze sent that same electric sensation through him he'd felt when he'd met her the other day, and he was frozen in place for a minute. Was she some sort of hypnotist? "Do you know Cecilia?"

"I just came out here to talk to her about selling her property," he explained. "I work for Anderson Environmental, and... oh, but I told you that. Anyway, we're trying to acquire the land to preserve it." He tried to recall their previous conversation, but he was too busy tripping over his own tongue.

She tipped her head to the side, and as a few more strands of her hair floated in the breeze, he felt a strong urge to touch them. She seemed to be a part of the wilderness around them. "How do you know that?"

"Know what?"

"That they actually want to keep it the way it is. I've heard some rumors that say otherwise." She wore a long yellow dress; the soft fabric fluttered in the breeze as her bare feet poked out from beneath its hem.

Finn had a hard time focusing on the actual subject of conversation. His body was doing strange things. He'd never felt the need to shift unless he was in danger, but at the moment, he couldn't quite figure out what state he wanted to be in. He was sweating, his internal temperature rising by the minute, not sure how much longer he'd be able to control himself. "Why would you say that? Our company is all about conservation. Sure, part of the reason we're trying to do this is for PR, but it's still something that's at the core of what we believe in."

She raised one slim eyebrow. "If I were you, I'd look into it a little more. I've learned not to trust anyone who sits behind a big desk. Come on, I'll show you the way out."

He followed her down the path, heading in the same direction he just came from. In most places, the trail was narrow enough that he had to walk behind her. Finn took the opportunity to appreciate the curve of her shoulder, the way her waist tucked in above her hips. He was fully expecting to end up once again at the lake, but they soon emerged near the cabin. Finn glanced over his shoulder dumbfounded, wondering how Aurora had been able to do that. "So, how do you know Cecilia?"

"We've known each other for a long time. I stumbled onto her property once and met her, and we've been friends ever since." Aurora's lips turned up at the corners into a genuine smile.

Finn wondered what it would be like to kiss those lips; so much, he could practically envision himself stepping forward and doing just that. He was standing next to his Jeep now, hardly even sure of how they'd gotten there. "Would you like to go out for dinner sometime?" he asked, the words exploding out of him as though they couldn't be helped. "Maybe tomorrow?"

Aurora's smile increased, and so did his heartbeat. "That would be great. I'm working at the university; you can pick me up just outside the library. Sound good?"

"Yeah. Sounds great."

Still buzzing from his surprise encounter with Aurora, he hardly felt the ruts in the road as he headed back toward civilization.

## 5

FINN STRAIGHTENED THE COLLAR OF HIS SHIRT FOR THE MILLIONTH TIME. "You really think this is all right? I think it makes me look too stuffy. I mean, I've never even seen Aurora wear shoes."

Elliot laughed from where he relaxed in an overstuffed recliner with one foot propped up on his knee. "Someone's nervous."

"I'm not nervous, I just don't want to give her the wrong impression. She's very granola. You know, the anti-establishment nature hippie type." He frowned at the button-down shirt, convinced he looked more like an insurance salesman than anything else.

"Then she must be right up your alley," Elliot commented. "You were always out running through the woods behind your parents' place, and by the time Leah could get you inside, you were hardly recognizable from all the mud. And women prefer it when you overdress, so just wear the freaking shirt already."

"Tell me again why you're here? I could get ready on my own, you know." Finn picked up his wallet, double-checking that he had his debit card as well as cash. He never did that, but he was suddenly worried about doing something stupid and not being able to pay for dinner.

"I'm not so sure. You've been yammering on about this Aurora chick for two days straight. I don't think I've ever seen you so affected by someone except for Phoenix."

*Oh, god, Phoenix.* A fresh wave of guilt washed over Finn at the idea of leaving his son just so he could go out on a date. It didn't seem like the right thing to do at all when he looked at his chubby little cheeks or smelled the fresh baby shampoo on his hair, but his Uncle Beau and Aunt Autumn had assured him multiple times they were more than happy to watch the child. "She's not just some chick," Finn grumbled, trying to refocus his mind. "She's not like anyone I've ever met before."

Elliot put both feet on the floor and leaned forward, his fingers dangling limply over his knees. "Do you think she could be..." He didn't finish the sentence, leaving the implications to hang in the air.

But Finn knew exactly what he meant, even without saying it. "I don't know, and I'm not ready to think about it yet." He'd heard everyone talking about fated mates and destiny his entire life. His parents claimed that was what had happened to them, even though his father was a dragon from a distant planet and his mother was a psychic Earthling. It only seemed more unlikely in light of the fact that Finn wasn't their son biologically, having been one of the last in a line of royal dragons saved from Charok. It was just a story, the kind of thing that didn't actually happen in real life when people had to worry about paying bills and holding down jobs.

Nora insisted that she and Kieran were meant to be together, and things weren't any different for Kaylee and Archard, who seemed practically glued at the hip ever since they'd gotten married. But was this the kind of thing that a man would actually feel? It sounded more like a princess story that women wanted to believe in.

Elliot threw his hands in the air. "Okay, but keep in mind that as soon as everyone else knows you're dating someone, they'll want to know everything about her. And it's only more complicated now that you have Phoenix."

"Why does it have to be like that? Huh?" Finn turned on his cousin, feeling a defensive flare of anger taking over his chest. "Why does anyone have to care who I date? Having dinner with her doesn't mean I'm going to ask her to be the mother of my child, or that I'll even see her again. Everyone needs to just stay out of it. I'm taking off." He snagged his keys from the side table and yanked open the door of his apartment.

Following him out into the evening, Elliot was unflustered by Finn's short tirade. "Think what you want, but you know I'm right," he said calmly as he unlocked his sedan. "Dating you is going to put her on trial. You're the golden boy, the one whose name and genetics will carry on to another generation." He grinned and got in his car.

Finn cursed his cousin under his breath as he got behind the wheel of his own car, but he knew Elliot was probably right. No pressure at all.

———

AURORA WAS WAITING for him on the bench outside the library. Her hair had been pulled into a thick side braid. A short, navy blue skirt revealed her long legs as she crossed them, waggling one foot, and her feet were clad in thin white sandals that matched her loose shirt. She'd made good use of her time as she waited for him, a thick book on her lap.

He could've just pulled up to the curb and let her hop in, but Finn instinctively knew that wasn't good enough. Aurora might not have cared, but he did. He found a parking space, hopped out and walked over to her. "Good book?"

She held up a battered copy of *Silent Spring* by Rachel Carson. "Very."

"Heavy reading for a beautiful day like this." As he said it, he realized it was always a beautiful day when Aurora was around. It wasn't just that he was so enchanted by her, either. The weather was literally just as stunning as she was. Her hair seemed to be made of the golden strands of the sun, her eyes the nut brown of the earth. Finn wanted to just stand there and stare. He cleared his throat, reminding himself of just who he was and that time was still passing.

"But necessary." She packed the book away in a messenger bag and stood. "I'm ready when you are."

Finn drove her to a restaurant he thought she might approve of, one with cloth napkins, no straws, and local food. She chose a large salad from the menu, and he suddenly wondered if she was vegan. She seemed like the type, but his body craved meat. He couldn't help that, and it didn't seem fair to either one of them if he pretended to be something other than what he was by ordering tofu. He asked the waiter for a grass-fed bison burger.

"Tell me more about your job," she said as she sipped her water. "Just how environmentally friendly is your company?"

"It's what we're all about. We specialize in creating products that people use every day but have a lower impact on the planet. Unfortunately, the public at large isn't going to be all that interested in conservation if it isn't easy for them. They need these items to be available at a reasonable cost at their local stores. The decision to throw something in a recycle bin instead of a trash can practically needs to be made for them. It's frustrating, honestly. I don' t know why people can't see what they're doing to this place." His face flushed as he realized what he'd just done. He found himself desperately wanting to please her, but he realized just how hard that was to do for someone he hardly knew. "I'm sorry, I didn't mean to get into all that. I shouldn't be on my soapbox already."

"Step right back up onto it," she replied enthusiastically. "Someone has to. But I have to admit I still have my doubts about your company."

"Where did you hear these rumors, anyway? About Cecilia's property?" He'd thought about the old woman several times since he'd left, wondering if she'd ever found her way back from that beautiful lake or if she was still out there, staring out over the water. At least he knew Aurora was around every now and then if Cecilia needed her.

She shrugged, a casual lift of one shoulder; the movement of bone and muscle under skin more entrancing than it should've been. "I'd rather not say."

"You know, there are quite a few people who believe that land is haunted. Other employees who've been sent out to gather information on the land or talk to Cecilia come back white as a sheet and ranting gibberish, completely terrified." He'd felt the sudden breeze kick up when he'd been out there on the trail. He'd felt the way the land seemed to mesmerize all who walked on it. He'd even experienced a very confusing pathway that seemed only to open up to those it approved of. It made him wonder if that was the kind of experience everyone else had, or if it was worse.

"That's because they're too focused on living in the city. They're used to having numerous people surround them, and they find safety in that. The truth is, they're probably much safer out there in the middle of nowhere. I know I feel that way."

The waiter arrived, and Finn dug into his burger, thinking. "Cecilia said there were spirits who lived there. I wonder what she meant by that."

"I think she has some Native American blood, and she still thinks the same way her ancestors did." Aurora stabbed a cherry tomato with her fork and plucked it off the tines with her lips, distracting Finn from all thoughts of land acquisitions.

*What else could she do with those lips?* he mused.

"Tell me more about your son." She dabbed her mouth delicately and looked up at him with those mesmerizing earth-tone eyes.

It took Finn a second to even understand how she knew about his son. Once he did, Finn found himself blabbering about the baby. He told her everything he knew about Phoenix, which was relatively little, considering how short of a time he'd been alive. Then he even told her about Mandy, and how she didn't want the baby, and how her mother and father refused to raise him for her but told her she needed to do the right thing; how he was still trying to figure out just what it meant to be a father and how he was going to deal with this for the next eighteen years.

"I'm so, so sorry," he said when he realized she'd finished her meal and he'd hardly touched his. "Here I am going on about myself, and I haven't even given you a chance to speak." It'd been difficult *not* to talk when he was around her. Finn never had a hard time hiding the truth from most people. He never slipped up and revealed his true heritage or explained how relieved his family was to see that Phoenix looked like a 'normal' baby and would have no trouble blending in on this planet. But with Aurora, he wanted her to know everything. It was as though one look from those deep eyes of hers had split him open, and he was perfectly fine with it. He wanted to share everything about his job, his son, and maybe even the truth about himself. He clamped his lips over the notion.

"I don't mind," she said, bracing her chin on her hand. "It's quite the story."

"The story of a woman abandoning her baby and leaving the poor thing in my care? Doesn't exactly sound like prime-time television to me." In fact, he was learning just how difficult it was to raise a child on his own, even with his village of dragons around him. His father had gone through the same thing when Finn was a child, and he'd given him plenty of advice, but no amount of talking could quite make up for the sleepless nights and the endless bottles.

"Maybe not, but it's real," she said, leaning forward a little and flicking her braid behind her shoulder. "It's nice to meet someone who isn't just trying to put up a façade to fool me into thinking something about himself other than the truth."

A new sort of guilt took over as he realized just how wrong that was. This poor girl had no idea what kind of beast was sitting across the table from her. What would she do if she knew? Jump up from the table and run screaming out into the street? Check him into a mental facility? Tell him she was into that sort of thing? He'd never been interested in testing those waters before now. "Still, it's not an easy thing to do. I don't usually have a lot of free time, and I'm usually dead on my feet. I never drank more coffee than I do now. Ethically sourced, of course."

"Of course," she replied with a smile.

"Anyway, tell me more about yourself. This has been entirely too one-sided." He picked up his burger and took a bite to force himself to shut up. And he truly did want to know more about Aurora, more than anything. She could tell him her parents were circus freaks and she was actually an international spy, and he'd still want to hear every detail.

"There's not much to say. My parents were hippies, and they practically raised me in the middle of the woods. My mother passed away quite some time ago. I spend all my time studying our planet and what we can do to help it. Most of the time, I'm just picking up trash along the hiking trails and chastising people for throwing cigarettes on the ground, but I'd like to think I could do something more at some point."

Finn swallowed, thankful he hadn't deprived himself of the meat. His inner dragon was fighting tooth and talon to get out, and it was going to take a lot of strength to keep him controlled. Finn had been able to suppress him for a while by talking about himself, but the beast seemed more agitated with every word Aurora spoke. The effect only amplified every time he glanced up at her. What was this woman doing to him? "I'm sure you will. Anyone who cares enough can make a big difference."

"But how far is too far?" she asked quietly, her eyes challenging him. "And how do we know that what we're being told is the truth? If a government agency tells you a body of water is safe to drink from or that they're protecting a certain species of bird, how do you know they're being honest? I mean, look at what's happened in Flint, Michigan."

As much as Finn thought he was into saving the planet, it was clear that Aurora was hardcore. "I guess we really don't know," he admitted.

"I like to think most people are honest. Other than that, I just have to do the best I can with the tools that are available to me."

"Do any of those tools include uncovering the truth about what your company is *really* doing?" she pressed.

Finn blinked at her, unsure of what to say. "I'll look into it," he said finally, "but I honestly don't think they're lying about this. It's too important to them."

Aurora seemed content to drop the subject and move on to lighter conversation like the weather or her studies at the university. When most of the other patrons had gone home for the night and the waiter was pointedly sweeping the floor just a couple tables away, Finn suggested they get going. "Do you want to head over to the theatre to see if there's anything good on?" He wasn't sure Aurora was even a movie type of person. He still knew so little about her.

"Thanks, but I'm a little tired. Can you just drop me off over at the university where you picked me up?"

It was fine with him if she didn't want to extend their date, and Finn knew he'd already stayed out late enough considering he had a baby to get home to, but he didn't want to leave her just yet. She was mysterious. She spoke her mind without worrying what he would think, yet she never really tried to start an argument. Aurora was unlike any other woman he'd ever met, and he felt his entire existence gravitating toward her, both physically and mentally. His body was harder to control as he stood up to gently pull out her chair. He was trying to be a gentleman, but his dragon didn't want him to be. He could smell the flowery scent of her hair, the softness of her skin, the tempting heat of her. "I don't mind taking you to your place. I'd feel better about that than just leaving you on the quad."

"Really, it's okay." She laid her hand on his arm as they walked to the car, squeezing gently. Finn felt a sense of peace mixed with something else. If he'd allowed himself to fully finish the thought, it was as though Aurora's inner strength was letting him know this was truly what she wanted. "I have a few things I need to pick up there, anyway."

He drove her back to the same bench where he'd picked her up, and once again, he parked and got out of the car. He longed to pull her into his arms, to feel the press of her body against his own, and run his hands down the smooth lines of her back. He wanted to shift right there on the sidewalk and show her who he truly was, knowing that

MEG RIPLEY

whomever he ended up with would have to understand the truth about him. His wingtips itched near his shoulder blades.

"Listen, I know it wasn't anything fancy, but I had a good time. I'd like to see you again." His words were polite, but the way he felt inside wasn't polite at all. He'd never felt as close to his roots as he did in that moment, wanting to scoop her up into his arms and fly off with her to some distant mountain where no other man could get his hands on her. He wanted to hide her away from the world until he could make her his own, hoarding her like a pile of gold.

She smiled at him. It was such a simple expression, but it meant everything when he saw it on her face. Even the campus street lamps could make her look good. "I'd like that."

"Can I call you?"

"Oh. I don't have a phone." She gave that casual shrug again, as if that was just the way everyone did it. "But we'll see each other around. I'm sure of it. Good night, Finn." She turned to walk away.

He only let her get a couple of steps before he couldn't stand it anymore. "Wait." He grabbed her by the waist and turned her around. The moment hung suspended there between them, frozen, their lips inches apart. Her deep eyes were surprised, but not afraid. Aurora was pliant in his arms, and he pressed a kiss to her lips.

To his surprise, she wrapped her arms around his neck and kissed him back, returning the emotions he'd been feeling flooding through his body the entire night. Finn wanted to focus on the way her lips moved softly against his, like velvet; the way her body felt in his arms. She was so much more real than he ever could've hoped for, like finding a dream was actually just a memory of the truth. But his dragon was fighting him hard now, lashing, snarling and demanding to be seen. It was a battle worth having. He could've kissed her until the sun rose and students began milling around them, and he wouldn't have even noticed.

But Aurora eventually pulled away, giving him a wink. "I'll see you around."

Finn padded back to his car, resisting the strong urge to go back for her once again. But he couldn't let the beast inside him scare her off, not now. That had been the best date he'd ever recalled having, and they hadn't done any more than have a simple dinner. They hadn't even gone to a fancy restaurant, but she didn't seem to mind. Finn practically floated home.

AURORA SIPPED A HARD LEMONADE AND GAVE FINN A SIDELONG LOOK. *Gods, he's gorgeous.* She'd known that the second she'd stepped out of the woods and found him with Nora, and at that moment, her mind demanded to know if the two of them were together. She was almost embarrassed to admit to herself how relieved she was to find out they were cousins.

She didn't feel these things about men, normally. Aurora was too busy helping her father run the fae kingdom and saving the environment to fuss over relationships. She simply didn't have the time. And, she had reminded herself over and over again, she wasn't here to look for a relationship. She was here to find out everything she could about the dragons.

The music tapered off as the singer strummed out the last bright notes on his guitar. The audience, small but enthusiastic, clapped and cheered. "Thank you, folks. You've been a lovely crowd. Be sure to grab a few drinks, and don't leave just yet because the The Dandelions will be out on stage in just a minute. Make sure you tip generously, too, since all proceeds are going toward solar panels for the high school. Thanks again."

"Pretty good stuff, huh? I wasn't completely sure what type of music you'd like." Finn turned to her, looking happy and hopeful. He held a beer in his hand, but he'd been sipping even more slowly than she was.

Aurora looked up at the lights strung overhead, noting they were fueled by tiny solar panels of their own. The entire event seemed to have sprung out of nowhere, in an empty field at the end of a country road. Aurora couldn't imagine people showing up to a fundraiser in a remote spot like this. But the folding chairs had been arranged, the bar made of old pallet wood had been delivered, and a small stage was set up. It was romantic and exciting.

"It's pretty good, actually," she admitted. It'd taken Aurora a while to get used to human music, but the acoustic guitars and harmonious folk tunes had been enjoyable. "And the drinks aren't bad, either. How did you even hear about this?"

He shrugged casually, still smiling as though his lips wouldn't let him stop. "I get word of anything like this though work."

"I see." She didn't like making him bring that up. She knew Anderson Environmental couldn't be trusted, even if Finn didn't know that. "Well, I appreciate you bringing me."

"What can I say? I enjoy spending time with you." He wrapped his free hand around hers.

Aurora looked down, not wanting him to see the sparkle of magic that swelled in her eyes. It didn't matter how many times she reminded herself this was all for show; her body was responding to his as though it had a mind of its own. Her magic surged inside her like ocean waves, pulsing, demanding, eroding at her willpower. She wanted to hold his face in her hands, stare into those spellbinding blue eyes of his, and tell him the truth about who she was.

Instead, she pressed her lips together demurely. "So do I."

"I know I shouldn't say this, but you're not like other girls." His thumb rubbed gently against the back of her hand, eliciting a frisson of electricity with each stroke.

"I don't know if I should take that as a compliment or an insult," she said with a giggle. Why was she acting like some smitten girl?

"Definitely a compliment." Finn's eyes held hers, once bright blue now the color of the night sky above them in the dim light, but they dropped to her lips for a moment.

Aurora's eyes did the same, studying the curve of his lips and his hard jaw. She'd kissed him before; it shouldn't have been a big deal at all. But her lips seemed to have forgotten, or perhaps they remembered it so well, they knew what they were missing. Their heads bent together just slightly, hesitating, trying to be sure.

But then The Dandelions struck their first chord of a rousing tune, breaking the mood of the moment, and Aurora turned to the stage. But Finn didn't allow it to happen. He squeezed her hand gently while his free hand cupped her chin and turned her back toward him, his lips gentle and seeking as they pressed and retreated. Aurora parted her lips, feeling that glow rise inside her once again as his tongue slid gently across hers. Her entire body was filled with light and sound energy, and the rest of the world had dissolved around her.

When they pulled away from each other, Aurora was surprised to find they weren't simply floating in the vastness of space. Her wings tingled inside her, itching to unwind. She pushed her back against the chair, reminding herself she had to keep them in check.

The rest of the concert seemed to fly by, with their hands still entwined between them. Aurora hardly listened to the music at all, concentrating only on Finn. It was so hard to remember that she was there on a mission, not a date. But the very sound of his blood inside his veins was enough to distract her.

When the concert was over and they'd picked their way through the grass to his car, Finn held open the passenger side door for her, always the gentleman. He'd been smiling at the concert, but his jaw looked harder and his eyes colder as he got behind the wheel and headed down the road.

"What's up?" she asked.

Finn pulled in a deep breath. "There's something I'd like to ask you, but it makes me a little nervous."

The statement alone made Aurora freeze. Had he figured out who she really was? After all, she and the other fae had no idea what kind of magic the dragons might possess. Could he sense her true self with the same intuition that told her he was a dragon? "What is it?"

He pulled his lower lips between his teeth and let it go again. He glanced at her before returning his eyes to the road. She'd never seen him look so hesitant. "I've been having such a great time with you, I tend to forget the real world is still out there waiting for me. I don't think about the fact I have to go to work the next day. And I also don't think of myself as a father with responsibilities."

Aurora stared at him for a long moment, unsure of where he was going with this. "I enjoy our time together, too."

He slowed the car to turn onto the highway. "Then I guess it's all right to talk to you about this. I mean, if I don't, it's not fair to either one of us."

"Go on..." She didn't like the slight tone of impatience in her voice, but she was dying to know what this was all about.

"Aurora, you know I have a son. I'm a single dad, and that's a huge responsibility in my life. I get so excited about seeing you, but I feel guilty about leaving him. What I'm trying to say is anyone I'm going to be with has to be okay with spending time with my kid, too. Not like all the time, and I'm not asking you to make some big commitment that you—we—aren't ready for, but I just want to know if you're okay with that."

Her heart melted. If she hadn't had a soft spot for this dragon before, it was definitely there now. He was a passionate man who just wanted to be a good father. "Oh, Finn. Of course I am."

Finn raised an eyebrow. "Okay enough that you wouldn't mind coming back to my place to meet him? Nora is there watching him."

So far, they'd been able to avoid anything that had to do with each other's homes. She'd always insisted that he pick her up at the university or meet her somewhere; obviously, he couldn't come into the fae realm. And it'd only seemed fair to Aurora to keep her own distance from his life, never asking what his place was like.

Her curiosity was stronger than the voice in her head cautioning her against getting any more involved in his life than she had to. "Sure. I'd love to meet the little guy."

As they pulled up in front of his apartment building and headed up the elevator, Aurora wondered just what she was letting herself get into. She hadn't been bothered by the fact Finn had a child, because it didn't matter in a relationship that wasn't even real. But did meeting his son make it real? Did that change what she was really there for?

Nora sat in a recliner in the living room, holding a bundle of blankets on her lap. She blinked sleepily at them. "I think he missed you," she whispered, standing and handing the baby to Finn. "He was a bit upset after dinner."

Aurora felt stiff and awkward, watching Finn with the baby after Nora headed home. He seemed to be a natural at it, folding his arms around the child, looking softly at his face. She was just starting to relax again when Finn held the infant out toward her.

It was one thing to see the little fae children in the nursery back home. They were the offspring of her own people, many of them cousins. But seeing this child was completely different. It shouldn't have been, because a baby was a baby. But everything about Finn was challenging her expectations.

She held out her arms for the warm weight, pulling it in toward her abdomen. Phoenix opened his sleepy eyes and looked up at her. They were the same blue as his father's, deep and revealing, with so many layers and levels, Aurora could get lost in them. But they were also sweet and innocent. She felt a warmth rising in her, mixing with that mysterious wave of energy she'd been battling all night.

"He's adorable, Finn," she whispered, holding her finger out to let the baby grasp it. "Absolutely adorable." There were better words to describe him, she knew; something to explain just how fascinating this tiny person was. But she was so flabbergasted by the way she felt when she held him, the way her magic whirled around her heart.

"Thank you." Finn was every bit the proud father as he watched them. The lights were dim to account for the sleepy baby, but he practically sparkled. "I'm sorry if I was a little weird in the car. It's just that I haven't dated anyone since Phoenix came along, and he's certainly changed things."

"Hey, don't worry about it." She handed him back reluctantly, feeling the emptiness of the lack of weight on her arms. Aurora had never enjoyed holding a baby that much. "I understand."

"Give me just a second. I'm going to lay him down for the night. I think he's ready."

"Of course." Aurora was grateful for a moment alone. Being near Finn was almost too much to handle. Now there was his son to contend with as well? She slipped off her sandals and dug her toes into the plush carpet. It wasn't the same as standing on the grass and feeling the energy of the Earth seep into her, but she could reach out with her senses, through the building below her, and still feel the pulse of it. She grounded herself in it, reminding herself that she was strong enough to keep herself together. Her tension settled as she pushed her power out and away.

Closing her eyes and feeling the sweet relaxation of it all, Aurora tried to remember when she'd had to do this last, but she couldn't. She'd only felt weak and out of touch since the wizards had invaded her land. Something had happened to her magic, though she didn't know what it was.

"Sorry about that," Finn said as he came back down the hallway. "I had to get him all tucked in."

"Thank you for letting me meet him," she blurted, saying what she'd been feeling before she had a chance to think about it too much. "He's a darling."

"I'm glad you came." Finn stepped forward, putting his hands on her hips and gazing down into her eyes. "You're something else."

When he kissed her, she felt all that energy she'd let drain out of her body come rushing back. She could barely contain the flux of power as their lips and tongues entwined, and her physical self was quickly taking over. She slipped her fingers under the hem of his shirt, feeling the smooth, hard muscle of his lower back.

Finn responded in kind, running his hands down her backside and pressing her closer. His fingers bunched in the fabric of her dress, telling her of his desire. She felt it, too, and she pushed that uncontrollable energy back down into the earth before it all became too much to bear.

On every date they'd been on, Aurora had concentrated on holding herself back. She knew she couldn't get too attached; this was all just a tactic to save the inhabitants of the fae realm. But now, in his arms, in the privacy of his home, she was no longer a princess on a mission. She was a woman, one who needed to feel everything this man could give her.

She pulled his shirt up over his head, grateful for the thin cotton of her dress that allowed her to feel the heat of his skin right through it. Running her hands over his chest, she bit back a moan. He was chiseled and strong, his wide shoulders encompassing her as he pulled at the fabric of her dress. It floated over her head and to the floor, and Finn's passion became more evident as he pulled her hips against his.

The next thing she knew, they were sinking onto the couch together, their arms and legs entwining around each other as the last of their garments hit the carpet.

"God damn," he breathed, pulling back for a moment to study her nakedness.

She burned delightfully, running her fingertips down his shoulders to feel the strength of his arms. There wasn't anything about him that she could complain about, from his wide chest and shoulders, to his chiseled abs, to his well-muscled thighs and the throbbing pleasure that awaited her between them.

He buried himself inside her, each of them gasping at the sensation. The way he filled her body reflected the way he filled her soul, a powerful force that rushed inside her most intimate places. Instead of overtaking her, he merged with her, their spirits twining around each other as they explored the new energy surrounding them.

Her hips moved in sync with his as they pushed themselves to the very edge. She knew now, with absolute certainty, that he was a dragon. He hadn't shifted. She hadn't seen so much as a claw or a scale. But she could feel it inside him just as surely as she could feel him inside her, that inner beast writhing and struggling against his human form.

And it was absolutely beautiful. Knowing that she lay with someone so powerful, so animalistic, so not of this world just as she wasn't, turned her on even more. The bubble of joy that had started in the pit of her abdomen raced up and exploded through the rest of her body. She cried out as she buried her face in his shoulders. Finn shuddered, tightening his grip on her as he thrust hard and fast. They lay together for a long moment, catching their breath.

Finn brushed her curls aside and whispered in her ear. "Stay here with me tonight."

Aurora could argue against the idea. She could make excuses about not wanting to interfere with whatever he might have going on with the baby, or she could claim she had plans for the morning. She could even try to tell herself they weren't ready for something like that.

But she couldn't help herself.

They'd picked up their clothes and padded over to his massive bed, where they'd made long, deliciously slow love all night long. He held her afterward, his fingers gently stroking the side of her breast, his arms heavy with sleep. Thoughts of what truly waited for her outside his apartment came swirling to her mind, reminding her that she had a duty. But she shoved them all away and concentrated on the way his body felt against hers, that determined heat that sank through her flesh and buried itself in her soul, a pleasant and addictive addition. That was the only thing she wanted to think about.

## 7

---

AURORA SAT IN HER QUARTERS, A SPACE SHE'D BUILT HERSELF SEVERAL years ago when she'd felt the need to get away from courtly life and find a place of her own. She'd found an old tree far from the castle, its massive branches thick and stately. She'd spoken with the tree for a long time, her palm resting against its bark as she explained what she was looking for. The tree hadn't needed any convincing; it was quite happy to welcome the king's daughter into its arms. Her little tree-house was quiet and peaceful, but she never felt as though she were alone. There was simply too much life in the fae realm for anyone to feel that way, and it gave her a sense of peace she always found herself missing when she ventured out into the human world.

At least that was how things had always been before.

Aurora leaned out her window. It troubled her to think humans covered their windows with glass and curtains to keep nature out. Now, she could see just how few fae were out on the pathways. Everyone was afraid to go about their business; the king had ordered them not to. He didn't want them risking their lives, and Aurora could understand that. But it didn't seem right that they should submit to these wizards, either.

She sighed, stretching her wings behind her and thinking about Finn. He was a dragon. She knew that for certain now, even without seeing him shift in front of her eyes. But she didn't need to see his wings, claws, or scales to sense the beast inside him, especially after the night before. She'd known he was different from other humans the moment she'd met him, and she had picked up a similar energy from Nora. She'd be able to use them to gather information for the wizards just as she'd planned.

But what she hadn't expected was the way she'd felt about Finn. Aurora slipped out the doorway and onto the outstretched branches of her tree, tiptoeing out to the very edge until she could sit where the breeze bounced her around on the springy wood. She'd never had a fear of falling, but now she was falling in a completely different way.

Finn was the sort of person she'd never expected to find in the human realm. He was kind and gentlemanly, opening doors for her and insisting that she be seated first. It wasn't the sort of thing that really mattered in the long run. Even in the fae realm, mated men didn't try as hard after a while. But Aurora still found herself blushing with pleasure every time the events of last night swirled in her mind, and she longed to be around him and experience it again.

Then there was the fact he cared about preserving the natural world. He was naïve when it came to his company's intentions for Cecilia's land, but that was only because someone had straight-out lied to him. Aurora had heard the men who'd trespassed there before, and she knew exactly what they wanted to do. That was why Cecilia was always more than happy to let Aurora scare away any unwelcome visitors.

And when the old woman had told her that yet another man was being sent out there, Aurora had been more than ready to stir up a little mischief. She just hadn't expected him to be Finn. She'd watched him from afar as she blocked his path, testing his patience and trying to discern just what kind of guy he was.

Aurora frowned, recalling how difficult it'd been to perform that little trick. In fact, it was getting harder to do what she'd been doing her entire life. Her body felt heavier, her connection to the plants and wildlife not as deep. She had to wonder if it had anything to do with that heavy iron chain around her father's neck and the other fae who'd already been enslaved.

She unfurled her wings as a particularly thick breeze made the branch bob frantically under her weight. The uncertain feeling she had out there on the limb mirrored the way Finn made her feel, only her problem with him was much deeper. She dove off the branch and headed for the castle.

King Oren was alone in his study, bent over several dusty tomes with ragged pages. He didn't hear her as she came in, and Aurora stood in the doorway to watch him for a moment. *When did he get so old?* she mused. Fae didn't age in the same manner as humans, but they did, in fact, age; she hadn't even noticed it happening in her father over the years. His hair, once the same dark shade as his eyes, had slowly streaked with various shades of silver until it was no longer brown at all. His eyes looked tired; his shoulders, slumped. He had once been so strong, so active; it hurt her to see him reduced to a mere shell of what he had been.

It hadn't only been the years that affected him. It'd been the wizards, too.

She cleared her throat. "May I speak with you for a moment?"

Oren looked up, startled. He slammed his book shut and shoved it to the side. "Of course. What is it?"

"What are you doing?" Aurora tried to take a peek at the volume, but her father only set another one on top of it.

"Don't you worry about it," he said with a scowl.

It wasn't like her father to snap at her, nor was it like him to hide what he was doing. He'd often prided himself on just how much of his work he'd involved her in, wanting to make sure she would be a capable ruler someday.

But despite his efforts, she'd caught the title of the book. "I thought you said there wasn't any amount of magic that could get that chain off your neck," she chided, but she allowed the bubble of hope that had risen in her chest. Was there some ancient spell he'd suddenly remembered? Some incantation his grandfather had told him that would set him free if he could only find the right words?

"There isn't," he said with a sigh. "At least, there isn't one I can find. These wizards have a completely different type of magic; it isn't of this world. They're incredibly strong. I've heard them reference someone named Tazarre, whom I assume to have been a great wizard leader of some sort. They use his name all the time, saying they do everything for him. Maybe I need to figure out who he is and ask him how to get this infernal thing off." He scratched at his blistered neck.

Aurora felt a sympathetic pain shoot under her own skin. *How could they have done this to him?* "You should let me talk to them," she said, already planning a trip to the far side of their realm where the wizards had begun to establish themselves.

Oren straightened, looking indignant. "Send my own daughter to sacrifice herself to those cretins? Nonsense!"

"They can't be that powerful," Aurora argued. "Just because we don't know anything about them doesn't mean we should let them get away with this."

The king sighed, his head bowing. "What do you expect me to do? They're already holding our people hostage, including me. If I push things any further, there's no telling what they'll do. I can't risk my entire kingdom falling to them. What will I do if they take you as well?" He flopped his hands uselessly at his sides. "As I've said, I don't even know how to help them."

"I do," she replied confidently.

He eyed her curiously, his hands folding in front of his belly.

She pulled in a deep breath, knowing he wouldn't like this. He'd asked her once already to stay out of it, citing her safety as the reason, but she'd refused. She was an adult, and she would be queen one day. If she found a way to help the kingdom, then she should have every right to do so.

"The wizards want the dragons, right?"

"That's what they tell me," he said.

"Well, I just happen to know a couple of them."

His eyes widened, and he pushed his head forward to study her more carefully. "Since when? You've never said anything about this before."

"I tried to, right after you explained what the wizards were really up to. But you were so determined for me to not get involved, you wouldn't even let me speak."

He lowered himself back onto the chair near his desk, weak and broken. "I'm sorry for that. I had no idea. But it's never been my habit to stop you from speaking your mind, no matter what I thought the consequences might be. I shouldn't have tried to start now."

"Don't blame yourself. You were trying to protect me." Aurora felt uneasy, but she had to push on with this. "And I owe you an apology. You told me to stay out of this trouble with the wizards, but I haven't been. I've been in the Earthen realm, talking to the dragons."

"Oh, dear." He picked at the cuffs of his robe. The fabric was starting to fray, and his thick fingers played with a loose thread. "You didn't tell them about us, did you? Just because the wizards have it out for them doesn't mean they're our allies."

"I know." Although she was starting to think Finn and Nora could easily become allies. They seemed like decent enough people. Then again, her father had initially thought that about the wizards as well. "I just thought they would be a good connection for us. I could learn more about them by befriending them, and in the process, I might be able to get the wizards the information they want after all."

"I see. If there are two dragons, then it's possible there are more. Maybe we can find out where they live. Then, the wizards can go harass them and leave us in peace. It's not the way I'd prefer to do things, but I'm not sure what other choice we have."

"I know." Aurora rubbed one foot against the other, thinking of the dates she'd had with Finn over the last few weeks. Time had flown by quickly, and still, he'd never given her any true indication of who he and his family were. She didn't press him, knowing it would throw up his defenses if he realized she knew the truth. But she could also tell how difficult it was for him to hold back, how much he longed to open up to her and explain everything.

There was something about Finn that was changing her as well. Every time she saw him, Aurora felt a cool stream of tranquility flow through her body. It carried an undercurrent of excitement with it, the kind of joy that came from seeing a dewy field at sunrise or watching a flower bloom. It was as though Finn's energies pulled at her own and made her a different person; stronger. If he went with her, she had no doubt she could put up a wall of protection around the perimeter of Cecilia's property, and those lying bastards from Anderson Environmental would never bother the old woman again.

But that wasn't on Finn's agenda, just as falling for him wasn't hers. She shook her head, reminding herself that it was only because her relationship with him was fresh and new that she still found it so thrilling. No other Earth being had tempted her like that before, and the excitement would wear off eventually.

"Originally, I thought I could simply pump them for information. I went to the woods just past our Earthen boundary when I sensed Nora was nearby. She goes out there all the time to make videos for her YouTube channel."

Oren squinted at her. "Her *what*?"

"It's a form of entertainment. Anyway, that part's not all that important. She had her cousin with her, a man who's a dragon as well. He can shift between his physical forms, just like she can. He was nice enough, and I realized I'd have twice the chances to find out more about their kind."

At the time, what she hadn't realized was what she'd been feeling for him, even when they'd first met. Finn was incredibly attractive, but in a completely different way than fae men were. His broad shoulders looked strong and all-encompassing, like he could pick up the world and carry it effortlessly. His shaggy blonde hair made him seem more boyish and playful, and combined with those deep blue eyes, she could gaze at him all day long.

And then there was the energy and the strength that radiated so clearly from him. Finn didn't seem to be aware of it, but she most definitely was. Aurora felt like a moth pulled to a flame, gladly dragged toward whatever her destiny might be as long as she got to be close to him. It was ridiculous and illogical, the kind of thing that humans would wax romantic about, but she couldn't help it.

"I see. And you've been spending a lot of time with these beings?"

Her father's question broke her out of her reverie. She swallowed. "Yes. Quite a bit, actually." She'd seen Nora occasionally, but she'd never pushed their acquaintance any further than running into each other in the woods or at the university. But Finn, on the other hand, had become a significant part of her life. She managed to "run into" him all the time, immediately sensing when he was in the area, unable to stay away. Their first date had gone well, and she'd agreed to let them continue. They'd gone for long walks, taken a boat out onto the campus lake, and explored the used bookstores in town. He hung onto every word she said as though it were the first time he'd heard a person say anything, watching her lips and leaning forward as she prattled on about her ideas. He never criticized her for caring so much about the land and the wildlife and what happened to them, as she knew most people would.

The real kicker was when he'd brought her back to his apartment to meet his son. Aurora hadn't wanted to go. It wasn't because she didn't like Finn or wasn't curious about where he lived. In fact, she found herself wanting to know more and more about him as time went on. But she knew that once she saw this child she'd heard of so many times, she'd have no choice but to carry on with her plan.

"And?" Oren pressed.

"And it turns out he has a very young child; an infant son. He's only a few months old, and I think it's the right set of circumstances I've been looking for." Guilt washed over her as she spoke the words, but she couldn't take them back now. As awful as she felt about it, she knew it was the one plan for saving her fellow fae that might actually stand a chance.

"A changeling..." Oren breathed, bringing shaking fingers to his lips as he contemplated this. "We can get more information from the dragons than they might ever give up to you. Parents don't usually worry about what they say in front of their offspring, so a changeling would make the perfect spy. He might even get to see them in their natural form. Then we can use that information to send the wizards out of our world and back to fighting their own battle." He turned slowly away from her as he spoke, gazing out the window in deep thought. "Perhaps we can even use the child directly, if necessary."

"What do you mean?" She swallowed the lump in her throat again, but it refused to go away.

"We'd have the child here, of course, while our decoy is in the dragon's den. When we've gathered enough intelligence, or if things get particularly bad and we don't have a choice, we can use the baby as leverage against the dragons. We can make them submit to us, and ultimately, the wizards."

She shifted uncomfortably as she thought about the babe's innocent sapphire eyes, his chubby little fingers, and the way he cooed in Finn's protective arms. "Father, I'm not sure this is the best idea after all. I—I never should've brought it up."

Oren turned to her, his eyes distant and sad. "I can't say it's the best scenario, either. We've lived here in relative peace for so long, but I suppose everything changes eventually. And what choice do we have? I don't have any doubt that the wizards will siphon every last drop of our magic and potentially even kill us, all under my reign. It's shameful, Aurora. That's not the kingdom I wanted you to inherit."

She hadn't missed the glint of tears in his eyes. "Don't talk like that. I'm not inheriting this place for a very long time. There's plenty of time to get the wizards off our backs. We'll be all right; we can do this."

The last sentence was for her own benefit as much as his. She needed to believe she could do this, as much as she hated it. She'd fought so hard to preserve the environment on Earth, and it was time she fought just as hard for her own world.

"Very well. Summon Basil. He'll be the right man for the job, and I think he'll particularly enjoy being young again."

The king was correct. Basil was a shriveled old fae with wisps of gray hair hanging limply from his spotted scalp. His knobby fingers and knees showed he'd had a long life of hard work, and even his wings drooped as though he couldn't quite hold them up any longer. But his cloudy eyes were alight when Oren explained the plan.

"How delightful!" Basil enthused, practically clapping his mangled hands together. "When shall I be sent on my way, your majesty?"

Despite Basil's eagerness, Oren was grave. "You must understand that we could be sending you into some very dangerous territory. We don't know much about the dragons or what they might do if they discover you. And of course, the wizards are a constant threat, no matter what world you're in. I want you to be sure about this."

Aurora wished she could be more sure. She knew it was the right thing to do for her people, for her kingdom. She was hopeful this would be temporary; that they wouldn't have to reveal what they'd done with little Phoenix. If they did, she knew Finn would never forgive her. But, as her father had said, what choice did they have?

Oren laid his hand on Basil's head, closed his eyes and pulled in a deep breath. Despite the iron weakening his innate powers, the king didn't need to speak the words of the ancient incantation to make the magic happen. The ancient fae seemed to melt, his body twisting and morphing before their eyes as his wrinkled skin became pink and plump, his hair shriveled to a cap of golden locks, and his rheumy eyes shone bright and clear.

The king picked up the newly-made baby and held it out toward Aurora. "Do you think he'll pass?"

She resisted taking the child into her arms for the moment, knowing it was Basil. But even with that knowledge, she didn't think anyone else would know the difference. The mental image she had passed along to her father had been accurately transcribed onto this old fae's face, and even Finn probably wouldn't know the difference.

Aurora held out her arms and took him, surprised by the warm weight of the child in her arms. It still felt wrong on so many levels, but there was no going back now. The sun was setting, and it was time to go. Without another word, she left her father's chambers and headed out. Fireflies buzzed along the path, but she didn't need their glow to find her way to the thinner part of the veil that kept the fae realm isolated from the Earthlings. She knew this path like she knew herself, and she walked it without paying attention to its twists and turns. Aurora was paying much more attention to the delicate baby bundled in her arms.

She had adored seeing Phoenix just waking up from a nap, rubbing his eyes with his little fists. Aurora had instantly felt her heart latch onto to him once Finn had eventually handed him over—after Aurora hadn't run from the room screaming—and she'd felt the child's own magic working on her.

And then there was the way Finn looked when he was interacting with his son. He was outwardly handsome, but he took on a whole new quality when he held the infant in his brawny arms. He was softer, yet stronger; sweeter, yet protective. Aurora liked it. A lot.

She slipped through the veil with ease, pausing for a moment to listen to the sound of the forest around her. It was almost completely dark now. She sensed no human presence in the area, as it should be. The deer, raccoons and other wildlife knew she was there, and she could hear them speaking to her, welcoming her. Aurora had to wonder if they would feel the same if they understood the true nature of her mission.

Though she'd made it a policy to never expose her true form while on Earth, she spread her wings and lifted into the air, flitting high over the heads of anyone who might still be out. She found Finn's apartment building easily enough, a massive brick edifice in the gentrified part of town. Landing softly on the fire escape, she slid the window to the nursery open. Outlined by a square of silver moonlight, Phoenix was sleeping peacefully in his crib. She could hear the muffled sound of a television in the other room, and her heart thumped, knowing Finn was just on the other side of the wall.

She nestled Basil down against the soft blue sheets, and he blinked happily at her. Aurora had no doubt the old fae would be living the good life there, resting on soft surfaces, constantly entertained by his family and caregivers, and well fed. It wasn't for him that she worried.

Phoenix stirred only a little as she lifted him away from his crib, away from his home. He snuggled in against her as she settled him in her arms, turning his face toward her as though she was who he'd been waiting for. The loving, motherly instinct that instantly captured her heart when she held him was even more difficult to understand than the way she responded to Finn.

She turned toward the window and paused. *Finn.* He was there in the apartment. Anyone could've been there to turn on the television, but she intuitively knew it was him. What would happen if she went to him and asked for help? It would mean revealing everything. But was there a chance he would step up and help her fight these horrid wizards?

She stiffened her shoulders as she become overwhelmed with uncertainty. She'd never liked this plan, but it didn't seem like a good idea to reveal her true nature either, subjecting herself to however the dragons might respond. Granted, her magic was strong, but she didn't know enough about the dragons yet to understand their full potential.

She took a long, slow breath as she slipped back out the window. The nighttime breeze was cool against her skin as she stood there for a long moment, examining the cityscape. This was how humans viewed the world, with its artificial lights and concrete buildings. They saw the hardness that they'd created for themselves instead of the soft, sweetness of nature. How could they think this was better? How did this not drive them crazy?

King Oren met her at the entrance, the concern clear on his face. He glanced at the child, and for a moment, Aurora wondered if he could tell the difference without using his magic.

"How did it go?" he asked nervously.

"Successfully."

She didn't tell him how horrible she felt taking Phoenix from his bed and from his father, as though she'd ripped him straight from Finn's arms.

She didn't tell him how she'd already made up her mind to ensure Phoenix got the best possible care while he lived there.

She found herself already trying to make up for the horror of what she'd done.

# 8

---

"What do you think of this one?" Finn stopped the stroller and pointed at a table full of fresh vegetables. "Do you like zucchini?"

Aurora smiled at him. He'd asked her to come to the farmer's market with him. From what she could tell from human movies, this wasn't a typical date. They were supposed to be eating expensive dinners, drinking wine, and blowing more money than either one of them ever had the right to. She couldn't expect Finn to be a normal guy, since he definitely wasn't, but he'd grown up here on Earth, after all. He continued to surprise her with the unique activities he'd planned, and some of them were completely spontaneous. He was showing her his real side, not just some censored version that was meant to impress.

"I do like zucchini," she said, looking them over. "What about you?"

"Honestly? I really only like zucchini bread. My mom makes it, and it's more like cake than anything. Tons of sugar and butter and things like that, and I know it's terrible for me, but it's so good. Especially slathered with a thick layer of cream cheese." His face flushed slightly, something that happened a lot when he was embarrassed. It gave him a boyish charm that she liked.

"Have you ever tried it sautéed, grilled, or roasted? Maybe with just a little olive oil, salt, and pepper?" She selected a couple of the green squash and paid the man behind the table. As she placed them in the canvas tote bag on the back of the stroller, she could feel Finn's warm gaze on her. There was a chemistry between them that they carried around like a rope tied from one to the other, keeping them from getting too far apart.

"They just taste bitter to me. And they get cold really fast. If a food is supposed to be hot, I like for it to be piping."

She smiled at that, figuring it made perfect sense. *A dragon would like his food hot, wouldn't he?* she mused. "I'll have to make it for you sometime. Maybe you'll like the way I make it."

What the hell was she saying? She couldn't bring him back to her house to cook for him, considering it was in a whole different realm. And, no matter how her body called out for his, she couldn't be involved with Finn any more than was necessary to keep this charade going. Eventually, he'd find out what she'd done. Eventually, she'd be turning him and his cousin—and probably the rest of his family—over to the wizards.

The true implications of what she'd done hit her like a wall.

"I'd like that. Hey, are you all right?" He put his hand on her shoulder, peering into her face with concern.

"I think, um, I think I'm just a little hot." The farmer's market had been set up on an empty parking lot out in the sun. It was definitely warm, although a fae was more likely to get too cold than too hot. But she felt sick to her stomach, and a sheen of sweat appeared on her forehead.

"Here. Come this way." He led her between two booths to a grassy area under the trees. Folding chairs had been arranged in front of a makeshift stage, where a small folk band sang old time songs and tried to get the audience involved. It reminded her of one of their dates, the fundraiser concert out in the middle of nowhere, but the jangly music only reflected the jangling of her nerves. The only people who'd really stopped to listen to the band seemed to be senior citizens trying to get out of the sun or young mothers whose little ones were content to toddle along to the music for a few moments.

Finn made sure Aurora was seated before parking the stroller next to her. "Wait here. I'll be right back."

Aurora wasn't interested in the music. It wasn't bad, for human stuff, but it was still a bit loud and obnoxious. Basil didn't seem to mind, staring at the band with his wide blue eyes that should've been

Phoenix's. "I hope you're enjoying yourself," she muttered. "And I hope this all ends up worth it in the end."

Basil couldn't respond beyond a drooly grin and slapping his hands against the side of the stroller.

Finn reappeared with a cold bottle of water and handed it to her. "This should help."

"Thanks." She took it and sipped slowly, knowing it would help, even though her real problem wasn't the heat. The water wasn't nearly as refreshing as what flowed through crisp, clear streams in her own realm, but it was good enough. Maybe her standards were slipping. Aurora figured that could eventually happen if one were to spend too much time on Earth.

The music rose to a crescendo and ended with a crash as the singer announced they'd be taking a break. Aurora breathed a sigh of relief. "I think I'm feeling a little better."

Finn sat next to her, his elbows braced on his knees as he looked around. She could feel the tension in him, and she immediately began to worry. He was going to tell her something; something he wasn't comfortable with.

He scratched his lip. "Listen, um, my family is getting together for a big dinner on Sunday. I'd like you to come. I mean, if you're free."

Somewhere in the back of her mind, she knew she should say no. She could pretend she had plans and couldn't make it. But being near his family would give her the chance to find out how many of them were dragons. Then again, Basil would be there as a changeling; he would find out eventually, so why would she need to be there?

She nodded and smiled. "Sure, that would be fun."

His answering grin made her heart flutter. "Where can I pick you up?"

*Shit.* This was the hardest part about pretending to date an Earthling, dragon or not. She had no home there. She could blend in with the other people, at least for the most part. She could conjure up the clothing needed to make her look like she'd just walked out of a trendy downtown shop, and she'd even figured out how to use her magic to create currency. But a house or an apartment was a completely different matter. That was a bigger illusion than she could keep up. The university grounds served as an easy pickup and drop-off point most of the time, but that probably wouldn't fly on a Sunday when there were no classes.

Aurora pressed her lips together. "What time does it start?"

"About five."

"Okay. I have a few other errands I need to run that afternoon, anyway. Just give me the address and I'll be there."

He looked disappointed. Finn had never outright asked to come to her place, but she knew he must have been thinking about it. "Sure thing."

An hour later, Aurora had escaped the clamor of the human world and was back in her own realm. She immediately headed for the nursery, located just behind the castle. Babies slept in beds of soft pine needles and fresh leaves, their cribs made of the sturdiest wood and wrapped in live, flowering vines. A few fae nannies flitted among them, checking them as they slept or woke, ensuring they had peaceful dreams.

At one time, before Aurora had been born, the nursery was a busy place. It was full not only of faelings, but human babies as well. Some of them had been rescued from hillsides and forests where their parents had left them, believing they were too sick to thrive. The fae had made it their business to take them in and care for them, eventually bestowing the infants to lonely couples who'd been longing for children of their own.

But then there was Phoenix. He smiled when he saw her, and she immediately scooped him up from his woodland crib. "Hello there, little one," she crooned, studying his face. The more time she spent with him, the more she could see the difference between him and Basil. They had the same blue eyes and the same sweet pink lips. It wasn't anything as obvious as that. Perhaps it was all in knowing the truth.

And then there was a difference in the way she felt around each of them. Aurora didn't particularly like being around Basil's changeling form, although she'd never had a problem with him in the fae realm. It was likely her guilt surrounding the whole situation more than anything else. After all, the plan was her idea; she couldn't hold anything against the elderly fae for taking part in it. On the other hand, when she picked up Phoenix, it was as though she carried the sun on her shoulders, warm and bright and elated.

"You're just a darling little thing, aren't you?" she whispered as she touched her fingertip to his nose.

He blinked, looking surprised for a moment, and then his smile widened.

Aurora did it again, thrilled at his reaction every time, even though she knew what to expect. Was this what it was really like to have a child? Did every mother have this sense of radiance and pride flowing through her as soon as she so much as thought about her baby? If so, she could see why there were so many of them in the world.

"Aurora."

She turned at her father's voice. He stood at the back door of the castle and leaned forward slightly, no doubt due to the weight of the heavy chain that still remained around his neck. His brows were drawn together, and the fae who worked in the nursery suddenly had work they needed to attend to elsewhere.

"What is it?" she asked, still holding Phoenix, dancing back and forth to keep him entertained. She didn't like the look on Oren's face.

He came close, peering down at the child, but not with the same interest Aurora did. "I'm concerned," he muttered.

"About what?"

The king gestured toward the baby, and then at her. "About all of this. I haven't had any definitive reports back from Basil. As far as he's told me, these people are just like regular humans. He hasn't seen any evidence of them being dragons; they carry their human forms constantly. I'm afraid you might have been mistaken, my child."

"I'm not," she replied, jutting her chin out indignantly. She didn't like being questioned, even by the king of the land. "I know what I saw the night I saw Nora and her mate flying, and I know what I can sense from both her and Finn. They have a different energy than the humans do. They're stronger, but there's something else, too." She wasn't about to explain how she truly knew for sure that Finn was a dragon. She couldn't attest to any of the rest of his family in the same way, but she'd felt it soul-deep when she'd slept with him. That dragon was inside him, even if he wasn't willing to let it out.

"But we still know virtually nothing about them!" he argued, his voice a whisper, despite the anger in it. He glanced around the nursery area as though he expected wizards to coalesce out of the foliage at any moment. "What if Basil never learns of anything? What if these so-called dragons don't even want their baby back? The wizards will have been slowly taking over our kingdom while we've just been sitting here on our hands. And what happens if they really are dragons, but we don't report that fact to the wizards before they find out on their own? There'll be no help for us then. We've got to find some other way."

Aurora instinctively turned away from him, suddenly afraid that Oren would take Phoenix from her arms. Even if the baby were returned to his father, she didn't want him to leave. The thought struck her, and she had to press her lips together to keep herself from saying anything about it. "Those foolish wizards aren't going to catch on," she growled.

"Sshh! They might be listening." He glanced to the side, where something moved in the underbrush, but it was only a squirrel. "I have no idea just how far their powers reach."

She felt herself getting impatient with her father. Aurora regretted suggesting the changeling idea in the first place, but she'd gone along with it because he seemed to believe it was their best shot at deflecting the wizards. She'd kidnapped a child and taken him off to another world, and he chose *now* to start doubting her?

"Then let them listen." She put Phoenix back in his crib, not wanting to upset him with the negative energy that was beginning to take over her body. She could feel her wingtips grow as black as her mood. "I'm getting past the point of caring what these wizards want. And yes, I realize it's easy to be brave when you're not standing face-to-face with the enemy. But you won't let me! You say you want me to rule this kingdom someday, but how am I ever going to be able to do it if you don't let me experience things first hand? I'm barely allowed to get my feet wet!"

His cheeks flushed an ominous shade of red, something she'd hardly ever seen in her permissive father before. "Don't you talk to me about the way I run things around here! I'm only trying to keep you safe, along with everyone else! You're too stubborn to see that, girl. And you can't exactly say I keep you sheltered. I've let you go flitting off to Earth any old time you want to for the last several decades and I've never argued against it. I know what dangers lie out there!"

She crossed her arms in front of her, regarding him coolly. "The dangers are far greater here at the moment. Most humans are too busy staring at their cell phones to notice what's going on around them. I could walk down the street with my wings out, dressed in my official regalia, and those who did happen to see me would think I was just in some elaborate costume. They don't believe in *magic*." It was something that angered her, usually because that lack of belief meant the humans were missing out on so much of their own world. Now it angered her because she felt foolish. She was a fool for thinking she could save the human world, and she was a fool for thinking she could save her own.

Oren's lips puckered, holding back an argument. His shoulders sagged and gave a sigh of capitulation. "I'll let this farce carry on for now. But bear in mind, things could change at any moment. You might just get your chance to dive in and see what it's like to be a ruler, whether you're ready and willing or not." Shaking his head, he turned on his heel and left.

Aurora wasn't sure how to take his last words. It was either a threat that she would be queen if he were killed, or that she wouldn't have a choice but to stand up and fight. Either way, she knew the coming times wouldn't be easy.

She turned back to Phoenix, who was exercising his little legs with vigorous kicks in the air. He exhaled with each one, panting his happiness at the movement of his own body.

"Whatever happens, I'll make sure you're safe," she said, bending to plant a kiss on his forehead. "I promise you that much."

# 9

FINN HAD ARRIVED EARLY AT HIS PARENTS' HOUSE, WANTING TO MAKE sure everything was perfect. He told himself it was because he didn't want to have to rush getting Phoenix ready and that his mother might need help with the food, but that wasn't the truth. Aurora was about to meet his entire family. It was a pressure he'd never experienced before.

He got Phoenix out of the car, along with his diaper bag. For such a small person, he sure required a lot of equipment. His feelings toward Aurora were completely different from any relationship he'd been in before. He'd brought a girl or two home for dinner when he was a teenager. It'd made him nervous, but now, the stakes were much higher.

This wasn't just a cute girl he wanted to take to the movies. Finn was a father, and he couldn't take relationships that lightly anymore. With Aurora, it was impossible to take it lightly, anyway. She was beautiful, on the inside as well as the outside. She always had something fascinating to say, and even if she thought someone might not agree with her, it never seemed to stop her from expressing her true feelings. He felt a deep connection with her, something he couldn't explain.

And of course, this poor woman wasn't just meeting his family. She was meeting an entire clan of dragons. Everyone was planning to be there. His parents, his aunts and uncles, his cousins, and even Lucia's family of dragons, who had come through a portal from Charok about a year ago. He hadn't yet figured out how to explain them. Lucia's biological son was Callan, but she'd practically raised her nephews, Archard and Kieran, as well. Finn's cousin Kaylee was now married to Archard, and Nora was in a serious relationship with Kieran. That certainly made them family, but Finn couldn't fool himself into thinking it was typical.

"Finn! I'm glad you're here! Come help me get this beast out of the oven!" Leah called from the kitchen.

Finn strode in and set Phoenix's car seat on the floor before grabbing a few pot holders and removing the ham from the oven. "Um, Aurora doesn't eat meat."

"I know that, silly. I listen when you tell me things. I made sure there are plenty of veggies, and I even did my research to make sure there was a vegan-friendly protein on the table." She smiled as she reached out to touch his cheek, a few soft wrinkles crinkling at the corners. It was because of her blue eyes that everyone easily bought the idea of Leah being his biological mother. Of course, as far as Finn was concerned, she was.

"Is there anything I can do?" He eyed the massive amount of serving dishes lined up on the countertop, waiting to go out on the table. His parents' home was the perfect place for a full family get-together since it was so big. Out on the edge of town where it backed up to large, country properties, it was big enough that Finn's friends always said he lived in a mansion back when he was a kid.

"No, you just take care of Phoenix. Everyone else will be here shortly, and they don't have a baby to fuss about, so they can do the rest of the work." She dipped her finger into a dish of gravy, tasted it, and then added more pepper.

But Phoenix had fallen asleep, and there wasn't anything for him to do at the moment. He shoved his hands in his pockets. "I wonder if I'm doing the right thing," he said quietly as he looked down at his son.

Leah set her spoon down and looked at him. "What do you mean?"

His throat was dry. "You know I wasn't expecting to have a child. This wasn't part of my plan, not that I really had a plan at all. But this is so much different than just dating some girl. I mean, if Aurora decides she wants to keep this going, to stick around for the long haul, then I'm going to have to tell her everything. She's going to know that I'm a dragon, and so is Dad, and so is practically everyone else I know. This isn't exactly a normal family."

Her face was soft as she wiped her hands on a kitchen towel, looking thoughtful. "Finn, you've never been a very serious young man. You were always adventurous. So first, I'd say not to look at any of this as settling down. It's just a new adventure; a different kind of adventure. And I also have to say that I've never seen you act this way about a woman before."

"What way?" He was suddenly very aware of his body, wondering what sort of cues he'd been giving away.

She laughed. "Like a deer in headlights? Like you've seen a ghost but you want to follow it? Finn, this girl means something to you. Just because you have a little one doesn't mean you're dead. Sure, there's a little more pressure because you don't want to expose Phoenix to anyone who might not be right for him, but that's only a good thing. I'm sure your father could tell you plenty about that."

"Yeah, he's tried." Finn scratched the back of his neck, remembering all the awkward conversations he'd had with Holden once he'd found out he was going to be a single dad. At the time, it'd been more about his father lecturing him than anything.

His mother picked up a serrated knife and began slicing a heavy loaf of homemade bread. "As far as her knowing the truth about us, you'll just have to wait and see how things go. You'll know when the time is right. Or maybe you won't get a choice and she'll find out anyway. It was a little hard even for me to believe that your father was a dragon, and I'm not what most people would call normal."

Finn glanced down at Phoenix, who stirred slightly in his sleep. "He hasn't shown any signs of his shifter side yet. You think it's possible he's just human?" It worried him, and at the same time, he was relieved by the notion. He liked the idea of a little person to carry on his legacy, to hold his DNA, to be a piece of him that would remain on this Earth, even when he was long gone. He looked forward to teaching him how to handle the shift from dragon to human and back again, how to fly, and how to control his fire.

But it would be so much easier for Phoenix if he didn't need to know any of that.

Leah arranged the slices of bread carefully in a basket, her head tipped to the side. She had that look on her face that said she was in deep thought. "You know, I can't say. But I have noticed something about him that I wanted to talk to you about."

"What is it?"

She sighed. "He doesn't seem quite as vibrant as he once was. He eats plenty, but he's not gaining weight the way I would've expected. He doesn't talk much, either."

Finn rolled his eyes. "He's only a few months old, Mom. He doesn't exactly have deep conversations."

"You know that's not what I mean. He used to babble all the time, and now he just lays there so quietly. It made me worry a bit about him, like maybe his formula wasn't agreeing with him. But then I picked him up, and I got the strangest energy off of him." She came over to stand next to Finn and stare down into the car seat. "I can't quite explain the change, but it was like... Well, it was like it wasn't really him."

Finn felt his stomach fall. He'd noticed some slight changes in Phoenix, but it wasn't anything he thought he should be concerned about. "That doesn't seem likely."

Leah nodded. "Neither does it seem likely that an infant could create such beautiful visions. I touched his forehead to see if he had a fever, and I saw the most beautiful place. It was filled with plants and wildlife, like something out of a fantasy movie. I saw him there in it, wrapped up in leaves."

"That doesn't make sense." Finn normally felt his mother's psychic powers were reliable. Everyone else seemed to think so, too, since she had a steady flow of customers on the days when she kept her shop open. The books she'd written on the subject were constantly out of stock. That had to mean something, but he suddenly had his doubts. "Could you have been getting it mixed up with a vision from some other source? I mean, babies don't have imaginations, do they?"

She shrugged. "I wouldn't think so, Finn, but it concerns me."

He had enough to be worried about with Aurora coming over and meeting his crazy family. "Maybe it just has something to do with the fact that he's a hybrid. None of us have ever dealt with a baby that's half shifter and half human before. He's bound to be a little different."

"Maybe you're right." Leah turned her attention back to the food, but she didn't look convinced.

The rest of the family began arriving, which distracted Finn from any more thoughts of why his son might be transmitting such images to his grandmother. He was too busy answering all the questions from his cousins about when Aurora would arrive, why he hadn't gone to pick her up, and if he was thinking about marriage. If this was how it was going to be, then maybe he'd just meet Aurora at the door and tell her to run away as fast as possible.

But then she did arrive. She was gorgeous; the top half of her hair had been tamed into a knot, showing off her delicate facial features. The lower half was long and loose, her curls spiraling everywhere like her wild spirit. She'd worn a pale blue dress with tiny white flowers, the detail of which Finn was sure he'd never notice on any other woman. He was glad to see she'd decided to wear shoes, the same white sandals she'd worn on their first date.

"Hi," he breathed, painfully aware of the numerous curious people standing in the living room. He wanted to step out on the porch, shut the door behind him, and just take off for a long walk with Aurora. It would be so much easier than having to bring her in the house and pass her around, introducing her to everyone and trying to explain why they were all there together. He wanted to pretend there was some good reason, like a birthday or a holiday, but really, everyone just wanted to meet her. This whole thing was completely for her. No pressure.

"I brought wine." She held up a brown paper bag. "A red and a white."

This, at least, gave Finn a reason to jump into action. He took the bag from her and held it under his arm as he opened the door to let her in. His cousins, aunts, and uncles had arranged themselves to look casual, but he could tell this was as far from casual as it could get.

Nora was the first to come forward with Kieran on her heels. "It's nice to see you again, Aurora. This is my boyfriend, Kieran."

Finn felt as though he had his girlfriend on parade as he introduced her to Kaylee and Archard, Uncle Julian and Aunt Naomi, Uncle Beau and Aunt Autumn, Uncle Xander and Aunt Summer, Lucia, her son Callan, and then Elliot. His parents were the last, still in the kitchen and putting the final touches on the food. His stomach turned as he escorted her through the doorway.

"It's nice to meet you," Holden said as he shook Aurora's hand.

"We're so glad you could come," Leah amended as she gave her the same loose but welcoming hug Nora had given her.

Finn's anxiety increased as he noticed his mother's spine stiffen. When she pulled away from Aurora, her smile was one that didn't quite touch her eyes. "We're just about to sit down. I hope you brought your appetite."

While Finn didn't imagine that anyone ever liked bringing their significant other home to meet the family, and he'd worried that his family was weirder than most, it was nice to have so many people seated at the monumental table. It would've been much more awkward if he'd had to sit there with only Aurora and his parents, the silence thick as they all tried to decide what to say. As it was, the dinner had almost a party atmosphere as everyone caught up with each other. Kaylee and Archard talked about their most recent adventure to China, which included an emergency landing on one of their flights. Nora had reached enough subscribers on her channel that she was now being asked to collaborate with other YouTubers, and that had only boosted her visibility even more. Elliot complained good-naturedly about the people he met while finishing up law school.

And while they each, in turn, had plenty to say about themselves, they also made efforts to include Aurora in the conversation. Autumn and Summer invited her to come check out their New Age shop and promised her a "friends and family" discount. Holden asked to hear more about her environmental studies and wanted to know what she planned to do with her degree. Callan passed along information about the best places to party in town, while Kieran scowled at him and advised her to be particularly careful at some of these places.

His advice came naturally, considering that he'd come from a long line of border guards back on Charok. As Finn watched Aurora scoop a helping of chickpea and edamame salad onto her plate, he realized how much more sense all of their conversations would make if Aurora knew the truth about them. He'd been so adamant about hiding it, but he was suddenly beginning to wonder. Maybe he could tell her. Maybe she would take it in stride. Maybe...

It was only Leah who seemed to keep a very careful eye on Aurora, although she made sure to glance away if there was any chance that their guest would see her. Finn noticed, though, and he felt sure that a least a few others did as well. He made a mental note to ask her later and then decided against it.

"So, Finn. How are things going with your job? I think you said something about a promotion coming up?" Elliot winked as he buttered his roll.

Finn supposed he should appreciate it. Elliot was trying to make him look good without bragging. But Aurora already knew more about his work than anyone else in his family did. "I talked to Mr. Anderson about it like you said I should. He said I was as good as in, but he gave me a special project to handle in the meantime."

"That's a good sign," Holden enthused. "What are you working on?"

"Acquiring land for conservation," he explained, reaching beneath the table to gently touch Aurora's knee. He knew this was a sensitive subject for her. "There's a large parcel adjacent to the property Anderson Environmental owns. It's privately owned right now, but they want to buy it out and turn it into a wildlife conservation area."

Summer clasped her hands together. "That's so exciting!"

"Sounds like a lot of work," Callan grumbled.

"It really wouldn't be, but the woman who owns it isn't interested in selling it. She doesn't care about any amount of money, and she doesn't want to live anywhere besides that property. I think, most of all, she's concerned that Anderson Environmental isn't being honest about their intentions." He hesitated a moment, wondering how much he should include Aurora in this story. But his encounter with her out there on Cecilia's property had been strange, almost magical, and it seemed wrong to cloud that up with a bunch of business. "I've heard a few rumors about it myself, so I'm checking with my boss to see what kind of details I can find out."

Uncle Beau nodded with approval. "And maybe if you can show her all the particulars, she'll change her mind. Sounds like a good plan. Not everyone is motivated by money, but if she cares enough about the land, she might really like to see it kept pristine."

Finn shrugged. "Mr. Anderson has been out of the office a lot, and I'm waiting to hear something back from him personally. We'll just have to see." It seemed that so much life had happened in the last couple of months, he'd hardly had time to think about his job in any capacity other than being what he had to do to keep himself and his son on their feet. He had been so happy when he'd learned he was up for a better job, and then Phoenix had come along. Once Mr. Anderson had asked him to work on the property acquisition, he'd met Aurora. There wasn't much else that mattered to him besides her and his son, not even his job.

When they'd cleared the dinner dishes and Finn had gone into the kitchen to help serve the pie, Kaylee pulled him aside with a wink. "She seems great, Finn. She's a little quiet, but I would be, too, if I were suddenly introduced to our loud family. And I see the way she looks at Phoenix. Do you think she might be the one?"

He'd experienced this line of questioning quite a bit, but at least Kaylee was doing it privately. "Everyone looks at Phoenix like that. I mean, check out your husband." He pointed through the kitchen doorway, where Archard could be seen holding the baby and feeding him a bottle. His face was alight as he murmured something to him, no doubt already sharing stories about what life was like back on Charok. A strand of his dark hair fell forward, and Phoenix reached for it. Archard bent further forward to let him grab it, the little fist holding on tight."

"That's adorable," Kaylee agreed, "but you didn't answer my question. Is the playboy finally settling down?"

"Would that make you happy? Knowing you're not the only one who's made the long trip down the aisle?" He picked up a dinner plate and rinsed it in the sink just to have something to do. "Not everyone has to be tied down, you know."

She laughed. "I'm not tied down. If anything, Archard lifts me up. He's interested in what I have to say, even when I'm yammering on about the same ancient tablet I've been studying for weeks. He always wants to go with me on my trips, and he gets just as excited about visiting new places as I do. It's wonderful. I couldn't be with anyone but him. I think finding someone who makes you an even better version of what you are is pretty special."

He felt the meaning in her words. She thought Aurora did that to him, even though she'd known his girlfriend for all of an hour. He glanced into the dining room once again, where Aurora was laughing at something Nora said. She was too beautiful to be real.

Her eyes slid up to meet his, provocative even from the next room. She glanced at him for only a moment before politely turning back to Nora, but it was enough. He easily remembered how her naked body had felt in his arms, how good it'd been to sink himself inside her, how their two bodies had so readily become one. His dragon slammed against the inside of his skin, daring him to deny it once again.

Finn held his breath until the feeling passed. "We'll just have to see."

## 10

"Come on, little guy. Just how much can you eat, anyway?" Finn watched as yet another bottle was drained. He picked up the can of formula and opened it, frowning at the small amount left in the bottom. Phoenix was ravenous, it seemed, and even with his good salary, it was hard to keep up with the sheer amount of formula the baby required. *Must be the dragon in him,* he assumed.

Phoenix responded by wrinkling up his face and curling his fists, his tiny mouth pulled down into a miniature frown as he prepared to launch into yet another one of his tirades. He screamed and wailed, his face turning bright red as he screamed for the lack of a bottle.

"Hang on, hang on. I'm working on it." Though he hated to put the baby down while he was crying, it took a lot longer to make up a bottle with only one hand. He'd seen women do it, on the times when he'd put Phoenix in the stroller and taken him down to the park or around the mall. In general, though, he was in awe of all the mothers he saw taking care of young children. He didn't know if they had any help with their little ones when they went home, but they managed them out in public with a quick efficiency. They changed diapers on their knees, they talked on the phone while chasing after toddlers, and he'd even seen one woman deftly braid a child's hair while keeping the younger sibling wrangled with her leg. He didn't know how they did it, and he knew that he'd never be able to keep up.

MEG RIPLEY

By the time he'd prepared another bottle and Phoenix had downed it like a teenager slamming a Mountain Dew, it was time for yet another diaper change. Finn wouldn't really have minded—he knew it was going to be a lot of work taking care of a baby—but he was supposed to be out the door ten minutes ago.

Finally fresh and ready to go, he strapped Phoenix into the back of his Jeep and set the diaper bag on the floorboard. Buckling his own seatbelt, he noticed the stain of spit-up on his shirt. "Shit! Oh, well," he muttered to himself as he turned the key in the ignition. There was no point in going inside to change when it was just going to happen again.

"We don't mind," his mother said. "We're just glad you could come. I thought it would be nice for you to have a homemade meal without having to fix it yourself, even during the week."

"Sorry I'm late," he said as he stepped in the front door of his parents' home. "It's been kind of a rough evening."

"Is work going all right?" Holden asked, holding the door wide and taking the diaper bag from Finn's shoulder to ease his burden.

"As well as it can. Things are constantly busy, but I can't complain about that. With this industry, if you sit still, you miss out." He set down the car seat, frowning to see that Phoenix had fallen asleep. If he took too many naps during the day, he was guaranteed not to sleep at night. Finn had to be at work in the morning, especially since Mr. Anderson was supposed to be back in the office.

Straightening, he noticed that he and his parents weren't alone. Varhan was seated on the loveseat, looking just as out of the place as the friendly wizard always did. He'd been living on Earth for quite some time, but he still wore the loose robes and long hair that were common among his kind back on Charok. Fortunately, the evil intent toward dragons that the rest of the wizards had wasn't alive in Varhan. He was a friend of the family who'd helped them through difficult times and was solely responsible for their escape to Earth. His wide, pleasant face rarely wrinkled with concern, no matter how bad things were. But his presence let Finn know that something was off.

He turned to his parents. "What is it?"

Holden and Leah exchanged a look. "Why don't we go sit down and eat," Leah suggested, gesturing toward the dining room. "I'm sure you're hungry. I've got a roast ready."

"That's nice of you, but you guys didn't just invite me over here to eat. I should've figured it out earlier, but I've been a little busy." He nodded toward the sleeping Phoenix.

"Yes, that's exactly what we'd like to talk to you about," Holden began. "But we really should sit down, whether it's here or at the dining table."

Finn was never one to turn down a meal, especially one he didn't have to make, but he wasn't hungry. He was certain he wouldn't be able to eat until he understood what was going on. And he didn't want to sit, either, but at this point, he'd do anything that would get his parents to get on with it. He plopped down on the couch and stared at them sternly.

Leah came to sit next to him, laying a cool hand on his back. "I told you on Sunday that I was concerned about Phoenix; about the energies I was picking up from him and his current behavior."

"Yes." He frowned down at the baby, wondering how they'd come to be talking about 'behavior' in an infant. But he couldn't deny the child was acting differently.

Varhan had slid off the edge of the sofa and was on his knees in front of the car seat, examining Phoenix with careful curiosity. It made Finn's stomach lurch once again. They knew something, and it couldn't be good, but the wizard's face gave nothing away.

"I know you weren't concerned about it, and I tried to let myself believe that it was something simple, like his hybrid background." She bit her lip as she looked at the baby and Varhan as well, and then her cool blue eyes looked into Finn's. "But when I met Aurora—"

"Oh, I see." Finn shot off the couch and stepped around the coffee table to the other side of the room. "This is about her. I knew you guys wouldn't like her. You've never liked anyone I've dated. Why? Have you thought every girl isn't good enough because I'm a dragon prince? Well, I've got news for you: I don't live on Charok, and I haven't felt as strongly about any girl as I do for Aurora. You think I'm going to ditch her just because you don't like her? It's not going to happen."

"Finn—" Holden warned.

"No. You guys have always been disappointed in me. You wanted me to have a higher college degree. You wanted me to get a better job than working for some hippie company who wants to save sea turtles. You were upset that I had a kid so young, and with no wife to boot. Now, for some reason, Aurora is just another mark against me." He could feel anger rising in his chest, mixed with fire, and his skin prickled.

His father stood, his jaw set and his face grim. "Why would you ever think we were disappointed in you?"

"How could I not? You were constantly pushing for me to do more, asking if I was sure I was satisfied with what I had and didn't I want to do more. I know my life doesn't seem like much to anyone else, but it's good enough for me." He was convincing himself of that just as much as he was trying to convince them. Things had been so crazy lately.

"We wanted the best for you," Leah said quietly, "but we've never been ashamed or disappointed. You're an incredible young man, Finn, and I think if you just hear what we have to say, you'll understand it all."

He frowned at her, seeing the love in her eyes, and his fury abated somewhat. "There have been too many changes over the last couple of months, and I don't know if I'm coming or going most of the time." He paced the floor, now far too full of energy to sit down again.

"I think that's perfectly natural for a new parent," Holden said, retaking his seat and folding his hands in his lap. "I know that's how I felt when I was in your position."

Leah cleared her throat. "Finn, honey... What I was trying to tell you is that when I met Aurora, I picked up the same energies from her that I'd been getting from Phoenix."

Finn stared at her, not quite comprehending. "What?"

"I saw that same mystical world," she explained, "and it was crystal clear. A lot of times, when I get a vision from touching a person or an object, it's obscured with shadows. It's blurred from their understanding of the picture as well as from being transmitted from one person to another. But it was as though I'd stepped into another realm. I could see Phoenix there as well as Aurora. I saw her bending over his crib, scooping him up and holding him in her arms."

Though he'd grown up with a human psychic for a mother, Finn still had a lot to learn about how it all worked. "So that's a good thing, right? Maybe it's a sign that she's supposed to be with me, if she loves him so much."

"When it comes to finding the woman you're destined to be with, you're the only one who'll truly know," Holden explained. "You won't need a psychic to explain it to you. Seeing the same thing from two people who shouldn't really have had much shared experience yet was a great concern to your mother, and we went to consult Varhan on the subject. Now, don't look at me like that! We wanted to have all the facts straight before we came to you." His brows drew together thunderously, warning him not to lose his temper yet again.

"And it might be a very good thing they did," Varhan said quietly. He'd unbuckled Phoenix and lifted him from his car seat, holding the limp body against his chest as he continued to study him. He even pulled off one of the baby's socks to examine his feet. "I only regret that I hadn't been feeling well the night of the dinner, or I would've been able to meet Aurora myself."

"Could you just tell me what the hell's going on?" Finn crossed his arms in front of his chest to keep from stepping over the coffee table and yanking Phoenix from Varhan's arms. The wizard wasn't hurting him, but he was looking at him as though he were an interesting rock and not a living person.

Varhan nodded, setting Phoenix back down for the moment. He stood, his grey eyes somber as they looked at Finn. "As I'm sure you know, humans like to share stories about beings they believe are fictional. There are plenty of fairytales about dragons, although they have no idea that you're living among them. They don't quite understand witchcraft in the same way that your aunts do, and while psychic powers are somewhat more acceptable, not everyone is convinced. I think there are other beings who fall into this same category. Including the fae."

Finn blinked. "Fae are real?" It shouldn't have been hard to believe, considering his own heritage, but Finn had never heard of them existing in reality.

"Oh, yes. They're not really *in* this world, more like adjacent to it. They have their own realm, a beautiful place that's protected with magic and kept secret. Most of them probably never even dream of venturing out amongst humans, but obviously, enough of them have over the years for humans to create the fairytales they've come up with." He smiled sheepishly, spreading his fingers as though it were all obvious.

"And what does this have to do with Phoenix?"

Varhan turned toward a tattered leather bag sitting on the loveseat and withdrew an ancient book. It's mildewy scent filled the air as soon as the wizard flipped open the pages. "Your child has suddenly changed his behavior. He eats far more than a baby his age should, and yet his body isn't growing and gaining weight; he's failing to thrive. He's quiet and reserved, not the same active child that you're used to. Yes?"

"Yes." Finn's impatience was growing again. Sometimes, it was easier dealing with humans.

The wizard pointed to a page in the book. "I believe he might be a changeling, a fae disguised as a human baby. It's a legend that goes back centuries, and the reason behind it seems to have changed over time. Some humans believed the fae were doing this out of malicious intent, stealing the babies to raise them as their servants. Others said the fae swapped their elderly relatives for the human babies so that they might live out their last days in comfort. Then, of course, you have to consider that a changeling was a good out for a parent who couldn't take care of a disabled child, in which case the child was never really a fae at all, and—"

"Varhan!" Finn's voice filled the room. Phoenix startled awake but instantly fell asleep again. "Get to it, already."

The wizard only seemed mildly startled by Finn's outburst. "Oh, yes. Phoenix's behavior, paired with the fact that Aurora is giving off the same energy and visions, not to mention the timing of her arrival and the change in the baby, led me to believe that she is a fae as well. I haven't found any evidence of the fae coming into this world to watch over the swapped children, but of course the human stories are often vague and distorted. There's very little literature on the fae, even from the perspective of wizards. Well, mostly."

"What do you mean?" Holden asked, his eyes narrowing.

"It appears the wizards just like to oppress anyone they can," he explained gravely. "There were a few references to them in some of my material, but only in reference to using them as slaves. I'm afraid the wizards weren't exactly performing anthropological studies on them."

"I don't understand." Finn came around the table to kneel in front of Phoenix. "Why would anyone do that? Why to Phoenix? And why Aurora?" He didn't like the unsettled feeling in the pit of his stomach. How could a beautiful woman, one who seemed to complete him and change his life in all the right ways, do such a terrible thing? He refused to believe it.

"We don't really know," Leah said softly.

Something about the tone of her voice made Finn look up at her. There were tears clinging to the corners of her eyes, barely held back.

"What?"

Holden cleared his throat. "The next logical step is to find out for sure if Phoenix is a changeling, before we say anything or do anything. Varhan has researched it thoroughly, and the most reliable test is to expose the infant to fire. It will cause a changeling to return to its original form and leave the home."

"*Logical* step? You're kidding. This is all a fucking joke, right? Someone's going to pop out from behind the couch holding a video camera, and we're all going to share a laugh. Because this can't be happening, and there's no way in hell I'm going to let it." That warm feeling was rising inside him again, the sensation of not being able to control himself. It wasn't the pleasant way that he felt around Aurora, when he couldn't figure out what form he wanted to be in. It was like a fever of rage taking over his body, something that wouldn't let him go until it was satisfied.

"Finn, this is for his own good," Varhan tried to assure him. "We can go about it very carefully and make sure that no harm comes to him if he's actually your son. You know we'd never want to hurt Phoenix."

"How can you claim this is harmless when we're talking about exposing him to fire? For fuck's sake, Varhan, this is completely barbaric! If there's not something simpler, like a little spell or putting the right kinds of herbs and gems or some shit like that near him, then I'm not going to do it." He instantly envisioned something from the Salem witch trials, where wicked old men who feared anything different from themselves would torture the young and innocent. He pictured Varhan tying Phoenix to a spit and roasting him.

Leah reached out toward him. "Finn, this isn't something anyone likes. But we have to find out the truth somehow. All we have to do is—"

"No!" Finn roared. The force of his words set his body free, and he could no longer control the shift that was coming over him. He felt his skin separate, splitting into a million tiny pieces that sent a shiver down his lengthening spine as they flipped over to reveal the brilliant yellow scales beneath. His wings erupted from his back, snapping out as they felt freedom from their confinement, and knocked a vase from the mantel. Finn didn't even hear the crash of the glass against the brick hearth. He only knew the anger and the determination that came with the deeply protective feelings he had for his son. No one would harm that child, not even people who claimed to be doing the best for him. His tail lashed with a thunk against the coffee table.

"Finn!" someone cried out, probably Leah.

But he wasn't really Finn anymore, not the Finn that they were all used to. He wasn't Finn, the college partier. He wasn't Finn, who thought he could save the planet. He wasn't even Finn the dragon, not really. He was Finn the father, the man who would keep his loved ones safe at all cost. The thought was more than his body could handle, and the furnace inside him could no longer be contained. He felt the fireball gush up his throat to explode from his mouth, passing his sharp teeth and his forked tongue to fly through the air and smash against the wall.

He hadn't meant to do it. Finn hadn't really been able to think at all with the raging emotions battling inside him.

But the fire from his own throat had been enough to prove Varhan right.

Phoenix's eyes bulged as his tiny body convulsed. His arms and legs grew long and slim, spilling over the side of the car seat until a set of hairy feet rested against the floor. The chubby little face was now long and haggard, a raggedy gray beard spilling down onto his belly. Blue eyes that were once bright and interested were now cloudy and terrified as the feeble being struggled to get free of the car seat.

The reality of it was simply too much for him. His son—a son that he'd never expected to have, but that he'd wanted with all his heart as soon as he'd met him—was gone. Finn threw his head back and let out a monstrous roar, a howl of grief that came from the very pit of his stomach and pulled the energy from his entire body. Hot tears ran down his saffron scales, and he didn't even care. He'd been a complete fool, and it'd cost him his child.

When he had gathered his wits together to look around, the car seat was empty. Leah and Holden were on their feet, staring in shock at the open door.

"He's gone," Holden said quietly. "He moves fast."

Leah reached up to touch Finn's cheek, not intimidated by his current form. "Finn, sweetie, we'll get this figured out."

"You're damn right we will," he hissed. Suddenly realizing that his current form wasn't going to do anything more than damage his parents' home, he shuddered and let himself fall back to his normal shape. His human hands felt dull and useless, and he almost missed the fire in his chest. How long had it been since he'd shifted? Forever, it seemed. And yet it had come on so strongly that he hadn't been able to control it. He brushed his concerns about that aside and tried to focus on facts.

Finn reached for the diaper bag and pulled his keys out of the side pocket, resisting the urge to kick the bag in anger. "I'm going to find Aurora."

His father put a hand on his shoulder. "You shouldn't go alone. We don't know what's really going on here and what her intent was. I'll come with you."

"No." He shrugged off Holden's grip. "This is something I have to take care of." Finn stalked out the door and got in the car. He felt like he was leaving something behind, knowing there was no car seat buckled into the back. Resisting the urge to turn around and double-check, he squealed out the driveway.

# 11

AURORA MADE HER WAY THROUGH THE WOODS, TOUCHING EVERY TREE and leaf she could get a hold of, seeking their reassurance. The plants in the mortal realm were as friendly with her as the ones back home, and she sensed they sometimes even communicated with each other. Everything in the universe was connected in some way; the challenge was finding out how.

Her heart still thundered as she remembered Basil flying back into the fae realm, his eyes wild and his body shaking. He was terrified, alternately screaming and muttering about the beast he'd seen.

"He was huge!" Basil had shrieked. "He took up the entire room, and he had the color and the heat of the sun. I thought I'd be burned up on the spot!"

"You're safe now," Oren had told him, laying a thick hand on the old fae's arm.

But Basil had been too busy glancing over one shoulder, then the other, to listen. "What if he followed me here? He's going to eat all of us! Those sharp teeth will be sinking into my flesh!" He plastered his hands to his face and wept.

The incident had horrified Aurora, but it also confused her. "Why is he acting like this?" she'd asked her father. "He knew they were dragons. What did he expect?"

"Ah, Basil will get over it in time. I hesitate to think what this has done for our plan, though."

Aurora knew something had to be done, whatever it was. She could feel Finn's presence whenever he'd been close to the woods, and as she neared the university, that sensation had heightened tenfold. She saw him only a few seconds before he saw her, and she could feel the vexation rolling off him in waves.

"*You!*" he roared as he stormed down the path. Plenty of moonlight filtered down through the trees, but she didn't need any light to see just how furious he was. "Who *are* you, and what the hell have you done with my son?"

She put up her hands defensively. She could feel his inner power now that he was angry just as much as she'd been able to sense it when they'd been making love. But it was a completely different sensation now. "Finn, I'm so sorry. I can explain everything."

"I don't want any fucking explanations! Give me my son right now, or else!" His hands were balled into fists; his arms shaking. In fact, his entire body seemed to be. Aurora wondered how long he would hold onto himself. She'd never seen him in his true form, but she could sense it just beneath the surface.

"I promise Phoenix is safe. I'll take you to him. But first, I just want you to listen."

"Why should I do that?" Finn's eyes were wild as he took another dangerous step toward her.

She shrank back instinctively. "I know you think I'm evil right now, but that's not how I meant for this to be. Please, just say you'll let me talk first."

His lips were tight, his jaw hard. But he gave her a curt nod.

"Come on." Aurora risked something that never seemed worth it any other time she'd been in the human realm. But even before she started her conversation with Finn, she wanted him to see she was willing to give something of herself. She spread her wings and flew down the path.

"Hey!" he cried angrily behind her.

But Aurora didn't stop. She knew he was more than capable of catching up. She floated along through the air, rising up through the treetops, feeling the leaves brush her wings. It was only a few more seconds before she could feel him in the air behind her. She risked a look over her shoulder, her breath catching as she took in the vision of him.

Finn was imposing, yet beautiful. She'd never seen anything quite like him before, and even though she'd had ideas of what a dragon would look like, it was nothing compared to this. His wings beat the air with the force of a god, his slim head on a long neck pulsing in time. His clawed hands gleamed in the moonlight, his amber scales shimmering. Aurora had to force herself to turn back around and face the direction she was heading before she ran into something.

Soon enough, they'd reached Cecilia's property. The old woman knew the truth about her, and if she happened to see her flying along with a great winged reptile at her heels, well, she probably wouldn't think much of it. Aurora needed someplace quiet, someplace where no one from either world was likely to see them. She had a lot to say, and her words tumbled over themselves in her mind as she settled on the rocky edge of the pond.

Finn landed behind her with a thump and a hot huff of breath. His eyes were narrow and questioning, and she wondered if he would keep his dragon form. But he quickly shifted back into the Finn she'd come to know. Aurora wasn't sure if she felt any better about that.

"Out with it," he snarled. "Now."

Aurora sank onto a boulder, her legs feeling weak. "It's complicated. I've got to figure out where to start." He had no idea just how hard this was. If he'd just been a pawn in the game of life, then it would've been different. But he'd been so much more, and right from the very beginning. She never should've tried to fool herself into thinking she could keep her distance from him.

"I don't give two shits where you start, but you'd better get to it. I don't have a lot of patience, Aurora."

She glared at him. "Yes, I know. I'm sure you're ready to throw out a talon and slice me open, but you don't understand what's been happening."

"Obviously."

Aurora ignored him and took a deep breath. "My world is attached to yours, but only a small piece of it. You could think of it like two different dimensions, existing side-by-side, but there's a door that connects the two of them when someone wants to use it. My people have worked hard to stay away from humans and most of everything on Earth because it's so dangerous." She could've gone into more depth on that, but it could wait for another day.

"The veil that keeps our realm hidden has been damaged, and we'd been struggling to find the right kind of magic to fix it for good. It's been in place for so long, the spell had been lost to time. But then a group of wizards came along to help." She heard Finn suck in his breath, but she kept her gaze over the water, placid in the moonlight. "They'd promised to repair the damage in exchange for a few herbs that we fae cultivate. My father, our king, agreed to this. But the wizards took much more from us. They've captured many of our people, shackled them in iron, and are draining their magic for their own use. I'm ashamed to admit I don't even know what they're using it for. I've been kept as far away from it as possible."

Finn kicked a rock. "That's terrible for you, but I still don't see what it has to do with my son."

She flinched at the force behind his last two words but nodded. "The wizards, as I'm guessing you probably know, aren't as interested in us as they are in you." Aurora turned to him then. "They're looking for dragons."

He was trying to keep his face neutral, but she could see the pain wrapped in fury beneath. It may have been a trick of the moonlight, but she swore she saw a glimmer of scales just above his left eyebrow. "So you were selling us out to them?"

Her throat felt tight, like the words wouldn't quite fit through. "Yes, in a way. It started out with us just trying to find out more information about you. When I ran into you and Nora in the woods that day, I already knew the truth about what she was. But I didn't expect to meet you."

"Now I know why you were so nice to me," Finn snorted. "I was stupid enough to think we had some sort of connection, Aurora, and I thought I felt it from that first moment. You were just working your woo-woo magic on me, and you've continued to. I'd ask how far you were planning to take this, but I'm not sure I want to know the answer."

"No, you don't understand. I'm not even sure *I* understand. I was doing this out of desperation; it seemed like the best way to save my people. And putting the changeling in for Phoenix was a good way to secure our position. He could find out more about you and your family." She jumped when something wet plopped into her lap, but then she realized it was a tear. Dozens more flooded after it. "I can't tell you how sorry I am. This all got out of hand so fast."

"Where is Phoenix?" he growled. "Is he safe?"

"Yes." She swiped away the tears, but they were only replaced by more. "He's getting the best care he could ever have. I spend lots of time with him, just to make sure he's happy. Oh, Finn, I can't tell you how awful I feel about this whole thing. I know you must hate me, and I don't blame you. But I didn't know what else to do. My people are dying." What she'd done was unforgivable, and Aurora knew it. She was losing Finn, and she already felt the cold space in her heart where he'd once lent her his fire. Even her magic seemed to react to the sudden deprivation of him, the last bits of it sinking away into the earth.

The silence between them was heavy, with even the gentle lapping of the water against the rocks sounding like crashing waves. "The wizards are a formidable enemy," he finally said. "I haven't had much experience with them myself, but my family has been fighting them for a very long time. Even when the dragons lived on their home planet, far from here, the wizards were their worst enemy. It's not easy."

"So you understand?" Aurora didn't want to ask him if he forgave her. That was too much to ask. Ever.

"I'm not going to say I'm all right with this, not by any stretch of the imagination, but I understand your motive. I just wish I hadn't been such an idiot." He stepped forward to stand over her. "I let myself fall for you, Aurora. I felt something for you that I'd never felt for anyone in my entire life. I thought you were the one person in this world who made sense to me, maybe even someone who could be a mother to Phoenix. I'm an even bigger idiot for telling you all that now."

She stood, feeling the close proximity of their bodies. She'd felt all the same things Finn did, but a wall existed between them now; one that seemed too tall and thick to ever overcome. "Come on. I'll take you to him."

"Into your realm?" he asked. "How do I know this isn't another trap? Just like getting close to me so you could steal my son?"

Her shoulders slumped. It pained her physically to know he didn't trust her anymore. "I deserve that, but this is no trap. You need your son back." She turned and headed away from the water, knowing that her people were doomed for certain.

## 12

Finn watched Aurora's back as they cut through the woods, leaving behind any semblance of a trail or civilization. He'd never minded being out in the wilderness. His father had taken him hunting many times when he was a kid, and there was something almost comforting about knowing you were the only sentient beings around for miles.

But he wondered if this was a trap. Aurora seemed genuinely sorry about what she'd done, but how could he know she wasn't just an amazing actress? She'd been carrying the farce this long, so who was to say this wasn't part of the master plan and that she wasn't preparing to hand him over to the wizards right now?

He wanted to forgive her, but Finn wasn't sure when his heart would be ready to, if ever. Aurora was stunning, and she'd made him think she might be more to him than any other woman had been before. But she'd put his son in danger, and no matter how sorry she might be, he wasn't sure that mark could ever truly be washed away. But the dragon inside him still seemed so attuned to her, as if it didn't understand what had just happened. It reached out, wanting to be closer to her.

"It's just over here," she whispered, ducking beneath a branch and holding it back for him. "Do you see where things look a little out of focus? A little shimmery?"

It looked like a trick of the moonlight, shiny leaves reflecting the pale illumination back at his eyes. "I think so."

"Walk toward it and see what happens."

Finn looked at her doubtfully. "I don't have time to play games with you."

"I'm not playing games, Finn. I'm trying to be as open with you as possible. No tricks. No games. No hiding."

It was clear he wasn't going to get anywhere with her until he complied. Finn stomped forward toward the patch of brush she'd indicated, but he never seemed able to reach it. The dark leaves were always just out of reach. The path curled around to the side, and as he followed it, he found himself right back at Aurora's side. "What the hell?"

"Pretty neat, huh?"

The elusive trail gave him a feeling he'd felt before. "Is that what you were doing on Cecilia's property that day? When the path was always blocked and never seemed to go where it was supposed to? You were there to trick me." The realization was one that only made him angrier.

"I had to do what I had to do. Just wait. When you find out what Mr. Anderson has planned, you'll be glad Cecilia is such a stubborn old biddy. Besides, it's not my fault most humans are so easily spooked. Come on." She gestured with a slim hand and led him toward the same brush he'd just tried to reach.

But when Aurora stood before it and waved her hands, her fingers twining through the air, the foliage shifted. It was a subtle change, one Finn probably wouldn't have noticed if he hadn't been looking. But the leaves were now a different shape, smaller and rounder, and the light hit them in a different way. When she took another step forward, she was among them.

Finn followed, the dragon inside him on high alert. *How many fae could a dragon kill?* he wondered. *Could dragons kill them at all, if they were to attack?* He'd suddenly wished he'd asked Varhan a few more questions before he'd left his parents' house.

The valley that lay before him was nothing like he'd ever seen. It was thick and lush with plant life, but among it, he could see the lit windows of small huts. Someone carried a torch slowly down a pathway. Frogs and crickets sang with such vigor, he could hardly hear himself think, but at least they sounded content. It was like a woodland paradise. "Wow," he breathed.

"You should see it during the day," Aurora said. "You can't imagine the amount of color we have here when all the flowers are in bloom." She touched the trees as she picked her way down a steep path toward the heart of the village, and Finn realized this was something he'd seen her do all the time. Even when they'd walked around the mall, she'd stopped to touch the philodendrons growing in planters.

"Why do you do that?" He didn't really need to learn anything else about her. He knew she was fae, and that she'd tricked him and kidnapped his son. There wasn't much need to know why she liked to be barefoot all the time or why she thought sunrise was better than sunset. And yet he felt the compulsion to ask anyway.

She looked over her shoulder at him, her thick hair bunching at the nape of her neck. "It's how we communicate. They can tell me a lot with just a little touch, and I like to let them know that I'm thinking of them." Aurora paused to press her palm against the bark of a willow tree to her right. "It's not as easy as it used to be, though. I've talked with some of the others, and they're feeling the same thing. Our magic is failing, mostly because of the thinning in our protective veil."

"Oh." Finn tried not to watch her as much as his surroundings as they reached the valley floor. The village was an interesting collection of oddly-shaped homes that looked to have been constructed out of whatever random natural resources the owners could find. Some were of stone, other of logs, and one seemed to be made of nothing but ivy. They stepped aside to let someone pass on the pathway: a male fae who hurried by them, his eyes darting up to meet Finn's and then looking away just as quickly. Finn turned to watch him go, noticing that his wings just barely dragged on the ground.

"Not very friendly around here, are they?"

The path was wider there, and Aurora dropped back to walk next to him. "It's not normally like this. Even at night, there would always be plenty of people out and about, carrying on with their business or visiting their neighbors. But I've heard rumors that the wizards are closing in, daring to come closer to the castle now that they've got my father under their thumb. No one is supposed to leave their home unless they absolutely have to, and when they do, they don't know who to trust."

Finn nodded. He'd heard similar stories from Lucia and her boys when they'd come from Charok. They'd kept to themselves as much as possible, even vacating some of the ancient lands that had always belonged to the dragons, because they never knew if they were safe or not. "What are you going to do now?" He didn't say the last part of it: now that he would be taking his son back and that the dragons could no longer be tricked by the fae.

The look on her face was a steely one. "I don't know. I'm not sure the original plan with the changeling would've worked anyway, but now that I've done it, I suppose I've thrown away any chance of an alliance with your kind."

Finn hesitated to answer. He had to admit he felt genuinely sorry for the fae; the people who'd once lived in a whimsical, perfect world, but now came to share a common threat with his kind. "I don't think it would be up to me," he finally said.

She nodded as she turned off to the left. Finn looked up and saw what must have been the castle she'd referenced, a massive stone structure. Even in the dark, he could tell how impressive it was. He expected her to lead him right up to the doorway, but she skirted around the wall toward the back until they stood at a curtain of thick vines. Aurora parted them easily, and Finn felt his breath leave his body completely.

It was a nursery of some kind, with several little beds wrapped in ivy. Sleeping babies occupied most of these, bathed in the warm glow of a hundred fireflies. The fae hadn't trapped these tiny creatures to use them for their light, though. The insects marched steadily around the inside of the ceiling, pulsing softly as they went. Finn was certain they were there of their own volition.

Aurora stepped inside and moved toward the back, where she stopped at the foot of one of the beds. Her lips puckered as she dipped her head toward its occupant.

As Finn laid his eyes on Phoenix—the true Phoenix—the rest of the world disappeared around him. He didn't care at all about this wild fairy land or how they'd gotten here. He wasn't even thinking about wizards and the threat they posed. All he knew was that his baby boy was right there before him, sleeping peacefully with his chubby fists laying on either side of his head. He was a little bigger than the changeling version of Phoenix had been, having grown like a healthy child would have, instead of failing to thrive.

Finn had learned early on that you never wake a sleeping baby, but he also knew every rule had exceptions. He swept Phoenix into his arms, a wave of warmth and tenderness sweeping over his body. Now that he held his true son once again, he could immediately see how Leah had been able to tell the difference between this sweet little boy and the changeling. This was real. This was love.

Phoenix stirred, blinked up at his father, and smiled before drifting off to sleep again. It was enough to bring tears to Finn's eyes. His inner dragon had calmed and quieted, circling up around his heart as he ran his fingers across Phoenix's pale hair. He'd missed this little face so much, and he hadn't even realized it until now.

"Finn?"

He glanced up at Aurora, almost surprised to see he was still there. "Hm?"

"I know you have no reason to help me, and I don't blame you. But if there's something you could think of that might save my people..." She trailed off, her eyes drifting down to study the child.

Finn could see the softness in her gaze. He could almost feel the way she wanted to reach out and take Phoenix from him; not to kidnap him, but just to hold him. Finn had no certain way of knowing how Aurora felt about him, but it was clear to him how she felt about the baby. It tugged at his heartstrings, awakening the dragon once again, but in a different way. Aurora had always done that to him, from the moment they'd met.

"It's not a simple thing. Even without this whole changeling business, I'm not the one to talk to. But my parents, my aunts and uncles, the others have done battle with them before... I think we'd have to talk to them."

There were too many factors he didn't know. How many wizards were there? Where had they come from? How many of his family members would be willing to stand up and fight for these people they didn't know? No, that last part he knew. They'd fight. They were always willing to stand up for what was right, even if they pissed someone off in the process.

She took a tentative step forward, her eyes glistening. "That means a lot to me."

"It's not a promise," he hedged, not wanting to get her hopes up too much. He looked down at Phoenix once again. How could ever forgive her?

"What's this?" came a voice from behind them.

Finn turned to see a short man with a pudgy belly and a moon face entering the nursery. Paired with his flowing robe and the wreath around his head, he reminded Finn of Dionysus. But he didn't look as though he were enjoying a glass of wine at the moment. His steely brows were pinched together on his forehead, and he regarded Finn with a combination of fear and contempt.

"This is Finn, Phoenix's father." Aurora gestured toward the newcomer. "Finn, this is my father, King Oren."

Finn struggled with the right words to say. The normal polite murmurings of how nice it was to finally meet someone didn't really seem to fit the mood. He gave a curt nod instead. King or not, this man still had something to do with this son being whisked off to another world.

But Oren didn't seem too concerned with the niceties, either. "Aurora, what have you done?"

"I'm sorry, but I couldn't exactly keep Phoenix here any longer. It was only fair to let him go home."

The king shook his head, closing his eyes and slowly opening them again. "No, my dear. I completely understand that. But you've brought him..." He gestured at Finn. "Oh, I wish you hadn't done that."

"You already know I'm not just an ordinary human," Finn said, suddenly realizing just how much taller and broader he was than everyone else there. Even the fae they'd passed on the pathway, who looked to be fully grown, was minute compared to him. "I'm not going to tell anyone you're here."

"That's not it. I'm worried who might know *you're* here. The wizards are looking for you; for anyone like you. They won't tell me why, but I know they're getting desperate. They've taken more of my people, and they could come again at any minute. Please, take your son and go back to your world." Oren flicked his fingers to gesture Finn out the doorway.

Finn started to protest. As angry as he'd been about everything, he knew leaving the fae to deal with the wizards on their own wasn't the right thing to do.

Aurora laid a hand on his arm. "He's right, Finn. You can't risk your own life for ours, and I never should've asked you to. Nor should I have ever taken your son from you. Let's get you out of here as fast as possible."

He looked helplessly from Aurora to Phoenix and back again. There were so many things wrong with this situation, so many things he wanted to change. But they were right. He couldn't put Phoenix in harm's way, no matter what else was going on. "All right," he finally said. "But come with me. I want you to talk to my family."

Aurora glanced at her father, who nodded gravely. "Let's go."

Oren held the vines aside for them to exit the nursery and they dashed down the path, Phoenix still asleep in Finn's arms. Maybe it was the desperation around them, or the sense of finally having something to fight for. He couldn't explain it, but he reached out to take Aurora's hand as they darted toward the edge of the valley and the passageway to Earth.

"We're almost there," she panted as they climbed the steepest part of the path. "Let's slow down for just a second. I don't think there's anyone following us."

But a brilliant flash of light and the crack of a tree trunk splitting in half told them otherwise. Finn instinctively spread his wings to protect the three of them. "You were saying?"

"I didn't think it would come to this," she gasped. "They've never outright attacked us before. They must've been able to sense you. I don't know what I was thinking."

They'd reached the doorway, and Aurora hesitated.

"What's wrong?" Finn flinched as another ball of fire hit the branches nearby. "I don't think we have a lot of time. Let's go."

Tears were running down her face, but this time, they were tears of anger. "I can't just leave them, Finn. I keep looking for a solution somewhere other than here, and I can't do it any longer." She turned to look down in the valley where complete chaos had broken out. The distant screams were filtering up to them. "You go, and be safe. My fight is here."

Finn envisioned her running back into the melee, sacrificing her life. She'd been putting so much energy into saving her people, but to no avail. How could she possibly defeat them when she'd already told him her powers were getting weaker? It seemed impossible. "We'll bring back help."

Aurora stepped forward, but it was only so she could run her fingers across the veil and pull it aside for him. "No."

Finn felt the same sensation he'd experienced in his parent's living room when he'd shifted; that same primal urge to defend. As Finn put one foot through the passage between the worlds, he wrapped his free arm around her waist and stepped through.

# 13

---

"FINN! NO!" AURORA TRIED PRYING HERSELF FROM HIS GRASP AND KICKED against his legs, careful to avoid landing any blows on the baby. She knew she couldn't hurt him, though. He was a formidable man, and now she'd seen the even bigger beast that lived within. But that didn't stop her from fighting against him, surging her body backward toward the opening that led to her home.

He only tightened his grip. "There's nothing you can do there, not on your own."

"I have to try!" She landed a solid kick on his knee, but that earned her no more than a grunt. "I can't just leave them all back there. You wouldn't do that if it were your people in danger."

"That's true. We stick together, which is why I know we're doing the right thing now. We're heading back to my parents' place to fill them in, and with any luck, we'll bring a force of them back with us and take down the damn wizards."

She put her palms against his side and pushed, but it was no use. "There's no time for that!"

"When it comes to wizards, they don't take much convincing," he grumbled.

Aurora collapsed against him, emotionally exhausted and wrung out from this pointless fight. She thought of her sweet father who always put his people's needs above his own. Her heart went out to all the babies in the nursery, wanting to protect the innocent children who might never be reunited with their parents until she breathed her last breath.

Finn's hold on her suddenly relaxed. "Maybe we won't need to head to their place to convince them after all."

"What?" Aurora noticed the direction Finn was looking and turned, finding the path clogged with people. They carried no flashlights, not needing them to see in the dark any more than she did.

Aurora instantly recognized Nora, whom she'd met in these woods so many times, with her hulky boyfriend, Kieran. Kaylee was there, her husband Archard at her side. Leah, Holden, Summer, Xander... all of them, some whose names she couldn't even remember at the time. The only face she didn't recognize belonged to a rotund, little man whose expression looked pleasant, even though everyone else around him was dead serious.

"How did you find us?" Finn asked, his voice sounding both relieved and exhausted.

Holden stepped forward. "We talked about it after you left. None of us believed Aurora could be that malicious, but we didn't like the idea of you heading out here alone." He spoke to Finn, but he glanced apologetically at Aurora.

"Wizards," Finn said breathlessly before Aurora could say anything. "They're taking over the fae realm. And they're looking for us, too."

"Ah," Holden said, nodding solemnly. "That explains a lot. We're here, and we're ready to fight."

"You can't," Aurora protested, stepping in front of Finn to stand before the crowd of dragons. "They're so strong. I can't ask you to do anything like that."

"You're not asking," Kieran said in a deep rumble, standing next to Holden. "We're offering."

Overwhelmed by such a thing, especially after what she'd done, she wanted to cry all over again. "But..."

"Aurora," Nora laid a hand on the fae's arm, her eyes soft. "We want to help."

Naomi, with her slim brown eyes, stood protectively next to her sister-in-law. "I should stay behind with Leah and the baby to make sure Phoenix is safe in case any of the wizards get through."

Finn looked relieved, and perhaps just as overwhelmed as Aurora felt.

Beau raised his fist in the air. "All right, then! We know what we're up against. Let's go!"

Aurora felt a surge of hope and resolution as she turned and headed back toward the fae realm. Parting the curtain of branches, she held it open as the thunder of dragons shook the earth beneath her feet. They'd shifted already, rocketing into the fae realm on leathery wings. There were only three of the group who hadn't transformed, and Aurora wanted to know what was different about Summer, Autumn, and the strange little man in a long robe, but there wasn't time to ask. She ducked through the portal behind them.

The battle had begun just before they'd left, and the devastation was already evident. The wizards had been shooting balls of fire, leaving the trees scorched and plants reduced to ash. Aurora finally spotted them in the valley. There weren't many, not nearly the army of evil sorcerers she'd envisioned, but their magic was powerful and malicious, this much she knew. And yet she had no qualms about buzzing into the air and taking off toward the fray just on the tail of the dragons. They were magnificent, the moonlight illuminating their scales, but hiding their colors so they were almost indistinguishable from one another. But she didn't need to look hard to know which one was Finn. She recognized him as though she'd always seen him in this form, his great head rearing back as he summoned his own fire in response to the brilliant red orb he'd just dodged.

A dark dragon dove toward the ground, his claws ripping at the robe of one of the wizards who stood on the path. The sorcerer fought back with a blast from the end of his staff, but he was concentrating so much on his spell, he didn't notice the explosion of dragon fire that ended up consuming him from behind.

Finn's aunts, Summer and Autumn, had been left to pick their way down the path on foot. They'd looked just as determined to fight as anyone else, but now they merely stood in a clearing and held hands. A wizard with a gaunt face headed toward them, his hands raised as he prepared to launch his attack. Aurora dove toward them, fearing for their lives, but she suddenly realized there was no need. The sisters opened their eyes and held their palms out toward the adversary, sending a shock wave that knocked the wizard of his feet and left him paralyzed on the path.

Aurora landed, wondering just what she could do to help. She knew her own magic wasn't nearly as strong as it used to be, and the wizards' powers were bolstered by the captive fae. Still, she couldn't sit back and let everyone else fight on her behalf. She touched a nearby tree, one that hadn't yet been affected by the damage, and sent her wishes into it. There was only a slim chance its connection hadn't yet been broken as she watched a dragon battle a wizard head-to-head near the creek. The dragon was falling back from the mage's onslaught of spells, his wings flung out as he fought to keep his balance under the brilliant globes of fire.

The trees heard her. They were more complicated than the requests she'd asked for on Earth; much more than simply moving a few young saplings. But the trees, the plants, and very dirt heard her and knew she needed them. The ground between the battling figures split in half as a full-sized oak erupted from it, knocking the wizard back and flinging him aside.

She next turned her attention to the odd little man who'd accompanied them, someone she now realized was much like the wizards they were fighting. He stood off to the side, watching the action with his hands folded peacefully in front of him. Her heart surged as she wondered if he was truly the enemy, but she then realized what he was doing. He was quietly observing, waiting for the right moment. He raised his hands and moved them in an intricate pattern, his lips moving slightly as he muttered an incantation.

Aurora didn't see the effect of what he'd done until her eyes landed on two wizards near the baking house. They'd been fighting several of the dragons, their magic pulsing from the palms of their hands. But it suddenly stopped flowing, and no matter how many wild gestures they made, they couldn't bring the fire back. The odd little man had bound their magic.

She shot to her feet in a surge of victory, knowing they were getting close to the tipping point. They just needed to push a little harder. There would be much to discuss later, but the moment only called for action. The ideas surging through her mind were ridiculous ones, and she had no idea where they'd come from, but she had to find out if they could possibly work.

"Finn!" Aurora found him easily. He'd just knocked a wizard back, but bowling them off their feet only kept them down for so long. She looked into his eyes, seeing the same man inside the dragon she'd come to know and love.

"Get back!" Finn cried, his voice even deeper in this form. "Get your people!"

"No, there's something we've got to try. Just trust me. Please." She felt hot tears burn at the backs of her eyes as she begged him to have confidence in her. She didn't deserve it. She didn't deserve any of what they were doing, but she reached out and placed her hand on his muscular shoulder. His scales were white hot to the touch, the heat from his fire radiating out between them. But Aurora pressed harder and closed her eyes, breathing deep as she searched for the thread of magic in him. It was different than what she felt when she touched the trees or spoke to the birds, but it was there. And it responded to her.

Finn grunted, but in surprise, not pain.

Aurora pulled harder at that small string of energy, asking it to join with her own. A bolt of lighting erupted before her eyes and shivered down her body, but she knew Finn felt it, too.

The wizard was on his feet once again. Finn's wings rose into the air as the bellows of his lungs built up his fire, now mixed with a new element. His claws dug into the ground with the force of the energy inside him. Aurora moved with him, knowing she had to keep the connection alive.

The fire that erupted from him was like nothing either of them had seen before. She knew because she was just as much a part of him at that moment, as if their minds were melded. The flames were brilliant, lighting up the night sky and calling the attention of the other fighters. It was thick and heavy like a stream as it burst out of him and slammed into the wizard.

His scream was barely heard as he was vaporized, crumbling to a pile of ashes.

Her breath had left her, and the shock of it all made her let go of Finn. She didn't even dare to look at him as she watched the ashes blow off into the breeze. "I've got to go tell the others," she gasped. "We can all fight. We have the strength."

Finn called for her as she ran away. She wanted to go back to him, to touch him and feel that link again. But she had to find her father and the other fae to let them know they had an alliance; the likes of which none of them had ever imagined. The wizards were weaker than they realized, and they could win. She would get back to Finn.

But she didn't see the wizard who stepped out behind her on the path, nor the iron chain in his hands until it was wrapped around her body, pinning her arms to her sides and her wings to her back. Aurora choked in pain as the metal burned into her skin. Her knees buckled and she collapsed, the world going dark around the edges of her vision as the man who held the chains yanked them.

"What's the matter, little fairy?" he asked with a cruel laugh. "We've fashioned some new chains, since you and your kind don't like to obey orders. They're a little stronger than what we used before."

She couldn't summon any words. They'd been so close. She'd lost so much hope and had allowed herself to restore that feeling when she'd united her powers with Finn's. But the iron wrapped around her body burned like the fires of hell, her wings wilting under its touch. Her flesh burned, and she swore she could smell the charring of it. The bindings stole the very breath from her lungs as they dug deeper and deeper.

The wizard yanked hard. "I think you're a fitting sacrifice to the great Tazarre, puny and pathetic as you are. Our great leader died in the process of eliminating the dragons, and here you are, fighting alongside them. You deserve the same death sentence they do." With another solid pull, the chains dug and pinched into her, burning like they were on fire.

From where she lay, Aurora could see the torch that burned proudly at the top of the castle. She whispered her apology to her father as screams broke out around her. She heard the cries of her people and wept, knowing they were about to meet the same fate. Aurora had fought as hard as she could. The dragons had joined them, but it just wasn't enough.

## 14

THE FAE HAD COME FLOODING OUT OF THE WOODS, THEIR BATTLE CRY A high and keening scream. Finn watched them as they came charging in. He didn't know if they had seen what happened or if Aurora had told them somehow, but they understood what they needed to do. The fae had been too afraid to fight before, and the few Finn had seen earlier were fleeing for their lives. He couldn't blame them. The wizards were much stronger; their power, more malevolent. The fae were used to magic that healed, magic that allowed them to speak to the world around them. No matter how strong it was, it couldn't compare to the power the wizards held.

That was, until they combined their power with the dragons'. They melted out of the forest, their hands reaching desperately for the scaled creatures. The dragons understood, knowing what was about to happen, and positioned themselves to send the deadly blasts toward the enemy. The fae touched the dragons and blended their magic, the wizards crumbling before them until the smell of scorched flesh filled the air. Even Varhan looked astonished, the idea not having come to him before.

The last of their enemies fell as the sun rose, and Finn suddenly became aware of his own exhaustion. The conflict was a long one, and it had been fought hard. His bones and scales rearranged from his dragon form to his human one, no longer wanting to wear the armor he'd battled in.

"That was unreal," Elliot said as he approached. "I had no idea we could do that."

"I don't think anyone did," Finn replied, taking tally of his family members. They were tired and dirty, but they were unharmed. He wondered if the other dragons had felt the same sort of bond with the fae who touched them as he did with Aurora, but he doubted it. A disturbing feeling twisted in his stomach as he realized he couldn't see her anywhere.

"The last time I saw her was right after you disintegrated that wizard," Archard said, nodding toward the castle. "She headed that way."

Finn followed the path, calling out for her every now and then. She didn't respond, and the feeling of victory he'd been carrying on his shoulders quickly dissipated. "Aurora!"

"Over here," croaked a tired voice from around a bend.

But it wasn't Aurora. It was King Oren, kneeling over her body. She lay twisted and broken in the path, her skin burned in great red welts. Her glorious wings had been reduced to little more than two glossy shards on her back, burned and brown on the ends.

"No!" He dropped to his knees next to the king. He tried to reach out to touch her, but there didn't seem to be a part of her body that was left undamaged. "Is she alive?"

"Barely," Oren replied, tears falling down his plump cheeks. "They bound her in chains. Fae can't handle iron, and the wizards had infused those chains with magic. It was a formidable enough weapon, but they used fae magic to make the chains even stronger." He pointed to the loop-shaped burns that made bands around her arms. "They'd already done it to me, and the chain fell away just after the fighting started. My best guess is that the wizard who created her chains perished as well, but not before he managed to inflict the damage."

Finn's heart shattered inside him. Only a few hours ago, he hadn't been certain that he could ever forgive Aurora for what she'd done. She'd stolen the most precious gift he'd ever been given, and there was no telling what might've happened to Phoenix if Leah hadn't discovered the truth. But he still felt his heart leaping out for her, his dragon raging at the sight of her in this condition. What was it about this woman that made him so unsure? Did fate know something he didn't?

Was this what it felt like to find the woman he was supposed to be with? He wanted to tip his head back and cry out at the unfairness and pain of it all.

He could no longer see her through his tears. "Aurora, please wake up. Everything is going to be all right. The wizards are gone, thanks to you. You can't leave us right now." He looked up at Oren, not even embarrassed to be weeping like a child. "Please tell me there's something you can do."

The king looked somber as he nodded. "I think so, but I don't know for sure. Our magic has been drastically weakened by the presence of the wizards. Yesterday, this would have been a completely impossible task; something I wouldn't even have attempted. Now, I have no idea."

"Is there anything I can do to help?" One of the fae Finn and Aurora had passed on the path to the nursery appeared behind Oren's shoulder. More fae showed up behind him, looking just as haggard as the dragons did, their wings bent and their narrow faces grim.

Their arrival seemed to bring some hope to Oren's face. "Yes. I'll need you; all of you. Join me; let's heal our princess."

"What about us?" Finn asked desperately. "We were able to blend our magic for the battle, maybe we can help with this, too."

A hand patted him on the shoulder, and Finn looked up to see Varhan. "I don't think that would be a good idea, my boy. The fae magic is much more delicate and refined, which is exactly what Aurora needs right now. Let's see what they can do."

Several of the fae glanced uncertainly at the wizard, but they stepped forward. They laid their hands on Oren's back and closed their eyes, the same way Aurora had communicated with the trees. The crowd had built, and those who couldn't get in to touch their king laid their hands on their fellow fae. They created a tangled web behind Oren as he bent forward and laid his hands on Aurora.

Finn was expecting something like a shimmering of light or an explosion of color. But there was nothing. His heart sank into his stomach as he watched, knowing this wasn't going to work. Slowly, though, the deep burns on her skin began to heal, fresh flesh sealing over the charred skin. Her breathing, which had been so shallow, became deeper and more regular. The stubs of her wings fluttered, and she opened her eyes.

"Finn?"

———

"I still just can't believe it all," Aurora said. They sat in her tree-house, which Finn had carried her up to once she'd regained consciousness. Her wings wouldn't grow back for some time, and she was keeping them tucked away for the time being. The rest of the crowd seemed to understand that the two of them had some talking to do, so they let them be. She'd settled on the end of her bed, and Finn had pulled up a stool to sit next to her; close, but not too close.

"I know." But Finn wasn't sure they were talking about the same thing. Aurora looked out the window over her kingdom, watching the fae mend the plants that had fallen victim to the wizards' attack. Others crowded around each other to heal those who'd been injured.

She turned to him. "Finn, I can't thank you enough for what you've done. I'm the very last person who deserved your help. I was horrible to you, and I lied to you. I don't think I'll ever forgive myself for that."

He reached out and took her hand. It felt different now than it had when they'd held hands on their dates; like each of them had changed, and they were two new people who had to get to know each other all over again. "But I forgive you."

"You do? How could you?" Tears glistened in her eyes in the early morning sunlight.

Finn longed to kiss her, to wrap his arms around her and show her what he meant. "You were desperate, and you were trying to save your family and your people. I can't blame you for going to great lengths for them. I'd have done the same."

They sat there for a while, just listening to the birds, each trying to summon up the right things to say. "Finn, I have to tell you something."

He pressed his lips together and looked at her. Her hair was still wild from the battle, her clothes ripped and stained with blood, yet she was still just as enchanting as she'd always been. "I'm listening."

Aurora swallowed. "When that happened down there, during the battle, I..." She paused and licked her lips. "I think there was some-thing happening, something more than just your magic mixing with mine. It was like I was in your mind, the same way I am when I'm communicating with nature. But there's so much more to it than that, and I don't even know how to explain it. I guess I'm apologizing, because I had no right to come intruding into your soul like that."

"My soul?" He lifted one eyebrow in surprise. Finn had been perfectly aware of what her intent had done to his fire. The change inside him had been a palpable one, and it made him feel like he could conquer the entire world. But if there was more to it than that, he had been too preoccupied to notice.

She nodded sadly. "I felt everything you felt. I knew what it was like to be covered in scales, to be a powerful dragon facing down an ancient enemy. I knew the heat in your chest as you vanquished him. But there was more."

"Are you saying you could read my mind?"

"I felt the love you have for Phoenix, that protective urge you have when you think there might be the slightest risk to him. I felt your anger at being betrayed. And..."

"Go on." Whatever it was, Finn wanted to know. They'd come this far, and there was no turning back now.

Aurora pressed her lips together, her eyes full of fear and hope. "I swore I felt that there was something between us, something more than just attraction or the union of our magic."

He couldn't stop the smile that spread across his face. When was the last time he'd smiled? It felt like forever. "I guess you know my secret, then."

"I didn't mean to—"

Finn stopped her protest with a kiss, a gentle one just to silence her. "It's all right. It shouldn't be a secret, anyway. In fact, I think I was keeping it a secret from myself. I didn't really want to admit that I could need someone as much as I need you. I felt so betrayed when Mandy threatened to give Phoenix away to strangers, like my destiny was being altered by someone else and there wasn't anything I could do about it." He pulled her other hand into his, twining his fingers with hers. "I had to wonder if you were changing my destiny, too; not that I really ever knew what it was in the first place. But Aurora, I do love you. I can't deny the pull between us, and now I don't see why I ever tried."

"Oh, Finn. I love you, too." She fell into his arms, pressing her lips against his.

He held her tightly, careful not to crush her too hard against him, even though he wanted to. There was no such thing as being too close to her; in fact, he felt he could never be close enough. He squeezed her hand, relieved to know she was healed and conscious again. To think that he'd nearly left her on her own to fight those damn wizards was shameful, but he knew they would both heal from the last of their wounds together.

Finn pulled his lips away from hers to trail kisses along her jaw toward her ear. Her curls tickled his face, but he didn't care. There was nothing that could bother him, as long as he was with her. "I can't wait until you're fully healed," he said as he kissed the side of her neck, sensing the pulse that throbbed just beneath her skin. "It's all well and good to tell you how I feel, but I'd like to show you."

"Mmm, I think I'm pretty well healed, and I've got a few things to show you, too." Aurora leaned back on the bed, pulling him with her.

The sensation of her smooth curves beneath him was making his head throb already. The beast inside him was going crazy, as it always did when he was with her, but it was suddenly much more focused. If he let himself go, he would end up hurting her. Finn was going to have to be careful. "Are you sure about that?" he muttered, even as he found the hem of her shirt and slipped his hand underneath, feeling the smooth planes of her back.

Aurora nodded, her hair splayed out behind her against the blanket. She was like his own personal goddess, radiant and deserving of his worship.

Finn felt his body surging with the invitation. He needed her desperately, in a way that drove everything else from his mind. The worries of the worlds—both his own and the fae realm—melted away as he braced himself on his side to lift her shirt over her head, revealing her pert breasts. He leaned forward to capture one nipple in his mouth, closing his eyes as he felt her arch her back toward him.

Her fingers trailed through his hair and down the nape of his neck. They explored his shoulders and his tattooed back, instinctively touching the delicate place where his wings broke free when he shifted. The sensation sent a surge of energy crackling down his spine and in between his legs, making it hard to concentrate on the pleasure he wanted to bring her.

Finn moved down to the softness of her belly, wanting to explore every inch of her skin, to taste her, to worship her, to know her in even greater detail than he knew his own body. He kissed her navel, surprised at how something so simple could be so beautiful. He pulled at her skirt and the panties, unaware of exactly where they ended up once he revealed the treasure underneath. He traced his lips against her skin until they met with her delicate folds, giving them the attention they'd been longing for.

Aurora wrapped her legs around him, her body rising and falling beneath him like an undulating sea. She gasped as his tongue flicked and his lips caressed her sensitive bud, and she held onto him as though he were the only thing that could keep her from drowning in a sea of pleasure.

Closing his eyes to focus on the sensation of her skin against him and the taste of her in his mouth, Finn ran his fingers down her ribs to her hip bones and around to the curve of her buttocks. He traced the sides of her thighs, memorizing every bend, every muscle. He felt as though they had all the time in the world, like the rest of the universe had stopped in its tracks to allow them this moment.

When he could take no more, Finn pulled away and ripped off his shirt. He—and his dragon—needed her. He needed to sink himself inside her and consecrate the bond they both knew existed between them. Sometimes, it was a white-hot heat; other times, it was a simple thread of a heartbeat that kept them linked. But he knew it was there, and he wanted to feel it at its core.

But before he could go any further, Aurora put her hands on his chest and pushed gently. He was twice her size, but the merest command from her was all it took. Finn stood up, his very veins vibrating. "What's wrong? Is it too much?"

Aurora stood as well, smiling up at him. "Not at all. I just want to make sure I get to enjoy some of you, too." She slid her hands over his sides and around his back, crushing her breasts against him as she kissed his chest. Aurora moved around him, trailing her fingers against his skin as she took him in from every angle. "You're not like any man I've ever met before."

"No?" he asked with a grin. She'd made it around behind him, and her fingers were studying his back. A naked woman standing behind him and tracing lines down his back was surprisingly sexy, but he wasn't sure how much longer he could stand the building tension.

"Not at all. And I like it." She finished her circuit and stood in front of him once again, her fingers working deftly at his belt. Aurora stripped him of the remainder of his clothing until he stood bare before her.

Finn pulled her close, feeling the hot press of their bodies together as he kissed her, running his fingers and then his palms against her back and buttocks, wanting her more than anything in the world. But she pushed away from him again and slid to her knees. He exhaled sharply as she took him into her mouth, reaching out to brace his hand against the wall as she brought a wave of rapture over him.

Her mouth was hot and wet, her lips soft, her tongue eager. She ran her hands up the insides of his thighs as she pulsed, sucking and releasing, licking and fondling. Her breasts touched his legs every now and then as she put her whole body into her work.

With his free hand, Finn brushed her hair back so he could see her lips wrapped around him, but it was too intense. He'd never enjoyed something that much, and his muscles clenched as he fought against the urge to bury himself.

"Aurora." His voice was hoarse. "I need you."

They fell on the bed together, their bodies colliding and entwining as they fought to get as much exposure to each other as possible. He sank into her as she wrapped around him, their bodies moving in unison. He was on top of her, and then next to her, and then beneath her. Every position felt exquisite, and yet none of it was ever enough. He clutched at the blanket as he wondered how they could possibly ever break apart again now that they'd become one.

Her legs on either side of him, Aurora sat up straight and tipped her head back as she rode him. He bent his knees to brace her up, still worried about her recent injuries despite how far they'd both come. She surged against him as he reached up to touch her, her hands clutching at his forearms for support as she bit her lip.

Finn gasped as he felt her walls clench around him and then let go. The pattern repeated, growing with intensity, and he swore he felt that same intertwining they'd experienced out on the battlefield, his very life force melding with hers as she cried out and sank her nails into him.

Rolling her over until she was beneath him again, Finn sank into her with a shudder that racked his bones. He held her tight as he poured his entire soul into her, knowing neither one of them would ever be the same again.

# 15

THE DELEGATION OF FAE THAT HAD COME TO HOLDEN'S HOME, HEADED up by Oren, looked particularly pleased. Both sides had been eager to get together, to learn about each other, and to create a pact between their peoples that would keep them both safe from future attacks. Everyone was interested in talking to Varhan and getting his take on the way the fae and dragon powers had combined.

Oren sat at one end of the large dining table, currently being used as a conference table. His hands folded in front of him, he looked solemnly at the dragons. "I can't thank you enough for everything you've done for us. My world was in great peril, dangling on the edge of complete destruction. You were incredibly brave to help us fight such a terrible foe. My only regret is that I didn't simply ask for your help sooner."

"We understand," Beau replied. "Things get very complicated when dealing with the wizards. It's never an easy task. And you must believe us when we say we're just as glad to have you as allies. We know we can learn a lot from you."

"I invite all of you to come visit us very soon. I'm afraid you only got to see what our world was like in the midst of battle, but nearly all the scars have healed. We've got our people back, and the plants and wildlife are making a solid recovery. In fact, I'd like to think we're about to be better off than we've ever been in my lifetime."

"Thank you for the invitation," Xander enthused. "We didn't exactly have time for sightseeing when we were there before."

Both sides of the table laughed.

Over in the corner, Kaylee and Archard were having a serious discussion with one of the fae about their language, and Nora had pulled someone else aside to discuss some of the unique flora of the fae realm.

Aurora sat back and smiled, watching the people she'd grown up with learn about this new world. It was one she had grown accustomed to over the past few years, so she wasn't surprised by televisions or cell phones. But the fae, including her father, were more than interested. They wanted to see and experience everything.

"Isn't it funny?" Finn whispered next to her as everyone began shaking hands and preparing to leave.

She leaned back against him, enjoying the steady hardness of his body. He was always so strong, so warm. Her spirit had swelled simply with knowing him, and being in contact with him made it double again. His power became her power, one they shared. "What's that?"

"The dragons aren't from this planet, either. We're just teaching your people what we've come to know, but the truth is, I still think we have a lot to learn." He held Phoenix on his hip, the little blonde baby watching all the hubbub with interest.

"Maybe so, but I think it'll all work out. Who ever would've thought we'd have an alliance like this? Fae, dragons, and even a wizard." Aurora smiled as she looked at Varhan. She'd come to know the stout man as a good friend of the family, someone who would fight just as hard to protect his friends as if they were of his own blood. In fact, the kind wizard had even taken the time to locate the spell needed to reinforce the veil around the fae realm permanently, restoring each of the fae's powers to their full capacity.

"And an alliance sealed with a ring, just like in medieval times," Finn replied, picking up her hand and kissing the delicate gold band he'd placed there during their marriage ceremony a month ago.

Their relationship had moved quickly, but not a single person on either side had questioned it. Finn's family had gone to the fae realm for the affair, with Oren playing host in the castle. Aurora still warmed when she thought of it. Her father had never looked happier, and indeed even the rest of the fae looked like they could float right through the open roof. Their fae princess was now married to a dragon prince, and even though she didn't live among them at the moment, they toasted and feasted throughout the night.

"Hold on, Oren," Holden said as the fae were finally heading toward the door. "There's one other thing I wanted to show you. It's called a debit card. I thought it was the silliest thing when I first came here, but now I can't believe I ever thought I'd live without it."

"Let's get out of here," Finn said in her ear. "Phoenix is tired, and if we actually wait for them to finish, we'll be up all night."

She turned in his embrace and touched a finger to the collar of his shirt. It was a subtle gesture, but it didn't take much. "I don't mind staying up all night if you don't."

"Fine with me as long as we can get back to our place," he murmured, pulling her by the waist toward the entryway.

They sped across town, their fingers entwined on the console and promises in their eyes. Aurora knew she would never quite get used to living there, with fast cars and highways, trash on the ground, and pollution in the air. But things were slowly getting better. She and Nora had teamed up to create a cleanup movement on campus and in the woods nearby. Students, non-profit groups, and families were joining in, suddenly taking up the cause as their own badge of honor.

Finn squeezed her knee gently. "You know, I don't think I ever thanked you."

"For what?" She imagined she was the one who needed to thank him, considering he'd helped save an entire kingdom, among other things.

"For getting me lost in the woods that day when I went to talk with Cecilia. I never would've believed that Mr. Anderson had anything but good intentions for that land, but you were absolutely right. The bastard was only going to keep it protected long enough to make a good public show of it before he sold it off piece by piece to make the most profit. He tried to deny it at first, and he gave me the run-around for a long time. It wasn't until I saw his actual plans for logging and a subdivision that I finally lost it with him." He shook his head, looking angry with himself.

"I'm glad you quit," she said quietly against the gentle hum of the car. "I know you thought you were making a difference there, and it wasn't easy for you to let go of that job."

He glanced over his shoulder, where Phoenix was sleeping in the backseat. "It was particularly hard, not knowing where my next paycheck was going to come from. But who ever would've thought my consulting firm would take off like it has?"

Aurora smiled again. Everything was changing, but only for the better. Finn and some of his coworkers who'd found out about the plan for Cecilia's property had created their own agency where they worked as consultants for companies wanting to be more eco-friendly. Instead of coming up with new products, they explained to businesses how they could use the products currently on the market to reduce their carbon footprint and save money at the same time. He worked long hours, often calling from his desk or from the road to explain he would be home late, but she didn't mind. She always knew he would come home, and that was what mattered to her.

They arrived at their apartment, a new place they'd rented together where they could start over anew. Aurora loved it for the large windows and the hardwood floors that reminded her of home, and Finn loved it because it made her happy. The large park nearby meant they always had a nice place to take Phoenix, and they were on the same side of the city as the woods, so she was never too far from her father.

"Why don't you let me tuck him in?" Aurora offered when they walked in the door. "You go relax for a while." She lifted Phoenix from his car seat, indulging in the weight of his head and the softness of his cheek against her shoulder. His fists curled in the fabric of her shirt, clinging to her.

"I know, sweet one," she said quietly, wrapping her arms around him. "You need me, and I need you just as much. You're so precious, and I hope you always know you mean the world to me." Aurora set him on the changing table to put him in his pajamas and a clean diaper, still in awe over this child, despite the months she'd known him. He gained more personality every day, and she couldn't wait to see what a fine young shifter he would grow into.

"Things are going to change around here soon," she whispered as she scooped him up. "But you need to remember that your daddy and I will always love you. You're our special little man."

He was out cold, and she could easily lay him in his crib and slip out of the room. But Aurora couldn't resist holding him just a little longer, swaying back and forth and enjoying the feel of him against her. She'd bonded with him so much when he'd stayed in the fae nursery, more than she ever could've imagined she'd feel for a child not of her own blood. She couldn't imagine what life would've been like if Finn had come to take him away, storming away from the fae realm and never looking back. The two of them had each been fools in their own ways, not wanting to believe what was happening right before their eyes. Fate had intervened, and thank goodness it had. She laid her cheek against his head and sang to him in the ancient language of her people, remembering words from when she was little and living in the nursery herself. Finally, she laid him down and pressed a kiss on his cheek.

She headed down the hall, expecting to find Finn with his shoes off, his feet up on the ottoman, and a beer in his hand. It was a Saturday night, after all, and he'd put in a lot of hours at work. But the living room was empty, the television off. She peeked through the kitchen doorway and found him there at the sink, washing bottles. "What are you doing?" she asked as she came up behind him, rubbing his back. "I can get those in the morning."

He rinsed the last bottle, drained the sink, and dried his hands before turning around. His face was soft as he looked at her. "But you deserve your rest, and maybe some time to sleep in." He put his arms around her and kissed her. "I think you might need your rest by the time I'm done with you."

A jolt of energy shot through her, something that was happening more and more often lately. She never failed to get excited at the prospect of spending time alone with Finn. "Yeah?"

Finn kissed her again before pulling away, rolling his eyes up toward the ceiling as though he were thinking about it. "Um, yeah. Definitely."

Aurora laughed, loving how playful the two of them had become. Married life and raising a child hadn't been boring at all. "You still think I'm sexy? Even with this?" She ran her hand gently over the slight curve to her belly that had only just started forming.

"Now that is incredibly sexy," he said, covering her hand with his own and shaking his head. "I still can't believe we're going to have a baby together. You don't know how happy that makes me, Aurora." He kissed her again, his hands in her hair and his arousal evident against her.

"I do know," she said when they pulled apart, their lips still only a fraction of an inch from each other. "I feel like Mother Nature, or a doe in spring. I can't wait." She felt full and proud and warm, and even more so because she was sharing it all with Finn. In this state, she felt her magic might be strong enough to send away an entire circle of wizards.

"It's going to be crazy, two babies running around here." Finn raked his fingers down her backside, sending a shiver up her spine.

"Yes. I guess that means we should enjoy ourselves while we can, huh?" Aurora touched the fine golden stubble on his face. He hadn't bothered to shave that morning, and he looked a little more like a wild animal than normal. And she knew just how wild he could be.

Finn responded by scooping her up into his arms and carrying her to the bedroom. He pulled off her shoes and rubbed her ankles, working his way up her legs to her knees, her thighs, and then under the skirt of her dress. "Definitely."

Aurora closed her eyes. "You spoil me."

"Do you mind?"

"Never." Aurora pulled him down to her. He could turn her on with hardly more than a glance or a touch, making her crave him constantly. Their clothes fell to the floor, the sheets and blankets tumbling after them. Soon enough, they'd only have time for a quickie while the children napped, but for now, they wanted to explore their love in every way possible.

She straddled his hips, and as she leaned forward, Finn buried his face between her breasts. They were already starting to get heavier with her pregnancy, something they both enjoyed. Aurora felt like a fertile deity as she took what she needed from him, feeling the waves of delight and womanly strength wash over her. Explosions of color erupted behind her eyes as her body buzzed.

"Tell me what you want," she whispered, the idea of turning him on keeping her going.

"I'll do better than that. I'll show you." Finn lay her on her back, getting to his knees. He sat back on his heels as he pulled her into his lap by her hips, piercing her once again but at a different angle. Her body was open for him to run his hands over her breasts, her ribs, her softening belly, and she wrapped her legs around his waist as she felt his girth increase inside her. Finn grasped her hips and pulled them hard against them as he came.

But Aurora wasn't done with him yet. There was something about knowing he was satisfied that aroused her all over again, and she grabbed his hands where they rested on her hips to keep him firmly in place. Her toes curled behind his back as she came, her nipples tingling as she bit her lip to keep herself from screaming out and waking up Phoenix.

Afterwards, Finn lay at her back with his arms around her, one hand softly stroking her belly. "You know, I never get tired of doing this with you."

She grinned and rolled toward him, looking up into his face. "Me, neither. You're very entertaining, you know."

"That's why you married me, right?"

"Yeah, and you're kind of cute, too." She picked up her head just enough to kiss his jaw. "Did you see the look on your mother's face when you told her this evening? I thought she would pass out."

Finn laughed, his chest vibrating against her shoulder. "I know, her and Dad both. And your father, too. I don't think I've ever seen him smile so much."

"I have to admit I wasn't sure what they would all think. I mean, they seemed to be supportive of us, but it's all a lot more real when there's a baby coming along. I didn't know what they would think about a half-fae, half-dragon shifter child." Her cheeks were getting tired of smiling so much, but she simply couldn't help it. They'd told their parents first, figuring they should have the privilege. But the word had spread quickly around the full house, and soon everyone was hugging them. Even Varhan seemed beyond delighted, clapping his hand with glee and giving her blessings that she didn't understand.

"It's going to be interesting around here, that's for sure. But I think they're pretty happy. I wouldn't be surprised if Aunt Summer is out buying yarn right now." He nestled his nose against her cheek.

"Yarn?"

Her husband laughed. "It's a closely-guarded secret, since she's always acting so tough and bossy. But just you wait, she'll have knitted the softest little baby blanket you've ever seen."

Aurora closed her eyes, sleep beginning to drift in and take over. It'd been a long day, and the days were only going to get longer while she grew this miraculous child inside her. But she loved the idea of having such a diverse family, of fae, dragons, witches, humans, and even a wizard. She'd heard an old human phrase that it took a village to raise a child, and they were lucky enough to have a giant, loving one of their very own to help support their growing family for years to come.

———

# ROYAL DRAGON'S WITCH

## SHIFTERS BETWEEN WORLDS

# 1

ELLIOT SPREAD HIS DEEP BLUE WINGS, A DARK SHADOW COMPARED TO THE sinking sun that had turned the sky the color of slate. He caught a good cross breeze and felt it shove his body further up into the sky. The turning season was bringing in colder temperatures, but he loved the way the cool air skimmed across his scales and cooled the heat that burned inside him.

"You look like you're enjoying yourself," Finn commented with a scaly grin. "I told you it would be good to peel yourself away from those books for a while." The yellow dragon rolled over in the air, his wings twisting around him and then snapping out again as he righted himself. "You can't spend all your time studying."

Elliot shook his head and sighed. "That's easy to say when you've already got a good job. I'm getting ready to take the bar exam. The results of this test could change my entire life." It had been weighing so heavily on his mind that he'd done little else beyond studying. The modest house he'd rented on the edge of town—far away from the temptation of cafes, bars, and women—had helped him somewhat. He'd also purchased a good pair of noise-cancelling headphones, so that even when he went to the university library to study, he wouldn't be distracted by the murmurs of other students.

"Sure. Because god knows you'll never get another chance to take the test if you fail," Finn remarked.

"Don't even say that!" Elliot spat, feeling a few hot sparks against his tongue.

Finn veered off to the left, further out over the woods. "Don't be so serious! You know I'm just messing with you."

"You're telling me not to be serious? You're the one who's married and has kids. Don't you think you should be the serious one?" Elliot grumbled, following his cousin. The sky was growing darker, but it didn't matter for them. Their vision was excellent, even in the darkest of circumstances.

"I am serious, when I need to be." Finn had recently married Aurora, a beautiful fae who was now carrying his second child. She'd readily adopted his young son Phoenix, and the three of them were living happily ever after, as far as Elliot could tell. "I get up every morning and go to work, even though I'd much rather wrap my arms around my wife and go back to sleep. But I know I've got to provide for my family, and that's all the motivation I need."

"I'm glad that works for you, but I don't know how you do it." Elliot looked down at the treetops as they skimmed along beneath him. He reveled in the beauty of nature when he had the chance, which hadn't been often lately. Laws and codes still simmered in the back of his mind, insisting that he remember them long enough to pass that stupid exam.

"You should give it a try," Finn suggested. "Find yourself a nice woman and settle down. You'd be one hell of a catch with that law degree and a three-piece suit. It wouldn't take long."

Elliot sighed. "You make it sound so easy, but you know just as well as I do that it's not that simple. If I just wanted to go out and find any woman, I'm sure I could. But a woman who could fall in love with a dragon? A woman who doesn't turn and run as soon as she finds out I'm a shifting prince from a distant planet on the other side of the universe? Not to mention a woman who's willing to put up with the rest of our family, who are dragons, witches, fae, and psychics. Yeah, I don't see that happening any time soon."

Finn dipped low and swooped back up again, giving his wings a firm snap to level out. "You're only saying that because you haven't experienced it. Elliot, I'm not even kidding. There's nothing better than waking up next to the person you love, except for knowing the other person you love more than anything in the world, your child, is right in the next room. Or that there's a whole new person growing inside your mate, one you haven't even had the privilege of meeting yet, but you unconditionally love already. It's...like magic. I don't know how else to explain it."

"You do you." With a flick of his tail, Elliot undulated through the sky. The first stars were just beginning to peek out, and he couldn't help but think of his place in the universe. He'd never been to the distant planet of Charok, where his father, Beau, had rescued him as an egg from the curse cast by the evil wizard Tazarre during the War of Storms. While Beau wasn't his father by blood, he'd vowed to protect and raise Elliot as his own. The Great Curse had wiped out most of dragon kind, including his mother, the queen. Even though they now knew there were still a handful of dragons alive on their home planet, Elliot knew it had only been a very special set of circumstances that had landed him on Earth and with a loving family. He was grateful for it, but he sometimes wondered what might've happened if he'd grown up somewhere else.

Finn swooped closer. "You know, I'm sure we could set you up with someone. Aurora might know someone in the fae realm, or maybe Nora or Kaylee have a friend."

"A blind date?" Elliot let out a roaring laugh, a deep noise as it crackled through his fire chamber. "I don't think so. I'm not asking anyone in my family to hook me up. I don't know what it is about all of you who seem so obsessed with finding a mate and making sure everyone else does as well."

"Dude, I had serious game when it came to the ladies before I found my mate," Finn reminded him with a snort. "I didn't see much point in settling down with just one woman, either. But then I met Aurora, and I'm telling you, there's no feeling like it. When you find the person you're meant to be with, it's like there's something inside you that's just been waiting to wake up. The whole world changes, along with the way you see it. I don't know if humans get that same reaction when they meet *the one*, but it's addictive."

"I'm sure." Elliot didn't want to argue about it any further. He knew Finn wouldn't give up. And now that his other cousins, Nora and Kaylee, had met their mates as well, it was only a matter of time before they started harassing him, too.

But Elliot had other plans for his life. He'd worked damn hard to get through law school, and that was no easy challenge. There'd been so many times he'd thought about giving up and going for something

easier, something that wouldn't require him to memorize entire text-
books of information or make arguments against much more experienced attorneys. But he saw court cases as one big puzzle to unravel,
like a maze he had to negotiate so that he and his future clients would
end up at the right exit.

And he'd invested so much time in his education that he wasn't
going to let himself get distracted by some woman. Elliot had a
detailed plan in place for himself, though. The first thing was to take
the bar exam, of course, and that involved a lot of studying. He could
afford to dedicate a few months of his life to nothing but books and
study groups if it meant securing a passing grade on the first try. That
would save him a lot of time, since it would mean he could go ahead
and start looking for a job. The firm he'd been interning at didn't
currently have any open positions, but the attorneys there had
promised to write him thorough letters of recommendation.

Once he got his foot in the door as a junior lawyer—hopefully
something he could do without moving away, so he could stay near his
family—Elliot would be working constantly to establish himself and
work his way up the ranks. It wasn't until he made partner and could
put some of the grunt work onto someone else that he would worry
about things like marriage and family, if at all. There was something to
be said for living life just for himself, where he wouldn't need to worry
about changing diapers or dealing with in-laws who wanted them to
come for the holidays.

The two dragons turned in silence, heading back for Elliot's home.
The chill air had thinned and the stars were standing out like brilliant
lights. The sun was gone for another day. They morphed as they came
in for a landing in Elliot's back yard, their wings acting as parachutes
just long enough to bring them near the ground before folding into
their arms, their claws retracting and turning once again to innocent
fingernails, their teeth dulling and gathering together.

"Ugh," Elliot said as he thudded into the grass, already beginning
to crust over with a layer of frost. "It always feels better to shift from
human to dragon instead of the other way around. It's like shoving
myself back inside a tiny box."

"You'd think we'd be used to it, but I know what you mean." Finn
shook his arms and legs before running a hand through his shaggy
blonde hair.

Elliot opened the back door. "Want to come in for a beer?"

"Can't. I promised Aurora I wouldn't be out too late. She tires quickly now that she's getting closer to having the baby. I felt bad about coming out at all, but she told me to go and have fun."

"Just not too much?" Elliot challenged, reaching into the fridge and grabbing a bottle.

"You're one to criticize. All right. I'll see you soon, man."

With his house empty, Elliot sat down and cracked open one of the numerous books piled up on his desk. He shook his head, feeling a little sorry for Finn. He would have to go home, probably rub Aurora's feet and assure her he would take care of Phoenix in the morning, and spend the entire weekend doing whatever his family wanted. For Elliot, he was his own man. He could drink a beer or two without anyone nagging him. He could watch whatever he wanted on TV, if he even decided to watch TV at all. And dinner? That could be a bowl of cereal if he wanted. Yes, there was definitely something to be said for bachelor life.

## 2

SIBYL SAT AT THE SAME DESK HER FATHER HAD USED AND RAN HER HAND over the smooth, worn wood. If she closed her eyes, she could almost imagine she felt the imprints of his quill as he wrote his proclamations, the documents that had completely changed their world. Tazarre had been a great wizard, the kind of man everyone worshipped. She only hoped she could live up to the name he'd established before sacrificing his own life in an effort to wipe out the parasitic dragons that had tried to take over their lands.

She rose from the heavy chair behind the desk, wrapping her fingers around the crystal that had been her father's at her neck. Being Tazarre's daughter had its advantages, but there were times when the burden was almost too heavy to bear. She crossed the vast room, her robes swirling around her legs as she headed for the window. The opening stretched almost from the ceiling to the floor, with the casement narrowing to a point at the top. Sibyl looked out over the land that surrounded the castle, noting that the place looked almost barren. Crops were difficult to grow in the red dust that covered Charok, especially up in the mountains. The lowland areas were more fertile, but even the ogres—long an ally of the dragons—had a difficult time keeping those areas safe.

A soft knock on the door made Sibyl turn. She cleared her throat so that her voice would reach across the vast room her father had used as a study; sounds often got lost in the vaulted ceiling. "Come in."

The heavy door swung open, but it didn't do so at the behest of a hand. Ganon stood in the doorway, his fingers still splayed in front of him from casting a spell at the door. His dark eyes penetrated the room and locked on hers. "I knew I would find you here."

"Is there some other place I should be?" Sibyl challenged. "The council is set to meet in less than an hour." She'd been awaiting this meeting with a mixture of excitement and dread. There was no greater honor than knowing the rest of the wizards had accepted her as their leader once her father was gone. But it wasn't an easy thing to do, not when she knew the fate of their entire kind rested on her head alone. Her position as lady of the castle didn't come without its challenges, either. And one of them was standing just on the other side of the room.

"Of course not, my lady," Ganon replied, sweeping her a courtly bow as he strode into the room as though it were his own. He flicked his hand behind him, making the door slam shut with a bang that echoed in the room. "It was merely a compliment that you should be here preparing for the council meeting. It's precisely what I would expect from someone as powerful and competent as you."

Sibyl rolled her eyes as she turned back toward the window. Darkness was beginning to descend over the castle, reducing visibility. Torches winked to life around the curtain wall and on the towers as servants lit them, throwing an orange glow on the sharp-toothed dragon skulls posted on either side of the barbican. "You don't need to grovel, Ganon."

"It's not groveling when I'm merely paying you an honest compliment." The other wizard had swept up behind her, his breath warm on the back of her neck. "We're incredibly fortunate to serve under a woman like you."

He was too close, making Sibyl wish she could jump out the window, sprout wings, and fly away. But no, that would be too much like a dragon, wouldn't it? The filthy beasts. Instead, she sidled away from him and headed toward her desk, tapping the parchment she'd been taking notes on. "We have a lot to cover tonight. It's been too long since I brought everyone together, but I wanted to wait until all our agents returned. Some of them have been working in the furthest corners of the land, and even in enemy territory. I'm eager to hear what they have to say."

Ganon came to stand in front of her desk, towering over her instead of taking a seat. His dark hair was slicked back, the glow of the lamp dancing in his eyes as he stared at her. "You seem anxious, my dear. There's no need for you to worry so much. You're doing an excellent job. Of course, if you find you need someone to share the burden with you, I'm sure it wouldn't be difficult to find someone."

Sibyl raised an eyebrow. "Find someone to do what?" As soon as she asked, she regretted it. She knew where this was going. Ganon had never made his intentions a secret.

"To stand at your side, of course," he said as he came around the corner of the desk and placed himself next to her chair. He trailed his fingers down the back of her hand. "To help you rule, to make your life a little easier, to rule as a lord by your side. You need me, Sibyl. Just admit it."

She snatched her hand away and stood. "What I need from you is to leave me alone."

He frowned dramatically at her. "You carve my heart in two with every rejection."

"And yet it always grows back together, doesn't it?" She faced him across the desk. Ganon was a handsome man, tall and broad-shouldered with a devilish smile. She might've found him appealing if she was a different kind of woman; the kind who liked manipulative, greedy men who were only looking to advance their own position.

And Ganon wasn't one to just give up, either. "Sibyl, I don't think you understand me. I just want what you want."

She arched an eyebrow testily. "And that is?"

He spread his arms over the desk as though the answer was obvious. "To get rid of these miserable dragons, of course. To show the rest of Charok who's boss around here. It's very simple, and you know I can help you."

Sibyl held out a finger. "Only part of that is right. Yes, I want to get rid of the dragons. And yes, I do believe you can help me."

"Oh, I know I can," he said before she was quite finished. He came around the desk once again. Sibyl remained firmly rooted, tired of this game of cat and mouse, but she regretted it as soon as he came to stand behind her once again, his lips dangerously close to the back of her neck. "I can help you in so many ways."

"That's enough!" In one quick movement, Sibyl turned and shoved him backward.

Ganon stumbled but caught himself against a bookshelf. Shock widened his eyes, but only for the briefest moment before he forced that overly wide smile across his face one again. "So you want to play rough? I'm game."

With a flick of her fingers, Sibyl erected a shield around herself and chuckled as Ganon bumped against it. "It's time for us to go."

He cleared his throat. "As you wish, my lady."

He followed her down the wide hall to the council room, but no matter how swiftly she walked, she couldn't gain any distance from him. Her cheeks burned, knowing there would be talk when they were seen entering the chamber together.

The other wizards and witches had already been seated at the long table. The wood had been sanded and waxed to a sheen that reflected the firelight from the torches around the room. Sibyl glanced down at her silhouette as it darkened the surface. "I thank you all for assembling here tonight. We have much to discuss. Welcome."

"Thank you, Great Lady," they intoned as one.

Sibyl felt the corner of her mouth tip up a little. "Now then, Avira has just returned from the furthest reaches of our territory in the south. I'm eager to hear what—"

The door to the chamber slammed open, rattling on its hinges. A thin man clung to the doorway, breathing heavily. His face was gaunt and his cheeks scarred, his beard singed away. Sibyl immediately recognized him as a wizard who'd been working in the neighboring region on the other side of the mountains.

"Ozelius! What is this intrusion?" Sibyl shot to her feet, offended that this man should barge in, disheveled and dirty, and interrupt her meeting.

"My lady, I beg your forgiveness." His attempt at a bow was more like crumpling to the floor. "I've only just returned, and it couldn't wait."

Two guards shouldered in through the door, snatching Ozelius by the arms. "Our apologies, Great Lady. He slipped past us."

But Sibyl narrowed her eyes, noting that the fear in the intruder's face wasn't from the guards. "Let him go. I'd like to hear what he has to say."

As soon as the guards let go of him, Ozelius fell to the floor once again. "Oh, Great Lady. It was so terrible."

"What?" she snapped impatiently. She knew the man had been working on transportation spells, a particular interest of hers since there were rumors some of the dragons had been able to leave for other worlds. It was only that curiosity that kept her listening, but all the groveling and moaning was going to get old quickly.

Ozelius took a deep, shuddering breath and wiped his mouth on the tattered sleeve of his robe. "We found a spell to use in conjunction with the crystals, and it brought us to the fae realm. It created a bit of a rift and we were having a hard time patching it, but in the meantime, we decided to use their world to the best of our advantage. There were numerous herbs and—"

"Get to the point!" Sibyl came around the table to stand before the man. "If you found some pretty little fantasy land, that's great. But I don't see how that warrants barging in on my meeting!"

He plastered his forehead to the stone floor. "It doesn't, my lady. I mean, not that part, but..." His next words were muffled by his position against the floor.

"Pick up your head so I can hear you, unless you want me to do it for you!"

Ganon was at her side. "This is ridiculous. Guards, get him out of here."

"No!" Her voice echoed through the room and stiffened the spines of all in attendance. "I want to hear this!"

Ozelius gulped. "We found dragons there," he whispered. "Not at first. There were just the silly little fairy people. But then the dragons showed up and we fought them! There was a huge battle, and at first, we were winning. Then something changed, some shift in power I could detect but I couldn't figure out. That traitor wizard Varhan was there, so maybe it had something to do with him. I got scared, and I transported myself out of there just in time. Unfortunately, the spell didn't put me where I'd started on Charok. I was miles and miles away, and it took me so long to get here. I'm so sorry, my lady. I'm so sorry."

Sibyl watched him sob for a long moment. "You found dragons in another world?" she asked quietly.

The wizard bobbed his head pitifully.

"How did they get there?"

Tears were streaming down Ozelius' face, leaving tracks in the dirt.

"There was a portal, a passage that linked with a planet called Earth. They came from there."

Silently cursing to herself, Sibyl nodded at the guards. "Take him out of here. Get him cleaned up and fed. I'll need to speak with him again later."

With a sweep of her robe, she returned to her place at the head of the table and the meeting proceeded. The information Ozelius had presented was vital, but she still needed to know what her other scouts had seen. They gave their reports, but she wasn't listening. Those damn dragons were everywhere.

———

"THERE IT IS. RIGHT THERE." Sibyl pointed to the swirling circle of golden energy. It had taken far too long to replicate the spell the other wizards had used to get to the fae realm now that most of them had been obliterated. Instead of going there herself, Sibyl had used the massive crystal ball in the heart of the castle to scan this fae world and see what she could discover.

"Interesting," Ganon muttered over her shoulder. He was once again too close, too eager to work with her.

But Sibyl knew she needed him. Cocky bastard that he was, he was one of the most talented wizards she'd ever met besides her own father. He'd helped her formulate a way to adjust the original spell they were working with so that it would take them to Earth instead. "Are we ready? I'd like to get started as soon as possible."

Ganon grinned. "I'll alert the others."

"No." She stayed him with a hand on his arm. "This mission will be just you and I. We need to stay quiet until we know exactly what's going on."

"Oh, I see." He waggled his eyebrows at her hand where it rested against his sleeve. "A vacation for just the two of us. How romantic, Sibyl."

"Stop it." She pulled her hand away and took two steps back from him as she pulled her crystal from the front of her robe. It was so familiar that it was like a part of her, and she'd memorized each facet of its pale blue surface. The tiny gold markings on it were hardly legible anymore, but she knew them all by heart. "Are you ready?"

Ganon held his own crystal. "As soon as you say the word, my lady."

They began, closing their eyes and focusing their energies. Sibyl felt the glow of magic in her crystal, and it sent a shudder of pleasant warmth throughout her body. She chanted the words she'd so carefully memorized, concentrating on the sound of her voice and the way it harmonized with Ganon's. The tips of her fingers and toes began to feel fuzzy, like they were emitting sparks of light. The feeling expanded up her arms and legs, the waves of power crashing together in her abdomen. Soon enough, her lips had turned to those same sparks of light that inhabited the rest of her body, and she could no longer speak the words necessary for the spell. But she didn't need them anymore. She exploded in a cloud of brilliant dust.

———

THE GROUND MUST HAVE COME up hard to meet her, though she didn't remember it. Her head pounded and her stomach churned. Her body was angry for disassembling it into a million pieces and then putting it back together somewhere else, and she couldn't blame it. But the nausea that bubbled up in the back of her throat was nothing compared to the heavy weight on top of her. "Oof. Get off me!"

Ganon propped himself up on his elbows to let her breathe, but he didn't get up. "I don't know. It seems the universe is trying to tell us something."

"Off!"

He rolled away and helped her to her feet. They were surrounded by trees, but to Sibyl, the place didn't sound like it was complete wilderness. There was an underlying buzz to the air. It was one she couldn't pinpoint, but she had a feeling it meant civilization. Her crystal was warm against her skin as she looked around.

"Let's head this way."

Ganon swept her an elaborate bow. "After you, my lady."

Her instincts had been correct, and they soon emerged from the trees. They stood on the edge of a forest, facing a collection of massive buildings. Humans walked from one to the other or lounged on the mowed grass between them, but nobody paid any attention to the newcomers.

"If this is truly a completely different world, then it's going to take some time to find the dragons. I suggest we split up. Concentrate on any heavily populated areas. I'm sure if the dragons are trying to take over this planet, we'll at least hear something about it." Sibyl charged forward from the woods.

"Hold on." Ganon's fingers wrapped around her elbow and pulled her back into the shade of the trees. He gestured at his robe and then at the people they could see out by the buildings. "We don't exactly fit in around here."

She rolled her eyes. He wasn't wrong, but she was ready to get this under way. Sibyl turned back to the gathering of humans and focused on a young woman lying on the grass with a book. She wasn't reading, since she was too busy laughing and flirting with a few young men. Sibyl flicked her fingers at her own robe, copying the striped top and denim pants the girl wore. "There. Is that better? I'm sure we can find something around here for you."

"You can't go marching around like that!" Ganon exploded, gesturing wildly at her new outfit. "You look like... like..."

"Like what?" But Sibyl already knew what he was thinking. She could feel the breeze wrap around her middle, where the top didn't cover her stomach and lower back. It didn't leave much to the imagination near her breasts, either, and the pants hugged her backside a little too closely. But if this was how women dressed there, then that was just the way it was.

Ganon glared at her but clamped his mouth shut.

"Find yourself some clothes and get out there. I'll meet you back here at the witching hour." Sibyl drew a deep breath and strode out into the crowd.

# 3

ELLIOT SAT BACK AND STARED AT THE SCREEN. HE ONLY HAD TO HIT THE "submit" button and he would be done. All those long nights of studying would finally be behind him. Maybe. It would take weeks to get the results of the bar exam, something that seemed entirely unfair. If he'd failed, then those weeks between would be completely wasted. There was no choice but to go back home and keep studying, just in case he'd need to retake the exam. In the competitive field of law, only those who truly had patience and dedication could be successful.

With a sigh, he hit the button and logged off the computer. His body was stiff from sitting in that hard plastic chair for too long, and he hadn't even realized just how stuffy it had gotten in the building. A few other students glanced at him as he made his way to the door, and just for a moment, it made Elliot wonder if he should've taken longer with the test. It wasn't always a good thing to be the first one done.

His footsteps echoed in the university hallway. It was a Saturday morning, and hardly anyone else was on campus. Perfect. He would grab his books out of his car and head to the library, where he could study in peace and doublecheck the work he'd done on his test. And maybe, he thought, rolling his shoulders and wishing he could spread his wings right then and there, he could go out for a long flight later. He deserved it, right?

But someone was waiting for him at his car. A blonde man leaned against the driver's side door. Three women rested against the hood. Two other men, far too hulking for their own good, stood on either side of the vehicle.

"What's all this?" Elliot asked, unable to stop the smile on his face as he recognized his cousins and their significant others. Finn and Aurora, Kaylee and Archard, and Nora and Kieran were all there waiting for him.

"You didn't think we were just going to leave you alone on your big day, did you?" Kaylee asked, folding her arms in front of her chest.

"But I didn't even tell you I was taking the test today," Elliot protested.

Nora rolled her eyes. "I guess you've forgotten that some of us work here at the university. Plus, your parents knew, and it wasn't difficult to get the information from them."

Elliot shook his head. This was just like his crazy cousins. They always spent time together, making sure they gathered for a dinner at least once a month to catch up. He'd secretly feared that those times would come to an end as each of them paired off. First, it had been Kaylee. She'd been so involved in her own life, jetting around the world on archaeological digs to translate ancient texts, that Elliot had never imagined she'd fall for one of the dragons that had accidentally been transported to Earth from Charok.

Kieran had been part of that group of dragons as well, and despite his quiet demeanor, he and Nora were soon in love. The last had been the impossible Finn, the ladies' man who would never settle down, tumbling head over heels for a fae woman.

But the four of them were still just as close as ever, and their arrival here proved it. Not only did his cousins still care about him, but so did the mates they'd found. "You know I won't even find out if I passed or not for a while. Today's not really a big day at all."

"Of course it is!" Finn argued enthusiastically. "It means you won't have your nose stuck in a book all the time! You can finally relax and let loose a little."

"Which is exactly why we're all going out," Kaylee said, her green eyes glittering and daring him to challenge her. "We haven't been able to get all of us together in a while, and I think we deserve it."

"Can we get some dinner first?" Aurora swept her golden curls away from her shoulder, resting her hand on her swollen belly with the other hand. "I'm starving."

"You're always starving," Finn teased, putting an arm around his wife.

"Only because this baby has your appetite," she shot back.

"Dinner it is," Elliot agreed. "But that's it. I don't have time to go out and party."

Nora grinned knowingly. "Right. We'll see about that."

———

DRAGONS ARE STUBBORN, and Elliot was reminded of this as his cousins dragged him out to one of the local clubs after dinner. He'd thought for sure he could satisfy them by having a few drinks at the restaurant and then excusing himself, but when he'd paid his part of the check and started heading toward his car, he found Archard blocking his way.

"Come on, man. I'm tired and I just want to go home."

Archard, his dark wavy hair combed back, gave him a broad smile. "Kaylee wants you to go out, and you know that whatever Kaylee wants, I make sure she gets."

Elliot slugged him on the arm. Archard and Kieran were just as much his cousins as the rest of them were. Even Aurora had won him over as soon as he'd figured out just how much she cared about Finn. Their family continued to expand, and it was good to know there were so many people who had his back.

"Fine, fine. I'll go. But just for a little while. I've got things to do in the morning."

"Sure, we all do."

The club was a popular one, but Elliot couldn't remember the last time he'd been there. It was much nicer than he remembered. "Is it just me, or did they remodel this place?"

Nora laughed. "Yeah, like a year ago. Seriously, Elliot, you need this. Let's go dance."

Heavy music pumped through the club, and the dance floor was just as packed as the bar and the tables that surrounded it. People danced and swayed, letting the music take them over as if in a trance. Nora tried to pull him from his chair and into the crowd, but he resisted.

"You got me here. You're going to have to be happy enough with that."

She sighed. "Fine. Be a stick in the mud." She headed out onto the floor with Kaylee, Aurora, Kieran, and Archard.

"What about you?" Elliot asked Finn, who'd seated himself at the same table. "Aren't you going out there to dance with your wife?"

His cousin grinned at his heavily pregnant wife, who'd kicked off her shoes and was twirling and gyrating as though she didn't have a dragon-fae hybrid growing in her belly. "Nah, this is really more of her thing. We dropped Phoenix off with Dad, who was more than eager to babysit. Truth is, she needs this night out just as much as you do. Once that baby comes, we're going to have our hands full. But she's a free spirit, and even as much as she enjoys motherhood, I don't want her to get burned out."

"Wow." Elliot took a swig of his whiskey, relishing the burn as it trickled down his throat. "You're really dedicated."

His cousin shook his head. "Don't make it sound like a chore. I want to do this for her. I want to do *everything* for her. She's amazing. You have no idea just how it feels when you find the one."

"Don't get started on that again," Elliot protested. "And don't tell me you guys brought me here because you think now's the time for me to meet someone. Whomever I do end up with—eventually, a long time from now—won't be some chick I've picked up in a club."

"And I didn't think I would fall for some woman who tried to get me lost in the woods, but here I am." Finn nodded his head toward his wife, the lights shining in her hair. "It's like nothing else."

But Elliot didn't want to think about that. He steered the conversation away from things like romance and marriage, focusing instead on work, his plans for the future, and how Finn was doing with the new company he'd helped start. He wanted to remain rooted in the concrete world, not distracted by the possibilities and strange feelings that everyone in his family were so damn focused on.

Still, he felt a strange feeling tingling down his back. It moved forward and gathered in the pit of his stomach, embracing his core. He brushed it off, thinking he was just excited about finally going out and relaxing after so many months of cramming. But it wouldn't leave him alone, and even a second round of drinks wasn't cutting it. His wings, claws, and scales itched just under the surface of his skin. Elliot looked around the room. He didn't normally feel that way unless he was sensing danger. But this was something else. Something else completely different.

"You all right?" Finn asked, tapping him on the elbow. He had to shout to be heard over the music, even right across the table. "You got real quiet all of a sudden."

"Yeah. I'm fine. Just thinking."

"It's time to stop doing that!" Kieran boomed as he stumbled back to their table. "You're not supposed to be thinking about anything. I'm going to go get a...a...what do you call it again? A Brooklyn?"

"A Manhattan," Nora said from just behind him. "And I think you've had plenty of them already."

"Don't be ridiculous! I'm a dragon! I can handle more liquor than anyone else in here." His roaring voice would have attracted the attention of everyone in the room if the music hadn't been even louder.

"Sure you can, big fella. Let's go get you some water." Nora pointed him toward the bar before turning back to Elliot and Finn. "I might need some help getting him out of here later. I underestimated just how much fun a Charokian dragon would have in a night club."

Elliot couldn't blame her, especially since Kieran usually had an aversion to crowds, but he was distracted by Archard and Kaylee as they returned to the table as well. "I'm telling you, that's just how it is. You have to ignore it."

"I can't! They're constantly bumping into me or I'm bumping into them."

"That doesn't mean you have to apologize every time." Kaylee rubbed her hand on Archard's muscled arm. "You've really changed a lot since you came here, you know?"

"Would you rather I start a few fights?" he asked mischievously. "I'm sure I've seen a few guys looking at you, and I don't mind reminding them that you're mine."

The odd sensation that had been taking over Elliot was now a buzz that vibrated into the very fiber of his being. He finished off his whiskey and slammed his glass back down on the table. "Excuse me a minute." He headed for the restroom. The music thudded incessantly against the walls, but it didn't quite reach him in there. The strange feeling subsided to a dull hum. Elliot turned on the cold water and ran his hands underneath it, focusing on the way it felt to distract him from whatever it was that was going on. He glanced up at himself in the mirror, just to make sure he didn't have any scales erupting unbidden on his face.

When he thought he was doing well enough to return to the crowd and he left the restroom, that feeling wrapped around him again instantly. He was going to have to get out of there. But as he headed back toward the table where his cousins were, his eyes locked on a woman in the corner.

She sat with her back to the wall, watching everything around her with cool, observant eyes. There were people all around her, and yet she seemed to be completely unaffected by the music and the noise. Elliot swallowed as the buzzing filled his ears and drowned out everything else as he studied her. She was a knockout, with irresistible curves under her tight crop-top and jeans. Auburn waves hung just past her shoulders and complimented the deep crimson of her lips. Her eyes changed colors depending on the pulsing of the lights, and Elliot was so transfixed, he found himself staring into them.

He didn't register that she was staring right back at him until he found himself standing at her table. Elliot had no recollection of moving his feet in her direction. He'd been planning to do something else, but his mind could no longer tell him what that was. This enchanting stranger had taken up his entire mind, and it was the most pleasant feeling he'd ever experienced.

"What's your name?" he asked, his throat suddenly dry and his tongue too big for his mouth.

Her answer was lost in the noise, but he still liked the way her lips moved as she said it.

"I'm Elliot." Why did his own name sound so stupid all of a sudden? "Do you want to dance?" He despised dancing, but somehow, it seemed like the next thing to do.

The woman scanned the swaying crowd, her gaze serious, and finally nodded. She stepped out with him onto the floor.

Elliot didn't know what he'd been expecting, but he couldn't tear his eyes away from her. She moved in such perfect timing to the beat, the music seemed to emanate from her instead of from the DJ booth on the other side of the club. Her hips and shoulders moved and swayed, hypnotizing him, and Elliot almost forgot that he was supposed to be dancing as well. He studied the delicate line of her jaw and where it met the sudden curve of her neck. He focused on the way the fabric of her shirt strained against her skin, and the way the lights changed her coloring with each flash. He was entranced by the contrast of her white teeth against her red lips, gorgeous red lips...

The next thing he knew, he was kissing her. The strange feeling inside him had slipped away, but the roar of his dragon was almost impossible to control as it surged against the underside of his skin. He didn't even want to control it. He wanted his wings to fly out from his back and wrap around this woman; to show the rest of the world that she was his and no one else could so much as look at her. He craved the release that would come from shifting, but short of that, there was another release that would work just as well. Given that she was kissing him back, with her hands exploring his back and neck and her tongue sweeping against his, he knew he couldn't stop now.

"You're amazing," he whispered as he pulled back just enough to look into her eyes. He could see now, as though the club had completely disappeared, that brown flowered around her pupils into green with just a hint of blue around the very edge. He'd never seen anything so mesmerizing in his life.

"So are you." He could hear her now, holding her so close, and her voice seemed to burrow under his skin and live in his body. Where had this woman been all his life?

The next thing he knew, Elliot was guiding her body off the dance floor. He didn't know exactly where he was going, just that he couldn't go anywhere without her. Kissing once again, their hands explored each other as their feet stumbled, leaving the brilliant lights of the dance floor and receding into the darkness of the hall where the restrooms were. Spotting a door off to the left, Elliot opened it and discovered a storage closet. The two of them tumbled inside, their desperate need for each other driving them.

He shut the door, encasing them in complete darkness and hiding them from the rest of the crowd. Elliot pushed her up against a wall, his hands roving over her body and slipping beneath the edge of her shirt. A tiny voice in the back of his head reminded him that this wasn't the sort of thing he did. He was a sensible guy, a reasonable guy, a serious guy. But his inner dragon quashed that tiny voice with a single puff of flame and it was gone.

"What was your name?" he murmured against her lips. "I couldn't hear you." The music hadn't completely left them alone in there, but it was just enough.

A laugh bubbled up from inside her, and Elliot thought he could feel it as much as hear it. "Sibyl."

"Elliot," he replied, just in case. His hands cupped the fullness of her breasts. He felt like he was sixteen again, his blood coursing and his head so light, it could float right off his shoulders.

But he wasn't the only one enjoying himself. Sibyl's leg was wrapped around his waist, her hands buried in his hair, her lips caressing his mouth, his jaw, his ear, his neck. "I want you," she purred against him.

That tiny voice tried to speak up again, the one that wanted to ask, "Right here? Shouldn't we go somewhere else? Someplace more private?" But there was no time for any of that. They wanted each other, and Elliot knew he needed her, too. She had made that strange feeling and the buzzing in his head shift and change into something pleasant and beautiful, as if those colored light from the dance floor were spinning and shifting in the pit of his stomach.

He reached for her waistband, frustrated to find that it was a button fly and it would take that much longer to get to her. By the time he shimmied her jeans off her hips, he found that she'd done the same to him and had her hand wrapped around his shaft.

Still keeping her back pressed to the wall, he lifted her off her feet so she could wrap both legs around him and he pierced her. As he sank into her warmth, he felt a shudder of pleasure ripple down his spine, a feeling like returning to a sacred place he'd known only in his dreams.

Sibyl's arms were around his neck, crushing his face into her breasts, her nails scraping against his skin. She smelled of honey and something else his brain didn't have the patience to identify. Her hair was cool against his temple as her head whipped back and forth.

Elliot felt her tighten around him as the air escaped her lungs in a gasp of pleasure. He thrust harder, clinging to the soft flesh of her hips to keep her aloft as he drilled away. A white heat exploded behind his eyes and lit the room as he came.

And then, just as suddenly as it had begun, it was over. He let her slip slowly to the floor, and the two of them began fumbling for their clothing. Elliot was grateful for the darkness, so that Sibyl couldn't see the heat that he knew flushed his cheeks. "Are you all right?" he asked quietly.

She cleared her throat. "Of course." She had a subtle but strange accent though her English was perfect, and this didn't seem the time to ask her about it.

"Can I, um, buy you a drink?" It seemed like the least he could do, and Elliot knew he couldn't let her go just yet. Whoever this woman was, he needed to know more about her.

"Maybe," she said slowly, a shadowy figure in the dark. "I just need to head to the restroom for a second."

"Of course. Right." They slipped out of the supply room. Elliot caught a glimpse of her back as she pushed open the door to the ladies' room, her hair still perfect. He would never have known what had just happened if he hadn't been there himself.

Pulling at his shirt to make sure it was straight, Elliot headed back for his original table. His cousins were talking and laughing, but their spines stiffened and the corners of their mouths jerked up when they saw him. "What?"

Kaylee pressed her lips together, but she couldn't stop herself from smiling. "We're just happy to see that you... had a good time."

"Score!" Kieran enthused, slugging him hard on the arm. The burly man had a bottle of water in his hand now, but was still swerving as he stood.

"Oh, don't start." Elliot waved them off, not wanting to be a spectacle just because he'd gone off and done something completely crazy. And the more he thought about it, the more he came to realize just what it was he'd done. He watched the little hallway where the restrooms were, waiting for Sibyl to emerge. He would buy her a drink, but not there. Maybe he could take her someplace quieter; one of the upscale bars, perhaps. They could talk and pretend they hadn't just had wild, impulsive sex in a storage closet of a night club.

But as he continued to watch and wait for her, he noticed that strange feeling coming back. It was different this time, and it opened a gaping pit in his stomach that made him nervous. It was the feeling of being without something; something he desperately needed. His skull vibrated with it, so much, he was surprised his teeth weren't chattering.

"What's wrong?" Finn asked. "You look like you're going to be sick."

"I, uh, I don't know. I don't feel right." He didn't know if he was going to hurl or shift, but his body had definitely been thrown out of whack.

Nora touched his arm. "I need to go check my makeup real quick."

"You look fine," Kieran enthused. "Mighty fine, if you ask me."

She rolled her eyes and disappeared into the bathroom. When she emerged a minute later, Nora simply gave Elliot a slight shake of her head.

Shit. Whoever this woman was, she had come into his life like a lightning bolt and left just as quickly. The only thing he knew about her was her first name, and that wasn't much to go on. She could've given him a fake name, for all he knew. Elliot raked his hand through his hair, regretting ever coming out in the first place.

"Where are you going?"

Elliot wasn't even sure who'd asked him, and he didn't remember getting up out of his chair. He was standing there, facing the door and ready to go. "I've got to find her."

"Come on," Finn tugged at his elbow. "She could be anywhere. Just sit down and have another drink. You look like you need it."

But there was something pulling much harder at him than his cousin was. "I've got to go." He headed out into the night, uncertain of what direction he even needed to go. He just knew that he absolutely had to find Sibyl. He closed his eyes and listened to his inner dragon, which was writhing angrily inside him. The buzzing was too loud inside his head to quite make sense of it all, but he knew he had to try.

# 4

SIBYL OPENED HER EYES AND IMMEDIATELY SHUT THEM ONCE AGAIN. THE light hurt all the way into her brain. The alcohol here on Earth hadn't tasted any stronger than what she was used to on Charok, but it definitely had a greater effect on her. Her head pounded and her stomach coiled like a snake inside her. She couldn't remember the last time she'd been hung over, but she couldn't say she'd missed it.

Cracking one eyelid, she gazed up at the yellowed ceiling for a long time, trying to make sense of exactly where she was. Her hazy mind searched, retracing everything that had happened over the last few days. She and Ganon had arrived on Earth. That, in itself, had wreaked havoc on her body, but she'd recovered quickly enough once she'd headed out on her mission.

It was a strange place with a very different sort of civilization than what she was used to, but Sibyl was determined to do her best. She explored the area in which they'd landed and soon discovered that it was a school of some sort. No one paid much attention to her as she roamed the enormous building, studying the architecture and watching the people. They all carried little devices that must have had a very strong magic in them. They spoke into them and poked at them, which made her think they were used for communicating, and the humans seemed to get quite a bit of satisfaction out of them.

She heard the sound of a door opening, and then Ganon was standing over her. "Good morning! Or should I say, good afternoon?"

Sibyl clamped her hands over her ears, even though the movement made her nauseous all over again. "Could you talk a little softer, please? My head is killing me."

"I would say I'd whip you up a potion to take care of it, except there doesn't seem to be anything on this planet that's useful for magic. I went into a place where they sell food—called a grocery store, apparently—and it was all just a bunch of packaged chemicals. I don't know how the Earthlings eat this stuff. Other than 'potato chips.' Those are delicious, and I bought a lot of them."

"I'll definitely need something to eat," she moaned as she sat up. The room twirled around her before it settled down again, and she hauled herself to her feet as she followed him to the kitchen. "Then we can catch up."

"We wouldn't need to catch up at all if you hadn't stayed out all night. I don't even think you remember that I was already here when you got back. Where have you been, anyway?"

Like a crashing wave, Sibyl remembered exactly what she'd been doing the night before. She'd wandered into the club because it seemed to attract a lot of people, and she knew it would be a good opportunity to observe and learn. There had been no mention of dragons, and no winged creatures had been in attendance other than a woman wearing feathered wings as some sort of costume. Sibyl had been fascinated by the way everyone had been entertaining themselves. They danced, completely letting loose and relaxing, stopping just long enough to chug some alcohol before heading back out into the crowd.

Until that moment, she'd never realized just how serious her life had been on Charok. Even from a very young age, Sibyl had known she had a lot of work ahead of her. She'd studied hard under the tutelage of her father, determined to prove her worth. She'd eagerly grabbed every book she could get a hold of, often reading deep into the late hours of the night. Sleep had seemed like a waste of time when she could have been learning something.

And even upon reaching adulthood, Sibyl had found that there was very little time for socializing and entertainment. She was aware that many of the wizards would spend their evenings around a fire, drinking and singing the low, old songs that were their heritage from so long ago. She had knowledge of duels and mock battles where young wizards and witches would test their skills against each other, but she'd only attended one before she'd decided it wasn't worth her time.

"Hello?" Ganon asked, bringing her back to the present moment with the crinkle of a potato chip bag. "I thought we were supposed to be reporting to each other, not staring off into space."

"Hmm? Right. Didn't you ask me something?"

He sighed impatiently at her. "I asked where you'd been. It's a very strange world out there, and I hope you've been all right without me around to protect you."

His worry was a false one, Sibyl knew. He only said such things because he was trying to ingratiate himself to her, although it wasn't a good method. "I'm fine. Of course you know that I spent yesterday securing us this house. After spending some time at the university and realizing it was going to take some time to find the dragons, I figured we would need a place to stay. I saw a man posting a sign out front here looking for a tenant, and I compelled him to let me stay, free of charge." It was a rundown rental on the edge of town. The landlord had asked if she was a student at the university, and she'd told him she was simply because it seemed like the right thing to say.

"What are you studying?" the man had asked as he'd shown her all the furniture and appliances that were included with the home.

Fortunately, Sibyl had already spent a lot of time at the library. She'd read books, listened to conversations, and studied the curious little pictures of students who'd completed their education. "History," she'd blurted out.

"Yes, but I daresay you could've found a better place." Gannon rapped his knuckles on the countertop. "I don't even know what this is made of. Humans seem to like flimsy materials, don't they? Hardly any solid wood or stone anywhere."

"You can't expect me to find a castle," she retorted, still feeling like shit from the night before. "This was the best I could do, and we're lucky to have anything with our limited knowledge of the place. We don't even have any coins, or at least not the kind they want around here."

"Well, I don't like it. And two bedrooms? We could've gotten by with just one. Not much of a lovers' vacation with this arrangement." He raised an eyebrow.

It was lost on Sibyl, who wasn't interested in combatting his advances at the moment. "Anyway, I started off at the library again. It's a wealth of information, even though it's not all relevant to our mission. I did, however, spend some time looking up dragons. Almost all the references I found were in fiction. There were a few historical accounts, but even those seem to be mythical in origin. I have to wonder if Ozelius was mistaken."

Ganon twisted his lips up in thought. "I don't think so. He described the portal between here and the fae realm so accurately, we were able to find it with very little effort. I don't think he would just make something up like that. If they were defeated in a battle, it also explains why several wizards of that circle are now missing. We can't just give up on this."

"I agree." Sibyl tentatively took a chip from the proffered bag and took a bite. It was thin and crispy, but incredibly salty. The snack was what she needed at the moment, but they would need to find some proper food before long. "That's exactly why I left the library, actually. I wanted to get out into the world a little more and see what I might find out for myself. I went to a place called a mall, which is like a big collection of shops where people exchange items in return for swiping little cards. From what I've read, it's some sort of payment method, although I haven't looked into it all that deeply."

"Any dragons there?"

"No. Nor did I find any walking down the street through the town. As the day went on, I ended up in this place called a club, where everyone was drinking alcohol and dancing and..." She trailed off, once again remembering exactly what had happened there.

Sibyl hadn't expected any real interactions with the humans. She wasn't here for them, after all. They were a strange and noisy species, but they weren't all that different from her own kind, except that they didn't appear to have any magical abilities. Or at least that was what she'd thought until she walked into the club.

From the moment she'd entered, she felt a strange bubble of magic that started in the pit of her stomach and bubbled up into the back of her throat. It made her hair stand on end and her skin prickle, but in a pleasant way. Sibyl recognized it instantly as the energy signature from a particularly powerful spell. At first, she'd looked around for Ganon. He was the easiest explanation, and it wasn't entirely impossible for the two of them to end up in the same place at the same time. But she didn't see any sign of him, nor had she seen anyone else who looked like they were performing magic.

"And what?" Ganon demanded, crunching noisily on his chips.

She glanced up at him, irritated but curious. "You didn't happen to go to one of these clubs last night, did you?"

He gave a callous laugh. "You're kidding me, right? No, not at all. But I suggest you tell me what happened."

"Nothing." That, of course, was far from the truth. Maybe too far, given the way Ganon was staring at her now. She wondered if he could see within her eyes the way she'd felt when Elliot came to her table. She hadn't seen him at all while she'd been observing the crowds, but when he'd appeared out of nowhere, it was as though something about the atmosphere had changed. Maybe even that *she* had changed. She couldn't be sure, but the way he'd drawn her in had been unbelievably thrilling.

That feeling she'd thought was magic had been coming from *him*.

Never had she met someone who had intrigued her so much. The wizards and witches she worked among on Charok were simply there as tools, part of her circle, and in some ways, part of her family. But she'd never been particularly close to any of them. Her mother had died so long ago, Sibyl didn't even remember her, and of course her father was gone as well. There was Ganon, but he was more like a force she couldn't get away from instead of one she couldn't resist.

Elliot was incredible. He had a fire in his eyes that pulled her in, and not only had she been unable to resist him, she didn't want to. She wanted everything from him, and he gave it to her. That wasn't the sort of thing she normally did. Sibyl knew she could've had flings with numerous wizards—and certainly Ganon—but she'd never wanted any of them as much as she'd wanted that human.

"Sibyl," Ganon intoned, his voice a warning. "Something most definitely happened at that club. Now I suggest you tell me what the hell it was. In case you've forgotten, we're on the other side of the universe together. We're the only wizards on this planet, except possibly one who's a complete traitor. You can't just leave me in the dark like this."

"Fine." She hadn't wanted to tell him at first, but now that she'd mulled it over, she didn't know why not. They were both adults, and despite what he might think, Ganon had no claim over her. Not only that, but it might drive home the fact he didn't have a chance with her. "I had a little fun with a human while I was there."

His brows had been arched in curiosity when he'd asked her, but now they fell flat and serious above his eyes. His lips, too, were a straight and hard line. "You're kidding me, right? You're joking with me because I haven't left you alone. Listen, Sibyl, I know you like to be stubborn. You get some sort of kick out of being independent and strong. That's fine, but you know you can't do this on your own forever. You need me, and you don't have to keep pulling me along."

She sucked a deep breath into her lungs in an effort to remain calm. "We've been over this. I do need you, but not in the way you *want me* to need you. I need your strength, power, and intelligence when it comes to creating new spells that ensure our cause is furthered in my father's name. But I don't need you or anyone else for anything beyond that."

Ganon slammed his palm down on the countertop, his dark eyes dangerous as he leaned forward. "And what about the human then?"

"That was different," Sibyl sniffed. And it most certainly had been different. With Elliot, there had been no talk of the evil dragons and where they might strike next or what spells should be chosen to develop further. Her time with him had been light years distant from the struggles of her life on Charok, and she'd enjoyed it. She deserved it.

Her explanation hadn't been enough for him, but Sibyl knew there was nothing she could say or do to make him okay with this situation. His hand curled into a fist, whitening his knuckles. "It is only because I care for you so much that I'm not transporting myself back to Charok right now and dragging you with me."

The mention of the transportation spell brought Sibyl's crystal to her mind, which rested coolly against her heated skin. "And why the hell would you do that?"

"Why wouldn't I?" he roared, flinging his hands in the air and then running them through his hair. "You claim that you're here for the betterment of our people, but you're spending your time rutting humans. Maybe I should just leave you here and go back on my own, and expose you for exactly what you are."

Sibyl lifted her chin and narrowed her eyes, straightening her shoulders and her back despite her throbbing head. "I see. So, in all these years you've proclaimed your interest in me and how much you care about me, with all the times you've said you want to rule at my side, your loyalty is shattered in an instant because I chose to do something for myself for once? I think you'd be hard pressed to find another person who hadn't been looking out for their own best interests at least every now and then."

Her words had softened his anger, but not his indignation. "You can't blame me for being upset," he finally replied after a long moment of silence. "After all, I've offered you everything. I've stood beside you even when our efforts have been met with failure. I come from a good family, and an alliance between the two of us would only serve to strengthen your power. You can't say that I'm a bad match for you."

She pursed her lips. Despite how angry he could make her, she also didn't particularly like hurting his feelings. Sibyl wasn't as cold-blooded as her father had been. Still, Ganon needed to understand his efforts weren't getting him anywhere. "I suppose I can't say that, but the point that matters here is I'm not looking for a match. I don't have time for things like that, Ganon. If there's anyone who understands that, it should be you."

He nodded, but she could easily detect the jealousy emanating from him. "Fine. I guess that means we need to get back to the matter at hand. What do you suggest we do?"

"I'm not sure." She turned away from him to look out the window. She needed a break from that intense stare of his. He always looked at her as though he owned her, and it got tiresome after a while. "From the research I did in the library, this is a big planet and there are billions of people on it. I'm concerned that searching the old-fashioned way isn't going to get us anywhere."

"I have to agree with that." Ganon opened the fridge—something Sibyl was impressed with—and removed a bottle of brown liquid. When he opened it, a layer of foam formed at the top. "Have you tried soda yet?"

"No, thanks. I'm not sure how much more Earth food my stomach can handle."

"Suit yourself." He took a big swig and grinned. "Such good stuff, and it goes perfectly with these." Ganon crunched on another handful of potato chips.

Sibyl sighed. "All right, let's think about what we know. The portal from this world to the fae realm is close by, and we know from Ozelius' account that the dragons used it. So it make sense that the dragons are still somewhere close by. But, if they're here, nobody is talking about them. I haven't heard a single mention of them, and given the lack of magic on this planet, I think someone would be making a big fuss over it."

"But not if they're in their human forms," Ganon pointed out. "If they behave like good little reptiles and stay on their own two feet, then none of these stupid Earthlings would know the difference between a dragon, a wizard, or a human."

"True," Sibyl admitted, "but why would they come here and not make themselves known? You've heard all the same stories I did growing up, about how the dragons came sweeping in, taking over our land, killing and eating children and trying to rule with an iron fist. Why wouldn't they do the same thing here?" When they'd first begun their search, Sibyl had been reciting spells in the back of her mind so she'd have them at the ready as soon as she needed them. She knew that encountering a dragon was going to be dangerous. But as more time passed without seeing one, she'd begun to question if their mission was on the right track.

"That's an interesting point, and it's one I've thought about myself. I'm not sure I know the answer, but I do have an idea as to how we might find them."

"I'm listening." Sibyl knew it must fill Ganon with all sorts of arrogant thoughts to know she was relying on him right now. But it was difficult to wrap her head around the problem when all she could think about was Elliot and the way the alcohol had made her feel.

"We'll create a new spell," the wizard said simply. "We don't have a lot to work with here, and it's going to take some time. But we do know that our crystals are very powerful. We might be able to formulate a detection spell that will help us find the dragons even when they're in their human form. Waiting for them to show up as dragons could take an eternity."

"It's brilliant," Sibyl proclaimed, ignoring the look of pride on Ganon's face. "We'll have to get started right away, though. I feel like we're already wasting time here, and I hate thinking about whatever might be happening at home while we're gone."

"They'll be fine," he assured her. "And they'll be thrilled when we come home with necklaces made of dragon teeth." Ganon grinned, showing his own teeth.

Sibyl nodded, but she couldn't get quite as excited as he had. She knew they had a lot riding on the line, but it just made her more nervous than anything. And Ganon hadn't been completely wrong when he'd questioned her loyalty to the mission, simply because she knew how distracted she'd let herself get. "I brought a few books with me. I'm going to my room to study for a while."

"I'll be doing the same. Just bring them out here and we can figure it out together." He crunched loudly on his chips.

"Another time. I just want to be alone right now." She closed herself in her room and leaned heavily on the door. Sibyl hated that she was even thinking about this as "her" room, considering the only things in there that truly belonged to her were her robe and a few books. The furniture had all come with the house, and since the previous occupant had left behind a lamp, some dingy curtains, and an alarm clock, she had those at her disposal as well.

She sank down onto the bed and lay back on the pillow, staring up once again at that yellowed ceiling. Deep down, she knew the only thing she should want was to find the dragons that were supposed to be there, take them down, and bring them back home to prove what they had done. It was part of the destiny that had been set forward for her from the very moment she came into the world, and she was determined to fulfill it.

But Elliot had been so much more than a distraction, so much more than a few minutes of fun sprinkled into her lifetime of work. Part of her had stirred when she saw him, and it had fully awakened once they'd touched. She could look through her spell books and try to devise some enchantment that would help her find the dragons, but she was much more tempted to find some way to locate *him*.

After all, no one had touched her like that before. If she closed her eyes and stilled her mind for a moment, she could still feel the warm gentleness of his hands on her breasts, the heat of his mouth on hers, the hard determination of his manhood as it thrust into her and brought them both to a crescendo of pent-up emotions that they needed so desperately to let go of. She wanted him again. Sibyl wanted to set aside all her thoughts about dragons and find Elliot.

No, that was stupid. No matter what that man had done to her or how badly she wanted to experience him again, it wouldn't mean a thing in the long run. She wasn't staying on this planet any longer than she had to for the mission, and once she went back to Charok, there was little chance of her returning. Elliot didn't mean a thing—*couldn't* mean a thing—and that was exactly why she'd risked using a little magic to whisk herself out of the club's bathroom and into the alley behind the building, where she slipped through the darkness and wound her way back to the odd rental house she shared with Ganon.

She'd looked back once, when she could just see the edge of the brilliantly-lit sign over the club, wondering if he was looking for her or if he'd moved on with his life already. Sibyl didn't know much about how human relationships worked, but as far as she could tell, it had been nothing more than a fling. No point in torturing herself over it.

Leaning her head heavily in her hand, she opened her grimoire.

# 5

ELLIOT SAT BACK IN HIS DESK CHAIR AND FOLDED HIS HANDS BEHIND HIS head, staring at the computer screen. He'd spent an eternity perfecting this resume, and yet it still didn't seem like enough. Sure, he'd gotten a good position as an intern at a prominent firm. He'd done very well in his classes at the university, and soon enough—hopefully—he'd find out that he'd passed the bar exam. But still, he knew there were others out there with more experience or better resumes, other men and women who would beat him out of the best positions and hinder his chances at living out his dreams.

His phone rang, startling him enough that he nearly knocked his chair over. Elliot recovered quickly and answered it. "Hey, Finn."

"You sound upset," his cousin said. The four of them had always had a knack for knowing when there was something wrong, even if they didn't know what it was right away. "What's wrong?"

Elliot switched the call to his headset. He'd found out a few years ago that if he had to be on the phone, he wanted to have his hands free to accomplish other tasks. Wasting time was one of his biggest pet peeves. He rested his hand on the mouse and once again scrolled through the document. "Nothing, really. I've just been working on my resume."

"Really? Didn't you already have to do that for one of those classes you took?"

"Yeah, but that was a couple of years ago. I've got a networking event tonight, and I have to make sure it's absolutely right. There can't be the tiniest mistake." Elliot knew that if there was one word missing or if the formatting wasn't just so, it could cost him a potential job. He planned to not only have a few printed copies folded neatly in an envelope in his jacket pocket, but to have it ready to email to anyone who might request it as well.

"So send it over to Kaylee. She's good with those things."

"Already did." Their cousin was technically good in any language, even ones that didn't originate from this planet. She had a natural talent for translation that nobody could quite explain other than it must've been handed down genetically. "I think she was a little bored to have to look over something in English, but she sent it back with her approval."

"That's all you need, then. If Kaylee thinks it's good enough, any attorney you meet is going to think the same thing."

"I'm not so sure. This is a huge deal tonight, Finn. Every lawyer in the county is going to be at the Heritage Resort, and probably some from outside the county as well. I'm beyond lucky that Mr. Dodson wrangled an invitation for me, since it's not the sort of thing interns usually get to go to. But he feels bad that he doesn't have room for me at his firm, and he's doing what he can to help me get a good position."

"So, does this mean when you're a full-fledged attorney, you'll help me sue all the companies leaching chemicals into the local creeks?" Finn asked hopefully.

Elliot sighed. He knew that had long been a dream of Finn's. His cousin had always been concerned about the environment, and even though his job as a consultant was already making a difference, it would never be enough for him. "You know I can't promise you that. Some of it depends on where I end up working, plus you'll have to wait until I'm experienced enough to take on a place like that."

"If your resume is perfect and your boss is practically pinning you up on a bulletin board for everyone to see, then what are you so tense about?" Finn pressed. "You've got this in the bag."

"Yeah, I guess." Elliot wished he could have as much confidence in himself as everyone else did, but he knew exactly what was on the line. His family just figured he would be fine no matter what happened. They were dragons, after all. They were resilient, stubborn, and determined, so things always worked out one way or another. But Elliot didn't want his future to be that random. He knew exactly what he wanted.

"Does this have anything to do with the chick at the club?"

Elliot took his hand off the mouse and glared at his phone where it sat on the desk, as if it was the device's fault that Finn had asked him such a thing. "Of course not. Why would you say that?" He could hear the defensiveness in his own voice and hated it.

"Well, you know."

"No, I don't know." Or at least, he didn't want to know. Elliot had been baffled by her sudden disappearance after their exchange in the storage closet. He didn't know if he felt guilty or abandoned or both, and the other men in his life seemed to think he was only supposed to feel proud. But Elliot knew this wasn't just some conquest. This was something almost otherworldly.

Finn's sigh came heavily through the phone. "Look, it's obvious there's something going on with you. You were having a pretty good time that night until that girl came along and then disappeared. Since then, I've hardly seen you or talked to you at all."

"I've just been busy."

"Doing what?" Finn challenged.

"Finding a real job, for one thing," Elliot retorted. But he knew that wasn't the entire truth. Finn was right, and something had changed inside him when he'd met Sibyl. He wanted to think he could ignore it and move on with his life, especially since it was obvious she was going to move on with hers. But he'd felt a heaviness in the time since that night, and he couldn't quite shake it. "Okay, maybe the girl affected me a little bit. But you can't blame me. I mean, I haven't had time for any sort of relationship since I started college. I've constantly had my nose to the grindstone, and the one time I looked up from it, I made a complete spectacle of myself."

"I wouldn't say that," Finn argued. "Plenty of people hook up at clubs and bars, and I'm sure most of those nights don't end in happily-ever-afters."

"Right." But that was easy for Finn to say, because he didn't know what Sibyl had done to Elliot. He didn't know about the way his dragon had writhed and squirmed inside him, the way he'd felt both physically and emotionally. Elliot hadn't told anyone about that, but he didn't see any need to start now. "Well, I need to get in the shower and get ready. I'll talk to you later."

"Knock 'em dead!"

Thirty minutes later, Elliot stood in front of the full-length mirror on his closet door. He had purchased a new suit just for this occasion, and he couldn't complain about the way it fit. He looked the part, and anybody might mistake him for a junior attorney instead of a humble intern. With his resume tucked away in his pocket and the document saved on his phone, he was as ready as he was going to get.

He got in his car and headed down the long driveway that led from his secluded house to the edge of town. It'd been a decent place to live for his college years, cheap and out of the way, but he couldn't help but hope that the job he might secure tonight would give him enough funds to buy the sort of bachelor pad he actually wanted for himself. Elliot had seen the expensive apartments downtown, the ones with floor-to-ceiling windows that looked out over the city lights at night, gleaming hardwood floors that paired beautifully with the exposed brick walls, and even parking garages.

But for now, he knew he would have to stick with what he could afford until he actually got that dream job. Out of habit—a habit that had only arisen within the last couple of weeks—Elliot scanned the sidewalks as he headed toward the hotel. He checked either side of the street, hoping to notice a woman with dark auburn hair. He looked sideways at the stoplights, casually taking note of the drivers in other cars.

He couldn't fool himself. He knew exactly what—or rather, who—he was looking for, but Sibyl wasn't anywhere. Their city was big enough that he couldn't really expect to just randomly see her once again, but he couldn't help but look. Eventually, he knew he would have to stop.

Slowing down for traffic, he leaned against the back of the seat and let out a sigh. He needed this event to go smoothly. He needed to rub elbows with the right people. He needed to get a good job and get on with his life, and then maybe everyone else in his family would leave him alone. He needed to... catch up with that woman on the sidewalk!

As soon as the light changed, Elliot smashed his foot on the gas pedal. He changed lanes to get a better look, and he knew he couldn't be wrong. Sibyl had just come out of a grocery store and turned down the sidewalk, heading in the same direction he was. Elliot flicked on his turn signal and swung over into a parking lot. He jumped out of the driver's seat, barely remembering to shut his door behind him as he jogged up onto the sidewalk. "Sibyl!"

She glared up at him with startled eyes as he grabbed her by the elbows, then quickly took a step back. "Elliot?"

"I'm sorry if I scared you. I just... I saw you on the street and I wanted to see you." His hands were shaking, and he removed them from her arms so she might not notice. "I wanted to spend more time with you at the club, but then I couldn't find you again." As he noticed the strange look in her eyes, Elliot suddenly began to wonder if Sibyl wanted him to find her at all. Maybe he'd made a huge mistake by practically tackling her on the street.

"That's, um, that's very nice of you, Elliot. It's just that I don't plan on being in this—in this town for very long." She wore a short white dress which was too summery for the cool autumn day, but the way the neckline dipped and the skirt flared accentuated her curves in the best way possible. Her deep auburn hair waved gently around her shoulders and contrasted beautifully with her creamy skin.

As far as Elliot was concerned, she could've been wearing sweats. He thought she looked stunning regardless, and he knew exactly what was underneath those clothes. He could've stared at something as simple as the curve of her shoulder for hours. The tip of his tongue flicked out onto his lip as he remembered the way her body felt against his. "I can understand that. I'm sure there are a lot of people in a university town that are just traveling through. But I haven't been able to get you off my mind, Sibyl. Not at all." He gazed into her eyes and felt his dragon thrumming inside him, pushing him to get closer to her once again.

She blushed, but raised her chin and showed him that cool, independent side he'd noticed when he'd first seen her sitting in the corner booth. "That's very sweet of you, but I don't really have time for a relationship right now. I have my...job, and as I said I won't be in town much longer."

Both Elliot and his inner dragon were getting frantic now. He wanted to be reasonable and logical about this, just like he had been about everything else in his life. Life got in the way of relationships all the time, and who was he to demand she drop everything she had going on just for him? He realized he didn't know what "everything" she had going on even was. They hardly knew a thing about each other except for their first names.

"Yeah, I totally understand." He raked a hand through his hair and then self-consciously rearranged it again. "Listen, I'm on my way to this networking event for attorneys. I know it's probably a little boring, but it's really a big deal to me. And I'm technically allowed to bring a plus-one. Why don't you come with me?"

She shook her head, one foot stepping to the side as though making ready for a getaway. "I don't know, Elliot. I'm not sure I should."

"Because of me, or because of the type of event it is? Because if you're concerned about the invitation part, it's really not a problem. Everyone else brings someone, and there's nothing saying I can't, either. And the drinks and the food are free." Shit. What was he saying? Elliot knew he sounded completely desperate. It probably didn't help matters any that he emphasized the free food and drinks. He didn't want Sibyl to think he was a cheapskate.

But she was watching him thoughtfully, her eyes slipping down to his chest and then pausing on his lips before coming fully back up to his eyes. "You're sure?"

The bubble of hope that had been rising in him ever since he'd seen her on the sidewalk was threatening to burst and leave him giggling like a kid in a candy store. He cleared his throat, determined to sound and act his age. "Yeah. Absolutely. Not a problem at all."

"I guess I could. Just for tonight. It would give me a chance to observe—meet a few more people while I'm here."

"Great." Elliot escorted her back to his car and opened the passenger side door, trying to disguise the thrill he felt inside him. He'd found her. She didn't want anything from him in terms of a relationship, but he could handle that. The important thing was that he'd found her and he even had a chance to spend time with her. "So, what do you do?" he asked as he pulled back out of the parking lot and into traffic.

"What do you mean?"

"For a living. You mentioned you were busy with work."

"Oh, right." She seemed almost startled by his asking, but maybe she was still recovering from him jumping in front of her on the sidewalk. "I'm a historian."

"Interesting. Is there any particular facet of history that you specialize in?" Elliot desperately tried to recall what he'd learned about history that didn't have to do with court cases.

Sibyl fiddled with her necklace, a long crystal with a point on the end, as she turned to look out the window. "Right now, I'm working on a project about ancient mythical creatures and how they've affected certain populations over time."

"Sort of like leprechauns in Ireland or bigfoot, right?"

"Um, yeah. Sort of like that. Have you seen any hanging around here?" Sibyl laughed.

Elliot shook his head, feeling strange. He knew several creatures who would be considered mythical by anyone else. He wasn't going to admit that part to Sibyl, but it made him wonder if perhaps someone had seen him and Finn flying out over the woods, or Nora and Kieran spending time at the lake in their true forms, or noticed the strange little man who lived with Julian and Naomi and imported rare herbs from distant places. He shook his head again, knocking those thoughts aside. If anyone suspected them, he would know about it. "I'd love to help you in your search, but I can't think of anything. No lake monsters, no hairy beasts in the woods, and no tiny people with gold coins. Have you been doing your research out of the university?"

"Yes. The library there is full of information."

"You might know my cousin, Nora. She works up in one of the botany labs."

Sibyl shook her head. "I don't think so."

"Yeah, of course not. That's not your kind of thing. There's also her boyfriend; he's a security guard there. You might have seen him around. Big hairy guy." Why the hell was he so determined to find some connection between Sibyl and the other people in his life? She'd already told him she wasn't staying. She probably didn't care that Nora and Kieran worked at the university, and it was a big place with tons of people.

"Maybe. No offense, but I can't say I've really paid a lot of attention." She adjusted the hem of her dress where it came down just above her knees.

Elliot had to drag his eyes back up to the road so he wouldn't stare at her legs too long. Damn. Even something as simple as her knees could distract him. He'd already missed the first turn into the hotel parking lot, and he had to slow down significantly to make the second one. Swinging into a space and putting the car in park, Elliot remembered he hadn't even gotten to the hard part of the evening.

"I'll have to introduce you to my boss," he said apologetically as he opened her door for her and straightened his suit jacket. "It's through my connection with him that I'm even able to be here tonight. You see, I've just taken the bar exam, so the next step is to secure a job I want."

She scrunched her eyebrows at him. "The bar exam? Does that have something to do with the club?"

He paused and stared at her for a moment, and then he laughed. When she wasn't laughing with him, Elliot stopped. He didn't know if she was being serious or not, and his cheeks burned with embarrassment over not wanting to embarrass her. "Let's head in, shall we?"

The ballroom where the meeting was being held was clearly marked with a massive sign on an easel that read, "Welcome to the Fifth Annual Assemblage of Attorneys! Please sign in." Elliot registered at the table near the door, where a white-haired woman carefully scrawled his name and the firm he worked for on a name tag.

"And your name, sweetie?"

"Oh." Sibyl took half a step backwards. "I don't need a nametag. I'm not important here."

But the old woman was persistent. "Everyone needs a nametag, honey, even the girlfriends."

He felt his face burning once again. "Oh, she's not...I mean we're just..."

"Sibyl," she said, saving him from trying to finish that awkward explanation. "My name is Sibyl."

"Very good, honey." The old woman's marker squeaked as she made the second name tag and handed it over. "You'll find the drinks on the right and the dinner buffet on the left. There are several tables in the very back with some silent auction items, and Mr. Peterson is scheduled to speak at seven-thirty sharp. If you have any other questions, I'll be right here." She nodded and smiled, confident in the words that she'd undoubtedly been saying to hundreds of attorneys every year for the fifth year in a row.

"I'm sorry about that," Elliot muttered as they stepped into the ballroom. "I just didn't quite know how to explain...us." He'd never been at such a loss for words before Sibyl came around. It was his quick wit that had caused his own father to urge him toward law school. Elliot had resisted for a short time, not sure that it was the right path for him. As soon as he'd understood that it fell in line with his natural talents, though, he'd been hooked. All those talents for witty repartee and debate seemed to fall by the wayside when Sibyl was around.

"It's fine. I get it. I think it's simpler if we just say we're friends. What do you think about that?' She gave him a look out of the corner of her eye, one that made him want to put his hands on her waist and pull her close.

Elliot settled for resting his hand gently on her back as he guided her toward the bar instead. "Works for me. Let's get some drinks and find a table." He knew he should be focused on the real reason he was there. He needed to pay attention to everyone else who'd come to the gathering, noting not just who they were, but what they said and how they acted. While it was true that his actual credentials were important, Elliot knew the impressions he made on anyone there that day would be vital as well.

"What do you like?" he asked her when they'd reached the end of the line and the bartender looked at them expectantly.

Sibyl's spine stiffened slightly. "Oh, um, just anything. Whatever you think."

It seemed a strange answer for a woman who was normally so sure and stubborn in the little he knew of her. "Wine okay?"

"Sure."

He ordered a whiskey for himself and a wine that sounded good for Sibyl before winding his way through the room to find a table. On the way, he spotted Mr. Dodson. "This is my boss," he turned to whisper in her ear.

That was a mistake. Being so close to her like that, with the scent of her perfume invading his senses and the warmth of her skin against his, he thought he might go crazy. Elliot tightened his grip on his whiskey glass and tried to get a hold of himself. He couldn't mess this up. His whole life might revolve around this meeting, and he couldn't let his dragon get in the way of that.

"Elliot!" Mr. Dodson called cheerfully, raising his own glass. "Glad to see you could make it. I hope you're fully prepared." He raised a thick eyebrow.

"Of course. Absolutely. No doubt about it. Let me introduce you to Sibyl. Sibyl, this is Mr. Deffrey Jodson. I mean, Jeffrey Dodson." He closed his eyes, feeling his face burn once again. What the hell was the matter with him? He'd never been unnerved around strangers before.

Fortunately, Mr. Dodson was an old pro, and he took the goof in stride. "Jeffrey Dodson," he said as he held out his hand to Sibyl. "It's nice to meet you. Elliot, could I talk to you for a second?"

Shit. "Sure. I'll be right back, Sibyl." He stepped away a few paces with his boss.

"Are you all right?" Mr. Dodson asked. "You're sweating."

He hadn't even noticed, but when Elliot swiped a hand across his forehead and it came away damp, he knew his boss was right. "It's just such an important night. Between this and waiting for the results of the bar, I guess I'm a bit of a mess." And wanting to get back under Sibyl's dress wasn't helping matters at all. He'd been a fool to ask her to come along with him, but in that moment, he'd been so desperate to keep her close, he couldn't think of a better option. He still couldn't, and he wasn't about to take her home.

"Just relax. Remember, nobody's going to hire a nervous attorney. Not a client, and not anyone in charge of a firm. You don't have anything to be nervous about, anyway. You're one of the most promising interns I've ever had in my office."

The compliment was enough to pull his mind away from Sibyl for a second. "Really?"

Mr. Dodson laughed, his eyes crinkling at the corners. "Yes, really. I'll be honest with you. I don't really like having interns around at all. People think it's great for us old dogs because we have someone to do the work for free, but that's not really worth it when the intern knows so little and keeps screwing up. You're not like that, Elliot. You're smart and you're very capable. Now tell me, what's the deal with this girl you've got on your arm? I haven't heard you mention a word about a girlfriend before."

"Oh, uh, we're just friends." His eyes focused on Sibyl. He'd felt strange about leaving her to talk to Mr. Dodson, but she seemed perfectly comfortable standing near the wall. Her eyes swept over the crowd slowly, taking it all in. She took a sip of her wine, frowned down at the glass, and then let it dangle from the tips of her fingers as she continued to focus on the people around her.

"Well, she seems great. Just don't get too distracted by her. And to be honest, you might want to keep an eye on her. Some of the old men around here have grabby hands, if you know what I mean. I know, I know." He held up his hands in defense as Elliot cast him a horrified look. "Things are changing, and that's not how it's supposed to be, but some of them are from an older generation."

"Thank you, sir." It took all of Elliot's self-control not to run back to where Sibyl stood before anyone else could approach her. Mr. Dodson hadn't been wrong. Elliot had known there were men like that, and certainly some of them were in this room, but he simply hadn't thought about them. Well, let them try. He'd fucking tear them limb from limb.

His chest tightened as he realized this urgent need to protect her. Elliot was acting as though Sibyl was his, as though he had some right to her that nobody else did simply because they'd hooked up at the club. It wasn't a rational way of thinking, but his body didn't care. He wanted to let his wings fly out and cover Sibyl up with them so nobody else could see her.

Instead, fighting against that wild beast inside him that had never given him so much trouble before, Elliot walked up to her calmly. "Is there something wrong with the wine?"

She frowned down at the glass again. "I don't really drink much. I wasn't sure what to expect, but I just don't like it. Sorry."

"There's nothing to be sorry about at all. Here." He held out his own glass. "Try mine."

Sibyl took the drink from him, her cool fingers sending a tingle up his arm as they touched his. She pressed her lips to the edge of the glass, looking up at him as she took a sip.

She was the one drinking, but Elliot swallowed. Her red lips against the glass and her gemstone eyes staring up at him were almost more than he could handle. It was just a drink of whiskey, but it was so incredibly sensual. He cleared his throat. "What do you think?"

Her lips parted and pressed together again as she tasted the heady liquid. She smiled at him, her eyes still locked on his. "That's good stuff."

His body was going insane, and he took a deep, controlled breath to put it back in check. "Then let's go get you one of those and some food."

Sibyl went through the buffet line in front of him, studying each offering carefully before putting it on her plate. When they found a table and began to eat, she attacked her appetizers with gusto. "What do you call these?" she asked, holding up her fork. "They're delicious!"

"Shrimp," Elliot explained slowly. "You've never tried them before?"

She shook her head emphatically as she chewed. "No. I think I would've remembered."

"Try them in some cocktail sauce." He spooned a little onto her plate.

Sibyl did as he suggested, closing her eyes in pure ecstasy. "This is amazing."

"I'm glad you think so. Sibyl, I know this was a strange place to invite you to. I'm sure you have much more exciting things to do than hang around with a bunch of boring lawyers. But I really appreciate you coming along with me tonight. I'd like to get to know you a bit better."

She stopped eating for a moment to take a large swig of whiskey. "I told you, I'm not staying. Your time would be better spent doing... whatever it is you're supposed to be doing here."

"Technically, my plan was to come here to mix and mingle, to gather a few names and hopefully hand out a few resumes. It's possibly my way into a job."

Her brows drew together. "Don't you already have a job? You introduced me to your boss."

"It's just an internship." He felt like a complete loser explaining all this. Who would want to date a guy whose job didn't pay anything and who had no guarantee of finding real work? "Mr. Dodson seems to think it won't be a problem for me to find a firm that has some space, though. But anyway, we don't need to talk about me."

"I'm sure he's right. Have you tried these?" Sibyl pointed to a mushroom stuffed with goat cheese on the corner of her plate.

She was distracting him again. Elliot was starting to wonder if she was doing it on purpose. "Um, no. I don't think so."

"Here." She delicately picked up the mushroom between her thumb and her finger, holding it out. She could've put it on his plate or simply gestured for him to take one, but she was placing it right up against his lips. The morsel was perfectly bite-sized, and as Elliot opened his mouth, her eyes lifted from his lips to lock with his gaze. The cheese was hot and delicious inside, the mushroom curvy and savory, and Elliot turned away, suddenly embarrassed to be chewing in front of her.

"Don't you like it?" she asked. "I thought it was good."

He swallowed, thinking he couldn't possibly finish the rest of the food on his plate now. He couldn't do anything without wondering what she was thinking behind those jewel-like eyes of hers. "No, no. It's delicious."

Her smile sent a ripple of electricity up from his stomach, retracing the path the mushroom had just taken. The ball of energy pulsed in his tongue, and Elliot remembered how much he enjoyed kissing her. He took a drink in the hope of suppressing it, since he'd never get a job if the lawyers here saw him sticking his tongue down a woman's throat. "So, where are you from?"

Sibyl tipped her head slightly as she looked at him, her eyes contemplative for a second before she smiled again. "I'll let you guess."

"Oh, no. I'm not good at that."

"I'm sure it won't be that hard," she encouraged.

Damn it. Elliot would do anything she asked if she just kept looking at him that way. "All right. I'll do my best. But you have to give me at least a few hints. You don't sound like you're originally from the States."

Her eyes rolled from side to side. "Not originally, no."

He wished Kaylee were there to help him. She could identify an accent from almost anywhere. "Okay. Let's see. Germany?"

Sibyl shook her head and smiled, her hair brushing alluringly against her shoulders.

"No, I can see how I'm not right on that." It was a familiar accent, but not a common one. "Maybe a little more eastern European. Romania?"

Again, she shook her head.

"This is going to be difficult. I didn't exactly worry about retaining what I learned in geography, since I didn't think I'd really need it." Elliot racked his brain for his next guess. He couldn't just give up, not when he was so desperate to learn more about her. "What about Bulgaria?"

"You've got it!" Sibyl took a bite of a chocolate-covered strawberry and rolled her eyes with pleasure.

Maybe they didn't have shrimp cocktail, stuffed mushrooms, and chocolate-covered strawberries in Bulgaria. He would have to ask Kaylee sometime. But realizing where Sibyl was from also made him realize just how far apart they would be once she left. "So, is that where you're going back to? When you're done here, I mean?"

She tipped her head. "There, and maybe a few other places, too."

"Yeah, I guess they have other versions of Bigfoot for you to chase."

Sibyl glanced at him quizzically for a second before laughing. "Yes. Right."

Fortunately, Mr. Peterson took the podium and began his speech, keeping Elliot from saying anything else foolish. He tried to listen to the man, a well-renowned attorney that he knew he could learn a lot from, but the words just drifted through his mind without any meaning. Elliot could only think of Sibyl. She was sitting right there next to him, the most gorgeous and intriguing woman he'd ever met. Sure, they'd met under less-than-ideal circumstances, but Elliot thoroughly believed that was something they could get past. Even with as little as he actually knew about her, she had to be smart and cultured to be flying around the world and studying the folklore of various places. Yes, she was a little strange, but he had plenty of strange things in his own background.

There was little getting around the fact that she would be leaving the country, though. That was a long-distance relationship at its worst, and she'd already told him she didn't have time for anything serious. But Elliot couldn't just accept that.

The roaring of applause thundered in his ears, and Elliot clapped for the speaker even though he didn't know a word Mr. Peterson had said. The attorneys and their associates began mingling in earnest then, and Elliot once again remembered that he'd come there for a purpose other than spending time with Sibyl.

He checked out the silent auction items, striking up conversations with the various men and women who lingered around the table as well. He handed out a few resumes and exchanged several emails, making sure to drop Mr. Dodson's name here and there so they knew who he worked for. He'd been so nervous about making sure his resume was correct—and then even more nervous knowing Sibyl was with him—but somehow, the two combined into a feeling of complete ease as he tried to make an impression on these other professionals. With Sibyl at his side, he could see the sense of approval in their eyes. And given the opportunity to do what he was good at in front of her—instead of rambling nonsensically as he had been—made Elliot feel he was now making a much better impression on her.

By the time the event was over and they were getting ready to leave, Elliot felt like he was on top of the world. He stepped out of the ballroom and into the hallway, abruptly aware that they were in a hotel, and pressed his tongue between his teeth. She'd already said she didn't want anything serious. But a night at a hotel didn't have to be serious, and they were already there, and he wanted her just as much if not more than he had when he'd first met her...

"It's getting late," she said with a knowing flash in her eyes as he slowed down on the way toward the parking lot. "I'm sure you're tired."

Was it the whiskey? Or was she good at reading minds? Or was she just thinking the exact same thing that he was and having a little more self-control about the situation? "Yes. I mean, yes, it's getting late. But I can't say I'm tired. I had a lot of fun with you tonight, Sibyl. Much more fun than I would've had on my own."

She slipped into the passenger seat of his car, peering up at him through her lashes as she did so.

Elliot walked around the back of the car so that she might not see him trying yet again to keep himself together. If she didn't want anything more from him, then why had she agreed to come that night? Why did she keep looking at him that way? Why did she have to make him feel so intensely excited about the tiniest thing? It was as though the entire world was embellished when she was around, and it was difficult to take.

Getting behind the wheel, Elliot realized he had no idea where he was going. He couldn't exactly drop off Sibyl in front of the store where he'd found her earlier that evening. "What's your address?"

Her mouth opened to speak, but no words came out. Her face turned a shade paler in the dim light of the parking lot. "You know, I have a little bit of research I still wanted to do today. Just drop me off at the university library."

He checked the clock on his dash. "It's after eleven."

"They're still open," she countered.

Elliot started the engine and pulled out of his parking spot, a sense of unease tightening the muscles in his shoulders. "I don't want to pry into your business, but do you have a place you're staying while you're in town?"

"I do." She was cryptic as ever, hardly answering him with anything more than was absolutely necessary.

"Do you feel safe there? I mean, I know sometimes the university puts people up in some pretty iffy apartments. I could find a place for you to stay tonight if you're not comfortable. I could get you a room right here at the Heritage Resort, actually. No strings attached." He was desperate to figure this out. Nobody would want to go to the library when it was almost midnight, not when they'd already spent the evening out.

Sibyl turned to him and laid a hand on his shoulder as she gave him a small smile. "It's very kind of you, Elliot, but I'm fine. I'll go back to my place later, but right now I really want to go to the library."

He didn't like it at all, but Elliot headed toward the university. "I can stick around if you'd like. I'll give you a ride when you're done."

She turned to him then, a hardness in her eyes. "I don't need you to do that. I'll be fine."

"I'm sure you believe that. I mean, it's easy to think a place like campus is perfectly safe. But you have no idea who might be hanging around there at this time of night. There could be vagrants lingering to get out of the weather, or people who see you as an easy target because you're a woman by yourself." He was beginning to feel desperate as he thought of all the horrible things that could happen to Sibyl if he just dropped her off like that.

Sibyl let out an exasperated breath. "It's very kind of you to worry about me. But I've traveled a long way without you as an escort, and I don't need you now." They'd reached the university, and she swiftly unbuckled her seatbelt and opened the door. "Thank you for a nice evening." She slammed the door behind her as she charged up the sidewalk toward the big brick building.

The further she got away from him, the more Elliot felt himself losing control. A strange buzzing—the same one that had haunted him that night at the club—was building at the base of his skull once again. He didn't understand who this woman was or why she was so damn important, but there was no denying that she was. His inner beast surged as he leapt from the driver's seat and stormed up the concrete after her. "Sibyl. Sibyl!"

She ignored him, her head high and the skirt of her dress swishing around her thighs.

He couldn't stand it. Maybe he was completely wrong and he would regret it later, but he just couldn't help it. "Sibyl!" He grabbed her by the elbow and turned her around, her body landing against his and his arms wrapping around her waist to keep her upright. "I can't just let you go like this. I know you don't want to get involved, and I respect that. I get that you're leaving. But if you think you're being kind to be by keeping your distance, you're completely wrong. I know this sounds crazy, but I'm practically sick without you. I can't stand not to be near you, under whatever circumstances that needs to be."

She stared up at him, her eyes wide as they reflected the starlight and continued to dazzle him with their everchanging colors. Her body, warm, soft and luscious, was pressed against his, and she made no move to get away from him. Her lips were slightly parted, velvety and inviting. "Elliot, I—"

He didn't want to hear what she had to say. Maybe it wasn't fair, and he could deal with all that later. But he didn't want to hear any more arguments or excuses. He knew what he needed, what his body demanded, and what he was certain she needed as well.

Elliot bent his head to kiss her fiercely, funneling all the need and frustration he'd been feeling into the way his lips pressed against hers. He splayed his fingers against the small of her back and curled them at the tips so that they pressed into her flesh, trying to let her know just how much he needed her. He felt sparks of energy as he deepened the kiss, her lips pliant under his as she parted them and let him explore the surface of her tongue and the ridges of her teeth. The world disappeared around them as she returned the motion, her fingertips clutching at his shirt under his suit jacket and her hips wedging harder against his.

Pulling away reluctantly, Elliot rested his cheek against her forehead and continued to hold her tightly. "Sibyl, you don't know what you do to me."

Her movement inside his embrace made him loosen his grip slightly. She looked up at him, her eyes earnest and determined. "I do, actually. But I've got to go."

He released her reluctantly. "If that's really what you want." Elliot didn't know how he was going to manage being without her, but he couldn't exactly throw her over his shoulder and put her back in his car."

"Goodbye, Elliot."

Watching her go, Elliot felt the buzzing start once again. It was nothing more than a bumblebee at first, but it swiftly increased to the noise of a swarm of hornets. There was no denying now that it was Sibyl who was creating these strange feelings in him. They weren't the same feelings his cousins had described, but they were similar enough that he had to wonder.

As the distance between them increased and the buzzing was so loud it seemed to make even his tongue vibrate, he knew what he was losing. "Can I at least get your number? Or your email?"

But Sibyl only walked faster, and soon enough he saw the dark, imposing front of the library split open in a rectangle of light that outlined her silhouette perfectly for just a moment before the door slammed shut once again.

He turned back to his car, shuffling his good shoes on the sidewalk, feeling like a kid who just lost his baseball. Why did this woman have to do this to him? Did she not feel it, too? Half of him wanted to run into that library, find her amongst the shelves, books, and desks and demand to know if it was just him. But she'd made it very clear she didn't want to be near him, and he already knew what the answer would be. This thing that was affecting him didn't affect her, and it wasn't fair to ask her once again to change her mind.

Elliot got into his car numbly, his hands and feet operating it without his consent because his brain no longer knew how to drive. He wound through the streets of the university campus until he ended up at the parking lot behind the security station. Kieran's vehicle was there, so at least Elliot knew there was someone on campus he could trust. That was something. He thought for only a fleeting moment about sending Kieran a text and asking him to check up on Sibyl, but that was once again not what Sibyl wanted. She didn't need his protection or his company. She didn't need him. It was time to stay out of her life.

Driving away from campus, he headed downtown. Most of the stores had closed for the evening, leaving only the bars and a late-night taco restaurant open. The lights were glaring and offensive against the darkness of the closed businesses that surrounded them, and Elliot found himself getting irritated about something as small as not being able to see the stars above the buildings. His car didn't sound right. The people gathered on the sidewalk in front of one of the clubs —fortunately not the same club where he'd met Sibyl—were being too loud. His one copy of his resume that still resided in his inside jacket pocket crinkled loudly in protest against the seatbelt. With frustration building inside him, Elliot headed home.

The long driveway that led to his house had once seemed like a blessing, keeping him secluded from the rest of the world that might distract him from his goals. Now, it was dark and lonely and far too long, stretching deep into the woods toward a house that was just as dark and lonely. Elliot swung the driver's side door open with anger, giving a dirty look to the passenger seat as though it was at fault for Sibyl leaving.

And cradled amongst the leather upholstery, he saw her necklace. There was no mistaking that it'd come from Sibyl. She'd been wearing it both times he'd seen her, though he hadn't paid all that much attention to it until now. Elliot scooped it up, feeling the cool length of the crystal against his palm in contrast to the warm leather of the strap. He could imagine the warmth there was still from her skin, but he knew he was being foolish.

Storming into the house, Elliot turned on every light in the humble bungalow, even the one over the kitchen stove. He had tons of family in the area, most of them living in big houses with plenty of spare room for guests. They probably wouldn't even bat an eye if he called them at this late hour and asked to come over, but they weren't what he needed. They weren't Sibyl.

Leaning against the kitchen counter, he held up the necklace and studied it in the brighter light. It was a pale blue, not quite clear, and the end of it had been wrapped in thick, bronze-colored wire that looped up to attach it to the leather string. It was the sort of thing he might find in The Enchanted Elm, the new age store his mother and his aunt owned. But none of the ones he'd seen there had writing on them quite like this.

It was small, so small that he hadn't noticed it at first, and the symbols were completely foreign to him. What alphabet did they use in Bulgaria? He had no idea. Elliot allowed himself the fantasy of running the necklace straight back to Sibyl to give it back to her. He would charge into the library and find her easily. When she saw what he held in his hands, she would touch the bare skin at her neckline and her eyes would widen, because she wouldn't even have realized it was missing. She would be touched that he cared to return it to her, and she would wrap her arms around him and melt against his chest.

But it was past midnight now. Elliot had wasted too much time driving aimlessly around town, and the library was now closed. Sibyl would already be gone, and he had no idea how to find her. He was right back where he'd started before he'd left the house that morning. He closed his fist around the pendant one final time before setting it on the kitchen counter and pouring himself a drink.

## 6

Sibyl gasped for air in the back of the cab. She didn't like this method of transportation, even though it seemed to be the most practical and reliable way of getting around town without a vehicle of her own. But the back of these cars always smelled like unwashed bodies and stale perfume, something she had come to understand was faded air freshener. It didn't make things any better that the drivers were always shady characters who either talked too much or too little and had strange auras around them that made her uncomfortable.

Elliot hadn't been completely wrong. She didn't think there was any good reason for a woman on her own to be a spectacle, but apparently, she was. The librarian had glanced up at her when she'd left the library, waiting until just before midnight to use up as much time as possible, stopping her before she'd reached the door. "It's late, honey. I can call one of the security guards to come escort you out to your car."

"No, thanks." The last thing Sibyl needed was another person asking where she was going and what she was going to do with herself all night.

As she'd trotted down the sidewalk toward the parking lot, she was both relieved and disappointed to find that Elliot wasn't still there waiting for her. There was something about that man that really got her, even though she couldn't explain it. He was charming and sweet, and he seemed to care about her more than anyone else she'd met before. Sibyl might even be able to set that aside if it weren't for the way he made her feel.

She'd had a hard time resisting when he'd asked her to come to his networking event. Sibyl knew she shouldn't go. She shouldn't encourage him, since she'd already told him she wasn't going to take this any further. But the idea of spending time with him had been more tempting than she wanted to admit, even if they were claiming they were nothing more than friends. She liked the way he got nervous about making sure she had what she needed, the way he stumbled over his tongue in front of his boss, and the way he could completely change his attitude and be professional when meeting new people at the event.

And then, that kiss! She'd been so angry with him when he'd insisted she needed his protection. It was sweet in its way, but she didn't want someone bossing her around, acting like she couldn't take care of herself; she had Ganon for that. But when Elliot had pulled her close and pressed his determined lips to hers, she'd nearly relented. She liked the way he towered over her, the way his arms felt so powerful around her, the way he genuinely wanted to keep her safe from the rest of the world. *If only he knew who he's dealing with,* she mused. *A witch from another planet looking for dragons.*

Sibyl picked at the hem of her dress and chewed her lip, wondering just what Elliot would think if he knew what she was. He was a practical, professional man who likely had no idea there were any such things as wizards, dragons, and other worlds. Just imagining his reaction reminded her she had no business getting involved with a man like him, and she'd done the right thing by leaving.

"Right here," she said, sitting up and pointing before the driver passed the dark driveway. The house wasn't anything special. It huddled on the edge of town instead of towering over the land like the castle she was used to. Sibyl couldn't quite think of it as home. The living room light was on, which meant Ganon was home. Her shoulders slumped. She didn't want to deal with him; not now. But what choice did she have? What choice did the child of any powerful leader have but to follow in his or her footsteps and do what was expected?

"There you are!" Ganon looked up in surprise as she came through the door. "I've been dying to tell you what I found this evening!" He had taken up a place in an armchair, his long legs stretched out in front of him as he watched television.

"Oh." She forced a smile to her face as she sat on the sofa, a sad little piece of furniture that sagged so badly in the middle, it made her knees angle back up toward her chest. She adjusted the skirt of her dress uncomfortably, feeling it revealed too much. "I'm here now, so you can tell me."

But Ganon wasn't so easily fooled. He clicked the button on the remote to turn off the television and leaned forward in his chair. "That can wait. I'd like to hear about your evening first."

"It really wasn't that special," she lied. It was incredibly special. She'd tasted food she'd never even seen before, and it was far better than the potato chips and hot dogs Ganon had become so attached to. She'd figured out that some of the human alcohol here on Earth was better than others, and that there was something shockingly intimate about sharing food with a man she found so attractive. And though it wasn't the first time, she'd also had one of the most amazing kisses of her lifetime, the kind that made her want to follow Elliot wherever he went.

"Really?" The wizard raised a dark eyebrow as his eyes raked over her dress and her nearly-bare thighs and back up again. "I'm no expert in human behavior or what they wear, but that dress seems a bit more, shall we say, flirtatious than the sort of stuff you've been making for yourself."

"I could say the same about you. I saw the way you dressed this morning." He'd put on a three-piece suit minus the jacket, but at the moment, he was wearing sweatpants.

"I was experimenting." Ganon rose from his position on the sofa and retreated into the kitchen, returning a moment later with a beer in his hand. "Have you tried these? Like soda, but a little better."

Sibyl had already experimented plenty with alcohol for the evening, and maybe without it, she wouldn't have gotten so far in over her head like she had with Elliot. "No, thanks."

"Suit yourself, but either way I'm waiting anxiously to know why you put on that dress. Or rather, who you put it on for." His obsidian eyes glowed menacingly at her.

That only made Sibyl feel more defiant. He didn't own her. He wasn't in charge of her. There was no rule saying she couldn't do what she wanted while they were on this planet. Still, it seemed wrong to share the details of her outing with Elliot, as though it would somehow tarnish the memory in the telling. "Not that it's any of your business, but I happened to secure an invitation to an event this evening where I could observe a large amount of people all at once." That was true, at least.

Ganon twirled his hand in the air, not distracted from the subject of her outfit. "And the event required this getup?"

"It was the best I could do on short notice," she retorted. The reality of it was that she'd seen the dress on a mannequin in a store window and simply thought it was cute. She'd created it for herself once she'd gotten around the corner, and it was pure coincidence that she'd run into Elliot after that.

He pulled a long breath in through his nose. "It seems to me that you could've found something a little more modest."

"And it seems to me that you often mistake chauvinism for chivalry," she hurled back. "Now can we please get off the subject and go back to what you were originally going to tell me?"

"I wouldn't dream of it, Sibyl. Not when you've clearly attended such an important event. Please, tell me about all the dragons you found this evening."

He'd cornered her once again. Ganon had to be the most irritating wizard in the entire universe. "I found plenty of interesting people, but I'm fairly certain none of them were dragons."

"Well, since you've failed in your mission tonight, I suppose I can tell you about mine. I'm sure it's not nearly as fascinating, even though I stumbled upon a rather interesting little magic shop." He grinned widely.

Sibyl rolled her eyes. "I told you, they don't believe in that stuff here. What they call magic is nothing more than slight-of-hand and illusions. Whatever trick cards they sold you aren't going to help us."

"No, no. Nothing like that. It was a real magic shop, or at least as close as I think I can get. It's called The Enchanted Elm. I was asking around a bit, and I heard the two women running it claim to be witches."

Sibyl sat up straight, or at least as straight as she could on the pitiful sofa. "Seriously?"

"Don't get too excited over that. They're not witches in the same sense that you are, I don't think. The woman behind the counter just wanted to prattle on about candles and incense. But there were a few herbs and stones there that I thought might further our cause." He crossed the room to the cabinet under the television and opened the doors.

"The spell?" Sibyl hoisted herself off the uncomfortable couch to see what he had.

"If we can actually pull this off, then this should be everything we need. I've done my best to find the equivalent ingredients here on Earth. Going by magical properties instead of actual names makes it a little more difficult than if we were back on Charok. But look at this." He pulled a small leather pouch from a shelf in the cabinet and dumped it out gently on the carpet. Ganon pointed to a translucent octahedron, like two little pyramids that had been glued together to form a diamond shape. "They call this fluorite here, and it's supposed to be very good for perception. This will be the crowning jewel in our detection spell. I have a few other stones to help reinforce and focus its powers, but the fluorite is the biggest player."

Sibyl studied the other stones. Some were crystal clear, and others had stripes and speckles of various colors. They were all beautiful in their own ways, but they were even more glorious if they would actually bring them victory. She blinked as she stared down at the stones, realizing just how far away from their goal she'd let herself get. When was the last time she'd actually looked for a dragon, or even thought about one? When Elliot had asked her to go with him to the hotel, she'd only really thought of it as a chance to observe people, but not specifically to find dragons. But what Ganon didn't know wouldn't hurt her. "Looks like you've been busy. Good deal. We should get started on it right away." After all, the sooner they found the dragons and got out of there, the sooner she could stop thinking about Elliot.

The work was time-consuming and difficult. In the days since they'd first decided to create a detection spell, they'd written and rewritten their incantation countless times to ensure its perfection. While it would've been very convenient to create a spell that would make the dragons immediately convert from their human forms to their true ones, they'd come to the conclusion that they couldn't even formulate a discernment spell that would allow them to see the dragons' true forms. If it worked, simply having the enchanted fluorite near a dragon would make the creatures emit a vibrant, radiant energy.

The two of them started by thoroughly cleansing the home of any energies, negative or positive. They couldn't risk having anything interfere with this spell. It was too powerful, especially considering they didn't know how it might differ when performing it on Earth instead of on Charok.

"Even the slightest shift in energy could change the outcome considerably," Ganon reminded her as he wafted a tight bundle of burning sage in the air, ensuring the smoke reached fully up into the corners of the ceiling and behind the curtains.

"I know." Sibyl bit her lip. She'd been worrying about this ever since she and Ganon had come up with the final formula, and she was starting to think she'd been letting her time with Elliot carry her away from her original mission just so she didn't have to think about the danger they were getting themselves into. "I'd really rather not think about it."

"Why not?" the wizard challenged with a mischievous grin. "You don't like the idea of potentially opening a rift in space and time that will leave us lost in the cosmos forever?"

"That's a very extreme and unlikely situation and you know it," Sibyl said with a roll of her eyes. He was just impossible, really. "But I still think we need to keep our thoughts focused on how we *want* things to go, instead of how they shouldn't. You know as well as I do that one's state of mind can affect a spell."

"Ah, yes," Ganon said, moving the smudge stick so that the smoke twirled in a spiral around the old light fixture. "Poor Strumaex." He said the words without any actual sympathy in his voice.

Sibyl shuddered at the thought. Strumaex had been a wizard of their own time, but he was now one who was only mentioned as a cautionary tale. When working on a spell that was supposed to summon a dragon from a long distance, Strumaex had been so nervous about what would happen once the dragon actually got there that he executed the spell incorrectly and zapped himself right out of existence. There was nothing left of him but a dark spot on the ground that leaked a thin stream of smoke for several days. Originally, the formula for the spell had been blamed. Further investigations revealed that Strumaex was simply emitting too much of his own negative energy for the spell to take hold correctly.

She cleared her throat. "Anyway. I think we've got the space prepared. Are you ready for this?" Sibyl looked up at him, asking not just with her voice, but with her intention so that she got an accurate answer. Ganon would never admit to being apprehensive about something, especially not in front of her.

His eyes sparked with delight. "I thought you'd never ask."

First, Sibyl prepared two pieces of the fluorite by winding a pure silver wire around the middle and leaving a loop through which they could tie a ribbon of silk. This would allow them to hold the stone out in front of them in the search for the dragons, allowing the magic to flow all around the fluorite. That was the easy part, though.

The remainder of the ritual took hours of calling energy into the fluorite and the other stones, placing them in specific patterns on the table to allow them to soak up the energy, moving them to new positions to receive different power, and then shifting those positions once again. Each movement, each breath, each word had to be precise. One wrong shift of a stone could throw the entire thing off.

When the sun rose and dared to peek through the curtains to check on their progress, Sibyl and Ganon each held out a completed amulet. The pale blue stones glowed softly, but not from the light of the sun nor from the ugly light fixture on the ceiling. They bore a light all of their own, one that pulsated with a gentle beat as it consistently searched for any nearby dragons.

Ganon's smile was pure joy. "I think we did it."

Sibyl blinked sleepily, unsure that this wasn't just a dream. "I think you're right. Now we just have to decide if we should get some sleep first or if we should head right out and test these." She watched as the fluorite spun in a lazy circle as it dangled from her fingertips.

He moved closer, holding the crystal away from his body as he grabbed her waist with his free hand. His thumb moved in suggestive circles against the fabric of her dress. "I think we could take the time for a little celebration, and if you want to call it sleep, then that's perfectly fine with me."

Sibyl stepped away and glared at him, angry that he had to ruin this moment. With a grunt of disgust, she pushed him away and dropped her stone into a small pouch. "I'm going to bed. Alone. I'll see you in the morning, and we can get started when we're refreshed." She didn't wait for his answer, turning and storming off to her bedroom.

If Ganon truly wanted to push the issue, he could obliterate the flimsy wooden door with hardly more than a flick of his fingers. Sibyl wanted to trust in the barrier between them, delicate as it was, simply because Ganon had never dared to intrude on her before. But as she sat on the edge of her bed, the pouch with the powerful charm clutched in her hand, she wondered just how far he might push things.

He was getting restless, and he didn't trust her anymore now that she'd had contact with humans. There was no good reason for him to be so upset about it, other than the fact that he wanted her for himself.

Flinging herself back onto the bed and slipping the charm under her pillow, Sibyl forced herself to go to sleep. She would need rest if she was going to get out into the world and search for dragons, and she would need even more energy if she was going to do this with Ganon at her side.

"I APPRECIATE YOU COMING OUT HERE TONIGHT." ELLIOT HELD THE DOOR wide, admitting Kaylee and Varhan. The pit of his stomach swirled like an angry storm, as it had been doing ever since he'd dropped Sibyl off at the library the previous night.

"It's not a problem," Kaylee assured him. "But I have to admit I was a little surprised by the invitation. You haven't been all that social for the last few months. I don't even remember the last time I was over here."

Elliot pressed his lips together. "Well, the bar exam and all that."

"Any word on it?" Varhan asked.

"Hmm? No. Not yet." Elliot had hardly even thought about it. Sibyl had taken up such a large amount of space in his brain that there was little room for anything else. He gathered the mail without much interest and only remembered to check his phone when its incessant beeping alerted him to a flurry of notifications. One of the attorneys he'd met at the Annual Assembly had already emailed him, but Elliot hadn't even bothered to reply. He had more important things to think about.

"If you were wanting to get together, I'm sure my father would've been more than happy to host," Kaylee said, running her finger through a thick layer of dust on the end table and wiping it on her jeans. "He hasn't said it directly, but I think he's been dying to get everyone together."

"I can confirm that," Varhan added. The wizard had been living with Kaylee's parents, Julian and Naomi, for the past year or so. "I keep telling him I should get a place of my own, because I don't want to overstay my welcome. But he won't hear of it. I think he was rather happy when he had a full house."

Kaylee counted on her fingers everyone who had come and gone from Julian's household recently. "He had all the dragons from Charok there for a time, and I think he loved it. But of course Archard and I have our own place. Jake has gone to college out of state. Lucia has that beautiful little house to call her own. Kieran's staying with Nora. Even Callan managed to get a good enough job that he could afford an apartment all his own. Everyone has moved on, which is great, but I think Dad's a little lonely. He's just got you, Varhan."

"I think I keep him well enough entertained," the friendly wizard laughed. "He's still very determined to learn as much magic as he can, but really he jumps at the chance to further any type of education. There was this documentary series he turned on the television the other night about the red-lipped batfish. Hideous little thing, and yet—"

"Guys."

Kaylee and Varhan turned to Elliot with surprise.

"Sorry, I'm just a little impatient. You see, I asked you here for a reason." Elliot twisted his fingers nervously in front of him. He knew some very smart and powerful people, but he knew these two were the ones who could help him the most. Of course, that also meant revealing more about himself and what was going on in his life than he was ready for people to know just yet.

"What is it?" Kaylee asked, her brow creasing with concern. "Is everything all right?"

"Yeah. Yeah, there's nothing wrong. Not really. I mean, um..."

"Let's have a drink," she suggested. "I've been so busy with work, I haven't had any time to relax. If I know you, I'm sure you've got some whiskey in here." Kaylee charged into the kitchen, rattling glasses.

Varhan guided Elliot to the sofa and pushed him down gently. "You know, my dear boy, whatever it is, you can always talk to us."

The words might have been what anyone would say at seeing a member of their family distraught, but Elliot knew Varhan truly meant it. The wizard had been a friend of his father's and uncles for a very long time, and even though the wizards and dragons on Charok were mortal enemies, Varhan was truly a part of their family now. "I know. And I've been thinking about saying something for a little while. I'm just not sure how to start."

"The beginning is the best place, usually," Kaylee advised as she returned to the living room, three glasses on a tray. She set it on the coffee table and passed them around. "We've got all the time in the world."

"You sure?" Elliot challenged. "I know how Archard can't stand to be away from you for more than five minutes at a time."

She punched him on the leg. "We're not that bad! Yes, we do spend a lot of time together. But he's out with Callan and Kieran tonight for a change. I've got at least a few hours before he starts missing me again." She smiled happily.

And Elliot was happy for her. She hadn't trusted Archard and the other dragons that had accidentally come to Earth from Charok when a spell went awry. But the two of them were fated, and anyone could see they were meant to be together. "Actually, you and Archard are a good place to start."

Kaylee glanced at Varhan and then back at Elliot. "We are?"

"Sort of. I mean, I guess I'll get to that part." He pulled in a deep breath, hoping he could actually get through this. "Okay. You remember that girl I, uh, met at the club?" He didn't want to bring it up. Everyone had seemed so happy for him, even though he'd gone and done something completely stupid. It bothered Elliot to be the center of attention in that matter.

His cousin smiled at him. "Kind of hard to forget, to be honest."

"Yeah, that's what I thought. Anyway, I had the strangest feeling that night. It was this weird humming, almost like the back of my skull was vibrating. It got worse and worse, and then when I got close to Sibyl—that's her name, Sibyl—it changed into something completely different." He rose from the sofa, uncomfortable with sitting still as he related the tale. "I didn't think much about it at first. I was too focused on wanting to find her again. And I did."

"You saw her again?" Kaylee asked excitedly, clapping her hands together. "How did it go?"

"I don't know how to describe it, really."

Kaylee reached out toward him, and it was when her hand settled on his arm that Elliot realized he'd been pacing. "Hey, you're going to need to be candid with us. It's clear you want some sort of help, but we can't give that to you if we don't know exactly what's happening."

"Yeah. You're right." Elliot picked up his glass and tossed it back, focusing on the burn of the whiskey in his throat. "Seeing Sibyl again was unbelievable. It's like she has a physical effect on my body and I start going through withdrawals if I get more than a few feet away from her. I just happened to see her walking downtown, and I stopped and invited her to the Annual Assembly with me."

Kaylee raised an eyebrow. "You invited her to that boring networking event? Sounds like the two of you are really hooked on each other."

Elliot gave her a look, but if there was anyone who was allowed to tease him like this, it was his family. "Yeah, I know. She made it very clear that she didn't want anything serious because she's only in town for a short time. I told her that was fine and that I just wanted to spend some time with her, but I'm not completely sure that's true. Hell, just the thought of someone else getting anywhere close to her made me feel incredibly protective, like I had some right to stand over her like a guardian. It's crazy, right?" He looked at the two of them for confirmation, though he wasn't sure what sort of reaction he was actually hoping for.

Varhan stood up and put a thick arm around his shoulders. "I know you've heard everyone else in your family talk about what it feels like to find their fated mate."

The words, though he'd been expecting them, sent a bolt of something akin to fear through Elliot. "But it can't be that. It just can't be. I've got plans for my life."

The wizard laughed. "My dear boy, our own plans rarely have anything to do with fate. I can't say it was in my plans to defy the rest of the wizards on Charok and risk everything to help save you, Kaylee, Nora, and Finn, the last eggs of our Queen. I remember when I was young, and the only thing I wanted was to rise among the ranks and prove myself as a powerful sorcerer. But life has a way of changing things for us and guiding us toward the path we're actually supposed to take."

"Even if that's true," Elliot argued, "what about the vibrating? I haven't heard anyone else describe a feeling like that when meeting their...mate." He had to force the word out of his throat. Elliot had certainly enjoyed the act, but to think he was meant to be with some-one, someone he didn't even get to choose but that destiny had thrust upon him, was so strange.

Kaylee looked at him softly. "It seems to be a little different for everyone, Elliot. I don't think that's much different for humans, either. Take it from someone who's studied a lot of different languages. There are numerous definitions of love, and often even within a single culture. I'm sure if you surveyed all the human couples you could find, they would each have something slightly different to say about love. It's not the kind of thing we can easily categorize in a tidy little box."

"Yes, language." He was feeling desperate now, and it was easier to focus on the part he knew they could help him with. "That was why I asked the two of you here instead of anyone else." Elliot retrieved the crystal from the little wooden box on the mantel where he'd stored it for safe keeping. "Sibyl dropped this when I saw her last. It has some symbols on it I don't understand. She wouldn't give me her number or any way to reach her. She won't even let me know where she's staying while she's in town."

Varhan frowned at the crystal, taking it gently from Elliot's grasp and studying it more closely. "Is there a reason you think this will help you find her?"

Elliot shrugged. "I don't know, really. She's from Bulgaria, and she wears this necklace all the time. I guess I thought maybe it would have her family name on it, maybe some clue about her that would help me. I know. I can hear it now. It's pathetic, isn't it?"

Kaylee's green eyes were entranced by the object, and she stepped closer to Varhan to get a better look. She held out her hand, and the wizard gave it to her. They exchanged a knowing glance before staring at the crystal once again. "She said she's from Bulgaria?"

"Yeah. I mean, she made me guess it, but yeah. She's got just the slightest accent. It's quite nice, really..." His mind wandered from the subject at hand, getting lost as he remembered the way words rolled off Sibyl's tongue. "She doesn't even say much, but when she does, I swear I could just listen to her for days."

"Elliot." Kaylee's voice, unlike Sibyl's, was harsh and demanding. She turned away from the crystal to make sure she had her cousin's attention. "This isn't Bulgarian. They use the Cyrillic alphabet, which I'm very familiar with."

"Oh." His shoulder slumped as he realized what a fool he'd been.

"I'm sorry. I shouldn't have wasted your time. I've seen necklaces like that at the Enchanted Elm, but I guess I just really wanted to believe it was something more."

Kaylee handed the crystal to Varhan before turning to Elliot. "It probably is, just not what you thought. You see, the writing on that crystal is Charokian."

A shiver of energy undulated beneath Elliot's skin, making a few scales shimmer to the surface. "You're kidding me, right?"

"Not at all."

The shiver increased as Elliot watched the two of them. Their faces were too serious, their shoulders too tense. "What? What is it? Does it say something?" He didn't know what to think. He'd been prepared for the writing to be complete nonsense, some cheap import that Sibyl simply wore because she'd liked it. It would've been disappointing, but it also would've been an acceptable and realistic alternative to finding out it was some great family heirloom.

"It does." Kaylee pointed to a line of script down the side of the crystal. "It says a lot of things, actually. Each line is a little bit different. But this one right here is particularly, ah, interesting."

"What is it? Come on! Don't leave me hanging!"

"*We are chosen, and our magic lives within us for a purpose,*" Kaylee read slowly.

Varhan cleared his throat. "It's an ancient and very common saying on Charok...among wizards, that is."

Elliot's eyes danced back and forth from Kaylee to Varhan, trying to understand just what they were telling him. "I don't get it. Why would Sibyl have something like that?"

The wizard's shoulder slumped with the burden of telling him. "Every wizard is given a crystal like this on the day of their Arrival. It's like a rite of passage, when their parents and elders deem them worthy of practicing their magic on their own. Wizards have to go through this process before they can marry, before they can hope to hold a spot on the council, things like that. The crystals are incredibly powerful. They hold a tremendous amount of magic in a very small package. They also serve as a family history, if you will. Since many of them are passed down through generations, a single crystal could hold an absolutely massive amount of information. Your modern computers are inadequate by comparison."

Elliot's backside hit the couch as he tried to absorb all this. "What about you?" he asked quietly. "Do you have a crystal like that?"

Varhan shook his head sadly. "Not anymore. It was taken from me when the council deemed me a traitor. If I did, then it would've made my job of transporting your parents from Charok to Earth much easier. And I'll be completely honest with you: it greatly disturbs me to see an item like this here. It could mean that the wizards who harassed the fae realm are back."

"But we haven't heard anything," Elliot argued. "Aurora would have told us. She would've heard of some sort of disturbance. Maybe this is just something Sibyl found, something that was dropped by one of the wizards when they were here."

"But they weren't really *here*," Kaylee reminded him. "They stayed almost entirely in the fae realm as far as we know."

Elliot knew. He simply didn't want to understand something that was so terrifying. "She's a wizard? From Charok?"

"Well, a witch. But not the same kind as your mother or your aunt. And it's a distinct possibility," Varhan said gravely. "Fortunately, we should be able to learn quite a bit from this crystal. It can tell us exactly who she is, and I may even be able to find the spells she's used."

"Is that something you can do right away?" Elliot asked. He was holding on to a desperate hope that they were wrong, that this was just some knockoff that happened to look like a wizard's crystal. He knew it couldn't be, but he wanted it to be.

The wizard sighed and bobbed his head from side to side. "It will take some time to extract all the information, but I can probably at least gather a little bit from it. Bear with me. It's been a long time since I've done anything like this." Varhan closed his thick fingers around the crystal, still holding it aloft. He gently shut his eyelids, though they still flicked with movement.

Elliot felt every atom of oxygen leaving his chest. He knew there was something strange about Sibyl, but he'd never expected her to be one of the greatest enemies of the dragons. This was just impossible. Any moment now, he was going to wake up and find out that this whole thing had been a dream. A nightmare. That even Sibyl herself wasn't real.

But Varhan's eyes flew open. He gasped and panted, nearly dropping the crystal. The wizard took a single step forward to set it on the table and then retreated from it as though it was contaminated, his eyes wide.

"Are you all right?" Kaylee grabbed the older man's hand to examine his palm. "Did it burn you?"

"I would be happy if that were the case," Varhan wheezed. He slumped onto the couch next to Elliot, his face pale. Beads of sweat formed a constellation on his forehead.

The dread that Elliot had been feeling only increased at seeing the wizard's distress. "Please tell me."

"Oh, my boy." Varhan leaned forward, pressing his hand over his eyes. "The crystal does indeed belong to Sibyl. And I can tell you that's her real name. It belonged to her father before her, and it still bears the name of its former owner. That crystal once belonged to Tazarre."

Elliot's ears rang, but it wasn't with the same sort of humming that he'd experienced when he'd been near Sibyl. This was pure horror. It was bad enough that the daughter of Tazarre was here on Earth, but he'd gone and fallen in love with her.

# 8

SIBYL'S STEPS WERE SLOW AND CALCULATED AS SHE CARRIED THE fluorite, watching everything around her as she moved through the shopping mall. It was a busy place, and fortunately one where nobody seemed to pay attention to much besides themselves or the bright sale signs that decorated every storefront. She was one of the few who explored the area on her own. There were young couples with their arms wound around each other, families who dragged children in and out of clothing stores, and knots of young girls who laughed and took pictures of each other with their phones.

If she'd been on Earth simply to observe human behavior, this would've been a good place for it. The mall had enough going on that it had attracted a massive group of people who wanted to shop, eat, or go to the movie theatre attached to one end of it. Sibyl had been there for hours, yet the crowd hadn't abated yet.

She spied a tall man with a dark head of hair on the other side of the food court, his ebony eyes watchful. Seeing him caused a lurch in Sibyl's stomach. Her life had been a little more pleasant while she spent the morning away from him, but she had no choice but to wind her way through the crowd toward him now.

"Any luck?" he asked casually as she approached, still watching the crowd instead of looking at her.

"Not a bit."

Ganon swung the charmed stone on its ribbon so that it made a small arc through the air and into his hand. He pocketed it. "Then either there aren't any dragons here, or we messed up. I'm not sure which conclusion I prefer to come to."

Sibyl nodded in agreement. Things had been even more awkward between them since he'd come onto her the previous night. It wasn't as though it was the first time he'd made an advance, but it was so much stranger for her now that she'd met Elliot. It shouldn't matter, and she knew that, but even with all the magic she knew, she didn't know how to stop herself from feeling that way. "I guess, if we have to pick, it's that the dragons aren't here."

He shoved himself off the low wall he'd been leaning against. "I'm hungry. Let's get some food."

They ordered their corndogs and french fries without saying another word to each other. Sibyl choked down the food, but only because she needed sustenance. It was horrible compared to the delights she'd had from the buffet when she'd been with Elliot. "Did you happen to go into the movie theatre?" she finally asked simply to break the silence. "It's a weird place. A whole room full of people, all sitting next to each other but making no attempt at getting to know at each other, and all just to stare at a screen for a couple of hours."

Ganon had been poking a french fry into a puddle of ketchup, but he flung it down and brought his ink-black gaze up to meet hers. "I have an idea."

She raised an eyebrow, figuring whatever venue he had in mind for their next stop would be one she'd already thought of. "Yes?"

"If we are forced to return to Charok without any proof that dragons are here, then you'll marry me."

"What?" There was a massive crowd of people all around them, but not a single person was paying attention to them. The lights were too bright, the chairs too hard, the food too salty. "Why?"

"You probably don't know this because you're always locked away in your tower studying, but there's been a lot of talk about you among the rest of the wizards. Some of them don't believe you're up to the task your father charged you with."

The lump in her throat was so big, Sibyl was sure it was visible from the outside. "They can talk all they want." She wasn't completely unaware of the rumors. Sibyl knew she was a strong leader, but there were some who were simply jealous or who didn't think she could do the job because she was a woman.

"Yes, and that's all fine until they decide to take action on those words. If there are enough wizards who choose to do so, you could be ousted with very little effort. It's not going to help your case if you return from this mission unsuccessful. That's why I offer you my help. I have some very influential people in my pocket, and no one would dare stand up against the two of us united." He spoke calmly and confidently, as though he'd been thinking about this for quite some time.

Sibyl looked down at her fries, trying to decide how to respond. She knew she didn't want to marry him. Ganon was a cocky bastard, and she highly doubted he would be good husband material. But she couldn't deny that he was powerful and influential, and his insights as to what might happen if they returned empty-handed weren't completely wrong. She didn't want to lose her position. Her father had done so much work, and she knew he was counting on her to continue it. "Ganon, I—"

But he held up a finger to stop her. "I suggest you take your time in coming up with a response. It has become your automatic reaction to reject me, over and over. But I won't extend this offer to you again. I've put myself on the line for you often enough, doing my best to help you understand what we could have together. But a man has to have at least a shred of pride, and you won't have another opportunity."

This warning caught her completely off-guard. Sibyl was thrilled to know she wouldn't need to worry about him hitting on her anymore. In a way, that alone offered her a great sense of freedom. But he'd done exactly what he'd intended and made her unsure of how the rest of the wizard community would receive her if they didn't find and kill any dragons, something she was increasingly unsure of.

"Fine," she finally said. "If we return to Charok without any dragons, then I will marry you."

His eyebrows raised slightly, and he nodded. "It's good to hear you've finally come to your senses."

"I'd like to be very clear about something, though," she continued. "I won't marry you out of anything but necessity. I don't love you, and I don't think you love me, either. I just don't think there's any point in fooling ourselves that it's any other way."

"Duly noted. Are you going to eat those fries?"

Sibyl shoved the little plastic basket of food across the table at him. She was no longer hungry anyway.

———

THE REST of the day went much as the beginning of it had. They went to the busiest areas of town they could find, often splitting up to cast their spell in as wide of a path as possible. They tested old women at the public library, young children at a playground, and middle-aged men who'd stopped in at a bar to drink in the middle of the day. They visited a butcher shop, wondering if the scent of meat might draw the dragons in, but the only thing they walked away with was a pound of salami. They had no luck at a farmer's market or at a coffee shop, even though Sibyl very much enjoyed the vanilla latte she ordered.

Sibyl was quiet as they turned for home, walking so that they might still have a chance to cast their spell along the way. She knew now that there was so much more on the line than just her reputation. "Do you think we did something wrong?" she asked quietly.

"What do you mean?" Ganon, despite the long day and the fact they'd walked over the whole damn town, didn't look tired at all. He walked erect and self-assuredly, still glancing from side to side at houses, parks, and small businesses along the way.

"You know exactly what I mean," she retorted. "Did we do something wrong with the spell? Was there an incorrect placement of stones? Or should we have used different stones entirely?" She eyed the fluorite skeptically.

Ganon sighed. "I told you, I researched everything thoroughly. The elements we used were as close to the ones we would find on Charok as possible. If they're not good enough, then there's nothing further we can do."

A nagging thought, one that had started forming earlier in the day but which she had purposely shoved aside, resurfaced once again. "Unless you messed it up on purpose."

He stopped in his tracks and rounded on her. Ganon was over a head taller than she was, and he loomed down at her menacingly. "Excuse me?"

"You heard me right. Maybe you botched the spell on purpose." She stabbed an angry finger into his chest.

"Are you seriously saying you would leave me in charge of gathering all the materials for a spell that we worked so hard on, a spell that could possibly change the future for our people, and then you would accuse me of spoiling it on purpose? Why the hell would I do that?" He flung his arms out wide, his voice rising. A woman on her porch went inside, not wanting to be witness to what she no doubt thought was a domestic squabble.

"You're making a scene," Sibyl pointed out.

"That's fine with me. I don't mind the rest of the world hearing you fling false accusations at me. It's the last thing I deserve after everything I've done for you!" His jaw was hard and tight, his eyes sparking.

But she wasn't afraid of him. She wasn't afraid of anything short of letting down her father's memory. "What you've done for me? You mean harassing me every day of my adult life because I wouldn't submit to your poor attempts at charming me? Or paying your way into a position with the council so you could pretend to be my ally? Or purposely messing up the spell and then getting me to agree to marry you if it doesn't work?"

"Oh," he breathed slowly, his voice suddenly and menacingly quiet. "That's low, Sibyl. That's very, very low of you."

She moved past him and charged down the sidewalk. They were almost to the edge of town and almost to the house. She couldn't think of it as their home, since she didn't intend to stay here any longer than she had to. For all she cared, they could return to Charok right then. Let the rest of the council throw her out on her ear. At least she would've done her best. "You haven't exactly given me a reason to believe otherwise."

Ganon, with his long legs, quickly closed the distance between them. "That's a mighty fine thanks, Sibyl. I'll remember it."

"You do that." She turned off the sidewalk and onto the little brick path that led up to their front door. "And feel free to tell everyone you know. I'm sure that's what you'll do anyway." Sibyl felt hot tears burning at the backs of her eyes. She wasn't crying over losing what little of a friendship she had with Ganon. He could go fuck himself. She wasn't even crying over the fact that she might very well lose her position when she got home. It would be terrible, but she could get over it.

No, she was crying about something much different, something she never expected. Sibyl had come all the way across the universe with the idea of defending her homeland against the plague of dragons that had haunted wizardkind for decades, but she'd found something completely different. She'd found a new world of people who were strange and different, but so nice in their own ways. Sibyl had encountered men and women who waved to each other on the street even though they didn't know each other. She'd learned of numerous charities that fought hard to help others in need, once again strangers. A young man at the grocery store had offered to carry her groceries out for her, and a woman who bumped into her at the pharmacy had apologized profusely. They were little things, but they'd made a big impression.

Even more disturbing was the way she felt about Elliot. If it was simply that humanity had earned her heart, then perhaps she could leave them behind to their own planet and be satisfied with thinking of them every now and then. But Elliot was much harder to let go of. She loved the way he stumbled over his words when he spoke to her, even though he could be smooth and professional when he talked to his associates. She loved the way he kissed her, and the way his eyes became azure velvet when he looked at her. She loved him.

It was ridiculous. She hardly knew him, and they weren't even from the same planet. From the research Sibyl had done, neither Elliot nor anyone else on this world knew they weren't alone in the universe. If she tried to tell him who she really was—and her true identity was an undeniable part of herself she couldn't live without—he would probably laugh at her or throw her in a mental institution. It simply wasn't meant to be.

And yet, could she actually return to Charok without him? Without knowing what might've happened between them? Or figuring out why her body reacted so strongly to his? Did he feel the same way? He was attracted to her, that much she knew for sure. But did he feel that same, strange intensity take over all his senses when she was around.

"Sibyl."

"Just leave me alone." She'd paused near the flower bed, empty of anything but weeds, and she reached for the doorknob.

But Ganon was, as ever, persistent. "Sibyl! Look!"

She whirled on him. "What?"

He pointed at her stone, still swinging from her hand. The pale blue surface had changed color on one side, a tiny dot in the very center of it glowing a brilliant red.

Sibyl nearly dropped it, and her heart jumped up into the back of her throat to compete with her sorrow. "I don't understand."

"Look," he said again, stepping closer. "It's only on this side. Whatever it's reacting to must be in this direction." Ganon examined the stone and then pointed off the north side of the house.

Retracing her steps back out to the sidewalk, Sibyl watched as the crimson glow faded and then disappeared altogether. When she approached the house once again, the little fire renewed its glow. Adrenaline surged in her blood. "Are they here waiting for us?"

"I doubt it, unless they also have some way of detecting *us*. And it's faint. I think we need to follow it."

All the anger and resentment from their argument forgotten, they pushed through the bushes that ran along the side of the yard. Sibyl was hardly even watching where she was going, she was concentrating so much on the reaction of the fluorite. She swore the glow was increasing, but it could've been a trick of the light.

"Hey! What are you two doing in my yard?"

Sibyl glanced up to see a man standing on his front porch. His skinny arms were covered in faded tattoos, and a thick beard clung to his chin. With his crooked teeth and the numerous beer cans that surrounded his lawn chair, he made quite the picture.

"Sorry! We're just looking for our dog. You didn't see him come through here, did you? About this big, black with a blue collar?" Ganon gestured the rough shape of a dog down near his knees.

"No, and I'd better not! If he comes through here and tears up the yard, you're going to be hearing from me! Landlord says we're not even supposed to have pets, and I've a mind to turn you in!"

Going along with Ganon's story, Sibyl smiled apologetically. "I'm sure we can work that out later. Thanks for your help!"

The two of them moved around to the alley on the other side of the skinny drunk's house. It was full of yet more beer cans.

"That was a good story back there," she mumbled to him, not wanting to give him credit but knowing it was due. "Even drunk, I don't think he would've believed the truth."

"I'm not sure I do, either," the wizard replied, looking at his own crystal and at the alley before them. "There aren't any other houses here. Unless the beasts are hiding in the woods, I'm not sure where we're going to find them. It's getting dark, though, and that will only help us."

"How so?" Sibyl had never actually battled a dragon face-to-face. So few of them had wandered onto wizard territory on Charok that she'd only seen them from great distances. Other wizards had quickly been dispatched to take care of them. She wouldn't tell Ganon, but she felt a great wall of hesitation form in front of her. Could the two of them handle one of the creatures on their own? What if there were a whole flight of them?

Ganon grinned. "Makes it easier to see the glow, both from the fluorite and from them." He charged down the alley.

They wound their way around behind the other houses in the neighborhood there on the edge of town, past old trash cans with litter spilled around them and tangling in the weeds. They passed barking dogs and half-naked children playing on tire swings. The few people that saw them only glanced up long enough to make sure they were harmless, if strange, and then went back to their barbecues, bonfires or marijuana pipes.

Soon enough, they ran out of houses completely, but the glow was building brighter. It was practically a flashlight at this point, and it continued to build as they pressed through the foliage in front of them. Sibyl felt the crunch of gravel against her shoe. "A driveway?" she said quizzically as she looked first one way and then the other down the back road. Grass grew in the center of it, indicating it wasn't well traveled.

"Let's find out." Ganon moved down the driveway, away from the rest of civilization.

"There's a house!" Sibyl's free hand twisted in the hem of her t-shirt. She was so excited, nervous, and electrified, she hardly knew how to handle herself as she studied the little bungalow. In the dim light that the setting sun hadn't quite taken away, she could see it was painted dark blue with white trim. The light next to the door wasn't on, but the glow of a lamp showed through the curtains in the front picture window. The yard was plain but neatly kept, converting quickly to wilderness and weeds as the woods took over around the edge.

"Yes," Ganon breathed. "Now let's see who's home."

"We really should've prepared for this." It was too late now. She should've thought about it a long time ago, when they'd first started their research for the spell. What to do with a dragon once they found it?

"What's there to prepare?" Ganon's face was a twisted visage of menace and bloodlust. He held his fluorite out at arm's length, his eyes flickering from the stone to the house and back again, encouraging the glow to increase. "We knock on the door, slaughter a few dragons, maybe leaving one or two so we can torture some information out of them, and then kill them, too. Only thing that's left after that is to gather a few mementos of our time here and head home."

Home. That was a word that had changed meaning several times over Sibyl's life, and she felt it was doing so once again. She touched the spot on her throat where her crystal was supposed to hang, the sacred object that had been handed to her from her father just before he cast the spell that obliterated the vast majority of the dragons. It would take her home, back to where she'd come from, back to the land where the rest of her kind lived. Or at least, it would if she still had it. Sibyl hadn't yet told Ganon that she'd lost it somewhere. A crystal was a wizard or witch's most sacred possession. He could use his own crystal to transport the both of them back to Charok easily enough, but she didn't want to hear what he would say when he discovered she'd been so careless.

She cleared her throat. "We need some way of getting in the door, first. We don't even know how many of them are in here."

Ganon sighed and shoved his charm in his pocket, still keeping his focus on the house. "Fine. What do you suggest?"

Sibyl's mind quickly flicked through everything she'd learned while on Earth. They needed a reason to be approaching a house. "I guess we could be selling something."

"Even I know they won't let us in if we say that," he spat.

"I know. I'm just nervous, okay?" Sibyl put her own crystal in her pocket. "We could say we're here on behalf of the landlord. Or we're distant cousins from another country. Or we're detectives."

"Yes, let's go with that one. I have plenty of complaints about this planet, but the crime shows on television are particularly intriguing."

There was no more time to discuss it, since they were stepping up to the door. Sibyl felt the frothing of her body's reaction to magic building up inside her as they approached. It sparked on the outer borders of her body and rushed inward, coalescing in her stomach. Whatever was going on inside this house, it was powerful. Her hand felt weak as she tried knocking on the door, knowing as soon as she did, it wasn't loud enough for anyone to hear. She tried again, willing her bones and muscles to cooperate. She couldn't fall apart now.

Vibrations in the floorboards of the porch let her know someone was coming. The sphere of excitement inside her intensified, and it was getting so strong, she thought she might throw up. She'd never experienced a reaction to magic quite like this before.

The door swung wide. Sibyl's eyes raised to the person in the home, expecting some hideous creature ready to pounce on them. But it was a man. A simply beautiful man, with carefully combed hair in a mixture of shades of light brown that reminded her of wood grain. His light blue eyes burned into hers as time froze. She felt the fluorite throb in her pocket, getting so hot, she thought it might burn her skin, and she pulled it out and flung it away from her as she fell to her knees.

"Sibyl!" Elliot's strong arms scooped her up and into the house. He laid her on a couch. "What are you doing here? What is this thing?" He reached for the silk ribbon that held the fluorite.

"Don't touch that!" she gasped. "I don't know what it will do to you." But as she looked up into Elliot's face, she could see the brilliant red energy from their spell reflecting off of him and around him, creating a glow that matched the pulsing in the stone. He was the one they were looking for.

Elliot, of all the people on Earth, was a dragon.

Her stomach surged and writhed, her body curling in on itself as she drew her arms and legs around her stomach. The feeling she'd mistaken for excitement or magic was now nothing but pain, and it rippled through her body with such a quick pulse, she thought it might break her bones. She dared to look at the offending area of her body, noting with a deep panic that the red beacon was shining from her own body as well. "I don't understand."

Two more people rushed into the room. Sibyl only knew one of them, and she wished she didn't. It was the traitor Varhan, the only wizard from among their ranks who had dared to fight for the dragons during the War of Storms. She'd heard of him, though he'd always seemed more of a myth than reality. Yet he was right there, standing next to Elliot. The woman next to him glowed with the same crimson light that had enveloped Elliot. She was a dragon as well.

"Oh, I think I understand perfectly well." Ganon strode into the room. He had pulled the fluorite back out of his pocket, holding it out at arm's length. From somewhere amongst the folds of his clothing, he'd produced his wand. He held both items at the ready. His eyes were on fire, the reflection of the magic glow brilliant against his dark irises.

"What did you do to me?" Sibyl sobbed. She didn't know if she spoke to Elliot, who may have somehow possessed her and caused this sexual attraction between the two of them and subsequently the pain in her stomach. Or was it Ganon, who had created the majority of the spell and gathered the materials for it? Had he used it against her in some way?

Nobody answered her. The dragons and the wizards stood there in the living room, everyone on alert and ready to fight.

# 9

ELLIOT FELT THE STRANGE SENSATION OF WHATEVER SPELL SIBYL AND this man were casting, but it wasn't hurting him in the same way it was hurting her. "Put that damn thing away," he growled at the dark man who took up the doorway. "Whatever's going on, we can talk about this."

"I don't think so, *dragon*," the wizard snarled. "You're what I came here for, and I don't intend to take you back alive."

Varhan stepped forward into the center of the room, holding up his hands in a bid for peace. "There's no need for anyone to do anything rash. I know things have been tense on Charok for the last several decades, but there's no reason to continue that here on Earth."

Sibyl screamed in pain from the couch, clutching her stomach.

Elliot didn't understand. Varhan and Kaylee had just confirmed for him that Sibyl was Tazarre's daughter. She was the descendent of the most evil wizard who'd ever existed, and yet this wizard standing over her didn't seem to care that he was causing her such pain.

The dark wizard hesitated for only a moment before putting the stone away. "Fine. I guess I don't need it any longer. I already know who you really are. But know this: I will slay you and anyone else of your kind, and the traitor as well. Sibyl and I are here for no other reason.

Sibyl seemed to recover somewhat. She sat up on the couch, her arms still clutched around her middle. "Ganon, there's something wrong here, something wrong with the spell."

He snarled at her. "Haven't you been paying attention? They didn't deny it! They're the ones we're here for!" Ganon flung out his arms in frustration.

Despite what he knew about Sibyl, Elliot couldn't just let this go. His body was fighting against him, urging him to transform. He'd been resisting it as long as he could, but it was all that he could do to keep himself from destroying everything in the room when he heard the way Ganon spoke to Sibyl. Something was about to happen, but there were still too many answers he needed. "Sibyl, tell me what this means. Tell me why you had Tazarre's crystal!"

"Give me that!" she demanded as she reached out with one hand. But she was still too weak from whatever that other stone had done to her to get off the couch.

"I don't think so." Elliot felt pity and rage and hope swirling in his heart. It was a heady mix, and he blew out a deep breath to try to keep control over himself. "I know what this thing does, or at least some of what it does. It's powerful. Tell me what's going on."

Her head slumped back against the couch cushion, her hair tangling against the upholstery. "He was my father," she breathed.

"You don't owe them any explanation," Ganon growled. "Now get off that couch and get ready to fight!"

"I can't," she gasped. She no longer kept hold of her stomach and was getting her breath back, but it was clear she wasn't completely all right yet. She reached out once again toward the crystal Elliot held. "My father was the great wizard, Tazarre. He fought so hard for our people, and he sacrificed himself to keep us safe. But you dragons, who have tormented us since before I was born, are everywhere. We received word that you'd come here, and we came to destroy you."

"Was this your plan the entire time? Is that what's been wrong with me? Did you cast some enchantment on me to seduce me to try to figure out where we were?" Elliot couldn't believe this was happening. How could he have been so stupid? He hadn't seen through her scheme at all.

Sibyl shook her head. "It wasn't like that at all. I thought you were human until just now."

Elliot wanted to believe her, but there was too much evidence against her. "I don't think I can believe you. The way I feel when I'm around you can't possibly be real."

"Yes, that's right," Ganon snarled. "She tricked you. She seduced you. And all in the name of our great Tazarre. Now, dragon, are you going to give me any kind of a fight on this? Or do I just take you down right where you stand? I don't mind, either way. Nobody on Charok will know the difference."

"If you want a fight, then I'm more than happy to give you one." Elliot felt a shiver over his skin as he allowed his scales to erupt. "There's nothing I'd like more than making toast out of you."

"Now, hold on!" Varhan roared, his voice far louder than Elliot had ever heard the soft-spoken man get before. "We all need to listen to reason for just a moment! I know how the wizards view Tazarre. You've heard of the supposed sacrifice he made for his people. You *thought* he only wanted the best for your kind. You grew up hearing the tales of how terrible the dragons were. But you have no idea that all of that was pure propaganda."

"Don't you dare speak that way about my father." Sibyl had produced her wand from somewhere inside her clothing, and she now pointed the tip of it at Varhan. "He did everything for us. Everything."

"I know. I know, my dear. And I'm so, so terribly sorry that you lost your father. But what you must understand is that he was not a victim, nor a martyr. He was a truly talented wizard, one who could have done so much with his power, but he was also deranged. Something inside him changed when he started playing around with black magic. It got even worse once he started getting involved with necromancy." Varhan clasped his soft hands in front of him as he plead with her to believe him.

"That's a lie," Sibyl hissed, but Elliot could see the fear in her eyes. "Even a traitor like you should know that necromancy is strictly forbidden. My father would have never gotten involved in something like that."

Varhan regarded her seriously. "He would if he thought it would help his cause. Tazarre learned early on that he had no limits when it came to getting what he wanted. That's also why he created all those terrible stories you heard about dragons. They were never there to attack the wizards. As a matter of fact, the territory that was being fought over during the War of Storms was occupied by the dragons long before anyone else even knew about it. I know that's a very hard pill to swallow, but I promise you it's the truth."

"No," she whispered, red blotches of color taking up residence in her cheeks. "You shut up, and you do it right now. You want to talk about propaganda, but that's exactly what you're trying to spread right now. I know how it was. I know how it *is*. The dragons have been attacking us for as long as I can remember. Sure, it might not be as bad as it once was, since we've been successful in decreasing their numbers. But what would you expect us to do to beasts who exist solely to burn down our crops, eat our children, and murder every living thing in their paths?"

Elliot stepped forward as his wings whipped out of his back. "Is that what you think of us? I suppose nobody ever bothered to tell you about the numerous dragons who lay dead or dying in the mountains, the poison your father created, slowly seeping into their bones and killing them from the inside out? Nobody told you how young dragons were left without anyone to raise them and teach them our ways, so the orphans died of starvation instead? And then of course there was the clutch of eggs laid by our Queen, who died on her throne without ever knowing her children? I was one of those royal eggs, Sibyl. Your father killed my mother, and almost everyone else around her! That deranged wizard changed my entire life." He'd never realized until he said the words just how much that fateful day before he was even born had impacted him. All the rage he'd felt toward the wizards was rising quickly to the surface, and he was more than ready to fight.

Recovering, Sibyl stood. As much as Elliot hated to admit it, he still found her attractive even with that spark of anger in her eyes and her chin jutting out. She was the enemy, and he knew that with his mind, but he didn't know it with his body or his heart. His instinct was to step in front of her and spread out his wings to protect her from whatever onslaught might come from those around them. It would piss her off, and it might very well make her attack him, but he still felt that strange sensation inside him that made him think of her as his.

"That's quite enough," Ganon asserted, stepping up next to Sibyl.

"Yes," she agreed. Her wand flicked to Kaylee and to Elliot but then quickly away again. "I'm not going to listen to these lies any longer!"

Varhan snatched the crystal from Elliot's grasp. The leather strap tangled in his clawed fingers, but the wizard was determined. He tapped his own wand on the tip of the crystal and drew it away slowly, bringing out a thin shaft of light. It twisted and writhed between the crystal and the tip of the wand, like a thin bolt of lightning, until Varhan threw it at the wall.

Like a movie projector, the entire gathering could see a little girl with dark red hair in two braids. She stood next to a much taller man, practicing with her wand. The candle she was attempting to light simply refused. The man crouched down behind her, wrapping his hand around hers and showing her just the right way to move the wand, and the candle ignited. There was no sound, but Elliot could easily hear the little girl squealing with delight.

The scene shifted, first changing to a multitude of colors that swirled on the wall and then coalescing to form a new view of the wizard that had been standing behind the little girl previously. He was a bit older now, and the glare in his eyes much darker. He used his own wand this time to draw up a column of black smoke from the floor. It smoldered and spun around him as he manipulated it with his magic until he tamed it into a bottle.

"Poison," Sibyl whispered.

"He did what he had to do," Ganon corrected her. "You know yourself that it's not easy being a leader, especially a great one."

But when the scene shifted again, there was little anyone could do to deny it. Instead of showing Tazarre, it showed the dragons. They were, as Elliot had described them, dying on the mountainsides. Their heads rolled to the side as their eyes looked up toward the burning sun covered in smoke, the last vestige of the Great Curse. Their tongues lolled on the hot red sand, and pink circular wounds showed where their protective scales had fallen out and left them vulnerable. Both adults and children had been struck down. The survivors weren't any luckier than those who had been taken quickly, their ribs showing through their thick hides as they wandered the land in search of a safe place and of food.

Elliot felt a shiver of horror down his spine as he watched. He'd known these things had happened. His father and his uncles had told him. But it was completely different to actually see it.

In the background, brilliant sparks of light began to show. As those sparks made their way forward, it became clear that they were balls of energy that expanded between the hands of wizards. They thrust their magic out at the dragons, slaughtering them where they lay dying.

Sibyl's hand covered her mouth and tears clung to her lashes. "No," she whispered. "This can't be."

"Don't let him fool you. The traitor created this vision to make you think poorly of your father." Ganon wheeled on Varhan, ready to let loose with his magic.

But Varhan lifted one shoulder in a shrug and held the crystal out, offering it to Sibyl. "Feel free to see for yourself. It took me a little while to work up the right spell to read everything inside, but you know as well as I do that crystals hold the memories of everyone who has possessed them. You just saw exactly what Tazarre saw. I can't manipulate or change that."

Sibyl gently folded her fingers around the crystal, staring at it. "My whole life has been a lie. It's just not fair."

Ganon gave an impatient grunt. "There's no time for worrying about it now. We have a mission, Sibyl." He raised his wand.

But Sibyl put her hand on his arm. "No, Ganon." Her eyes drifted around the room, landing lastly and lingering on Elliot.

He felt her gaze as though it were a physical thing as she studied him. Elliot was suddenly and incredibly aware of her taking in his deep blue scales, the cobalt leather of his wings spread behind him. He knew in that moment just how different the two of them were, but he also knew that he'd been completely wrong about Sibyl. He'd been shocked when he'd discovered who she really was, and her mission on Earth had been the logical next step. But she hadn't put a spell on him. He didn't feel the way he did about her because of any magical charm or manipulation. It was just the way the two of them worked together.

Sibyl turned to her cohort. "Ganon, you saw what I just saw. We can't let our people go on thinking they're doing the right thing just because my father made them think they were."

"Are you listening to yourself?" he roared.

Elliot started forward, but Sibyl put out her arm to stop him. "Yes, I am listening to myself. And that's exactly what I need to do. I'm tired of listening to you all the time, and I've been listening to what my father wanted my entire life. But I know what's right now, and so do you. We need to go back to Charok and explain the truth."

"We have to go back to Charok, all right, and bring an army back here with us! If there are two dragons here, plus this pitiful excuse for a wizard, we need to make sure there aren't any more. We can't allow these parasitic beasts to exist!" He lifted his wand. "One final battle!"

"Stop it!" Energy glimmered off her fingertips. "Don't you see how many people have died in vain? All over something so ridiculous? We have to tell them the truth and stop the fighting! Think about all the good that could happen if the wizards and the dragons actually worked together?"

"So you're on their side, huh?" Ganon shoved her backwards and pointed his wand at her, the tip glowing a menacing shade of red. "I shouldn't be surprised. I've tried so hard to train you, to mold you into the leader and the witch that you're meant to be, but you've constantly refused. And now, not only do you refuse to do what's right, but you sympathize with the dragons. It's not a surprise, given that you've got one of them growing in your belly!"

"What?" Elliot knew he couldn't have heard that right.

But Ganon had retrieved the detection stone from his pocket. He threw it at Sibyl's feet, and it glowed a brilliant red that matched the bright pulse once again coming from Sibyl's abdomen. She kicked it away, shattering it against the brick fireplace, but it was too late. They'd all seen.

"Sibyl, is this true?" Elliot took a tentative step toward her, a small part of him still wondering if this was all part of some elaborate trick on her part. But his mind flashed to that night at the club, to the way their hot flesh seared together as they coupled, and the fact that there hadn't been anything else between them. It made sense. If the two wizards had created a spell to detect dragons and the child inside her was a half-breed, then the stone would pick that up, too.

She pressed her hands to her stomach and looked at him wide-eyed, just as surprised as he was.

"Well, I know, and I'm tired of standing around waiting for you to do something!" Ganon roared. "Don't worry, Sibyl. When I get back home, I'll give them a lovely account about how I tried to save you. With your dying breath, you assured me that you wanted me to carry on your work for you." He whisked back his wand, prepared to cast a spell that would end the whole charade.

But Elliot snatched it out of his hand. The wood shattered in his grip as he finished his transformation, his fingers and back and legs lengthening and strengthening, his wings unfurling to their full capacity and knocking a framed print off the wall. He was only vaguely aware of the crash of glass behind him. His teeth reached for the back of Ganon's neck, eager for blood. Elliot wasn't about to let this evil wizard hurt the woman he loved—or the unborn child they shared. Protection and anger swelled inside him.

But Ganon was too quick. He whirled on Elliot as he fell to the ground, their arms locking as they fought to get to each other. The wizard curled his fingers, building up a ball of energy between them and flinging it in Elliot's face.

The magic burned, sending Elliot backwards as he fought to clear his vision. He could sense that Kaylee had shifted behind him, but he didn't want her to get hurt. He was the one who'd gotten them into this mess, after all.

As the gleaming streaks cleared from his eyes, Elliot saw that Ganon had grabbed the crystal around his neck. He muttered words to himself that Elliot didn't understand, but he didn't need to know their meaning to comprehend what was happening. Ganon was about to transport himself back to Charok!

But Sibyl flung herself at him, her hands clawing for the crystal. "You're not doing this!" she screamed. "I won't let you do this! I won't let you kill any of the others!"

Whether by magic or by physical force, Ganon was too strong for her. He flung her aside like a rag doll, her body making a dull thud against the couch.

Elliot's body moved of its own accord. He snatched Ganon up by the collar of his shirt and shoved him with such force toward the open front door, they both crashed through the wall. In an explosion of wood and insulation, they tumbled into the front yard. Elliot lost his grip on the other man as they rolled down the porch steps.

Ganon jumped to his feet, a wound on his temple leaking a thick trickle of blood down his cheek. "Come on, then!" he roared. "You wanted this, dragon!"

Elliot had been feeling his fires burn for far too long. He shoved out a ball of flame with force, determined to see it obliterate the man.

But Ganon hopped easily to the side and let it pass, watching the tree behind him go up in flames. "Is that the best you can do?" he laughed.

Infuriated at his arrogance, Elliot sent another ball of fire and then another, shooting them out as quickly as his body could produce them. There was no way he could avoid all of them.

But Ganon pressed his knuckles together, one hand over the other. His fingers spread wide as he drew them apart, one hand lifting and the other falling. A transparent shield like a clear wall grew between them, and all of Elliot's efforts bounced right off and to the ground.

"I've been spending a lot of time studying, especially while Sibyl was out fucking around with you." the wizard called over the roar of the flames, which now began singing the grass in the yard. "I know how you dragons are. You fight with your bodies instead of your minds. You rely on nothing but brute strength to defeat your enemies, but that doesn't work when you're battling someone smarter than you." Ganon dropped the wall he'd created and worked a different magic between his fingers instead, one that pulled in the power of the flames that burned all around them and created a massive fireball no dragon could ever produce.

Just as he was about to cast it at his adversaries, a shimmering green dragon came charging from behind Elliot. She moved swiftly, using the element of surprise to her advantage as she rushed the wizard. Elliot, not wanting her to get hurt on his behalf, dove into the fray after her.

Momentarily caught off-guard, Ganon lost some of his control over the fire. It rolled away from him, setting whatever grass, weeds, and flowers were in its way up in smoke, but the wizard wasn't about to stop yet. He cast spheres of energy at close range toward his attackers, screaming nonsense as he did so.

Elliot felt the injuries to his scales as he bit and clawed. His weapons were sharper and more concrete than the wizard's, but he simply couldn't move as fast as Ganon could. He'd knocked Kaylee back, sending her tumbling through the weeds so he could focus on Elliot.

"Get out of the way!" called a voice behind him. Varhan was flinging his own spells toward the wizard. "I should have done this a long time ago!"

Elliot ducked around a crystalline disk that spun through the air. It ripped at Ganon's flesh, leaving a shower of blood in its wake, but it only managed to leave a surface wound at the man's elbow.

"Give it up, traitor!" Ganon cried. "I've trained under Tazarre himself! I've absorbed the magic that Charok has living within its core. You can't possibly defeat me!"

"But perhaps I can."

The gathering turned to find Sibyl standing at the door. She looked calm and collected, the fire reflecting in her kaleidoscopic eyes as she slowly descended the porch steps. Her hands were hanging at her sides instead of up and at the ready.

Elliot didn't care whether she looked ready or not. "Get back in the house," he growled, backing up towards her so he could protect her and still keep an eye on Ganon. "You can't be out here fighting, not in your condition."

But Sibyl easily slipped around him. Her fingers trailed against his scales as she walked forward, her steps as sure and even as a queen's. "Elliot, you don't own me. Nobody does, and I'm not going to let anyone think that any longer." Her eyes turned to his, mesmerizing and deep.

Elliot was so hypnotized, he didn't even see Ganon's attack before it was too late to react. But Sibyl did, and she repelled the blast of energy with a shield that flew out from her fingers with the slightest motion of her wrist.

"You think you were the only one studying?" she challenged him. Sibyl's left arm was straight out in front of her to hold the shield, but she swiveled it to the side as she lobbed a brilliant firecracker of light at her new enemy and then quickly replaced the shield. "You've always underestimated me, Ganon. You were constantly coming to my side, thinking you were aiding me, but the only thing you did was stop me from seeing the truth. You only want the side of the story that works for you instead of worrying about what's right."

"Sibyl, be reasonable," Ganon warned. Even as he spoke, he generated a new attack at each of his fingertips, the orbs of light growing slowly and deliberately. "You've come a long way, and you've let these derelicts exploit your softer side. I'll give you one more chance. We can go back to Charok. We can use my crystal. I'll hold up my end of the bargain."

She tipped her head to the side, her face neutral. She didn't even look like herself, having suppressed all the light from her eyes. "I don't think so."

In one fluid motion, Sibyl dropped her shield. She held her fingertips together, her elbows out and her palms facing Ganon. Forcing her hands apart created a wave that rippled through the air, bending the light that shone through it so that Elliot saw the trees behind Ganon flex and quiver.

She didn't stop, her slow and careful steps continuing as she sent wave after wave over Ganon until he was crushed so hard against the Earth, he couldn't breathe.

Elliot stood at the ready behind her. He didn't want her to fight; he wanted to do it for her. But it was clear that Sibyl wasn't going to listen to anyone else at the moment, and she seemed to be doing a good enough job on her own.

As Ganon lay gasping on the ground, Sibyl stepped forward and pressed her foot against his ribcage. She bent down to grab the crystal at his chest and it glowed in her hand. "I'm sending you back, but not as a free man."

The wizard disappeared in a puff of smoke the precise shape and size of his body, letting Sibyl's foot fall to the ground.

## 10

SIBYL SLIPPED HER FINGERS INTO ELLIOT'S AS THEY FACED ALL HIS cousins, aunts and uncles, and extended family at his parents' house. The crush of dragons made the house seem much smaller than it was. She needed his strength now as she waited for them to absorb everything they'd just told him. Elliot was certain they would all understand, but she couldn't be so sure. She'd never encountered any dragons before Elliot, and though she now knew their persecution had been unjust, she also knew there was still plenty of anger in the world. A heavy silence had descended over the room.

A tall woman with straight red hair, whom Elliot had introduced as his mother, Autumn, watched them closely. He'd explained that while his birth mother was the dragon queen, Autumn was the only mother he'd known, raising him here on Earth since he was a toddler. She chewed her lip, looking like she was going to say something, but no words came out.

The man at her side, his blonde hair graying at the temples, stepped forward. This was Elliot's father, Beau. He put a hand on his son's shoulder and then pulled Sibyl into a tight, squeezing hug. "Welcome to the family, Sibyl."

As if that was the only thing they were waiting on, the rest of Elliot's family came rushing forward. Autumn's arms were wrapped around them, followed by the rest of the aunts, uncles, and cousins;

even the tiny fingers of children. Sibyl felt a tear of relief and joy slip down her cheek. It had been so much to take in, knowing she was bearing a child who was half-dragon and half-witch, a child who was partially of two worlds, yet entirely of both. There was plenty more work to do, but this was the best first step she ever could've imagined.

Eventually, the crush of dragons abated, leaving Sibyl feeling warm and loved.

"I told you it would be all right," Elliot whispered in her ear as he pulled her close, his arm wrapping around her waist so that his fingertips could just touch her lower abdomen where their baby grew.

"What's the next step?" Autumn asked.

Sibyl took a deep breath and fingered the crystal that had been returned to its rightful place at her throat. "I have to go back home. As I said, Ganon is imprisoned there and no doubt spreading numerous lies about what actually happened. But I want everyone to know the truth. I can't guarantee that they'll listen, but I have to try. I can't let anyone else die because of what my father did."

"And I'm going with her," Elliot asserted, "as an ambassador for the rest of us."

"You can't just walk into a wizard's castle alone," Archard pointed out. "I'll go with you."

Kieran stepped forward. "So will I."

"I wouldn't mind taking a look at my old stomping grounds," Callan volunteered.

Lucia, a noble woman that Elliot had said was like an honorary aunt to him, stepped forward. "Boys, you can't do that. Not unless you're taking me, as well."

The rest of the crowd clapped and cheered until almost everyone was going. Only Finn insisted on staying behind as he gestured to his very pregnant wife. "I have business here."

Sibyl blushed. "It's very sweet of all of you, really, but there's no need. I have all the proof I need right here, and the wizards might think I'm under duress if I show up with so many dragons at my heels."

"Then we'll go, but only to speak to our own kind," Julian said. "The dragons on Charok need to understand what's happening, too."

"That sounds like a good plan," Sibyl said with a nod. She liked the idea of knowing she would have other allies on her home planet in case something went awry.

"I'm afraid there's one thing we're overlooking," Varhan said quietly, and the rest of the room hushed to hear him. "Sibyl, my dear, you're going to get very sick traveling while pregnant. I'm not saying you can't, but you need to be prepared for that."

"Will it hurt the baby?" Elliot asked, his fingers squeezing a little tighter around hers.

Sibyl felt that same warm flush on her cheeks as she looked at him. Nothing was more adorable than seeing how much he cared for her— except seeing how much he cared about their child. The little one wasn't even born yet, was hardly even formed, and yet he seemed to spend every minute fussing over the babe. The baby's dragon form surged to the surface, the same part of it that had triggered the detection spell and gave its existence away to everyone else. It already loved its daddy.

"No, no. No need to worry about that. But you'll want to give yourself some time to recover before you try to speak with the council."

She nodded at him and smiled, wondering how this poor, good man had been treated as a turncoat for so long.

---

THE DRAGONS DIDN'T POKE around when there was something they wanted to do. With Varhan's help, she was able to use the crystal to transport everyone to Charok. Her stomach reeled as she watched the majority of the dragons head toward the mountains to the west to find their own kind. Some of them shifted instantly, with Archard and his deep charcoal wings leading the way.

"They look happy," Sibyl said to Elliot as she watched them go, their vast silhouettes taking up the skyline. "Are you sure you aren't upset about not going with them? I could delay the council."

"No. Don't even think about it." Elliot kissed the back of her hand, looking softly into her eyes. "I don't want to be anywhere but with you. Are you feeling all right?"

"Not really, but I'll make it," she assured him. Her belly revolted against the trip through space and time, but Sibyl was determined to get this done. "The sooner I speak with them, the sooner we can end this war."

As they approached the castle, Sibyl tried to remember the last time she'd really seen it from the outside. She'd spent so much time inside its walls, working on spells and talking to her people, she rarely got the chance to get outside and go on any real missions. She smiled to herself at the irony of finally getting to leave, only to come back with a friendly dragon in tow.

"Great lady!" A guard knelt before her, bowing his forehead so far forward, it almost touched his knee. "We've been anxiously awaiting your return."

She raised him back to his feet. "Thank you for keeping the castle safe for me. Please, tell me where Ganon is."

The guard's face darkened and he looked away. "He's in the prison, as your spell indicated. But I can't say he's very happy about it, and there are many among us who aren't pleased, either. It doesn't seem right to hold such a prominent council member against his will."

"I understand completely, and I promise everything will make sense soon enough. I need to gather everyone. Please ready the great hall."

The guard's grey eyes snapped up to hers. "The great hall? My lady, we haven't used that area in ages."

"I know," she said with a warm smile. "Don't worry about it being a little dusty. Just make sure there's enough room, and tell everyone to come. I'll be in my chamber." Sibyl dismissed the guard. Her heart fluttered as she led Elliot up to her room. The place had always been so familiar, but after her trip to Earth, she felt as though she were returning to it as a completely different person.

"Are you all right?" Elliot worried over her, touching her ribs as she stared out the window. "I know this can't be easy for you."

She leaned against him, taking comfort in the way he made her feel. She still hadn't come up with a word to describe it, though the two of them had spent a lot of time discussing it ever since they'd defeated Ganon and finally had some time to be honest with each other. They knew now that it wasn't any sort of spell or sickness. It was the universe's way of letting them know they were supposed to be together. It didn't matter that she was a witch and he was a dragon, or that their parents had fought against each other in the War of Storms. And who was she to argue with fate?

"I'm all right," she replied. "I'm happy to be back. I just hope everyone is willing to listen."

She needn't have worried. The gathering of wizards in the great hall was restless and curious, their eyes studying Elliot for long moments before returning to her with questions. They wondered why

Ganon had been locked away, and they probably even doubted that Sibyl had been successful in her quest. Deep down, she knew there was even a possibility that her information could start a new war entirely.

"I thank you all for gathering here," she said, standing at the end of the great hall on a dais. It felt too formal, even without the ceremonial candles lit. The last thing she wanted to do was remind the people of Tazarre.

The hall fell to a hush as they listened.

"I have a lot to tell you about my journey to Earth. Some of it's not going to make a lot of sense. Most of it, you won't be prepared to hear. Please understand that I'll do everything in my power to make it clear, because your lives are about to change."

There were gasps of disbelief, snorts of derision, and pants of excitement as she told her story. Sibyl didn't give them all the gory details, since they didn't need to know exactly what had happened between her and Elliot. But she knew, and she also knew that he was right there behind her. It was strange, since she'd always been so independent, to know that the other half of her wasn't inside her own body. He was just a couple of feet away, waiting for her to need him.

Sibyl's hands shook when the time came to not only tell the wizards and witches in attendance what had happened, but to show them. It seemed a violation of her father and the sacredness of her family to put the crystal memories on display the same way Varhan had for her. But she needed to.

"I would never have believed it all if I hadn't seen it with my own eyes," she explained as she twisted her wand in just the right direction and at just the right angle, as Varhan had shown her. "It's not easy to watch, not even for me, though I think I've seen it a dozen times now. But everything you've known to be true is false."

She kept her eyes averted, studying the stone floor underneath her feet as the gathering watched it all play out. Sibyl didn't need to see it, nor did she need to study the faces of those in attendance to determine what they thought about it. They would make their own decisions, no matter what she did.

When she noted a flicker in the memories that indicated the worst of it was over, Sibyl stepped back up onto the dais. "What we've done to the dragons is wrong," she declared. "And there can be no winners when it comes to war. I call upon you—each and every one of you—to put an end to this. Tell your families. Tell your neighbors. Leave your grimoires shut unless you plan to use your work for good, and be sure you think about that long, hard, and deeply before you do. I consider everyone pardoned, since we've all done some terrible things that we can't be proud of, but from this point forward, I will also consider anyone who continues the war against the dragons an enemy."

Silence fell once again. Sibyl forced her hands to remain relaxed and calm against the fabric of her robe, though she felt like balling them into fists. This was it. This was the culmination of her existence. She'd always thought she had a different calling than most of the others around her, but she knew for certain now. This was what she was meant to do.

The hall erupted in a crescendo of cheers and praise. Wizards and witches swarmed the dais to congratulate her or tentatively shake hands with the dragon that was now in their midst. Others leaned against each other and cried, grieving for loved ones who'd died uselessly or sobbing for their own deeds. It was a new day in Charok.

"You did great," Elliot said that evening when they returned to her chamber. "I'm so proud of you."

Sibyl pressed her lips to his, letting her hand linger on the side of his neck. "I couldn't have done it without you."

"I don't know," he said. "I have a feeling some of them aren't pleased with me."

"We'll always have the extremists," she allowed. "There will be dragons who hate wizards until the day they die, and wizards who will feel the same about dragons. There's only so much I can do about it, and I'm not going to worry myself over trying. Some people just don't want their minds to be changed."

"Like Ganon?" he asked with an arched brow. "He doesn't seem like the kind of guy who'd want to hang out with me on the weekends."

Sibyl had to laugh a little at that. She felt bad for Ganon, though. He thought he was doing the right thing when he wanted to slaughter Elliot and anyone associated with him. It was the way he'd been raised and trained. If only he'd been willing to listen, he might be starting a new life right now instead of letting the old one rot away in a prison cell. "I still have some hope for him," she finally replied, "but right now, he's where he needs to be."

"And what about you?" Elliot caressed her cheek with the backs of his fingers. "Where do you need to be?"

She started to tell him that she didn't know, and maybe they should just turn in for the night. But she realized she finally had the chance for something that had always been too far out of her reach. "I've always had this dream of flying right out the window," she said, a small smile perking up the corners of her mouth. "I've never really felt free, you know."

"Oh, this window right here?" Elliot eased the glass open on its hinges and looked out over the castle walls before glancing back over his shoulder at her mischievously. "Let's go." He dove over the windowsill.

Sibyl gasped, but Elliot was flying instead of falling. He's shifted in midair, and his dark blue wings held him aloft easily. She almost hissed at him to get back inside before anyone saw, but then she had to remember that things were different around the castle. If anyone were to look up at just that moment, it would likely be the first time they'd seen a dragon in that vicinity in decades.

"Are you sure about this?" she asked, putting one foot on the window sill.

His smile was different when he was in his dragon form, but it was there all the same. "I've never been more sure of anything in my life until you came along."

She hopped on his back and they took off. He was being gentle with her, she knew, not wanting to hurt her or the baby, but even an easy ride was exhilarating as he swooped past the walls. The cliff faces of the mountains dropped away beneath them, the setting sun burnishing them a deep shade of crimson. Sibyl clung to his back and felt her worries melt away, as though they'd been attached to the castle and weren't capable of making the journey with her.

It seemed like she was seeing her homeland in a new light. "See that section of woods over there?" she called as she pointed to a clump of trees that used to look much bigger. "I used to play there all the time as a little girl. That was where I cast my first successful spell on my own, actually. I turned a muskrat into a mushroom and back again."

Elliot's laugh was a low rumble between her legs. "I'm sure the muskrat was a little confused by that."

"Probably." She took a deep breath, inhaling the thin clean air over the mountains. "It's so beautiful here. And it's only going to get even more beautiful if we can actually convince everyone to remain at peace."

"I think we very well might have," Elliot said, gesturing with his great head off to the north.

Sibyl followed his gaze, seeing first one dragon gliding along in the air and then another. A third joined them, and as their numbers multiplied, Sibyl realized they weren't just the dragons that had accompanied them to Charok from Earth. These were dragons who'd never left or been forced to leave; dragons who knew this place as home. Sibyl could appreciate the beauty in their wings that seemed so delicate, yet were so strong, holding them aloft as they zoomed over the mountains.

"What's that sound?" she asked. It was faint, but she knew it was there, a humming that pulsed through the air.

Elliot listened for a moment before making that same noise himself. "They're happy, Sibyl, and they're welcoming you. You've restored peace to Charok."

# 11

SIBYL HELD UP A TINY PIECE OF CLOTHING. THE TWO OF THEM HAD finally found some time to sort through the numerous toys, clothes, and blankets that Elliot's relatives had been showering upon them. "It's impossible to think we'll actually need all this. And it's even more impossible to think that any creature is small enough to wear this."

"And it's going to be our little creature," Elliot reminded her, reaching out from his place on the sofa, touching her now-rounded belly. "I can't tell you how happy I am that you decided to come back with me. Seeing you speak in front of the council and how good you are as a leader, I wasn't sure you would."

"I'm just glad you still wanted me, knowing who my father was," she replied, leaning into his caress.

"Are you kidding me? Of course I want you. I'll *always* want you." His pale eyes looked up into hers with such softness and sincerity, Sibyl could've fallen into them. "And just for the record, I felt that way long before I knew about the baby. That's just an added bonus."

Sibyl grinned at him. "You're something else, you know that?"

"So are you, which is exactly why I can't live unless we're on the same planet. I hope you don't regret leaving Charok behind for a while."

Settling down into his arms, Sibyl let out a happy sigh. It hadn't been an easy decision. Charok was the only thing she'd ever known.

But given that she didn't have any true family there, and that she'd taken some time to help the council set up a more democratic leadership before she left, Sibyl knew she was safe to finally take charge of her own life. "No, I don't regret it. I'll miss it, and I definitely want to take our child back there so he or she knows exactly where they came from. But Earth is so vibrant and full of life. I've gotten so attached to it. And there's no doubt in my mind this is where you belong."

"You think so?"

She twined her fingers through his hair as she looked down into his face, wanting to memorize every gorgeous detail. "I do. I think it's where all three of us belong.

She laughed as she heard the rumble of a truck coming up their street. It paused for a moment before trundling on, stopping again further down the road. "The mail's here. I'll get it." She trotted out the front door in her bare feet to check. The sidewalk was cold in the December air, but she didn't care. She didn't know why, but there was something Sibyl truly loved about the mail coming. None of it was addressed to her yet, but she didn't care. She liked the excitement of it, even when it was junk mail.

"Here you go." Sibyl handed Elliot the majority of the mail, setting aside a catalog to look through later. She liked those best.

"Oh, god. Here it is." Elliot stood up, an envelope in his hand. He pressed his other hand to his forehead as he stared at the lettering on the front. "I'm not sure I even want to open it."

"What is it?" Sibyl came to stand beside him. With everything they'd been through, she was ready to settle down to a life of relative ease. There would be plenty to worry about with the baby, and she might want to get a job later down the road, but all of that was nothing compared to being at war. Now, whatever was in that envelope had Elliot all upset.

"It's the results of my bar exam," he explained breathlessly. "I've been so caught up in us and in Charok that I'd hardly thought about it at all."

Sibyl didn't know a whole lot about being an attorney, but she knew it was important and that Elliot had to pass this test if he was to get a job in his field. "Well go ahead! Open it!" she encouraged. It wasn't even her exam, but she felt her heart lifting in excitement.

Elliot extended one claw with a flick of his finger and neatly opened the seal. His hands returned to human form instantly as he pulled out the thick sheet of paper. His eyes scanned it, then whisked back up to the top to start again. "I passed," he finally breathed. "I actually passed!"

"Of course you did!" Sibyl threw her arms around him as he shot to his feet.

He grabbed her by the waist and swung her around, laughing. "Do you know what this means?" he asked, his words punctuated by his laughter. "I've got several firms who said they'd hire me as soon as they knew my results. I'll have a real job in no time, and that means no more of this rental house. We'll get a nice place, any place you want, with plenty of room for the baby and maybe a dog and even a pool table! And we can make sure there are good schools and a park nearby, and I'll be gone during the day for work but I'll make it up to you every night when I come home." He pressed his lips to hers.

He hadn't been making much sense with his ramble, but this last part she most definitely understood. Sibyl kissed him back, pleased to know that every time they got close, the magic between them was still there. "Seems to me like we have a reason to celebrate," she murmured against his neck.

"You think so? We can't exactly open a bottle of champagne."

"We won't need that." Sibyl slid to the floor and immediately reached for the waistband of his jeans. "But we can celebrate this way, if you'd like?"

His whole body relaxed as he heard the words, that velvety look in his eyes returning. "You don't have to ask me twice." Elliot lifted her shirt over her head, exposing her swollen breasts and letting out a gasp of pleasure. "Have I told you how gorgeous you are when you're pregnant?" he asked huskily.

"Does that mean you won't like me anymore once I've had the baby?" she teased, closing her eyes as his warm hands caressed the fleshy mounds, gently pinching her nipples with his thumbs.

"I think I can find a way to handle it." Elliot's mouth closed over one pert bud, taking her breath away as he pushed her leggings and panties down her legs.

"You're distracting me from what I was going to do," she argued gently, straightening up and reaching for his waistline once again. Sibyl slipped his jeans down until he could step out of them, removing his boxer briefs that he looked so hot in when he was trying to find something to wear in the morning. She knelt before him, naked and vulnerable, yet knowing she still had all the power she needed in the world. Taking him into her mouth, Sibyl used her actions to let him know just how much he meant to her.

His hands gripped her hair as he fought for control. "You're too good at that."

"Don't you deserve it for passing your exam?" she asked, glancing up at him for a second before pulling him all the way to the back of her throat. She got off on knowing he was turned on, and there was no doubt about it when his hardness was in her mouth.

"I won't argue with that. But let's go to the bedroom." He pulled her to her feet and down the hall, leaving their clothes behind to be retrieved later.

Sibyl stopped short as they entered the room, making Elliot turn around. That was just what she wanted; she could just push him backwards onto the bed and climb on top. He bounced slightly on the mattress and smiled. "You really are going to treat me, huh?"

"That's the plan." She continued what she'd started in the living room, working Elliot up into such a frenzy, his fists balled in the sheets beneath him. She lifted her head and moved her hips forward to take him inside her, but Elliot was faster.

He'd grabbed her thighs and brought her forward while scooting himself down toward the foot of the bed, lining up her most secret spot with his mouth. He returned the favor, licking and sucking her silky folds as his fingers squeezed the flesh of her backside.

"Hey," she panted as she felt her inner walls contract. "This is supposed to be a celebration for *you*."

Elliot broke away from laving her with his tongue for only a moment. "And maybe this is exactly how I want to celebrate," he argued before stroking the tip of his tongue over her clit, faster and faster under her knuckles were white on the headboard.

Sibyl screamed her pleasure as he brought her to the edge and over. They'd coupled numerous times once they'd reunited, and yet he always knew how to make her feel like it was completely new.

When she'd had enough, he let her settle her hips down over him, burying himself as deep as he dared. Sibyl rocked gently back and forth, relishing the feeling of him sliding in and out of her. She swore she could feel his tension building as her own wound up again, and then like a spring that had been pushed too far, it unwound with a fury and speed she could hardly keep up with. Sibyl tightened her thighs around him as she pulled everything she needed from him and gave him her own in return.

———

SIBYL AWOKE in the middle of the night. The pain in her abdomen was strange, unpleasant, and completely different from anything she'd experienced before, but it was also telling her something very important. Her sleep-addled mind couldn't figure out what it was at first, and when the pain subsided, she thought perhaps it had all been a dream.

But it returned again several minutes later, stabbing through her body. "Elliot," she whispered harshly. "I think it's time."

He was out of bed in an instant, flicking on the lights and grabbing her robe. "The suitcase is already in the car. Let's go."

"Are you sure about this?" she asked as he settled her gently into the passenger seat. "We don't know exactly what it'll be like when he or she is born." She'd had numerous nightmares of going to the hospital to have the baby, only to have the entire world watching when she gave birth to a dragon.

"It'll be fine. I promise." Elliot shut the door before dashing around to the other side of the car. He tumbled into the driver's seat, firing up the engine before he had his seatbelt on. "Aurora already gave birth to a half-dragon, remember? Phoenix looked like his human side, too. It seems that they come out looking human, and I have no doubt that ours will do the same. Even Varhan believes it."

Sibyl knew that Varhan's words meant a lot to everyone in Elliot's clan, and they were beginning to mean quite a bit to her, too. "If you say so."

The hospital was a blur. She didn't understand all of what the doctors and nurses said to her, even though they acted as if they were having everyday conversation. Sibyl had studied human childbirth thoroughly and found that the general idea of it should be the same for her. But the big difference lay in going to a hospital and relying on doctors and nurses instead of friends and family members. She'd even talked about having the baby at home, but Elliot assured her they were better off around medical professionals in case there should be an emergency.

"No, she definitely doesn't want any," Elliot said forcefully as they settled her into a private birthing suite and a nurse offered her painkillers once again.

"You're sure? She's pretty far along, and this might be her last chance for it."

Elliot looked down at Sibyl, and she gave him a firm look. They'd discussed it extensively, and Sibyl said she wanted this to be as natural as possible. Even with a forceful pain rocketing through her body and making her grit her teeth, she shook her head.

"She's sure."

Less than an hour later, Sibyl was holding a warm bundle of blankets in her arms. She peered at the perfect face with its chubby cheeks and dark blue eyes. "He's absolutely gorgeous," she breathed. "I think he looks just like you."

Elliot put his arm around her to gaze down at their son. "And I see only you in him. Time will tell."

"Do we have a name?" the nurse asked, pen and paper at the ready.

Sibyl looked up at Elliot for confirmation and then back at the nurse. "Tristan Draco."

The nurse raised an eyebrow, but she wrote down the name after confirming the spelling. "I can get all the information put in on the birth record, then. Meanwhile, you have a visitor if that's all right?"

Elliot stiffened. "I hadn't even called anyone yet," he whispered to Sibyl. "I've been too busy."

"I haven't either, but I guess we don't have much choice other than to see who it is." Sibyl's body had been through hell and back. She hurt, but she also felt the thrum of excitement and motherhood in her veins. She could deal with Elliot's family showing up unannounced. "Send them in, please."

The face that peeked in the door a minute later was a familiar one, but not one she'd been expecting. "Ozelius?" Sibyl sat up a little in bed, though the effort was painful. "What are you doing here?"

The wizard approached the bedside, wringing his hands. He'd copied someone's outfit in an attempt to blend in, but the polyester shirt and ill-fitting pants wouldn't have suited anyone. His crooked mouth tweaked nervously at the corners. "I was doing a routine scan of the planet to check for any signatures that might indicate trouble. I knew something had happened to you, and I had to come and see for myself."

"It was very sweet of you to come, Ozelius."

He stared down at the child for a long moment before lifting his fingers and holding them in the air over the babe's forehead. "May I?"

"Of course."

Ozelius fluttered his fingertips in the air until a silvery light descended from them. When they touched Tristan's forehead, they revealed the scales that lay just under the surface of his skin. "Wonderful," the wizard breathed. "Absolutely wonderful. I didn't even need the spell, to be honest, but I had to be completely sure before I took word back to Charok. Half wizard and half dragon."

"You think they'll approve?" Sibyl asked quietly. She'd contemplated this moment for a long time. Things on Charok had been peaceful, but things could change in the face of reality at a moment's notice.

Ozelius bobbed his head emphatically. "To be sure! They'll be drinking and singing well into the night, both the dragons and wizards alike. I'll tell everyone, Great Lady! Everyone!" He practically skipped out of the room, still shouting to any random hospital workers in the hall over what a miracle it was.

Sibyl looked up at Elliot. "And what about you, love? What do you think?"

He kissed her forehead, and she could see the happiness in his teary eyes. "I think the two of you have made me the proudest dragon in the universe."

As she looked at Elliot and then again at Tristan, her heart soared, knowing the sweet infant cradled in her arms was a symbol of the peace restored between the dragons and wizards for all of eternity.

THE END

# ALSO BY MEG RIPLEY

ALL AVAILABLE ON AMAZON

Book 3: Captured By The Soldier Wolf

Book 4: Christmas With The Soldier Dragon

Werebears of Acadia Series

Werebears of the Everglades Series

Werebears of Glacier Bay Series

Werebears of Big Bend Series

**Dragons of Charok Universe**

Daddy Dragon Guardians Series

Shifters Between Worlds Series

More Shifter Romances

Forever Fated Mates Box Set

Shifter Daddies Box Set

Beverly Hills Dragons Series

Dragons of Sin City Series

Dragons of the Darkblood Secret Society Series

Packs of the Pacific Northwest Series

Early Short Stories

Mated By The Dragon Boss

Claimed By The Werebears of Green Tree

Bearer of Secrets

Rogue Wolf

# ABOUT THE AUTHOR

Meg Ripley is an author of steamy shifter romances. A Seattle native, Meg can often be found curled up in a local coffee house with her laptop.

Download Meg's entire *Caught Between Dragons* series when you sign up for her newsletter!

Sign up by visiting www.redlilypublishing.com or Meg's Facebook page:
https://www.facebook.com/authormegripley/

Printed in Great Britain
by Amazon